RISING DAWN

THE GUARDIANS OF THE MAIDEN

RISING DAWN

BECK MICHAELS

PLUMA PRESS

TRIGGER WARNING: this book contains sexual situations, strong violence and gore, foul language, violence against women, mutilation, death, death of animals, heavy grief and loss, self-harm, captivity, torture, suicide ideation, alcohol and drugs used to cope with depression and PTSD.

PLUMA PRESS
P.O. Box 341
Camby, IN 46113
Visit Us at PlumaPress.com

Published August 2024

First Edition

Author: Michaels, Beck

Title: Rising Dawn / Beck Michaels

Series: The Guardians of the Maiden; 4

Genre: YA Fantasy Fiction

Identifiers:
ISBN 978-1-956899-16-0 (hardcover) | ISBN 978-1-956899-17-7 (softcover)
ISBN 978-1-956899-18-4 (ebook)

www.BeckMichaels.com

Printed in the United States of America

Printed in the United States of America

For my father.
Thank you for coming to say goodbye.

And for all those who have lost a loved one,
may you find solace in these pages as I have.

JERASH

GLACIAL OCEAN

SKATH

UNITED CROWN

THE THREE
RIVERS

EDYM

XIAN
JING

HARROMAG
MODOS

DRAGON CANYON

Le

LANGSHAN

RED
HIGHLANDS

THE VALE

LEVIATHAN OCEAN

SUN
GUILD

MA

MOUNT IDA

LUNAR
GUILD

AND OF URN

TEZUMA

ARGYLE

DWARF
SHOE

OATING ISLANDS
OF NAZAR

GREENWOOD

HE ELVES

PIRE

HERMON
RIDGE

AZURE

HILOS

SAXE SEA

MISTY
ISLES

EARTH
GUILD

THE SEVEN GATES

Each soul passes through the gates at their beginning and their end.

HEAVEN'S GATE

LIFE'S GATE

SPATIAL GATE

TIME GATE

MORTAL GATE

NETHERWORLD GATE

DEATH'S GATE

Seek the Maiden with emeralds for sight and tresses of fire,
for she holds the key to the Unending thou desires.
Beware the Guardians who come to shield her from thee.
She will be protected by one of divine blood
and a dweller of the moon howling to break free.
Thus follows a warrior bestowing his vow,
and a sorceress grants her sorcery.
A familiar face vies for vengeance,
and a creature with the strength of ten eradicates the forgery.
Great peril in the venture thou art pursuing.
Be not swayed by love, lest it be thy undoing

PART I: MIRROR

PROLOGUE

Kāhssiel

The sky was burning.

Smoke wafted over the barren ground, charred black from scattered fires and littered with burnt feathers. Kāhssiel's chains clinked as he lifted himself up on his knees. The dried blood on his lips cracked as he coughed and pressed on his aching ribs.

The *Hyalus* tree's leaves rattled softly, and he briefly closed his eyes as he heard her faint voice in the wind. It echoed back the promises they made right here.

Sheli...

The back of his eyes ached with unshed tears, and his veins hummed with his trapped flame.

My Sheli ... can you feel me? I'm here.

But there was only a vacancy in his chest. It had been empty since the day she was cut out of him. His heart thudded weakly. *No more,* it begged. It didn't want to keep beating. Not without her.

"All this death and bloodshed, only to end defeated. All for what? For some witch?"

Kāhssiel lifted his tired eyes to where Raziel stood before him, clad in armor. His white wings looked gray in the dull dawn. "Am I defeated?"

"You are in Skath chains, Kāhssiel. You have no power now."

He laughed, enjoying how stupid they really were. "They will not hold me for long, Raziel. As soon as I am free of these chains, I will come for you. For all of you." He snarled at the traitors standing with him and lurched at them. The guards held onto his chains, jerking back his manacled arms. "Each of you has betrayed me, and nothing will inhibit me until I have melted the flesh off your bones. I will return you to the Gates and raze the Realms to the ground. As soon as I am free, I will fill this world with a sea of flame and consume it all until there is nothing left of it!"

Seraph fire blazed in his eyes, searing them with his promise.

"I WILL BURN IT ALL!"

CHAPTER 1

Dynalya

Much could be said about one's name. It marked where you came from, where you belonged, and where you may go. As the sound of Klyde's true name settled in the silent room, Dyna knew what it meant.

Canting her head, she studied the Captain of the Skelling Mercenaries hovering in the air in nothing but his trousers, bound in purple magic. Klyde's dark blue eyes looked back at her calmly. The sunrise shone through the windows, highlighting the edge of his jaw and dark blond hair. Now that she knew who he was, Dyna could see past his thick beard to the face he had tried to hide.

He was a Morken, brother of her enemy. And he had hidden his identity from them the entire time they were in Skelling Rise.

The air in Klyde's bedchamber charged with electricity. It prickled against Dyna's skin, and she glanced at Lucenna beside her. The furious sorceresses' lilac eyes glowed brightly as her Essence wound tighter around Klyde, making him grimace.

"Easy." Zev crossed his arms over his broad chest and leaned against the wall. "You'll kill him before we can learn anything useful."

Lord Norrlen's kind gaze fell on her. "We owe the captain a chance to explain himself, my lady. He has done much for us in our time of need. We very well may not be alive if not for him."

Hmm, Dyna supposed he had a point. He had come to their aid with the trolls and against the Vanguard.

"We don't owe him anything," Lucenna hissed. "Everything out of his mouth has been nothing but lies." Her eyes flared brighter as she glared up at him. "I told you what I would do to you if you *lied* to me."

Klyde's brow tightened. He didn't seem afraid of her, but he did seem regretful. His eyes flickered to Dyna next, and she read his silent request for a chance to be heard.

Leader to leader.

The bedroom door slammed open. Eagon and Tavin burst in, armed.

The boy aimed a loaded crossbow at her face. "Put him down or this bolt goes straight through your eyes."

Oh, she almost found him endearing, coming in here to rescue his uncle. Her Guardians braced themselves with magic, claws, and bow.

"That would be a poor decision on your part," Dyna said.

Eagon had his throwing stars ready. "You're sorely mistaken if you believe you'll make it out of here alive, lass. The manor is crawling with mercenaries. Hurt him, and nothing will deter us from taking you down."

Tavin fixed her with those pretty, pale blue eyes. They weren't hard or sharp, but they were the color of frosted ice. "Release him! I won't tell you again."

Familiarity washed over Dyna as she studied his youthful features. The truth had been in front of her since they arrived, but she was too preoccupied with frivolous matters to see it.

"Well, well." She smirked at Klyde. "You have been keeping many secrets, haven't you, Captain?"

Things were now beginning to get interesting.

His eyes grew wide. He strained against his gag to say something. Dyna nodded to Lucenna, and she removed the magic covering his mouth.

"Get out and shut the damn door," he ordered Eagon while still looking at her. "No one is to disturb us. That's an order."

"What?" Tavin gaped at him. "But—"

"Aye," Eagon cut him off at Klyde's look. He hooked an arm around Tavin's chest and hauled him back out the door. It closed after them, and the lad's angry voice faded as they left the hall.

Now what was she to make of this new knowledge? The others glanced at each other questioningly as she and Klyde stared at one another in stony silence.

"Set him down," Dyna said.

Lucenna's mouth pinched in disapproval, but she relented by placing Klyde in the chaise. With a wave of her fingers, she bound his wrists and ankles with glowing ropes of magic.

"It's not what you think," he told her as she worked to secure him to the chaise next.

"Spare me your breathing."

"Lucenna," Klyde said, a warning in his tone. "You know I enjoy it when you're mean to me."

"Be quiet before I strangle you," she snapped, tightening the bonds around his neck. "I should kill you right now."

"If you keep flirting with me like that, I'm going to fall in love with you."

Lucenna turned bright pink, though her fury overshadowed it. Electricity sparked around her ominously.

Humor may have been Klyde's way of dispelling tense situations, but now wasn't the time to test them.

Zev shook his head. "Either you truly have a death wish, or you don't know when not to make a jest out of everything. She is seconds from sending you through Death's Gate."

Dyna's patience was beginning to thin with all their bickering. "Leave me with him."

They all looked at her as if she had gone mad.

"That wouldn't be wise, my lady," Rawn said.

"I am not leaving you alone with him for a second," Zev added.

Dyna tried not to let their overprotectiveness annoy her, but it reminded her too much of the absent presence she was working hard to ignore. She squeezed the velvet sachet in her fist tightly, releasing the scent of sage in the air.

"Then stand back and let me speak to him. Don't interfere." They obeyed her curt order and silently moved to stand by the door. Dragging a chair over, Dyna sat across from Klyde. Warmth from the hearth pressed into her back, the burning wood crackling gently as they studied each other. "Does he know?"

"As far as Tavin knows, his father died a hero during the overrun, and I'd rather keep it that way."

Chuckling, Dyna crossed her legs. "I wasn't speaking about your nephew, Captain."

The drag of quiet was heavy as a muscle in Klyde's jaw flexed. Slow realization crossed the faces of her Guardians as they finally understood.

"I suppose your silence is answer enough," she said. "Interesting."

All amusement had long since faded from Klyde's expression. It was now hard and cold, resembling his brother's almost perfectly. Instead of ice, a severe hurricane churned in his gaze. One that promised retribution if she tried anything against his family.

This was a monumental secret that could serve in her favor, but for now, she would play nice.

"Don't worry," Dyna continued. "I don't care about Tavin or why you kept his existence a secret. I'm sure you have your reasons. What I want to know is why you kept *your* identity hidden and what your intentions were with us. As you can see, naturally we assumed the worst."

He opened his mouth, but Dyna held up a finger. She glanced at Lucenna. The sorceress drew the rune for truth in the air. It pulsed bright purple above the captain's head before fading away.

Klyde shivered as the spell fell over him, and he scoffed. "I would have told you the truth regardless, lass."

Dyna shrugged. "It's merely to dispel any suspicions. I hope you don't mind."

He already had his chance to reveal everything before, so why would she believe him now unless spelled to speak the truth?

"I don't work for Tarn if that is your concern," Klyde began. His gaze flickered to Lucenna. "I had no intention of turning you in for the bounty. But you're right about one thing. I did intend to use you."

A muscle flexed in his jaw as he let that confession settle. Otherwise, he was completely still.

"To do what?" Dyna pressed when he fell silent.

"To find him," Klyde replied tightly. "That was the only thing I wanted from you. The means to track Tarn down and stop him—by whatever means necessary."

That was the last thing she had expected to hear, as had the others, by the silence that crept back into the tension between them.

Klyde's attention drifted past her to the hearth, and the firelight shone in his distant gaze. "Aye, our father was Lord Morken, earl of this manor. Regardless of our nobility, there was no warmth in these halls, but my sister, brother, and I, we had each other. Until the Horde came." Klyde's brow furrowed, his mouth thinning as he remembered.

Dyna easily recalled it, too. It wasn't difficult when she had borne witness to the slaughter. The hair stood on her arms as the picture formed in her mind. The screams of the men as they died, the stench of swamp trolls in the summer heat, her feet slipping through the mud drenched in blood.

"All the knights were called to arms that day. As a squire, it was my duty to gather the others and evacuate the women and children to the dungeons. So many died … devoured and torn apart before our eyes." Klyde's throat bobbed. "But I noticed Aisling was missing. She was…"

"Tarn's wife," Dyna murmured.

"Aye…" He blinked at her, surprised she knew. "My brother was out fighting back the Horde. It was my duty to protect her, so I returned to his estate … but … a troll had broken through the door." Desolation weighed down his expression, and he rubbed his face. "Her death was instant. There was nothing I could do to save her, but…"

Dyna's memory flashed with the image of Aisling's wounded stomach. Not torn but *cut*. Her eyes widened. "You saved Tarn's son…"

This was another part of the story. One she had not glimpsed when Dream Walking through Tarn's past. She imagined a frightened boy, finding his sister-by-law dead, shaken and afraid of what he had to do to save his nephew.

Lucenna's soft gasp came from behind her.

"What happened next?" Dyna asked.

"Nothing." Klyde's tenor hardened, and the muscles in his arms flexed with the clench of his fists. "There was *nothing* left of our town but a graveyard. When I reached the square, I found my father with a gaping hole in his chest and my brother's broken sword. The viceroy told me Tarn had killed him with magic, but I didn't…" His gaze lowered to the ground, his jaw clenching. "I didn't believe it. No one was left alive, so I assumed Tarn had fallen as well, but he returned that night. Not for us. He didn't care about us." Klyde laughed drily, shaking his head. "He only came to sack the coffers and steal my mother's jewels. When I asked him what he had done to our father ... I saw the truth in his eyes. Then he left with Von. They abandoned us without ever looking back." Klyde's face was expressionless, but she could feel his ire and misery. Or perhaps Dyna simply knew it was there because those same emotions now lingered beneath her own mask. "Over the years, I heard of all the wicked things Tarn had done. He escaped justice time and again because no one could ever find him. So I waited for his return. And finally, after fifteen years, he came back..." Klyde's eyes lifted to her. "For you."

Rays of the morning sun rose higher and cast an orange hue in the room. It reminded Dyna of that evening in Landcaster when she met Von. That led to Tarn learning of her existence and her map to Mount Ida. How different would things be if fate had not brought her there?

"I think it's only fair that you tell me the truth now," Klyde said. "Why is my brother hunting you, Dyna? Why did he risk returning to Azure merely to put a bounty on all your heads?"

She leaned back in the chair, linking her fingers. "I am not the one on trial here. My business is my own."

Revealing the existence of the map had brought enough conflict to her life. Klyde might not seem like a greedy man, but she was finished being naïve.

A look crossed his face, a knowing one that made her tense. "Aye, don't tell me. I don't really care why he wants you. The only thing I care about is finding him."

There was only one way to do that.

"You want to join us," Dyna concluded.

Lucenna scoffed. Her heels clicked on the floor as she drew up to her side. "You think we would allow that after all of your lies?"

Klyde searched her face. "I kept the full truth because I needed to, love. But I didn't outright lie."

"The truth spell is not perfect," Zev said gruffly. His tall frame came to Dyna's other side, and he crossed his arms, making his white tunic tighten across his broad chest. Sharp fangs peeked past his lips as he spoke. "You may have told us the truth now, but how are we to know what else you have omitted? You're a *Morken*. You could easily change your mind later about whose side you're truly on."

"I am only on one side." Klyde looked out through the window at Skelling Rise. It offered a view of farmhouses on distant hills past the forest, smoke drifting from the many chimneys. The snowy landscape glittered beautifully, like a blanket of diamond dust in the morning. "The side that protects this town and its people. Tarn deserves to be brought to justice for what he has done." He met her gaze again. "But as of now, no one has the power or the strength to defeat him."

And they never would if Tarn gained immortality. It was his ultimate ambition, and she had made it her purpose to defeat him.

"You are quite right about that," Dyna said. "Tarn is dangerous, and you have no idea how much so."

His mouth curved in a harsh smirk. "Oh, but I do. The viceroy told me enough before his death, and I learned the rest from my mother's journals. Tarn is a descendant of the Ice Phoenix. And I know *exactly* what he used to put that hole in my father's chest."

Something about the way he said it made Dyna go still, because she sensed there was far more to Klyde than they fathomed.

"What makes you believe you can inhibit him, Captain?" Rawn asked.

Klyde's smirk widened into a sharp smile. One that was callous and cunning. Confident. "Because, mate, he isn't the only one with a powerful ancestor."

The statement drew a pause as Dyna took in his meaning.

She glanced at his mercenary coat draped on the chaise, the firelight gleaming over the white sigil of a bird's skull. It was a symbol that represented more than their town, but who they were.

She inhaled a faint breath. "You're a Skelling."

CHAPTER 2

Lucenna

Lucenna hated liars. Hated it even more when they fooled her. She felt utterly stupid for not seeing Klyde for what he was. It made her so angry she choked on it, and looking at him only made it spew from her pores.

Dark blond hair had fallen around his jaw in rumpled waves, still tousled from his sleep. A light sheen of sweat glistened on his bare chest beneath the light of her purple Essence that contained him.

She leaned down until they were eye to eye. This close, she got a full view of his scars and his familiar scent that reminded her of the sea. Klyde looked back at her silently as she searched his eyes for *something* to support his claim. Yet all she saw was a man.

A useless, lying man.

Lucenna narrowed her eyes. "The Skellings are extinct."

"Or so they say, love," Klyde replied in his smooth, brogue accent.

"I am not your *love*," she hissed. He winced at the tightening grip of her magic.

Lucenna had long misplaced her book on the Ice Phoenix, but she had read it several times over. And once she had been told about these Skelling creatures who were as large and powerful as dragons, she had done some research of her own.

"The Skellings became extinct during the Dark War," Lucenna told the others as she straightened. "He is no more a Skelling than I am compelled to believe him."

Zev's eyes bled bright yellow with his wolf, and he took a deliberate sniff. "He smells human to me."

Rawn canted his head, making one of his pointed ears poke out of his hair as he studied the captain. No doubt listening to his heartbeat.

Klyde frowned at her. "We can discuss Everfrost history at another time. You and I both know I can speak nothing but the truth."

Even as the power of the truth spell hummed in the air, Lucenna couldn't help but distrust everything he said.

"What does this have to do with Tarn?" Zev asked.

"The Skellings were said to hold King Jökull's only weakness," Dyna said, watching Klyde carefully, fingers leisurely drumming on the armrests of her chair. Her crimson locks were braided back in a coronet. She wore black boots and black trousers, a fine blue redingote on her frame. Her green eyes were indifferent yet piercing. Looking every bit like a woman in power on her impromptu throne. "Their existence brought about his downfall."

Lucenna remembered quite clearly the passage on Jökull's death. He had been an immortal, one of the Seven Gods of the Seven Gates, yet he had been killed by his own creation.

Dyna crossed a leg over the other. "Do you know what Tarn is after?"

Klyde's gaze met her cool one. "Aye, I do. After years of following his exploits, I probably know more about him than anyone. And I assure you, I have the means to stop him."

"Slay him, you mean."

His jaw clenched. "If it comes to that."

The statement left Lucenna momentarily stunned ... because it wasn't a lie. Klyde was prepared to kill him. To come to terms with spilling his family's blood, he had to have thought about it for a long time. Was it out of hate for his brother or out of love for his nephew? Because she had seen a storm rage in Klyde's eyes when Dyna taunted him with Tavin.

He would do anything for that boy.

"I am not your enemy, lass. You can trust in that."

Dyna ground her teeth as if offended by the vile word. "I have given you the chance to explain yourself, Captain. But make no mistake, *I do not trust you.*"

And she probably never would.

A disquieting feeling fell over Lucenna and the others. She glanced down at the sachet clutched tightly in Dyna's fist, made of dark green velvet, embroidered with flowers in golden threads.

In the center lay the rune for dissipation.

A powerful rune.

A spell breaker.

They had each sewn one the night Dyna expressed her worry about protecting her mind. She had carried the sachet everywhere she went for fear King Yoel would attempt to erase her memory again. But never could any of them have ever imagined Cassiel would be the one to do so.

What would that damn Celestial think to know his compulsion never lasted more than a few minutes? Even in her confusion, Dyna still found her sachet and regained her memories the moment he stepped out into the courtyard. She had watched him shoot into the sky in a plume of blue flames, leaving her with the reality of what he had done.

Naturally, they were all furious with him, but how Dyna felt, Lucenna could only imagine.

"I know…" He searched Dyna's face a moment before saying softly, "I understand the pain you feel, and I am sorry for that."

Not only because Klyde was also left behind, but because he had never fallen under Cassiel's compulsion. The magic imbued in his mercenary jacket had protected him.

Dyna's chair screeched on the floor as she jerked to her feet. She turned away for the door as if needing to flee the crack his words had cleaved through her carefully formed armor. The barrier on her magic was stronger than the last one had ever been, but her emotions were so potent right now, Lucenna thought she almost felt a flicker of her Essence.

Dyna paused when she took the doorknob. "When you say you have the means to kill him…"

"It's the only weapon that will, no matter how powerful he becomes," Klyde said. "I hope that will be enough to buy my way into your fellowship."

"Show it to them. If they can confirm what you are implying, I will consider allowing you to join us." Then Dyna slipped out of the room.

Lucenna wanted to go after her, Zev too, but Rawn shook his head slightly. She probably didn't want them around her right now.

They had a task to focus on.

Lucenna crossed her arms as she studied the captain. He kept his expression neutral. During the questioning, Klyde had been perfectly still, but he couldn't quite prevent one of his knees from restlessly bouncing now. The only sign he was nervous about being left to her devices.

"I like you like this," Lucenna said. "All tied up."

His mouth lifted in a half smile, making one of his dimples appear. "Oh, I'm quite sure. Would you like me to beg you to release me?"

"Perhaps I'd like to torture you a bit first."

"Oh? *Tempting.*" He flashed her a wry grin.

The sight of it only infuriated her more. Gods, it was humiliating how close he had come to seducing her.

It didn't take much.

Only a smile and the kind of attention that made her feel seen. He knew how to say the right thing to get his way, and he was doing it now.

Electricity danced along her arms at the thought of singeing that ridiculously handsome face.

But Rawn frowned at her disapprovingly. "My lady."

She glowered. *Honorable elf.*

"You're angry with me," Klyde stated the obvious.

"Oh, I am far past angry," she hissed through her teeth.

At least things between them were now clear.

Lucenna flicked a finger to release him from his bonds. Though she took her time and made sure the magic chafed him a bit.

Once freed, Klyde rubbed his wrists. "Thank you."

"Thank Lord Norrlen. If it were up to me, I would have given you a few new scars."

He still had the nerve to laugh. It wasn't a jest.

Lucenna worked her jaw. "Well? Show us this weapon that can kill an immortal."

"I'm still not convinced he's a Skelling," Zev growled, the words rumbling in the back of his throat.

Rawn canted his head. "Looks can be deceiving, my friend."

13

"I suppose you can say I am human. Mostly. Like the wee lass, my ancestry is somewhat … peculiar." Klyde headed for the unused bed and crouched by the old wooden chest set by the footboard. "Skellings were powerful dark fae in their time." His eyes flickered to Lucenna. "And they were known to have a penchant for murderous women."

She gritted her teeth, containing the urge to murder him for saying such a thing in front of the others.

"What happened to them?" Zev asked.

"It's not really known for sure." Klyde lifted the chest's lid and sorted through whatever was inside. "Most believe they died out during the Dark War against the Shadow God, also known as the Endless Night. Others believe the Skelling tribe retreated deep into the Frost Lands when their chief died. They were powerful, wild things, especially when they shifted into their hawk forms. But the half-breeds with human blood, who couldn't shift or fly, joined civilization."

"Humans mated with Skellings?" Lucenna asked incredulously. She imagined them as ugly, bird-like creatures with beaked faces and feathered bodies.

"It's not mentioned in most of Azure's history books, but the first union came to be over a thousand years ago," Klyde said, his tone taking on a mysterious note. "When the Queen of the Everfrost, wife of the Ice Phoenix, married her sister, Ansa Morkhàn, to the son of the Skelling Chief." Klyde bore a satisfied smile at the shock on their faces. "It was to bring peace to the land. But Ansa's grandchildren were not born with wings and couldn't survive with the tribe, so they returned to the Morkhàn clan. That's where their descendants remained, to one day become the heirs of Old Tanzanite Keep." Standing, Klyde faced them, holding a large object wrapped in a frayed white cloth. "And from there comes my family line."

Despite the fire in the hearth, she suddenly felt colder, like whatever secret hid beneath the cloth made the temperature drop in the room.

Lucenna didn't move, and her heart beat faster as she watched Klyde slowly unwrap the cloth. Nestled inside was a long black blade, but not one made of steel. It was curved, fashioned with a rough handle. The circumference thinned along its length toward the sharp, pointed end.

A Skelling talon.

CHAPTER 3

Dynalya

Dyna stepped out into the hall, and the door thudded shut behind her. It took every effort to control her shaky breaths. Why was Klyde apologizing for what *that one* had done to her? Gods, she couldn't even think of his name without her entire body spasming with pain. She shut her eyes and willed away the tears threatening to spill.

Stumbling down the hall, Dyna headed toward her bedroom but paused at the threshold.

She hated that room.

Her mate was gone. He had erased himself. He took everything that was his and everything he ever gave her. Her crown was gone, her gowns, her ring, her sword, even the headboard with his scorched handprints. He removed every trace of himself, including his scent.

But her memories? She still had those.

Leave you? That will never happen...

Liar.

Dyna took a step in but could go no further. The curtains were drawn against the sun, leaving the room dark and gray. His ghost remained, regardless of all his efforts. Because she saw him in every corner and heard his voice in the shadows as if he were still there.

"All but a dream," she whispered to the empty space. *Now we have to wake up.*

Soft light shone from the edges of the nightstand drawer. Dyna pulled it open, finding her crystal necklace glowing on a bed of black feathers.

The feathers were the one thing he hadn't known she kept. Dyna banished away the reminder of how she got them, refusing to think about the last night they were together. But the necklace—that had been left behind on purpose. He had fabricated a new memory of her father giving it to her instead.

How absurd.

She couldn't stand to wear it anymore.

Dyna slammed the drawer shut so hard it rattled.

Glancing at the scorched floor, she smirked bitterly at the false memory used to explain it. What other memories had he planted?

Dyna retreated into the brightly lit corridor. Golden sunlight streamed through the tall windows and spread across the floor. It was a new day and a new life.

Her only purpose now was to reach Mount Ida at any cost once the snow melted. If that included a tentative alliance with the Captain of the Skelling Mercenaries, she would do it. Because nothing else mattered.

The steady clack of her boots rebounded against the walls as she wandered down the corridor. Whatever the past, her focus would only be her future. That required recovering her magic first.

Dyna looked down at her hands as she tried to call on her Essence. But it was contained tightly behind a thick wall. Solid and heavy, without a single crack.

She broke the barrier before. She would do it again.

Eventually, Dyna found herself on the fourth floor in front of King Yoel's bedchamber. The door was slightly ajar. Icy air whistled past the thin opening, caressing her cheeks.

She didn't know why she came here.

Maybe she subconsciously searched for signs of him. Maybe she only needed confirmation that some part of the dream had been real. But what could be more real than the remains of her shattered soul?

All the pieces had scattered like glass at her feet, and she would never put them back together again.

Dyna hesitated before pushing on the door. It creaked loudly as it slowly swung open. The harsh wind wailed through the broken windows like a tortured spirit, sending a shiver down her back.

The room was destroyed.

Furniture lay broken, tattered curtains billowed in the wind, with strewn glass and torn books everywhere. Her eyes fell on a dark red stain on the floor by the open balcony doors.

Dyna's aching heart withered further as she imagined King Yoel cut down. Zev had told her Amriel had killed him. But she had no false memory of this room. There was no attempt to hide what happened here.

He had been in too much of a hurry to leave.

Or he hated this room as much as she hated theirs and couldn't stand to be in it, even to clean up the evidence of his father's assassination.

If Yoel had lived, would things have turned out differently?

Sighing, Dyna turned to go, but she noticed something at the foot of the bed. A long rectangular box wrapped in brown paper. An envelope was tucked in the twine. She knew immediately what it was and who it was for.

I'm sorry, King Yoel. I won't be able to give him your gift after all.

And yet Dyna knelt to retrieve the box when something else caught her eye. Beneath an overturned chair, the edge of something glinted in the light. She moved the chair and sucked in a soft breath at the sight of a flat silver bowl, scalloped like a seashell. Dyna carefully picked up the water mirror. It felt heavy in her hands as she turned it over. Iridescent mother-of-pearl lined the inside.

How could Lord Jophiel leave this behind?

Dyna stood at the rush of footsteps thudding down the hall. Soon her friends entered the room.

"Here you are," Zev said with a sigh of relief. It wasn't as if she could go anywhere else. "What are you doing here?"

"I'm not sure..." Dyna replied, thoughtfully frowning at the mirror. But coming here may have been a good thing, after all.

"What is that, my lady?" Rawn asked her.

"Nothing of importance." Dyna turned to them. "Well? Does he have it?"

They nodded, though Lucenna looked furious.

"He has a dagger honed from the talon of a Skelling," Rawn confirmed.

Dyna looked out to the sleepy town of Skelling Rise and smiled. "Good."

17

Tarn wasn't immortal yet, nor did he have Jökull's full power, so they may not need the talon. But it would be her contingency plan in case he made it to the island before her.

It was about time she got ahead of her enemies.

"Don't tell me you're truly considering his request," Lucenna said.

"I am."

Zev frowned. "Why?"

"Because he may help us turn the tide against Tarn," Dyna said, watching the snow flurries drifting down.

"I don't like it."

She closed her eyes against the sharp wind streaming through the windows, letting it blow against her numb cheeks. "You don't have to like it, Zev. This is happening whether you agree or not."

Before, others told her where to go and what to do. They told her what she was capable of and what she lacked. Letting others decide her path is what brought her here.

Well, she was making the decisions now.

"This is a bad idea," Lucenna said. "We can't trust him."

Dyna whirled around, snarling through her teeth, *"I trust no one."*

It didn't occur to her how venomous the words sounded until she saw the hurt and shock on their faces.

"I'm sorry." Her voice broke, and she rushed to them with her arms extended. "Of course, I don't mean you. You're all I have."

They gathered her in an embrace, and she buried her face in Zev's chest. His warm arms wrapped around her. "You won't leave me, will you?" she whispered.

Because she couldn't withstand losing anyone else.

He squeezed her tight. "Never."

Come back... Dyna cried out, but she couldn't give sound to the words. *Please stay!*

Her voice was locked away in her throat as he walked away from her. She threw out her hand, but her fingers missed the edge of his black wings by inches.

Don't leave me!

He walked away and not once did he look back. Her blurred vision stayed on his retreating form, her cries echoing around her.

His wings caught the fading light as he stepped out of their bedroom into the hallway, and the door began to creak close. Once it shut, it would be the end of them.

Wild desperation took over, and Dyna scrambled to her feet. She ran after him, begging and weeping, reaching for him. But the room stretched and stretched, and everything tilted.

Cassiel!

She tore open the door and skidded to a halt. The threshold ended at the edge of a cliff. It stood hundreds of feet high, with only blackness at the bottom. Something rammed hard into her back and shoved her out.

There was no one left to catch her. No hope. No safety. Nothing but a void as she plummeted through the dark.

Her body slammed into the ground with a sickening crack.

Dyna jolted up in bed. Frantic screams tore from her throat as she clawed at her head, checking for breaks in her skull and the blood that wasn't there. The sensation of every bone and organ in her body bursting had followed her to consciousness.

And she felt those hands.

Firm and ruthless against her back. Thrusting her into the darkness. Over and over again.

Someone grabbed her, and she shrieked, swinging at them.

"Dyna! Dyna, it's all right!"

"No!" she wailed.

"You're all right. I've got you." Lucenna wrapped her arms around her tightly and rocked her as she sobbed. "Shhh ... it was a dream. Only a dream."

Dyna shook her head, her eyes brimming with tears. It wasn't. It wasn't merely a dream. Because it kept plaguing her every night for the past week.

It always ended the same.

With her falling to her death.

Dyna sucked several gasping breaths, shaking violently, sweat slicking her clammy skin. No matter how hard she tried to wake herself, she couldn't suppress experiencing the fall.

Not even the crystal could stave off her nightmares.

It glowed softly in the open drawer of their shared nightstand, completely useless.

Zev and Rawn stood outside of Lucenna's bedroom door, their faces grim and exhausted. None of them could have a good night's rest because of her. She couldn't bring herself to tell them what her nightmares were about.

But they knew.

Growling, her cousin stormed away. Glass shattered in the other room. "Damn him!" The walls rattled with another crash. "Damn him!" Zev's enraged shout broke at the end. "Damn him…"

Dyna curled on the bed, shutting her wet eyes. She wasn't the only one … left behind.

"I am sorry, my lady," Rawn said softly, then he went to calm Zev. But any attempts to pacify the situation were drowned out by another bang.

Lucenna cursed under her breath and quickly stepped out. "Stop it! This isn't helping her!"

"What would help her?" Zev shouted.

"Oi," Klyde joined in. "Keep your voices down. Do you mind not destroying the manor—" A crack of splitting wood cut him off.

"Tell me what would help her, Lucenna? He haunts her every hour of every damn day, and I can't protect her from it! How is she supposed to forget this?"

Maybe it would have been better to forget. To forget about Cassiel, to forget who he had been to her, to forget what he had done.

Yet she put a spell in place to remember.

And she … she regretted it. Dyna buried her face in her pillow, soaking it with her tears.

"Please," Rawn cut in. "We must calm ourselves—"

"I have no mind for your lectures right now, Lord Norrlen. I want to tear him apart for what he did to her, but I can't!"

"Oi, put the chair down. Don't break the—"

"When she's not screaming from her nightmares, she sits in her room like a ghost! She doesn't move, doesn't eat. She only stares at the sky. We all know what she's waiting for, but he's never coming back."

Dyna flinched.

Never coming back.

Another crash of glass came, with it the rise of angry shouts. Each one battered against her head, and she couldn't stand it anymore.

Snatching up the crystal necklace, she sprinted out of her room and down the hall.

"Dyna!" Zev called after her as she darted down the stairs.

Her legs pumped with every beat of her heart. She burst out of the backdoors of the manor, running into the courtyard. The harsh cold pricked her skin, the wind tugging at her nightgown and hair. The call of voices sent her sprinting into the woods. Sleet whipped past Dyna's eyes, blinding her, as she fled through the trees.

It was the same as nine years ago.

Back then, she had run toward the *Hyalus* tree.

Where was she running to now? She didn't know.

She simply had to run.

Her bare feet slid over the snow as she ran and ran from the emptiness in her chest. From the well of anger and pain. From every damn memory in that manor. She ran from the fact that she couldn't sleep without him. Couldn't breathe without him.

Dyna kept running until she reached the lake.

And she screamed.

The sound tore out of her throat as she simply let it all out with a heart-wrenching cry. Pitching back her arm, she flung the crystal necklace with all her might. It sailed through the night sky like a shooting star and plinked into the black depths of the lake.

It belonged with the version of her that died there.

With the girl who had been so in love, who had yet to be betrayed by the one person whom she thought never would.

Cassiel deserted her.

He left her stuck in a place where she couldn't follow him because he thought her too weak. He had always thought that. And every single word he had said to her that day was branded on the crushed pieces of her heart.

You don't belong in my world. I don't want you in it...

I don't want you.

I don't want you.

I don't want you.

Dyna tripped and fell against a tree, breaking down in the snow. The harsh winter air coated her lungs with every gasping sob. How could she let go of the one person who felt like home? Because without him, she was dying.

Everything hurt. Getting out of bed hurt. Every beat of her heart hurt. Living. Breathing. Time. It was all so painful, she wanted to crawl into a hole, deteriorate into the earth, and fade away.

Yet life went on, even for her.

CHAPTER 4

Zev

Zev found his cousin curled up against a tree with tears frosted on her lashes. Her lips were blue, her skin pale as snow. He wrapped a blanket around Dyna and gently picked her up. She was limp in his arms and frozen to the bone. That divine light that used to glow on her skin had dimmed to nearly nothing. It was the bond, he realized. It was deteriorating like she was. Dyna was breaking before his eyes, and he had no way to stop it.

It enraged him.

He blinked back the sting in his eyes and focused on getting her back to the manor. Lucenna and Rawn waited for them by the courtyard doors.

"Is she hurt?" Lord Norrlen asked softly.

Zev didn't answer. It was an irrelevant question because they all knew that she was. These wounds simply hadn't appeared on the outside.

Yet.

He carried her upstairs to Lucenna's room and tucked her in the extra bed. Dyna's lashes fluttered open. She didn't say a word, but her hand reached out and clutched the end of his shirt before he could take a step.

"I'm not going anywhere," Zev murmured. "Sleep. I will watch over you."

Zev settled in the wingback chair beside the bed and held Dyna's cold hand. She shivered beneath the blankets, tears rolling down her cheeks. He counted each one until her breath evened out when she fell asleep.

Would the dreams end if he stood guard over her all night? What could he do to keep her from falling apart? It was his turn to be the anchor now.

Exhaling a heavy breath, Zev leaned back. But he stilled, his nostrils flaring with many scents.

Dust, despair, and divinity.

His claws extended, his wolf eyes surfacing as he studied the shadows dancing with the balcony curtains billowing in the night breeze.

A low growl rumbled deep in his chest. "If you come near her again, I will *kill* you."

The shadows fell still, departing behind him with the faint flutter of the wind. Moonlight streamed in through the balcony doors.

And nothing about it was bright.

When Zev woke in the early dawn, Dyna's bed was empty. He leaped out of the chair. Panic rushed through his half groggy mind until he heard a distant thudding coming from outside.

He went to the balcony and saw her.

Zev rushed out of the room and made it downstairs to the courtyard doors, where Lucenna, Klyde, and Rawn were watching with concern. He pushed past them and went outside.

Dyna was fighting a tree.

Her fists beat into the bark, leaving behind red stains in the grooves. Blood dripped from her torn knuckles and down her arms. Every brutal thud echoed in the courtyard, but there was no change to her blank face.

She was trying to break through to herself, and he could see every fissure left behind. He had done the same damage, ripped at the same wounds, and drowned in the air. Because pain was better than grief.

Zev caught her wrist. "If you want to hit something, then hit me. All that hurt. That anger. Give it to me, Dyna. I can take it."

And she did.

Dyna fell into perfect formation and sparred with him.

"You're not living," Zev said as he deflected her blows. "You're floating through your days, trying to bury what you feel inside. When you do allow yourself to feel something, it's anger, but even that is stinted." He

24

took her shoulders and shook her. "Scream. Cry. Rage. Release everything you are holding inside. And live. Because I see you dying, and I know how that feels. Don't let this break you. Don't let it knock you down. Get up and fight for it!"

She knocked back his hold and hit with all her might, screaming with every attack and blow. Her powerful hooks carried everything she had. Zev bore it all until she couldn't move anymore.

Her feet staggered, and Zev caught her. He braced for more tears, but there were none left. Dyna steadied herself with a deep breath and straightened up. Her chest labored with heavy breaths, and there was only fortitude on her face. Laced with determination.

That strength made him so proud.

She wouldn't sink into the waves like he did.

She wouldn't bend.

At the same time, seeing her like this made him sad. Because his sweet cousin was no longer the same. She had endured so much pain it had sharpened her into a blade. The softness was gone, and so was her innocence. It's what Zev had wanted to protect her from, but he couldn't prevent the hardships of life any more than he could prevent time from stopping.

And he also didn't need to.

He saw the predator growing inside of Dyna, and his wolf surfaced to acknowledge her.

"We are a Pack," he said. "All we need is each other."

She nodded.

The others came to join them outside.

"All right." Lucenna's eyes glowed with magic as she faced off with Dyna. "My turn."

CHAPTER 5

Dynalya

The door to Dyna's new chambers creaked open as she stepped inside. She brought her pack and knapsack to the chair by the fireplace. The room was dark and chilly, covered in dust, but it was hers. It wasn't tainted by any memories. There were no familiar scents here but stale air.

Here she could rest.

Or maybe that was what she pretended. Because no matter how much Dyna pushed herself to forget, there was no mistaking the vacancy in her soul. How odd that in such little time, she had become dependent on it. That the presence of another could change the very essence of her being.

Her life had transformed so much since she left North Star. She had been a different person before she met him. Then there was the person she became with him. That bond had felt so permanent she hadn't imagined who she would become without him.

Dyna still didn't know.

She looked down at the object in her hands. It was wrapped in a cloth, hidden away as her own little secret. Dyna brought it to the round table set up in the corner and placed it in the center. With a gentle tug of her fingers, the cloth fell away, revealing the water mirror. There was much she could do with something like this.

She could speak to whoever she wished.

Spy on whoever she wished.

What remained of her conscience warned against going down such a path, but Dyna hardly heard it. She no longer worried about being good. Would it be so wrong to take advantage of this ... *advantage?*

She stared at the water mirror for a moment, taking in the beautiful reflections of the iridescent plating. She poured water into the bowl and added a sprinkle of salt. Her fingers slowly stirred the surface, creating several rings as she let her mind wander to the one she wanted to see.

Maybe because she was lonely or spiteful or simply reckless, she thought of *him* first. The spiraling water clouded with color until it cleared to reveal a room she'd never seen before.

And it was destroyed.

Broken furniture, torn books and scrolls, and shattered glass were scattered across the floor. Her gaze fell on the one sitting against the wall, with his head in his hands, his hair and clothes a rumpled mess. Her pulse drummed at the sight of him, her mind struggling to accept he was truly there. But he was.

His head lifted, and he looked up.

Right at her.

Dyna jerked backwards from the mirror. Her feet tripped on the edge of the rug, and she caught herself on a chair, her heart hammering against her ribs. She didn't move, didn't breathe or dare make a sound, but there was no pretending.

He saw her.

"Now, don't be shy." The sound of that cool voice sent a tremble through her chest. She inched toward the mirror and met his wintry eyes. The edge of Tarn's mouth lifted in a faint smirk. "Hello, Maiden."

THREE MONTHS LATER

CHAPTER 6

Dynalya

"Clear your mind," Rawn said as he circled her in the courtyard. "Allow your instincts to guide you."

After weeks of relentless training, Dyna had long learned to let everything else fall back beneath the surface. Her body was one with her blades. She readied her short swords and nodded.

Klyde launched at her.

She deflected his attack and spun around to parry Rawn's sword. Their blades clashed as she met them, hit for hit. A blast of purple magic came for her. Dyna ducked and rolled out of the way, leaving it to hit a tree behind her. Her blades crossed, blocking Klyde's next blow, and she spun away.

All three came at her at once.

But she had been anticipating that.

Dyna spun and delivered a kick to Lucenna's stomach, throwing her back. She dodged Rawn's next attack and fought Klyde at the same time. The sound of their blades clashing echoed through the courtyard as she advanced. She parried, knocking Rawn's weapon out of his hand. But it left her back exposed. A blade flashed at her neck, and she paused, breathing heavily.

Klyde's knife hovered a needle pin away from her pulse. "You need to watch your back, lass."

"And you should watch yours," Dyna said, prompting him to glance down at her blade fixed against his groin.

Barking a laugh, the captain stepped away, and she sheathed her weapons.

Zev came over clapping, a grin on his face. "You're ready."

The confirmation settled over them as they looked at each other. The courtyard was free of snow. Winter was over, and it was finally time to move on. They collectively decided to leave once they were ready to face the Horde waiting for them on the Bridge.

After three months of non-stop training, Dyna was confident they would make it out alive.

"When do we leave?" she asked them.

"As soon as the scouts confirm that the snow has melted from the gorge," Klyde said, wiping the sweat from his face with a towel. "Shouldn't be long now."

He took a drink from his waterskin and handed it to Lucenna, but she ignored him. Her anger hadn't thawed yet, and Dyna was beginning to suspect it was due to more than lying about his identity.

"We'll need to prepare provisions," Zev said.

"Aye. Put together a list, and I will take care of it, mate."

Eagon showed up with Tavin. Klyde went over to join them, and Zev followed as they discussed what would be needed for their departure.

"Were you trying to make me spew all over the courtyard?" Lucenna asked, rubbing her stomach. "That last kick winded me."

"Next time be quicker with your shields," Dyna shot back teasingly. "You really should learn your way around a weapon."

"You're probably right." Lucenna frowned thoughtfully at the purple currents of Essence hovering at her fingertips. "Are you able to access any more of your magic?"

Dyna sighed. "No..."

A couple of days after she woke with half of her soul, all traces of her magic were gone. This barrier was thicker and sturdier than Yoel's had been. No matter how hard Dyna tried, she hadn't been able to make even a dent in it. Lucenna had confirmed she could sense faint traces of her Essence, but the barrier hid it so well, Dyna felt as if she had none at all.

"Do not be discouraged, my lady. You have been trained by all of us," Rawn said as he approached. "You are well equipped now, regardless of magic."

She offered him a polite smile. He meant well, but their sympathy only reminded her of its absence. Spending all of winter without feeling the warmth of Essence in her veins had been like learning how to walk with only one leg.

31

Dyna glanced up at the manor. Melting snow left rivulets on the windowpanes. With the feathers she found, it gave her the means to bring down the barrier, but only temporarily. Best to save them for when she truly needed it.

"Shall we go wash up?" Lucenna asked her. "It will be dinner soon."

"Go ahead. I will meet you in a bit."

While Lucenna headed inside, Dyna retrieved her quiver and bow and moved on to target practice. She felt Rawn watching her, and she sighed.

"Lord Norrlen, I can feel you thinking again." She aimed and let loose. The arrow zoomed away and hit the center of the target perfectly. "What is on your mind?"

"Pardon. I wanted to ask how you were feeling."

"I'm fine." She shot another arrow, and it plunked next to the first.

"My lady, your hands are bleeding."

"That happens when training."

This was nothing. After everything, she had to make herself strong. Strong enough not to be left behind again.

"It will do well to rest. You've torn the calluses on your fingers. It must sting."

"The ability to endure pain is a warrior's true weapon." She nocked another arrow. "Master that, and nothing will ever hurt you."

"Who told you that?"

Dyna paused, then shot the arrow. "How about we discuss what you truly wanted to ask, Lord Norrlen?"

Rawn's hand gently rested over her grasp on the bow, and she allowed him to take it from her. From a pocket at his belt, he drew out bandages and began wrapping her bloodied fingers. "The question is the same. How are you?"

She watched him work, not wanting to look into those sympathetic eyes. "I am fine. I don't think about him anymore, if that is your worry. I have moved on."

"Have you? Or have you found a way not to think about him anymore?" Rawn looked at her knowingly, and it only made her more annoyed.

Throwing herself into training was the only thing keeping her standing now. She needed it. "Does it matter?"

He fastened the bandages in place. "The state of your heart matters, my lady. Ignoring it does not heal you."

She pulled her hand away. "Why bring this up now?"

Rawn's brow furrowed. "I know it is a difficult subject to speak of, but I am concerned about what will happen once we leave this place. Your life could still be in danger. While in Skelling Rise, we are hidden, but only because Cassiel—"

Dyna flinched.

Her entire body spasmed at the sound of his name. It had not been said aloud since he left. Hearing it now had wrenched the air out of her.

"Do not ever speak his name again," she said tightly.

Rawn dipped his head. "Forgive me..."

The silence filled the space between them, and her eyes burned with anger and humiliation. With a mere group of syllables, he had proven she wasn't as well as she claimed. Her nightmares came sparingly now, but only because she worked herself to exhaustion and limited how many hours she slept.

She could only *pretend* here.

"No, I am sorry, Lord Norrlen." Dyna rubbed her face and sighed. "When we leave...?"

Rawn cleared his throat. "When we leave, we will face many uncertainties. Tarn. The bounties. And most importantly, the Realms. He ... declared your death to his people. If they learn that you are alive..."

She inhaled an exasperated breath. "Why would my existence be of any importance to them anymore?"

Rawn blinked at her. "My lady, you are the High Queen of Hilos and the Four Celestial Realms. We know now that Lord Raziel is the perpetrator behind your attempted assassination, but we know nothing of what happened to Lord Hallel and Lord Jophiel once the Celestials retreated. The Realms may very well be in chaos as they fight over the throne, which could still hold repercussions for you. Due to, well, for..."

"Because of whom my mate used to be?" Dyna scoffed and shook her head. "I'm not part of that world anymore. I am *not* his *Queen*. He left me, so he can deal with it himself. I don't care about who sits on the throne. I was never supposed to have anything to do with their conflict."

She gathered her arrows and slung the quiver's strap over her shoulder. What became of the Realms had nothing to do with her now.

"I appreciate your concern, Lord Norrlen, but as far as the Celestials know, I'm dead. And I plan to keep it that way. The only thing I need to worry about is retrieving the Sol Medallion from Mount Ida and returning to North Star before the Shadow returns by the next winter. I have no time for anything else. I have lost too much of it already."

Rawn bore her curt response in stride. "I understand."

It was wrong to allow her agitation against someone else to fall on him. Anything that reminded her of the past only seemed to fuel her deep resentment. Still, it wasn't his fault.

"Thank you for caring about me," Dyna said in a softer tone. "There is no need to worry, though. I'll be fine." Rawn nodded, but she sensed his concern remained. "Well, I am all finished here. Shall I help you bring in the gear?"

"No, it's all right. I will see to it," Rawn said as his horse cantered over to them. He stroked Fair's white mane, murmuring to him in soft Elvish.

The wind swept through the courtyard, rippling his loose green tunic. It lifted one end, and Dyna glimpsed a marking on the right side of Rawn's lower back. A tattoo of an open bloom that matched the sigil on the pommel of his sword.

A dynalya flower, the emblem of Greenwood.

She recalled Elon's scar on the back of his hand.

"That tattoo…" Dyna said. "Do all elves have one?"

Rawn adjusted his tunic. "Yes, my lady. It serves to represent which kingdom we belong to, as there is nothing else to truly distinguish us. Most red elves tend to have dark hair, but such a thing is easily disguised with magic. Therefore, the Vale came up with the means to … mark us."

He seemed uncomfortable speaking about it, though, so she didn't ask more.

As if sensing his restlessness, Fair bumped Rawn's shoulder with his head, making him smile. *"Ot'norp asac'ne someratse, Osom'reh."*

Whatever he said seemed to make the Elvish stallion happy. She went on, listening to Fair's cheerful neighs as she strolled toward the manor.

"Good morrow!" Gale said, coming through the courtyard doors. She carried baby Gwendolyn on her hip.

"Good morrow," Dyna replied, smiling at the wee thing.

Gwendolyn had grown. She had her father's gray-blue eyes, and they lit up when she saw him.

"There's my big girl." Eagon took her from Gale's arms, swinging her up in the air.

"Be gentle with her!" his wife chastised, going after him.

Dyna passed through the doors and made her way down the hall. The sound of soft sniffling caught her attention. She found Edyth in the grand hall. The older woman looked out the windows with tears on her lashes.

"Edyth?" Dyna called. "Everything all right?"

The woman jumped a little at the sound of her voice. Her cheeks grew rosy, and she chuckled, wiping her eyes. "Oh yes, I'm fine. I've been feeling a little sentimental as of late."

Dyna hesitated to go to her. That room ... It held too many memories as well. But she ignored the thought and went to stand by her.

Edyth gazed at her son as he sparred with Klyde in the courtyard. "As long as there is a sword in Tavin's hand, he's happy. He lives for it. My first son was also a knight, but he hated it. I thought him too soft, that perhaps I had spoiled him. But I see now his heart wasn't in it. I sometimes wonder if our lives would have been different if we didn't force him to serve. But Von died out there defending the town, alongside his father and sister."

Dyna stilled at the name. She met Edyth's sea-green eyes, and it all became clear. She wasn't Tavin's mother, but his *grandmother*. It shouldn't have shocked her the way it did. She merely had not considered who the woman was to the boy.

"I've been told you know who Tavin's father is." Edyth faced her. "Can I ask a favor of you, Dyna? Please ... please make sure he never finds out."

The woman gently squeezed her hand without waiting for a response and went outside to join her family.

The request circled Dyna's mind as she took the stairs to the third floor. It was a dire secret to keep. But it wasn't only Tavin they wanted to keep it from.

But they didn't need to worry.

She had other plans.

Entering her room, Dyna locked the door behind her. She leaned her bow and quiver against the chair's backrest by the fire and went to her small round table by the windows. The sunlight spilling past the curtains gilded the water mirror's iridescent plate. Dyna opened the small wooden container set beside it, revealing white grains of salt. After pouring some water in the mirror, she sprinkled in a pinch of salt and stirred with her finger. Rings spread across the surface as it clouded with color. Eventually, it cleared. She studied the image of a room with a view of the sea and a man sitting at a desk.

"I have no time for conversation right now, Maiden. I'm busy," Tarn said as he flipped through a thick tome.

Dyna couldn't see the pages from her position. It must be something important to hold his rapt attention. Perhaps he was researching another detail of his elusive plan.

She leaned back in her seat and crossed her legs. "Oh really? Has your search at last been fruitful?"

Tarn frowned as he straightened. "I don't know why I told you about that."

"Merely admit that you enjoy these conversations. They are the best part of your day."

"I think you're the one who looks forward to them," he retorted. "Not much to do on Hermon Ridge while stuck in mountains of snow, I gather."

That's where he assumed she was. There was no need to correct him.

"You're right, there isn't." Dyna propped her elbow on the table, leaning on her fist. "And there isn't much for a wanted felon to do but stay out of sight while trying to search for this mysterious Druid." Tarn may have had a little too much wine on the night he told her about that, but he had not been drunk enough to tell her more. And she knew better than to tell him she knew exactly how to find Leoake. "If you share with me why you need him, I may be able to help." Tarn looked up from his reading, and she shrugged. "The snow is melting."

"And?"

"You have something I want, Tarn, and I have something you want."

"Pray tell, what is that?"

Dyna arched an eyebrow. "Mount Ida's location," she said pointedly. "Release Von and the others, and in exchange, I will tell you where to find it. That's the deal."

Tarn returned to flipping pages. "Odd how adamant you were about never telling me where it is. Yet now you're willing to trade that valuable knowledge for mere slaves."

"My priorities have changed."

"So have mine."

The statement made her brow furrow. Did he not care about Mount Ida anymore?

Tarn canted his head as he observed her. "I think the one you really want is Von. Why is he so important to you?"

"I'll buy out his life-servant contract. I have the gold," Dyna said, ignoring the question.

Well, her fortune was stuck at the bottom of the cascades, but they would retrieve it soon enough.

"He is not for sale," Tarn said nonchalantly, flipping another page.

"Not even for the map?"

"You think I would give up my commander for a piece of parchment?"

"I think you would give up anything to accomplish your goal. At the moment, our interests coincide."

Tarn shut the book. He stood, eyeing her a moment, then moved on to rummage through a stack of scrolls in a chest, letting her words hang in the air.

"Well?" she pressed. "Do we have a deal?"

"No."

"At least let me speak to him." She inwardly groaned, instantly regretting saying that. Her desperation was showing.

Going all winter without catching sight of Von left her with an odd restlessness. It was unusual not to see him around, and she couldn't help but feel worried.

Tarn's pale eyes narrowed. "We may be cordial, but you will not make demands of me."

Dyna glowered. "Then I suppose you will continue to search aimlessly for the Druid. Goodbye now."

"Maiden."

She paused.

Tarn set down his papers. "Why don't we end this little dance and tell me what you truly want?"

Dyna shifted in her seat. "What do you mean?"

"For what other reason are we having these *conversations?* You didn't contact me at random merely to pass the time. You want something, yet you are too prideful to admit it." His piercing eyes held hers, and she felt the air thin. "Say it."

Dyna grew serious as they stared at each other. He was right. There was something she wanted. It had been forming in the back of her mind since the day she spoke to him through the water mirror, festering like her own dirty secret.

"I want to join you."

CHAPTER 7

Lucenna

"When do you leave Skelling Rise?"

Lucenna tossed another pair of boots into her enchanted bag, and they vanished into the depths. "At dawn tomorrow. Rawn and the others are discussing it now."

Lucien looked at her worriedly from her orb resting on the desk. "Please be careful. The journey through the Bridge is perilous, and I fear the Enforcers catching wind of you."

"We plan to leave Urn before they notice me. We are more than ready to face the trolls now. Once we reach Dwarf Shoe, we will set sail for Mount Ida."

What could possibly go wrong? She wouldn't dare ask it aloud, lest she curse herself with bad luck.

"Good. That eases some of my worry."

Lucenna heard something in his tone that made her pause to look at her brother as he kneaded his temples. Lucien looked tired, and shadows had formed around his eyes.

"How are you, though?" she asked.

"I'm fine." Lucien leaned back in his chair with a sigh and ran a hand through his short, white hair. He had cut it recently. She liked the new look but couldn't help but feel it was his way of starting anew.

"How is Princess Ava?" Lucenna asked softly.

Lucien's lilac eyes dimmed. His past love was a sore subject, but he offered her a faint smile, regardless. "She's well. Ava and Ender ... well..." He took a deep breath and expelled it slowly. "They're expecting."

"Oh!" Lucenna exclaimed excitedly but caught herself and said more nonchalantly, "Oh..."

"It's great news," Lucien said with a feeble chuckle. "For us especially. As first to bear an heir, this means Ender will ascend as the Archmage once his child is born. The hunt for you is nearly over."

Lucenna bit her lip so she wouldn't smile so much. She thought of her freedom first, before a distant thought reminded her Everest would no longer be obligated to the throne. But there were others who were desperate to keep him on it.

"Not necessarily." She straightened. "How far along is she?"

"Three moons."

Lucenna placed a hand over her medallion, and she grew anxious. "Father won't give up while there is still time. He will send many more Enforcers as possible to bring me back."

Her brother nodded. "It's best if you leave the country quickly."

"I will."

Lucien got to his feet as he slipped on his blue robes. "You're doing well, though?"

"Yes."

"And how is Dyna?"

Lucenna sighed and pressed on the growing tension pinching her forehead. She had been doing that a lot lately. Her worry for Dyna weighed on her mind. She was different now. Naturally. Zev said to give her time, but Dyna only seemed to worsen. She was more irritable. Quieter. And she didn't seem to be sleeping. Sometimes Lucenna heard her at night, muttering to herself.

"As well as she can be."

Lucien looked at her knowingly, having been jilted himself. It wasn't Lucenna's place to tell her brother everything that had transpired between them. All she could share was that Cassiel had left, and it had been hard on Dyna.

"The captain will be joining you, then?"

She was grateful for the change in subject, but not for the topic. "Unfortunately," Lucenna grumbled as she slammed grimoires into her bag next.

She, of course, did her best to convince them otherwise, but Dyna was set on letting Klyde join them. Lucenna suggested stealing the Skelling dagger, but the others had warmed up to him. Apparently, Dyna thought he could be useful.

"Is he so terrible?" her brother asked.

A knock came at her open door, and she scowled at the man in question. "Beyond reprehensible."

Klyde's blue eyes danced in the low light, and he leaned against her door frame, crossing his arms. A half smile played on his lips, making those damn dimples appear.

"Did something happen between you two?" Lucien asked.

Lucenna flushed, and she ground her jaw. "Nothing worth mentioning." But Klyde didn't leave, so she hissed at him quietly, "What? I don't have time to waste on you today. I'm busy."

"I see that." His smile widened at her glare. Lucenna hated that it made her stomach knot.

"Well, I would like to meet him before you leave," Lucien continued.

Klyde swept into her room before she could answer. "I suppose now would be a perfect time to introduce myself," he said, approaching the orb. "Hello, there. I'm Klyde Morken, Captain of the Skelling Mercenaries."

"Oh ... hello," her brother replied, blinking at him in surprise. "I am Lucien Astron, Lucenna's brother."

She rushed to him, hissing under her breath. "What are you doing?"

"A pleasure." Klyde took a seat at her desk, ignoring her. His serious expression was perfectly composed. "I have been meaning to speak to you for some time now, Lucien."

"Have you?"

"Lucenna has made me aware of the situation in the Magos Empire. I am sorry to hear of the prejudices your people are suffering through. There is not much that I can do about that; however, I would like to offer you aid by way of sanctuary."

Lucien's eyes widened. Speechless, Lucenna stared at Klyde, too.

After their near kiss during the party, they hadn't broached the subject again. She had forgotten about it, assuming the offer had been part of his ploy to seduce her.

"Well, that is a generous proposal, though very unexpected. My sister has made no mention of this to me," Lucien said, looking at her questioningly.

"We had discussed it in passing..." Lucenna said distractedly. "I didn't think he meant it..."

Klyde met her eyes. "I do not give my word lightly, lass. I will never say something I don't mean." There seemed to be a second meaning in there only for her. He faced her brother again. "My town is well secluded on Troll Bridge with a stone wall over sixty feet high, and it's been spelled to cloak magic, thanks to your sister. We have plenty of space to take in refugees. Now that winter is at an end, ships can make their way to Skelling Rise through the northern bay through the Saxe Sea. Your people will be safe here."

"I don't know what to say."

"A thank you is enough."

Lucien cleared his throat and schooled his expression. "Of course, the Liberation thanks you, as do I. But I assume you wish for compensation, Captain. What is your price?"

"That is not necessary."

Wariness crossed Lucien's face. "You are a mercenary. Surely there is a price. We wouldn't feel comfortable accepting such a significant offer without offering something in return."

Klyde glanced at her again, and a sly gleam entered his gaze. Heat rushed through her cheeks. Lucenna gave him a scathing look, silently warning that if he dared to make an unseemly comment to her brother, she would—

"Then, if it's not too much to ask, perhaps Lucenna wouldn't mind casting a warding spell over Skelling Rise," Klyde said to Lucien. "Keeping our presence hidden here is a top priority for us both. It would do well to visibly cloak the town as well."

Lucenna smiled at him sharply. Of course. He had asked about a warding spell before. She had warned that he wouldn't be able to afford her services, yet here he found a way to get them.

What else could she expect from a mercenary? All he cared about was getting what he wanted.

"That's fair." Lucien looked at her questioningly. "What do you think?"

She crossed her arms and shrugged. "I suppose."

In the end, it didn't matter as long as her people were safe.

"Captain, thank you. This is great news. It has been years since we have been able to allocate our people safely. This will bring new hope. I must inform the Liberation at once so they may begin preparations. I will be in contact again once we know more." Lucien stood and nodded to her. "Take care, Lu."

The glowing orb cleared. She and Klyde held a long stare.

"You have some nerve," she finally said. "You ambush me in my room and go around me to bring your offer to my brother, knowing he would accept. Merely to get your town warded."

Klyde frowned. "I suggested the warding spell, but we both know you would have placed one for the safety of your people."

That was beside the point.

"Let's not pretend this isn't what you wanted. It's all about gain for you," she snapped.

"Oi." He lifted his hands placatingly. "Calm down, love."

"Don't tell me to calm down," she hissed.

"If I wanted a reward, I could have easily requested a fortune from your brother." He sighed. "I don't understand. Last we spoke of it you were grateful for the offer."

"Exactly. *Last we spoke.*"

He shook his head. "Did you assume everything we discussed was a lie?"

She didn't answer. Didn't need to.

Klyde leaned on the desk and rubbed his face. "Look—"

"No, *you* look. I don't care what you have to say or whatever excuse you wish to construct. I don't trust you, Klyde. You flirted and seduced me with your stupid jests and flimsy charm to get close to us and learn our secrets. You *lied* to me." Lucenna clenched her teeth as magic sparked on her skin. "I will never believe anything you have to say again."

His blue eyes softened as he searched her face. "I thought if I gave you some time, your anger would have lessened some, but I see now there was something I should have done from the beginning." Klyde stood, his height towering over her. It reminded her of the night they were both right here in this same spot together. "I am sorry, Lucenna."

She stared at him, completely taken aback.

He stepped closer. "I am sorry I wasn't honest with you. I didn't enjoy hiding myself from you or the others. The truth is, I find it difficult to speak about my past. If you can understand that."

Lucenna looked away, because she of all people did understand.

Klyde sighed as he surveyed the room, and his eyes fell to the bedpost against the wall, where a name had been carved. "This was my bedroom once. I shared it with Tarn during my youth. Our father was a hard man, and this place might have been the only sanctuary we had from his wrath on the days he had too much to drink. Sometimes ... it wasn't enough, but Tarn had been there to protect us from the brunt of it ... until he decided he was finished with that."

He stared blankly at the walls, and she sensed he had fallen back into that time. Sharing that part of himself softened Lucenna's anger. She imagined what it was like for him as a boy, bearing his father's beatings.

Klyde rubbed his face again. "I share no kinship with him anymore, but admitting we share blood isn't something that is generally taken well.

It kept me from revealing the truth, because, well, I wanted to evade the confrontation that inevitably happened."

They fell quiet for a moment, and she could almost feel the memories here. Maybe that was a reason the room always felt so cold.

"Does your family know?" Lucenna asked him.

His brow creased questioningly.

"That Tarn is alive."

His mouth thinned. "Everyone knows ... except Tavin. It must remain that way."

"Because you don't want him to know you plan to kill his father?"

Klyde stared blankly at the twin beds. "All I want is to prevent Tarn from accomplishing his plans. If stopping him requires taking his life, then so be it." He faced her. "Regardless of all the lies, my intentions were never impure." He took her hand. "Not with you. I ... wanted to tell you that before we leave. So you know where I stand."

Lucenna looked down at their linked hands, and her pink diamond ring caught the light. She pulled away. "But it's irrelevant, isn't it? You are who you are, and I am who I am."

He was only a stranger, joining them for a brief time. She had her mission and ... a betrothed awaiting her return. It didn't matter what she might have felt or what his intentions were, because nothing could come of it.

Lucenna turned away and resumed packing in the silence. Sighing, Klyde turned for the door.

"I understand why you lied," Lucenna said without looking at him. His footsteps paused. "But as of today, that is the last lie you will ever tell me."

She hadn't fully forgiven him yet, but it was a start.

"You have my word."

She didn't move until Klyde's steps retreated into the hall. His voice had been faint, only four words to bridge the gap between them.

But somehow, she had heard his smile all the same.

CHAPTER 8

Rawn

R awn knew he was dreaming when he found himself listening to Aerina's dulcet voice as she read aloud to herself. He stood at his post in his Castle Guard uniform in the courtyard below, near her terrace. King Leif, his Kingsguard, and his father walked past, discussing the garrison report. Generally a topic of interest while he was bored on duty, but his attention had focused on something else now.

"Princess," Aerina's lady's maid called. "It's time for your Magi studies."

"Coming!" Her soft footsteps padded away as she went inside.

He sighed.

A sudden force swept Rawn's legs out from under him. He hit the ground with an *oomph*. Pushing up his helmet, he glared up at his sister.

Nisa grinned, looking rather pleased with herself in her imposing Royal Guard uniform. Her blonde hair was pulled away from her face in a coronet braid, exposing the Greenwood emblem of a dynalya flower tattooed on her cheek.

When an elf came of age, they chose where to place their tattoo, and his sister had proudly chosen her face.

The sound of boisterous laughter had him glowering at his best friend standing behind him. Sylar held his stomach as he laughed, the sunlight catching over the golden embroidery of his grand velvet green Magi apprentice robes.

"Oh, find this amusing, do you?" Rawn tripped him, and Sylar fell beside him, still snickering.

Nisa helped them up. "If you had been on alert, instead of swooning over the princess, you would have heard me coming."

"I think you mean I would not have noticed Sylar using magic to conceal your presence." Rawn brushed the dust from his armor and shook out his dark green cape. "Nor was I swooning."

"He was swooning." She nudged Sylar. "Was he not?"

"Desperately."

Rawn feigned to strike him, and Sylar ducked behind Nisa, snickering. As annoyed as he was, it was fortunate they didn't tease him in front of the princess. Worst yet, their father. God of Urn, he could only imagine how his father would react to learn Rawn dared pine after her like a lovesick fool.

But he was never confused about his place in the world.

"How long do you plan to remain a castle guard, Rawn?" Nisa leaned against the wall next to him. "You should be a captain in the army now."

"At best, second lieutenant," Sylar added. He posted beside him on his other side. His warm brown eyes caught the light as he shrugged, his hair resembling the color of acorns. Sylar had more delicate features that gave him a graceful beauty the court ladies both envied and admired. "You surpassed all of us during training. You don't belong here."

"If that were true, I would not be here." Rawn tried not to show how much it bothered him. To be demoted from a sergeant to a low rank castle guard in front of his entire unit was a great shame, but even more so for it to be done by his father. "The General deemed it so."

"You *allowed* Father to send you here." Nisa crossed her arms. "You are a fine warrior. It is clear to all who have seen you wield a blade. One day you will be a part of the Ranger Regiment, but until then, you belong with him on the battlefield."

The irony was that Rawn had never dreamed of becoming a soldier. Nonetheless, that was the card he drew in life when born to a military family who loyally served Greenwood for centuries.

His father had already deemed him a disappointment when he entered the world at the expense of his mother's life. Rawn had worked hard to please him, to train until the blade was an extension of himself. But when he had been at last promoted to lead a garrison, it had been at the expense of many lives.

Rawn shook his head. "Soldiers died, Nisa..."

The garrison had only stood for one day beneath his command. How could he have known that red elves would attack in the middle of the night? Most of his men died in their beds before ever realizing what had happened.

Nisa looked out at the sky. "We all die one day. A warrior's wish is to die well."

Sighing, Sylar leaned his head against the wall. It exposed the edge of the emblem tattooed on the back of his neck. "Such is the life of a soldier. The cost of war is always blood."

Better it had been his own.

Rawn had been the only survivor, simply because the spear had missed his heart by two inches. Sometimes, he dreamed of that black spear coming for him, yet he couldn't see the face of the one who threw it. "If the General believes I best serve the King guarding the castle, that is what I will do. I will not disgrace the Norrlen House again."

His sister scowled. "The only disgrace I see is—"

She and Sylar abruptly stood at attention at the approach of Princess Aerina, prompting Rawn to do the same. She strolled past the open veranda that faced the garden with her lady's maid. Rawn and the others quickly bowed.

He listened to the soft sounds of footsteps as they entered the courtyard, her slippers coming to a stop before them.

"Good morrow," Aerina's light voice greeted. "How is your mare doing, Nisa? I heard she gave birth to a colt a fortnight ago."

"She did, your highness," Nisa said. "A strong one, too."

"That's wonderful. I see you're back on your feet after your magic skirmish in the training yard, Sylar. Has the burn on your leg healed?"

"It's healed up perfectly thanks to your poultice, princess. Thank you."

Rawn felt it when Aerina's gaze landed on him next. "Good day, Rawn."

A shallow breath caught in his lungs at the sound of his name. He bowed deeper. "Princess."

A long pause followed as he felt her gaze linger on his down turned head. He didn't dare look up.

"I will escort you to the study hall, princess," Nisa said after a pause. "Magi Master Eldred must be waiting."

"Right, of course. Will you walk with us, Sylar? Tell me more about your studies on the Melodyam Falls."

"I would be glad to." He joined her. "I was able to retrieve samples last week. I aim to prove those waters have absorbed the natural magic found in the earth there. I believe it has to do with..."

As their voices faded, Rawn straightened. But to his surprise, Aerina had lingered by the archway into the hall. Her light green gown fluttered in the passing wind as she looked at him, waves of gold-spun blond hair pinned beneath her circlet of gold undulated in the wind. The sunlight danced in her blue eyes with her smile, leaving him frozen there like a fool.

"Sir Norrlen." A guard marched forward and saluted to him as though he still held rank. "You have been summoned."

Rawn frowned, wondering what for. He pondered on it as he walked through the castle and worried what it could mean. The scent of the dynalya flowers wrapped around the terrace columns kept him company until he came upon the heavy doors of the throne room. The castle guards posted there opened the doors for him. His father stood by the short set of stairs leading to a platform of stone that faced the room. Upon the throne, was the King of Greenwood.

Rawn woke up with a soft start.

He slowly straightened up where he had been napping on the dining room table. Speaking about Greenwood and emblems had stirred up old memories. That had been so long ago. He had barely been a man then.

Rawn sighed down at the page filled with script. It rested beside two envelopes.

He took a deep breath and rose to his feet, feeling some weight lift off his shoulders. His pack was already prepared in the chair beside him. He had been up early before dawn, too restless to get much sleep. So he had come down to write one more letter.

He stared at his handwriting. The last line was heavier than all the rest. *Sincerely yours.*

Were letters truly enough anymore?

One year, he had told her.

It would only take him one year to find the Dragon's Fang.

How naïve he had been.

Time was plenty for their kind. Rawn had assumed he would return before harvest, right as his son would take his first steps.

It was that heedless confidence that led him to accept such a mission. Or perhaps he was eager to show his gratitude toward King Leif for allowing him to marry Aerina.

Whatever his reasons, Rawn had given an oath to not return until he found the sword. He never imagined it would inadvertently force him away from home for this long. His wife was left with the burden of their estate, left to raise their son alone. Raiden was a young man now. If he lost his place in Aerina's heart, she had good reason.

The door to the dining hall creaked open, and Lucenna peered inside. "Ah, I found you, Lord Norrlen."

"Pardon, were you looking for me?"

"Yes, we are ready to go."

That was all he needed to hear for the damper on his thoughts to lift. He was at last leaving Skelling. He would make it home this year. Even if his wife and son resented him, he would *see* them again.

He would come home.

Rawn couldn't help smiling at the thought.

"You're happy to leave, aren't you?" Lucenna said.

"Aren't we all?" Zev stepped in with Dyna.

"Enough time has been spent here," Rawn said, and they all glanced at the large open windows displaying the forest behind the manor, clear of snow. When they arrived, they were different people. After nearly four months here, they were leaving stronger. "Skelling Rise gave us shelter when we needed it, and we are thankful for that. Nevertheless, it is time to continue with our journey. There is much to be done."

"Then why are we standing around here?" Zev chuckled. "Let's go!"

Lucenna laughed. "Right behind you."

Rawn gathered his belongings and tucked the envelopes away in his cloak. After what happened last time, he didn't want to risk opening another portal. It was best to get a hold of a crystal so he could open one himself.

They headed out into the hallway together. Zev and Lucenna stepped out the front door, but Dyna lingered behind. She gazed into the grand hall for a moment. Rawn assumed she was perhaps remembering the day King Yoel had arrived, or another memory of the one she regretted remembering.

No ... it wasn't that.

Leaving this manor behind was the last connection she had to Cassiel. It was where so much happened. Good and bad. It was bitterly nostalgic.

Because he'd known, secretly, some part of her must have been waiting for his return. But Cassiel knew they would eventually leave this place when spring arrived. So if he didn't return by now, he never would.

Dyna wiped all emotion from her face and turned toward him. She was dressed in her leather armor, strapped with a short sword, knives, and her bow.

Gone was the Maiden.

In her place stood a warrior.

Dyna strode past him and went outside without looking back.

A weight settled in his stomach like a stone. The indifference on her face, the remoteness of her presence, saddened Rawn to see it shadow the spirit of the one who used to shine like the sun.

This should have been a good day. A happy one even, but the cloudy sky matched the mood.

Gale, Tavin, and Edyth were waiting to say goodbye. They each hugged Klyde.

"When will you return?" Tavin asked him.

"Only the Gods know, lad. Perhaps within the year, at best."

Rawn heard an echo of him saying the same and inwardly winced. At least Klyde had not made any promises.

"I don't understand why I can't go with you."

Klyde mussed his hair. "You're not finished with your training yet."

His nephew jerked his head back. "This isn't a mercenary mission, uncle. You're not off to fight in someone else's war, so it's hardly dangerous."

"It's the trolls I'm worried about, Tavin."

The boy's mouth pursed. "I'm the best cadet on the squad. You've said so yourself. I can hold my own out there."

"One day you'll be ready to cross the Bridge, but not yet. For now, I need you to keep the town safe while I'm gone, aye?"

Tavin stormed away into the manor.

Edyth smiled apologetically. "That is his way of saying he will miss you."

"I know," Klyde sighed. "Keep an eye on him."

"We all will," Gale said, handing Eagon a sack of food when he approached. He kissed her temple and the sleeping baby in her arms.

A unit of mercenaries on horses waited for them by the path into town. Zev helped Lucenna and Dyna climb onto two spare horses as Klyde went to Onyx.

At Rawn's whistle, Fair cantered over, and he mounted the saddle.

"We will escort them to the west gorge," Eagon told his wife. "I will return in eight days."

Crossing the bridge on horseback would significantly cut down their travel time. It would also make it easier to escape the Horde if needed.

She smiled at him shakily. "Don't keep me waiting too long."

They shared a long embrace before the lieutenant pulled away and mounted his horse next to Klyde's. At his signal, the men rode out, and the girls followed with a black wolf on their heels.

The captain spared one last look at the manor. Rawn followed his stare to the window where Tavin watched them.

The boy's pale eyes were hard. Resentful.

For a moment, he saw the shadow of his own son standing there in the window, scorning him for leaving him behind.

Klyde lifted his hand in a wave, but Tavin turned away and vanished into the shadows.

Sighing, he gave Rawn a nod. They rode quickly to catch up to the others, kicking up mud as they took the main path through town. The mercenaries on the wall blew the horn in farewell as they rode through the gates, at last leaving Skelling Rise behind.

They rode steadily and quietly on the Bridge, careful not to make more sound than they needed to. The mercenaries were on constant alert, communicating with nothing more than a look or hand signal.

Klyde had warned them that spring was the most dangerous time to cross Troll Bridge, for the beasts had woken and they would be famished.

The captain led them on a detour an hour south to the cascades where Rawn had fallen to search for their lost gold. They would need it to fund the rest of their journey. Unfortunately, when they arrived, there was nothing left but a few scattered coins.

"Bad luck, mate," Klyde said. "The current must have carried it off. The sea has laid claim over it now."

Dyna sighed. "We are out of funds, then?"

Rawn rubbed his jaw, exchanging worried glances with his companions. He had some gold left, but it may not be enough to purchase seats on a boat for everyone to the west coast.

"We will pull our reserves together once we camp," he told them. "It will have to make do until we reach Dwarf Shoe."

They nodded and continued with their journey. There was a second option, but it was risky. Rawn had plenty of gold he could request from the bank, but as a wanted man, he stood to be caught before he ever received it.

However, Dwarf Shoe didn't permit extradition. That would provide them protection from bounty hunters.

If they could make it to the free state without further trouble.

Trouble found them by the second day.

Rawn woke to find Klyde crouched beside him. He brought a finger to his lips. Feeling his pulse climb, Rawn sat up on his bed mat. The black wolf to his left growled faintly, bright yellow eyes staring off into the trees. The hour was early, dawn not yet on the horizon.

The mercenaries were all awake and quietly arming themselves. The captain crept to the girls and gently woke them, motioning for them to keep quiet.

They held still, bracing themselves to fight. Nothing surfaced other than the rattle of the trees, but Rawn felt eyes on them.

Watching.

"What is it?" Lucenna whispered after a long stretch of stillness.

"There is something there," Klyde said faintly.

"I don't see anything."

"Trust me, they are there." He glanced at his lieutenant. "There are three in front of us. How many are behind me?"

Rawn perked his ears, listening as closely as Zev was. His sharp sight locked onto the still shapes in the shadows.

"Five, Captain," Eagon whispered.

Klyde drew out his blades. "Ready?"

They all nodded.

The mercenaries leaped to their feet with a cry, yanking out their weapons.

Trolls burst out of the trees.

CHAPTER 9

Zev

Zev's fangs tore into a troll's throat. Another came bellowing toward him, roaring so loud, it rang through his skull. Dyna slid across the mud in front of him, shooting off arrows as she did. They pierced the troll's third eye, and it crashed at his feet. The creature was large, its scaled body covered in bony spikes. He had forgotten how unsightly they were. Its swamp stench overwhelmed his senses.

Dyna charged forward, and Zev sprinted after her.

She leaped up and shoved her blade through the neck of another troll. Dark blood sprayed, and it fell backward with her on its chest. She landed as Zev bounded past her with a snarl and leaped on the back of a ten-foot troll.

Running for a tree, Dyna leaped off its trunk, and she lifted her blade as her body arced for them. Steel flashed in a rapid slash through the troll's throat and the head landed by her feet.

Zev stared at her a moment, shocked by how deftly she moved. How swiftly she killed them. No hesitation at all.

Dyna turned around, her face speckled with blood like war paint. Her hard green eyes scanned the area for any more beasts, but the others had already finished them off.

He couldn't have been prouder.

But disquiet hovered around Lucenna and Rawn as they exchanged a look.

"Well done, lass," Klyde said with a low whistle. "But let's not take any further risks, aye? Best to leave the trolls to those who have experience in disposing of them."

Dyna rolled her eyes. "I had no trouble taking them down, Captain. If I need your aid, I will let you know."

She flicked the blood off her blade and sheathed it as she marched on, Zev following behind. Only confidence radiated off her petite frame, layered in leather armor.

The mercenaries watched her pass warily.

Lord Norrlen called his name under his breath. Zev met his gaze and was made to step aside with him and Lucenna.

"The captain means well," Rawn said quietly, enough for only them to hear. "There is no need for Lady Dyna to take unnecessary risks when we have employed the mercenaries to escort us."

Zev sat on his haunches and yawned. He was finished with overprotecting her. Dyna was strong enough to defend herself now, and they had all seen to it through months of training. He wasn't about to let others disparage her abilities.

Lucenna narrowed her eyes. "You don't agree."

He watched the mercenaries make sure the trolls were all dead by stabbing through their skulls.

"Zev." Lucenna stomped her foot. "This is a serious matter. Dyna has been pushing herself more and more, and we're worried about her."

There was no need to be.

It only bothered them because she didn't need their protection anymore. They had to accept it like he did. Of course, Zev would always stand by her side, but she could finally stand on her own. They should commend her for that.

"She's not sleeping. Haven't you noticed?"

Zev blinked at Lucenna. No, he hadn't.

Once Dyna no longer woke up screaming from her nightmares, she told him he could go back to staying in his own room again.

Rawn nodded in confirmation, his expression grave.

"Sometimes I hear her speaking late at night," Lucenna continued. "Whenever I ask her about it, she merely explains it away. She's unraveling, Zev. You know what I mean. It's easy to shroud ourselves in lies while hiding the truth we ignore inside."

He knew exactly what that was like.

The impression of the Madness was still there, like the grooves of an old scar. It showed how deeply ingrained it had been a part of him for all the years he had tried to hide how wrong he was. Zev had not had the time to think about who he was now without it. All his attention had been on Dyna.

On making her stronger. Better.

Had he underestimated how deep her scars went?

Zev scanned the camp for her, but she was nowhere in sight. Springing up on his paws, he sniffed the air. He swiftly caught Dyna's scent. He turned to go after her but growled at Rawn and Lucenna in annoyance when they tried to follow.

They stayed behind with the mercenaries as Zev ambled through the bushes. The scents of the forest were strong beneath the damp coating of rain from last night and the arrival of spring. He noticed the faint tracks of her boots in the mud, and they led him a few yards away from camp until he heard her faint voice.

"We aren't far from Dwarf Shoe now," she said. "The journey may take perhaps a fortnight."

There was a pause as the wind picked up, loudly rustling the leaves .

"Of course, I will. They wouldn't understand."

Zev came through the bushes. Dyna yelped, jumping to her feet with a start. Her pack dropped from her lap and splashed into a silvery plate.

"Zev, you startled me," Dyna said, sounding rather annoyed.

Who was she speaking to? A sniff of the air proved there was only them. He canted his head.

At his visible confusion, she glowered and gathered her things. "I came here for a moment to myself. You don't need to follow me around like my constant shadow. I'm fine."

He lowered his ears at her sharp tone.

She sighed down at her soaked satchel and lifted it off the shiny plate. It caught the sunlight as she dumped out the water. It was a rather fancy dish to drink water out of. The Celestials had left it behind.

Why keep it?

Dyna shoved it into her satchel and slung the strap onto her shoulder. "Forgive me for snapping at you. I'm a little tired, is all."

She did look tired, now that he was finally looking for it. Exhaustion lined the purple shadows beneath her eyes.

Dyna petted his muzzle, and he licked her fingers, tasting the salt on her skin. "We should go back before the others come searching for me, too."

They returned to find the mercenaries hanging up Wendigo pelts from the trees.

"To repel the trolls," Klyde explained.

The stench would repel anyone. Zev laid by the fire so he could hinder some of the smell beneath the burning wood.

"According to the map, we are two days away from the gorge," Rawn told them quietly as Dyna took a seat beside Lucenna.

"Good," the sorceress replied. "May our luck hold up until then."

Dyna frowned. "Well, don't wish misfortune on us now. How far is the Morphos Court from Troll Bridge?"

"The Morphos Court lies at the center of the Wyspwood, my lady," Rawn said. "Perhaps fifteen miles from the gorge."

"The detour won't be too far," she said. "We must stop by to gather Princess Keena on the way."

"You are assuming she will want to join us," Lucenna said, arching a brow.

Dyna shrugged. "She's one of my Guardians. Why wouldn't she want to join me?"

Again, taken aback by her harsh tone and how easily she was open to adding another to their group, Zev shifted out of his wolf form. "Dyna, we've yet to discuss the princess or if she's even trustworthy," he said, quickly tugging on a pair of trousers. "She may know more about Leoake than she's let on."

He glanced down at her arm where her geas in the shape of an oak used to be. Dyna mentioned the Druid had moved it, but she was still bound to an unknown promise. He would come to claim it soon, and Zev sensed its imminent arrival like the incoming rain. Whatever favor Leoake wanted, it was bound to carry a heavy price.

"Even if she does know more about the Druid, it doesn't change the fact that she is one of my Guardians. She's part of my prophecy."

"Tarn's prophecy, you mean," Lucenna corrected with a frown.

Dyna gave her a look. "It may have been given to him, but it's mine, too. I need all—" She grimaced and amended, "I need to gather what Guardians I can before we make the voyage to Mount Ida."

"My lady, does that include Commander Von as well?" Rawn asked.

Zev stiffened.

When Dyna had revealed that Von was the sixth Guardian, he didn't want to believe it. He would have preferred it to have been Klyde. A familiar face seeking revenge? The captain fit the mark.

Why would Von join them when he still served Tarn?

Dyna avoided his gaze. "I know he's done wrong against us ... but it's only because he had to. Von is meant to join us."

It stung Zev a little that she would decide that without discussing it with him first.

"And how do you plan to take him away from Tarn?" Lucenna asked her next. "We don't even know where they are."

Dyna was quiet for a pause. "Our paths will cross again."

The conversation ended as the mercenaries gathered for their evening meal. They ate stale bread and dried meat.

Discreetly traveling the Bridge would only get them so far.

That night, Zev took first watch with Klyde. He remained on constant alert, sniffing the air for that telltale troll stench. But all he heard was the whisper of the breeze and the chatter of nature among the steady heartbeats slowing as the others fell asleep.

But one stayed awake.

Dyna's eyes shone in the moonlight as she stared blankly at the leaves above them, lost in thought.

Was it the darkness that kept her awake?

Was it *his* absence? She never cried for Cassiel again after that day in the courtyard.

Zev thought it was because Dyna had moved on, but there were five facets of grief. And he remembered exactly which one he had fallen into before he went mad.

CHAPTER 10

Dynalya

Something lurked in the trees.

It had been hunting them since they left Skelling Rise.

Dyna lay still on her bed mat, staring at the canopy above her. Their stalker was so quiet, she sometimes didn't know where they were until a branch faintly creaked. They were skilled at hiding, though, for not even Zev and Rawn had noticed them yet.

But she knew they were there.

The sky rumbled with a coming storm as the night wore on until the sky lightened with the beginning of dawn. A light drizzle of rain fell, pattering on the leaves. Lightning flashed in the distance, exposing a faint shadow passing overhead among the branches. It was so quick, she nearly missed it. Her heart hammered wildly in her chest.

She heard it.

The flutter of wings.

Rawn eventually took his rest when it was Lucenna's turn to take watch. She joined a mercenary named Alasdair on the perimeter, a polite bulky man with unruly brown hair. Dyna waited until they were distracted before quietly standing and slipping away in the direction the shadow went.

They had trained her in many things over the winter, and learning how to move soundlessly was one of them. The rain picked up, cloaking her rapid steps further.

With each strike of lightning, the canopy lit up, helping Dyna search for her stalker. A winged silhouette flew past with a rustle of feathers. Then she was running.

Was it...?

It had to be.

She could almost smell it. That divine scent that belonged only to their kind. Her boots splashed through a puddle, and in the center of it floated a black feather. The sight of it sent her heart leaping into her throat, her chest rising and falling sharply with shallow breaths. Something in her chest rose past the poisonous anger. Past the fog of exhaustion.

Something she didn't want to give name to.

Dyna entered a clearing and shouted, "Are you there, coward? Come out!"

Her shrill voice reverberated through the still trees. A murder of crows burst from the leaves, cawing loudly as they took flight.

Dyna stared at the scatter of their little black feathers left behind. She sank to her knees. Her vision blurred as she cried over her stupidity for daring to hope.

Cassiel wasn't coming back.

Long had she accepted it, yet why did she continue to hallucinate his presence?

Dyna choked back a sob and punched the reflection of the weak, weepy girl in the puddle before her. How pitiful.

Her mind was crumbling because she couldn't sleep anymore.

The nightmares never stopped.

She simply learned how not to wake up screaming.

Every time she closed her eyes, it was the same. Cassiel turned his back on her, then hands pushed her off a cliff. When she hit the ground, it was the most horrible sensation. She not only felt her body breaking, but she also heard her bones snapping and the echo of an agonizing scream.

The dream must represent her soul shattering when her mate betrayed her. And somehow, her mind couldn't let go of that.

Maybe it had been a mistake to remember.

Wiping her cheek, Dyna got back to her feet.

She couldn't fall to her death if she stayed awake. Sleeping only an hour at a time kept the dreams at bay, but that would only work for so long.

"Dyna?" Lucenna called behind her. "What are you doing? You shouldn't be out here."

"Nothing." She moved past her. "I came to relieve myself, if you must know."

Lucenna grabbed her arm. "Don't dismiss me like that," she said tersely. "What is wrong with you? You know how dangerous Troll Bridge is. We never go anywhere alone."

Dyna jerked her arm away. "Well, I needed a moment alone, all right?" she snapped. "I have had enough of all of you hovering around me like I am made of glass. I'm already broken. Nothing you do now will prevent that."

Her voice broke on the last line, and she angrily wiped her tears away before they could fall.

Lucenna's glowing eyes softened. "Dyna … we do it because we care."

"I know." She exhaled a heavy breath and rubbed her face. "I'm sorry. I'm exhausted."

"Did you have another nightmare?"

Dyna nodded, merely to move on from the conversation and because it was partially true.

With a wave of her hand, Lucenna cast a shield above their heads. Rain pattered on it as she wrapped an arm around her. "Come. Let's get you to sleep. We have another hour before daylight."

They walked away together towards camp. The distant flutter of wings passed overhead again, but Dyna didn't bother looking up. Her mind must be on the brink of unraveling, because the faint sound of a flute emerged from deep in the forest, but Lucenna showed no signs of hearing it.

Her side ached where the geas was, and she pressed on her ribs.

When they passed by a thicket, Dyna considered searching for Phyllon roots for a sleeping draught but spotted another plant she recognized. The dark purple leaves stood out among the others. Perhaps it was chance or perhaps fate mocked her, but she no longer cared. She picked a handful of stems. Their bitter scent filled the air as she tied them together with twine and stuffed them in her cloak.

"What's that?" Lucenna asked.

"Medicinal herbs I will brew later," Dyna said, continuing onward. "They will help me with my sleep."

CHAPTER 11

Cassiel

Ash rained down, landing on Cassiel's face. The smoke-choked sky kept all sunlight at bay, not that he could see it anymore. His body ached. He was used to it now. It was a constant pain rooted deep within the pit inside of him, serving as a daily reminder of why he did this.

"I have surrendered, My King. Please, I have told you everything I know. Spare me, and my Realm will be yours."

Cassiel's gaze lowered from the dark skies to Lord Hallel, kneeling at his feet. Soot and blood stained his pallid face and armor, his weapons long broken. It took all winter to track him down. Here, Hallel made his stand with the full force of his army.

And lost.

He was the last Skath warrior on the battleground scattered with feathers and fire. Every soul he had destroyed forever marked the land. Including his own.

"You have misconstrued me, Lord Hallel." Cassiel's eyes flamed. "I didn't come for your surrender."

Lord Hallel begged him, but Cassiel couldn't hear his voice anymore. He only saw a reflection of his past. Lord Hallel had been one of his generals, and he had been among those who betrayed him in both lives. He wouldn't return to do so again.

For Seraph fire destroyed all, including souls.

The vivid blue flames fell over the Lord of Skath, and his screams echoed in the field as Cassiel watched him burn. The only thing left was a black husk of ash, his mouth frozen in a scream. The next gust blew it away.

Two Lords down.

Two more to go.

Cassiel felt how the brutality of every death he caused marred his soul further. So many he had consumed with his flame. His heart was no longer stone or glass. It was now charred wood. And pieces of himself continued to fall away, carried off in the wind. He shouldn't want anything now ... but Cassiel hoped somehow ... they would land wherever he used to belong. Maybe then that dead part of himself would be at peace.

He blinked blearily at the scattered fires. His sins weighed down on his chest like a bolder, compressing his lungs. His body sagged, and he stumbled. Strong arms caught hold of him and held him up.

"Are you all right?"

"No ... this weight..." Cassiel pressed on his chest. "It's so heavy. I'm afraid it will crush me before the end."

"Turn back. You don't have to do this."

Turn back? It was too late for that. Yet an integral part of his being begged him to return to where he had left the other half of his soul. If only he could catch a glimpse of her. Go to where she was and tell her he was sorry.

That he missed her.

But what they had was gone now.

"Yes, I do." Cassiel straightened up. "I must continue what I started. And you must remain unseen and unheard." He turned to the male Celestial standing beside him. His black hood hid his face, something Cassiel had commanded him to do. "There is only one purpose for a spy, especially for one who is supposed to serve as my support during this trying time. It's the reason I called you here, Netanel."

His spy bowed his head. "I know."

Netanel was special in that regard. He could move and act in ways the Valkyrie couldn't. The Realms would be on the lookout for half-breed female warriors, but no one would expect a pureblooded male from Hilos.

"Go," Cassiel told him. "Return to scouting the skies. Anything you hear on the wind, I want to know."

Netanel nodded. He crouched and shot into the air with his gleaming white wings, disappearing behind the smoky clouds.

"My King." Yelrakel and his golden Legion stood behind him.

Their expressions were cautious, careful. Only his general kept her expression blank, but he sensed her concern. Perhaps she disapproved of how he killed Lord Hallel without a trial, or how brutal he was when he wiped out the Vanguard. But he couldn't take any chances now.

He wouldn't let history repeat itself.

In his past life, they had won.

But Cassiel had made them a promise of what he would do once he returned. And he had every intention of seeing it through.

"Where to next?" she asked.

"To our next target, General." Cassiel spread open his wings. It would be a long way to the south. A fortnight of travel at the very least, if not longer, but he was looking forward to this part of his plan. "Let us give Lord Gadriel a visit."

CHAPTER 12

Lucenna

They reached the end of Troll Bridge on the fourth day. Lucenna had held her breath all the way across until they came out onto a high ridge overlooking the isthmus that connected the land to the rest of Urn. The air was refreshingly brisk. On the left stretched on the glistening horizon of the Saxe Sea, carrying brine on the wind. Ahead, a section of marshes expanded about half a mile wide, and at the end of it lay the gorge.

Two steep rock walls hundreds of feet tall, coated in bright green moss and surrounded by waterfalls. A shallow creek cut through the narrow passageway like a trail. She could hear the rush of water from here. The view lent the feeling of standing in a world apart.

"We made it," Klyde said, bringing his horse to a stop beside hers. "A mile upstream lie the cascades. There is a passageway hidden behind them large enough for a small troll to slip through. Fortunately, they haven't discovered it yet."

Fortunately.

"Come, we must prepare." He clicked his tongue and tugged on the reins.

Lucenna followed him back into the cover of the trees where the mercenaries had dismounted. They removed their jackets, detaching their grappling gear and checking their weapons.

Rawn and Zev exchanged confused frowns.

"The marshes from here to the gorge are the most dangerous part of the Bridge," Klyde told them. "There are no trees to filter a horde attack or to hook on to, greatly deterring our advantage against trolls. Not to mention the muddy terrain makes it difficult to ride through. It's easy to get sucked in and makes for easy prey. From here, we need to be on high alert and ready to fight. Secure your boots and remove any heavy clothing. Once we reach the gorge, we must swim part of the way."

Lucenna's heart jolted. "Swim?"

"Aye. We'll hike the creek bed for about a mile, but it does get deep at one point, especially at this time of year."

Her stomach sank.

Klyde winked. "Don't worry, lass. We've done this many times before. We'll make it across fine. The one thing trolls hate is water."

"And how big is this Horde?" she asked. There seemed to be hundreds the last time they faced them.

"We exterminated more than two-thirds of the eastern Horde last summer out of necessity. They're nasty buggers, but they don't tend to rut in the winter. Against fifty of my best mercenaries, I don't anticipate any casualties now." Klyde gave her a nod of assurance and went on to speak to Eagon.

It did little to ease her worries, though. She glanced at the cascades. The trolls were one thing, but they were not her main concern at the moment.

"Are you all right?" Dyna asked her. "You look pale."

Lucenna forced a smile. "Only feeling a little cold. The air still clings to winter's chill."

"Can you cast a warming spell?"

"I can, but it's best to conserve my power in case we're confronted." Lucenna buttoned up her black leather redingote. "I will simply keep on my coat."

"Are you sure, my lady?" Rawn asked as he and Zev joined them. "It may weigh you down." He had already removed his cloak and Zev didn't need one.

"I will wear it at least until we reach the gorge."

Rawn held out his open pack to them. "We will need to have our wits about us at this point. Allow me to carry our belongings during the crossing."

"Thank you, Lord Norrlen," Dyna said.

She and Lucenna put their satchels inside, then Zev added his. Already enchanted to conserve space, Rawn's pack appeared as if it carried nothing at all. He tied it to Fair's saddle.

"Be careful out there," Zev told them.

Lucenna smiled, warmed by their care. "You two worry too much."

"I'm ready," Dyna said, resting her hand on the hilt of her short sword.

Tugging off his shirt, Zev shifted into a massive black wolf. He rose to his full height, nearly as tall as Lucenna's horse.

The mercenaries had already mounted on their rides, the forest littered with their grappling gear. Two others collected them into enchanted packs. The sight of that made her nervous. Removing their gear meant they didn't want anything weighing them down.

The men settled down as they lined up in formation. Klyde and Eagon took the lead along with Olyver, Cam, Sigrid, and Alasdair. Her group took up the center, and the rest of the mercenaries covered the rear.

"Listen up," Klyde said, his eyes sweeping over the younger mercenaries, then falling on Lucenna and her group. He kept his voice low, and all held quiet to hear him. "Some of you have not faced the west end trolls. They are slightly different from the trolls on the east end. These trolls are bigger, faster, and *intelligent*. Once they attack, move quickly. Don't hesitate and strike true. Right and left flanks will create a barrier to hold them back as I lead our guests to the gorge, with the last flank covering our backs. Once we are through, the first and last flank will unite with the unit to make for the sea. Go with your God."

"And may he receive me," the mercenaries murmured in quiet unison.

The younger mercenaries paled but did their best to hold their courage.

Nerves buzzed in Lucenna like a hornet's nest. She briefly shut her eyes and sent a prayer to the God of Urn that they would survive this.

Klyde gave a signal, and they rode on.

"Steady now, *Osombre*," Rawn murmured to Fair.

They cantered ahead at a quiet but steady pace. Lucenna and Dyna kept close, keeping an eye on their surroundings. They clomped through the muddy marshes without trouble until they reached the middle of the glade.

Trolls sprung out of burrows in the ground. The mercenaries reared back on their horses. Mud coated the three-eyed beasts, but they ran on all fours. They were lithe with spiked hides, and they were incredibly fast. Their frightening roars echoed across the land, thrumming against Lucenna's heart.

The mercenaries fought with Klyde in the lead. She cast out spells, Rawn unleashed a rain of arrows, and Zev tore into any trolls that got too close to them. They kept Dyna shielded in the center. The men fought all around them and soon killed them all.

A Horde burst out of the trees and charged after them. They poured out in an endless stream. There were so many, it completely ruined their initial plan.

Klyde yanked on his reins and rode to the front lines with Eagon.

"Stay back, my lady, please," Rawn said to Dyna, and he gave Lucenna a look to watch over her.

She nodded.

The mercenaries fell in formation as they rode after their captain, with Rawn and Zev following close behind. But they were severely outnumbered.

The sound of clashing blades came from all around her as Eagon and Klyde called out attacks. Lucenna knew their luck wouldn't last for long, but she also didn't expect the trolls to find them right when they reached the gorge.

"The Horde will swarm them," Dyna said. "We need to cut off their attack at the neck."

She shook her head. "What do you mean? You don't have magic."

Dyna reached into her pocket and took out a black feather, giving her a sly smile.

Lucenna gaped at it. It was one of Cassiel's feathers. "Where did you get that?"

"Never mind that," Dyna said, yanking her horse around. "You take right, I'll take left."

"What? Wait! You're supposed to stay with me!"

But Dyna kicked her heels and rapidly galloped away. She rode low and fast, arcing around the two units to race straight for the Horde.

Lucenna cursed and galloped in the opposite direction. She called on her Essence, feeling it crackle on her skin. She rode across the marshes and circled to the right as the Horde passed between them. A Violent charge in the air, but it wasn't hers.

A brilliant green light flared across from her as Dyna's hands filled with magic. Storm clouds rolled across the sun as Lucenna called on her power. Green fire roared across the marshes and exploded into the left flank of the Horde. Lucenna reached up to the sky and drove down her fist with a cry. Bolts of lightning rained down and tore through the screeching beasts.

The air filled with thick smoke and the stench of scorched flesh. Lucenna couldn't see a thing. She coughed violently and blinked her watering eyes. It was quiet. Too quiet. Her heart raced wildly, and she felt the world closing in.

"Dyna?" Lucenna called, tugging on her reins as she turned in place. "Rawn?"

A troll crashed into her horse, and she went down. Her horse neighed wildly as the troll tore into it. Lucenna stifled her whimpers as she tried to pull herself out from beneath it.

The ground rumbled with incoming riders, and she fought desperately to break free. The mercenaries burst out of the smoke with the Horde chasing after them. Klyde charged for her and swept his skull blades through the air, beheading the troll. Its hot, reeking blood splashed her in the face.

"On your feet, lass!" Klyde jumped down and dragged her out from under the dead horse. Taking her waist, he tossed her up onto Onyx's saddle and leaped up behind her. Trolls came screeching through the smoke, more than ever before.

Klyde cursed. He kicked his heels, breaking into a gallop across the marshes. "Head for the gorge!" he shouted at his men. "We will make our stand there!"

The narrow passageway would make it easier to fight them back.

Lucenna cast out spells left and right, taking down any troll that got too close. They caught up with Zev and Dyna riding with Rawn on Fair. The rumble of racing hooves and beasts came from all round them.

They made it through the veil of smoke onto the end of the marshes, the gorge within sight. But this Horde was as fast as the horses. They leaped onto the last flank and men started to go down.

Olyver and the first unit rounded to defend them.

"Keep riding!" Eagon yelled to Klyde as he yanked on his reins. "We'll cover you!"

Klyde gritted his teeth but kept going, and they raced for the gorge.

When they reached it, Rawn called out, "Above us!"

Lucenna whipped her head up. Trolls growled from the edge of the steep rock walls of the gorge, some already leaping down. They landed between them and the mercenaries riding to their aid, Eagon in the lead. It was an ambush.

Lucenna looked up at the desiccated trees in the soft earth at the top of the gorge and threw out her hand.

"No, lass!" Klyde shouted.

But her power flared out and hit the ledge. Trees came down in a violent slide. The ground shook as they rained down like massive spears, falling through the Horde. After several seconds, when all was still, she took in the newly formed dam at the base of the creek. The barricade was at least twelve feet high, constructed of splintered wood and twitching limbs. Dark blood seeped into the water.

Lucenna shook with trembling breaths. *The mercenaries...*

"Eagon!" Klyde bellowed out frightfully. He listened for a pause, his chest heaving. *"EAGON!"*

Only silence answered.

CHAPTER 13

Lucenna

Lucenna's mother had taught her to win her battles with strategic intelligence, not rash desperation. But that's exactly what she did. Her legs shook as Klyde's cries for his best friend filled the gorge. *Gods ... no. Please no.* She had only wanted to counteract the ambush.

"I'm sorry," she said, her eyes welling. "I didn't mean—"

Klyde dismounted and ran to the logjam. "Damn it, Eagon, answer me!"

"Aye, Captain, I'm here!" the lieutenant called back from the other side.

He stumbled to a stop, his entire body sagging heavily as if the relief almost knocked him over.

Lucenna closed her eyes, thanking all the Gods.

"Is anyone hurt?" Klyde called earnestly. He continued to the barricade and climbed up some of the logs. He reached the midway point, looking through an opening.

"Some injured," replied the echo of Eagon's voice, sounding much closer. He must have climbed the wall on the other end as well.

"Any dead?"

The silence was a breath too long. "A few fell in the marshes to the trolls..."

Klyde dropped his head against a branch for a moment. "Climb over, mate," he said. "Leave the horses."

"You know we can't. It's too dangerous for the injured, and we have obligations in Skelling Rise. The men were only meant to escort you this far."

"Can we remove the barricade?" Dyna asked her.

Lucenna checked her Essence. She had drained perhaps half of her power, but her hands still crackled with electricity. She might...

"Not in time before the trolls regather," Rawn said somberly. "The mercenaries could be cornered if they stay."

Zev growled and looked up at the ridge again. His ears twitched with sounds they couldn't hear. More beasts were coming.

Lucenna led Onyx to the wall. "Klyde," she called softly. "We can't stay here."

Klyde gripped the branches tightly, releasing a harsh sound of frustration. His gaze stayed on his friend. "This Horde, Eagon ... it's as big as the one that tore through Azurite all those years ago."

"Aye, I think we grew overconfident. We should have known they were too quiet for a reason," Eagon said. "Thanks to the girls, their numbers have reduced drastically. We can still fight our way out of the marshes. Go, and don't return until you have finished what you left to do. I will take it from here."

Klyde's expression tightened. "Don't get yourself killed, Lieutenant. I expect you to make it home to my sister."

There was a pause before he replied, "Aye, you have my word."

But as firm as his voice was, Lucenna heard the false confidence in it, because he couldn't promise his life wouldn't end out there.

Klyde nodded once in acknowledgement, understanding that, too.

"Go with your God." Eagon's boots thumped on the sleek logs as he climbed back down.

Klyde watched him go a moment longer. "May he receive me," he murmured, his voice faint enough that she thought he also said, *And you...*"

The sounds of clashing metal and screeches filled the gorge. The rumble above was getting closer.

"They will be upon us soon, Captain," Rawn called. "We must keep moving."

He reluctantly climbed down and mounted Onyx in a smooth leap. Taking the reins, he kicked his heels, and they rode at a fast pace across the creek bed. The water grew deeper until it reached their knees.

"We need to swim from here," Klyde said, sliding off.

Lucenna gathered her courage and climbed down as Dyna did. She shivered as they waded through the frigid water for several yards. This wasn't so bad. They had already ridden half the mile through the gorge. They were almost there.

The ground unexpectedly dipped, and Lucenna yelped as she sank half two feet down. The water reached their knees now.

"We're crossing the deep end," Klyde said behind her. "We're close."

She nodded and kept moving, trying to stay calm as the water kept rising to her neck. Dyna hung onto Zev, and Rawn swam beside Fair. Lucenna tried to keep up, but she was walking on toes now and losing hold of the creek bed. She searched for Onyx, but the horse had moved too far to her left. Water sloshed up her nose, spiking her panic.

Magic. Use magic, she told herself.

But her heart was racing, and she couldn't think of a spell to use. Her satchel. Where was her satchel? She forgot she had a boat in there.

Lucenna tried to call out to Rawn but choked on a mouthful of water and coughed violently.

"Oi." Klyde grabbed her waist, hoisting her up. She sucked in gulps of air, and her shaking hands gripped his coat. He turned her around, staring at her. "Are you all right?"

Lucenna was shivering so hard, she wasn't warm enough to blush or even have the energy to be angry that he caught her. "I-I can't swim," she admitted between her chattering teeth.

"Why didn't you say so?" he growled.

Before she could answer, he swung her around, bringing her legs around his waist. She quickly latched onto his neck.

"Keep your head up." He sounded colder than usual. He must be upset with her over the jam.

The guilt already growing in her chest weighed heavier.

After another ten minutes, they rose out of the water again, thank the Gods. Soon they were back in the shallow creek, and she slid down Klyde's back.

"Thank you..."

He nodded without looking at her. They came up past another curve of the path and at last reached the cascades. It crashed down in a small, beautiful pool on the bottom, a soft mist brushing against her cheeks.

"This way," Klyde told them as he recovered Onyx's reins.

They followed him on a path of moss curving against the wall to come behind the fall of the water and found a narrow cave opening. It was dark, but there was light ahead. A curtain of vines covered the exit.

Klyde pushed them aside. He went in, and Lucenna followed. They entered a thick, vibrant forest. It was bright with sunlight, peaceful, as if they had not fought their way through Death's Gate to get here.

Slowing down, Klyde stopped in the glade with his back to the gorge. His clenched fists shook at his sides, his posture rigid. He wanted to go back.

They will be all right, Lucenna wanted to say, but it wouldn't be welcomed from her.

"Come." Klyde turned away. "We have a ways to go before we can make camp."

Klyde led them through the forest for several miles before bringing them to another ridge. He dismounted and said it was safe now. Lucenna sighed with relief. The day had drained her.

Opening up her satchel, she called out her enchanted tent. It spun out with a twirl of pixie dust, enlarging as it went. They were quick to set up camp and light a fire. Lucenna and Dyna went into her tent to change out of their damp clothes first. When they came out, Rawn went in next. Zev laid by the crackling campfire in his wolf form, already dried.

But Klyde was missing.

Dyna went to the pot hanging over the campfire and stirred the contents, the air wafting with the scent of mushroom soup.

"The captain?" Lucenna whispered to Zev.

The wolf pointed his nose east.

Lucenna went in that direction, passing by a crop of bushes and coming out onto a clifftop. Klyde stood there, staring at the edge of the gorge in the distance. The brisk wind blew against him, rustling his hair and coat.

"Klyde," Lucenna called hesitantly. She twisted her hands together. "Are you all right?"

"No," he said gruffly.

She lowered her gaze at his tone.

"I am not angry about the logjam," Klyde muttered. "You likely saved our arses. I am angry with myself for being so arrogant. I never expected…" He rubbed his face. "Merceries died today. The weight of that fault lies on me alone. Now I don't know if my best mate made it out. But I believe in him. That must be enough."

He turned around and glowered at her. "However, I am angry that you didn't tell me you couldn't swim until you were guzzling down water. For what? Pride, or because you simply refused to accept my help? Is that worth drowning for?"

She glared back, ignoring the flush filling her face. "Why would I tell you that?"

"Stubborn woman," Klyde growled and stormed to her, taking her arms. "Why is it so hard for you to ask for help, Lucenna?"

She stared up at him, taken back by his eyes. They were so scorching blue they simmered. His hands were firm and warm on her arms. But instead of restraining, they felt supportive. Holding her up as if she might fall.

That only infuriated her more, because Lucenna didn't need support. She stepped out of his hold. "You were raised with family and friends there to watch your back. I didn't. I have relied on myself since I was a girl. There was *no one* there to ask for help."

Klyde's anger softened. "And now? You're not alone anymore, Lucenna."

She looked away to the ground. "I know ... but..."

He sighed. "But habits are hard to break?"

Lucenna closed her eyes. She made herself strong because she needed to be. She had friends now, but it felt too incapacitating to rely on anyone, though she knew it shouldn't.

"It's difficult," she admitted faintly.

"Because you think it makes you weak."

Lucenna looked up at him, embarrassed and surprised he understood.

Klyde gave her a half smile. It was faint and kind. "Far from it, lass. I think it makes one brave to admit they need help. Even if you can't admit it to the others yet, I hope you will come to me whenever you need to."

As Lucenna studied the Captain of the Skelling Mercenaries, she found there were many sides of Klyde. The ridiculous part. The solider part. The calculative part. The part that was violent like a rogue tidal wave. Then there was this unanticipated soft side she had only seen in these stolen moments when their walls unexpectedly dropped around each other.

She arched an eyebrow. "Free of charge?"

Klyde's smile widened into a grin, and he winked. "Only for you, love"

Lucenna rolled her eyes, pretending she wasn't glad to see him in a better mood. "I'm not your love."

"Right." At his nod toward the trees, they headed back to camp together.

"I am sorry about the gorge though," she said. "The mercenaries won't be able to cross into the west now."

Not without a full force to fight back against those beasts.

"It's a good thing they won't be leaving Troll Bridge while I'm gone," Klyde said as he moved a low-hanging branch out of her way. "They are taking the year off to build new homes in Skelling Rise and prepare for the refugees coming from the Magos Empire."

She halted. "What?"

"Your people are going to need places to live, lass. The manor will be used as a command center for them to gather, with rooms for them to stay meanwhile. The logjam was a fortunate accident, as it assures outsiders won't be making their way in, and those damn trolls won't escape either."

"But how will you get back in with Onyx?"

"I suppose I will figure that out when the time comes." His casual statement seemed too indifferent towards how he reacted before.

Was it to hide his worry?

"Why did you offer to take my people in without compensation?" Lucenna asked instead. "The truth."

Klyde sighed and came to a stop, facing her. "I couldn't accept any sort of recompense, for my reasons are not entirely unselfish."

Lucenna had suspected as much. She braced herself for whatever he was about to say.

"Opening our doors to outsiders is something I should have called a town meeting to discuss first. But I chose this because when you cried about the suffering women endured in the Empire, I couldn't stand not doing whatever necessary to make it stop." His hand reached for her cheek, but he caught himself and pulled back. "But I must admit ... I do have another reason. Our population hasn't grown much because there are more men than women in Skelling Rise." When her eyes narrowed, Klyde gave her a look. "You know what kind of town I run and the laws we have in place, lass. I promise, your people will always be respected, valued, and protected."

Lucenna crossed her arms. "What if I told you sorceresses and mages are prohibited from mixing their bloodlines? To have a human love-mate is unheard of and very unlikely to happen."

Sighing, Klyde shrugged. "Well, we hold no expectations. Most of the men have resigned themselves to never having a family, and the life of a mercenary tends to be a short one. Every day our town survives is a miracle. We hope opening our doors will bring in a new strength to continue that survival, even if it's only with magic. And if by some rare chance a sorceress should choose a mercenary for herself, they would consider it a blessing from the Gods." She stared at him, and he smiled, making those damn dimples appear. "Did you expect me to change my mind? We are stubborn folk, if you haven't realized it yet."

Her heart dipped at the way he was looking at her, sensing there was a double meaning behind his words. "I have noticed," she replied faintly.

Klyde chuckled as he continued, and she watched him go.

Choose...

The word circled her mind around and around.

Her people would have the right to choose in Skelling Rise. They would have *rights*. To use magic if they wanted. To marry who they wish or not marry at all. To choose how to live their lives, no longer fearing that the Archmage and his Enforcers would come to take it from them.

With the warding spell in place, her people now had their own sanctuary.

She did that.

With his help, but she did it.

Lucenna looked up at the sky, wishing her mother were here to see it.

"Are you coming, lass?" Klyde called from up ahead, passing through the bushes. "Or do you need me to carry you again? Please say yes."

Lucenna snorted. She blinked back the wetness in her eyes and quickly wiped her cheek. "Relish that moment, depraved fool. It's the last time you will ever feel my body pressed against yours!"

His warm laughter drifted to her, and she secretly smiled.

CHAPTER 14

Dynalya

"Are you sure it's around here, Lord Norrlen?" Dyna asked. She drew out the rolled-up page from her cloak and opened it, revealing the blank page, and quietly murmured, *"Tellūs, lūnam, sōlis."*

A spark of purple and green light rippled across the page. Black ink swirled on the surface next as the enchanted map took form. It glowed purple, outlining the entire country of Urn. She tapped on the crop of trees outside of Troll Bridge, and the enchanted ink spiraled until a forest called the Wyspwood filled the page. But it didn't reveal the location of the pixies.

"My only knowledge is that they reside in these woods," Rawn said beside her. He frowned thoughtfully, studying Azeran's enchanted map. "I'm afraid I have not had the pleasure of visiting it yet."

"Nor did Azeran, by the looks of it." Otherwise, it would have been marked. Dyna sighed and rolled up the map.

"We have been searching for Morphos in these woods for the past two days." She observed their surroundings and the mystical forest. There wasn't a sense of danger, but she did sense magic here. "Why do I get the feeling we are going in circles?"

"Why are you searching for the Morphos Court?" Klyde asked suddenly from behind them.

Dyna jumped and discreetly hid the map behind her back as they turned, passing it to Rawn.

Klyde held on to Onyx's and Fair's reins. They had asked him to take the horses to a nearby creek to drink with Lucenna and Zev while they filled their waterskins.

The captain's brow pinched. "Are we not headed to Dwarf Shoe?"

"We are, of course," Rawn replied. "There is someone we must see first."

"And I imagine you can't find it on your map," Klyde guessed, and she stiffened. "Nor would it be on any other. Most fae courts keep their territories hidden, as they prefer it that way, the Morphos Court most of all."

She discreetly released her held breath, and the others eased.

Klyde continued. "The Wyspwood is enchanted to keep uninvited guests out of their territory."

"Then we *have* been walking in circles." Dyna groaned, pressing on her left side beneath her chest. She always felt sore there now.

"Makes sense. I have not been able to pick up their scent," Zev added. "I thought it was due to the rain."

"They keep their court hidden because of their wealth?" Dyna asked Klyde.

"Because of their flowers."

"Flowers?" Lucenna's brow furrowed. Zev shrugged when she glanced at him questioningly.

"That is the source of their wealth," he said. "And much more."

"How do we find them?" Dyna asked.

"They find you." Klyde handed Fair's reins back to Rawn. "There are several ways to draw out the fae. Filling your pockets with posies, rolling in a patch of four-leaf clovers, stepping into a ring of toadstools, drinking fresh rainwater from a tree hollow. Even requesting to make a deal with them, which I do not recommend, or..."

"Or?" Dyna pressed, all of them keenly listening.

"Or I can simply take you there."

She gaped. "You know where the Morphos Court is?"

Klyde grinned. "Aye."

"Why didn't you say so before?" Zev growled.

"You didn't ask."

Lucenna reached out as if to strangle him and stifled a scream of frustration. She spun away and started jamming her belongings into her satchel. "He has a death wish, this man. One of these days, I will grant it. Mark my words."

"I look forward to it, lass," Klyde said, and he laughed when she gave him a foul gesture. He turned to Dyna. "I didn't offer my assistance since it seemed you didn't want me privy to your plans?" At her wary expression, he shrugged. "Well, it's no business of mine. I don't care which path we take as long as it eventually leads to Tarn." Klyde strode ahead, walking his horse beside him. "I will take you to Morphos but keep close. The deeper we go into their territory, the stronger the magic works to lure you. Once we find the path, do not leave it. For there is no telling where the woods will take you. It's called the Wyspwood for a reason."

A shudder crept down Dyna's spine, and they followed behind the captain quietly. When had he come across the Morphos Court?

Zev murmured under his breath. "He's human. The least of us to likely resist enchantments. How do we know he won't get us lost here?"

"He descends from Skellings," Dyna reminded them. "He has fae blood in him, albeit distant."

"And that coat of his reveals spells," Lucenna added. "He has seen through my glamor before."

Rawn shook his head as he studied Klyde confidently walking through the woods. "It is not his coat that reveals them, my lady. The captain may have the Sight, and if so, he will know the way."

"The Sight?" Dyna whispered questioningly.

"He is referring to unveiled eyes." Lucenna's own eyes widened with realization. "The ability to *see* spells. It's a rare ability among the fae, nearly unheard of in humans."

Well, it seemed Klyde wasn't finished surprising them. Keena had that ability too, if Dyna recalled.

Rawn nodded. "Look there."

They stared at the dirt trail Klyde had been taking that none of them noticed until now. It widened into a path with every step they took.

A faint flutter of wings passed overhead, and the shadow of a figure passed through the faint daylight streaming through the branches. Dyna stifled a gasp. *Don't look.* She kept going, but Zev whipped his head to the right, his eyes shining bright yellow.

"Hold on to him," Rawn instructed her, and Dyna quickly took Zev's hand.

Lucenna halted, staring into the dark trees on the left.

"Do not look at the trees, my lady," Rawn warned, taking her arm. "The forest easily deceives."

Klyde paused on the path, looking over his shoulder. "He's right. Don't listen to it, lass."

Lucenna's eyes welled. "But that's my mother."

"No, it's not."

"I hear her..." She tugged out of Rawn's hold.

"Lady Lucenna, don't leave the path." He released Fair's reins to grab her.

"Let me go! She needs me!"

Klyde swiftly yanked Lucenna backward into his arms before her foot landed outside of the path.

Dyna clung onto Zev's arm, but he made no move to follow whatever called him. She stared in the direction he did, seeing nothing but still trees. "What do you see?"

His reflective eyes were pained and glassy. "Only dreams of things that once were and never will be again..."

Perhaps he saw his father, or the early part of his life when he had been truly happy. She squeezed his arm tighter.

Shaking himself out of it, Zev patted her hand. "I'm all right."

Klyde had managed to calm Lucenna down, but she continued staring at the trees, shaking her head. "Oi, look at me." He cupped her teary face, his bright blue eyes holding hers earnestly. "The forest will show you anything to lure you off the path. It's not real, but I am." He put her hand on his cheek. "Feel that? Pure pompous mercenary. Come back to us, Lucenna."

Zev and Rawn gathered on either side of them, making sure she didn't try to escape again.

In the distance, Dyna heard the soft trilling of a flute. The gentle melody made her breath catch. She knew that song.

This damn forest.

It only played tricks.

A laughing young woman with dark hair ran past, holding onto the hem of her gown. A male with white wings chased after her, laughing too. Dyna's pulse drummed. What was a Celestial doing here? She followed, watching him corner the woman in a gondola made of white stone. She squealed with laughter as he nuzzled her neck.

The young woman noticed her there and her green eyes met Dyna's. They stared at one another, both too frozen to move or say anything because she was looking at a woman with her face.

A perfect mirror reflection.

Then the male turned around. Dyna stumbled backward with a sharp gasp. *No, no, no.* She ran away, only to find herself alone in the forest. The path had disappeared. When had she left it?

"Dyna, where are you?" Zev's faint cry echoed in the far distance.

"Zev, I'm here!"

"Lady Dyna!" Rawn called out in the opposite direction. The others called for her, and their voices came from everywhere all at once.

Dyna's breath was loud in her ears as she ran towards the closest voice, but the trees seemed to stretch beyond her. Everything looked the same. She whimpered at the sharp pain stabbing her side, and she continued to run into the fog. Lost before she ever knew what was happening.

No.

Dyna refused to let the forest take her. She stopped and stilled her heart, listening to the voices.

Find me. Find me. Cassiel...

The world snapped into focus, and a firm hand clamped around her arm. It hauled her out of the trees, and she collapsed on the ground, heaving for air wildly.

"Thank you," she said breathlessly.

But the quiet only stirred with a passing breeze. Her murky vision cleared, and she found no one. Who had pulled her out?

"Hello?" Dyna called.

The bushes rattled loudly as her Guardians burst out, running to her.

"Gods, Dyna." Zev hauled her up. "Are you all right? One second you were behind me, then you vanished."

"The forest." She stared at the trees. The mystical haze that had hovered over it before was gone. "It ... tried to take me away." Dyna studied them, seeing the enchantment had left their eyes, too. "What happened? How did you manage to leave the path?"

"We had some help."

"Oh dear," a voice said with a soft, bell-like laugh. A glowing yellow butterfly fluttered around Rawn's head. "Thank the Gods, I found you in time."

With a burst of glittering gold dust, a dark-haired girl in a dress made of pale pink petals appeared before her. Dyna stared at the beautiful, pointy-eared girl with dusky skin and a diadem on her brow. Translucent yellow wings fluttered behind her, dispelling golden dust into the air.

"Princess Keenali..."

The fairy gave her a bright smile, her hazel eyes glittering. "I wondered when I would see you again."

CHAPTER 15

Dynalya

"I'm sorry you found trouble in my court," Keena said as she led them through the dark forest. Having returned to her pixie size, she was no larger than three inches. She left a trail of shimmering gold dust in her wake as she flew ahead. "The Wyspwood is only meant to confuse outsiders and lead them off our land, not harm them. But the magic here has been unruly lately."

Dyna kept close, but the fairy's presence seemed to be all that was needed to settle the woods. She looked back at the trees behind them. Nothing called out to her anymore.

"We are fortunate you came to our aid when you did, Princess," Rawn said.

Keena brought them to the same path Klyde had originally found. "I came as soon as the wisps informed me you were here."

"What are wisps?" Dyna asked her.

"They are the spirits of the fallen fae who still lurk here, becoming part of the forest like moss on a tree. They are but a wisp of smoke or a pin of light to a mortal's veiled eyes, and they are naughty things."

They glanced at Klyde. He kept his gaze fixed on the path, clutching Onyx's reins tightly.

"Can you see them?" Lucenna asked.

He shuddered. "Aye."

Dyna squinted at the canopy. Nothing seemed to be there at first, but she caught glimpses of blue lights. Like little bulbs of fire ... or souls. The wisps had given her those strange visions. Why? And why make him look like a pureblood?

"They're harmless, or rather, they're supposed to be." Keena frowned at the trees worriedly.

Zev brushed against Dyna's side and growled at whatever his yellow eyes had noticed up in the canopy. He had shifted as soon as they reunited. Likely he felt safer that way. But there was nothing they could do to defend themselves against spirits.

"Ah, wolf! I remember you." Keena flew down to him and poked his nose, making him sneeze. Her laugh sounded like a chiming of bells. "Zev, right? But there is one missing. Where is Prince Cassiel?"

Dyna's heart squeezed at the sound of his name, and she fought the invisible weight of a boulder that pressed into her chest.

"He was crowned king over the winter," Lucenna commented indifferently. "He has gone to attend to the Realms."

Dyna gave her a grateful look. It was too difficult to talk about him yet. She ignored the stares of the others while pretending the mention of Cassiel didn't knock the air out of her. Was this how it would always feel like?

"Oh, I see," Keena said elatedly. "That is great news. The High King of Hilos, imagine that."

A dour feeling settled over Dyna again. "Are we far from your court?" she asked to change the subject.

"We are already here." The path ended abruptly at the edge of a glade. In the center of it was a large ring of toadstools with blood red caps spotted white. "This is a fairy ring. Enter and your eyes will be unveiled." Keena turned to them with a sudden seriousness. "But I must warn you, not all fae are the same. Should you come across another ring in another wood, do not *ever* enter without invitation. Lest you are never to be seen again."

Dyna felt a sudden chill in the air, and she shivered. That discouraged her from entering at all. Her friends stared back at the fairy princess with dread.

Keena burst out into tinkling giggles. "Your expressions are hysterical."

She flew for the ring.

"Was that a jest?" Lucenna asked nervously. "I cannot be sure if that was a jest."

"Fae cannot lie, lass," Klyde muttered under his breath.

Well, that didn't make Dyna any less nervous. They looked to their Guidelander, and Rawn nodded, but she wasn't sure if it was out of agreement or encouragement.

The black wolf chuffed at them in annoyance. He jogged ahead for the fairy ring, catching up with Keena. Both crossed the ring of mushrooms at the same time—and vanished.

Dyna gasped. "Zev!"

Fear for her cousin jolted her into action. She ran after them and leaped over the line of redcaps.

The eerie forest winked away and the Morphos Court appeared as if out of a dream.

An enormous tree rose before them with sprawling branches and dark green leaves and pale pink blooms. The small hollows in the trunk or on the branches held tiny homes. Hundreds of glowing butterflies fluttered among the branches. No—*pixies*. They worked either to gather pollen, flowers, or tended to the roots. A shimmer of gold dust hovered in the air like living magic. The flowers seemed to twinkle with the light of the sun.

Dyna gaped up at it with wonder. Rawn, Lucenna, and Klyde appeared beside her next, staring with equal bafflement.

"Welcome to my court," Princess Keena said, holding out her arms proudly. "This is our Aurora Tree."

"This is … incredible," Dyna murmured. "This tree is the Morphos Court?"

Lucenna nodded. "All small fairy folk like pixies and sprites rely on some sort of source of magic grown within nature," she reminded her. "Their kind survive off of the Aurora blooms."

That's right. Dyna did remember Keena mentioning their court's wealth was based on their perfume trade with the rest of Urn.

An alluring fragrance of flowers filled her senses. It was sweet and indulging, but beneath it lingered an odd scent. One that reminded Dyna of decaying plant matter.

The breeze blew a few Aurora petals by her boots. They were blemished with brown burns, as if held too close to a candle. She picked one up, inspecting it up close with a frown. Whatever it was, more browned petals lay scattered around the tree.

Keena's hazel eyes saddened at the sight of the petal. "Our Aurora Tree has stood in these woods for hundreds of years. It has fed us. Clothed us. The perfume created by its blooms is our source of our fortune. But this tree is also our home, and it's dying."

Dying? How could their tree be dying?

82

Keena flew over to the tree roots, and Dyna followed. Up close, she noticed they were blackened with rot, and it had spread into the earth. Dyna knelt by the tree, inspecting it with dismay. How could this have happened? The tree otherwise looked healthy. She placed a hand on the trunk, hoping to feel something, but couldn't with her magic trapped behind a barrier.

"What happened here?" Rawn asked.

"A mystery yet to be solved." Another fairy flew down to join them. He bore a crown over his long braids, and an elegant robe woven from leaves. In his hands, he held a scepter made from a branch of the Aurora Tree, a tiny blue gem embedded at the top.

"Father." Keena greeted with a soft smile. "This is Dynalya Astron, the girl I told you about. Dyna, this is my father, Kalan, King of Morphos."

She quickly rose to her feet and lowered into a curtsy. "It's a pleasure to meet you, Your Majesty."

"Please, the pleasure is mine." Kalan dipped his head. "I am honored to meet the girl who saved my daughter's life."

"She saved mine first." Dyna exchanged a smile with Keena. "May I introduce my companions?"

Holding out her hand to the others, they quickly exchanged names and greetings.

"I wish you could have come at a better time," King Kalan said with a sigh. "I would be most pleased to bring you up into our tree, but that may be detrimental to your health. If you can smell it, there is a sickness in the air. Many of my court have already become ill."

Zev and Rawn nodded to confirm they could smell it. Was that what Dyna had smelled?

"What sort of illness?" she asked. "I am a Herb Master. I could—"

Keena shook her head and took a seat on her shoulder. "I am afraid there is no remedy that can heal them. We feed off the nectar, and if it's contaminated, so becomes our food. They will only heal when our tree is healed, or die when it does..."

That was awful.

She wanted to help but didn't know how. If only she had her magic.

"We are connected to the Aurora Tree," Kalan said as he motioned for them to follow him. He brought them to the other side of the tree, not visible when they first entered, and Dyna found more decay climbing up the trunk. "Its magic keeps us alive, and it gives life to the Wyspwood. Without it, we will not survive, and wisps in the woods will either fade as well or become sluagh—dark wicked things. I have sent for all healers and those knowledgeable in plant magic. Druids, Magi Masters, Earth Magus. They all say the same thing. Our tree will not survive the year."

That was a horrible thing to face. They were losing their home and dying because of it. She had never seen such an illness fall over a tree before.

"What could have caused this?" Dyna asked.

Lucenna frowned at the tree thoughtfully and placed her palm on the trunk, closing her eyes. Soft purple mist flickered around her fingers. "I sense odd magic here. Did you cast any spells on your tree recently?"

Keena and her father shook their heads.

The sorceress's brow pinched. "It feels almost like a…"

"A hex?" Keena suggested.

Lucenna quickly drew her hand back.

Dyna inhaled a soft breath. "Has someone placed a hex on your tree? How? When?"

The fairy shrugged her small shoulders with a sad sigh. "We have never seen this happen to a fair folk tree before, but no one in our court would ever do this. The Aurora Tree showed signs of failure the night after we held a feast during the Summer Solstice. Many courts were in attendance that day."

Kalan sighed heavily. "Perhaps it was done out of envy, or a grudge unbeknownst to me. Regardless, we have no proof of who did it or why—" He cut off with a wheezing cough. His daughter quickly flew to him, supporting him against her. Oh, no. He was ill too. "We are running out of time."

Who could have been so cruel as to do this to them? And why? Did Morphos have enemies they didn't know about or was it merely jealousy?

"I am sorry this is happening to your court, King Kalan," Rawn said. "Have you contacted trustworthy courts for aid? Perhaps there is another Aurora Tree you can find or grow a new one."

"That is where our problem lies, Lord Norrlen. There may not be a court who can take us, for the Aurora Tree is not of Urn. The first tree grew on an island half a world away, and its seeds were brought here to plant." Kalan held out the scepter to show them the tiny kernel within the jewel. "This is the last seed, and it requires the pure soil from which it was born. But that soil does not exist in Urn."

Dyna knew then why they were here. There was only one place that held pure, untouched soil that could grow enchanted trees. She glanced at her Guardians, and each nodded their approval. Lucenna and Zev had the foresight to distract Klyde by taking him away to watch the fairies turn pollen into nectar.

"We can help," Dyna said.

In a whirl of gold dust, Keena appeared at full size beside her. "That night in King Dagden's court, Leoake told me one day you would come and help us."

The mention of the Druid made Dyna's geas throb. She took Keena's hands. "Princess."

"Call me Keena, please. We're friends." She looked at her worriedly. "It's all right. Tell me the truth."

It was the only thing Dyna could offer her now.

She gently squeezed Keena's hands and gave her a small nod. "I am sorry to say the other healers were right. Your tree cannot be saved, and the soil here has been festering with some sort of rot that has infected the land. It's no longer viable for any Aurora Tree to survive here."

Tears welled in Keena's eyes, and her wings drooped. "I don't understand. Leoake said you would come when I needed you."

Dyna hugged her. "I came here for you, Keena, my Guardian of Strength. I can take you where you will find pure soil untouched by anyone. The same soil that birthed that seed."

They told Keena and her father about the prophecy and Mount Ida. The fairies listened with uncertainty at first until Rawn brought out Azeran's enchanted map. Keena's eyes lit up with awe as the ink swirled across the page, revealing Mount Ida.

The first spark of hope filled the court like the coming of spring. Dyna had missed that feeling. The optimistic belief that good things were still possible.

"Join us," she told her. "And you will find what you need."

But the fairy's hope faded beneath apprehension as she looked up at her tree. She clutched her arms around herself, worrying her lip. Rotten petals coasted on the wind, tainting the air with a sick sweetness.

"Go with her, Keenali," Kalan said softly.

"But Father, I am needed here. You have fallen ill. We don't know how long we have left. What if..."

"What if you don't return in time?" He cupped her cheek. "Then that is fate, daughter. But I have faith. The Aurora Tree has always been protected by the Queen of Morphos. Your mother protected it, and now that task falls to you." He handed her the scepter, and Keena's tears spilled as she accepted it. "Find the soil we need and plant it. If the seed takes root, you will have saved us all."

Maybe there was no such thing as hope anymore. Dyna looked up at the glowing blooms against the night sky. Their light seemed to dim in and out like struggling breaths. She felt her own lungs struggle to fill for the past three months. The tree was fighting to live, but it didn't have long.

The soft tinkling of bells hovered from the branches where the pixies slept in their tiny homes. Kalan invited them to stay for the night as Keena debated on what she should do. They laid out their bed mats a couple of yards away from the tree. No campfire tonight, but Lucenna set up an enchanted flame for Dyna to use as she stirred a sticky mixture within a bubbling pot. The scent of sap and pine masked the scent of flowers and decay. She didn't know what she had expected to find in Morphos, but it certainly wasn't this.

Rawn, Lucenna, and Klyde slept soundly, tired from their trek through the woods. Only the wolf was awake. He sat on the edge of the fairy ring, his yellow eyes fixed on the dark trees.

"He can rest," Keena said, flying over to her. "No need to stand guard tonight."

Dyna perked up at her presence, hoping it meant they had an answer. She still carried her father's scepter, and the blue stone glinted in the light. "Zev sees something in the forest that is keeping him on alert."

"He must see the wisps, but they won't bother us." Kenna landed on Fair's saddle where the horses grazed beside them. He whinnied softly, giving the fairy a sniff. She patted his muzzle. "Hello, handsome Fair. Do you remember me? What is your friend called?"

"The other is Onyx. He's Klyde's horse," Dyna said, removing the pot from the fire. It released steam into the air.

"You have gained new companions since we met last." The princess sailed down to her and sat on a stone covered in moss. She canted her head, making one of her pointed ears poke out of her hair as she watched her stir the pot curiously. "What is that?"

Dyna lifted the ladle, letting it drip a thick sticky substance the color of honey. "I have brewed a special phloem. It's a sap full of nutrients to create energy for your tree to grow and strive. Aerate the roots and apply this nourishment to the rot. It won't heal your tree, but it will delay it from dying and prevent anyone else from falling ill."

"Oh!" Keena flew up excitedly to look inside, her wings releasing sprinkles of gold dust. "How long will it last?"

"At least two seasons. It can be applied as often as needed."

The fairy hugged Dyna's cheek and gave her a kiss. "Thank you, Dyna."

"Of course."

Releasing her with a sigh, Keena returned to her mossy seat and sat down. Her sad hazel eyes looked up at her, and Dyna held her breath, waiting for what her tiny Guardian had come to say.

Keena looked up at the Aurora Tree as a gentle wind rustled the branches. Its steady light cast a warm glow over her dusky skin shimmering with pixie dust. "I thought about your offer ... but ... I cannot join you. My father needs me now more than ever."

Her wings drooped, and so did Dyna's shoulders. That was disappointing, but she understood. It wouldn't be fair to ask her to leave her court behind when it was in such dire straits.

"But I brought you this." Keena reached into a small woven bag made of grass that hung from her shoulder. She pulled out a green berry. "I noticed your geas is burning. Eat this. It will help relieve the pain."

Well, that was unexpected. Dyna accepted the little offering in her palm. It looked like a green raspberry. "You can see Leoake's geas?"

Keena stiffened, and her fingers brushed over her parted lips. "Only the geas, not who cast it. Why would you make a deal with him? Fae deals are tricksy, but everyone knows not to make deals with *that one*."

If only she had gotten that notice.

Dyna grimaced and ate the berry, finding it sweet and tart. "I admit, I was foolish when I struck a deal with him. I received only half answers in trade for a favor of his choosing."

The princess sighed. "Oh, Dyna."

"I know. The burning means the time has come to fulfill it, right? Should I be worried?"

"Knowing Leoake, it really could be anything. I can't say much of his character. Mischievous. Mysterious. Sly. A courtier that makes it his business to know everyone's business, while never sharing his own. I can't imagine what he would want. I have not known him to necessarily be cruel, but..."

That dastardly Druid may not have shown her cruelty yet, but he wasn't kind either.

"You couldn't command him to release me?" Dyna asked sheepishly.

The princess shook her head. "I'm afraid not. Leoake is not of my court. He does not answer to me. Regardless, a geas is a powerful spell. Such things cannot be easily broken, at least to my knowledge."

Dyna groaned. Well, she knew as much.

"If you want to be rid of him, you must either give him what he wants, or trade for something else that he wants more."

Dyna wouldn't know where to start. Leoake didn't reveal his secrets. He had already gained his freedom from King Dagden. What could be more valuable than that?

Perhaps a sweet little fox might know.

"I wish you luck on your journey," Keena said, looking down at the scepter on her lap. She rubbed the stone. "If it's not too much trouble, could I ask you to bring us pure soil?"

Dyna nodded. "I will do my best. But if you change your mind, we are on our way to Dwarf Shoe. We will catch a ship there in Kelpway."

The princess rose into the air and gave her a small smile. "Thank you for coming, Dyna."

Then she flew away toward her dying tree.

Zev ambled over to her and glowered. Well, that was the expression Dyna thought she could read from his wolfy face.

"We came all the way here for your fifth Guardian, but we are leaving without her?" Dyna guessed, deepening her voice to sound like his. Zev rolled his glowing eyes, and she smiled. "Yes, Zev." She stroked his furry ears. "We must continue our journey. When it's time, we will see Keena again."

It was already foretold.

All Dyna had to do was wait.

CHAPTER 16

Zev

Raindrops beaded on Zev's fur as he breathed in the scent of the earth and listened to the gentle trickle of rain on the leaves. It calmed his spirit, allowing him a rare peace he only found in the forest. They had trekked for two days across the wilds towards the south. The forest eventually ended when they neared the first signs of civilization.

Zev shifted back onto two legs and dressed before they moved onto a paved road. There were a few people traveling by, and with it came the hum of voices. A castle appeared atop the rocky peaks. It was a stronghold of stone overlooking the city below, bordering the coastal shores of the Saxe Sea. The deep maroon flags on the battlements flapped in the wind.

"The Kingdom of Argyle," Rawn said as they came to a pause. He held Fair's reins while Dyna sat in the saddle. "There be Hydell, the capital."

"Aye, and a patron of ours," Klyde told them as he tugged on Onyx's reins, slowing his canter. "I need to make a short stop to see the king. Go on, I will catch up to you."

Without waiting for a reply, he kicked his heels and cantered down the western road for the castle.

"To do what?" Lucenna wondered aloud as they watched Klyde ride away.

Zev wondered the same. "Should we wait?" he asked next to her.

"Of course, we'll wait," Dyna said thoughtfully, canting her head as she took in the view. Klyde was the holder of the Skelling dagger after all, so naturally she wanted to remain nearby. "Could we go closer? I want to get a better look if it's safe."

"Yes, my lady. It is safe." Rawn led Fair followed along the paved road.

"Have you been here before?" Zev asked him.

"I passed through perhaps five years ago. Argyle is a peaceful kingdom, though it has not always been so."

"Due to war?" Lucenna guessed.

"Not quite."

They reached the drawbridge where merchants had gathered to sell goods. Not too many people were about beneath the overcast weather, though enough to notice them. Merchants called out, offering their wares. A few men lingered near an outdoor pub, watching them narrowly, but made no attempt to approach. Perhaps because of his intimidating size or Rawn's weapons, or even the Hydell Guards patrolling the road.

There was a theme, Zev noticed. The wares, clothing, even the kingdom sigil on the breastplates of the guards, all bore the effigy of a black dragon.

"They tell a tale among these parts about the curse once placed upon Argyle," Rawn told them. "There are many versions of the tale, but all recount the same thing. At the beginning of the second age, a powerful dragon, who lived in the Montezuma Mountains, met with the Argyle King. It declared this land as his but would permit the kingdom to remain under one condition. The dragon wished to wed the eldest princess. When the king denied him, he placed a dark curse that draped them in shadow for decades, keeping them trapped from the rest of the world. Against all odds, the princess broke the spell and slayed the dragon. In so doing, she stole his power and became the new dragon in the mountains, where she now eternally watches over her home."

Lucenna exchanged an awed look with Dyna, and Rawn chuckled.

"Sounds more like a fantasy than truth," Zev said, crossing his arms. "I thought dragons lived in the west."

"Most do," Rawn said, pausing deliberately before adding. "In some versions of the tale, the dragon was the God of Shadows."

Now Zev was certain the story was merely a fairytale. Though, for some reason, a chill prickled his skin.

"I thought the Shadow God was defeated by Kāhssiel and the Celestials?" Dyna said curiously. "And it took them many years."

"Yes, that is so."

"Then how could a simple mortal girl slay him?" Lucenna asked next, her eyes widening with interest.

Lord Norrlen smiled. "I cannot say for sure, my lady. There also once existed a race of fae dragons who could take human form, living in both land and sea. One of them once ruled the seas north of here. Perhaps that was the dragon she slayed. Nevertheless, whether the tale is true or not, Argyle has declared it their history, and many believe it. No other kingdom has dared to rise against them, for fear of rousing the dragon princess from her long sleep."

Dyna smiled at a child who offered her a wooden charm painted dark red with the carving of a dragon. She handed him a few russets in return. "Well, I like that story," Dyna said as she tied the charm to her satchel. "I hope she gave him a good death."

Zev smirked, and Lucenna frowned at him. *What? It's not as if she hasn't expressed the same sentiment against her enemies.*

They bought hot food from a vendor and waited on the side of the road for Klyde. He appeared a few hours later with a frown on his face.

"You waited," he stated disapprovingly.

"We did." Dyna stood. "We had an agreement, didn't we?"

"Aye..." He shook his head. "We were offered a place to stay for the night, but I think it's best to keep going."

They agreed. Zev handed him a roll of bread, and they went on their way.

"What was your business in Argyle?" Lucenna asked. "Did they need another dragon slayer?"

Klyde grunted with an amused curve of his mouth. "I have faced many beasts in my lifetime, lass. But I draw the line at enormous beasts with wings who have teeth larger than I."

"Mercenary business, then?"

"Bounty business. You would be wise to pull up your cloaks, mates. Attracting any attention now would hinder our efforts. Many bounty hunters lurk in these parts, and many more are looking to score easy coin." Klyde narrowed his eyes on the two impoverished men watching them as they rode past. They all obeyed, and Zev switched to high alert as he now noticed the few who had been keeping track of them. "The King of Argyle knows me well, as I have worked for him in the past. I came to request for his soldiers not to detain us if we are recognized in his territory. He agreed, yet that's as far as his clemency goes. Others not serving Argyle are free to collect your bounties if they wish."

Zev growled in annoyance. He had nearly forgotten about their high bounties, thanks to Tarn.

"Meaning we need to reach Dwarf Shoe as soon as possible," Lucenna said.

The free state was a refuge away from wars and kings.

Klyde nodded for them to follow him off the road into the forest. "It's well known people flee there for freedom, and they do have an impressive military in place to protect their citizens, but the best hunters are very determined. They enter Dwarf Shoe discreetly, and once they capture their targets, they are taken out of the state to claim the bounty in the next city. So we need to be careful."

Well, wasn't that simply grand?

Zev debated if he should shift now, so all his senses were fully heightened to catch any prowlers.

"How far are we from Dwarf Shoe, Lord Norrlen?" Dyna asked.

"Third River marks their border, my lady. I would say about three days away."

"Third River?"

"It's the last of the Three Rivers," Rawn explained. "They are the longest rivers in Urn, and they cross nearly halfway through the country."

Curiosity lit her eyes, and Zev suspected she was itching to look at Azeran's map.

Klyde pulled out his map for her instead. "Neat fact," he pointed at a large lake in the center of Urn. "The Second River appears to end in Naiads Mere, but it continues as several underground waterways that cross beneath the Anduir Mountains and emerge into the valley of Greenwood."

Rawn frowned. "Who told you that? Not many know about the hidden waterways."

The mercenary grinned. "A little water nymph told me. When I found myself at the bottom of the lake."

Lucenna rolled her eyes. "Do we even want to know how that happened?"

"Only if you're not squeamish."

Zev slowed down, letting them walk ahead as he adjusted his pack. He kept his eyes on them, pretending he wasn't aware of the new scents on their trail.

He continued, letting his keen sense of hearing and smell do the work. A branch snapped. It was very faint, but enough. Rawn glanced at him, communicating with only a look. Klyde laughed at something Lucenna said, but his shoulders grew tense, and his hand rested on the knife strapped to his thigh. He looked back at Zev and subtly nodded.

Well, they were in for a night.

Zev lurked in the night, unseen and unheard in the cover of the bushes. He kept his eyes fixed on Dyna's form straight ahead. She sat with four of the others around the campfire, conversing idly over their evening meal. After some time, she motioned having to relieve herself and went into the woods.

Dyna hummed to herself as she made her way into an open glade, stopping to forage for plants.

The bushes rustled as men appeared from the shadows. The same men that had followed them in Hydell, and others they had called.

Dyna gasped and spun around as they fully circled her.

"I told you it was her," a dwarf said. "Mighty prize for such a pretty thing. The others have rewards on their heads as well."

"Aye, but this one is nearly worth all of them combined," said a familiar voice.

A large burly man ambled out of the trees. He carried with him a large ax, the rest of him wrapped in leather armor. Four long, jagged scars ran down half his face through one eye, leaving it milky white. Zev bit back a growl once he recognized the poacher they met in the Port of Azure.

"Do you remember me, little minnow?"

Dyna's eyes widened. "Draven..."

A leer played on his mouth as his men took out their blades. "You're a hard one to track down, lass, but I always get my catch. Come quietly now. Don't make me cut that pretty neck. Not until you pay back every cent you swindled from me."

Zev was reminded that Jophiel mentioned Draven had attempted to enter Hermon several times to capture a Celestial of his own. When that failed, he came after her.

"No, please," Dyna whimpered, slowly backing away. Her quick shallow breaths clouded in the brisk night.

"Tie her, Galen."

A young man with Draven's features stepped forward with a ring of rope and a sneer. "That half-breed of yours isn't around, is he? This will teach you not to wander into the woods alone."

"Alone?" Dyna's frightened expression changed from terror to cold indifference. "Who said I was alone?"

Zev prowled out of the night behind her with a rumbling snarl. The men stiffened and he heard the wild beating of their hearts. He focused on the poacher. That was his target.

"I'm afraid you've got it all wrong." She smiled sharply as Lucenna, Klyde, and Rawn appeared from the forest next. "I'm not the one being hunted here."

Dyna slashed at Galen's stomach with her blade and twisted around, whipping out her sword in time to parry Draven's ax. But the force of the man's weight bent her legs, and her arms shook with the effort to hold him off. Zev leaped over her head and took down the large poacher. He tore out

Draven's neck and blood gushed free. A fight broke out all around him, screams and clashes of magic and blades filling the forest.

It was over before it started.

"This wasn't a very fair fight, was it?" Dyna said, wiping her knife. Zev's heart sank to see her sweet face now harsh and cold as she studied the bodies at her feet.

Galen stumbled away, holding his bleeding stomach.

"What about that one?" Lucenna crossed her arms. "He's getting away."

"Let him go," Klyde said, sheathing his weapons. "He will bleed out by morning—"

Dyna flicked up her knife and threw it at Galen's retreating back. They froze, watching it spin through the air. Rawn whipped out his bow and released a shot. The arrow hit the knife, and both whipped past the young man, missing his neck by inches. Galen fled into the trees, out of sight.

She scowled. "Why did you do that? You're letting him get away."

They all stared at her mutely in shock, and perhaps a little dismay. Zev would have been the first to attack an enemy without mercy, but to witness it from Dyna, he didn't know how to react.

Noticing their stares, she frowned. "What?"

"You tried to kill him..." Lucenna said.

"He was running away. Why give him the chance to inform others of our whereabouts?" Dyna shot back. "Klyde said so himself. Galen will die anyway. I'm merely ensuring he does not become a problem later."

"It's one thing to defend yourself, lass, but stabbing a fleeing man in the back is generally frowned upon," Klyde said uneasily.

She took in all their expressions of disapproval, then met Zev's gaze. He offered no defense because ... he agreed. Taking a life left its mark, and he didn't want that for her.

Dyna scoffed in disgust as she turned away. "All of you have blood on your hands, and you've gained it without questioning your morals, because it was done to survive. How dare you question mine?"

Zev whined and tried to follow.

"Stay," Dyna snapped, pointing at him. He halted, lowering his ears. "All of you. I have nothing else to fear in these woods but your judgment."

Her wet eyes caught the moonlight as she stormed away. Guilt sank in Zev's chest. It wasn't her anger that made him feel ashamed, but the hurt behind it.

Because he was the one person she always expected to be on her side.

CHAPTER 17

Dynalya

Dyna trudged through the woods, furiously muttering to herself. When she found a small clearing, she leaned against a tree and closed her eyes. Her tired legs trembled, drawing her to sit and rest among the roots. She only attempted to kill Galen because he reminded her of everything and everyone she'd been up against.

She looked down at her shaking hands stained with blood.

This was what it took to survive in this world.

But she couldn't help remembering the way Tarn had killed the fleeing Azure Knight in gold blood. Was she like him, too?

Dyna's stomach twisted and she pushed the memory away. It didn't matter what it made her. She had already decided to become whatever necessary to get what she needed.

Reaching into her satchel, she called upon the water mirror, and its cool weight landed in her hand. She pulled it out and brought it onto her lap. Rain pattered into the bowl, creating soft music as it slowly filled.

With a sprinkle of salt, Dyna focused on the one she wanted to see. The swirling water fogged until an image appeared. Tarn sat at a chair by the fireplace, nursing a cup of wine.

"How close are you now?" he asked in greeting without looking up.

"I should reach the border of Dwarf Shoe in three days and arrive in Little Step."

Tarn picked up a book. "It will take you perhaps another day to reach the Port of Kelpway."

"Has your search been fruitful?" she asked with a hint of mockery.

Tarn's cool eyes narrowed on the book he was reading. "It's only a matter of time before I find the Druid. He may have already moved on. Whether you arrive here by the fourth day or not, we will continue. So make haste."

Dyna forced a smile to disguise her bout of nerves that he would disappear before she could catch up with him. "A gentleman would be patient and wait."

His mouth curled. "Maiden, we both know I am anything but a gentleman."

Something foul stirred in her stomach, lodging anger in her throat. It sent a rush up her nose.

"Would it really trouble you to wait?" Dyna demanded. "I am right here. You wanted me to join you, and I am finally on my way to you, yet you cannot be bothered to stay." Her voice shook. She scoffed to mask it, rolling her burning eyes up to the trees. "Well, I won't beg you. Leave. See how well you do without me."

An awkward quiet stretched between them, and Dyna inwardly cringed at how pathetic she sounded. So much for not begging him. After a minute, she reluctantly looked at him again and found Tarn staring at her.

"I am not sure whether I should be more perplexed by the blood on your face or the tears in your eyes." He canted his head. "What happened?"

She wiped her cheek. "Nothing."

"I very well doubt that. Where is your prince?"

Dyna scowled. "That's none of your concern. *Nothing* happened."

He smirked and closed his book. "Now, Maiden, if you expect me to believe you, then you must become a better liar. Since we have spoken, not once have you mentioned your—what did you once call him? Oh, yes. Your *mate*." Her withered heart sank. "Nor have I seen him or any of your other Guardians, for that matter. I take it that means they do not know about us, and I doubt you could keep me a secret this long unless you were alone. I can only assume *he* is no longer with you."

Her pulse pounded loudly in her ears.

"That spark of fire that I once saw in you was a candle flame. Now it burns like a bonfire, but not with love. Where is your Celestial?"

"Gone," she said tightly. "And I will say no more about that. Speaking of those absent, where is Von? I have not seen him either."

Tarn's attention returned to his book. "He's preoccupied."

She narrowed her eyes. The constant deflecting was making her suspicious. "I want to see him, Tarn."

"Then I suppose you better arrive within four days, Maiden," he said dismissively. "Time holds for no one, and neither do I."

"Wait," she blurted. "I'll be there. What is the name of your boat?"

"*The Somnio.*"

The water mirror cleared, leaving Dyna to stare at her reflection … along with the shocked faces of her Guardians standing over her shoulder. Including Klyde.

She spun around.

"Oh, you little liar," Lucenna hissed. "I knew you weren't simply speaking to yourself at night. You were communicating with that man this whole time!"

"Is that true?" Zev asked, staring at her wide-eyed. "You plan to join Tarn in Dwarf Shoe?"

Dyna quickly stood. "It's not what it looks like."

Electricity crackled around Lucenna. "It looks like you're consorting with the enemy. Why else keep it from us?"

"Because I knew you wouldn't like it."

"With good reason," Zev said gruffly. "What is the meaning of this? I don't understand."

Rawn lifted his hands placatingly. "All right, we can address this in a calm manner. Let's allow Lady Dyna to explain her motives." He turned to her with a worried frown. "I am sure there is a valid reason for her actions."

They fell quiet as they waited.

She closed her eyes and took a deep breath. "I plan to steal Tarn's ship."

They stared at her as if she were out of her mind.

Dyna groaned. "I didn't share this with you for the very thoughts I can see spinning in your heads right now. You weren't meant to know until we arrived in Dwarf Shoe. My plan is to arrive in Port Kelpway under the guise of joining him. The rest of you could sneak onto the ship to help me take Tarn down."

Klyde scratched his cheek, "Well, lass, I am no stranger to reckless plans, but this one may be out of the question…"

"What do you mean take him *down*?" Zev asked, flabbergasted.

Dyna straightened her shoulders, clenching her jaw. "I intend to finish him." A long drag of silence followed, and their skepticism only angered her. "We could have been on our way to Mount Ida by now if I had done the right thing and let him die from the start!"

He rubbed his face. "How long have you been planning this?"

"Probably for as long as she has been speaking to him in secret," Lucenna said.

"How long?"

Dyna sighed. "Three months past."

Zev shook his head. "I thought we agreed to no longer keep things from each other."

A twinge of guilt sank in her stomach. "It will work, Zev. The time I have spent talking with him was to gain his trust. He is waiting for me to arrive."

"Because he wants your map. Once he knows where Mount Ida is, he will kill you, Dyna."

"No, he won't. When I was in Tarn's camp, he had me trained and tried to convince me to join his side." Dyna crossed her arms. "He collects those with abilities he wants. In this case, my magic."

"Which you can no longer wield," Lucenna stated, and Dyna tried not to show how much that stung.

"Yes, well, he doesn't know that yet," she said sharply. "I only need him to allow me onto his ship. I have friends among the Raiders who will help us fight him. Those who weren't as fortunate as me to escape." She still needed to go back to set them free, too.

"You mean like the Minotaur," Zev said.

Klyde's brows shot up. "He has a Minotaur?"

Dyna nodded. "Sorren would be more than ready to take down some of Tarn's men to gain his freedom. As well as Geon, Yavi, and Von. They will join us. I know they will. Once Tarn is dealt with, we will commandeer his ship and sail with no threats of warrants or check points at any ports."

"Well ... I understand how that would be to our benefit," Rawn said, clearing his throat. "However, if we somehow achieve this plan, none of us have experience in navigating a ship."

"Von does." At their silence, Dyna groaned frustratingly. "Regardless of how you feel about him, Von is a *Guardian*. We need him."

Klyde's brow furrowed, and Dyna reminded herself to be careful.

"You speak as if this will be easy," the sorceress snapped. "We don't know how many men Tarn has on board or what we are walking into. And you are assuming Von will simply turn on his master after fifteen years of servitude. Your plan is foolish and reckless, and if you had told us about it from the beginning, I would have told you as much."

The very statement was a slap to her face.

"Remind me when I need your permission to make plans," Dyna hissed.

Lucenna's eyes flashed purple in response, and thunder rumbled overhead. The static of her power charged the air, crawling like ants on her skin.

"Easy," Zev growled. "Come with me. Let's take a breather." He took Lucenna's arm, leading her back to camp with Klyde.

Dyna turned away with a sharp exhale. She scowled at the trees, angry that they had to question her decisions about everything. She also didn't want to look at her Guidelander yet. Somehow, his opinion always weighed on her more.

"My lady," Rawn called gently.

"What is it, Lord Norrlen?" she sighed, shaking her head. "What more could you have to say that they have not?"

"Are you all right?"

A knot immediately formed in her throat at the question. No judgment. Only concern for her wellbeing. This wasn't about the last three months or even about her plan. She knew why he was asking that now.

Dyna clenched her shaking fists, feeling the dry blood crease in her palms. "We fought … and we won."

"That is not an answer." Rawn came around to face her, and he looked down at her with those kind eyes that she couldn't stand. "The feeling you are trying to ignore right now is your soul speaking to you. The way we fight, why we fight, and how we win all matters. If we chose to sacrifice our morals in order to win, then we have already lost."

Her vision stung as it blurred. "Why should I be kind and merciful? It's gotten me nowhere. The world is violent, and if I want to survive, I need to be *ruthless*. I need to tear into them before they do, because *no one*, not even the ones I love…" Her voice cracked. "…will show me mercy…"

It came to him.

It always came down to *him*.

There was no starlight in the sky. Not anymore. Yet why did Cassiel's faint scent strike her whenever she was reminded of him? Why did her withered heart always stir at the flutter of bird wings? No matter how much she burrowed into herself, his absence still haunted her. Had she not suffered enough?

Why couldn't she rip him out the way he had done with her?

"I feel as though I am hitting a wall," she said.

"Sometimes walls are there for us to lean on and rest."

Her tears spilled, and she dropped her head. Why did she feel so weak? After all the training she had done, she couldn't turn her heart into steel.

Rawn brought her to sit on a fallen log and sat with her beneath the rain as she silently cried. "I lament for your pain, my lady. And for the loss of who you used to be."

"He ruined me..."

"No," he said softly. "You are hurting, and rightfully so."

They looked out at the forest, listening to the drizzle patter on the leaves.

"I am stumbling in the dark..." she admitted. "It makes me feel so lost."

"To be lost does not mean one is lost forever. It merely means we need to find our way back. The most worthwhile path is seldom the easiest, but I have faith you will find your way again. For after darkness falls, the dawn will arise." As if the fates had to agree with him, the clouds parted at that moment, spilling the first rays of morning light through the trees, and he smiled. "If you need help with that, I will be right here to guide you."

He was kind to her and always a warm guide to turn to, but Dyna couldn't take any comfort right now. It only made her feel worse. Maybe she had forgotten how to be a good person.

Dyna wiped her cheek. "Thank you, Lord Norrlen."

"Of course, my lady." Rawn took out a handkerchief from beneath his cloak and handed it to her. "Now, shall we discuss the other matter at hand?"

She sighed. "Regarding Tarn, I take it. You don't agree."

"I have given you an oath that wherever you go on this quest, I will guard your steps and shield your life, to the end of the world and back. I am doing so now."

"You're saying I should be careful."

"I am saying we must be wise," Rawn clarified. "I fear the true reason you are doing this is rooted in your pain."

Dyna looked away. Pain was merely a sign of weakness. She would move on without Cassiel and prove she didn't need him anymore. "This has nothing to do with him, if that's what you think. It's a solid plan. It makes sense."

Or was she fighting too hard to convince herself of that?

"You have learned to defend yourself and how to wield weapons. Now you must learn strategy for when to attack and when to retreat. Regardless of how perfect a plan may be, they never go as planned, for they are carried out by imperfect people."

She made a face. Clearly, she wasn't perfect.

"I do not question your prudence. I merely worry about the state of your heart, for I know the pain you feel."

She looked back at Rawn in surprise, not expecting that.

"A dear one I loved also left me behind, and I too became lost. Anger wrought me into something I never wish to be again." Rawn looked down at his sword. The crest of a blooming dynalya adorned the pommel. "My actions had grievous consequences I could not amend, forever marring my name."

Dyna searched his kind face, finding it hard to believe he could ever harm another out of anger. But his eyes were sad and remorseful.

She inhaled the crispness of the fresh air as they continued to sit in silence, simply watching the light make the forest glitter.

Cassiel was her True Bonded. The other half of her soul.

His absence left her with a wound she may never heal, and she hated that. She hated the *helplessness* of it. Hated that she couldn't forget what he did. He had planted a seed of fury in her so deep it may never fade, and if so, there was no hope of ever finding her way back.

Perhaps she should thank him.

Rawn's advice had always helped her in the past, but she would never win against bloodthirsty demons, scheming fae, and men like Tarn by being the girl she once was. It was time to find a new path.

"Who left you behind?" Dyna asked, needing to take her mind off herself. "If you care to share…"

Rawn's teal eyes lowered to the signet ring on his forefinger. It bore his family's crest: a rearing horse in a shield, framed by laurel. There were other symbols she couldn't quite distinguish.

Lord Norrlen opened his mouth to answer, but Fair trotted through the trees. He nickered at them, giving Dyna's cheek a nuzzle.

"He sensed we needed comfort," Rawn said.

She smiled and petted his mane. "Fair, the noble steed, a great horse with the equal measure of his master. Kind, calming, and wise."

"He has seen me through everything since he chose me when I was a boy."

"Fair chose you?" Dyna asked curiously.

"He did. Elvish horses are special creatures. Very intelligent and magical in the sense that they bond with their rider for life. A deep connection forms between a horse and his master that allows us to move as one when riding into battle." Rawn's brow furrowed with that far away sadness as he stroked Fair's muzzle. "The loss of one is a loss of the other," he murmured.

"The one who left you … was it a previous horse?" Dyna was almost afraid to ask.

"No, not mine." He sighed and rested his head on Fair's neck. "My sister. Her horse was killed during a mission, and she could not..."

Withstand the loss.

Fair stood between them like a wall that hid him away, but Dyna didn't need to see Rawn's face or to hear the words aloud to know that his sister was no longer alive. And she sensed it led to the dark period when he had lost himself.

"I'm sorry," she whispered.

"Such is the life of a soldier, my lady." Rawn came around Fair, taking the reins. His gaze drifted south, as it always did when he was missing his home. His family.

"We are close to Greenwood, Lord Norrlen. Once we have the ship, why don't we..."

He shook his head. "By the oath I made to my king, I cannot return home until I have completed my mission. Our word is sacred, considered a covenant with the God of Urn. I have not been this close to Greenwood in years. It is a great risk to be in this part of the country."

"Because of Red Highland?"

"Not only them. There are elves who move through the shadows. They sever lives for the right price, and there is a substantial one for mine."

Dyna stilled at that, but he didn't seem to want to discuss it further. They made their way back, with many things circling in her mind. It was unfair that Rawn couldn't return home because of a promise he made. And at the same time, it made her hate for the one who willingly broke all his promises to her grow more.

CHAPTER 18

Cassiel

Cassiel soared across the open sky. The setting sun painted the horizon a vivid orange, washing out all blue. Flying used to be the only time he found a shred of relief from the burden of his life, but now all it held was a reminder of her.

"My King," Yelrakel called to him. "We are being followed."

He came to a halt on a bedding of Seraph flames, and his Legion braced themselves. A group of armed Celestials flying on a flock of Pegasi were headed his way. He focused on the one who led them. It was perhaps the last person he expected to see on this side of Urn.

Asiel.

The Valkyrie braced to fight, but Cassiel signaled for them to stand down. While armed, there were not enough of them to deem this an attack. Even if it was, they would be no match for him.

Asiel and his unit of male Hermon guards came to a stop. He dismounted and slowly flew to him. They sized each other up in the windy silence before Asiel clanked a fist over his heart and bowed his head, as did the others. "Pardon our unexpected arrival, Your Majesty."

Cassiel let the heavy title hang between them for a moment. "Why have you come? Speak freely. I care nothing for your false deference, that of which you never cared to show before."

Asiel straightened, and his expression grew guarded. "You know why I've come, Cassiel."

"Whether it's to question me or challenge me, both are one and the same."

Asiel shook his head. "I came searching for you in hopes you would hear my plea. On behalf of the Realms, desist this."

"Desist what?"

"Please do not insult me, cousin," Asiel said tightly. "The entire Legion of Valkyrie has rallied to your side. Even the Watchers have joined your ranks, leaving Hermon without protection. Then you destroyed an entire Realm, which we came to learn from the survivors fleeing your flame. We know nothing of what happened on Troll Bridge besides the note that was given to me. The High King and your mate assassinated. By whom? The people have yet to understand what is happening. We saw the *Hyalus* tree glow. We know what it means. You are now our High King, but months passed without any further word or sign from you. The only news being the loss of Skath ... and rumors."

Rumors about *him*.

"All I am left with are questions that plague me. I fear the answers." Asiel took a breath but hesitated.

Cassiel smirked. "You want to ask if I am Kāhssiel reborn?"

He shook his head. "No, I don't care if you are reincarnated or not. I want to know why you killed Lord Hallel and his people." His voice grew anxious, raw. "I want to know what happened to my father. *Where* is he?"

Cassiel gazed at the horizon as the last of the sunlight dipped beneath the clouds. Thinking about that day made his skull feel as if it were being crushed. He didn't want to remember his uncle's betrayal.

"Is he...?"

"Lord Jophiel lives," Cassiel said, looking back at him.

Asiel's shoulders sagged with relief. "Then why has he not returned home?"

"Your father is being held for crimes against the crown."

His cousin stared at him with angry incredulity. "He would never."

"And yet he has," Cassiel replied coolly as he turned away.

"No, I will not accept that." Asiel grabbed his arm, and the Valkyrie immediately drew their weapons. Cassiel motioned with his other hand, silently ordering them to stay back. "That is a lie," his cousin continued. "My father would never betray his brother, or *you*, for that matter. Because he *always* placed you above me. Whatever happened, there must be a reason. You have taken him from me time and again." His voice cracked. "Give him back, Cassiel. Please."

The plea stirred in his chest, but Cassiel ignored the feeling. "Let go."

"I can't." Asiel's grip on his arm shook, and he lowered his head. "If I let go, I know what you will do."

He wasn't the only one who had changed. Asiel seemed different, too. Now Lord of Hermon, he was here because he felt the duty to protect his people, even if it meant coming here to defy him.

"And you think you are enough to stop me?" Cassiel asked.

"I know that I'm not. None of us are. But that will not bar the Realms from doing everything to fight you. They believe the throne was stolen. Most accuse your mate of killing your father to make you king."

Cassiel's eyes flamed blue.

Asiel sighed. "It was not I who said it, but it is not the only rumor spreading amongst our people. Others say you have committed regicide and are now making your way through the Realms, killing each Lord who does not bend to your will."

They would say that. But Cassiel was no longer surprised by what those against him would concoct.

At his silence, Asiel's eyes widened. "Don't tell me it's true. Did you take the throne at the point of a sword?"

"You insult me with a question I will not dignify with words."

Why bother defending himself? No one would believe the truth. Not from a half-breed.

"If it's not true, why didn't you come to Yoel's funeral?"

The question made Cassiel clenched his jaw. "I had no reason to go."

Bewilderment crossed Asiel's face, and he shook his head. "I understand and I'm sorry. But whatever your torment, you must halt this army and return to Hilos to address the Realms, Cassiel." He grabbed his shoulders. "After what you have done to Skath, Edym and Nazar are preparing for battle. They will fight to defend their territories. Think of your people. The children who are innocent, made casualties of war. Dyna would not want this."

Her name was a hot iron searing into his very soul.

Cassiel shoved him off. "You know nothing, Asiel."

There was only frustration and distress on his cousin's face. "You're right. I don't. So *tell* me! What happened that night?"

Memories flashed in Cassiel's head. Blood. A bright light. A caress against his cheek.

Sharp pain pierced his skull, and Cassiel grimaced. He turned away with a shallow breath and pressed on his temples. "The only thing you need to know is that I am righting wrongs."

"If you go to war for vengeance, it will not fill the hole inside of you. It will consume you."

It already had.

"This is not what your father would have wanted for you."

Cassiel leaned his head back and laughed. The harsh sound echoed through the sky, tainted by his madness as he faced his startled cousin. "*Oh.* Did you expect that to change my mind? I no longer have a heart for you to sway. If you search for sympathy, you will not find it. If you hoped for compassion, I am free of it." Seraph fire flamed in his fists, coursing up his arms. "Choose a side, Asiel. You either stand with your king, or you die with those I intend to *burn*."

Asiel's throat bobbed as he stared at him. "All of our lives, you and I have never been on the same side. Do not force me to stand against you now."

He didn't want to fight. Of all times, he was choosing now to be noble. Maybe Cassiel should have told him the truth, but he didn't trust anyone anymore.

As far as the Realms knew, the High King was on a rampage to eradicate them and didn't care what innocents died. It had been true in his past life. Let them believe it in this one. All the better that assumed him a mad king.

Only then would his true enemies appear.

"Whether you live or die, it will be by your will alone."

His cousin's face fell. Cassiel saw the struggle there, but it wasn't a question of who Asiel would choose. He had to stand with Nazar for Sarrai's sake. His mate came first.

As Cassiel's did.

Asiel flew back and mounted his Pegasus. "I would have followed the man you used to be, Cassiel. Not the tyrant you have become."

He soared away with his unit of soldiers for the south, leaving Cassiel with the weight of his words. They caught the wind quickly, and soon fell out of sight as they vanished through the clouds. With his new strength and speed, Cassiel could keep up with the Pegasi, but the same couldn't be said of his Valkyrie.

Asiel had a head start, and they both knew it.

Yelrakel came to his side. "Sire, if you let him go, he will inform Lord Gadriel of our impending arrival."

"I look forward to it." Cassiel was prepared to become the monster the Realms believed him to be. For his mate, he would swallow up the darkness and let it consume him whole.

His soul be damned.

CHAPTER 19

Rawn

It was a calm evening around the campfire as Rawn worked on fletching more arrows. Zev lounged on his bed mat while the others wandered the open field searching for four-leaf clovers. The evening air carried an earthy scent. Lightning flashed in the distance, then came a faint rumble.

"Smells like rain again tonight," Zev muttered.

"Yes," Rawn agreed, a droplet landing on his cheek. The wind picked up, shaking the wet branches of the tree above them. A few more droplets landed on the golden ring on his pinky. It bore the sigil of his House and the sight of it pulled him back to memories he would rather not remember. He had been dreaming a lot of his past lately. It started a while ago after the magical explosion when Dyna's barrier had first broken.

"Rawn?"

He blinked. "Pardon?"

"I asked what that ring was," Zev said, sitting up. "You were staring at it."

"Oh, it is the signet ring of my household." Rawn twisted it around his finger, watching how it glinted in the firelight. "It was passed down to me by my father, and one day ... it will belong to Raiden."

"Raiden?"

"My son ... I have not shared his name, have I?" Rawn smiled faintly as he looked out at the girls still searching for clovers. "He would be about your age now."

At times, Rawn liked to picture his son here among them, but he couldn't place his face.

"I found one," Klyde announced, spinning a little clover stem in his fingers.

"Splendid," Lucenna groused as she moved on to another green patch.

"If you want it, I'll trade it for a kiss."

"Attempt it, and no amount of clovers will protect you."

Klyde's laughter resonated across the field.

Zev canted his head as Rawn picked up another set of feathers to fletch. "You haven't told us much about your family."

"I regret to say I left the day after my son was born. My wife, however, was the grace that changed my life." He glanced at his other gold ring, the one that Aerina put on his finger the day they were wed. "I am alive today because of her ... and I am sorry to have been parted from her for so long."

How much his life had changed since he accepted that mission. Where would he be now if he had turned it down?

"I am sure she is eagerly waiting for your return," Zev said. "How did you come to meet her?"

"It's a long story..."

Dyna returned to sit on her bed mat beside them with a huff. "I give up," she sighed.

"Already?" Zev asked with a chuckle.

"It's too dark to see now. Perhaps in the morning ... oh, look!" Dyna exclaimed. "You have a bit of luck, Lord Norrlen."

Nestled within the tuft of grass by his boot was a small stem with four heart-shaped leaves. "It appears I have." He plucked the clover and handed it to her. "Take it."

"I can't. It belongs to the one who found it." She placed it inside of a small leather pouch no bigger than two inches and fastened it to the inside of his tunic with a pin. "There. Four-leaf clovers have magic of their own. It will provide protection against any spells cast against you."

"I remember," Rawn murmured, pressing his hand over it. If only he had had a bit of luck when he had needed it.

TWENTY-FIVE YEARS AGO

When he had entered the throne room, Rawn dropped to one knee and bowed. He took a shallow breath to calm his hammering heart, his hands trembling. Not once had he been in the presence of the king before today, now he was only a few feet away from him.

King Leif's calm voice drifted over him. "Please rise."

Rawn stood, but kept his head lowered. He had too much reverence for the King of Greenwood to meet his eyes, but Leif wasn't having it.

"There is no law against meeting my gaze. I must look upon the one I am entrusting with this very important mission for the crown."

Mission?

Rawn took a breath and looked up.

His previous teacher, Magi Master Eldred Lothiriel, was present along with his father. Eldred's silver hair caught the sunlight streaming in through the windows behind the grand throne. He stood silently in robes the color of lichen, white staff in hand. Sylar's father offered him a kind nod.

Rawn's father, however, stood tall and commanding in his green armor veined in silver. The General's harsh eyes fell on him from his post at the foot of the stairs. Only disapproval swam in his gaze. Rawn could sense his father didn't think he was right for this mission, so why had the king called him here?

Then Rawn met King Leif's steel-gray eyes. His long ash blond hair was braided at his temples, a circlet of gold and silver adorning his forehead. He appeared young, though he was a few hundred years old. He wore light gray robes trimmed with gold, the long sleeves coming to a tapered end on his middle fingers.

"Before I tell why I have called you here, Rawn Norrlen, I must ask for your sworn oath of secrecy," the king said.

Rawn immediately gave it. "Of course, sire. Before the eyes of the God of Urn, I swear no word of this day will ever be spoken to another."

The king nodded. "You know the history of my family and the blood spilled for the throne. There are yet those who seek to replace me, and now a reason has surfaced."

Rawn had heard the rumors about the queen having not yet borne an heir for Greenwood. It put into question Leif's reign. His relatives were circling, their fingers itching to snatch the crown.

"It may soon come to light that the one who cannot produce an heir is I..." King Leif said, and Rawn stilled. "Some time ago, the last king of Red Highland placed a curse upon the males of my family, and now that curse has fallen upon me. I am unable to continue my line. However, I am not the last of House Silva, and many know it. I have reason to believe my sister is now in danger."

Rawn's pulse spiked at the news. "Who would dare, Your Majesty? Give me a name, and I will remove them. No one will ever touch her."

King Leif's mouth twitched at his passionate declaration, and Rawn flushed when he exchanged a look with his father. "I am pleased you are willing to protect her, Rawn. However, I fear the threat also comes beyond our walls. It is no secret Red Highland wants to return the kingdoms in the Vale under one rule again. *Theirs*. If not by marriage, then by war."

The threat of war was the last thing Rawn had expected today, yet when was anyone ever prepared for it?

Then Rawn realized the implication in his statement. "King Altham has asked for Aerina's hand, sire?"

"Altham has proposed that she marry his eldest son. I refused him, of course, but now we hear rumors of radicals who are sympathetic to Red Highland's cause. Some believe he is the true heir of Greenwood, and others merely have grown weary of bloodshed. I fear our borders may no longer be properly protected."

Rawn's mind spun. His garrison was attacked not a short time ago. If Red Highland soldiers could ambush them so easily, perhaps they were being helped.

If it was a question of heredity and who could have rights to the throne of Greenwood, even Red Highland had a claim. For at the end of the first age, it was two princes of the Silva bloodline who had split the Vale into two.

God of Urn, if a red prince managed to abduct a green princess, to abduct Aerina...

The world was tilting.

"You understand my concern." The king watched him soberly.

"Yes, sire." Rawn glanced between him, Eldred, and his father. "Have you received word from your spies that our enemies mean to infiltrate our borders? If they attempt to kidnap our princess, that will put an end to the current ceasefire between Greenwood and Red Highland."

King Leif leaned back on his throne with a sigh. "A calamity I would prefer to avoid. We have hardly recovered from our last war. I do not wish for another. Alas, until we find out who is aiding them, Aerina is not safe."

Rawn clenched his jaw at the thought of anyone harming her. To think that some of his people were secretly sympathetic to Red Highland after all the lives that had been lost sickened him.

"Then I will go and find where the threat in our borders lie before they have a chance to enter—"

"I am afraid it's too late."

He stilled. "Sire?"

His father shifted on his feet, resting a hand on his sword's hilt. The scar on his lip pinched with his frown. "The garrison at West Wall was infiltrated three days past, and no survivors were left behind. They could not have crossed our walls without help, but one thing is for certain. They are *here*."

Rawn's pulse climbed as he thought of the night a spear took him down. His garrison had not been attacked at random. They had been planning this.

To think red elves were in his home with the intent to do harm angered him.

"I have made an attempt to track them," Eldred said, "But they are cloaked. One among them is certainly a Magi Master, and a dangerous one."

King Leif leveled him with a look as he stood. "Aerina is the only hope for our kingdom now. Protecting her life may come at the cost of your own."

But Rawn didn't hesitate again. He lowered to one knee and bowed his head. "What will you have me do? I am at your command, whatever it may be."

King Leif climbed down the steps to him, and he looked outside to the courtyard. At the center rose a particular tree split in two at the base that had grown into a perfect circle.

"Your mission is to take Aerina away from the palace tonight at high moon through the Elder Tree's gateway. It will take you as far as the highlands of Erendor, and from there, escort her to the convent in Galadir. A week's travel at best. You will remain there and guard her. Do not return until you have received word that the threat has been eliminated or that my wife has borne an heir. The future of Greenwood is at stake, Rawn. Can I trust you to keep my sister safe?"

"I swear upon my life that no harm shall fall upon the princess." Rawn clanked a fist over his heart, and it shook with the weight of his oath.

Should he fail, the cost would be his head.

"Good. Then you may take two others to help you. Is there anyone who you can trust with this mission?"

Rawn didn't need to think long on it. He glanced at his father and Eldred. Both could guess his thoughts, and neither spoke against it.

He rose to stand. "Nisa of House Norrlen, sire. She was a Ranger before becoming part of the princess's personal Royal Guard. As well as Sylar of House Lothiriel, Magi Apprentice. I trust them both with my life. I would like to request them to join me."

King Leif dipped his chin in a nod. "Granted."

And that was perhaps the greatest regret of his life.

Aerina giggled over a funny story Sylar told her by the campfire as he played a silly tune on his lyre. Rawn preoccupied himself by checking their horses and bags again, making sure they had enough provisions for the second leg of their journey.

They had finally reached the borders of Erendor. They had perhaps twenty-five more miles before reaching their destination. They kept to the forests, avoiding the main roads. His hand paused on the flap of a bag as he gazed at Galadir far below the range. Moonlight reflected over the roofs of the tall stone buildings, windows flickering with candlelight.

Only one more day left.

Time had passed by too fast for his liking.

"What are you doing?" Nisa appeared by his side suddenly. "Come sit by the fire and celebrate the summer solstice with us. The fireworks will start soon."

"I am preoccupied here."

She groaned and crossed her arms. "You won't be condemned merely for speaking to her, brother."

He frowned. "What are you implying?"

"Rawn." Nisa arched an eyebrow. "Since we left the castle, you have hardly spoken three words to the princess. She believes you dislike her."

He balked. "She said this?"

Nisa grinned. "No, but now that I have your attention, why do you elude her?"

Groaning, Rawn returned to checking the belts of his saddle.

"What do you think of that, Fair?" Nisa teased as she stroked his horse's muzzle. "Rawn can finally speak to his beloved, but he hides away like a child." Fair whinnied and she snickered. "He agrees with me."

Rawn shushed them desperately as he glanced at Aerina, but Sylar's music was thankfully on his side tonight. "Will you cease?" he told her sharply. "Do not pretend to sense Fair's opinions. He is not bonded to you."

"I do not need to be bonded to him to comprehend him." Nisa went to her own bonded horse grazing beside Fair and began brushing down her beige coat. "Horses are easy to understand. They do not complicate things like we do. Lowenna chose me as her rider as she chose Fair for her mate. He did not fight it either, did he, girl?"

Lowenna chuffed, nibling at Nisa's cloak brooch in the shape of a horse. His sister grinned.

With a sigh, Rawn shook his head. "We are here for a reason, and it's not so I can yearn for her, let alone be her friend."

Nisa's face softened. "So you do yearn..."

He continued his work, if only to ignore the statement, but the silence made him have the urge to fill it. "I am a lowborn soldier, Nisa, and she is a *princess.* One I am tasked with escorting to safety. Nothing more. To even imply it, to even speak of it..." Rawn shook his head as his gaze returned to Aerina.

He knew his place. Yet in his heart, she was a wish.

A forbidden one.

"You were once friends."

"That was before I understood who she was," Rawn replied faintly as he recalled the time they spent together during their schooling years. Life had been more innocent then, not yet encumbered by duty and status. "We are not children anymore."

"We are taking Aerina to Galadir tomorrow," his sister said softly. "Once this mission is over, you may never see her again. I think you can afford one night where you forget about her status and the lack of yours. Tonight, you are not a soldier on a mission. You are simply Rawn who will ask a girl for a dance. What is the worst that can happen?"

The worst?

That would be to reveal the secret he had buried somewhere in his heart a long time ago. That Aerina would see past the carefully built wall he constructed around himself, concealing how hopelessly in love with her he was.

To entertain such a thing went far beyond any realm of acceptability. Especially while aware of the reason he was escorting her in the first place. King Leif trusted his honor. What kind of elf would he be to betray that?

Before Rawn left the castle, his father had given him the signet ring with a word of warning. *Take this so all who meet you know you are a progeny of our House. This mission holds many lives at stake. Do you understand? Do not fail your king.*

Not again.

They all looked up at the sky as it burst with fireworks. The colorful lights flashed in Aerina's eyes, making them sparkle. They met his gaze and she smiled.

The power that action had on him made his heart pitifully tumble into his stomach. If only she knew how much it broke him. He had already crossed so many lines by simply experiencing such a thing.

Those feelings were dangerous.

Because what if...

"Princess!" Nisa called cheerily. "Would you care for a dance? Sir Rawn is at your service."

"What? I—"

Nisa pushed him hard enough that he stumbled a few steps forward until he found himself standing in front of Aerina. He felt a rush of heat shoot up his pointed ears, and his heart shot back up into his throat.

Aerina stood and said with the sweetest smile, "I would love to."

Rawn couldn't do anything more but take her offered hand. Sylar immediately began a new song as he led her into a dance. But Rawn had been trained in everything except that. Aerina laughed at his clumsy attempt, yet he didn't care, because she was still smiling at him.

His sister and his best friend had their fill of ale as he endured their teasing at his lackluster dancing. They eventually fell asleep. But Rawn stayed up late into the night, talking with Aerina by the fire about everything and anything.

Well, she mostly talked, and he listened. He could fall asleep listening to her voice.

And he had.

A grave oversight, for Rawn woke to a distant scream.

He stumbled to his feet, his mind on alert and disoriented in the gray dawn. Sylar and Nisa jerked awake. The highlands were coated in a veil of fog.

And Aerina's bed mat was empty.

"Princess!" Rawn shouted.

The scream came again from the trees.

He bolted for his horse, Nisa and Sylar running close behind. Leaping onto Fair's saddle, Rawn kicked his heels. They chased the echo of Aerina's cries and the beat of retreating hooves.

Rawn raced into the forest, his heartbeat thudding in his ears. This couldn't be happening. He couldn't fail. He had to reach her.

A group of riders galloped ahead. They wore black armor, their dark red cloaks flowing behind them like veils of blood.

Force Sentries of Red Highland.

They were fleeing with a carriage, and Rawn heard Aerina's cries.

Rawn galloped for the carriage through the forest, determined to reach it before he lost her forever. Nisa and Sy caught up on his flank. A fight broke out of steel and magic as they fought sentries guarding the carriage and every rider who appeared from the trees.

Rawn leaped off Fair's saddle onto the back of the carriage and climbed onto the roof. A blade came for his head. He ducked and rolled out of the way. Rising to his feet, he whipped out his sword and met his opponent. The sentry was covered head to toe with black armor. The only thing visible were his amber eyes through his helmet.

Their weapons clashed as they fought.

His opponent muttered a spell in Elvish, and blue electricity spiraled around his blade. Rawn rolled out from under the sentry's next attack and kicked him off the roof.

Climbing down the side of the carriage, Rawn yanked open the door to find Aerina inside. She cried out in relief and rushed to him.

"We have to jump!" he told her.

"What?" she said frightfully.

"Now!"

Aerina latched onto him, and they were yanked away by the force of magic. Sy tossed them on soft ground, and he murmured a second spell. A yellow hexagon with glowing runes blasted toward the carriage. It erupted with a deafening *boom*, taking down the remaining soldiers.

Aerina shook against him with quiet sobs.

"Are you hurt?"

She shook her head but touched her stomach. "He … he cast a spell on me." She cried harder.

Rawn's eyes widened and a chill sank through him. "Did he…?"

Aerina shut her eyes. "I don't know."

He couldn't think of anything else now but to get her to safety.

"We need go," Rawn murmured as they sat up. He looked her over, brushing the hair from her face. "Are you all right? Can you stand?"

She nodded, and he helped her to her feet.

Nisa kicked up dirt with the jerk on the reins, bringing her horse to a halt in front of them. "We need to find high ground. It's not safe here. Move—"

It was the whistling he heard first. The high pitch cut of wind that he had heard before.

"Down!" Rawn shouted.

The black spear zipped through the trees with a crackle of orange magic. It pierced through his shoulder, and he hit the ground with Aerina. She cried out his name. He tried to move. His vision spun and his ears rang. He gripped the shaft of the spear, but it struck him with a spell. He couldn't pull it out. Embossed on the socket was the sigil of a red maple leaf.

"Prince Anon," Aerina gasped. She gaped up at an elf standing on the rise above them within the trees.

The morning sun glinted over his black armor, his red cape fluttering in the wind around his feet. He had short dark hair and dark eyes, a silver circlet on his forehead. Anon smiled at them, cold and sharp.

He lifted another black spear.

"Get down!" Rawn yanked Aerina to him.

The second spear came, and Nisa screamed.

She screamed so terribly, Rawn thought she had been hit.

A body dropped heavily on the ground beside him. He shut his eyes for a moment, gathering the courage to look. Lowenna. The beautiful beige horse lay dead with the spear through her neck.

His sister's cry ripped through his ears as their bond broke. His vision welled as he felt her pain. Her loss.

And her rage.

Rawn desperately searched for Fair and shuddered with relief when he heard his horse's neigh.

Anon's laughter floated to them, and he darted into the trees. Any remaining Force Sentries followed. Good, they were retreating.

But his sister snarled and snatched up her fallen sword.

"Nisa!" Rawn desperately clutched her green cape. "Do not follow. It's a trap."

"I will not besmirch my honor by allowing him to escape," Nisa said, her furious eyes blazing above him. "He owes me a life. If I do not return, you must take over the hunt. Slay him, Rawn. Even if it's the last thing you do."

She bolted into the forest.

"No, Nisa!" Rawn tried to get up, but the sharp stab of pain in his shoulder left him immobile. "Sy!"

"I'm here." Sylar scrambled to him on his hands and knees. His wide eyes looked him over as he inspected the wound. "The spear missed anything vital, but I need to take it out. This is going to hurt." He placed a thick piece of leather in Rawn's mouth and Aerina's small hand clutched his. Bracing, he inhaled a sharp breath. Sylar yanked it out. Rawn screamed through the tearing of his flesh, and the pain began to drag him under. "Take this, princess. Clean the wound and apply the waters," Sylar instructed Aerina quickly as he handed her a glass bottle. Pale pink liquid sloshed inside, swirling with red petals.

"Stop her..." Rawn rasped as his eyes drifted shut.

"Don't move, Rawn," Sylar told him. "Stay with the princess while I will fetch Nisa. You have my oath. I will bring her back!"

Then his best friend sprinted after his sister.

And neither of them returned.

CHAPTER 20

Lucenna

Lucenna stepped out of her tent and was greeted by a clear sky. Thank the Gods. She was sick of the spring rains. The others conversed idly as they ate their morning meal by the campfire. Rawn nursed some tea while Dyna was out in the field with Fair, practicing her sword drills.

"Good morrow, my lady," Rawn murmured. "Sleep well?"

"As much as I can without a bed," Lucenna said, rubbing the sleep from her eyes. But she could tell from Rawn's face he didn't sleep well at all. His eyes were red and his face haggard. He looked pale.

"Here, break your fast," Zev handed Lucenna a bowl of cooked oats sprinkled with cinnamon and wild berries. "We'll be on the road soon."

"Thank you." She sat beside him on a log by the fire and couldn't help but notice someone missing. "Where has Klyde gone?"

"The captain woke before dawn to scout ahead," Rawn said. "We will meet him on the road later."

"Hmm." She narrowed her eyes on the trees. "Have you noticed he no longer questions who we are and what we are after?"

"Aye, we have," Zev said as he rolled up his sleeping mat and stored it in his bag. "It seems he has lost interest."

"Or perhaps because he already got his answer."

Even with all of Dyna's posturing, Klyde had to notice her whispering to Keena in secret.

"Do you suspect he knows the truth?" Rawn asked.

Lucenna wasn't sure. They had been careful with the map. Every day it changed hands, so Klyde wouldn't know who held it. But he was never looking either way, and he no longer asked about them or their plans.

It seemed his only interest had always been to catch Tarn.

"Klyde is an intelligent man." They all looked up at Dyna, where she stood against the sunset, sweat glistening on her forehead. She sheathed her weapons. "I suspect he knows where we are going, but I don't think he cares. He made his priorities clear. Perhaps our caution is necessary."

Lucenna frowned. "I remember how secretive you were when I first joined."

"Well, you have a reason to go to Mount Ida," Zev said. "He doesn't."

"If the plan goes awry, he might have one." Rawn set down his cup and pulled out the map.

They all huddled around him as enchanted ink swirled across the page and the Land of Urn appeared. He tapped on the coast of the Saxe Sea. The map augmented for a closer view of Dwarf Shoe and the northern region of Greenwood. A brief tightness crossed his brow before he adjusted the spelled view to only focus on their next destination.

"If we continue on the main road, we will cross Tertius Bridge over the Third River by midday. It leads to Little Step, a border city in Dwarf Shoe."

"Tarn is in Kelpway." Dyna pointed to a port on the coast that was about thirty miles away. "He's been tipped off that Leoake is there."

Lucenna's brows rose up. "What does he want with the Druid?"

"He has the other half of the Unending Scroll."

Zev curled his lip. "Why do I have the feeling that's not a coincidence?"

Dyna crossed her arms, glowering at the trees. "With Leoake, nothing ever is."

"If we travel by carriage on the morrow, we could arrive in Kelpway by the evening," Rawn said.

They had leased a carriage before, and it helped to cut down their travel time. Lucenna wished they had a more convenient way of travel the majority of the time.

Once they finished their morning meal, they packed up their belongings and set on their way. Lucenna walked behind Rawn and Zev, glancing every so often at the forest. Where did that mercenary go?

Dyna cantered beside her, riding Fair. Things had been strained between them lately. Lucenna didn't know how to talk to her anymore, but she didn't like this distance between them.

"Dyna," she started hesitantly. "I'm sorry if I am overbearing sometimes. I'm only worried about you."

Dyna glanced at her for a moment, then at the road again. "I'm sorry for my manner lately, too," she muttered. "I think ... I secretly resent you for having your magic, while mine is once again locked away. That isn't your doing. I don't blame you. I am simply ... envious."

Lucenna's frown softened. "I should have known that was how you were feeling." She took Fair's reins, bringing her to a stop. "But this plan, is it because you want revenge against Tarn, or because you have something to prove ... to Cassiel?"

Dyna glared at her. "And why are you so distrustful of Klyde?" she demanded, immediately defensive. "Is it because you're embarrassed that he wooed you with his charm or because he made you question your feelings for Everest?"

Electricity crackled around Lucenna, and she smiled tightly. "I know you are not in your right mind right now, so I will let that pass. This once."

Dyna slid off Fair's saddle. She strode past her, moving ahead on the road.

"Brat," Lucenna groused under her breath.

Fair snorted disapprovingly.

"She is." Lucenna threw out her hands in exasperation.

The horse lowered his ears and pushed his head against Lucenna's back, nudging her forward.

"You want *me* to apologize? She started it." Fair swatted her with his tail, and Lucenna sighed. "What am I to do with her, hmm? I can't reach her anymore. She's too hurt. Too angry. She's changed."

And it reminded Lucenna of herself.

She had also been in a dark place when her mother died. Heartbreak sometimes made others hurt others, because they were hurt themselves.

Fair nuzzled her cheek.

"Go on." Lucenna shooed him away playfully. "You're the only one she likes right now."

With a soft whinny, Fair's hooves beat on the path as he trotted ahead. When he reached her, Dyna patted his muzzle and mounted the saddle again to catch up with Rawn and Zev waiting for them at the top of the knoll.

With how unpredictable Dyna's emotions were, maybe it was a good thing she didn't have access to her magic.

Lucenna snapped out of her thoughts at the sudden rustle in the bushes on her left. Purple Essence crackled in her hands, but it was only Klyde. "What were you doing lurking in the woods?"

"Bounty hunters tend to stake out the roads to catch any potential targets before they can reach the city. I went to make sure we wouldn't be ambushed."

Lucenna's eyes widened, surprised she had not thought of that. "Did you find anyone?"

Klyde joined her on the road. "I did."

He said no more, and the answer was enough. She swept her gaze over him, finding nothing out of place but a singular drop of blood on the cuff of his coat.

How many hunters did he ... eliminate? Why not mention it to them before?

"Did they deserve it?" she asked next.

A look crossed his face that reminded her of the day she went into his parents' chambers.

"Good," she murmured as they continued. "I hope this won't be a problem for us later."

Klyde stuck his hands in his coat pockets. "Bounty hunting is a trade with high risks and high rewards. Often, hunters are as vile as their targets. They won't be missed." That's not what she had meant, but then he said, "Thank you for allowing me to use your orb last night."

Lucenna nodded. They had used it to check on Eagon. She was glad to find he and the Skelling Mercenaries had made it home without any more casualties. Klyde seemed more relaxed now that he knew his friends were safe.

They reached the others at the top of the knoll, and Lucenna forgot all else when they took in the view.

The state of Dwarf Shoe was settled cozily into the bay. The capitol building rose in the center as a pointed needle. Beyond the shores of the Saxe Sea, ships sailed into the wharf. The surrounding islands were separated by a small strip of sea, more homes going into the distance.

Lucenna basked in the warm sunlight and clear skies. A bell tolled in the distance, marking the afternoon hour. Now this weather was perfect.

Rawn's gaze moved past it to the south, toward Greenwood. She followed his stare to the profile of gray mountains in the distance, the peaks nearly hidden within the thick clouds. They were so large they seemed to tower in the sky.

"Your home," Lucenna commented.

Rawn nodded. "On the days of rain, a morning fog rolls over the range, giving the impression one is walking amongst the Heavens." His gaze grew distant, as if he could clearly see it. "The Anduir Mountains are renowned for their beauty, with a lush forest evergreen. At the foothills lies my home in the Valley of Sellav. The land is full of rolling hills and fields of dynalya flowers that fill the air with their sweet scent. The rivers are so clear you can see to their depths as they sing to you." Rawn faintly smiled, and she thought his eyes looked wet. "To stand in Sellav is to discover peace, for you will find no other place like it."

"You miss it." She could hear it in his voice.

"I miss those who live there more." He took a breath and turned to the others. "We are losing daylight. We must find shelter before nightfall."

They all nodded and pulled up their hoods. Dwarf Shoe may be a free state, but that didn't mean they shouldn't be careful. Lucenna, especially. Mages were everywhere. The closer they moved to the Magos Empire, the more it unsettled her nerves. She had not been this near the south in years.

With a wave of her hand, Lucenna cast a glamor spell. Deep purple robes enveloped her small, hunched frame. She covered her white hair with a matching turban and pulled out a sash to tie it over her eyes. It was thin enough to still see through.

Klyde inched up his brows curiously and chuckled. "Whilst I understand avoiding mages, what is the purpose of hiding behind the disguise of an old hag? Why not simply appear like another fair maiden?"

"I prefer to be an unfair one. It averts *unwanted* attention," Lucenna said, stabbing his chest with a long-yellowed nail. "But if you insist." She snapped her fingers and changed her appearance to resemble Gale.

He reared back. "Gods, that's worse."

"Why?" Lucenna simpered as she moved closer to him. With a flirty smile, she flipped her new blonde hair over her shoulder. "This is the *perfect* disguise, according to you."

"Please." He shuddered. "You torture me."

Grinning, Lucenna changed back to her wrinkly appearance.

They trekked for several more miles, passing stone markers at each intersection. The dirt path switched to a paved road, and it became more crowded as others joined them. Many had traveled from afar, some on foot, others on horseback, or by carriage. At least half were dwarves.

Eventually, the road led to Tertius Bridge suspended over the Third River. It was a massive body of water, serving as a border between Argyle and Dwarf Shoe. The wind whipped against Lucenna, carrying the scent of brine and kelp. Several fishing boats idled on the clear blue surface, with seagulls squawking as they circled above.

Beyond the shoreline, the city of Little Step appeared. The stone structures with domed roofs spread throughout the land.

"I take it this is your first visit?" Klyde asked as he paused beside her. He smiled at the city, the wind ruffling his hair around his eyes that shone like the sea. "Little Step was the first town founded before it grew into a city. As more people from all over gathered here, their land expanded until it became the first free state in Urn. Without a king to rule it, the wealth generated by the people is for the people, and it reflects in the advancement of their state. Cleaner roads, well-structured buildings, schools, running water, transportation, and food for all. There exists no social class. No war. Poverty is unheard of here."

Like Skelling Rise.

She had a feeling Dwarf Shoe had served as Klyde's inspiration for the progression of his town.

As they fell in line to enter the city, standing guard at the gates were several armored dwarves dressed in gold cloaks. Embossed on the badges pinned to their cloaks was Dwarf Shoe's sigil: two crossed double-headed battle axes. Each of them carried shields and the same weapon in hand.

"The Shieldmen," Rawn said when Dyna asked about them. "Merely to keep the peace and assure no hunters attempt to capture fugitives on the bridge. They may not be interested in war, but they are quick to end any hostilities. Regulations are well kept here."

A Shieldman standing on a barrel barked out instructions through an enchanted amplifier on repeat as people passed. "Herbs and opiates are not permitted without a Herb Master's license. The sale of outside provisions and other goods requires a merchant's license. Weapons are barred to those with category five crimes. No exceptions. Surrender all illegal contraband to the Shield Guard. You can recover your belongings from the Bailiff's Office once a license has been granted to you..."

"Category five?" Lucenna muttered questioningly.

"Anything regarding murder, assault, or high theft," Klyde said. "But don't you worry about that, lass. That won't apply to us." He pulled out a brass badge with Azure's interwoven seven-pointed star and pinned it to the lapel of his blue coat. He nearly passed for a member of the Azure Guard.

A nervous jitter grew in Lucenna's stomach with each step they took closer to the gate. When it was their turn, Klyde confidently approached a bearded Shieldman with bright red hair and handed him a small leather folder with paperwork inside.

"You work for the Azure King, eh?" the dwarf said as he squinted at him suspiciously. "What is your purpose here? Business or refuge."

"Refuge."

"Name?"

"Veron Moreland, Commissioner of the Azure Guard," Klyde replied nonchalantly.

Lucenna's insides jumped at the name. She had met the commissioner in the Port of Azure before. By the looks the others exchanged with her, they remembered him too.

The other Shieldmen also reacted to the name and saluted.

"Commissioner, welcome," the Shieldman said, his eyes nearly sparkling. "We hold you in high regard for the many refugees you have saved, and your charitable donations to the state. Is this the first time you have made a trip to our city?"

Klyde nodded, folding his arms behind his back. "This is a special case. You will see my paperwork is in order with listed weaponry permits, rank, and identification."

"Right, of course."

He motioned to Lucenna and the others as he handed the dwarf their wanted notices. "I am escorting these fine folk to safety. They were unfortunately marked with category two crimes by association." He leaned down to whisper, "Completely false allegations, I might add. Used merely to catch another criminal wanted by the crown. You and I both know how selfish kings can be, caring nothing for what lives their actions destroy."

"Aye, we know that well." The Shieldman returned the paperwork and saluted again. "Welcome to Little Step, Commissioner."

Klyde winked at her over his shoulder, and Lucenna rolled her eyes. Well, it seems he was of some use, after all.

CHAPTER 21

Lucenna

Little Step was an advanced city ripe with magic. Lucenna saw it in the floating lanterns lining the shops and even felt it beneath the cobblestone streets. They followed the crowd into the marketplace. A blend of exotic spices and the smell of fried fish filled her nose. A chorus of accents from all over the country blended in a hum. Stalls lined the streets, merchants selling and auctioning a panoply of wares. Their hawking shouts blurred together in a roar.

Orange flags fluttered from the lampposts, displaying the state's sigil.

All manner of fairies zipped past in a colorful array. Besides dwarves, there were so many elves. None wore any livery, but they must be from both kingdoms from the color of their hair, a mix of both blond and dark.

When Lucenna saw a Lunar mage, her heart stopped. He was tall, lean, slicked back white hair, no beard. Her heart raced, sweat sprouting in her clammy palms. She couldn't see his face, but somehow he looked exactly like...

Uncle?

The lunar mage paused in the street, and his head began to turn.

Klyde jerked her backward.

A massive creature strolled past, blocking them out of view. It looked like a cross between a horse and a deer, with a coat of sea-blue scales. It had a long tail, and a white mane that lined its back to its head, moving like mist. People gave it a wide berth, wary of its sharp antlers.

"What is it?" Dyna asked in awe.

"A Kirin..." Rawn said. "They tend to roam the western lands, my lady. I have not seen one this far out of Xián Jīng before."

Lucenna searched the crowd once the creature passed, but didn't see the mage anymore. It wasn't him. The mind sometimes saw what it feared, and sometimes what it wanted to. Thank the Gods it was only her imagination, because although her father was Head of the Lunar Guild, her uncle was more frightening—and far more ruthless.

"All manner of creatures are here," Zev said, sniffing the air. His eyes flared to yellow when he spotted two women with pointed, furry ears. Their feline eyes flashed a bright green as they sauntered past him.

"I suppose it's to be expected in Dwarf Shoe," Lucenna said.

They eventually made it to the street for the inns. It was packed with people, as expected. Lucenna had little hope they would snag one. They followed Rawn into the first inn. There were way too many people inside, so only Rawn, Zev, and Dyna went to the counter to inquire for lodging. They soon returned with relieved smiles.

"Well, we are certainly fortunate today," Rawn said.

"Very," Zev laughed, tickling Dyna's cheek with a lock of her hair.

She blushed and elbowed him. "Bugger off, Zev."

"What happened?" Lucenna asked.

"The innkeeper said he had two rooms left and he saved them for the next pretty girl with red hair to arrive," Zev said with a chuckle. "We didn't have to pay a single russet."

Lucenna arched an eyebrow at that. Innkeepers were notorious for price gouging, yet she must have made an impression to get two rooms for free.

"He was being kind," Dyna grumbled as she handed Rawn a key and Lucenna the second. But even she looked puzzled by the unusual luck.

"What now?" Klyde said. "Shall we find something to eat? I'm famished."

"Please do," Rawn said. "I must see to something first."

"You won't join us, Lord Norrlen?" Lucenna asked, confused. It wasn't safe for him to be out and about, either.

Rawn paused as he thought of it. "I must lease a carriage to take us to Kelpway, my lady. And perhaps find a courier to mail another letter."

"Then, if you'll allow me..." Lucenna waved her hand over Rawn's face, and his features changed into another male elf with dark hair. His eyes remained the same, the only thing she couldn't change. "To be safe."

He rubbed his cheek. "Thank you."

"I'll follow you out," Zev said. "I need to visit the smithy to tighten my chains before we leave tomorrow."

"I'll come with you, too," Dyna said. "We need to replenish our provisions. We can stop at an outdoor vendor for a meal instead."

All the food they brought with them had been confiscated at the gates. Not that it had been much. They had to ration their meals with their gold so limited. But the Shieldmen gave them some coin to replace what they took.

"Are you staying?" Dyna asked Lucenna.

She nodded. It was for the best.

"Today we replenish, rest, and report any news we may hear," Rawn told them. "Keep your heads low. This may be a free state, but you never know who is watching. Let us meet here in the taproom tomorrow at dawn, then make our way to Kelpway. However, if we are separated, or if any of you are compromised, leave the state immediately and head for White Woods in the south."

They all nodded in agreement. A light shudder went down Lucenna's spine.

Nothing will happen.

The nerves must have showed on her face, because Klyde gently squeezed her arm in assurance.

"What's in the White Woods?" she asked Rawn.

"It is merely a place of sanctuary on the border of Greenwood, my lady. A good place to lie low and to send for aid if needed." Then he excused himself, with Zev and Dyna following him out of the inn.

The crowd soon swallowed them up.

"Wouldn't you rather go with them?" Klyde asked.

"I would, but I cannot risk being spotted." She took a seat at a dirty empty table, and he sat across from her. "There are far too many mages here. I can feel them."

More than she was used to sensing, and it left an anxious buzz on her skin.

"Do they live in Dwarf Shoe?"

She shook her head. "If they do, it's not permanent. Mages cannot gain citizenship in other kingdoms. They may travel for work and apprenticeship, but they belong to the Magos Empire and can be summoned back without notice. And sorceresses..."

"Are never allowed out," Klyde guessed. "If a mage sees you?"

"He will attempt to detain me or report me to an Enforcer. I told you of them and their purpose."

"Capture and siphon."

Her stomach churned, and she shrunk in her chair. "Exactly. I'd rather not hold a mage battle in the middle of the city if I can help it."

A muscle in Klyde's jaw flexed, and his blue eyes fixed on the crowd. "Are you cloaked right now?"

"Of course."

"These Enforcers, what do they look like?"

"They are powerful mages, and the elite are the best in their guilds. You will know them by the sigil embroidered on their clothing, and they always carry amplifier crystals in their staffs."

"Like that one?" Klyde subtly motioned with his chin to two men in black cloaks.

On their shoulders was the triad symbol of the Magos Empire, along with the mark of their rank. And leading them was her uncle. They idly passed through the crowd, headed for the front.

Lucenna's entire body went cold.

Quietly, Klyde took her hand and led her back outside. It was a good thing, too, because she had frozen. He led her into a shadowed alleyway and moved her behind stacked crates, bracing his arms on either side of her head as he peeked over them.

She couldn't even care that he had her back up against the wall. Sound muffled, and all Lucenna could hear was her heart pounding in her ears.

Magnus was in Dwarf Shoe. *Why?*

It was a stupid question, really. She knew why. Her father had failed to capture her, so they sent someone far better. And she feared Magnus far worse. She had seen him kill mages with a snap of his fingers. He should have been Head of the Lunar Guild but chose to work directly for the Archmage instead.

A fight against him wasn't one she would win. Lucenna shut her eyes, forcing herself to calm down. Klyde stepped closer, and the shield of his body helped even her breathing.

"Lucenna," he whispered.

"Yes?" she whispered back.

"Can you please change your face? This is really disturbing."

She glowered up at him. "Casting glamor might have attracted them in the first place."

Yet to her absolute horror, the glamor began to peel off.

Klyde glanced past the crates again and cursed. He pinned her to the alley wall and braced his hands on either side of her head.

Lucenna froze. "What are you doing?"

"Don't kill me," he whispered as his nose grazed her cheek, lips hovering so close to her mouth. "They're coming."

Her heart stopped when she heard footsteps and voices tinged with the Magos accent. Klyde angled his face to hide hers out of sight. His hand slid up her neck, cupping her face as his lips faintly brushed her jaw. Light as butterfly wings, only a sliver of space between them. Their eyes met and held. Her heart was pounding so hard, she imagined he could feel it.

If they were to sell this illusion, Lucenna told herself it was fine. She looked at his lips, deciding she would kiss him. Klyde stilled a split second, then his other arm snaked around her waist and hauled her tight against him. Heat spread through her from his touch. It warmed her skin, curling up her spine, revealing to her how close they stood to each other. Her hands landed on his chest, feeling the warmth through his shirt.

His eyes were bright and focused. "Your glamor completely dissolved."

Lucenna gasped, touching her face.

"Don't worry. They have already gone."

Heat rushed through her cheeks, and she shoved him off. "You better not have lied about them coming merely to kiss me," she hissed.

Klyde frowned. "I would never subject you to anything for my own pleasure."

"If you ever did, I would cut off your favorite appendage with a dull knife."

"I suppose that's fair." He grinned, his dimples appearing. "But let it be known, *you* were going to kiss me first."

She sputtered, her face going red.

He grinned and leaned in close. "Love, you can assault me all you wish."

Turning away, Klyde whistled as he strolled out of the alley. Lucenna was left staring after him dumbly. The fool wanted to test her patience today. She recast her hag glamor and followed him.

He led her out to another street, the opposite way they came in. "The inn may be compromised. I don't think we should stay there."

Lucenna sighed in exasperation, but he was probably right. She didn't know if her uncle was searching for her or if he merely sensed magic. Better not stay to find out. What should we do?"

"First, I want to see you fed, then we will catch up with the others."

She had no mind to protest when her stomach grumbled in agreement. Klyde led her confidently across the city until they arrived at a restaurant. The air smelled so delicious it made her mouth water.

Klyde ordered mutton stew for both of them, and they ate in silence, keeping an eye on the front door. She was glad to be out of view and to have her stomach filled.

The ground suddenly rumbled, and the chandeliers overhead rattled. Lucenna tensed.

"It's only the train," he said, nodding to the windows.

"They have a train?" she asked incredulously.

Lucenna couldn't see much past the wave of people passing by, but most were leaving or going towards a large building with smoke trails rising above it.

"This state knows how to manage their wealth," he said. "There are two trains. One that runs north to south through the state, and it stops at a station in each of the major cities. The second one runs east to west across Urn, from here to Xián Jīng. Should we fail to steal Tarn's ship, we could take a train to the west coast and attempt to board a ship there. They recently added a new track to Ledoga last year."

Lucenna had heard of the great train that traveled from the Saxe Sea to the Dragon Canyon, but she didn't know it originated here. She was curious to see what the trains looked like. "You seem to know a lot about Dwarf Shoe, and about Urn, for that matter."

Klyde shrugged. "I have traveled a lot."

"And on these travels, do you make a habit of using the commissioner's identity?" She arched an eyebrow.

His smirk grew, obviously waiting for her to ask. "Only when necessary. I don't make a habit of announcing myself if I don't need to."

"Hmm. And have you met the commissioner?"

"In passing. He is a good man with a reputable reputation. I knew his name would serve to get us through the checkpoint."

Well, if it was only for that, Veron may not mind. Whatever happened to him after they had escaped the port?

Once they finished eating, they went on their way.

"Could we see the train?" Lucenna asked.

He winked. "Where do you think I was taking you?"

They came to the station with a train already on the tracks. The metal beast hovered with an invisible force above a set of tracks. She felt the magic thrumming through it as if it were a living creature. Whoever had created such a mechanism was indeed powerful.

The train departed the station as another arrived behind it on the platform across from them. All manner of fae, creatures, dwarves, and humans spilled from the doors, swarming the platform.

Klyde took her hand. "We need to go."

His cautious tone immediately had Lucenna on alert as he pulled her away. "What's wrong? Did you see mages?"

"Worse."

What was worse than mages?

She peered over her shoulder. A group of elves in black armor and deep red cloaks stepped out of the train. The sigil of a red maple leaf marked their shields.

Red Highland soldiers.

CHAPTER 22

Zev

Zev wasn't fond of crowds. It was difficult to focus on one of his senses when there was so much commotion around him. The faint drone of magic, the clack of movement, and the roar of voices swarmed his ears in a constant hum. He tensed every time someone or *something* brushed against his skin. His sensitive sight struggled to adjust to the colorful streets and the writhing crowd. Then there was the smell. Strange new scents swung from pleasant to unpleasant on a pendulum. His nose twitched at the lingering scent of bitter herbs. It was beginning to give him a headache.

The quietness of Skelling Rising had been a gift.

Dyna normally enjoyed discovering new places, but she didn't seem to enjoy the trip through the market either. She walked silently beside him, not bothering to browse the merchant stalls or shop for the provisions they needed.

Her gaze was fixed on the east.

But he had already guessed why she chose to accompany him. There was no time to explore when the only thing on her mind was how to enact her plan to find Tarn.

Zev had overheard the last of Dyna's conversation with Lucenna that morning, and he worried.

Because he had wondered the same.

Was this all to prove she didn't need Cassiel? Or was her recklessness need to spite him? The questions made him feel guilty, so he decided not to question her anymore.

As Zev paid a merchant for a sack of potatoes, he told her, "I am finished here, unless you would like to visit any of the shops?"

Dyna shook her head.

He asked the merchant where he could find a blacksmith and was pointed in another direction. They eventually reached the smithy street. Bright fires glowed from the forges. The familiar beat of hammers and billows of steam greeted him, heating the air.

It stirred a bit of nostalgia, reminding him of the beginning of their journey. He inhaled a breath and halted in the middle of the busy street.

"What is it?" Dyna asked quietly. She reached for her sword's hilt, studying their surroundings.

"That scent..." Zev's wolf stirred inside of him as he sniffed the air. His eyes widened. "It's her."

"Who?"

"Lara..."

It was faint, but enough for him to identify it, or maybe because the memory of her scent was still so potent in his mind.

Zev eagerly followed the trail until it brought him to a forge further down the street. The scruffy blacksmith there beat his large hammer over a plate of metal.

He paused, sensing Zev. His eyes flared blue with his wolf in acknowledgment. Setting down his tools, he studied Zev and smirked. "I have been waiting for you, pup."

Zev frowned. He hadn't been called pup in a while, nor did he recognize the Lycan. He never forgot a scent, and he certainly had not smelled the musk on this one before. But Lara's scent was here, too.

It rose above all the others, so starkly out of place, like a flower in a barren field.

Zev glanced around, expecting to see her walk around the corner.

"She is not here." The blacksmith wiped his dirty hands on a soot-stained rag. "Hold a moment. I have something for you."

For him?

He soon returned and handed Zev a wrinkled envelope smudged with soot. "I was told to give this to a Lycan who fits your description."

Zev stared down at the envelope a moment, his pulse stirring. He lifted the flap. The sweetest scent drifted to him from the folded page inside, and he knew what it was.

Dyna gave him a small smile and went to sit on a nearby bench to wait, giving him privacy. Careful not to tear the page with his claws, Zev took it out and read the black scribbles.

Dear Zev,

I hope my letter makes its way to you, because if you are reading this, it means you chose to live. Forgive me for assuming, but I caught the scent of silver on you at our first meeting. Wayland is a skilled blacksmith. He will tend to your chains well.

I must share the wonderful news that the Lupin Pack survived due to Dyna's medicine. Please pass on our thanks. We owe her a great debt.

As for my brother and I, we arrived in Little Step before the first snowfall. The train will take us home. Should you ever come west, you are always welcome in Lángshān.

Yours,

Lara

On the bottom of the page, she added:

Ronin insists that I mention the Garou Pack is nearly complete. Whatever that may mean.

Zev's eyes lingered on the word *yours*. There was no connotation behind it but a means to sign off a letter. Yet it made him smile all the same.

He read each stroke of ink again while imagining the words in the timbre of her voice. Lara had written to him at the start of winter, yet the page still smelled of her. Zev subtly inhaled her scent from the air once more before carefully returning the letter to the envelope and tucking it safely in his pocket.

Wayland leered knowingly. "Good news, I take it, eh?"

Zev removed his thick chains from his pack, and they clanked loudly as he set them on the service counter. "Only that I don't need to come up with some explanation for what these are for. You come highly recommended."

Wayland chuckled and crossed his hairy arms. "Our kind recognizes good smithing when they see it. Worry not, I will see that your pup chains are reinforced."

Zev's wolf growled, the sound rumbling in his head.

Now he understood why Wayland had taken to calling him that. A Lycan should have outgrown the use of chains by now.

"How much do I owe you?" He reached into his pocket.

"The payment is covered. Call it a pack courtesy."

Zev paused, not expecting Ronin to pay for the work in advance. "Thank you." He placed a couple of coins on the counter anyway. "For the letter and for your haste. I will come for the chains before dawn."

"Aye, fine that, pup."

"I am called Zev," he snarled, his eyes flaring yellow. The wooden counter cracked beneath the force of his claws. Wayland held his ground, but the stale scent of fear joined the smoke. Zev smiled tightly, bearing his fangs. "And I am much too old to be a pup, wouldn't you agree?"

Wayland nodded meekly. "Your pardon," he said quietly. "I haven't seen a fully grown Lycan who still uses chains. At this point, it's too..." He looked away and cleared his throat. "Aye, it's no business of mine. Have a good night."

A heavy feeling sank in Zev's chest. He stared mutely at Wayland's retreating back before he could make himself leave.

Dyna rose from the bench, eyeing the blacksmith stand. "I hope he apologized."

"More or less."

She smirked as they strode down the street together. "I feared you were going to tear out his throat."

"He should know better than to antagonize another wolf," Zev muttered. Especially one who wasn't in control of his Other.

"So, what did the letter say?" Dyna asked, giving him a teasing smile. "Did Lara confess her undying love?"

Zev choked on a cough. "Hardly."

She laughed. "Well? What did she say?"

"Not much." He shrugged, scratching the side of his neck. "She says the Lupin Pack survived."

"Oh, that's wonderful!"

"And I am invited to visit them in Lángshān."

Dyna's smile grew wider, and he couldn't help being glad to see it. "Then she *did* confess."

He scoffed. "You're having a laugh. I don't know why you're assuming there's anything of the sort between us."

"Zev, I saw the way you looked at her."

He walked faster to hide how red his face felt. "What you saw was fascination at discovering there were others like me."

"I know what I saw," Dyna said. "As I know, you didn't see the way she looked at you when you weren't looking."

He stopped in place. A tangled mess of emotions wrangled in his chest. Surprise. Confusion. Hope. All overshadowed by denial and resignation. "It doesn't matter. I'm not going to Lángshān."

"What? Why?" Dyna came around to face him, frowning incredulously. "You know why."

She shook her head. "Because of the Other? For that very reason you should go. They can help you."

"I will not put her at risk, Dyna. It's too late." Because Zev knew that's what Wayland had attempted to say. It was possible to control the Other— *if* he had been taught as a pup. But his Other had been untamed for years, grown too wild and too strong.

During their stay in Skelling, Zev had tried to connect with his Other. He thought perhaps he could teach himself how to control it. But when Zev did, he felt it rush to the surface and almost take over him. He inwardly shuddered now at the thought. It easily could have been released in the town and torn into any prey that crossed its path.

It had come out on its own once, when he had been cornered by the Lykos Pack. It must have been the instinct to survive that set it free.

But if he called on his Other again, what if he couldn't call it back?

The full moon was near, and he sensed it there beneath his skin. Eager to be released.

Goosebumps scattered over his arms. "There is no controlling it, Dyna."

Zev tried to move on, but she moved in his way. "No, I don't believe that. It's never too late, and I refuse to let you say so. We are going to Lángshān someday. Whether it be on this journey or thereafter. Because you promised to learn how to fight for yourself, too, remember?" Her eyes lowered to the thick scars on his wrists. "A life bound in chains is not living."

Her words reminded him of the last dream he had of his father. *I never taught you to give up.*

To do so would make the Madness return. That wasn't what he wanted. He was finally free, and he had to put in the effort to stay that way.

Sighing, Zev mussed her hair. "You're right." As the wind brushed against him, he caught that bitter herbal scent again. It had been following them around since before the city, so he had assumed it was some plant in the region, but he still smelled it. Zev subtly sniffed Dyna and reared his head back, wrinkling his nose.

"What is it?"

"You smell ... odd."

She pulled away from him, giving him a strange look. "What do you mean?"

His nose twitched. "What is that scent? Are you taking a tonic? Are you ill?" He attempted to check her forehead, but she dodged him.

"I'm fine. You're smelling the balm I used last night." Dyna continued, and her pace picked up. "Let's go find the others."

Frowning, Zev followed, but he wasn't going to let her change the subject that easily. "Your balms usually smell of honey and eucalyptus. This new one smells of rank weeds."

"Well, that happens when it's made with a sedge flower that grows in these parts. It has a bitter scent instead of floral, but I find it works quite well."

His brow furrowed. "What is it for?"

She was quiet a moment before saying, "It keeps the nightmares at bay."

There was something in her voice that made Zev slow. "Dyna, you know you can talk to me, don't you? I'm right here. Simply talk to me. I know you're not all right. We all do."

His cousin paused in the middle of the street, but she didn't look at him. The last rays of sunlight casting off the roofs lit up her tresses as they blew around her face.

Her emerald eyes fixed on the towering clouds above them, and he could almost see a hint of Nazar's floating islands. "Can you do me a favor?"

"Of course. Anything."

"I need you to go on pretending that you don't know that."

Zev's throat tightened at the emptiness in her expression when she looked at him, and he nodded. Aye, he could do that, but only for so long. Because he couldn't be the only one who fought to go on living.

Sighing, Dyna leaned against him, her entire body sagging as if she needed that support from him. "Shall we return to the inn, or wander about until we catch up with Rawn?"

Zev wrapped an arm around her shoulders, and they made their way down the street together. "Hmm. Let's see where fate takes us."

CHAPTER 23

Rawn

Many had gathered in Little Step's courier office. Voices swarmed all around Rawn as he waited in line for his turn at the counter. The crowd made him nervous, but he couldn't lose another opportunity to send Aerina a letter again.

After an hour, he at last reached the front.

"Good afternoon," Rawn greeted the dwarf postman as he placed a crumpled envelope on the counter. He added the carving of a wolf figurine with it. "To Greenwood by portal, please."

"One silver." The postman poured a dollop of red wax on the envelope, and Rawn pressed his signet ring into it, sealing it closed.

"Province and size?" A sun mage beside the dwarf asked in a bored tone. He sat in a stool at the service counter, playing with a wisp of flame between his fingers.

"Sellav Province." Rawn placed a silver coin on the counter to cover the postage. "Standard size. Instant delivery and confirmation, if you will. No expected letter in return."

"Orbital address?" The mage held out his palm where he carried a dark green crystal patterned with stripes in lighter green. Malachite. The *porta* rune was carved on the surface.

Lucenna had mentioned he would need to acquire such a crystal to open his own courier portals.

Rawn gave him the address and lightly tapped his ring against the crystal. Both lit up with magic, a sign the crystal had connected with the enchanted letterbox located in his home. The mage's eyes glowed orange as a spiraling portal with white light about five inches in diameter formed between them. The dwarf inserted the letter and the wooden wolf statuette inside.

The mage's gaze went distant for a moment. Rawn held his breath, always nervous at this part. "Delivery confirmed."

The portal winked closed out of existence.

Rawn exhaled with a smile. "Thank you."

"A pleasure," the mage replied drearily. "Have a fine day. Next!"

Slipping past the waiting line, Rawn strode out the double doors of the courier's office. Fair waited for him outside.

"First order of business is complete," Rawn told him, untying the reins from the hitching post.

There were a few things to pick up from the market before returning to the inn. If they managed to set sail tomorrow, they would need to be well equipped for a journey at sea.

After traveling discreetly for so long, it made Rawn nervous to walk among so many Elves. But no one paid attention to him. He was merely another face in the throng, and the glamor spell had held well. Rawn inserted some beeswax in his ears to dull the constant din of the market. By his third purchase in the mariner's street, the tension eased out of his shoulders.

"Lemon linctus, milord?" an old herbalist offered, holding up a dark brown bottle. "A spoonful a day keeps the scurvy at bay."

"You'll need salt to keep your fish unspoiled at sea." The elderly woman beside her thrust a burlap sack in Rawn's face next.

"Oh, um…" His response was drowned by the women instantly bickered over who should have the sale. He quietly slipped away.

A flash of yellow flitted past the edge of his vision. Instantly, he thought of Princess Keena, but when Rawn looked, his eyes locked on another standing a few feet away from him.

He recognized the elf's cornflower eyes and long, acorn brown hair, but his mind was slow to understand. Because it couldn't be possible. He had not seen this face in over twenty-five years. Two small Elven boys with dark brown curls clung to each of the male's hands.

"Pardon…" Rawn took a step forward, a part of him waiting for the illusion to vanish. His throat tightened when it didn't. "Sy?"

The male gasped and spun around, confused at first by the stranger he appeared to be, until his gaze settled on Rawn's eyes. Recognition flashed through him.

Rawn peeled off the glamor and whispered. "Sylar?"

As if the sound of Rawn's voice struck him, his old friend flinched back. He snatched up the boys in his arms—and ran.

"Sylar!" Rawn called in confusion. "Wait, Sy!"

He sprinted after him. But trying to maneuver the thick crowd with Fair made it difficult to keep up. Rawn soon lost sight of him. He couldn't have disappeared that quickly.

Rawn spotted him darting into an alley, and he followed him inside. "Sy?"

Sylar whipped around, and his eyes went wide. "Rawn..." Fear marinated his name. He clutched the boys tightly to his chest. "Whatever my fate, I accept it. But please, do not harm them."

Rawn's brow furrowed further at the plea. "I—" He stilled at the cold press of a dagger at his throat.

"It's unwise to follow another into an alley alone, Lord Norrlen. Many dangerous folk about." It was a voice he had heard only a handful of times, but Rawn recognized Elon all the same.

He stilled merely out of further utter confusion to find them together. He didn't understand what was happening or why Sylar was terrified of him.

Rawn held out his hands in surrender. "I am not here to hurt you."

Sylar's wide eyes flickered from him to Elon, then to the boys. They couldn't have been more than four years old. They whimpered, their teary eyes warm brown.

Red Elves.

"Who is he, papa?" one asked Sylar.

Rawn's mouth parted with a shallow inhale. "They are yours?"

"They are," Elon said icily in his ear. "So you understand why I cannot let you live."

The possessiveness behind the claim answered Rawn's questions all at once, while striking him with new ones.

A containment dome slammed down around Sylar and the boys. They cried out and Elon hissed. Lucenna appeared from the other end of the alley, with Klyde at her side.

From behind Rawn, footsteps idly approached, followed by a feral growl.

"I'm afraid I cannot allow that," came Dyna's cool voice, and he felt Elon stiffen. "Step away my Guidelander, Lieutenant. I will not ask twice."

Elon slowly lifted the blade from Rawn's neck and moved back. He wore a dark heavy cloak over his armor. His amber eyes fixed on Dyna, surprised to see her as well.

She came up beside Rawn on his right and nodded at Lucenna. The containment dome trapping Sylar disappeared. "I have never seen you as my enemy, Elon. Am I wrong?"

The spy didn't answer.

Nor did he reach for the sword at his hip, but Rawn felt the tension of his magic gathering in the air as he backed toward Sylar and the boys, keeping them within his sights. Lucenna and Klyde moved to join Dyna's side. Zev growled steadily on Rawn's left.

"How did you find me?" Sylar asked shakily. He stepped closer to the Lieutenant. One of the Elvin boys reached for Elon, and he took him in his arms without taking his eyes off them.

As Rawn studied them together, he finally understood.

They were a family.

It was no wonder Sylar ran and why Elon was ready to slaughter him. The union between a red elf and a green elf was forbidden in the Vale of the Elves.

Rawn sighed, offering Sylar a faint, confused smile. "By chance, Sy. I never expected to see you again. I thought … I thought you were dead."

Sylar lowered his gaze.

"God of Urn as my witness, I give you my oath that I mean you nor your family any harm."

There was a pause as Elon and Sylar exchanged a look. The violent energy in the air slowly faded. Sylar took a breath and closed his eyes. An elf's word was his bond. They both knew that.

"Then what is your business here?" Elon demanded.

Dyna's smirk grew as she crossed her arms. "I'm here to kill Tarn."

They couldn't be out in the open. A group gathered would draw the eye, and when Lucenna mentioned seeing Red Highland soldiers arrive at the station, Elon wanted to leave immediately. Rawn knew it was best to hide too, but he had questions that only Sylar could answer.

His old friend reluctantly brought them to their home in a more secluded rural area on the edge of the city. It was a hovel, really. A place to lie low.

Rawn sat with Sylar at their small table. Elon stood beside his mate like a sentinel. Both held onto the boys, sleeping in their arms. Zev, Lucenna, and Klyde had gone out to stake the area in case they were followed. Dyna stayed with him. She leaned against the wall beside the door with her arms crossed, looking out the window. It was too dark to see anything except what the moonlight allowed.

The long silence was awkward, neither of them knowing where to start. Rawn let his eyes wander around the small hut. He could cross it in ten strides. There wasn't much but a sturdy bed of straw in the corner, a wardrobe for clothing, a threadbare couch by the hearth, and the kitchen where they sat now.

The small kettle bubbling over the fire broke the quiet with a low whistle of steam. Sylar poured them both a cup of tea, and the scent of nettle and honey warmed the chilly air.

"Thank you." Rawn accepted the cup as they met each other's gazes across the table. "It's good to see you."

Sylar's expression softened, though it was shadowed by remorse. "It is good to see you as well. How ... how is my father?"

"I have not seen Eldred in some time, but I believe he is well." Rawn hoped he was.

Sylar nodded, and they fell into another lapse of silence.

"What happened?" he finally asked. "Why didn't you come back?"

"How could I? I gave you my word that I would return with your sister, and I couldn't keep it." Sylar looked down at his son, and his eyes welled. "By the time I arrived, it was too late. They had already ... what they did to Nisa..." His misted eyes met his. "I heard your screams when you found her, Rawn. I felt your pain as they dragged me away. Even if I had not been caught, I didn't have the courage to face you."

Rawn shut his eyes with the horrid memories of the day he found her.

The rage he felt, the sorrow. It was like something had taken over him. He had hunted down any remaining red elves that he could find and ... slaughtered them all.

A tear rolled down Sy's cheek. "If we ever met again, I was sure you would..."

"Kill you for it?" Rawn guessed. He had been so lost after his sister died, drunk on the bloodshed, perhaps he might have. His gaze swept over the sleeping boys Sylar held, then to Elon standing guard over them. "It was more than guilt that kept you away."

Sylar's throat bobbed. Elon laid a hand on his shoulder. Both a silent claim and a warning. His hard amber eyes held his.

Eyes—Rawn finally realized—he had seen before. "I understand now where you have heard of me. You and I, we have met before, haven't we, Elon? The day outside of Willow's Grove was not the first time we crossed swords."

141

"What?" Dyna straightened. "You have met him before."

"He is a Force Sentry," Rawn said. "Elite Red Highland soldiers specially trained to conduct secretive operations for the crown." He clenched the cup of tea in his hand, feeling it burn against his palm. "You were there in Erendor, when your prince came for my princess."

Elon remained silent and completely still. But if Rawn knew anything, the elf had already calculated all the ways to kill him if he made any move he deemed threatening.

"He no longer serves King Altham," Sylar said quickly. "He took no part in your sister's torture ... only mine." That broke the stark tension in the small room. Emotion at last crossed Elon's face as he looked down at Sy. It was hardly visible. They spoke no words, but Sylar's eyes saddened at whatever was communicated between them. "I was held in the dungeons beneath the Blood Keep for weeks."

Rawn's stomach pitched. He had heard stories of the torture captured elves endured there. All prayed for a quick death, and most didn't find it.

Sylar's gaze went distant as he stared at the wall blankly. "I refused to divulge any information about my kingdom, not that I knew much. The time I spent there..." His voice dropped low. "I would not wish it upon my worst enemy."

Elon lowered himself to his knees, looking at him in a way that could only be described as remorseful.

Sylar smiled at him faintly. The turn of his head exposed the large scar on his neck where his tattoo had been cut off. "You did as you were bid, El. At first it was your duty, then you did it to spare me, so others would not do worse. But you saved me. Here we are, safe and free, with our boys."

Elon wiped the tears from Sylar's cheek, exposing the warped circular scar on the back of his hand. A self-inflicted burn.

"You defected," Rawn concluded. "When you escaped Red Highland with Sylar, you chose him over your king."

Elon stood. "What do you intend to do?"

"Do?" He frowned. "I have no intention of reporting you, if that is your concern. The way you chose to live is no business of mine. I am also a wanted elf, if you recall." He looked at Sylar. "As far as Greenwood knows, you died with Nisa."

Sylar's shoulders slumped with relief. "Thank you, Rawn."

"He is here on another mission," Dyna supplied.

"For King Leif?" Sy grew concerned again. "Against Red Highland?"

Rawn nodded.

"What does that have to do with Tarn?" Elon asked next.

"Only that we are headed to the same place," Dyna replied. She canted her head as she studied him. "I always sensed you served Tarn out of duty as well, but not out of loyalty. As you are here now, I suppose that means you no longer serve your old master, either."

Elon didn't reply, though the answer was clear.

"Where is Von?" she asked next. "Is he with Tarn?"

No answer again. Man of little words.

Dyna's mouth hitched. "You won't tell us because you are loyal—to *Von*. Well, he is one of my Guardians. I am on his side, too."

There was a perceptible pause after that reveal, though it didn't seem to surprise Elon.

"We leave for Kelpway tomorrow," Rawn said.

Elon's eyes narrowed. "Tarn is there."

Dyna crossed her arms. "We know."

A quiet knock came at the door, before Klyde, Lucenna and Zev reentered the hut.

"We weren't followed," Zev confirmed, shaking off the raindrops in his hair.

"But we cannot return to the city," Lucenna said. "I saw them, Rawn. A squad of Elven soldiers coming into the square, clad in red. They might be travelers, but…"

"They are not travelers." Elon met his gaze. "They know, Lord Norrlen. Red Highland knows you are here, and they have come."

CHAPTER 24

Dynalya

"You cannot go to Kelpway. It is far too dangerous." Sylar's statement filled the stifled silence. "If Red Highland knows you are here, they will hunt you, Rawn. They care nothing for Dwarf Shoe's laws."

Klyde looked out the windows. "How would they know he is here?"

"Red Highland has spies everywhere," Elon replied.

Lucenna frowned. "But I glamored him before entering the city. He must have been seen before coming here."

"He was." Everyone looked at Dyna at her cool answer. "Galen. The poacher that you allowed to escape. Clearly, he survived and spread the word that we are here."

Zev's eyes widened as he exchanged a look with Rawn.

Dyna turned away from them and scowled at the moon outside. She had been right after all. This was what mercy bought. Another obstacle in her way.

"We need to abandon the plan," Zev said.

She shook her head. "I can't."

"We can't go through with it anymore, Dyna," Lucenna said sharply. "Going will put us all at risk."

"They are searching for Rawn. He can remain in hiding until the danger passes. Stay here to glamor him and cloak the area. Meanwhile, I will go. Klyde and Zev can come with me."

"My lady," Rawn sighed. "I understand why you wish to go after Tarn, but now may not be the time. Splitting up is never wise against such an opponent."

"I have to agree, lass," Klyde said, and she gritted her teeth. "Together, aye, we have a chance of taking him down and commandeering his ship. But meandering in there alone, let alone with half of the manpower, will get someone killed."

"As I told Von before he left."

Dyna whipped around to Elon. "What?"

He took a seat beside Sylar. "Von also defected, Maiden. He no longer serves the Master."

She took a shaky breath, relieved, happy, but worry knotted in her chest. "When?"

"Three months past. He escaped the ship once it left Indigo Bay."

"And the others?" She eagerly stepped forward. "Yavi, Geon, and Sorren. Did they make it out?"

Last she saw Von he mentioned Dalton had already escaped.

Elon's expression was answer enough. "No."

Her heart sank. They were still captive with Tarn. "Tell me where he is."

"Von is on his way to Kelpway." There was something in Elon's tone that Dyna didn't like, and she had the sudden urge to leave.

"Von must be going back for Yavi," she said to the others. "We must go. He will surely die if we don't help him."

"*You* will die," Lucenna said, exasperated. "How many times must we tell you, *think* before you leap."

"That is rich coming from you," Dyna hissed. She stormed out of the door and went outside into the chilly night. Lucenna followed her out. "I will not be lectured by the sorceress who acts first and asks questions second. What happened to not allowing anything to stand in your way?"

"What happened to the compassionate girl who had a kind heart?" Lucenna demanded. "Who thought of others before herself?"

She stopped with her back to her, the center of her chest shaking. "You know what happened to her."

"Dyna..."

"How much did you change after you were betrayed by all that you knew? What filled the hole in your chest when you lost your mother?" Dyna asked. At the drag of silence, she said, "You do not get to judge me, Lucenna. We both know if you had a chance to right the world by defeating the Archmage, you would take it."

"Not like this..." Lucenna came to her stand beside her. "Why is going after Tarn so important to you?"

She shook her head up at the sky. "I am tired of others making my decisions. I am tired of always losing and being out of control of my own life. I need to take him down, and take down everyone who has ever hurt me, so they cannot do it again." Dyna turned to her. "You used to be brave. I idolized you, Lucenna. I aspired to *be* you. To be someone who wasn't afraid to fight against whoever stood in your way. What changed? Why are you so afraid now?"

"Because of you!" Lucenna exclaimed. "I am afraid for *you*. We all are."

She noticed Zev and her other friends standing at the door. Watching her with the same solemn look Lucenna was now.

"You're angry and violent, and so lost. I wish I knew how to help you," Lucenna said, her voice breaking. She hugged her tight. "I want my friend back. Please come back."

Dyna closed her eyes, fighting the tears welling behind them. The girl she used to be was gone. Why did they keep hoping to see her?

"I'm sorry..." She exhaled shakily and slipped out of her hold, looking away. "I need to be alone. Please..."

There was a pause before she heard Klyde say, "Come, lass. Give her a moment. You have cloaked the area enough."

Lucenna walked away toward the hut. The others went inside, and the door closed quietly behind them. Dyna sank to the wet grass and pulled up her knees, wrapping her arms around them. She listened to the chatter of the forest as her vision blurred.

What they didn't know was that Dyna missed the girl she used to be, the one who trusted the good in people, who loved unreservedly, and still believed in hope. But how could that girl live with half of her heart missing?

At the gentle snort and brush against her head, Dyna hugged Fair's muzzle. He lowered onto the grass beside her, serving as the only thing holding her up as her tears soaked his mane.

Fair didn't judge her. He never questioned her, no matter how distraught and angry she was. Maybe it was silly, since he was a horse and couldn't speak, but he was her only comfort now.

Dyna laid there with him in the grass as she looked at the half-moon. The wispy clouds parted, bathing the field in soft light. The stars seemed distant without her dreams beneath them. And she wondered where the other half of her heart had gone.

Sitting up, she rolled her eyes at herself.

Crying was pointless. She didn't need these types of thoughts holding her down. Reaching into her satchel, Dyna took out a pewter bottle and sipped the tonic. It tasted awful, but it did the trick to vanish the ache in her chest. She sighed down at the bottle.

She really was pathetic.

A flick of blue flashed in the corner of Dyna's vision. It was a familiar aquamarine shade. She whipped her head to the left in time to see the tip of a tail dashing into the bushes.

Azulo?

She leaped to her feet and ran after him. Fair trotted close behind her as Dyna followed the streak of blue darting through the forest. Where was he leading her?

The trees eventually receded to a clearing with a small pond with a short waterfall. The rush of water joined the sounds of the night, and somehow, Dyna sensed that held a purpose. A fully grown blue fox with a diamond-shaped patch on its forehead waited for her by the edge of the bank. He sat on his haunches, wagging three fluffy tails.

"There you are, sweet one." She smiled and gently scratched his head. "You have grown over the winter, Azulo. How big are you now? Perhaps, to my shoulder?"

A golden light flared around him, and he rose up way past her shoulder. A young man with furry ears grinned at her. He looked about twenty years old or so now. Only in a pair of black trousers, she got an eyeful of his well-built form. Bright cerulean hair fell around Azulo's handsome face in soft waves. The sapphire gem on his forehead glinted in the moonlight.

"Much bigger than that, Mistress." He chuckled at her shocked face, flashing his fangs. Muscle had filled him out well, his new height a good foot above her. He gained some new tattoos on his shoulders and chest. They pulsed blue faintly with magic.

Dyna gaped at him a moment, then laughed in surprise. "Dear Gods. You surely have grown."

Azulo puffed out his chest proudly. He scooped her up in his brawny arms and hugged her tight, spinning her around in a circle. "I have missed you."

"As have I." But her smile wavered when his did, and he set her down. "You didn't lure me here for a visit, though, did you?"

His furry ears lowered. He glanced away, and she followed his stare to the crop of trees on the right. A shadowed form moved forward and stepped into the moonlight, revealing the beautiful green-haired male she met a season ago.

The Druid's golden eyes glowed eerily in the night. "It's time, clever mortal."

"For what?" Dyna asked, but she knew. It had been coming since the night her geas began to throb.

"To complete the deal we agreed upon. A favor for a favor of my choosing." He circled her, grinning like a cat toying with its meal, and he leaned in intimately close. "No amount of scheming will exempt you from it."

CHAPTER 25

Dynalya

Dyna's pulse drummed as she waited for what came next. Leoake took a seat on a boulder and snapped his fingers. Azulo kneeled beside him like an obedient puppy, or better yet, a slave. It was at that moment, she noticed the geas on Azulo's ankle. It was in the shape of an oak tree with interwoven branches.

What did Leoake have on him?

Dyna crossed her arms, Fair standing beside her like her own guard.

"So we at last meet again, ye fair maid."

She cut to the point. "What do you want?"

He laughed. "I want many things, but at this moment, I desire a key."

She arched an eyebrow. "A *key*?"

"Well, parts of a key." With a twist and flick of his hand, Leoake conjured a cylindrical case about a foot long made of dark green leather, gilded with leaves on the ends, and tied with gold twine. On it was a sigil she had not seen before. He handed it to her. "It's a bronze key from the First Age. Broken into two pieces a long time ago."

Opening the cap, Dyna poured out the scroll. The parchment was very old. She unrolled the page and looked upon a faded drawing of an ancient elaborate key.

Leoake's ringed finger traced the long stem of the key from the bow to the shoulder. "The shank is your priority."

"You only want one piece?"

"Both pieces, but you only need to find one."

Dyna furrowed her brows at that odd explanation. "Then the geas will be removed?" she reiterated, leaving no chance to be tricked again. "I will owe you nothing after?"

He steepled his fingers, a sly smile on his lips. "That is our agreement. Retrieve the key, and our deal will be complete."

Dyna exhaled a breath. Sounded easy enough. She had feared his demand would be much worse. May as well do this so she could be done with him.

"A broken key," she mused, studying the page. "What is the point if the bit is also missing? Without both pieces, the key won't be of any use."

"The bit will be safe in your pocket by the time you retrieve the shank."

She narrowed her eyes. Because of course he must have planned out everything perfectly. It was a beautiful ornate key, yet otherwise unremarkable. But she wasn't stupid enough to think it was worthless. "What does the key open, Leoake?"

"A lock," he said matter-of-factly.

"Dyna clenched her jaw so she wouldn't kick his shin. "What kind of lock?"

"A rusty one."

She stifled a groan. Whatever. He wouldn't tell her what the key would open. The tricksy fae could keep his secrets. For now. "All right, and where is this key piece I must find?"

Leoake's smile grew, and Dyna knew she wouldn't like the answer. "Red Highland. The Blood Keep, to be exact."

"Are you mad?" she exclaimed. "The Blood Keep is a prison. It's as guarded as the border, if not more. Entering the Vale of the Elves to steal from them is foolhardy, even I know that."

He waved his hand with a chuckle. "Yes, well, that is beside the point."

"Are you hearing yourself? You want me to sneak into a warring kingdom with a high chance of death to retrieve a broken piece of metal. How will I ever cross their borders?"

"Oh, ye of little faith." The Druid pouted, clapping his hands together. "I am most affronted that you have so little trust in me."

"I do not trust you at all," Dyna growled.

Chuckling, he said, "Worry not. All will be clear soon enough. Aye, to do this, you must put your life on the line, as you like to do. Nonetheless, I believe in you."

"You mean you have seen it."

He waved his hands in a flamboyant display and bowed mockingly. "That is what Seers do, clever mortal. We *see*."

Dyna rolled her eyes. "No one else could have done this for you?"

"You are the perfect one for the task."

"How so?"

Leoake's eerie gold eyes glowed as he grinned at her knowingly. "Teeth that bite and stem that binds, through love and hate, the key realigns." She shuddered at the otherworldly tone his voice took. "The two pieces of the key can only be fused by one with a broken heart full of rage, my dear. Hatred and love go hand in hand, wouldn't you agree?"

Dyna worked her jaw, feeling something spoil in her stomach. It shouldn't surprise her that he knew Cassiel had left her, and the damage it wrought.

He had always known.

She almost laughed. "You didn't request your favor in Willow's Grove because you had to wait for me to be heartbroken first."

It wasn't a question. She knew it was true. More so confirmed by his cynical shrug. Instead of punching him like she wanted, Dyna returned the scroll to its case and tucked it into her satchel. The key must be more valuable than he let on.

"Hmm, I used to wonder..."

Leoake rose to his feet. "Pray tell?"

"On whether there was a worm-eaten heart beating in your chest. Now I'd wager there isn't one in there at all."

His head fell back as he cackled. "Oh, you have become quite cheeky. I like it."

Dyna studied him for a moment, trying to gauge his schemes. He was connected to Tarn, to her, and to other things she hadn't figured out yet, but she would. "Very well, dastardly Druid. I will retrieve your key."

"Splendid." He headed for the trees, apparently done with their conversation.

It was in the opposite direction of the city with no paths to be seen. Dyna already knew how he traveled, because Keena had mentioned it, and she had seen Azulo do it before.

Fae traveled through the trees.

Leoake knew how to appear wherever he desired, and she, too, had places to be.

"But you will have to do something for me first," she called after him. "Take me to Kelpway."

Leoake chuckled. "Sorry, that is not how this works. A favor for a favor as we agreed. I already held up my end of the bargain." He flashed her a grin over his shoulder. "And I have no intention of stepping foot in that port."

Of course, he knew Tarn was looking for him. Did that mean he indeed had the other half of the Unending Scroll? Shifting back into a blue fox, Azulo rubbed against Dyna's leg before reluctantly following his master.

"Well, once I have the key, I will call you through my mirror."

"Best not." Leoake shooed the idea away, pursing his mouth. "Don't toy with enchanted mirrors, clever mortal. You never know who is listening." He turned away. "I will come when it's time. Until then."

He waltzed into the forest without looking back, whistling that same tune that always seemed to tug at something in the back of her mind. He would soon disappear.

She had seconds to catch up.

Dyna released Fair's reigns. "Return to the others, Fair." He whinnied in protest. "I must do this. If you can communicate with Rawn, tell him to meet me in the White Woods."

She ran after Leoake.

Dyna kept her steps light and soundless as she had been trained. She slipped into the forest without disturbing the brush. It was dark inside, the moonlight struggling to peek past the canopy.

She ignored the darkness. Her only focus was the faint whistling in the distance. Moving swiftly, Dyna soon caught up to them. She slowed her steps, hiding behind a shrub as she peeked out. The Druid stopped before an oak tree. It was massive, with low-hanging branches. With a glowing fingertip, he drew several unfamiliar runes on the bark.

They pulsed with golden light. The trunk split and snapped, and the tree groaned as it reformed itself into a perfect circle. Leafy branches framed it like a crown. A golden light spiraled in the center, falling brighter.

She stifled a gasp. He made a portal.

Azulo darted in, vanishing through it. Hands in his pockets, Leoake followed.

She bolted after them.

"Dyna, no!" a voice shouted behind her.

Her foot caught on a root, and she crashed into Leoake from behind. He yelped, toppling through the glowing portal with her. The world seemed to split and spin. Everything went downside up and right side down. Every strand of what made her unraveled as she was blown away like threads in the wind.

Then she was nothing at all.

Gasping for air, Dyna jerked awake. She smacked away the pouch of smelling salts held to her nose.

Golden eyes glared down at her. "How dare you come through my Door!"

Sharp nausea swept through her stomach. Dyna rolled to her knees and grabbed a pretty clay pot in the corner as all the contents in her stomach were expelled out of her.

"Oh, that's simply perfect. That pot is now ruined." Leoake gagged as she continued to heave. "Do you know how old that is?"

"Sorry," she croaked before vomiting again.

"Deal with this before I toss them to the Void!" Leoake snapped, storming away.

Her blurred vision struggled to take in her surroundings, and her head ached terribly. At first, it looked like a cave, but she realized they were in a den carved out of a tree. It had round wooden walls covered in vines and a stone hearth built into the corner. A small bed of moss was on one end and on the other a desk with all sorts of trinkets, including a blooming blue rose in a crystal vase.

But Dyna's eyes fixed on the round door, or rather what Leoake called *his* Door.

It was painted green with a brass knob in the center. Painted with the design of a tree formed in a perfect circle. Ancient runes had been carved in the frame. She couldn't read them except one.

Raido.

The rune for journey.

"It's enchanted, isn't it?"

A cool cloth pressed on Dyna's forehead. "Yes, Mistress."

She weakly smiled at Azulo, now in his human form. "Magic not meant for mortals, I take it."

He nodded. "Your stomach will settle in a bit. Though your horse is handling it much better."

"What?" Dyna snapped her head up and gaped at the white stallion standing in the middle of Leoake's house. "Oh, Gods. Fair, no! You were supposed to stay!"

He nuzzled her clammy cheek.

Dyna moaned, slumping against the wall. "Send him back."

"If I could, I would send you both back," Leoake said coolly. He sat in a chair at his messy table and glared at her. "My Door can only be used twice in one day. Once to cross and once to return. That allowance is met."

Groaning, Dyna pressed on her aching head. She vanished with Rawn's horse. He would be terribly worried.

But someone saw her jump into the portal.

Who had called her name? Her mind was still too groggy to place the voice. She didn't even remember if it had been female or male. It may have been Zev. Someone had gone in search of her when she didn't come back.

Whoever it was, they would logically guess where she was headed. Tomorrow was the sixth day. Tarn wouldn't wait for her anymore. She had to find him, but she prayed her Guardians wouldn't come after her. It was too unsafe for Rawn and Lucenna.

"I must arrive in Kelpway by dawn," Dyna told Leoake. "Geas or not, I will not retrieve your key until I go there first."

His golden eyes churned with anger. "Actions have consequences, clever mortal. Remember that when you find yourself standing alone in the rain."

Leoake wasn't much of a host. He commanded her not to touch anything or eat anything. Then he left, putting Fair outside in whatever forest they had landed in.

It gave Dyna time to study the Door.

A series of rope levers hung above it from the ceiling. Each one was braided with different colored sashes and decorative beads: Red, green, blue, and black. She stared at it all night until dawn broke the sky through the window.

"What are the levers for?" Dyna murmured to herself.

"They determine where the Door opens," Azulo replied in a groggy tone. He rose from the moss bed with a yawn. "Did you sleep?"

"I'm not tired." She scooted closer to him. "What do the colors mean?"

"Blue for Azure, black for Arthal, green for Home, and red for the In Between." Azulo studied them warily. "The first three will only open with any portal. The In Between can only be accessed with an Elder Tree."

"What is an Elder Tree?"

Azulo motioned to the drawing carved on the door. "*That* is an Elder Tree. It happens to any tree whose roots have grown in the veins of magic that run deep within the earth. Their magic can create a means to cross certain distances. But Leoake can turn any tree into an Elder Tree. He manipulated *this* tree to function without limits. From it, he created a door that can cross continents and appear at any point he wishes by traveling through the In Between." Azulo shuddered, and Dyna stared at him, her mind whirling. "But it's dangerous. There are creatures that lurk there. They protect the bridges between worlds created by the Spatial God. Master can evade their attention, but so long as he does not cross more than twice."

"Are you speaking of portals?"

"*Gateways.*" Azulo clarified. "The In Between is the world between worlds."

A sudden thought whipped through Dyna sharply, and her eyes widened. *Worlds.*

As in more than *one.*

His next words broke goosebumps on her skin. "It's filled with countless bridges that open to many doors ... and some open to worlds we're not meant to see."

Dyna's mind was reeling. "Can this Door take us to Mount Ida?"

He shook his head. "That is the one place Master's Door will not open."

She gaped at him. "Why?"

Azulo glanced at the window and dropped his voice to a whisper. "There is another door there. Many dire treasures hidden inside of it. The Gods wish them to remain hidden. If they knew Master could freely travel the In Between ... he would be punished."

Dyna could hardly fathom all of this. "That's why he was so angry that I came through his Door?"

"Because he didn't predict that happening." Azulo fidgeted with his claws, suddenly nervous. "His most prized possession are his eyes, but even those are flawed. The Druid can see all fates but his own."

"Why?"

"The God of Time does not permit it..."

Dyna pondered on that and what else Azulo could tell her. "Azulo ... what does the key open?"

An anxious expression flitted across his features. He opened his mouth, but he couldn't answer. Not that he didn't want to, but he couldn't. He must be under some sort of spell to protect his Master's secrecy,

"You have the scroll," Azulo blurted, and sweat sprouted on his skin as if it cost him to say even that.

Dyna withdrew the green leather case and took out the key's scroll. He gave her a look, then glanced at the fire. Hesitantly, she held it over the flames. Letters slowly appeared on the page.

Seek a key and make your claim but beware the door untamed.

Cross into realms of old, in the loom its secrets unfold.

Once a bridge of finder's luck, now a curse to madness struck.

What did that mean? Azulo's wide aquamarine eyes flickered to the window again, and he rapidly shifted back into a fox. Dyna put away the scroll as the den's green door opened.

Leoake stepped through, letting Fair in. "It's time. Here, take this." He shoved something in her hand. "To keep you from retching again."

"Thank you..." Though Dyna doubted it was because he cared. She studied the glass vial with a translucent pink liquid. "What is it?"

"Water." He shrugged at her skeptical frown. "Healing waters with the power to cure nearly any ailment, even on the brink of death."

Her eyes widened. "Am I ill?"

"The In Between wasn't made for humans to use. The air is poisonous to you." Leoake shut the door and drew the curtain over the windows. Returning to the door, he yanked on the red lever. A crackle of dark energy crawled over her skin.

Dyna quickly drank the potion. It tasted of sweetened rose water. Whatever was in it seemed to settle her stomach.

"Let's get on with it then," Leoake grumbled as he reached for the doorknob, and she clutched Fair's reins.

Normally, he was so nonchalant. Cynical. But only in situations, she realized, when he knew what was going to happen. That meant he couldn't see everything. Deviating from his little game had irritated him, because it changed his plans.

"Leoake."

He paused.

"What are you scheming?"

A smirk played on his lips. "Chaos in order and madness in reason."

She glowered. "Do you always speak in riddles?"

"Only on special occasions."

"You want something on the island, don't you?"

The Druid flicked away the accusation like swatting a fly. "I care nothing for gold and jewels."

Of course not. His fingers were bedecked in fine rings, and a pink pearl glinted on his pointed ear. With such lavish clothing, it was clear he had no need for wealth when he already had it. Many have paid well for his services.

"And yet I didn't ask if you wanted gold."

His expression danced with amusement. The fae could speak no lies, but they found ways to twist truths. He pulled open the door, revealing a spiral of golden light. "Ladies first."

Dyna clutched Fair's reins. But now that she would get what she wanted, she hesitated to go through. Every warning that her Guardians gave her, every time Cassiel accused her of recklessness, surfaced in her mind. She was headed straight for the most dangerous man alive.

Why did she expect to survive this?

"You have seen my future," Dyna said. "Tell me the truth. If I go after him, will I die?"

Smiling sharply, the Druid leaned in close and murmured in her ear, "Not today."

An icy current swept down her spine. There was no point in considering what that could mean. He was only teasing her.

Even if he wasn't, everyone would meet their end one day. But this was her life, and only she would decide how it would end.

Taking a deep breath, Dyna stepped through the Door.

CHAPTER 26

Lucenna

A light cover of fog rolled across the quiet platform of the train station. Only a few people mingled about, waiting for the next ride out of the city. Lucenna wearily looked to the road. As soon as Zev and Rawn had realized Dyna and Fair were missing, they set out for Kelpway during the night.

Lucenna shifted on the stone bench. Her body felt cold and stiff from waiting here since dawn. Leaning back against the wall, she closed her eyes. She hated this. She hated being left here out of the fight. Nothing good ever came out of separating. She should have gone after her, too.

But it was no longer safe for her here.

There had been no more sightings of Magnus. He probably moved on from whatever business he had here. Lucenna was still holding onto the hope his sighting was only a coincidence, but she had to risk glamorizing herself as an old hag. Sighing, she adjusted the sash over her eyes, making sure they were covered. When she told Lucien about their uncle last night, he urged her to leave Dwarf Shoe immediately before anyone else spotted her.

The mages weren't the only thing to worry about. The map to Mount Ida was tucked away in her satchel like a secret. Rawn and Zev felt it best she kept it with her, far away from Tarn.

But Lucenna couldn't help feeling to blame for this mess. She rubbed her eyes beneath the sash and sighed. "I shouldn't have been so hard on her. I drove her to do this."

"The lass was determined to go. You couldn't have stopped her." The detached tone in Klyde's voice made Lucenna look over at him. He sat leaning forward with his elbows resting on his legs. His jaw was clenched, his cool blue eyes fixed on a crack in the wooden floor.

"You shouldn't be here," she said. "You have waited years for the opportunity to confront your brother. Why are you still here?"

Klyde inhaled in a harsh breath and rubbed his face. "I am tasked with taking you to safety, Lucenna."

Yet she could read the frustration on his face and the restlessness of his bouncing knee. He wanted to go. Though it may be difficult since he lent his horse to Rawn.

"I can find my way to the White Woods. This may be the only chance you have to find Tarn."

He straightened, and his tired gaze found hers. "You're probably right. This may be the only time he and I are within the same province. But if something were to happen to you, if you were taken by mages because I went after him, I could never bear that."

They looked at each other in the quiet morning, and a drizzle began to fall. He put her first, before his own vendetta, but it somehow made her feel worse.

Klyde leaned his head back. "At the moment, helping you leave the state takes priority over everything else."

She glowered. "I am not a defenseless woman, Klyde. I have been battling mages for the last three years, and I held my own perfectly well. I don't need you to protect me."

He chuckled, but it didn't sound amused. "Aye, I know. Fine, that. But allow me to take you where you need to go, then I will leave you be."

Lucenna frowned, taken aback by his response.

But as easily as it appeared, Klyde's irritation faded with another breath. "Do you know how to travel by train and how to get to where you need to go?" he asked in a softer tone.

Unfortunately, he had a point. At the look on her face, he nodded and returned to staring at nothing. She studied him, trying to understand the unsaid things behind his words. He was upset, but it was more than merely not going after his brother.

A crowd slowly gathered on the platform as the hour drew near. They perked up at the vibration beneath their feet as the floor rumbled with an incoming train. It let out a piercing whistle, spitting out steam into the early morning. The brakes hissed and screeched as the train came to a halt at the station. She rose from the bench with Klyde.

The gathered crowd swarmed forward in a rush toward the many entrances of the attached carriages for passengers. Conductors in dark blue uniforms stepped out.

The one assigned to the carriage in front of them was a grumpy dwarf. He barked at them to form a line and make room for the passengers disembarking the train. "Mind the gap," he announced on repeat once the line started moving.

Eventually, it was their turn to board. Klyde went in first and took her arm, towing her past the opening between the platform and the train's stairs. He led her to the back of the carriage, and they chose the empty wooden booth at the end. Lucenna sat, and he took the seat across from her. It wasn't long before all the seats were taken. The train sputtered a whistle, and the carriage rattled as they rolled away from the station. Lucenna stiffened as the train picked up speed. It was a marvelous experience, even if a little unnerving.

"Rest," Klyde murmured. "It will be a long ride until the next stop."

She wouldn't sleep, not whilst riding this metal beast.

"Don't worry. I'll keep watch." Klyde appeared laid back with his arms crossed. But his alert eyes studied the crowd. He had taken the seat that gave him a full view of the carriage.

Lucenna almost retorted something about having a personal guard, but she yawned instead. They fell into a comfortable silence as she watched the city of Little Step sweep past them out of the window. The rising sun cast a golden light over the rooftops. Eventually, the rocking of the train pulled her into a dreamless sleep. She seemed to float on a warm cloud, enveloped in the rich scent of sea salt and cedar. For whatever reason, it made her feel safe.

She woke to the soft rumble of Klyde's quiet voice. "Evening."

It was close. Right beside her. Lucenna almost thought he was speaking to her until another spoke.

"Tickets, please," came a nasally response.

She peered through her lashes, finding herself laying against Klyde's chest. He had his arm securely wrapped around her waist with his mercenary coat covering her. Her first thought was annoyance, followed by embarrassment that she fell asleep on him. His coat partially hid her view, though she saw the dwarfs' small boots in the aisle beside them.

"One moment." Klyde slightly shifted, careful not to wake her as he reached into his coat pocket.

"Traveling with your wife?" the dwarf asked him.

Lucenna tried not to twitch at the question. She remained still, pretending to be asleep.

"Aye," Klyde answered gruffly as he handed the conductor their tickets.

"Where to?"

"South."

"Hmm. Silver hair. I've never seen a lass with pretty hair like that. Where does she hail from?"

"Is that your business to know?"

She inwardly smiled at Klyde's unusually brisk tone.

"All right, sir. I meant no offense." The dwarf stamped their tickets and returned them. He went on his way, muttering to himself about tetchy mates.

Wait. He said *silver hair*.

Lucenna sat up with a gasp. She looked down at herself, finding her glamor had dissolved again. Why did it keep doing that?

"Sit back." Klyde quickly pulled her toward his chest and tucked the loose locks on her temples beneath his mercenary coat. He must have put it on her to cover her hair. "The spell broke a little while after you fell asleep," he whispered, peeking over his shoulder. "My coat deflects magic, but I don't know how well it serves to cloak it. I wouldn't risk casting another spell."

Lucenna stiffened at the wariness in his tone. "Why?" she whispered back, listening to the rapid beat of his heart. Her pulse climbed with it.

"I am quite sure there is a mage on this train."

"What?" she hissed.

"The next town is in Oreville. We'll get off there and take the next train out."

Lucenna glanced at the evening sky outside of the window. She had slept most of the day. "When?"

"Soon," Klyde murmured, his breath drifting over her scalp.

Lucenna shivered. Both from the sensation and from nerves. "You saw him?"

"Aye. Spotted him in the next carriage when the conductor crossed through. He's wearing gray robes."

The tension eased out of her body with a heavy exhale. "He's not an Elite Enforcer. Only an earth mage."

"No cause to worry, then?"

Lucenna peeked past his shoulder to the door that separated the carriages. It had a window to see into the other side. She couldn't see the mage, but she did see part of the green crystal on his staff. The little Essence hovering around him was hardly of any note. Must be a boy still learning the craft, and by the charcoal color of his robes, he was of a middle-class House. The earth mages from a noble class dressed in brown.

Like the Celestials, the mages wore their colors according to their Guild and power level. The darker the color, the more powerful the mage, but most liked to inflate their power level by basing their robe colors on their nobility. Black was the highest status of all. Only worn by Enforcers and the Archmage's household.

"Every mage is a risk, but if I am spotted, this one will more than likely report me to an Enforcer rather than confront me," she said.

"Because it's not his duty to capture you?"

"Because I can sense his little power." Lucenna turned back around. "Once he senses mine, he won't wager his life."

Klyde chuckled. "I admire your confidence, lass." He switched to the bench across from her again to keep his sights on the carriage door. "Once we reach the station, we'll go somewhere to lie low for a while. The next train arrives in two hours."

Rain pattered against the carriage roof, filling the silence as they waited. When the train began to slow, Lucenna could finally breathe easy. They were already standing when the train came to a stop. Klyde took her hand and pulled to the exit before anyone else could beat them to it. The conductor berated him for opening the door. Klyde jumped out and lifted her by her waist, promptly setting her down on the platform.

Her legs wobbled from the unexpected solidity of the floor and the shock of how easily he moved her.

The spring wind blew against them, and the sash hanging loosely around her eyes lifted. Lucenna reached for it, but the wind snatched it away. And at that same moment, she looked up and met the gaze of the mage from the train windows. He was hardly a young man, perhaps sixteen.

But there was no shock on his face.

Because, she realized, he had wanted her to think that.

The air rippled with a burst of powerful magic, so strong it weighed on her like a heavy blanket. It had been completely hidden away until he dropped his cloaking spell and the glamor he wore peeled away.

The boy mage vanished, and in his place was a fully grown lunar mage. Tall as he was lean, with short white hair and glowing purple eyes.

Her lungs seized.

Magnus.

"Shite," Klyde cursed. He grabbed her hand, and they ran.

The hum of the train station faded behind them as he led her through the darkening streets of Oreville. Their boots splashed in rain puddles, their heavy breaths fogging in the cool, misty air.

Gods, how could she have been so careless? Of course, he came to find her. He was a skilled tracker. Her father must have swallowed his pride to ask his younger brother for help. The Archmage was finished waiting.

Static crackled in the air, and she knew Enforcers were already after her. Magnus must have had them waiting in each station along the railway.

"You really shouldn't have stayed with me," Lucenna said as they loped around another street. "We need to split up."

"What?" Klyde demanded. "I'm not leaving you, woman."

She gritted her teeth. "This is not your fight. I can feel the Elite Enforcers tailing me now. They are almost here. Go now before it's too late."

He stared at her a moment, shaking his head. "Lucenna—"

"Get out of here!" She shoved him. "I am trying to save your life, you fool." But he wouldn't budge. His jaw clenched, eyes burning. Lucenna shook her head, swallowing the lump in her throat. "Stop it, all right? Stop behaving as if I need you. *I don't.*"

Her feet stumbled as she backed away from him. She couldn't allow herself to need him, because if she did, she would come to rely on him. And she knew that would be when she lost him, too.

"Stay away from me, Klyde. While you still have the chance."

Lucenna sprinted away into an alley. The thud of her running steps and the rapid beat of her heartbeat filled her ears. When she looked back, Klyde was gone. A knot formed in her chest. It was better this way.

If he stayed with her, she would only get him killed, too.

CHAPTER 27

Dynalya

The streets of Kelpway were quiet in the early morning, the port beginning to wake. Fair's hooves clomped on the cobblestone as they wandered east for the pier. In the market, the smell of fresh baking bread made Dyna's stomach growl. One necessity at a time.

She stopped to barter for some apples, cheese, and rolls to break her fast. Well, Fair preferred the apples. Taking a seat on the edge of a fountain, she soaked in the sun and breathed in the ocean breeze as she ate. But after a couple of bites, her appetite seemed to disappear.

Water sprites in the fountain swam to her curiously, eyeing her food. They chirped at her, blinking their big oily eyes. She tore up the bread and cheese in smaller pieces for them, and they took off with their prize.

She needed a plan.

Would it be better to sneak onto Tarn's ship or approach him? She peered at the tips of the sails peeking beyond the roofs. Was he even still here? He didn't exactly give her time. Maybe she should look for Von instead. He would know how to find Tarn, but Von could be anywhere.

Dyna rubbed her dry eyes and yawned. Exhaustion was catching up to her sooner than expected. Falling sick last night didn't help either. But when she pulled out the tonic from her satchel, it felt near empty. What she had left wouldn't last long. She should visit the apothecary across the street before continuing to the docks. Tipping the bottle back, Dyna drank the last drops to the dregs. A sigh of relief slipped out of her as her energy returned and her worries faded.

She could do this.

After wiping her lap clean of crumbs, Dyna took Fair's reins and crossed the street. But when she headed for the apothecary, a hand snatched her into the shadowy alley and pinned her to the wall. A man's gloved hand clamped over her mouth, the other pinning her shoulder in place. Her pulse sped with adrenaline. Her hood covered her vision, so there was no telling how many were in the alley. She had been in this situation before, but they had no idea she had months of pent-up rage ready to release on the next person to try her.

Dyna thrust her hand against his elbow, breaking his hold off her mouth. She reached for his sword, but he caught her wrist. Twisting, she wrenched free. Her body fell in perfect formation as she whipped out her blades.

A low chuckle echoed in the alley.

Dyna stilled, because she recognized that sound. She yanked back her hood and met a pair of pale blue eyes that matched a winter sky.

His mouth curved in a faint smirk. "Maiden."

She blinked in surprise. "Tarn..."

After pushing and waiting and demanding to get to him, here he was. Her first instinct was to drive her knife into his heart, but no matter how much she trained, she knew her limitations. Tarn was an opponent she would have to defeat when he least expected it.

Dyna forced a small smile and sheathed her knives. "It's improper to sneak up on a lady. I could have killed you."

"Doubtful." He tucked his gloved hands into the pockets of his long coat. The lapels were pulled up, partially obscuring his face. "Though I see your reflexes have improved."

Tarn continued walking through the alley. She took Fair's reins and followed. It was odd to find him in public. The king's ransom on his head forced him into hiding, but perhaps he didn't need to worry in Dwarf Shoe. Or he had a pressing reason.

"Did you come looking for me?" she teased.

"Hardly. I came on another errand. Fortunately for you, as I am about to leave."

Dyna glanced behind her to make sure no one followed. "No luck meeting the Druid?"

"It seems my information was false."

She bit back her grin as they entered a quieter street with hardly anyone passing by. They made for the sea. "Well, he isn't another trinket you can simply gather for your collection, Tarn. You do not find him. *He* finds you."

Tarn stopped, eyeing her. "You speak as if you know him."

Dyna schooled her expression and shrugged nonchalantly. "I don't. I simply know how tricksy the fae are."

The crease in his scar deepened as he studied her. Her expression remained blank, fortifying her lie.

Tarn walked on. "How did you manage to come here alone? I half expected your Guardians to appear."

"I slipped away in Little Step." She needed to tell him some truths to make her story believable. "I rode through the night."

"Just as well." The pier came into view, and there was Tarn's ship. It was a fine black vessel with *SOMNIO* painted in elegant gold letters on the side. No sigil marked the black sails. "Leave the horse."

"What?" She slowed as they reached the docks.

"Did you think a ship was a place for animals?"

"But I can't leave him."

"Sure you can." Snatching the reins from her, Tarn tossed them aside and pulled her along. As if it were easy to leave something behind.

That made a thorn dig into her chest.

"Wait." Dyna tugged against Tarn's grasp. Fair whinnied and trotted after her.

"I already told you I am not waiting." He forced her into a quick pace toward the ramp. "You chose this, remember?"

The statement tangled the words on her tongue. She had chosen this.

Tarn led her up the gangway onto the ship's deck. Fair neighed in protest from below. His hooves beat on the deck as he spun in circles. Her heart tumbled, and Dyna had a sense she should be crying. She didn't want to leave him, but Tarn was right, he had to stay. Who knew what was going to happen next? It was too dangerous to bring Fair onto the ship.

"Find your master." Dyna shooed him. "He's looking for you. Go on, Fair."

As she walked away, his neighs carried on the wind. All her life, she acted on a whim and hoped for the best, because she was following her heart. It had been bleeding inside of her, dying, but it still spoke. And it was telling her now to go back.

Pressure built behind her nose and eyes. She halted, feeling conflicted, but she came here for a reason.

To stop Tarn.

To find her remaining Guardian and to free her friends held captive here. It would work out in the end. It had to.

When Dyna looked back, Fair had galloped away for the harbor. He would reunite with Rawn soon enough, because she was fooling herself if she thought her Guardians wouldn't come for her as soon as they realized she was missing. Zev would probably catch up to her first. She only needed to wait. Once they arrived, she would make her move.

Dyna allowed Tarn to lead her onward. The Raiders watched her pass silently. She searched for her friends, but they weren't on the deck. Well, Sorren and Geon were probably working in the kitchen.

"Where is Commander Von?" Dyna asked. She had to maintain pretenses, though she was looking for him, too. Elon said he had come to Kelpway. "I want to at least greet Yavi."

"They are below deck tending to their duties," Tarn said, without looking at her.

The spies weren't in sight, either. But she did spot new members among them. A man from Xián Jìng idled in the crow's nest, his dark eyes watching her. There were a few dwarves, foreign men, and a female elf coming out of the doors to the galley.

All eyes watched her as she walked with Tarn. The atmosphere felt strange. As if the Raiders were holding their breath.

Olsson stood by the steps. She was at least glad to see another familiar face, though he was surprised to see her.

"Lieutenant Olsson," she greeted. "You look well. Could you send word to Yavi or Dalton that I am here? I would like to see them."

She had to pretend to be oblivious to Dalton's escape, but what about Clayton?

The Raider's eyes widened further. He shifted on his feet, clearing his throat. He glanced at his master.

Tarn's cool eyes settled on him. "Gather the men."

Olsson immediately turned away and quickly marched down the steps. Dyna frowned at his lack of response. He probably didn't know Tarn had invited her here. She looked around the ship, taking in the black sails. It was an elegant vessel but held no character other than its name.

"*Somnio...*" She mused. "That's an interesting name for a ship."

Tarn glanced at her.

"It means to dream." Dyna faced him, and they shared a long stare, both thinking of the time she had spent in his dreams. She canted her head. "How quaint."

He scoffed. "Don't think I named my ship after you."

Dyna smiled wryly at the churning waves. Oh no. She knew exactly who it was named after.

In her pocket, she rolled the pewter bottle in her clammy palm. Attacking Tarn in his sleep wouldn't work since he never slept. Recalling the way he caught Rawn's arrow out of the air reminded her of his reflexes. Not to mention he had magic. How does one kill a powerful man who never let his guard down?

A plan had been in the back of her mind for months, though she had not let herself really imagine it because it made her skin crawl.

Footfalls lightly tapped on the steps as the she-elf joined them on the quarterdeck. She was beautiful in a childlike sort of way, with waves of dark hair and brown eyes. A white dress fitted her lithe body, but otherwise she wore no weapons or uniform. With a soft round face, pouty lips, and dewy skin, she looked sweet and pure.

Innocent.

The sight of her made Dyna angry, and she didn't understand why.

The she-elf bowed her head to him.

"Dyna, this is Lumina."

"You have been enlisting new members for your army," Dyna said, crossing her arms as she eyed Lumina. "Why hire her? She's too soft to be a Raider, and you have enough mages."

"She serves a purpose," Tarn said. "Don't let her appearance fool you. Lumina is a Magi Master, and in this instance, my recruiter."

"Recruiter?" Dyna furrowed her brow. If she was to fight her way into his inner circle, why not put her up against Len?

His mouth lifted in a cool smile. "Everyone must pass initiation, Maiden. No exceptions."

Lumina began to circle her. Vivid pink light spiraled around her palms as they faced off. She lifted her hands into position, making her bracelet of white shards clink softly.

"You have one minute," Tarn said.

Dyna frowned. "For what?"

"To survive." He snapped his fingers.

Lumina thrust her palm into Dyna's chest with an Elvish word.

Pink light clashed against her fae armor. It absorbed the brunt of the spell, but the force sent Dyna sliding backward. She braced her legs, her boots skidding to a stop.

Tarn leaned against the banister and crossed his arms. The Raiders gathered on the deck below, jeering and hooting. Money passed hands as they made their bets. Tarn arched an eyebrow at her, awaiting her response. This was more than a recruitment. He wanted proof of her abilities.

Dyna took out her blades. "Until I draw first blood or until one of us is left standing?"

His silence left that up to her interpretation.

She faced her opponent, inhaling a low breath.

Lumina muttered a spell and cast out a stream of magic. It rippled across the deck in pink waves. Dyna ran toward her. She leaped over the attack spell and launched herself off the banister. Her blade sliced past Lumina's arm. She yelped and dropped to the deck. Her magic vanished.

Lumina gripped her injured arm and wobbled to her feet, blood seeping through her fingers. This fight wouldn't last long. It was clear from the way she moved that Lumina wasn't a warrior. She relied on her magic.

"Zuled sadapse," Lumina said, her voice light and sweet.

Essence tugged against Dyna like static. The sky crackled, and spears of pink light lifted in the air. Crouching, she readied her weapons.

Lumina swept her arms, and the blades came for her one at a time. Dyna parried the first attack, pivoted away from the second, and flipped to dodge the third.

Pink streaks, like stars, spun around Lumina. She brought her fingers together, forming a circle. *"Rinuer."*

The enchanted flares spiraled out and formed a ring around Dyna. She had a split second to drop to the floor before the stars clashed into each other above her head, nearly taking it. A few severed strands of red hair floated down by her boots.

A fight to the death, then.

The Raiders hollered, thrusting their fists into the air. Tarn looked away to the horizon, unimpressed.

Dyna ground her teeth. A soft she-elf wasn't going to beat her.

Pink light glowed in Lumina's eyes. *"Orto ramalcer aram nev."*

The water churned around the ship. The waves rose like a living thing, and the Raiders exclaimed in fear. Well, Lumina had some grit after all.

But Dyna smiled back. She would win this without using a single spell but one. She waved her hands in a cast and said in Elvish, *"Orum ed erb'mul."*

Lumina's eyes widened. She dropped her hold on the ocean and prepared for the fire called against her. Except, her opponent forgot one thing.

Dyna wasn't an elf.

She sprinted forward, blades drawn. Lumina tried to counter, but it was too late. Dyna ducked under her next attack and slashed her across the stomach. She screamed. Dyna swept her second knife up for the killing blow.

The blade halted against Lumina's delicate neck. They both breathed heavily, aware of the edge pressing into her racing pulse. A drop of blood leaked down.

Dyna glared up at Tarn. "I had her."

Inwardly, cool relief secretly flooded through her. It had been a gamble if he would intercept her in time.

"You did." He flexed his tight grip on her wrist, and ice sank into her bones. "But I'd rather not have blood on my deck."

Yet Tarn said so while looking at Lumina. It was her life he valued, and Dyna was beginning to wonder who she was.

"Then you should have given me a challenge."

He searched her face, perhaps taken aback by the indifference in her tone. One end of his mouth lifted.

The Raiders broke out with wild cheers. The man from Xián Jīng dropped from the masts above them and landed beside Lumina. He wore deep blue traditional robes in the style found in his country. His expression was blank, his black eyes regarding her indifferently as he helped Lumina her feet. She stared at her, pressing on the shallow cut above her navel. It wasn't deep enough to require stitches. She would live.

Tarn released his hold on Dyna's wrist.

The blades spun in her palms as she returned them to the sheaths strapped to her thighs. "Did you find the fight entertaining?"

"Mildly." His pale eyes roved over her toned body, and they stirred with something she couldn't name. "It seems you did not sit idly these past months."

"Not much to do in the winter."

He led her to the banister where the Raiders had gathered and lifted up her hand. They cheered wildly. Their voices were like a roar, thrumming against her chest. It stirred her pride, feeding the victory she earned. It was small, but it secured her place in their circle.

And it brought her one step closer to her goal.

"I only have one question," Tarn said as they walked away together toward the captain's quarters.

"And what is that?"

Tarn pulled her inside and shut the door, trapping her against it. Dyna's heartbeat fluttered wildly beneath his cool stare. Placing his hands on the wall on either side of her, his icy breath drifted down her nape as he leaned forward. "What happened to your magic?"

CHAPTER 28

Dynalya

Dyna refused to answer that question. She slipped past Tarn and strode further into the captain's quarters. A dance of purple lights from the spinning amethyst crystal on the ceiling greeted her. Besides the Forewarning Crystal and the red Crystal Core, new wards dangled from the ceiling. Their purpose was the same, but they didn't prickle on her skin anymore. He didn't bother to put bangles on her this time.

She didn't need them.

"Well?"

Dyna wandered around the room. "Well, what?"

"While that exhibition out there was interesting, I couldn't help but notice you didn't call on your magic once. Nor does it glow in your eyes, but more importantly, I do not feel it hovering off you as I did before."

"I don't see why that's relevant."

They were interrupted briefly by Olsson. The burly man came in to set their meal, tasted it before serving Tarn, and promptly stepped out.

She arched an eyebrow at him questioningly. The security of Tarn's meals was Von's job, but she had to continue pretending she didn't know he wasn't here.

Dyna joined Tarn at his table and frowned at her questionable meal that didn't look appetizing in the least. "Surely, you don't expect me to eat this. It's unlike Sorren to burn food."

Tarn steepled his fingers. "You're deflecting."

"And you're prying," Dyna replied sharply. She didn't owe him any answers to her private life. "Did I come here for an interrogation? If so, drop me off at the next port."

"Testy." His fingers slowly drummed on the table in a pensive rhythm. "I was merely curious. I find my mind is full of ... questions."

Tarn's eyes caught the sunlight from the windows, turning them icy white. Dyna held still as she waited for his next question. For his next demand. But what he asked next was the last thing she expected.

"Why didn't you take my hand?" It took her a moment to understand Tarn referred to the first time he asked her to join him.

Dyna swallowed before she could make herself answer. "I did," she admitted faintly. "Want...to take it."

The truth rune that had been burned on the wall lit up the cabin, bathing the edges of his face in blue. The ship creaked on the waves as neither of them moved. It was the only sound in the silence that took up all the space between them.

Dyna reached into her cloak, but he snatched her wrist. "So fearful I will betray you?"

"The only people who can betray you are those you trust." Tarn's gaze darkened, and the intensity behind his stare sent her pulse racing. "I trust no one."

"Then don't expect me to trust you."

They fell quiet again as they measured each other. He pulled her hand out of her cloak, revealing the red apple in her grasp. Dyna arched her brow pointedly, and he released her.

Leaning back in his seat, Tarn crossed one leg over the other. "Tell me this: why did you contact me with your water mirror? I will suffer no lies from you, Dyna."

He wouldn't trust her, nor believe her without the truth.

Dyna took a bite of the apple to buy some time. She had to tell him that much. Suddenly, her chair felt too uncomfortable. Getting up from the table, she wandered the cabin, stopping to examine the artifacts on his desk with false interest. "At first, I contacted you out of spite. Speaking to you..." She worked her jaw. "It felt like revenge."

"Against who?"

"That doesn't matter," Dyna said coolly as she faced him. "I'm here now. Is that not what you wanted?"

"Better question is, why *now*?" Tarn asked, watching her intently. "You had your chance to join me before, and you did all you could to escape, including taking a life. I am no fool. Over these past winter months, something changed. In you or your situation. Therefore, I will hear your intentions plainly. *What* do you *want?*"

His head on a spike.

His boat.

His resources.

Him—out of her way.

But Dyna couldn't lie here without giving herself away. The longer she was silent, the more her heart raced. Tarn rose and prowled forward. She walked backward as he approached until her back was against the wall.

Tarn stood inches before her, forcing her to meet his icy eyes. His substantial height made her feel small. "Why are you here, Maiden?"

He demanded an answer. There would be no way around it. She had to lie.

But the only way to lie in front of the truth rune was without words.

Dyna rested her palms on his chest, holding his gaze. His white brows furrowed. "I'm no longer a maiden," she whispered.

Then Dyna stood on her toes and kissed him.

It was like pressing her lips to cold marble. He was stiff and unmoving. She felt his shock, but Tarn's moment of hesitation lasted only a second. His arms wrapped around her and his mouth invaded hers. Dyna closed her eyes and pretended. She imagined who she wanted it to be, but it was impossible. Cassiel was a gentle kisser.

Tarn was not.

Kissing him was demolishing. Bruising. Immobilizing. He pinned her to the wall, consuming her air. There was no love behind the kiss. Only a heated attraction fueled by something that felt like possession. Perhaps Dyna had been lying to herself. It wasn't only out of spite or anger. Her body was starved for touch, and some part of her needed to feel wanted.

Even if it was by him.

Tarn's hands traveled around her waist, sliding up her spine. She shivered as his other hand took her throat, holding her in place as he took control. The beat of her heart raced with every intimate stroke, stirring heat in her stomach.

Dyna might have liked this form of wild kissing. If her lips did not burn. If guilt did not chastise her. If tears did not gather behind her eyes. The shriveled bond shook violently as if to recoil. Her entire body rejected the man who wasn't her mate. But her mate *left* her. He rejected their bond and tossed her away.

They were nothing anymore.

So Dyna endured it.

If she was to gain Tarn's trust, she couldn't back out now. Dyna wrapped her arms around Tarn's neck and made herself kiss him back. Let it burn. Let it hurt. Let it peel back every layer of her skin. Maybe then it would sear Cassiel out of her memory for good.

Tarn's fingers threaded through Dyna's hair at the base of her neck, and he tugged her head back. She choked back a gasp at the sting as his mouth moved over her racing pulse.

"Wait," Dyna panted. This was too much. Every kiss he planted on her skin made her feel like she was sinking to a place she may never surface from. "Tarn, stop."

But he kept kissing her. She put herself here, so she had to get herself out.

Dyna yanked on his hair, and that only seemed to encourage him. Incorrigible man. She was about to knee Tarn in the groin when his icy tongue swept against hers. He froze, and his hands halted on her back. He pulled back a few inches, staring at her incredulously. The cabin was quiet, only holding the sound of their soft panting and the crash of waves.

Dyna blinked at him in confusion, coming out of her daze. Clarity struck when he smelled her breath. A flush rushed through her face. She slid back to her feet, but he grabbed her before she could get away and riffled through her clothing. His hand came away, holding the pewter bottle. He flicked it open, and the scent of bitter herbs wafted between them.

Tarn's quiet, mocking laugh made her stomach turn. "*Oh*, we're not so different after all, are we?" Humiliation and anger churned inside of her, and she flushed. Dyna tried to move past him, but he grabbed her arm. An arrogant glint shone in his eyes. "Call me curious, but I must know what changed."

Dyna shoved against his chest, but she may as well try to move the ship. Panic rushed through her. "Let go!"

Tarn released his grip at her next push, and the force sent her sprawling backwards onto his bed. Fury crackled through her like hot oil on water, and the mood rune blazed red.

She gripped her dagger's hilt. "Hold me down again, and I will bury this in your throat!"

Tarn smirked as he wiped his wet lips. He leaned against the end of the bed, not looking inclined to continue what they started. "I like it."

She clenched her jaw. "Like what?"

"You—showing some teeth."

Dyna glanced past him to the mirror on the wall. Through that reflected surface, she had communicated with him for the past three months. She saw herself now, couched on the bed like an animal ready to spring.

"Fangs … and claws…" she retorted to herself. "Odd, how not too long ago I despised myself for lacking them. And now … I hate that it's all I have left…"

Dyna sat back and folded up her knees, wrapping her arms around them. Her eyes bitterly stung as her vision blurred. "I … lost my magic. It was taken from me."

The temperature dropped in the cabin suddenly. "By whom?"

The seething behind the question made her meet Tarn's gaze. His eyes were orbs of ice, but he was listening, truly listening, as he watched her with a focused attention that made her want to tell him everything.

Dyna opened her mouth to answer, but she couldn't say *his* name. Her tongue refused to form the letters.

She closed her wet eyes. "The one I was bonded to. He left me … because he believed me too weak." Her voice wavered at the word. "He was right. I *was* weak. I was completely helpless as my magic was stolen from me. Now all I am left with is a pit of hatred and nightmares I cannot escape." She gritted her teeth as she glared up at Tarn. "So yes, I suppose you and I are the same. Is that what you wanted to hear? That I am a hypocrite for taking Witch's Brew? That you were right about the world? Does it please you to know I am now as deranged and violent as you are?"

"Yes." Tarn's low reply settled in the vacancy of her chest.

The bitter tears she'd been holding back rolled down her cheeks.

Taking her chin, Tarn was surprisingly gentle as he lifted her face. "The most painful betrayal is from the people we trust the most. Yet that pain is a lesson we never forget. For it hardens us and teaches us that the only one you can ever trust is yourself."

As much as Dyna wanted to deny it, a part of her couldn't help but agree.

"That faltering you once had, the naïve notion that everyone is good— it's gone now. You are ready to spill blood and fight for what you want, for at last, you understand there is no other choice. The girl you once were is dead, and you have risen from her corpse to become the woman you are now." Tarn wiped away the last of Dyna's tears with a faint swipe of his thumb, leaving a trail of frost behind. "And as I once predicted..." he murmured. "She is *glorious*."

The atmosphere seemed to dim with the confirmation of what she had long suspected. She had become him.

A cold, cynical person who was quick to violence and mistrust.

"What if I don't like her?" Dyna whispered.

"There is no need to like her. To survive, you don't have to be stronger, only deadlier. And that is what she is. Your truth—unleashed. You are here now because you know it's the only place you will not be judged for it. Because you know exactly what you can achieve at my side." His expression shifted to a half smirk. "I assume that's why you attempted to seduce me. Unless it was also revenge against your Celestial."

Blushing, Dyna jerked herself away. "I am here because I need to find Mount Ida. And as much as you pretend, you waited for me because we both know you still need my map to get there."

But there was no reply to that. Tarn moved on to the sideboard and took out two goblets. The drag of silence made her realize something. He had yet to ask for her map. In all their secret conversations, he had not asked about it once.

Her eyes widened. "You don't need it anymore...do you?" One end of his mouth lifted as he poured the wine, and a chill washed through her body. "You know where Mount Ida is. How? When?" No one else in his camp knew the location of the island except her. He had tried to take it from her mind, but—her breath caught. "Clayton."

When he hit her with the desolate spell, he had been rummaging in her mind and found exactly where it was.

"He was of some use to me," Tarn said. "Before I slit his neck."

He watched her carefully, gauging her reaction.

"Good. He deserved it," Dyna said with such frostiness, she wasn't sure if she was still acting. Inside, horror bubbled in her chest. The one advantage she had over him was gone. "If you have Mount Ida's location, why wait for me?"

Tarn walked back to her, and Dyna's pulse climbed with every step. She instinctively wanted to move back, but her legs were pressed firmly into the side of the bed.

"You may have forgotten, scarlet flower." He handed her the goblet. "I still have plans for you."

She narrowed her eyes. "What plans?"

"We will discuss that in a moment. Drink."

Dyna glanced down at the ruby liquid. The scent of bitter herbs hung in the air beneath the fruity aroma of wine. Her mouth watered with a craving to drink Witch's Brew again and dilute all the emotions tearing through her now. But she knew what would happen if she didn't stop.

"I don't want to be a monster..."

Tarn brought the goblet to her lips. "Virtue and kindness are useless qualities. Why fight what nature has made us?"

Maybe he was right. Why fight it?

She wouldn't beat him by being who she had been. He already told her as much. *Sometimes, to defeat a monster, you must become one.*

"What do you want most in the world?" Tarn asked.

Dyna considered the question. "To take back everything stolen from me," she replied. Her magic. Her dignity. Her control. Over everything, including him.

The truth rune glowed blue and cast a gleam on the walls.

Tarn held out his hand. "Then you will have exactly that."

She took a breath as they gazed at one another. There was that look again, the one he had in the tent the last time he offered his hand. The genuine desire that she would accept it ... and him.

"Put all your trust in me, Dyna, for you will also have mine. Join me and nothing will ever stand in your way."

"Join you as what?" she asked. "As I already told you before, I will not be a slave or your spy."

"You will serve a purpose far grander than that. A place at my side as I conquer Azure. Not behind me or in service to me." He closed the space between them, lifting her chin so she saw nothing else but him. "*With* me."

Dyna's heart raced wildly at the proposal and the heated insinuation behind it.

How ridiculous.

How enticing.

She evaluated every honeyed word, listening to what he said and what he didn't. Tarn may not need her map, but he was a collector. A user of people. He needed her for *something*.

He made no promise not to betray her, and she wouldn't promise that either. Because she had a mission, and the outcome garnered no loyalty. He would never trust her, but she could, however, wait until he lowered his guard.

Sliding her hand into his cold palm, Dyna gave him a sly smile. "Does this mean you intend to make me Queen of Azure?"

Tarn returned the smile. "Why else do you think I waited?"

An answer without an answer. He was good at those. Well-practiced when he was constantly in the presence of a truth rune. It reminded her very much of Leoake.

"I will toast to that." Dyna tossed back her head and drank every drop of wine.

Every useless emotion was buried in a dark pit inside of her, and every weakness faded. Her worries. Her exhaustion. She felt strong. Clear of mind. All that weighed her down faded away.

For once, she was sure of herself.

Tarn smirked as he drank from his cup. "Cheers."

She smiled, determined to beat him at his own game. "So, about these plans—"

A knock at the door interrupted her. Lieutenant Olsson came in with the man from Xián Jīng. "We are ready to set sail, Master."

Tarn nodded and took a seat at his desk. He eyed the map with a crease forming in his brow. "Set a course for the Misty Isles. We will replenish provisions there in Hager's Port before making our way to Mount Ida."

Dyna's heart sank into her stomach. "Hager's Port? I thought you were still searching for the Druid." Her tone was inquisitive but perfectly innocent while inside she tensed.

If they left Kelpway before the others arrived, it would throw off her plan. Her heart rate started to climb at the thought of going out to sea without her Guardians. Lucenna may not be able to track her that way.

"After three months of searching Dwarf Shoe, it's clear he is not here. I have been stagnant in this town long enough," Tarn said as he read over a chart. His cold eyes narrowed on the quiet man. "Remind me, Sai-chuen, what purpose do you serve?"

The Xián Jīng man tilted his head. "I did say the Druid would be a challenge to find. He must have caught wind of me, but I have received word he was last spotted in Little Step."

"And you are telling me this now?"

"He is either departing the state or taking the train. Both would require leaving the ship."

Which Tarn preferred not to do. He didn't want to call attention to himself.

"I disagree." Dyna crossed her arms as she sat on the edge of his desk. "The Druid won't be lurking in cities of stone. He will be in what feels safe and familiar, like the forest. If you ever want to find the fae, find a crop of trees first."

They were random facts. Her last statement was vague and, in some ways, true with her experience, so the rune couldn't call her a liar. She needed to stall for time and stay in Dwarf Shoe.

Sai-chuen's black eyes lifted to her, his expression unreadable.

"Trees…" Tarn repeated skeptically.

Dyna shrugged. "Do what you wish. I am only saying it's worth looking into. There happens to be a small woodland in Argent Cove near the coast."

And it was the next port over. A day away.

She slid off the desk and strolled outside, lingering by the railing as she looked out at the city of Kelpway. Zev wouldn't make it in time, but luring Tarn to the next port was the next best thing … if he took the bait.

The breeze blew against her as Dyna held her breath, waiting for his decision.

After five minutes, Olsson left the captain's quarters. "Weigh anchor and hoist the sails!" he barked to the men. A swarm of action broke out. His heavy steps climbed the stairs to the quarterdeck above her, and she overheard him say to the helmsman, "Chart a course for Argent Cove. The master wants us flying on water with the next wind."

Dyna hid a smile. Soon the sails inflated, and they were out on the sea.

Unleashed, Tarn had said.

She would show him unleashed.

CHAPTER 29

Zev

"We are too late." Rawn's defeated words crashed in Zev's ears like rogue waves as he watched Tarn's black ship sail away. He sat on his haunches and howled at the sky. How could Dyna simply leave him that way? His paws scraped the planks as he restlessly paced at the edge of the dock. How would they catch up to her now? Where was Tarn taking her? Was she safe?

Another howl ripped from his throat.

Rawn rubbed his face. He was rumpled and windblown from a long ride here, worry settling on his exhausted features. "Would she have taken Fair with her on the ship?" he asked him.

Zev whined. He didn't have an answer, but Fair and Dyna's scents were all over the dock.

Closing his eyes, Rawn took a breath. "I pray they are together. If not, then Fair will find me."

Zev hated this. Having their group separated felt as if they had been split away from him somehow, as if he was walking on only three legs.

He huffed, and the inhale of air uncovered another familiar scent. It faded beneath all the others, mingled with the sharp smell of...

Zev rapidly shifted back on two legs, startling Rawn. He heaved heavily, staring after the ship vanishing over the horizon in horror. "Gods..."

"Zev, what is it?"

He yanked on a pair of trousers Rawn handed him and stormed away. "Von was here."

"Here?"

"We have to go after them."

"Yes, well—wait, Zev. What is wrong?" Rawn tugged him to a stop.

"I caught Von's scent," he exclaimed. "Along with the scent of saltpeter, charcoal, and sulfur."

Rawn's eyes widened. "*Huyao.*"

Xián Jīng gunpowder.

They turned to Elon, where he waited on the shore with his brown stallion and Onyx. He accompanied them here, per Sylar's insistence. But that may not have been the only reason.

"You knew, didn't you?" Zev growled.

The red elf's expression didn't change from its permanent stoic state. His black cloak cast his face in shadow as it rippled in the breeze. "Von is the Guardian of Vengeance. This is his purpose."

"Vengeance?" Rawn repeated. "For what?"

"When Von tried to escape, his wife was killed." Elon looked out to sea. "He lives now to rectify that."

Zev's chest heaved with rapid breaths, and he snatched the front of Elon's cloak. "And when were you going to tell us Von planned to blow up Tarn's ship?" he shouted. "Dyna is on it!"

Elon broke Zev's hold with a swift sweep of his arm, and the next blow to his chest knocked him back a few steps. Zev wheezed, gasping to recover the air knocked out of him.

Retrieving the reins, Elon returned to the road. "We cannot stand in the way of fate."

What did that mean? Did he say that because they didn't reach the boat in time, or because Von was meant to do this?

"Where are you going?" Zev demanded.

"Home," Elon replied without looking back. "Once I put you on a train in Little Step."

"We cannot go with you," Rawn said.

That made the elf stop and fix his amber gaze on him. "Your Maiden is now accompanied by a Guardian. Von will assure her safety. *You,* however, have put yourself at further risk, which grows with every hour you are here."

"Regardless, I am bound by oath to protect Lady Dyna. I will not leave until we are reunited with her and my horse."

Elon's jaw worked. "You do not have the means to find them."

"But you do." Zev crossed his arms. He hadn't forgotten that spell he cast at the Kazer Cliffs, nor the battle between him and Rawn in Willows

181

Grove. "You have magic. Cast a tracking spell for us, and we can go our separate ways from here."

The elf fell silent for a pause. Then he reached into his cloak and drew out a small glass orb that fit comfortably in his palm. On the polished surface appeared a glowing map of the region and a speck of white light that rhythmically pulsed.

"What is that?" Zev asked.

"A locator orb." Rawn moved closer for a better look. "They are used to hold locator spells on one individual at a time. The pin is moving south. I presume this one is linked to Von?"

"It is," Elon said.

Zev narrowed his eyes on him. Did he want to know why?

"Thank you," Rawn said.

"Do not offer your thanks, Lord Norrlen." Elon tucked the orb away. "I am not here merely because Sylar asked it of me. If you are captured, I will not allow you to reach Red Highland alive."

They fell silent at the cold statement.

Now Zev saw the real reason he came. To guarantee Rawn would never speak of his family's existence.

"Attempt it, and you will not return home alive either," Zev growled, moving to shield Rawn. "You want your family safe, as do I. The sooner we find Dyna, the sooner we leave Dwarf Shoe. So lead the way."

Elon met his yellow eyes a moment, then mounted his horse. He cantered ahead.

"I don't trust him, but right now, he is our only damn option."

"Possibly not our only one." Rawn mounted Onyx's saddle. "Lady Lucenna taught me how to cast a location spell during our stay in Skelling Rise. I am unsure if I can locate Lady Dyna past Cassiel's barrier, but if I can, it will only work if she is on land."

"Let's hope she steps off that boat soon."

Zev stripped away his clothing, and a familiar ache went through his body as he shifted back on four paws. He shook out his fur to rid himself of unease. There was something off in the air. Either it was the constant hum of magic in this province, the lurk of danger hanging over them, or simply because their group had split up again. Something was surely coming their way.

Gods willing, he found Dyna first, before it did.

CHAPTER 30

Lucenna

The stream of magic chased Lucenna through the darkening streets of Oreville. She pressed her back against a brick wall in a dark alley, panting to catch her breath. The charge of energy in the cool air prickled against her skin. She could feel them closing in on her from across the town in every direction. After hiding and battling throughout the day until nightfall, clearly there were too many Enforcers for her to fight them individually. If she was to survive tonight, it would take one last stand.

She had to hit them all at once.

The storm clouds gathered above, rumbling with thunder. Lucenna smiled as her veins hummed with her element. "Yes, that will do perfectly."

Once the coast was clear, she bolted for another street. Her running steps carried in the quiet, splashing in rain puddles. Reaching the town square, she stopped in front of a flowing fountain. Colorful bulbs of lights glowed from the alleyways as Elite Enforcers surfaced from the dark with their staffs. They had her surrounded on all fronts. Thirty of them this time. By the force of their Essence pressing against hers, they were from all three guilds.

"There she is."

"We've got you cornered now."

Their laughter swarmed around her, taunting her bad luck.

Lucenna might have been intimidated last season, but she had been training over the winter. It was about time she tested her new abilities. The mages moved forward, striding through the puddles in the cobblestone.

They circled her as a sun mage said, "There is nowhere left to run anymore."

Purple Essence flared in Lucenna's hands. "I wasn't running."

She had only been searching for an open space. Here was as good as any.

"This does not need to go any further, Lucenna" A lunar mage in dark blue robes offered her a kind smile. His white hair reached his jaw. He was young, perhaps sixteen or seventeen. Not an Enforcer, then, but clearly a noble. "After four years of running, you must be tired. Allow me to escort you back home in peace, all right? I wouldn't want to be on ill terms with your brother if you get hurt."

She narrowed her eyes. He was an acquaintance of Lucien?

At her silence, the young mage chuckled. "You remember me, don't you? Well, it has been some time. I'm—"

"I don't care to know your name. You won't be alive long enough for me to remember." Lucenna clapped her hands together, conjuring a violent surge of purple electricity.

She cast it to the ground, and bolts of lightning shot across the wet stone like living eels. The mages not quick enough to block the attack were struck, and their screams rang out. Ten down.

The mages fanned out, and the crystals in their staffs flared with light. Their magic crackled violently in the air.

"Only subdue her!" the lunar mage commanded. "Our orders are to take her alive."

Lucenna would rather die fighting. She had come too far to allow a mage to capture her now.

Running forward, Lucenna cast out spheres of fire at them. The mages blocked or dodged, some conjuring spells of their own. An earth mage waved his staff, and the water from the fountain rose up in a torrent. Lucenna spun and took hold of it, hurdling the burst of water toward the mage. It crashed into him, tossing him across the square where his body smashed into a building.

One more.

Two sun mages sent a sweep of fire at her. Lucenna threw up her shield, and the flames clashed against the protective barrier. Reaching for the skies, she yanked down her arms with a scream, and a barrage of lightning fell from above.

The lunar mage threw out his hands, catching the lightning before it hit him. Three Enforcers were not so lucky. Their smoking bodies joined the rest.

Lucenna sneered. "You need to move faster than that."

A roar of flame crashed into her from the left. The searing heat sent her flying back, but she wove her Essence through the flames, turning them purple. Lucenna landed in a crouch, and the fire flared in her hands, building into a spinning maelstrom. The Enforcers gaped at her in bewilderment. They either weren't warned she was a Transcendent, or they didn't expect her level of power.

Lucenna released a tsunami of flame. It blasted through them and crested over the square, disintegrating everything. The charred buildings rumbled, debris crashing. Embers drifted down amongst the bodies. She panted, her veins throbbing. As powerful as that blow was, she had only taken out six more. Ten were still left.

Another mage stomped his foot, and frost crackled across the ground. Ice shot toward her like spears. Lucenna yanked her fist up, and a wall of cobblestone lifted at her feet, taking the hit. She snapped open her arms, flinging the stones out like cannons. The earth mage halted them in the air—leaving himself open. Lucenna flicked her wrist. Spears of ice went through him and the next four mages beside him. Their gurgled cries fell behind her as she faced the remaining five.

"Lucenna, that's enough." The lunar mage held up a hand, taking a step back. "Stop. It's me, Artem."

She halted, staring at him. "Artem?"

He was Magnus's only son. The last time she had seen her cousin, he'd been a little boy.

Whips of orange Essence snatched her feet out from under her. She hit the ground, and another mage captured her hands with bindings of green light, tying them behind her back.

Enraged, Lucenna screamed, and thunder boomed overhead.

"She can still cast!" Artem warned. "Put her to sleep!"

A sun mage holding a staff with a yellow crystal marched toward her. She shut her eyes and fell into the *Essentia Dimensio* for some manner of escape. But her heart sank when many colorful lights lit up in the dark void all around her like bulbs of falling stars. Essence of the Enforcers. Much more than she had originally counted. So many more were lying in wait in case they were needed.

Lucenna looked up at the glowing crystal above her head, her breath shuddering. Then her mother's voice swept through her memories. *Show them what it means to be a sorceress.*

She burst open her Essence Channels, drawing the full force of her power to the surface like a storm. It blasted out with a powerful burst of light, throwing the mages back. Her magic cleaved through the enchanted bindings on her wrists. Rolling to her feet, coils of purple electricity spiraled around her as she faced them.

Thunder boomed overhead, and lightning flashed, lighting up the square.

Artem stepped back, his eyes widening. "We need reinforcements!"

More Enforcers flooded the square. She decided at that moment, none of them would leave Dwarf Shoe alive. For every sorceress they hunted and siphoned, she would end them all.

The mages began conjuring spells, but one jerked, blood spilling from his neck. His body dropped, and the remaining mages stumbled back, staring at Lucenna. But it wasn't her.

A black shape cut between the Enforcers, blades flashing in the firelight. Cries and gurgles broke out as blood sprayed in the air and bodies rapidly dropped. The mages forgot about her as they directed their power on the unexpected opponent.

A flash of lightning caught the edge of his face, the bottom half covered in a black mask. Klyde. Lucenna's breath caught as he leaped through the Enforcers, severing lives faster than they could realize what was happening.

They threw a barrage of spells at him, and she cried out. "Klyde!"

But every single spell clashed against an invisible force field around him. It wasn't his shield or his coat. Attack magic couldn't touch him.

The four-leaf clover, Lucenna realized.

His blades cut through half of the Enforcers before they realized he was no ordinary human. Leaping into the air, Klyde hooked his legs around a mage's neck and brought him to the ground in one fluid motion. He twisted his knee, and she heard the crack of bone.

Gritting his teeth, Artem threw a powerful purple Essence last. He crossed his arms, protecting his face. The spell hit, but the clover took the brunt, sliding him across the wet ground. Artem backed away as more Elite Enforcers streamed from the shadows.

One ripped debris from the ground and hurled it at Klyde. Magic couldn't touch him, but physical objects could. Lucenna snatched him out of the way with her Essence and yanked him to her side, placing him on the fountain.

He nodded his thanks. "Nearly got me there."

"I told you to stay out of it," Lucenna hissed as rain began to fall. "I don't need you to protect me. Now stay off the ground."

Lucenna strode toward the Enforcers. Her Essence made the air vibrate and crackle with ferocious energy. They readied their glowing staffs.

"Careful," Artem said, standing further away from the battle. "She's dangerous."

But they didn't listen. They never did.

Purple electricity crackled off her as she conjured whips of light. With a snap, they struck the wet ground. Screams rang through the square as the mages too slow to throw up shields were electrocuted to death. Her whips slashed through them, tearing through their bodies and their staffs. She would kill them all.

A force collided into her. It flung her back, and she rolled, crashing into the fountain.

"Lucenna!" Klyde rushed to her, taking her face.

Groaning, she sat up with her vision spinning.

Slow clapping snatched their focus to a dark figure walking into the square. The scattered burning debris revealed him in the firelight. Magnus.

Her uncle's eyes shone vivid purple, his white hair stark in the night. A thick shield glowed around him and Artem. The only mage he had bothered to protect.

"Father, don't underestimate her—" Artem cut off at his sharp look. He ducked his head.

"I see you have started tapping into the magic of other elements," her uncle said coolly. "I am tasked with stopping you before you master all three."

Lucenna got to her feet and wiped the blood from her nose. Power flowed to her glowing fingertips. "You can try."

Magnus's magic rippled through the air, making her faintly gasp from the potent force. It was heavy, powerful, and fully charged. Oh, that bastard. He sent a full company of Enforcers after her. Not because he thought they could take her down, but merely to drain her first. They had finally learned, after four years of hunting her, that it would take a lot more to bring her down.

Klyde moved in front of her.

Magnus's brow creased, his glowing eyes flickering back and forth between them. "What's this?"

"No one." Lucenna yanked Klyde out of the way and hissed at him, "Stay back."

She could feel her uncle's Essence crawling through the air, filling every breath she took. He was far past the level of any mage she had faced, including her father.

"Halt!" A group of Shield Guard dwarves in golden cloaks came running into the square with their battle axes drawn. "Detention of refugees is illegal in Dwarf Shoe. Stand down or be—"

Magnus idly flicked his hand. The awful sound of bones snapping rang clear as all their necks broke at once. The dwarves dropped dead.

Lucenna stifled a curse. She knew her abilities, as well as her limitations. And she wasn't ready for this fight. With the little Essence she had left, her only option was to detain Magnus. For a moment in time.

And it was going to take everything she had.

But Lucenna had to distract him first. "Did my father send you?"

"No."

She chuckled drily. "Ah. So your *master* did."

Magnus' electricity crackled around him, his mouth pursing. Yet the insult had made him fall still, and that was all she needed.

"What did he promise you, uncle?" Lucenna canted her head as she subtly wove her magic through his. It was slow, like water trickling through the thin fissures in the ground. Unnoticed until the damage was too great. "A place in his council? Or my father's seat as Head of the Lunar Guild?"

His glowing eyes stayed on her. Cold and unwavering.

"Something more? I wonder how generous the Archmage will be once you return forty Enforcers short."

The tension eased from Magnus's expression, and it was his turn to smirk. "Why do you assume the Archmage sent me?" His glowing eyes dropped to the ring on her finger.

Her heart dropped. No, it couldn't be. Magnus would say anything to make her falter.

"He sent me here for you, Lucenna. Is it not time for this to be finished?"

Her magic dimmed, her thoughts tangling as she went still.

When it's finished, I will find you...

That's what he promised on the eve of their wedding when she was caught escaping out of her bedroom window.

"Prince Everest is waiting for you."

Her chest heaved with a shallow breath.

Magnus stepped closer, and his voice dropped to a lulling tone that made her vision sway. "All obstacles in your path will be removed. You don't need to run anymore. Return to Magos and take your rightful place beside him—as his queen."

Klyde's hand closed over her arm, and the haze in her mind instantly cleared.

Lucenna hissed at Magnus, fury rising in her blood. "You attempted to use cognitive magic against me."

And it almost worked.

Magnus's eyes narrowed on his hand. "What are you doing?"

He couldn't understand how a non-mage had broken his spell.

"He killed half of the Enforcers, father," Artem told him.

Magnus stared at Klyde with furious outrage and said to her, "Are you with *him*?"

"He is the least of your concern." Lucenna snapped her fingers.

The world came to a standstill.

The crackle of magic and patter of the storm vanished. The flames were still in place, rain droplets hovering in the air. Klyde muttered a low curse at the streak of lightning unmoving in the sky. Artemis and Magnus stood frozen in front of her, but only for a split second.

Essence rippled around her uncle, and he lurched forward with a spell blazing in hands. "Lucenna, stop!"

"Enjoy your stay." She snapped her fingers again, and the world flashed a blinding white.

They fell backward onto the fountain ledge. Magnus and his son were gone, along with any remaining Enforcers. *Gods, it worked.*

Klyde held her against him as she breathed heavily, feeling her strength wane. "Are you all right, lass? What happened?"

"I'm fine," Lucenna rasped. "I need a moment to gather my bearings."

He nodded as they looked at the mess she had made of the town square, bodies strewn all around. "Gods," he muttered. "I still don't quite understand what happened."

"I've trapped them in a rift within the Time Gate. But it won't hold Magnus for long, and I am out of magic."

"All right. Let me know when you can walk." He supported her against his chest so she could rest on him. He was firm and warm.

She blinked blearily up at him. "You came back..."

"Did you really expect me to leave?" The intensity of Klyde's storming blue eyes rendered her speechless. Shifting his position, he took her arms, and she felt his hands trembling. "You can't do that, Lucenna. You can't toss me aside like I am some rubbish to forget in the rain. Damn whatever comes. I am with you. From here to the end."

Lucenna couldn't do anything but take in a shaky breath. She had always fought her battles alone. But with him, she no longer felt alone. Fighting back the knot in her throat, she gave him a short nod.

"Are you injured?"

"No, but you are," Lucenna said when she noticed the blood dripping down his arm.

"I'm fine."

"Let me see."

He slipped his mercenary jacket down his arm enough to reveal the gash on his shoulder. It was shallow. Must have happened during the fight. She tore off a piece of her blouse and wrapped it around his arm.

"You're not as mean as you pretend to be," Klyde murmured.

Lucenna rolled her eyes as she fastened the bandage in place. "Then what am I?"

Klyde's gaze searched hers, and the rare lack of humor in them made her still. "Angry. You're angry that this is your life and how helpless it makes you feel. So now you must prove to the world that you're not."

She gritted her teeth. "I am not helpless."

He brushed the hair from her temples, and the gentle stroke of his fingers eased the rigidity from her body. "I know, lass. You've never had to prove it to me."

Why did he have to say things like that to her? Her eyes stung, and she blamed it on the smoke.

She managed to stand without falling over. "We need to leave before anyone else arrives."

"Aye." Klyde sheathed his short swords within the scabbards strapped to his back and slipped his hand around hers. "Follow me."

They left the remains of the mage battle behind and ran into the night. She looked down at where he held her, perplexed at the way he did so with ease. His hold comforted her more than it should have. He led her to a street of inns where they stole a beige horse from a stable.

"We should take the next exit out of the state," Klyde said as he helped her up onto the saddle. That meant leaving the others behind again.

We are stronger together, Rawn had once told her. It was about time she started listening.

"The Enforcers will expect that," Lucenna said. "We need to join the others. Our only way out of Dwarf Shoe is to finish the plan and steal Tarn's ship."

Now that Magnus was on her tail, putting a league of water between them was her only chance.

Klyde paused, looking pleased by that suggestion. "To Kelpway, then?"

Drawing on the last of her power, Lucenna shut her eyes and cast a location spell. She searched through the void until she spotted a faint green light. The glowing bulb of Dyna's Essence faintly flickered in the *Essentia Dimensio,* hiding behind a veil. Cassiel's damn barrier. Lucenna could hardly see it and sensed she wouldn't be able to for long.

But she managed to cast a tracking spell on Dyna, and the light moved rapidly away. To go at that speed, she must be on Tarn's ship.

Lucenna's eyes opened, and the path of purple flames sprouted through the streets ahead. "Dyna's not in Kelpway anymore. The others won't find her there. They will have to move on. What's the next harbor?"

"Argent Cove." Klyde climbed up behind her, taking the reins. "About a day's ride ahead. Rest so you can recover. I will get us there."

With a snap of the reins, he galloped away down the path of flames. His free arm pulled her close to the shelter of his warm chest. Lucenna didn't have the strength to object. The fight had left her magic spent, and her mind was too preoccupied taking apart what Magnus had said.

Obstacles...

The word left her with an unsettling feeling. Lucien must have sensed something because his call drummed against her temples like an insistent tap, but Lucenna couldn't answer the orb now. Her heavy eyes drifted shut. Tomorrow. She would contact him tomorrow and share what their uncle said. It had to be a lie. Or maybe she didn't want to believe that Everest could be involved. But she was too tired to question it more.

Lucenna fell asleep as soon as they crossed the edge of town.

CHAPTER 31

Dynalya

Unlike its name, Argent Cove was a dreary place, or it may have been the dark storm clouds gathering overhead. It banished the late morning sun, casting the town in shadow. The crowded stone buildings looked dim, damp, and unwelcoming. The only color was the crop of trees on the rise above the beach. Dyna stood with Tarn by the wheel as he steered them into the wharf. His hair was stark white against the backdrop of gray skies. Olsson barked orders as the sails were lowered and the anchor splashed into the dark sea.

Dyna didn't like the feel in the air. She rubbed the chill from her skin. It felt ominous, but that may have only been her nerves. If the others didn't show up soon, she would have to find a way to enact her plan herself.

At Tarn's command, the Raiders lowered a gangway to the dock below. A small group of Raiders gathered, which included Olsson and Sai-chuen.

Tarn took her arm when she moved to join. "Stay with the ship."

Dyna frowned. "Why?"

"We won't stay long."

"Do you think I will run away again?" She sighed dramatically at his silence and rolled her eyes. "I came to *you*, remember? I want to be here."

Tarn tucked the red tresses fluttering across her face behind her ear, making her face warm by unexpected touch. It left a tingling current on her skin as his fingers trailed down her jaw. "Then wait for me."

The focus of his gaze held her captive. Apparently, she wasn't the only one above using seduction to get what they wanted. But he didn't fool her. She had already learned her lesson when it came to him.

Tarn was always planning.

Well, so was she.

Glaring, Dyna moved away. "Hurry back. Another storm is coming." But Tarn didn't leave yet. His pale blue eyes studied her a moment longer. "What?"

He arched his scarred eyebrow. "I am waiting for you to tell me how to call on the Druid. I have long suspected you know him, Dyna."

Her stomach clenched. "How would I know him?"

Tarn leaned down, bringing them eye to eye. "Don't play coy with me." He trailed a finger down her arm where her geas of an oak tree used to be, making goosebumps break out on her skin. "You have dealt with him before."

By his cool tone, she was treading on thin ice.

Dyna crossed her arms and smirked playfully. "Oh, fine. I admit I know him."

Tarn straightened and tucked his hands in his coat pockets. "Continue."

"To call on him, you must place a circle of stones in the forest with an offering inside. Whatever you think may strike his fancy. It's merely a payment for his appearance. But he will only come if he is interested in bargaining, Tarn. I must warn you. Whatever deal you make, it will carry a heavy cost, and not for him."

"I have no intention of making a deal." Tarn turned away for the stairs. "Don't leave the ship."

Dyna leaned on the railing as she watched him cross the deck. She didn't bother telling him that the Druid was a seer. Whatever Tarn had planned, she doubted Leoake would show up, but that didn't matter.

Because her real intention was to get him *off* the ship.

Tarn glanced at his Magi Master as he stopped by the hatch, and she bowed her head. Then Lumina's soft brown eyes locked on Dyna.

Ah, left behind to watch her. *How grand.*

He climbed down the gangway with his men, and they went on their way.

Lumina chanted something in Elvish, and a swarm of pink magic flared outward, falling over the ship like a rippling dome. Dyna stiffened at the static of magic against her skin. The ship became invisible as the rest of the world outside of it became dull in color.

They were in a veil.

Her breathing sharpened as she was reminded of her time in captivity. Closing her eyes, She took several deep breaths until her hands stopped shaking. A passing thought reminded Dyna she already knew how to remove the veil if needed. She shouldn't have put it past Tarn to place precautions.

Dyna held Lumina's gaze as they measured each other silently. A Magi Master. And a skilled one to cast a veil on her own. Well, elves had no limit to how much Essence they could use. Nevertheless, Dyna saw her for what she was.

A replacement for the mages that used to serve Tarn.

Dyna smiled to appear friendly, even if she had almost killed her. "If you don't mind my asking, are you from Greenwood or Red Highland?"

Lumina hesitated before saying in her sweet voice, "I am from here. My parents defected several years before I was born."

She conveniently left out which kingdom, but Dyna could guess from the color of her features that Lumina was a red elf.

"I see." She climbed down the steps. "And how did you come to serve Tarn? Or do you owe him a life-debt?"

Lumina linked her fingers together. "No … I–I work for pay, or well, I work to..." She looked away, clutching her arm to herself.

"To keep him from hurting your family?" Dyna guessed.

"They are Magi Masters who teach in Dwarf Shoe. He wanted my father to serve him, but they are old and near the end of their lifespan. Therefore, I volunteered."

Interesting. Dyna canted her head, wondering how old Lumina truly was. Likely older than she looked to have cast such spells. "What kind of magic do you specialize in?"

"I know healing and combat magic. Tarn said if I serve him loyally on this voyage, he will release me from my service by the end of the year." Lumina smiled at her meekly. "I'm not mistreated, and Sai keeps watch over me. My only position here is to provide magic when it's needed."

But Dyna couldn't help but question why. Tarn didn't like weakness, and Lumina was soft. It had to be something more about her magic that enticed him, something worth hiring *her* instead of a mage.

"Like with the recruitment?" Dyna asked.

"Oh, no. I cast cloaking spells and tend to the wounded. Sai oversees recruitments. Tarn only had me step in to test your magic." Lumina frowned at her thoughtfully. "But you have none. I was told you are a great healer who would be able to assist me with my current patient, yet I don't see how."

Dyna smiled at her tightly so she wouldn't grimace at the blatant statement of her lack of Essence. "What patient?"

Lumina led her to her cabin, which was a makeshift apothecary and healer's bay. The distinct smell of several herbs tickled Dyna's nose. She studied the organized glass jars on the wall, spotting the dark purple leaves used for Witch's Brew.

Someone was lying in one of the beds.

"Len..." Dyna murmured in surprise as she drew closer. The Versai native appeared to sleep; her black hair splayed on the pillow around her face. But there were no other injuries. The once vicious spy looked thin and frail, the X scar on her cheek more pronounced on her pallid complexion. "What happened to her?"

Lumina went to her desk to stir the elixir burbling in a small pot hovering above a candle. The white shards on her wrist tinkled lightly with her movements. "She is the only survivor from a mission dispatched to Beryl Coast in the early winter. But they were ambushed, and her entire team was slain."

Dyna's breath caught. "Including Novo?"

"Everyone." Lumina sighed as she looked at Len. "Her head was struck during the confrontation. She has not woken since. I have tried everything."

Dyna sank into the chair beside the bed, her mind reeling. Her heart saddened for Len. To lose Novo that way, and Bouvier was gone, too. She said *everyone*. That must have been how Elon left—by faking his own death.

"If they died, who brought Len back?" Dyna asked.

"Sai did," Lumina answered brightly. "He saved her and brought her to Tarn. It was how he joined."

That was *suspicious*. Tarn was very distrustful, and it was unlike him to welcome a stranger who allegedly helped his adopted daughter. Losing all his spies must have forced him to make an exception to fill the role. But Dyna had an unpleasant feeling whenever she looked at the quiet man.

"What did Commander Von think of Sai?"

Lumina's brow furrowed. "Who is Von? Do you mean Commander Olsson?"

Ah. Well, that answered some of her questions. Lumina must have joined after he defected.

"Von used to command the Raiders. There was a skirmish before I left, and some were lost." Dyna rubbed her temples, making her voice crack.

"My injuries from the battle have made me forget who fell that day. The faces I expected to see here haven't come to greet me yet, and I fear that..."

Lumina's expression softened with sympathy. "Well..." She lowered her voice as she glanced at the door's round window. "They may be in the brig. I heard there were prisoners there."

Dyna smiled, and this time it was genuine. "You're probably right." She motioned to the pot. "You're brewing an elixir for her nourishment, right? Add mugwort to stimulate her brain. That should encourage her to wake."

"Oh! I had not thought of that." Lumina turned away to sort through the glass bottles on the shelves.

Dyna leaned down and whispered in Len's ear. "I know why you won't wake up, but I hold too much respect for you to let you waste away like this. *Get up*, Len. And make the one who took Novo from you pay." She got to her feet. "Well, I will leave you to it then."

"Oh, all right." Lumina nodded.

Exiting the cabin, no one paid attention to Dyna as she wandered the deck. She passed the galley, hearing the Raiders inside sing some bawdy song as they made a mess in the kitchen. No wonder the food was awful.

Dyna made sure no one was watching before descending the steep steps into the lower deck. It was dark, the gray light from above hardly illuminating the barrels of cargo. Something thunked on the floor, as if dropped or *someone* bumped into it. Dyna held still, listening. There were no other sounds but the creak of the ship as it swayed on the waves. She went quickly, checking over her shoulder constantly until she reached the door to the brig. The rank air hit her first, making her stomach heave.

Every cell was empty except for one in the back.

A bulky form was slumped against the wall in the shadows, the tip of a horn catching the limited light coming from the single window.

"Sorren." Dyna ran to him. The Minotaur blinked at her blearily, and his cracked lips twitched. His fur was matted and patching, his ribs protruding. They had starved him. "That cruel—" She bit back her curse. "Sorren, can you hear me?"

Reaching in her cloak, she pulled out the set of cell keys that she had nicked from Tarn's cabin. She inserted each key into the lock until one clicked. The cell door creaked loudly, and she rushed inside.

"Here, have a drink." She held a waterskin to his mouth. Sorren guzzled down the water and coughed wretchedly. "Slowly now."

He breathed heavily, his head lolling. "Dyna?" he called, his rough voice weak.

196

"Yes, it's me. I need you to stand. Tarn has left the ship. Now is the perfect time to run."

"I can't…" he rasped. "There is no running."

Sorren's hooves jerked, and his witch bangles clinked, reminding her that they were trapped in more ways than one. And she didn't have keys for those.

"The Crystal Core," Dyna said. "Once I break it, you can run. You're getting out of here, Sorren."

He scoffed faintly, almost smiling. "I must be near death to hallucinate of freedom."

"You're not dreaming." Dyna took his face. "I am real."

His dark eyes blinked at her until they cleared, and he took several gasping breaths. "Dyna?" His voice cracked. "You're really here."

"I am."

Tears spilled from his eyes and down his fur. "Why did you come?" He sobbed. "Why? Why did you come now?"

"What do you mean?" Dyna smiled in confusion. "I came to set you free. To set all of you free." She looked around but found only empty cells. "Where are the others?"

Sorren laughed wetly, and it switched to a broken sob. The sound heaved through his body, making him shake. "They're dead," he croaked. "Dalton … Geon … Yavi … Von. They are all dead!" Sorren pushed her shoulder roughly, throwing her to the ground. "You are too late to save us!"

Dyna shook her head, refusing to believe it. "What?"

"You left us!"

Dyna's chest tightened. She did leave.

When she had a chance to run, she took it without looking back.

Sorren slumped against the wall, sobbing. "They're dead. All dead…"

A fist squeezed the air from her lungs, and Dyna felt like she couldn't breathe. Jumping to her feet, she stumbled backwards for the cell door and ran out of the brig.

CHAPTER 32

Lucenna

Lucenna held onto Klyde's waist limply, clutching the damp fabric of his coat. The hooves of their horse clomped over the cobblestone as he rode past the glowing windows of homes and establishments in Argent Cove. They had ridden all night. Her body was sore, as were her Essence Channels.

Voices and music drifted from an inn as a dwarf stepped outside. The swinging doors released the smell of cooking meat, and her stomach clenched from hunger. Hopefully, they would find the others soon.

The tracking spell finally led them to the seashore. The crash of waves joined the squalling of seagulls.

"Let's get down here," Lucenna said.

Klyde helped her dismount. Her sore legs wobbled, and she stretched her tense muscles. He left their stolen horse tied to a tree before they climbed over the rocky hill that overlooked the beach.

The field of sand was empty due to the coming rain. Up ahead was the pier. A few ships idled in the wharf, but they also looked unoccupied.

"I don't see anyone," Klyde whispered where they hid.

Lucenna peeked past him. "Dyna is here." The purple flames of her tracking spell traveled over the sand and continued over the surface of the sea, leading to a vacant spot by a lonesome dock. "There," she said, motioning with her chin. The ship was veiled.

"You're sure, lass? I don't see anything."

"Magic doesn't lie."

He gave her a half smile as he studied the spot. But the flames that had been flickering all night now completely winked out. Her magic was spent. Lucenna used what she could to search for Dyna's Essence, but the barrier completely blocked her.

"I can't feel her anymore."

"The lass is all right," Klyde assured her. "Come. Let's move closer."

They climbed down the rocks and onto the quiet dock where the ships idled beneath the stormy sky. Lightning flickered above. They ducked behind a stack of crates, attempting to listen beyond the crash of the waves.

"I'll try an amplification spell," Lucenna said. She waved a hand and focused on the spot where the ship hid but caught nothing. "I can't hear anything. That man has her contained behind a veil again."

"Or she's not on the ship," Klyde guessed. "Only way to know is to sneak onto it."

"That will be difficult when we can't see it." Lucenna peeked behind her. "I don't like this. We shouldn't be doing this without Rawn or Zev."

"Aye, but they should be here by now. Trouble on the road?"

"I hope not." She glanced at the sleepy town of Argent.

Something felt off. An odd sensation that carried a foreboding, but she didn't know for what. Odd, since this place was supposed to be a haven for refugees and those searching for safety. Yet she couldn't shake the feeling that they were all in danger in this place.

The murmur of distant voices drew her attention to a small woodland on a rise past the rocky hill on the beach. Men dressed in black appeared from the trees.

She gasped. "Raiders."

Klyde yanked her down behind the crates as the men tracked down the hill path to the beach and made their way to the dock. He motioned for her to keep quiet, then peeked past the crates at the men. No, at the one leading them.

The tall man had a distinct scar running across his pale face, from his eyebrow to his chin. White-blond hair was slicked back out of his face, his eyes the color of ice. His long black cloak fluttered in the wind as he strode for the dock.

Tarn.

Lucenna knew it was him by the way Klyde froze at the sight of him. As if he had waited all his life for this moment, yet now that he was faced with it, he couldn't do anything but stare. He slowly got to his feet, his chest rising and falling with shallow breaths.

"Klyde," Lucenna whispered incredulously. "Get down!"

But it was as if he didn't hear her.

"The Maiden must have lied," one of the Raiders said as they approached them.

"Or the Druid wasn't interested in coming," another said.

"Maybe we should have offered up someone in service to him."

"Are you volunteering?" Tarn said, his frosted tone making the hair rise on Lucenna's arms.

The men quickly quieted and bowed their heads to him. The largest Raider barked at them to get to the ship. Recoiling, the men rushed off at the command, their heavy boots beating on the wooden planks as they rushed for the empty spot on the dock. Magic rippled in the air, and a massive ship with black sales appeared.

Tarn strode for it, moving past them with his hands in his coat.

A sudden chill wafted over her with his presence. Lucenna's heart pounded wildly, shock trembling through her at the power she felt lurking in that man. Klyde blinked, his mouth moving with soundless words. He took a step to follow, but Lucenna snatched his hand, and her magic rippled over them like static.

Tarn halted on the dock. His head turned, and he peered over his shoulder—right at them.

Lucenna held her breath.

Tarn's eyes swept over the crates and the pier, a slight frown flickering across his features. He continued down the dock and climbed the gangway onto his ship.

"He ... didn't see me," Klyde said faintly.

"I made sure he didn't," Lucenna hissed. "Are you mad? You could have ruined everything!"

Klyde looked down at where they held hands. "You ... cast an invisibility spell." He exhaled a breath with a strange look on his face. "Here I thought..."

"That he didn't recognize you?" Lucenna's glower softened. "It's been fifteen years, Klyde. You were only a boy when he left. There is a possibility he might not recognize you now."

He rubbed his face. "You're probably right. It's not as if I should expect a wholesome reunion."

"What *did* you expect?"

Klyde's tired eyes lifted to the ship, and his brow furrowed a second before hardening. "Nothing. I didn't come here for answers." He drew his short swords with the grinning skulls and marched for the gangway. "I only came to kill him."

CHAPTER 33

Dynalya

Dyna's boots thudded on the steps as she ran back onto the deck. The Raiders stopped to stare as she bolted past them. Her heart pounded, her breath shaking. She didn't let herself think of anything but one thing.

Bursting into Tarn's quarters, Dyna snatched her satchel off the bed and shoved her hand inside. "Mirror!"

The weight of the cool scalloped plate landed in her palm, and she yanked it out. It nearly slipped from her fingers with her haste. It clattered heavily as she set it on the floor. Grabbing a flagon of water, she dumped water inside and most splashed out of the plate. Sweat coated her skin as she tossed in some salt and quickly stirred it with her finger, thinking of Yavi. Dyna stared at the rippling rings, waiting, hoping—praying.

Nothing.

The mirror didn't even glow.

"No." Dyna stirred again, picturing Von's wife in her mind. Her vision stung as the water settled, but no tears fell. She searched for Geon next. No image appeared. Maybe there were no reflective surfaces around them, or it was because they didn't have magic. But one of them did. Her hands shook as she added more salt. "Show me Dalton..."

The only reflection on the surface of the mirror was her own.

That day in Hallows Nest, when she asked Von about Dalton, he had not looked at her. *I'm afraid I won't be able to pass on your message, lass. The lad is no longer with us..."*

Nausea and disbelief tangled in her stomach. No matter how much Dyna stirred, the salt settled down at the bottom as the water fell still. She felt the shock, but no pain. No tears came, even though they should have. She had taken away her ability to feel the pain, grief now muted behind a wall of magic.

The door to the captain's quarters creaked open. Dyna hung her head, her fists clenching on the wet floor.

"The water mirror will not show you what you seek." That confirmation sank a chill through her body.

Did the others make it out?

No.

Elon had told her the truth. She simply hadn't been listening.

Standing, Dyna dumped the water into the chamber pot and calmly returned the mirror back to her satchel. Her voice was measured, unattached. "What have you done?"

"What needed to be done," Tarn said.

She made herself look at him, feeling something dark brew inside of her. "You killed them."

It wasn't a question. It was a statement her mind needed to hear to allow herself to accept it.

"Yavi was with child." Dyna searched for a reaction, but Tarn's expression didn't change. It wasn't news to him. "That didn't matter, did it? She convinced Von to escape with her, and you couldn't stand it."

He tucked his hands in his pockets. "I do not suffer traitors in my midst. You know that."

Witch's Brew dampened emotion, but it didn't remove morals. He knew right from wrong. He merely didn't care.

She may not be able to love or mourn, but there was one emotion that did surface, because it was the strongest one of all. The mood rune burned red with her rage. It pulsed on the walls like a heartbeat, bathing over them.

"Are you a traitor as well?" Tarn watched her intently with his icy eyes. "You didn't come to join me."

Dyna smiled as she drew her blades. "I came to kill you."

She flung a blade.

It sailed through the air—but not for Tarn. His eyes widened as it hurled at the Crystal Core. Her knife shattered the ruby, shards raining down. She sprinted forward and tackled him. They crashed through the doorway and hit the railing, the momentum sending them toppling over.

They landed on the deck with Dyna on top of Tarn. She whipped out a second blade to his throat.

His Raiders quickly had them surrounded. Even if they cut her down, she didn't care. He had to pay for what he had done.

A smirk played on Tarn's mouth, as if he enjoyed this. Enjoyed how truly violent and enraged she was now.

Tarn's low voice filled the mere inches of space between their faces. "Look at what became of your sweet, innocent heart. I think I quite like this version of you better." Hissing, Dyna pressed the knife harder against his pulse and his smile grew. "Careful, Maiden. Your monster is showing."

"You think I won't kill you?" she snarled through her teeth.

"It's not a matter if you will, but if you can." He didn't look worried though, as if this were merely a game to him. "Do you regret saving my life?"

"Yes, I do. I won't do so again." Dyna moved for the killing blow. Thick ice plated over his neck like armor, and it took over her hand, fusing them together. She jerked to free herself, but he had her trapped.

"I may be a monster, but I draw the line at killing children," Tarn said as he sat up. "I wanted Von submissive. I cared not that his woman escaped. I assumed she would die on her own at sea, but I failed to predict what Sai-chuen would do."

Dyna's eyes widened. "What did he do?" she asked, her heart racing. "Show me."

Tarn's jaw clenched, and an emotion crossed his face. It was only a flicker. There and gone in a blink, but she saw it.

Guilt.

He had that same look on his face when she first contacted him through the water mirror ... three months ago.

"Show me!" Dyna shrieked. Yanking out a black feather from her pocket with her free hand, she slapped it over his forehead beneath her palm. Green light flared out, and daylight vanished.

The dream walking spell yanked her away. It moved her through Tarn's memories with speed, fueled by the maximum force of her power. Dyna knew she found the correct memory when the bitter winter air slammed into her.

She stood on the ship's deck in the night, watching Von beg at Tarn's feet to spare Yavi. Dyna's eyes welled up when he embraced his wife, telling her how much he loved her before throwing Yavi onto the rowboat. He fought with everything he had so she could escape, but he was outnumbered. The Raiders quickly subdued him.

"You could have ended her life quickly, Von," Tarn told him. "Remember that."

He walked away for the stairs, but his head whipped around to Sai-chuen when he snatched an oil lantern hanging from the mast.

"Stop!" he commanded, but the man didn't obey.

Sai-chuen threw the oil lantern. Von's cry tore through the sky, throwing out a hand. Dyna covered her mouth in horror as it sailed through the dark night and shattered at Yavi's feet.

Dyna screamed.

The smoke ripped her away. She crashed onto the deck so hard the world shook, and her ears rang. Commotion stirred around her as raiders fled. The floor thudded dully against her ear with their running steps. A rumble shook the ship again and a violent hot wind smacked into her. Dyna fought to make her eyes focus.

The sails were in flames.

Fire raged all around the ship. Raiders either fought to put it out or they jumped into the sea. She choked on the smoke as she tried to stand. Her ears were still ringing, and her vision spun. A hand grabbed her arm and hauled her up. She stumbled against Tarn's chest as he pulled her from the spreading flames.

"What happened?"

"Something blew in the cargo hold," Tarn said as they made their way through the thick smoke. "The ship is going down."

"What do you mean?" She needed his ship!

The floor dipped on the port side with a groan. They were sinking. Olsson barked at the men to abandon ship. Sai carried Lumina on his shoulder as he headed for the gangway. Damn that man!

Gritting her teeth, Dyna reached for a knife with every intention of digging it into his back. But a rippling explosion threw her against the steps. She winced at the pain shooting up her back. Sitting up, she choked on the smoke, and it made her eyes water.

"We need to go." Tarn scrambled up from where he had fallen and hauled her up with him. "Hold on to me."

"Wait, what about Len!" She turned to the healer's bay.

"Olssen got her out."

"But Sorren—"

Explosions rocked through the ship, and it tossed them down again. Bodies were flung through the air and screams cried out. Fire consumed all around them. Oh Gods. Dyna stumbled to keep up, coughing as her vision continued to water. She needed to get to land.

A knife came spiraling out of the smoke.

Tarn ducked, and it missed him by inches. More came. He shoved her down out of the way and snatched a fallen blade.

A bearded man strode forward out of the flames. Both Dyna and Tarn froze at the sight of him. He was dressed in a dark red coat that flared around him with the rippling wind and smoke. Several glinting knives were strapped to the bandoliers on his chest. He looked very different, but she recognized him all the same.

Von.

His hard face was carved like stone, his eyes burning with rage. Von drew out two more knives. "You are going to burn on this damn ship, even if it means I go with you!"

Von sprinted for him. The clash of steel rang out as Tarn's blade deflected every attack with swift agility.

"I knew you survived," Tarn said as they circled each other. "You returned because we both know your place has always belonged with me."

"I came for your head," Von snarled. His knives cut through the air, inches from taking Tarn's neck.

But he was too fast, too skilled. Tarn dodged Von's next attack and delivered a kick that threw him into a stack of barrels.

"I didn't order her to be burned alive, Von." Tarn stalked toward him. "I didn't need to. She never would have made it on her own."

Von rolled to his feet. "Nothing you say matters. She still died because of you."

"Was it really because of me? Or was it because you once again disobeyed the holy law?"

The question stumped Von. He froze among the roaring flames, and the knives shook in his hands.

Dyna ran up and grabbed his arm. "Don't listen to him."

Von flinched back, staring at her with wide eyes. "Dyna?"

"Tell her, Von." Tarn sneered. "How did Dalton die?"

Pain and anguish crossed Von's features. She held her breath, but his answer was blown by another detonation. A hot wave threw them all back. Her back slammed hard against the mast. The ship let out a horrid groan, and the wooden planks cracked in half.

Dyna wheezed for the air knocked out of her. Her ears rang again. She almost thought she heard a distant voice shouting her name.

She pushed up on her hands and knees with a cry. Her shoulder was dislocated. Bracing, Dyna slammed herself against the mast and bit back a scream as it went back into place. She stumbled to her feet, searching for Von.

"Dyna," Tarn groaned as he sat up where he was slumped against a cabin wall. A large splinter of wood had pierced his leg. He slipped on a pool of his blood as he struggled to stand. "Help me."

But she didn't move.

His pale eyes looked up at her, his jaw clenching at the heartless look on her face. "You're a healer. Leaving me to die goes against your oath and everything you stand for."

It did.

Dyna went to him. Tarn's answering smirk faded when she clutched his head with another feather in her hands. "My healer's oath does not apply to you."

With a violent snatch of her magic, she tore the memory of Mount Ida's location from his mind.

Tarn's chest heaved, furious. But as she walked away from him, he laughed. "What did I tell you? Isn't she glorious?"

Dyna paused by the railing and looked back at the man who had plagued her life for the past six months. It should have been her who defeated him. It gave her a sick satisfaction to leave him to burn, and she hated that a part of her condemned her for it.

"Jump!" Von sprinted toward her. "The ship is going to blow!"

He tackled her over the railing. An explosion ripped through the air, hurdling them into the sea.

CHAPTER 34

Lucenna

Lucenna!" Hands patted her cheeks, and she focused her blurred vision on Klyde's frightened face above her. "Are you all right, lass? Can you hear me?"

She wheezed, gasping for air. The back of her head throbbed painfully. Gods, what happened?

The last thing she remembered was chasing Klyde through the pier, calling his name. He had run up the gangway of Tarn's without a plan, and she tried to stop him. But when they reached the top, a flash of green light flared out.

And then—

Lucenna gasped and jerked up on the pier's dock. Tarn's ship was on fire. Something blew, and the explosion had thrown them off. Her Essence, she must have softened their fall.

Screams and running feet swarmed around her as Raiders fled or jumped into the sea. Flames flared into the sky, filling the air with smoke. The burning ship groaned loudly as it tilted on one end.

"Oh Gods, Dyna!" She pushed to her feet.

Klyde hooked his arm around her waist. "Lucenna, don't!"

"Let go! Dyna is on that ship!" She shoved him off and sprinted for the gangway, shouting her name.

The world ripped away with a roar.

Heat hurdled Lucenna and slivers of wood through the air. Klyde caught her as they crashed into the sea. Rogue waves dragged her under, tossing her around like a rag doll. She gagged on mouthfuls of salted water and panic set in. Her arms and legs flailed wildly as she tried to locate which way was up. Something rough scraped her leg. Lucenna whipped around, and a burst of pain beat her skull.

Her vision went dark.

She could see nothing. Feel nothing. Except her soul falling through the depths.

A force punched against her heart. Lucenna jerked with a gurgled gasp, choking on water. She rolled over and vomited the rest of it onto the sand. Her lungs burned with the effort, her body shaking.

"Oh, Gods, thank you." Klyde slumped beside her on the beach.

"What happened?" she rasped.

"You hit your head on the reef and nearly drowned." He brushed away the wet strands clinging to her face, stained pink with her blood. His face was deathly white, his blue eyes prominent against his wet lashes. "I thought I was too late."

She touched her bruised chest. He must have...

Her wide eyes flicked past him to the burning sea. Tarn's ship had cracked in half, already sinking into the depths.

"No!" Lucenna leaped to her feet, stumbling.

Klyde caught her hand. "The ship blew, lass. I don't think—"

Another explosion ripped through it and rocked the harbor.

"Dyna!" She tried to yank out of his hold, but he pulled her back to his chest.

"Lucenna, stop."

"I have to get her!"

"Don't get any closer! Lass, please!"

The air burned, and heat knocked them down on the sand with another massive eruption. Fire and wood tore through the air like a wave. Klyde yanked her around, and they crashed onto the sand. Fire was everywhere, and the sea was burning.

Lucenna sat up with a sob to find the ship gone. All that remained were the sails on broken masts. She cried out for her cousin as her vision blurred with tears and smoke. No, she couldn't accept that Dyna was gone. She got out. She had to.

"Lucenna," Klyde rasped. "We can't stay here."

He helped her up, but she whimpered at putting pressure on her foot. Damn it. She must have sprained it. Lucenna took another failed step before Klyde lifted her onto his back.

"Klyde—"

"Aye, you can complain about it later, lass. We need to go." He broke into a jog, carrying her from the beach. Shieldmen came running onto the dock at the commotion. But Klyde's steps seemed stunted, and his breath came in heavy.

"I should have left our ride closer," Klyde muttered.

"Klyde?" Lucenna looked behind them, seeing the trail of blood left behind each of his steps. "You're hurt."

"I'm fine."

She shifted her hold on his shoulders and felt something poke her arm. There was a piece of wood pierced into his shoulder.

"Oh, Gods."

"It looks worse than it is," Klyde grunted. "I'll pull it out later. For now, we need to get out of here."

That thing would have gone straight through her back if he hadn't jumped in the way.

"Put me down," she said angrily, her eyes welling again. "You can't carry me like this."

"You can't walk on that foot either. It's all right. I got you. Relax, Lucenna."

As though she was merely waiting for that command, her body slumped against his, her cheek resting on his other shoulder. She allowed herself to be carried off, because he felt safe. It was a foreign feeling.

And it clashed with her worry for Dyna.

Thunder cracked overhead, making her flinch. The sky opened as rain poured down.

"She's alive, right?" Lucenna's voice was steady, even as tears rolled down her cheeks. She looked back at the ship and felt her heart break all over again as she watched the flames rise. Zev was going to be devastated.

Please, Lucenna prayed to any God listening. *Please don't tell me she's dead.*

"Many people jumped ship," Klyde said. "The lass must have made it. She has survived worse."

He was right. Dyna was more resilient than anyone she had ever met.

"Then we should go back."

"We can't. The Shieldmen are coming, and likely Enforcers will arrive next. We don't want to draw attention to ourselves. Rawn told us what to do if something happened. It's best we take the next road out of Dwarf Shoe and wait for the others in the White Woods."

He was in his mercenary role, thinking logically instead of emotionally. Lucenna was glad of it, because she was a mess. She looked back at the burning ship, wanting to search for Dyna. But a large crowd had gathered on the pier, and some used magic to put out the flames.

"Aye, you can't be here anymore, lass. This will surely draw the mages. Do you feel any in Argent?"

Lucenna closed her eyes, searching for any telltale signs of magic beyond the harbor. They nearly fell over when the town shook with a *boom*. Cursing, Klyde gripped her legs tightly as he braced.

But it wasn't fire that tore through the buildings. It was blue electricity. The charge of Essence crackled in the air.

"What was that? Enforcers?"

"No..." Lucenna's eyes widened as a flash of blue lightning crashed down from the sky. "Elves."

CHAPTER 35

Rawn

They were everywhere. Rawn dashed into a dark alleyway, with Zev and Elon following on his heels. Red Highland soldiers marched past them, their dark red cloaks fluttering in their wake. He hid behind a set of broken barrels and crates as he listened to the voices on the wind past the prattle of rain.

"First unit, take the east. Second unit, cover the west. The hounds tracked him here. Find him!"

Rawn closed his eyes while the thud of boots splashed into rain puddles and beat against the roads, along with the snarls of the Bloodhounds. Ugly, massive dogs from the Erdas Mountains in Red Highland, and the best hunters to track down prey, even through the rain. They would eventually be found, no matter the cloaking spell.

The voices of the soldiers faded. Rawn remained still, attempting to listen past the patter of rain. He looked to Elon, who had his back to him as he kept eyes on the alley's other end, his hands alight with magic.

They never did make it to the pier.

"I think here we part ways, Lord Norrlen," he said under his breath.

Rawn stood. "I agree. Return to your family, Elon. Thank you for coming with us as far as you did."

Elon glanced at him over his shoulder with unreadable amber eyes.

"They're here," Zev snarled, immediately alerting them.

Bloodhounds filled the entry to both ends of the alley. The enormous hounds were about seven feet tall, with thick, bulky bodies and ruddy fur that matched the sands of Red Highland. Their sharp teeth dripped down drool as they stalked forward, their short ears twitching. Each one carried an elf rider.

One shouted, "Here—" Rawn's arrow pierced his gullet.

Elon cast out a bolt of blue lightning, taking out the second rider.

But it was too late.

The charge of horses and cries of their pursuers echoed in the streets.

Both he and Elon chose a hound to take down. They sprinted toward their targets, swords in hand.

Elon dropped and slid on the ground beneath the Bloodhound, the greaves on his knees and shins screeching. He lifted his hand, bracing it with the other, and blue magic shot from his hands, spiraling into a rune filled hexagon. The air ruptured as power blasted outward in a blazing detonation that threw the hound and rider back. Rawn shuddered under the impact, bracing against a wall.

The Bloodhound, now headless, toppled over dead. Elon rose to his feet with ease.

Zev dashed past him and leaped into the air, falling on another hound prowling into the alley. His claws tore out its nape, but the creature was double his size and had a hide too thick. Rawn slid on the ground beneath it, driving his sword into its chest. Blood splattered on the ground as he came out from behind it. Elon flicked the blood off his blade, a hound's head at his feet. But it was a short victory.

More were coming.

"Flee north," Rawn told Elon. "Too many are coming from the south. Let us take them."

A charge of power crackled in the air as blue magic sparked around Elon's weapon, reflecting the glow in his eyes. A rare hint of a smirk lifted his face as he glanced at him over his shoulder.

"It is you who should flee." He confidently strode for the oncoming swarm of Red Highland soldiers.

"Surrender in the name of King Altham!"

"I have no king." Elon broke into a sprint and leaped into the air, breathing one word. "*Ogap'maler.*"

A surge of electricity sprouted from his hands and wove around his blade in brilliant vines. He fell upon the red elves and hit the ground with a *boom*. A massive barrage of thunderbolts blasted in a violent wave. The force threw Rawn and Zev backward out of the alley.

He rolled to his feet and ran with Zev beside him. Buildings shook and screams rang out. Magic swarmed through the air with another pull of massive energy. It was Rawn's only warning before a beam of blue light flared beyond the rooftops and buildings crumbled where they stood.

The Blue Scythe.

Rawn kept running, realizing Elon may not need his help at all.

Growls rumbled from up ahead. Three Bloodhounds were on their tail.

Zev skid to a halt and looked at him with those bright yellow eyes. "Let's split up. You go left, I take right."

Rawn shook his head and shot two arrows, taking down a hound. "We stay together."

Zev cursed under his breath as six more Bloodhounds surrounded them on the street. He kicked off his shoes and peeled off his tunic. "Go, Rawn. Get out of here while you still can. I will find Dyna and meet you in the White Woods."

"There are too many, Zev. You will die if I leave you to face them alone."

"Don't worry about me," he said, his voice a deep rumble as his wolf began to take over. "If I have learned one thing, when outnumbered by beasts, *it* won't go down without a fight."

Rawn stilled at the implication. Did he mean to call out his beast as well?

"Go," Zev snarled as black claws extended from his fingers. "You cannot be around me when the Other appears."

Then his yellow eyes rolled as his body warped and grew. He cried out with every brutal snap of bones, black fur sprouting across his skin. A long snout extended from his face as he rose on two legs. A beast that was part man and part wolf. Howling, it sprang on the hounds, ripping the head off one and disemboweling another.

The Other tore into them viciously.

Its feral eyes fixed on him.

Rawn quickly backpedaled and sprinted down the alleyway. He knew better than to stay. The sounds of carnage and keens followed him.

It did no good to keep running like this. It was best to leave Dwarf Shoe first and regroup with the others. As if by some miracle, Rawn spotted a ladder resting against the wall of a distillery. He rapidly climbed up to the roof and kept running. The roads were full of soldiers. He kept low on the roof, using the shadows and crevices for cover. He wasn't far from the ocean—

An explosion tore through the air. It rocked through the town of Argent Cove in a sharp wave and knocked Rawn back into the building.

His ears rang from the sound, and he shook his head to focus. Flames flared high from the docks at the pier. A ship was on fire. *What happened?*

"Roof!" Came a call from below, and an arrow zipped past his head.

A unit of Red Highland archers stood below with loaded bows pointed at him. Rawn threw himself out of the way as arrows rained down. Scrambling to his feet, he ran across the rooftop and leaped for the next. He kept going, loading his bow as he leaped. He spun around and released his arrow. It shot through the shaft of another that would have taken his back. He landed on a cloth canopy over a merchant stall and bounced off to land on the ground in a crouch.

Whickering called from a distance.

The familiar call had Rawn spinning around. Fair came galloping around the corner, and he smiled with such immense relief, his eyes welled. Rawn sprinted toward his horse. Fair greeted him with a head bump to his shoulder.

"It's good to see you, old friend." Rawn patted Fair's neck and leaped up onto the saddle.

The rattle of horses and shouts of soldiers interrupted the reunion. Red Highland soldiers were spilling in from every street and crawling over the roofs like ants.

There were too many.

A mist stung Rawn's eyes, and he took a breath as he accepted one thing.

He wouldn't make it out.

After twenty years of running from his past, it had finally caught up to him. The image of his wife carrying their son surfaced in his mind. If it was his time, that was his fate. But when she received word of his death, it would be said he fought to the death and took as many Elves as he could with him.

"What do you say, old friend?" Rawn asked as he took Fair's reins. "One last ride."

Fair reared with a neigh in what could only be a war cry. Kicking his heels, they raced down the street. Rawn shot arrow after arrow at the archers posted on the roofs, hitting every mark. Arrows came for him in return. Fair galloped with the speed of invisible wings. They managed to dodge as close as they could. A couple nearly took his head. An arrow sliced past his arm, but his adrenaline took the pain. He kept shooting every target that came his way until his quiver was empty.

Magic came next.

Spells blasted through the air for him. Rawn dropped his bow and whipped out his sword. He may not have learned new spells, but he certainly learned how to move faster. His blade cut through each attack until one got past his defenses. Rawn was too late to react, but the spell bounced off an invisible shield and disintegrated.

The clover Dyna had pinned to his shirt was still there.

Rawn almost laughed from the shock.

The elves were startled, some not moving fast enough to dodge the attacks he sent right back to them. Blasts roared through the town as the shocks destroyed buildings and black smoke spiraled into the sky. Bodies were scattered in their wake.

Rawn moved and fought on pure instinct now. There was no reason to think; he only needed the action of swiftly ending as many lives as possible.

He waited for a blade or for an arrow to finally hit him.

Yet he rode through the burning streets and left the veil of smoke alive.

Rawn tugged on the reins as they came to a crossroads. His heart hammered in his chest; his breaths ragged as he saw no one else pursued him.

Had he made it?

But as his eyes swept across the demolished streets, he heard the steps of a lone figure striding through the smoke. He squinted, trying to make out if it was friend or foe. The answer came when he recognized that face.

The male elf strode forward in black armor, his red cloak rippling in the wind. Dark hair, dark eyes. A face Rawn would never forget.

"You..."

Prince Anon smiled sharply. He paused there on the street and canted his head. "We met like this once before, and here I am chasing you again. Yet there is only you this time." He stroked the pin in the shape of a horse, pinning his red cloak to his shoulder.

Nisa's brooch.

"The road is clear behind you," Anon continued, a mocking glint in his gaze. "Please run. I find the chase more enjoyable if you do."

There would be no running. Not when Rawn had waited years to face his sister's killer.

Kicking his heels, Rawn charged for the prince and readied his sword.

The infuriating smile didn't leave Anon's face. His body glowed muddled red as a charge of power filled the air. The ground rumbled with

Anon's incantation, and cobblestones tore free from the ground, blasting toward him like cannonballs.

Rawn dodged and ducked. More of the ground tore away, opening holes to impede him. Fair leaped and bounded at quick speed. Anon jerked up his fist, and a barricade of rock formed between them. Rawn kicked his heels, and they broke into a burst of speed. There was no hesitation or break in his gallop. Fair was one with him at that moment.

They had both been waiting for this.

Nisa's voice murmured in his ear with the rush of the wind. *Slay him, Rawn. Even if it's the last thing you do.*

Fair leaped. They soared over the barricade in a perfect arc.

Anon waited right behind it.

It all happened so fast.

Rawn saw only a flash of black, and a burst of pain tore through his chest. Fair crashed, and his body went flying. Rawn hit the ground hard. All he knew was pain. The force of the fall sent him rolling across the street until he came to a breathless halt against some barrels. Rawn wheezed for air, pressing on his chest for the wound he felt, but there was none.

Fear stopped his heart for a split second. Rawn pushed himself up, gasping. "Fair?" he called shakily, searching for him in the smoke. "Fair!"

His eyes locked on the rivulets of blood filling the cracks in the cobblestone. The soft keens of a horse led him to spot Fair laying on the ground ... with a black shaft jutting though his chest.

"FAIR!"

Rawn scrambled up. The smoke cleared, revealing Anon standing above his horse. He took hold of the spear's shaft and met Rawn's gaze.

Anon twisted it with a brutal snap. Fair's keening cut off, and he felt a brutal agony slice him through the center of his being. A sound caught in Rawn's throat. A cry. A scream. A choking gasp for air. His entire body spasmed as the death of his friend tore through him.

Anon ripped out the spear. "You should have run."

Rawn dropped to his knees. Dark blood dripped down the edge of the spear's blade. He heard each drop echo as they splattered on the ground. The world seemed to darken around him with the pelt of rain.

Anon laughed. "You look as if your soul has died. As your sister did that day in Erendor." He stalked toward him. Sparks scattered out with the drag of his spear over the cobblestone.

The mention of his sister carried him back to that summer day. The night around the campfire, beneath a sky lit up with fireworks. Rawn heard the merry sound of Sylar's lyre. He felt Aerina's hand in his. He saw Nisa toast to them as she laughed. That was the last day they were all together.

The last day his sister smiled.

"It's true what they say about green elves," Anon said above him as he lifted his spear. "To kill one, simply kill their horse."

...if it's the last thing you do.

Rawn snatched up his sword and swung. His blade clashed with Anon's spear, and he parried the blow. Rolling out of the way, Rawn stumbled to his feet.

Metal rang with the drawing of Anon's sword, and he grinned. "Ah, there is still fight in you left, Norrlen."

Rawn attacked. The clash of their swords rang out with each meeting of their blades. But the fight had been drained out of him, his speed and strength stunted, as if he moved with weights on his body.

Anon overcame him with three moves and slashed Rawn across the stomach. He stumbled back with a wince. Anon came at him, and Rawn barely blocked the next blow before it took his head. He was too slow. Anon's elbow rammed him in the face, and Rawn staggered back, his vision swaying.

"Inept," Anon sneered. Their swords crossed, bringing them face to face. "Disgraceful." He head-butted Rawn, and he dropped. Anon's knee rammed into his jaw. "*Pitiful.*"

Rawn dropped to the wet ground. This elf killed his sister and his horse. He would not yield, even if he died here.

Snatching his sword, Rawn lunged to his feet. A blow knocked the air out of his lungs. Gasping raggedly, he looked down at the arrow embedded on the left side of his chest. His wavering sight lifted to the archer standing behind Anon with a unit of Red Highland soldiers. Another arrow whistled through the air and pierced him in the stomach. He stumbled back as blood spilled down his tunic. A third arrow took out his leg, and he plummeted to his knees.

Rawn reached for his weapon, but his trembling fingers couldn't grasp his hilt. There was no strength in him left.

"How disappointing." Anon kicked the sword out of the way, and it skittered across the ground beneath a wagon. "You neglect to live up to your legend, Norrlen."

Red Highland soldiers came forward and seized his arms. They dragged him away to a wheeled cell and threw him inside. He slumped against the wall, blinded by pain and on the verge of unconsciousness as he bled out.

Nisa had asked of him only one thing, and he failed.

Her. His wife. His son.

His Fair.

He failed them all.

"Rawn!" A faint voice gasped his name. In the alley across from him, he spotted Lucenna and Klyde, their eyes wide with horror. She took a step, but Rawn shook his head.

He wouldn't repeat the mistake of involving others in his troubles again.

This wasn't their fight.

And it wasn't one they could win. Red Highland soldiers marched past in a stream. So many sent to capture him.

Surely, he was off to his death. All he could ask of them now was to let his family know he would never come home.

The realization nearly killed him. Slipping off his signet ring, Rawn let it roll out of his cell. It clinked faintly on the ground.

Reins snapped and wheels creaked as they took him away. His waning sight peered past the bars to the smudge of white in the rain.

Forgive me...

CHAPTER 36

Von

Von's stomach burned as he heaved up sea water on the beach. Sand gritted in his teeth and stung his eyes. Pushing the sopping wet hair out of his eyes, he searched the shore for the Maiden, but she was nowhere in sight. When they fell into the water together, a rogue wave had wrenched them apart.

Von pushed up on his knees, wincing in pain. He stumbled to his feet, wounded and disoriented. Blood leaked from the many cuts on his face and body.

The pier glowed with fire. It teemed with people and Shieldmen working hard to put it out. He glimpsed a Minotaur with an auburn coat running for the town.

Sorren was at last free.

Von clutched his broken arm to his chest as he called out for Dyna. But she wasn't amongst the faces that passed him. She must have made it out and fled the pier. Or…

His eyes lifted to what remained of Tarn's ship.

The flames burned high, glowing brightly in his sight. No. He had to believe she made it out as well.

Von closed his eyes as an echo of Yavi's scream crashed with each wave on the shore. "He is gone, my love," Von whispered to the sea. "Rest now…"

That monster was dead.

Now that it was finished, he didn't know what else to do but disappear. Into the bottom of a barrel of ale, into some decrepit town across the world where no one knew him, or into some hole in the ground.

It didn't matter now.

He had completed his purpose.

Von turned away from fire and went against the current of the crowd. Bodies and voices surged around him. He wandered to the end of the beach, where it was empty. He wasn't looking for anyone anymore. If he had, he would have seen the blade before it sank into his stomach.

He jerked to a halt, gasping for breath. His trembling hands clutched the hilt. It was made of ivory, carved elaborately with some design he couldn't make out through his blurred vision. Distant cries filled his skull as he looked up at Sai-chuen.

"There is a proverb in my clan," the Xián Jīng man told him idly in a thick accent. He herded Von backwards towards the shore until the sea splashed around their boots. "To kill a beast, you must first cut off its tail. When it loses balance, cut off its legs. When it can no longer move, cut out its eyes. When it's blind, only then can you cut off its head." Sai-chuen twisted the blade and tore it out. Von jerked back a step with a ragged gasp of pain. "You were your Master's legs, Von. But I had to cut off your tail first."

The world lost balance, and Von dropped. His knees splashed into a wave rolling over the shore. The metallic taste of his blood gushed into his mouth and spilled down his chin.

Cut off your tail...

Yavi.

That wasn't right. She had been everything. All of him. He now may as well be blind.

Why? Why did he hurt her?

Von didn't understand. This was part of Sai-chuen's plan. Tarn was the beast in his proverb. Yavi had been merely a casualty.

Who was he? Why did he do this?

But Sai-chuen gave him no answers. He strode away to where a she-elf waited for him. She looked back at Von with an expression mixed with concern and confusion. Sai took her arm, and they vanished into the crowd. Thunder shook the skies as rain began to fall.

Von reached out with a trembling hand, "Why?" he rasped, his faint voice lost beneath the crash of waves. "Why?"

The last of his strength faded, and he fell face first into the wet sand. Waves washed over him, running red as it rolled away and returned. They smothered his mouth and nose.

Why! The question screamed in his head. He had to know before he passed through the Gates. Why did his wife have to suffer?

Rain beat down on him as his vision began to darken. His injured body wouldn't move off the cold ground, not that he cared to go on anymore. Von couldn't hope for more than the quiet sadness of this ending.

He would die here without ever knowing why.

Running steps faintly thudded on the beach toward him. Another wave crashed on the shore and rolled over him. It rushed up his nose and burned his eyes. He blearily blinked up at the blurred image of a young woman with hair the color of flames.

Hands grabbed his arms and hauled him onto dry sand.

Dyna crouched down and smiled at him sadly. "There's a familiar face."

CHAPTER 37

Dynalya

A thick veil of black smoke hovered over Argent Cove. Dyna didn't know who survived the blast and whether anyone was looking for her, but she had to get them out of view first. Dyna reached into her satchel and called on the last of her Celestial feathers. Two appeared in her hand, one black and the other...red.

Still wet.

Dyna ignored that one.

She tossed it back in and kept the black one. It glowed bright gold as it dissolved, and her barrier dropped. It wouldn't stay down for long.

Casting it out over Von, she lifted his unconscious body. She moved quickly off the beach and took the crude steps on the rocky hill. They needed shelter out of this cold and rain. Von hovered beside her in a mist of Essence until she found an abandoned cargo bay on the far end of the pier and went in. It was dark inside. Not much there but broken crates, wheelless carriages, and rope hanging from old, rusted pulleys. Rain beat on the leaky roof as she laid Von down on a dirty pile of canvases. He was unconscious, pale, his breathing shallow.

Dyna removed his bandoliers and pulled up his tunic to assess the damage. A hiss passed through her teeth at the deep wound. He'd been stabbed. She placed her hands over it and his blood seeped through her fingers as she called on her Essence to heal. It surged forward with eager intent, and she had missed that warm feeling of her power. She took her time repairing the damage to Von's organs. Piece by piece, the tissue and muscle sewed back together until all that was left was a fresh scar.

Dyna got a fire going to warm them up. She hung up her cloak and Von's coat above it to dry. He had traded his black coat for one of deep auburn. It reminded her of the color of Yavi's hair.

By the time she finished cleaning his wound, he woke up.

Von looked around them weakly, finding her. "Dyna..."

"I'm here." She moved closer. His shaking hand reached toward his stomach. "You're healed. I closed the wound in time."

Von shut his eyes and laid an arm over his eyes.

"Von? Are you all right?"

He began to shake, and she saw the tears rolling down his temples. "Why did you keep me here?" He wept. "Why didn't you let me die? I was ready to die!"

Dyna's vision stung at the pain she heard in his voice. "I'm sorry ... for Yavi. I saw what happened in Tarn's memories."

Von looked away from her to the ceiling. "Why were you there?"

"I suppose for the same reason you were." Dyna sighed. "You had stowed away in the cargo hold, hadn't you?"

"I intended to blow them all to the Netherworld, but I wanted to see his face when he realized death was coming for him. I wanted to see the fear in his eyes, knowing he would never accomplish everything he desired." Von sat up. "If I had not gone up there, you would have died as well."

"That wasn't our fate." Dyna held up a waterskin to his lips for him to drink. "Our paths were meant to cross, Von. I came for you as well."

He sat up, wiping his mouth as he stared at her. "What you said at the beach ... I thought I had imagined that."

She shook her head. "You are my fifth Guardian, Von."

"Guardian?" He retorted with a bitter chuckle. "I'm your *Guardian*?" Rising on his knees, he laughed so hard it shook his body. "No, see you're wrong, lass. Guardians *protect*. The one person I wanted to protect died before my eyes, and in the most brutal way possible." His laughter turned to wretched sobs. Von fell forward on his hands, and the sounds he made, the heartbreak was so strong Dyna felt it. Von beat against his chest as the sounds of his broken sobs filled the space. "She's dead because of *me*. The fates predicted it. They warned me, and I got her killed!"

He truly believed it. Tarn had chained him to the belief that turning his back on his holy oath towards his life-debt caused Azurite to fall, and now Yavi. But none of it was ever his fault.

"No, Von. That wasn't your doing." Dyna reached for him, but he pushed her hands away.

"I am not your Guardian!" he shouted, making her flinch. "I am *nothing!* My only purpose was to kill that man. I should have killed him a long time ago."

And she knew they were both thinking of that day the Horde came.

"He's dead now," she said quietly.

Tarn went down with his ship. And for some reason, it didn't give her any satisfaction.

"Then I can die in peace."

"Von..."

"Leave me! I serve no purpose now." He curled up on the dirty floor. She didn't know what else to do but go as he asked.

Dyna stood. "You do have a purpose, Von. Meet me in the White Woods if you want to find out what it is. If you don't arrive by the third dawn from today, I will assume your answer." She walked away to the doors and paused. "I hope you come."

She closed the rickety door behind her.

Taking a deep breath, Dyna ducked into an alley and went west. And soon found that the fire had spread through Argent. People screamed, fleeing from the burning buildings. Shieldmen swarmed the streets, calling for them to evacuate.

At first, Dyna thought the ships' explosion had somehow cast burning debris onto the roofs and spread. Until she saw the bodies. They were armed elves with red cloaks.

Red Highland soldiers.

Dyna gasped and looked around her wildly. "Zev!" She shouted into the chaos. "Rawn!"

She ran against the swarm, following the trail of destruction. They would have come after her, and they did. But Red Highland found them first.

Dyna shouted louder for them, but with no reply. She coughed on smoke and covered her mouth with her sleeve as she kept searching. "Lucenna! Klyde!"

They had to be here.

But if they were, they would have reunited with her by now. Dyna tried to connect with Lucenna's Essence, but she didn't know that spell, and the barrier had already fallen into place. Stamping down her panic, she kept going.

Her feet skid to a halt when she came across the body of a massive doglike creature in the middle of the street. Many more of them lay dead, either with missing heads, torn out throats, or gutted. Blood leaked from their brown fur where claws had slashed through them. She looked down at the puddles of blood and noticed the tuffs of black fur and arrows at her feet.

"Zev!" Dyna called again, her voice breaking. "Where are you?"

Black smoke spiraled from the sky as rain came down hard on her, slowly putting out the fires. She kept running and calling for her Guardians.

It was raining so hard it was impossible to know if she was blinded by her tears or the rain. Fear of what she would find made her hands shake as she kept running. The town had been destroyed by spell and fire.

A unit of Shieldmen in their orange cloaks had gathered ahead. She ran toward them, catching their voices.

"Damn elves."

"They disregard our laws and tear apart our town without a care."

"All of this to capture one elf?"

"Excuse me." She pushed past them. "Please let me through!"

Dyna made it through the wall of spectators and came out into the crossroads. She stilled at the destruction. At the blood painting the streets. It poured from the one left lying there.

"No..." She stumbled toward the white horse. "It's not him. It's not..."

But Dyna already knew.

She came around and choked back a cry at the sight of Fair. Blood still leaked from the gaping hole in his chest.

Her legs gave out, and she fell beside him. "Fair..."

Dyna shook her head and reached out shakily for her dear friend, but she already knew Fair was gone. Tears rolled down her nose as she brushed his mane away from his blank eyes.

"Is this your horse?" one of the Shieldmen asked. "Do you need help to move it? We must clear the road."

Help? There was no one to help her. Dyna trembled as she at last met her reflection in the puddle of blood and rain at her feet. And she couldn't stand what she saw.

Clutching Fair's head on her lap, Dyna held him as she sobbed.

Every action has consequences.

This one was hers.

PART II: DREAMS

CHAPTER 38

Zev

He was dead. That was Zev's first thought when he found himself in a white forest. It was perfectly serene. Everything seemed to glow in a soft, silvery light. He winced against the stinging in his eyes and shut them again. But his body ached too much to be dead.

How did he get here? The last thing he remembered was telling Rawn to run before he let the Other take over. He wasn't sure if it could come out that way without the full moon, but he had done it before.

Zev simply ... let go.

The Other's memories surfaced as if they were his own.

He had fought the Bloodhounds. Many had fallen to his claws and fangs, but Red Highland soldiers came and took him down. Zev had shifted back, left bleeding on the ground with his back full of arrows. His vision darkened as he waited for the end.

The last thing he remembered was a yellow butterfly in the rain.

"You're awake," a voice like tinkling bells said.

Zev smirked faintly to himself and rubbed his face. Dyna had been right. "You decided to join us, after all."

"It was a good thing I did." A faint tap landed by his head, and he peeked at the tiny fairy with golden wings who beamed at him. "Does this make it twice now that I have come to your aid?" Princess Keena asked, crossing her arms.

He sat up on a plush mound of soft pale moss and looked around at the strange forest of white trees. "What happened? Where are we?"

"Well, I stopped them in time before you were struck down dead," Keena said proudly. She held up her hand when he opened his mouth to respond. "And there is no need to offer me a life-debt. I have repaid the one I owed Dyna. Besides, I am sure you would do the same for me."

Zev smiled wryly. "I was going to ask how you defeated a group of Elven soldiers?"

"I am stronger than I look, remember?" Keena winked. "And I was also accompanied by my guards. They have returned to Morphos."

He spotted a cluster of fairies flying away within the trees. "Where are we?"

"The White Woods. You must not remember. You were bleeding out and delirious, but you asked to be brought here before you succumbed to your wounds. I found Onyx wandering the streets and used him to bring you here." Keena sat on a log beside him, her tiny legs swinging. "You've been unconscious for a day."

Wincing, Zev rose and staggered to a small pool of water. He had new scars marking his chest now. His Lycan blood had worked to heal him. He looked out at the weeping cherry trees with white bark and white blossoms.

"Rawn said this place is a haven of sorts." Zev stilled, suddenly realizing he was alone. "Where is he? The others?"

"Come with me." Golden dust spiraled around Keena, and she rose to life size height, reaching barely his elbows. The fairy princess strolled through the forest and brought him to a circular stone platform built into the ground. A podium rested in the center.

There, Lucenna and Klyde waited, sitting on mounds of moss as his horse grazed.

Leaping to her feet, Lucenna ran over and hugged him. "Thank the Gods."

"Glad to see you alive, mate," Klyde said.

He nodded back and looked down at Lucenna. "Are you all right? When did you arrive? Is Dyna here?"

She shook her head, her eyes welling up. "We arrived today. The mages came after me when we tried to take the train. So we decided to risk joining you in Argent instead ... but when we got to the pier..." Zev waited for her to continue, but she couldn't.

Klyde sighed heavily and said, "Tarn's ship blew."

An ice-cold feeling sank through his body. "Don't tell me she..."

"I don't know." Lucenna said faintly.

"What do you mean?" Zev demanded, gripping her shoulders. "You can't sense her?"

"I think it's Cassiel's damn barrier. Something has changed. It's grown stronger somehow, and it has completely hidden all traces of Dyna's Essence now. Not even I can track her."

That must mean she was alive. But why was the barrier stronger? Zev glanced up at the sky. Was Cassiel nearby?

"That's not all..." Klyde said, and the despondency in his expression made him stiffen.

Someone has died...

Zev's stomach sank. "Who?"

"Rawn."

The air knocked out of him. "What...?" he whispered.

"Red Highland soldiers captured him," Lucenna said. "There were too many of them. He couldn't fight them ... not ... not after..."

"Not after what?" Zev demanded.

"Rawn couldn't fight after the death of Fair," Keena said sadly, shrinking down again and coming to land on Lucenna's shoulder. "The death of an Elvish horse is a great blow indeed."

Zev's breath hitched at the news. They had killed Fair? Because they were bonded, he realized. Killing Rawn's horse must have both weakened him and devastated him.

He sighed heavily and rubbed his face. "I need to find Dyna."

"I'm here..."

They all whipped around to see her standing at the edge of the platform behind them. She was dirty, clothes torn, her face covered in soot and marked with scratches.

But alive.

"Gods, Dyna." Zev rushed forward and yanked her into his arms, hugging her tight. "What happened? Why did you leave us?"

Dyna clutched him with shaking hands. She was murmuring something he couldn't hear clearly with her mouth pressed against his chest. "I'm sorry. I'm sorry. I'm so sorry..."

Zev exhaled heavily, wrangling with his relief and the need to chastise her for running off, but he knew that wasn't what she needed right now. So he merely held her.

Her eyes welled. "Fair..."

"I know," he murmured.

The sounds of her quiet weeping in the dark forest made his eyes sting.

"Rawn is still alive," Lucenna said, her voice cracking. "I'm tracking his Essence now. They are taking him west."

"To Red Highland." Dyna stepped back and wiped her eyes. Straightening her shoulders, she said, "I am going after him."

Silence filled the glade with only the rush of water to accompany it.

"Red Highland?" Zev repeated. It was a warring country, as guarded as the Magos Empire.

Dyna faced him and all her Guardians. Klyde and Keena drew closer to their circle. "I did this," she told them, her eyes shining with tears. "Because I was reckless and selfish, and I didn't stop to think about what I was doing when I left on my own. Now Fair is dead, and Rawn will be if I don't save him. I'm so sorry for all that I put you through these past months..." She sniffed, taking a shaky breath. "I must fix this. I have to because I cannot allow another member of our family to die in vain."

Lucenna took her hand and squeezed it. "And we won't."

Zev nodded because he couldn't imagine turning his back on Rawn either. "We're not leaving him behind."

"Aye," Klyde exhaled a long exhale. "I've grown fond of the elf. Of course you can count on me, lass. But I do hate to be the one to say it..."

"I will." Keena piped up, fluttering around Zev's shoulders. "It will be near impossible to infiltrate Red Highland on our own. This will require aid."

Lucenna reached into her coat pocket and held out her palm for all of them to see. In the center lay Rawn's gold signet ring. The top was flat and circular, embossed with the sigil of House Norrlen. "He left this behind. I assume to let his family know what happened to him."

Gods, Zev could only imagine how they would take this.

"There is one thing we must do first," Dyna said, meeting each of their gazes. "We must go to Greenwood."

Zev liked that plan. "To inform King Leif and the Norrlen family that Rawn was taken."

"We are going to need their help to get him back," Lucenna added.

"Good." Keena smiled as she flew up the stone steps of the circular platform. "Then we must call on House Norrlen."

"Call?" Dyna followed her.

Keena landed on the podium and nodded to the small golden plate in the middle, affixed with a perfect circular groove. "The White Woods is a haven to all elves, and here they call for aid."

"How?" he asked.

"With their signet."

Gasping softly, Lucenna glanced down at Rawn's ring.

"Put it in, lass," Klyde suggested.

Zev held his breath as they watched her press the ring into the groove. It flared green with magic and lit up the runes carved into the stone circle. The light pulsed three times before fading away.

All fell silent but the trickle of water and the distant chirp of birds.

"What now?" he asked.

Keena nodded. "Now we wait."

Zev had been thinking a lot about fate lately. He questioned the future and how much of it was determined by what steps they took versus divine intervention. As they sat around the fire listening to Dyna share what she had been up to since she jumped through the Druid's Door, Zev didn't feel as though he was any closer to an answer.

He traced the faded illustration of an ancient key on the scroll she had shown him. The Druid knew this would happen. He knew Rawn would be captured and that they would go after him. But was it because he gave this task to Dyna, or had he merely taken advantage of this outcome?

Thinking about it only made Zev's head spin.

The others had not known how to react to it either. Klyde and Lucenna had long fallen asleep after their meal as the sun began to descend. Keena had flown off somewhere to sleep in the trees.

Zev was too restless to sleep, but he could see the exhaustion weighing on his cousin. It hovered over her slumped shoulders and in the line of her features. "Rest," he told her softly. We will need it for the journey to come."

Whoever they were waiting on was going to arrive by sunrise.

Dyna laid down on her side in the plush bedding of moss and stared at the fire. "Tarn is dead," she whispered.

Zev had wondered. That meant Von succeeded.

Good riddance.

"I ... tried to kill him," Dyna continued. "I wanted it to be me. After everything he had done, I wanted to watch the life bleed out of his eyes. I thought if I took his life, I could become something different. Someone stronger. Someone who wasn't afraid of ever being hurt again. It took holding a dagger at his neck to realize Tarn's path wasn't my own. Yet I still left him to burn alive ... because a quick death would have been too easy."

Well, he couldn't fault her for that. Zev wouldn't have made a dissimilar choice.

"I'm a monster now, aren't I?" She stared at the fire blankly. "I have claws and fangs, and it's made me bloodthirsty."

It wasn't that it made her bloodthirsty, but that she had to fall back on the part of her that was pure preservation.

As Zev had to do when he brought out the Other. A prickling sensation crawled over his skin at the reminder. He had yet to really process that he had been able to do that.

To call out the beast from within.

And it had answered.

"You're not a monster, Dyna," Zev said, draping a blanket around her. He sighed, and she read the guilt on his face. He should have known she was suffering. "You want to kill something inside of you. That perhaps will be your greatest enemy ... and your best friend. With time, you will come to realize it's the one thing that is keeping you going."

That's what his Madness had been, in a sense.

It kept him alive.

"I shouldn't have let myself fall in love with him." She shut her eyes. "When I learned of the bond, I should have accepted it as merely an accident."

"Dyna."

"You tried to tell me Zev. Now I understand. We never belonged together."

He sighed. "You cannot let this break you."

She scoffed softly. "What is it you said to me before?"

You cannot fix what is already broken.

Dyna laid down onto her back, staring up at the canopy. "My whole life I studied to heal nearly any wound but this one." Her small fist pressed against her heart. "It hurts. This pain, I cannot see it, but I feel it. There's a hole in my heart where he used to be, and there is nothing I can do to fill it. And I despise it." Her lashes fluttered closed. "I try to imagine myself as the person I once was, and not what remains of her. But all I have left are shards of who I used to be." Her next confession made him fall still. "I had been taking Witch's Brew to cope. Because if I sleep, I see him, and when I don't, I hear him. Every time I hear the flutter of wings, I think he has returned."

It broke Zev to hear that. How did he not see her suffering so much? Enough that she felt the need to drug herself.

Silent tears rolled down her temples, glinting in the firelight. "He took a part of me with him. How do I get her back?"

Zev didn't have an answer.

He wasn't who he used to be, either. Maybe it wasn't possible. With enough bruises and scars, life left its mark.

Dyna's breath evened out as she fell asleep. His brow furrowed as he watched her. Seeing her suffer like this enraged him. He didn't know how to fix it.

With a sigh, he slipped her arm under the blanket, but he noticed something clutched in her palm. It was a small leather pouch. He carefully slipped it out of her fingers and opened it.

His stomach clenched at the sight of the red feather inside.

The wind blew gently against the trees, making the leaves rattle. It carried the earthy smells of the forest and the sweetness of spring. Beneath it hovered a distinct scent he had come to loathe.

Zev silently stood and walked away from the campfire into the shadowy trees. He heard fluttering wings and kept chasing them down until the woods receded. He came out onto a high crag. A soft orange hue fell over him with the sunset.

He spun around, searching the dark branches of the woods where the light didn't reach. "I know you heard me that night when I warned you to stay away from her," he snarled.

"I do not take orders from you, wolf," a voice replied.

"You serve no purpose here. Leave!" His shout echoed over the rocky hill.

"Her life is bound to the life of the High King. My purpose is to make sure she stays alive."

Zev growled. "That is not your place anymore."

The branches creaked, and Zev's eyes snapped to a dark figure standing in the trees.

"You have been lurking around her, haven't you? You kept out of sight all these months, but you've been daring to come closer. Working up the nerve to show yourself," he realized. "Why now? What do you want?"

Silence filled the brush of the wind. The longer he stood there waiting, he eventually realized she wouldn't say.

Zev turned to leave. "I meant what I said, Lieutenant. I will not warn you again."

But he halted in place when he noticed Dyna standing behind him.

CHAPTER 39

Dynalya

Shock stole Dyna's breath. She rushed forward, ignoring Zev's sputtering. Yet who he spoke to quickly retreated into the growing darkness before her eyes could truly confirm who it was. She may not have gotten a good look, but there was no mistaking what she had overheard.

Pushing past Zev, she shouted up at the trees, "Sowmya! Come out. I know you're there!"

After a pause, a tree branch rustled, and a figure dropped to the ground, landing in a crouch only a few feet away from her. As it rose to its full height, wings stretched open behind them, then rested. Sowmya stepped into the light.

Dyna's pulse drummed at the sight of the Lieutenant. Lowering to one knee, Sowmya bowed her head, her sleek red feathers gleaming in the moonlight.

"I am sure now it was you, wasn't it?" Dyna said, her eyes widening with a sudden realization. "You followed us on the Bridge. You released me from the forest's spell in Morphos, then you paid for our stay in Little Step, and it was your voice who shouted for me when I jumped through the Druid's door. And I know you pulled me from the sea after the ship blew because I found one of your feathers on the beach where I washed up. This whole time I thought I was hallucinating the sound of wings, but it was *you*. How long have you been following me?"

"I never left your side, my lady."

She stared at her incredulously. "This whole time? Why?"

Sowmya lifted her head. "Did you truly think my king would leave his greatest treasure unprotected?"

Dyna heaved a breath, and her eyes immediately filled at the sharp ache in her heart. Her mind rebelled with anger, and she scoffed. "If he treasured me, he never would have left."

With a sigh, the lieutenant rose to her feet. "I will deny this if asked, but I do not agree with his actions."

Because it was wrong, even his Valkyrie knew that.

"It doesn't matter now."

"It does." Sowmya took a step, but Zev snarled at her in warning, and she halted. "I was never supposed to reveal myself to you. He wanted you to live without any memory of him or the Realms, so you both may go on with your lives."

"And how well has that worked out for him?" Dyna hissed.

"Far worse than you know."

The reply stumped her enough to pause. "What do you mean?"

The lieutenant dithered for a moment. "Cassiel is lost, my lady, and the Realms have turned against him. You are the only one who can make right what was made wrong."

Scoffing, she shook her head. Cassiel was the one who wronged her.

"He is on his way to Nazar."

Dyna looked up at the gathered clouds above the mountains where the floating islands hid. Then it hadn't been her imagination. She had sensed him near. *He was coming.*

But it had nothing to do with her.

"Return to him," Sowmya said softly.

"Why should I?" Dyna gritted her teeth, ignoring the burn behind her eyes. She wouldn't chase after the one who left her mindless and contained. "I am not his mate. He made that quite clear. The Realms tried to have me assassinated, if you recall. Why would I return to give them another chance to succeed?"

"Because you are the High Queen." The breeze blew loose tendrils of dark hair past Sowmya's somber gaze. "Whatever happened between you, whatever prejudice my people hold, that does not change. Go to him, my lady. Remind him who you are. He does not know how much he needs you."

The words embedded into her chest like molten iron as Cassiel's soft voice echoed in her head.

Leave you? That will never happen.

Without you, there is no sun.

A tremor ran through Dyna, and she shook her head.

You are the other half of me, Dynalya.

It was a dream. Now we have to wake up.

A violent shake went through her.

I don't want you...

Fresh tears spilled down her face. He didn't want a weak human.

The physical pain of that day was buried in the deepest crevices of Dyna's being. The words Cassiel said when he rejected the bond had torn her open, and she heard the sound her soul had made when it shattered. The agony and heartbreak. The betrayal of the compulsion taking over. It was all there. Planted the moment he left her on the floor as he walked away.

"Where was he when I needed him?" Dyna wrapped her arms around herself as all the broken pieces of her soul shuddered. "Where was he when I needed him!" she screamed, choking on a sob.

The question tore at her like hooks peeling her skin. She doubled over from the pain, holding her stomach as she wept.

The lieutenant reached for her, but Zev blocked her. Lucenna was suddenly there, and she wrapped Dyna in a tight embrace. They were the only thing holding her up now.

Eyes closing, Dyna felt her throat shut with the words she had to say. "Go, Sowmya, and do not return. I want nothing to do with him anymore."

Dyna's days were filled with pretending. She pretended she was fine. She pretended she had told the truth. She pretended her eyes didn't burn with unshed tears when she heard the lieutenant fly away.

She pretended not to be afraid when the nightmare came again.

But this time, it was different.

Cassiel wasn't as she remembered him. The face was the same, but he had golden hair and eyes the color of a clear sky. With a crown of Seraph fire and pearlescent white wings that glowed in the light. She heard sounds of distant laughter as he playfully chased a young woman with silken brown tresses. Her gown swished past the flowering bushes as she ran through a garden until he cornered her in the gondola ... below a *Hyalus* tree.

237

He tilted her chin as his lips gently pressed into hers. *"You are the one I choose. In this life and in the next one."*

Those words resonated through Dyna like a beat of a drum.

He lifted a necklace with a glowing iridescent crystal. The young woman smiled at him, so hopelessly in love. Her golden crown caught the sunlight, as did her bright green eyes. Dyna's breath caught sharply. The unnamed queen looked past his shoulder, right at her.

Horror rocked through her chest at the sight of her own face. Dyna stumbled backward, but her foot found only open darkness, and it dragged her into an abyss.

She jerked up awake in her mat with a gasp.

Her heart pounded wildly, a sheen of sweat on her skin. God of Urn ... what was that?

She had seen that garden scene before, in the Morphos Court, when she had been trapped in the Wyspwood.

And the male who looked like Cassiel ... matched the face from the portrait in Lord Jophiel's Hall. Was that ... King Kāhssiel?

Dyna stared at the mossy ground blankly. The shock subdued her, tangling her thoughts. King Yoel had never clarified if the rumor held any truth. Yet ... it gave reason as to why Cassiel had such gifts.

If it's true ... then the young woman with her face ...

Dyna shook her head. "It was only a dream."

"Was it?"

She jumped at the voice. Dyna looked around the mossy clearing they slept in, and her gaze landed on Leoake standing atop a ledge of earth beneath a white tree. A soft glow seemed to hover off the atmosphere, and Dyna questioned if she was indeed awake. Her Guardians were all soundlessly asleep in their mats around the campfire that had long died before the light of dawn.

"Sometimes, our minds know more than we do, and it chooses how and when to show us such things." He smiled down at her slyly. "Yours is speaking to you."

"Then why does it only show me nightmares?" Dyna asked faintly.

"Are they nightmares?" Leoake canted his head, making one of his pointed ears peek out of his green hair.

"I don't know."

His smile sharpened. "Oh, but you already know the answer ... *dream walker.*"

A hand shook her awake, and Dyna blinked up at Zev.

238

"You were talking in your sleep," he said.

She sat up, staring at her surroundings in confusion. The White Wood no longer glowed, and that dastardly Druid was gone. A dream within a dream.

"What is it?"

"Nothing." Dyna rubbed her face. "The Druid, he is not a normal fae is he?"

Zev blinked at her unexpected question. "I have had that impression myself." He got back to his feet. "We have to go."

"Why? What happened?"

Everyone else was awake now, standing together as they stared at something past her shoulder.

"A member of House Norrlen is here."

Dyna leaped up to her feet.

Her vision swayed, and Zev grabbed her arm before her legs gave out. Stumbling past the others, she met the stern gaze of an elf. He was older than the elves she had met, with age more prevalent in his features and with short ashy blond hair showing streaks of gray. He wore dark green robes and held a white staff.

"I am Eldred Lothiriel, Magi Master of the Sellav province, in service to the Norrlen Household," he said, his tone distrustful and curt. His eyes reminded her of a ghost fern, and they narrowed as he studied them before his gaze fell on her again. "Was it you who called for aid with the stone circle? To do so, you would have used a ring."

Lucenna held it out as proof.

His jaw clenched. "That signet belongs to Rawn Norrlen. How did it come into your possession?"

"He gave it to me."

"Let it be known, to lie about a member of the King's court is a grave offense."

Lucenna crossed her arms. "Why would I lie?"

"Why would you not?" Eldred countered coolly. "Lord Norrlen is a wanted elf with a substantial bounty on his head. He has not been seen in over twenty years. To claim he has given you his signet ring is either a lie, or you have somehow captured him to secure your fortune."

Princess Keena huffed. "They are telling you the truth, Master Eldred."

"I will hear proof of that first."

A surge of anxiousness and sorrow flooded Dyna's chest as she looked at her Guardians. How would they prove it? His Household didn't know them. But she knew Rawn.

"Lord Norrlen is the kindest person I have ever met," Dyna said faintly. "He taught me how to shoot a bow and how to swing a sword. And he taught me what it means to be strong without them."

Eldred stilled at whatever he read on her face.

"Rawn has a son who he carves wooden toys for," Zev said next. "Even if he is much too old for them."

The Magi Master's expression changed, his suspicion wavering.

Lucenna then added, "Every single month since Rawn has left home, he has written a letter to his wife so she would know he was alive."

"Rawn is our friend." Dyna's voice wavered with the lump growing in her throat. "And so was Fair..."

Eldred heard the meaning in her statement. "Was?"

Klyde sighed. "We have come here to bring unfortunate news to his family ... regarding his capture."

His face paled. "Capture? Who has him?"

Lucenna handed him Rawn's ring. "I think you know."

Eldred's hand trembled as he accepted it. "Was he alive when they took him?"

She nodded.

The Magi Master briefly closed his eyes, and Dyna saw the pain there. "This ring..." He looked at it somberly. "It has been passed down from heir to heir of the Norrlen House, and only at the predecessor's death. If Rawn has given this to you..."

It's because he didn't expect to survive. Knowing that alone draped a heavy despondency over them all.

"I don't intend to let them keep him, Master Eldred," Dyna said. "We didn't only come here to deliver bad news. We are here to help."

Eldred searched her eyes a moment and turned away. "Come. The estate lies at the other end of the foothills of the Anduir Mountains. I want to arrive before sundown."

"Across the mountains?" Dyna repeated incredulously. "That would take days to hike, if not more."

"Yet I arrived here in one." Eldred paused on the path and turned around.

Dyna followed his stare, as did the rest of them, to the bearded man entering the mossy glade. Von had come after all.

240

Everyone else immediately tensed, but all Dyna felt was relief. He looked tired and beaten down by life, and yet when he looked at her, they exchanged a nod. She didn't say it when they last spoke, but she needed him as much as the others, and he had sensed it because of who he was.

At last, she had gathered her Guardians. Well, save for one.

"Who is he? Another friend of Lord Norrlen?" Eldred asked.

Dyna smiled faintly. "He is a friend of mine."

CHAPTER 40

Lucenna

The sky was clear for once. It offered warm sunlight as Eldred led them on a hike through the woodland. Lucenna tried not to wince on her sore ankle. It had mostly healed, but the uneven terrain wasn't helping. Klyde stayed close so she could lean on him when she needed the support, but she tried not to, aware of the stitches she had sewn into his arm.

After what seemed like an eternity, they reached the bottom of the mountain. Immediately, Lucenna sat on a boulder with a groan. Her ankle was throbbing.

"Take a minute to rest," Eldred told them.

Only a minute?

The others sat and took out waterskins for a quick drink. Only Klyde remained standing beside her, his cool eyes trained on Von. The Commander, or former Commander, she supposed, stood away from them leaning against a tree. Only Dyna spoke to him in quiet tones, offering him water and something small to eat. Perhaps to make him feel welcome, since he clearly wasn't.

The hike had been a quiet one, with the strong tension circulating in the atmosphere from Zev and Klyde.

"We must continue," Eldred said.

"To where?" Lucenna asked, grimacing as she got to her feet. The others gathered up their packs again. "Not up the mountain, I hope."

Otherwise, she may need Keena to sprinkle her with fairy dust so she could float on, because she was finished with hiking.

"No, not up the mountain. We will go through it."

Through it? She exchanged a look with the others.

But the Magi Master offered no other explanation. They gathered around Eldred as he faced a solid wall of rock.

Lifting his staff, he tapped on the surface of it in a distinct pattern, murmuring in soft Elvish, *"Anat'nom narg at'reip'sed."* With each tap, glowing gold runes appeared, lighting up to form a large hexagon about ten feet in circumference. Placing his palm flat in the center, he said, *"Ellaval emai'ug."*

The mountain groaned.

The center of the spell vanished, creating the opening that revealed a deep, dark cave. Lucenna's mouth parted open in awe. The old elf turned to them and held out an arm, indicating they should enter. They all hesitated, but it surprised her when Dyna went in first. The crystal in the Magi Master's staff glowed white as he entered after her. Zev went in next, then Klyde. Well, Lucenna had to go, too. She cast out orbs of light to illuminate the cavern. It led to a deep tunnel, and the distant rush of water echoed inside.

Her heart started to pound with dread.

Eldred continued onward. "This way."

"Where are you taking us?" Lucenna asked.

"To the waterways."

She halted. "Excuse me?"

"The rivers of Naiads Mere have formed waterways beneath the mountain in the caves. We have learned how to navigate them through the kingdom. Some lead to the Saxe Sea, one to the White Woods, and others as far as Ledoga. The waterway we are to take will lead us to Sellav."

She really didn't like the sound of that at all.

"It should be safe," Dyna told her.

Swallowing, Lucenna nodded, though she couldn't make herself follow the elf.

Dyna and Zev continued behind him. Keena fluttered after them with her glowing wings. Lucenna glanced back at Klyde to find him and Von eyeing each other silently. She thought they were going to take out their knives and have a go at each other, but Klyde marched on.

Von removed the harness and saddle off his grey horse. Patting it's back with a soft word, it trotted away for trees. He was releasing his horse since it couldn't come with them.

"Keep close, lass," Klyde said under his breath. He offered his arm, but she muttered she was fine.

Lucenna limped after him, briefly glancing at the Commander. He let them move several yards ahead before continuing behind them. She had overheard Von tell Dyna he heard of Rawn's capture in Dwarf Shoe, so he came to help.

Why? It's not as if he owed them anything.

Funny, she had almost killed him once, if not for Dyna. And she was the reason he was here now. But Lucenna didn't trust the man, Zev ignored him, and Klyde seemed to hate him.

She would have to ask him about it later.

Keena flew over to her, fluttering around her head before settling on her shoulder. "Lucenna, can I ask about the Celestial in the woods yesterday?" she whispered. "I am mighty curious."

Lucenna eyed her and said under her breath. "How much did you hear?"

She smiled sheepishly. "Everything."

Naughty fairy.

"She called her a queen. Does that mean Dyna and Cassiel were married?"

"They were."

Keena's eyes widened. "And now?"

"They aren't anymore. It's not my place to speak of it."

"Hmm. Well, could you spare some gossip about our new companion?" Keena glanced behind them. "The others fell quiet the moment he arrived."

"His name is Von," Lucenna whispered. "He used to serve Tarn, Klyde's brother."

"Oh..."

Up ahead, the others conversed with Eldred. Their voices bounced through the cavernous channel, amplifying them. Zev tilted his head to catch other sounds with his keen hearing.

"He also stabbed Zev in the stomach with a silver knife while abducting Dyna for his master," she mentioned next. "They said it nearly took his life."

"Well, that certainly puts a damper on things." Keena peeked back at Von, past Lucenna's hair. "Why don't *you* like him?"

"Other than the fact that he tried to steal my medallion from me, I don't care for those who try to hurt my friends." She grazed her fingers over the diamonds in her medallion, checking it was still hanging from her neck.

"Hmm. Since he's here, does that mean he's not an enemy anymore?"

She didn't know what he was now. Only that Dyna had invited him along. "Apparently, he's a Guardian."

Keena canted her head. Her wings fluttered with a soft tinkling of bells, casting out a swirl of gold dust. "Why does he look so sad?"

Lucenna sighed. "His wife recently passed."

Dyna had told them last night what she'd seen in Tarn's memories, and even she felt sympathy for the man. How cruel of the fates to make him the Guardian of Vengeance, knowing what misfortune needed to befall him for it.

"Now I feel terrible for him," Keena said. "I should at least say hello."

"No, stay with the others. Go on."

The fairy princess pouted. She flew away and landed on Zev's head, taking a seat in his hair.

It was best to keep their distance—

Lucenna's boot caught, and she almost went sprawling if not for the hand that caught her arm. She looked up at Von.

Klyde tore his hand away and slammed him against the cave wall faster than she could blink. "Don't give me a reason," he growled.

Von didn't react. He didn't even move to defend himself. Klyde looked ready to kill him, and the man didn't care.

"Captain," Dyna called.

The men didn't move. Klyde's fists were white from how tight he clenched the front of Von's coat.

Lucenna rolled her eyes and tugged on his arm. "Leave him. He didn't do anything."

Klyde scoffed derisively. "That's the thing, isn't it? He's done plenty, and nothing at all."

She didn't understand. He marched on, leaving her confused as she followed.

The rest of the trek went quietly with only their soft steps in the dirt echoing off the walls. They reached two tunnels, and Eldred chose one with stalagmites on the ceiling. The rush of water echoed loudly as they were led to an underground river. The current moved rapidly through a narrow tunnel. Slender, wooden rowboats rested against the wall of the cave.

Lucenna tensed with sudden dread. She prayed they didn't have to get into the water.

"Two per boat," Eldred announced. "Be careful not to tip over. The currents are extremely strong. I have seen the best swimmers drown in these waterways."

Oh. Splendid.

"Lass, you're with me." Klyde nodded at her to follow him. He grabbed a boat and brought it near the edge. She didn't argue. He knew she couldn't swim, but she rather not let it be known to the others.

Zev had Dyna and Keena pair up with him. And because no one else seemed inclined to join him, Eldred ended up with Von. They climbed into the boats, and with a push of the paddle, they were off. Lucenna gripped the sides tightly as Klyde rowed. A cold spray misted her skin, the roar of the river echoing in the cave. One by one, they entered the dark, narrow cavern. Her heart raced wildly at the sudden darkness. But the ceiling was lit with glowworms. Their vivid green light glittered against the rocky surface as they passed.

"Brace yourselves," Eldred warned.

They dipped around a bend and were swept rapidly away along the current. They went so fast, Lucenna grabbed onto the back of Klyde's coat with one hand and gripped the boat with the other. She prayed it would end quickly.

Klyde's laughter floated to her.

Likely at her expense.

She scowled at the back of his head. "Why are you laughing?"

"This is fun."

The boat suddenly plunged down a short waterfall, and she choked back a scream. "You and I have two distinct understandings of fun!"

He laughed again, and the sound surprisingly put her at ease. She liked him better this way. Jovial rather than tetchy.

The rapid river continued to take them away. At the speed they were going, the journey would certainly take them through the mountain within the day. The waterways altered between winding tunnels and dangerous lanes with obstacles of sharp rocks they had to navigate, but Klyde had no problem dodging them. Eventually, she relaxed, choosing to trust he would maneuver them safely. It was hours before the current slowed and brought them to a wide cavern with still green waters. Lucenna slumped with relief at the sight of daylight pouring in from the opening ahead.

Thank the Gods.

They rowed out of the cave onto a steady river passing through a picturesque forest. At the cusp of a ridge appeared two statues of enormous rearing horses carved out of stone. The statues arched over the river, facing each other. They passed under as Lucenna gaped up at them

246

in wonder. They stood hundreds of feet high, their hooves easily dwarfing them.

The river led them through a canal with walls of bridges built into the stone, draped with vines and moss. They crisscrossed over each other, above the river, and along the ridge leading to who knows where. The rush of waterfalls tumbled down the rocky terrain into the river with a trickle that was almost musical. Evening sunlight poured in past the ledges, casting rainbow refractions in the mist.

Leaving the gorge, the landscape opened before them, and she was rendered speechless.

"The province of Sellav," Eldred announced.

A valley spread wide, resting within the protection of the Anduir Mountains that were coated in a light fog. A clear blue river cut through the land, breaking off into many streams along the homes that had been exquisitely carved from the natural white stone of the rolling hills. And field upon fields of dynalya flowers fluttered gently in the breeze.

It was exactly as Rawn described it.

Lucenna's vision misted. She couldn't help but appreciate the beauty of this place. There was a peace here she didn't feel anywhere else. As if this little pocket of life was free of all that was dark and wrong with the world.

An estate rested on a peak within the center of the valley on the edge of the main river. It was a beautiful, four-story structure made of white stone coated in ivy, with several towered peaks and arched windows catching the golden rays of the sun. Nestled within a vibrant garden, stone steps led to an open courtyard with a glittering fountain and more stone bridges that led to the following floors.

"There stands House Norrlen," Eldred said.

Lucenna gawked at it. "Rawn lives *there*?"

Klyde let out a long whistle. "I thought he was only a general."

Eldred frowned at him. "*His Grace* owns the entire province. Lord Norrlen is the Duke of Sellav."

"A *duke*?" Zev repeated from the boat beside her, exchanging a surprised look with Dyna. "Well, he certainly kept a few things to himself."

"So it would seem," Dyna said thoughtfully.

Eldred led them toward the estate, and they passed through a busy town. Green flags billowed in the wind with the golden sigil of House Norrlen: a rearing horse atop a shield, framed in laurel. Elves stopped to watch them row past. They reached a harbor where they moored their boats with the help of the shoremen.

"Who is with you, Master Eldred?" one of the boys asked.

"Guests," he replied. "Send word to the young master to meet me at the front gates. I bring dire news."

The boy nodded and took off in a run toward the town.

"Follow me," Eldred told them next. "I must introduce you to Her Grace."

Rawn's wife...

From the little they heard of Lady Aerina she was very special to Rawn. Lucenna had felt it the day they cast a locator spell, and saw it whenever he spoke of his wife.

Taking his staff, Eldred motioned for them to follow him to the stone bridge that curved over the river, with a path that led up the peak to the estate. Lucenna's heart raced with every step. Clouds passed over the sun as they reached the top and shadow fell over the land.

They arrived at gates guarded by Elven soldiers. Hooves beat on the path behind them as another elf came galloping up the road on a white stallion.

Yanking on the reins, he came to a stop in front of them, startled and confused.

So were they.

"Rawn...?" Lucenna gasped.

He was nearly the exact image with the same horse. He had the same long blond hair braided away from his ears, dressed elegantly in a fine, dark green doublet trimmed in gold over a long-sleeved white tunic and brown trousers. An elegant green cape was pinned to his left shoulder.

For a moment her heart leaped with the hope that Rawn was safe, and Fair had survived. But she took in the shade of his indigo eyes and the youth to his features, and she knew it wasn't him.

"No," Dyna said faintly beside her, astonishment lining her expression. "That must be Raiden ... his son."

"Who are you?" he demanded. It was his voice that finally made it real for Lucenna. It was curt and sharp, nothing like Rawn's. "What is the meaning of this, Eldred? Who have you brought to us?"

"My lord." The Magi Master bowed his head. "Forgive me for the unexpected intrusion. They are acquaintances of your father."

"Acquaintances?" Raiden's eyes widened at that, and he dismounted. Eldred took the reins from him while he removed his riding gloves. "How do you know my father?"

Before they could answer, the guards at the gate opened the doors as a female elf in a pale green dress came running out of the estate's front doors.

"Mother," Raiden rushed to her, putting himself between her and them. "Stay back. I don't know who they are." He motioned at an elf with long copper hair wearing green leather armor. His chest bore the sigil of House Norrlen. "Halder, take her inside."

Halder stepped forward with a bow of his head. "Your Grace, allow me to escort you to the estate."

"No, I know them..." she said, her face falling to amazement as she took them in.

Aerina was beyond what Lucenna would describe as beautiful. She had waves of pale blonde hair the color of the dawn gracing the surface of the horizon, and her eyes matched the aquamarine stone on the circlet resting on her brow.

Inhaling a shaky breath, her gaze fell on Dyna. "Lady Dynalya..."

"You know my name?" Dyna asked in surprise.

"Of course." Aerina smiled brightly. "Oh, how wonderful! In my husband's last letter, he wrote about all of you. Of the tale of how he met the Maiden and her Guardians."

Raiden turned to them with a mix of astonishment and recognition as he took them in again.

"Now you are all here ... but..." Aerina searched among them, and her smile wavered. "Where is my Rawn?"

Lucenna tried to answer, but the words wouldn't come. Zev lowered his head, and Dyna couldn't keep the sorrow from her face. Lady Aerina looked at Eldred. He bowed his head. Her smile slowly faded as realization landed.

She covered her mouth with a trembling hand. "I knew it ... I felt something the other day. I knew something was wrong." Voice shaking, she said, "Tell me..."

Dyna took a step forward. "I am so sorry to have to convey such difficult news ... Red Highland captured him three days ago."

The sound Aerina made came from deep within her chest. A tortured cry that was part whimper and part gasp. Turning away, she held her stomach as if she had been struck with a blow that took all her air away. She stumbled, and Raiden caught her as she fell to the ground.

Aerina broke down there in the dirt, falling into the arms of her son. The sounds of her cries brought instant tears to Lucenna's eyes. She took Dyna's hand as they silently cried with her.

"God of Urn, please take him with," Aerina begged as she wept.

That confused Lucenna, not sure if she heard her right.

Holding his mother, Raiden looked past them to the land, his expression caught between disbelief and shock. "If you knew what Red Highland does to their prisoners, you would wish for the same," he murmured. "He will be locked in the bowels of the Blood Keep in the dark, without food or water, enduring the unimaginable. Death would be a mercy."

Lucenna didn't have the nerve to say, "stay strong" or "don't worry". She wanted to say something comforting but couldn't find the words. Because she could see herself there on the ground as well, utterly distraught when her mother had been taken.

Because she knew they would never see each other again.

Aerina's tear-filled eyes looked up at the Magi Master. "Tell me he is dead."

"They have taken him alive, Your Grace," Eldred said softly as he knelt beside her. "For only one purpose. To break him until his mind gives up the secrets it holds."

Aerina's cries echoed over the valley.

And like the vanishing sunlight, that peace that had once laid in the wonder of Sellav was gone.

CHAPTER 41

Dynalya

A quietness filled the Norrlen Estate. They were in the grand hall as they waited for Eldred. The Magi Master had gone into the other room with Aerina as they spoke with King Leif through her orb.

Lucenna sat on a chaise with Keena on her shoulder, soaking in the warmth of the fireplace. Behind them stood Klyde and Zev, keeping an eye on Von, where he lingered on the opposite side of the vast room. He paid them no mind. His tired, bloodshot eyes fixed on a random spot on the stone floor, lost in thought.

Dyna sighed. She hated the tension between them. Hated more that she could hear Aerina's soft cries, knowing all of this was her fault. She looked up from the wingback chair she sat in, to the open courtyard doors where Raiden stood outside on the terrace. He stared blankly at the gardens, motionless.

He had yet to cry or show any other emotion, but that didn't mean they weren't there.

Rising to her feet, Dyna walked over to join him. A soft breeze rustled the bushes. The air was sweet with the scent of flowers and herbs. "How are you feeling?"

Raiden blinked down at her, as if surprised she was suddenly there. "I'm…" A thoughtful curl formed between his brows, as if confused by the question. "I'm fine," he said feebly. Clearing his throat, he turned to face her fully. He reminded her so much of Rawn she had to lower her gaze out of guilt. "I'm all right. Please pardon me for my curtness at your arrival. We have had ill guests as of late. Thank you, Lady Dynalya, for coming all this way."

A knot of emotion tangled in her throat at remembering Rawn's kind voice when he referred to her with a title. "I'm sorry to bring this to your door," Dyna said quietly.

"It was necessary..." Raiden glanced at the estate where his keen hearing could undoubtedly pick up the sound of his mother's weeping. "My father, he had a bonded horse with him."

She tried to hide the shakiness from her voice, but it was futile. Her vision welled as she looked down at her satchel. "Fair was lost during the confrontation."

A soft sigh slipped past Raiden's lips. He held out a folded handkerchief to her.

She accepted it with shaking fingers and wiped away the tear that had escaped. "I'm sorry."

It was all she could say.

"I would not fault someone to show their care, more so when those tears are for my family."

That wasn't what she was apologizing for. She wanted to confess that she brought about Rawn's capture, but the words lodged in her throat. The only way to make amends was to fix what she had done.

"I suppose this must be your first visit to Greenwood. Have you ever seen your namesake?" Raiden asked.

Dyna blinked, taken aback by the question. "Only in herbology books. Well, and today when we arrived."

The last of the evening light caught his eyes as he glanced away to the gardens. He nodded for her to follow him.

Raiden led her through the gravel paths and brought her to a fountain obscured by hedges. Adorning the circumference were flowerbeds of beautiful red blooms. The wind carried their sweet fragrance around her. The petals were truly the exact shade of her hair.

"I see why that name was given to you."

For a moment, an old memory surfaced of her mother brushing out her hair by the fire as she sang to her of crimson fields.

"There. No more tears," Raiden said at her small smile.

Had he brought her here to make her feel better? She was the one who should comfort him.

"And your name? Who were you named after?"

Raiden frowned at the fountain, crossing his arms. "Tradition, I suppose. In Greenwood, you will find the first-born son tends to take the first letter of his father's name. It started several centuries ago with the noble families to bestow honor. Now every family does so as a sign of love and respect." He looked back at the estate. "And my mother certainly loves my father."

His fingers drifted over a wooden pendant he wore around his neck. It was squared with a convex surface, whittled with an intricate weaving in the wood. He faced the fruit trees that were beginning to blossom.

"There is one missing among your group," Raiden said, canting his head. "There was mention of a Celestial in his previous letter."

Dyna's pulse jumped at the sudden change in subject. "Yes..." She fidgeted with a loose thread in her sleeve. "He is not with us anymore. He had other matters to attend to."

"Oh." Raiden's tone hardened. He held out an arm to shield her as he gripped the hilt of his sword at his hip. "Then who is lurking over there?"

Dyna whipped around. A winged shadow lingered within the trees. The leaves rustled as her red-winged guard stepped out.

She scowled. "Sowmya, I thought I made myself clear the last time we spoke."

The Valkyrie knelt on one knee and bowed her head. "Forgive me, my lady. I bring word that the High King will arrive within the hour. I came to plead with you once more." She looked up at her. "Save him."

Dyna frowned, a sense of worry and wariness coming over her at the beseeching in Sowmya's voice. "What do you mean? What is happening?"

"More than I have told you. A storm is coming to the Realms. They are revolting against him, my lady. Lord Gadriel awaits the High King at Nazar's Citadel with an armed force ready for battle."

Her stomach sank, and Dyna looked up at the shroud of clouds. The Realms would battle Cassiel merely because they refuse to accept him as their king?

"Nazar..." Raiden repeated. "A Celestial territory is hidden there."

"There is." Dyna looked back at Sowmya. "I don't understand. Do the Realms reject him so much they would rather wage war than have him take the throne?"

"Who?" Raiden said. "Who does she speak of?"

Dyna closed her eyes. "The first Guardian."

"The one who is absent? *He* is the High King of Hilos?"

"Yes." She pressed on her chest, feeling the brittle bond ache. "I cannot be a part of this, Sowmya. I have nothing to do with his legitimacy to the crown or claim to the throne."

"This was never about his legitimacy, my lady." Sowmya stood and looked up at the skies. "He does not come for the sake of his crown, but to eliminate a threat. Why do you think he left?"

The question made Dyna's heart start to pound, and she took a step back on instinct because she didn't want to hear this.

Sowmya looked at her again. "You have seen that instinct when it surfaces, the uncontrollable flames that erupt when his only focus is to *protect*."

The memory of Hermon came swiftly. It was vivid in Dyna's mind. A sea of blue Seraph fire and the screams of Celestials fleeing, Cassiel standing at the center of it all. A scatter of cold currents swept down her spine.

I care not who it is. Whoever comes after you will burn, even if that means I turn on them all.

"He is not well, my lady. Without the other half of his soul, Cassiel is lost."

Dyna held her breath, sensing something dire had happened from the look on Sowmya's face before she said the words.

"Skath has fallen."

Dyna gasped. "What?"

The lieutenant lowered her gaze, and Dyna felt she would be sick. "He has nearly been overtaken by the flame. With such power unchecked, the Realms fear another genocide, and they are banding together. He comes now to Nazar to eliminate those who conspire against his True Bonded. That instinct is seeded in the very root of what made him. What do you think the High King will do when he arrives in Nazar, and they defy him?"

She remembered Cassiel's reactions when any threat came near her. The visceral beast that rose behind the flame.

The words fell like smoke from her lips. "He will destroy it."

"How do you know that?" Raiden asked her.

"Because he was once my husband," Dyna whispered. Once her love. Once her soul. Once her heart. "I know him better than anyone."

Raiden stared at her mutely.

"Nazar has prepared weapons to fight him," Sowmya continued. "They will either kill him, or history will repeat itself, and he will annihilate us all."

History...

Dyna stumbled back, and Raiden caught her arm. "What are you saying?" she demanded. "Are the rumors about him true?"

The lieutenant's grim gaze was answer enough.

King Kāhssiel reborn.

The wispy image of the couple kissing in the garden passed through her mind. That was real?

Sweat beaded on Dyna's skin, and the sound of her racing heart thudded in her ears as the world skewed. No, it couldn't be.

"He has been down this path before," Sowmya said, snapping her back to clarity. "I beg you. Stop him. You are the only one who can."

Dyna didn't bother asking why *her*. No one else could withstand Cassiel's flame. She rubbed her face. "You asked me to save him."

"To do one is to do the other. If not for him, then for the promise you made to his father."

That statement punched her in the gut. It sent the sting of tears to her eyes as she remembered King Yoel's last wish. *Take care of him for me when I'm gone...*

To stoop so low as to throw that in her face.

Dyna seethed. "How dare you?"

She had to turn her back to compose herself. Lingering by the entrance of the hedgerow were Guardians. They looked back at her somberly.

None of them disputed this. It wasn't their place. Yet everyone knew there was no real choice here. Because she couldn't live with the blood of others on her hands while she had the power to prevent it.

Within the confines of Dyna's chest, past all the anger and resentment, deep within the cavern of her soul, lay the unraveled threads of their bond. They stirred with the instinct to protect her mate, even if he wasn't *hers* anymore.

To do what she must, required defying Cassiel in front of his people. Sowmya had to know that.

Dyna wanted to run, but her heart wouldn't let her. She gazed into the sunset, allowing the last rays of the sun to blind her watery vision. "Why have you come to me? Are you not loyal to your king?"

"I'm here because *I am* loyal to my king," Sowmya said. "He needs you."

Inhaling a shallow breath, Dyna finally allowed herself to see him.

Cassiel came out of the shadows as real as she remembered him, as if he had never left. He was in the garden, his white robes rippling in the wind, where he sat in a tree as the gentle melody of his flute drifted around her. He glowed like the magic of a dream from another world they had long ago parted from.

Oh, how she wished they had never left it. He smiled at her, his silver eyes and black wings gleaming in the sunset, same as they had the day they met.

The wet blur of Dyna's vision distorted him until the image faded away. She wiped her tears away.

Maybe it had been foolish to think she could forget him. He left without looking back, so why were the broken pieces of her soul fighting so hard to go after him?

Dyna looked up at Raiden standing silently beside her. "I must beg your pardon, Lord Raiden."

His brow furrowed slightly, and a faint smile rose to his face. Taking her hand, he kissed the back of it with a bow. "Lady Dynalya, your presence is needed elsewhere. Please do not feel you do me an unkindness to attend it. Go, and know you are welcome to return."

The touch was too gentle for her sharp edges. She carefully retrieved her hand, hesitating before saying, "I may not return alone."

He dipped his head. "I understand."

Dyna turned to her friends next.

Sighing, Lucenna crossed her arms. "You're going after him."

"I must."

"Then we are coming with you," Zev said, and they all nodded, including Von.

Their support brought warmth to the chill on her skin. Dyna could only offer them a slight smile as she shook her head. "Not this time. This is something I must do alone." To Lucenna she said, "Before I go, there is a spell you must teach me first."

Dyna tightened the belts of her greaves as she strode to the crop of trees where Sowmya waited. The short swords at her hips clinked softly against her fae leather armor. She had changed out of her dress for form fitting black leather trousers and boots that reached her knees. She checked that her braids were properly pinned back and would keep the hair out of her face.

The soft flutter of wings led her past the thicket, and she halted at the sight of the white Pegasus. Like Sowmya, it wore gilded armor. The fading sunlight glinted over the plates of gold adorning its head, the edges of its wings, chest, and legs.

Sowmya held the reins. "Do you still remember how to ride?"

"Yes..." Composing herself, Dyna approached the beautiful creature. It nickered quietly, eyeing her. It was the same one she had ridden to Hermon.

"Here." Sowmya reached into the saddlebag and pulled out two objects. "These are yours."

In her hands rested the sapphire tiara and her white opal dagger. Both had been lost the day the Vanguard came. And both were no longer hers.

"Keep them." Dyna mounted the Pegasus. "The only thing I need are Celestial feathers."

"How many?"

"As many as you can spare."

Without hesitation or even a wince, the Lieutenant ripped out a handful of red feathers from her left wing and tucked them in the saddlebag.

Dyna took the reins as Sowmya strapped her in. "Are you coming with me?"

"I will meet you there, my lady. I cannot fly as fast as Shira."

"Shira." Dyna repeated, and her ride nickered in response. She smiled, petting the Pegasus' neck. "I am putting my trust in you, Shira." Dyna looked up at the sky, and she called out the same command she heard Cassiel once say in the Celestial language. *"Lashamayim."*

To the sky.

Shira whinnied and took off in a gallop. Her massive white wings flapped, stirring the wind as they went. Dyna kicked her heels into Shira's flank. They flew for the ridge and leaped into the open air.

Shira soared over the land of Sellav as she made for the Anduir Mountains. She called out another command, and the Pegasus's wings worked harder to climb the sky. Dyna tugged on the reins and leaned back sharply. They shot into the covering of clouds, which gently misted on her skin. Closing her eyes, she breathed in the fresh air.

Dyna told herself the only reason she was going to see Cassiel again was to end his rampage, because she was the only person who could. She told herself it was the right thing to do. They may no longer be husband and wife, but their marriage remained valid before the Realms. So regardless of who hated her, regardless of him leaving, she was still the High Queen.

This involved her whether she wanted it or not.

Shira abruptly swerved, and they narrowly missed an obstacle hidden in the clouds. Dyna peered past the thick veil as it slowly parted, revealing three massive, floating islands.

It was a world above the world.

The two smaller islands bore cities with lush landscapes and aerial gardens with rivers that cascaded over the sides. Bridgeways connected them to the largest island in the center. On it rose a towering stone fortress with rounded blue domes, the spires flying the gold flags with the sigil of a sun fanned by wings. Extending from the foundation of the island itself were six imposing wings of stone, as if it carried the Realm through the sky. The courtyard continued outward past the wings, and there rose a great white *Hyalus* tree with translucent leaves.

The Realm of Nazar.

For a moment, wonder and awe stole Dyna's next thoughts. Until she rose up higher and noticed the army of Celestials in silver and gold armor in the courtyard. They stood perfectly in formation, a sea of white wings, ready for battle.

That structure had to be the Citadel, and Lord Gadriel would be with his army. He had little regard for her in Hermon, but she had to at least try to speak to him first before Cassiel arrived. Yet even she knew to tread carefully.

There was another gathering on the second island where they had evacuated the citizens. Better to land there first. Higher chances she wouldn't be shot down.

They looked up at Dyna as she circled around. Arrows whizzed through the air, and she ducked before they struck her head. Shira dove out of the way of the next shot.

She judged too soon.

"Stop!" a distant voice shouted. "Don't shoot!"

Circling around again, Dyna searched among them and noticed Prince Asiel waving back the guards. She tugged on the reins and aimed to land. He motioned for them to make way. Shira's hooves beat on the square as she landed, stirring up the dust. Guards dressed in Hermon blue and Nazar gold drew their weapons.

"Stand down," Asiel commanded. They hesitantly obeyed. Once he was sure no one would move, he turned and stared at her in amazement. "You're alive."

Although unexpected, Dyna was relieved to see someone she recognized. "I continue to be surprised by that myself," she said. He held onto the reins for her as she unfastened herself from the saddle and dismounted. "Has Lady Sarrai come with you?"

"She has remained in Hermon."

Dyna nodded. "Good. Then she's safe."

"Who is this?" demanded a male Celestial behind them. A noble by the make of his golden robes. Every Celestial gawked at her with astonishment and disgust.

Whispers hummed among the crowd.

"Why is there a human here?"

"How does she know of us?"

"Who is she to ride a Pegasus?"

The nobleman gripped his sword's hilt. "Answer human, or I will behead you where you stand."

Dyna arched an eyebrow at his reedy arms. She could probably break them before he ever drew his sword.

Asiel frowned at him. "Calm yourself, Nuriel. Show some respect. You owe her your allegiance."

"What?" Nuriel balked, gaping at him as if he were mad. "What do you mean *I* owe *her* my allegiance? To this filthy human who has trespassed into my father's Realm? If you weren't Lord of Hermon, I would have you detained for that insult."

Lord? Well, they had named Asiel both heir and Lord Protector of Hermon before leaving. Naturally, the position was passed to him once Cassiel became king.

"Hold your tongue." Asiel loomed over him. "Or you may lose it if you continue speaking of her that way."

Nuriel shrunk back, confirming her assumption. He wasn't a fighter. His shifty gaze flickered to her with new wariness, and she almost smiled. Asiel had changed a lot since she last saw him.

The sky ruptured with a *boom* that rocked through her being.

They all looked up at the bright blue light breaking through the clouds like a comet of flame. The Celestials cried out, and most of them scattered. Mothers and fathers grabbed children, fleeing in the opposite direction.

It was probably wise of them to leave. If what Sowmya said was true, Dyna came prepared for the worst.

"Why do you flee?" Nuriel shouted at them. "Your Liege Lord will protect you!"

"Not against Seraph fire," Dyna said. "You should go as well."

Opening the saddlebag, she gathered the crumpled red feathers, and they glittered gold as they dissolved in her hands. She closed her eyes, feeling the barrier fall away. The flood of Essence filled her veins with warmth. A current of energy filled her being with such delightful power, her lungs expanded with a full breath she had not taken in months.

Her Essence wasn't as it was. It had grown in strength, as her body had. And she instinctively knew she was capable of so much more. "Make sure no other interferes. I will take care of it from here."

"When I prayed for a miracle, I did not expect *Elyōn* would answer, let alone in this way." Asiel folded an arm across his chest and deeply bowed. "Thank you for coming."

Nuriel recoiled in disgust. "Why are you bowing to her? What is she doing here? You have yet to explain who she is!"

"I am Dynalya Astron," she said, taking the steps of the bridgeway that led to the Citadel.

"You say that name as if I should know who you are!"

Pausing, she trained her glowing green eyes on him and the citizens of Nazar.

"You will."

CHAPTER 42

Cassiel

Cassiel landed at the peak of the Citadel's courtyard like a comet. The force of his power cracked the stone beneath his feet and wisps of blue flame scattered out. His army of Valkyrie hovered behind him like a shroud of gold, filling the skies. He instructed them to watch from above first.

His black coat flowed around his legs with the wind as he strode forward, climbing up the steps to the circular planform that held the *Hyalus* tree. Each step left behind coils of flames in the stone, and his gaze leveled with the gathered army of Nazar.

Leading them was Lord Gadriel, flanked by two warriors who shared his squared features. The eldest of them stood tall, well-built with a broad chest and short blond hair. The other was more slender but confident in how he carried himself.

Cassiel circled the tree and stood before it. All was quiet as they stared up at him, perfectly still. The only sound came from the soft crackling of wood from the torches and the wind. It tugged at his clothing and wings, making them ripple.

As the sun dropped beyond the clouds, the *Hyalus* glowed with glittering white light through the leaves.

The Lord of Nazar looked upon Cassiel's crown of Seraph fire, and his throat bobbed a bit before he composed himself. He tipped his head in a slight bow. "Your Majesty."

"Lord Gadriel. I would say it is a pleasure to greet you again, but I don't think the feeling is mutual." Cassiel narrowed his eyes pointedly at his army.

Gadriel had yet to put on his winged helmet, but he didn't waste time with small talk. "I know why you have come."

"Do you?"

"Hallel was a fool. He had always been too ambitious and reached for more than what was his to take. That earned him a passage through the Gates, but that was his undertaking, not mine. I have no intention of challenging you."

"Hmm." Cassiel climbed down the rest of the platform steps to the courtyard as he played with a petal of flame between his fingers. "Is that so? Then what do you say about the army behind you?"

A muscle jumped in Gadriel's clenched jaw. The arrival of twilight exposed the sheen of sweat on his forehead. But his blue eyes remained cool and focused. "I am told you have usurped the throne from your father and executed two Lords when they did not bend to your will. Skath has been razed to the ground beneath a shroud of Seraph flame." His gaze shifted up at the three thousand Valkyrie watching from the sky. "Now you have arrived with your Legion. Am I mistaken to believe that you came here to do the same?"

Fear.

It lingered so strongly in the air Cassiel could taste it. He had learned its weight, its shape. He could read it now on their pallid faces and the tension in their bodies. They were terrified of him.

But they need not fear him as long as they didn't get in his way.

"I have come for only one thing," Cassiel said as flames slowly licked along his palms. "Justice."

Confusion flickered across Gadriel's face. "Sire?"

"Hallel's coup did not begin with him alone. These elitists have conspired against me and mine. Traitors of the crown lurk amongst your people. Give them to me, and no harm will befall your Realm."

It wasn't an empty threat. He didn't come to destroy them, but their streets wouldn't be spared of ash.

Denial furrowed Gadriel's brow with anger and disbelief. "I have always held fealty to my king. There are no traitors here."

Cassiel sneered at that statement. He could still see very clearly Gadriel standing among those who betrayed him so long ago. "Oh, but there is."

"Lies!" His tallest son bellowed. "To accuse us is to sully our honor. Nazar has never defied the crown, even when it has been usurped by the likes of *you.*"

Cassiel's veins bled blue. Flames burst out of him in a tornado and tore into the sky as a column of pure Seraph fire. The Nazarians gasped and quickly recoiled several steps back, nearly falling over each other to escape him. Blue light bathed the courtyard and over their frightened faces.

"Do not speak to me of honor when your Realm was founded in defiance!" Cassiel's bellowing voice echoed over the Citadel. "These bricks were laid upon your exile decreed by *Elyōn* a millennium ago for the actions of your ancestors that you now bear in shame." A red flush colored Lord Gadriel's face as he looked at him. "Your High King is here now declaring there are traitors in your midst. Do you deny me?"

The Lord of Nazar paled. Cassiel glanced down at the puddle at his feet. It held his reflection. He looked like a creature of obliteration with his eyes glowing a menacing blue with a massive pillar of fire behind him.

He cast his flame away. "Answer."

The Lord of Nazar straightened his shoulders, his expression pinching with acceptance and unease. "No."

"Then bring them forward, or I will go through you to get to them."

Throat bobbing, Gadriel nodded. "Name them, and they shall be called to an inquisition, sire."

At last, some shred of respect.

But could it be considered respect when done out of fear?

Letting his gaze pass over the silent army, Cassiel tapped against his thigh pensively. Before his untimely death, Lord Hallel had provided a few more names that had not been on the original list.

The only punishment they would meet would be his.

"Azael Sa'ar," Cassiel called out.

An older soldier from the crowd jerked back.

"Ah, there you are."

Azael tried to flee but Cassiel snapped his fingers, and the Celestial's wings snapped. He crashed on the courtyard hard, scrambling to his knees. Azael barely looked up when the fire swarmed into his helmet and set him ablaze from the inside. Screams echoed through the courtyard.

"Samiel and Serrachiel Goral," he announced next.

Two male brothers stepped forward. One with waves of blond hair and the other with braids. Sneering at him, they readied their spears, and they flew at him. Their weapons froze inches from Cassiel's face.

He tucked his hands in his pockets as they trembled against the force of his compulsion. "Who gave you permission to move?"

Fire unfurled at their feet and consumed them. Their screams cut off as they burst into ash. Embers scattered in the wind. Whatever divinity had made him dimmed like a dying candle. Cassiel was sullying himself with each death, but he did so with purpose. Because he could live with being a murderer. The only thing he couldn't live with was repeating his past.

Sighing, Cassiel said the next name. "Thaniel—" He whipped his head aside, narrowly dodging the arrow slicing past his cheek. Warm blood seeped from the cut and dripped down his chin.

Thaniel, the little sneak, had climbed up onto a low tower of the citadel. He aimed and shot more arrows. With a flick of Cassiel's hand, a wave of his fire shot forth. But the arrow cut right through it and grazed his arm.

Hmm. They had weapons forged with Skath metal.

Yelrakel threw a flaming spear, and it went straight through Thaniel's heart. He dropped dead from the tower.

Lord Gadriel's chest heaved with ragged breaths as they waited for the next name. "Are you finished slaughtering my people without trial?"

"No. I saved the best for last." He turned to him, and Gadriel stiffened. Then Cassiel shifted his gaze on the lean Celestial standing beside him. "Akiel Nephele."

His brother and father jerked, their mouths gaping wide with disbelief.

Akiel, however, wasn't surprised. His blue eyes sharpened, cold and calculative. A little smile on the edge of his lips.

"No," Gadriel growled. "My son is no traitor."

"He is."

Gadriel drew his sword, as did all of Nazar. "You didn't come for justice. You came for revenge." To his son he shouted, "Go!"

Akiel shot into the sky.

The Valkyrie attempted to make chase, but a unit of Nazarian soldiers flew up to defend him. The sky filled with the sound of clashing swords and cries, scorched feathers raining down.

Lights flashed as the fallen vanished.

"You have brought Death's shadow to my Realm," Lord Gadriel said.

So he had.

Death had clung to Cassiel with invisible claws since winter, following him around, sweeping away lives by the hundreds. No matter if he wanted to keep the losses minimal to only his targets, events continued to spiral him down a path he had walked before. The further he went, the less he'd be able to turn back.

In his first life, he killed to avenge his love.

In this one, he would kill to protect it.

Yet Cassiel still gave Gadriel one last chance. "If you choose to fight, you choose to die. End this, or I will. Who does Nazar stand with?"

Sneering, Gadriel put on his helmet. "I did not wish to fight you, but I will not allow you to annihilate the Realms with impunity. I see now it is *Elyōn's* will that you be stopped. You were never meant to be here ... Kāhssiel."

Celestials flew at him.

Lifting his hand, they all halted in place. Cassiel flickered his finger, and the sound of bone crunched as their necks sharply twisted. He slew every soldier who challenged him by sword and flame.

A blade swept through the smoke. Pivoting, it clashed against his weapon, bringing him face to face with Gadriel. The Lord twisted his sword and shoved Cassiel back a step. His foot sunk into a stone, and he heard a latch click before the sound of a sharp *clank*. At the touch of icy metal, he looked down at the manacle wrapped around his left ankle. It was attached to a chain coming out of the ground.

He had narrowly missed triggering the second snare that would have taken his right ankle. Divinity hummed in the manacle. His seraph fire died away,

They had shackled him in Skath metal.

The battle halted as all stopped to watch.

Cassiel took the chain in his hand, squeezing it tightly in his fist. "You set a trap."

Lord Gadriel smirked. "Are you so arrogant to assume I wouldn't be prepared to capture you?"

Cassiel broke out into a laugh. A dark maniacal sound that echoed through the quiet courtyard. "Capture me?" he growled. "I am the true High King. You are no one to capture me!"

With a jerk of his hand, the ground gave way, releasing the chain. The metal may block Seraph fire, but it couldn't hold up against his newfound Seraph strength. Cassiel grabbed the manacle and snapped it clean off as if it were merely a dried branch.

Eyes widening, Lord Gadriel flew back. His army fell into formation again and readied their weapons. "Take him down!" he bellowed.

That command echoed through Cassiel's memories, taking him back to that field of ash and bone as those he trusted came down upon him.

His generals.

His brothers in arms who arrived with him from the Heavens. They took everything from him, then butchered him when he was on his knees.

Fury swarmed Cassiel, and fire ruptured from his body. He became the beast of flame they so feared, and he heard another voice in his head.

BURN IT ALL!

A sea of Seraph flame roared through the courtyard like a living, violent thing, hungry for retribution. But Cassiel didn't feel in control of his fire anymore. It came from inside of him, from a deep well of pain and rage. From the remnants of Kāhssiel who demanded his enemies pay in blood. The flame rose in a massive wave into the sky and crested over the frightened citizens of Nazar, who had nowhere to run.

He would render it all to ash.

The wave collided with a beam of golden light.

The fire fell over an enormous dome and went no further. Confusion stunned Cassiel enough to take hold of himself again. The flames dispersed, a few scattered embers left flickering on burned bushes and debris. Thick smoke obscured his vision. It slowly cleared, revealing what had blocked him.

A transparent golden wall stood before him, as tall as the Citadel.

Crackling with magic.

It curved like a dome over the Celestials cowing on the floor, some still frozen in place with their weapons. All eyes fixed on the figure standing in front of the shield.

Smoke tinted by a green light veiled them, but he could distinguish the slender shape of a woman. A path of broken brick led to where she stood, as if...

As if she had caught his flame and withstood it.

Two orbs of menacing green light appeared in the night. She was encompassed with flames in the same color. All was quiet, save for her soft steps. She moved like a cat as she strolled forward. He drew his sword as she rose into the air, bracing to fight.

But something stirred in Cassiel.

His veins hummed.

His heart pounded.

A roaring filled his ears.

His opponent came forward, glowing like a living flame.

She brought her hands together, one above the other, and a crackling sphere of fire formed between them. Her power violently charged the air, lifting the hair on his arms. She hurled her spell.

Cassiel was too slow to react. Her spell hit true and hurled him back with the force of a firestorm.

He crashed into the stairs below the *Hyalus* tree. Hard enough to make it rattle and send glass leaves raining down. Cassiel groaned, gasping for air. He blinked up at the smoky sky. Past the branches, Yelrakel argued with another Celestial with red wings.

That spell.

It held massive power, as if the Heavens had struck him down. He wouldn't be surprised if *Elyōn* had sent someone to punish him for his deeds.

The goddess landed lightly a few yards away.

Her magic dimmed to reveal her face as she strode forward. A beautiful terror that had come to vanquish him. And that wrath that had been seeded in the fragments of Cassiel's soul faded as all of him fell still.

Her boots clacked against the stone floor, the firelight catching on the black leather fitting her body like a second skin. Her red tresses fell free from her coronet and flared around her face in the wind.

A face he had dreamed of for the past three months.

Her cheeks were now speckled with a constellation of freckles, yet all the more enthralling with a fierce beauty that left him speechless. Because she was different.

Strong.

Powerful.

Dangerous.

Cassiel stared at Dyna with a stunned reverence as she strode through his flames. Silent words caught on his tongue like barbs. He was stuck between begging for her to truly be there and fearing she really was.

A part of him was sure it was a dream. He couldn't get up. Couldn't breathe. The sound of his beating heart drummed in his ears.

Cassiel's throat bobbed, words falling from his lips like a wisp of smoke. *"Lev sheli..."*

Dyna crouched in front of him, her expression cool and impassive. Bindings of green Essence ensnared him tightly and pinned his arms to sides. Yanking him up, she brought them face to face. He couldn't move, and it had nothing to do with the magic immobilizing him.

A shiver coursed through him at the sensation of her breath against his skin. His eyes widened further.

She was real.

Her beautiful lips curved in a cold smile. "Hello, darling."

Lifting a glowing green finger, Dyna tapped his forehead.

A blow whipped through Cassiel's skull. He fell through a black void, sinking into the darkness.

And the world vanished.

CHAPTER 43

Dynalya

With a wave of her hand, Dyna lifted Cassiel's limp body into the air. She encased him in a swath of her Essence and layered it with a shield, in case anyone else tried to attack him while he couldn't defend himself. Standing, she gazed at her former love as he soundly slept.

Cassiel's hair had grown. It floated around his handsome face, almost to his shoulders. Black wings cushioned his back. He looked like an innocent young man with the messy locks on his forehead and the perpetual soft glow to his skin. Like a being who had stepped out of the Heavens. Not like the creature of annihilation who had almost demolished this Realm with his power.

Her barrier was beginning to rebuild.

It was time to go, and quickly.

Dyna dropped her shield on the Nazarian army as she turned to face them. "Forgive the king's misconduct. He has a temper in need of minding."

"You..." Lord Gadriel gaped at her with large, angry eyes. "You are supposed to be dead." He caught himself. "I mean, I heard you had been assassinated during Hallel's coup..."

She arched an eyebrow. "Well, I am sorry to disappoint you."

"Who is she, Father?" the bulky Celestial beside him asked.

Dyna didn't have time for this. She searched among the shocked faces until she spotted Prince Asiel coming through with her Pegasus. "Excuse me. I will be on my way."

"I don't think so," Lord Gadriel sneered.

His army drew out their swords and pointed their arrows at her. The Valkyrie dropped behind her and drew out their weapons.

"Halt!" Asiel came out of the crowd with Shira and stood between them. "It is treason to draw your weapons against her. You know who she is, Lord Gadriel."

"It's not her I draw them against." Lord Gadriel's hard eyes fell on Cassiel. "I cannot allow you to leave with him."

Dyna narrowed her eyes, and magic crackled on her skin. "You do not have a choice. *Move*."

"Who is she to speak to us this way?" Nuriel appeared from the crowd beside his father. "I still don't understand."

"Don't you?" Asiel faced the crowd. "You all bore witness to what occurred here today. She is the one who walks through Seraph flame, unburnt and unchallenged." He turned to her, holding out an arm in display. "I present to you the wife and True Bonded mate of Cassiel Soaraway, the sovereigns of Hilos and the Four Celestial realms. Your Queen of Fire."

He dropped to one knee and bowed his head. The Valkyrie beat against their golden breastplates three times and did the same. Dyna tried not to blush at the grand show. It was completely unnecessary.

The Nazarians, however, didn't bow. They still looked unsure of her. Afraid and cross.

"It's her power that keeps the High King from decimating you all," Asiel said. "It would be wise not to defy her."

Dyna shrugged and began to lower Cassiel to the ground. "If Lord Gadriel would rather keep the High King's company, I will happily wake him from his nap. I can't say how well Nazar will survive it, though." She canted her head. Gadriel's mouth thinned, and she lifted Cassiel back into the air. "I thought so. Now make way."

Asiel held onto Shira's reins as she mounted the saddle. Sowmya strapped her into the harness again.

"What of the charge against my son?" Lord Gadriel demanded. "He's been wrongfully accused of treason."

Dyna looked up at where Akiel stood on the tallest balcony of the citadel. She didn't know him, but she recognized his expression. The one of hatred and amusement. A mirror of Zekiel's.

"Keep him here under watch," she said. "Until he can be summoned to a proper inquisition."

"Is that your *command*?"

"Do mind your tongue, Lord Gadriel." Dyna smiled, allowing her eyes to glow. "You are speaking to your High Queen. When a decision has been made regarding your son and Nazar's defiance to the crown, you will be called on again."

She held out her hand for the reins and Asiel placed them in her palm. He looked up at her hesitantly. "You have done more than enough, but..."

"What is it?"

"My father never returned since he left Hermon," Asiel said. Dyna frowned. That couldn't be right. Lord Jophiel had survived the coup. "I have heard no word for him. If you could..."

Dyna glanced down at Cassiel, now suspecting the true reason she had found the water mirror.

"I will look into it." Then she noticed the chain left on the ground. "However, I may need your assistance with one more thing."

Once Dyna had what she needed, she flew away with Cassiel. She ordered the Valkyrie to linger behind in the sky to assure no others attempted to follow. Only Sowmya and Yelrakel shadowed her.

She rode fast for the province of Sellav. Her magic was waning. Her veins began to cool, and the light of her Essence flickered around Cassiel.

"Come on," Dyna grunted, trying to keep him in the air. But her magic winked out, and he plummeted through the clouds out of sight.

Choking on a cry, she dove after him. Her heart pounded wildly as she squinted through the cold mist. They broke through, and she saw him falling through the sky.

"Fly, Shira! Faster!"

They dove. The ground was coming in fast, and Dyna's heart raced wildly. She called on her magic, and it beat desperately against the reformed barrier on her power. Cassiel fell further away. He was going to drop to his death.

Her heart cried out, and she felt it all the way to her soul.

Throwing out her hand, Dyna let out a scream fueled by her desperation. A splinter cracked in her barrier, and her Essence caught him. Yanking back her fist, the green light hauled Cassiel back to her, and she lugged him onto Shira's back. Dyna panted as she closed her eyes in relief.

The barrier fell back into place, locking all her magic away.

So many emotions wrangled through her. She wanted to punch him and embrace him at the same time. Instead, Dyna placed her shaking hand on Cassiel's back between his wings, feeling the soft pulse of his heart. It made her vision welled.

"Stupid Celestial," Dyna murmured. "Look at what you made me do."

"Your Majesty!" Sowmya and Yelrakel flew to her. "What happened? We saw him fall. Is he all right?"

She turned away. "He is now."

Murmuring to Shira, the Pegasus flew for Sellav at her command. The cool breeze blew against Dyna, and she was grateful it dried her eyes. As they glided among the clouds, her mind spun with what she had seen Cassiel do and what he had almost done to his people.

The fire had taken over.

Sowmya told her it had, but to see him become a creature of pure flame with no thought or reason other than to destroy frightened her. Because she knew that wasn't who he had been.

She wasn't the only one who had changed.

The estate appeared on the horizon. Tugging on the reins, Dyna led Shira to it. They flew past the streams and the town before they landed outside the courtyard gates of the Norrlen Estate. Her Guardians and Raiden were already waiting outside.

Yelrakel landed beside her. "Will you wake him now, Your Majesty? We are far enough away from Nazar. What are you doing?" she asked next when Dyna motioned for Lucenna to take Cassiel.

"He will sleep for a little more." Dyna dismounted. "Join the Valkyrie and take position in the Anduir Mountains. I will call upon you when I release him."

"Release him?" Yelrakel's eyes widened as Lucenna lifted Cassiel in a mist of purple Essence and carried him away. "But you cannot hold the High King captive. I am his guard—"

Dyna held up a hand. "I am his *High Queen*." The words felt false on her tongue, but she said them with every note of authority. "And this is my command. It's not up for discussion, General. Now leave us and keep watch. I will send Sowmya if you are needed."

Clenching her jaw, Yelrakel stiffly bowed. Her angry eyes glanced at Sowmya accusingly, then she spread open her gray wings and leaped into the sky.

"You know why I am doing this," Dyna said. Sowmya watched as Cassiel was taken away, her Guardians following. Only Raiden and Zev lingered behind to wait for her. "Stay near."

"Yes, Your Majesty." With a bow of her head, Sowmya flew away toward the roof of the estate.

Sighing, Dyna turned to Zev and Raiden. She couldn't quite look at her cousin yet, so she addressed the young lord first. "I am sorry to bring my troubles to your door, Lord Raiden. With your permission, I will not keep him here long."

He nodded with a furrowed brow. "Of course."

"Is there a ... holding room I can place him in until he and I have a word? Preferably away from others. I want to assure he is not a danger first."

Raiden glanced at his home. "Well, he can stay in the old wine cellar. It's in the back of the estate, away from the main quarters and fortified well. I will see to it."

"Thank you."

It was far more than she could ask of him. But Dyna had nowhere else to take Cassiel. They had a few things to sort through before she could finally move on.

Dyna expelled a heavy sigh. "Was there any word from King Leif?"

"It seems he had already been notified," Zev said, crossing his arms.

She frowned at that. "He knew of Rawn's capture? Since when?"

Raiden dragged a hand down his face, and she saw the weight there. "He had already received the word from Red Highland three days ago. He didn't wish to alarm my mother."

Dyna clenched her fists, her stomach turning with anger for the poor woman. "What else did they say? Is he...?"

Raiden's throat bobbed a bit, and she braced for the bad news she didn't want to hear. "The King only mentioned that he has dispatched an armed escort to bring us to the palace in Avandia, Greenwood's Capitol. It will arrive in five days."

"Five days?" She shook her head. "There is no time to waste! When we reach the palace, it may be too late to save Rawn. I say we leave tomorrow. I can sort my business with Cassiel tonight, and we will be on our way."

Zev put a gentle hand on her shoulder, a gesture of calm she didn't feel. "That is what I said as well, but we have to wait."

"Why?" Her throat tightened. Time was passing them by. The night breeze swept over the land, making the dynalya fields dance beneath the coming moonlight. "Every hour hastens Rawn's death. What could be so important to delay us?"

"My mother," Raiden said, and he took a breath as if coming to a decision. "She is the younger sister of King Leif."

The news struck Dyna silent. Lady Aerina was a *princess*. Her mind spun as things now started to make sense. Why Rawn had kept silent about his past and his status as a Duke.

"Over a score ago, my father had been assigned to my mother's protection detail. His mission was to take her away to safety, for she was a very valuable pawn when my uncle's hold on the throne was weak. Red Highland made plans to force her hand in marriage so they may bring the Vale of the Elves under one rule again. *Theirs*. My father thwarted their plans, of course. I will spare you the details, but in the end, they were wed instead. This has protected her, but recently suitors from every province far and wide have been coming to our door to bid for her hand in marriage. And they are becoming ... insistent."

Dyna's mouth fell open. "But she is married to Rawn."

"Lord Norrlen has been absent for far too long," Zev said. "Most have assumed him dead, and once the news of his capture spreads..."

"My mother will be in danger again," Raiden said, looking out at the land of Sellav. She noticed the Norrlen guards on duty had doubled on the fortifications of the estate and on the road.

Lady Aerina was a prize.

With her hand, her next husband would gain a dukedom, wealth, this province, and a line to the throne of Greenwood.

They had to wait for the escort.

Rawn would want his family safe first.

Raiden crossed his arms as the wind tousled his long hair. In the moonlight, he resembled Rawn so much it gave Dyna goosebumps. "The Red King will keep my father alive."

"How do you know?"

"It stands to reason, for Red Highland to notify Greenwood of who they hold, it's for a purpose. They seek to exchange an elf of great value for something far more crucial." Turning away, Raiden marched for the estate. "I intend to find out what it is."

Dyna and Zev watched him go.

"How are you feeling?" he asked her softly.

She closed her eyes. "I don't know if I can put it into words yet."

Her body was tense. A ball of emotion writhed in her chest, tangled with the strands of her frayed bond that had not stopped pulsing since she confronted Cassiel.

"I assume there is a reason why you didn't permit them to reclaim Cassiel."

Dyna looked up at the moon gleaming in the starry sky. The Legion circled above, awaiting their king's return, and they wouldn't wait long.

"I must do something, Zev. I am not going to like it, and neither are you."

CHAPTER 44

Rawn

The echo of Aerina's voice brought Rawn back to consciousness. He blinked up at the wooden ceiling, not sure if he was still dreaming. The throb of pain in his body settled that question. The overcast sky past the bars of the carriage cell was dark and dreary. He was slumped awkwardly against the wall, and his vision struggled to clear as the cell rocked over the uneven earth. The emptiness in his stomach made him feel nauseous. To feel that meant he was alive.

"I thought you'd never wake."

Rawn turned his head limply and spotted another sitting across from him, with his hands bound in chains. "Elon?"

The red elf narrowed his amber eyes. "I should have killed you in Little Step."

Rawn looked over the bruises on Elon's face and dried blood on his torn clothes. "You were apprehended."

Elon's magic had not been enough to fight his way out of Argent. It was clear he was a powerful soldier, but so were the elves of Red Highland. He couldn't fight against so many.

The air smelled of mud and incoming rain. The clomp of horses, distant voices, and the creaky wheels of the carriage cell were a steady hum in Rawn's ears. Two soldiers on horses guarded the rear. Their snarling Bloodhounds watched them closely with eerie yellow eyes.

"How long have I been unconscious?" Rawn asked faintly under his breath.

"Four days." The elf regarded him indifferently. "Death nearly came for you."

He had been ready for it to take him. It nearly did when Fair died.

The reminder of his horse being struck down made Rawn's chest ache. Struggling to sit up, he winced at the pressure on his leg. It had been bandaged with a poultice of Elvish herbs, as well as the other wounds where he had been shot. The fabric used for his bandages matched Elon's tunic.

"You treated my wounds." He blinked at him. "Why?"

Elon made clear his only priority was his family.

"Anon needs you alive." Elon tossed him a waterskin. Beneath the slosh of water, he added so quietly Rawn barely heard him, "So do I. We are escaping the next chance we get."

That shook Rawn to full alertness.

When he had been captured, there had been no hope of escaping, but there was now that he wasn't alone. Rawn looked out at the grassland they were traveling through. Twilight had come, obscuring the land, but he knew they were headed west.

He took a drink, and the cool water soothed his dry throat. "How far are we into Ledoga?"

"Midway. A day or two from Naiads Mere." Elon's amber eyes looked back at him knowingly and a stretch of quiet fell between them.

"You know of the waterways..."

Naiads Mere was a kingdom in and of itself, and it had many underground caves with waterways that flowed southeast, most crossing into his homeland. But it was supposed to be a Greenwood secret, and Rawn didn't know how he felt about a red elf with that knowledge. Or how he came to have it.

"Sylar," he realized. That must have been how they had escaped Red Highland. The waterways were dangerous, and it would take two to navigate them.

Elon looked away to the nearly full moon rising in the sky. "Do we have an understanding, Lord Norrlen?"

"A plan, you mean." Rawn's chains jostled as he moved closer to the bars.

Past evening's veil, he could distinguish the silhouette of the Anduir Mountains. He pictured the day he left Sellav, Aerina watching him go with their boy in her arms.

If they could reach the waters of Naiads Mere, he would make it home.

TWENTY-FIVE YEARS AGO

Once Rawn had brought Aerina to safety, he spent five days pursuing Anon's trail across Greenwood. Each waking hour, he prayed to the God of Urn for speed, holding on to the hope that he wouldn't be too late.

In the hills of Lothia, Rawn found Nisa's body.

They mutilated and defiled his sister nearly beyond recognition. Her nude body had been drained of blood. The letters of Anon's name were carved into her chest. Her cheek had been flayed open, removing the tattoo she once proudly bore.

And they took her eyes.

Falling to his knees, Rawn filled the hills with his ragged screams. He screamed until his throat was raw and he had no more tears to give.

Then he hunted.

He didn't sleep. He didn't eat.

Rage drove him as Rawn down every Force Sentry he could find before they ever reached the East Wall. Each one suffered the pain his sister suffered threefold. Their blood seeped into his pores. It coated his armor and soaked his cloak. To the point, his people now called him *Isemrac Arabmos.*

The Red Shade.

For all of Rawn's efforts, Anon had slipped through his fingers, and he never found Sylar. Perhaps it was a blessing not to see what they had done to his best friend. The mission was an utter failure. He didn't protect the princess, and it cost the lives of the only two people he had in the world. Rawn could never forgive himself for this.

"You have honored your kingdom," King Leif said. "Now I will bestow an honor on you. Whatever position you wish to have here in the castle or in my army, it is yours."

Rawn didn't look up from where he knelt at the steps of the dais. He felt Aerina's eyes on him, but he stared blankly at the runner.

Honor?

Whatever shred of honor he had was lost during his rampage of vengeance. He was filthy. Rawn felt it in his soul. He wasn't worthy of any honor.

The distant chimes of bells came from outside, where all of Greenwood feasted and reveled, celebrating their victory over Red Highland. All the while, his sister and best friend rotted. What kind of victory was this?

"The king awaits your answer," his father said.

Even the sharp edge was missing from his tone. Shadows lined the General's face. The only signs of any grief he felt for his lost daughter. Eldred had taken a leave of absence to mourn his son.

"I ask for nothing, sire…" Rawn murmured.

"You have completed your mission and deserve a reward. Ask of me any position. Be it a knight or a Ranger, even a Crown Sentry as my Red Shade. Whatever you desire will be yours."

He had no more desires. They died with his sister.

Sighing at his silence, King Leif rose from his throne and came down the steps of the dais. "Well take some time to think about it. You have been through a trying time, soldier. Greenwood's princess is alive and well, thanks to your efforts. We are celebrating your great deeds tonight. Go and enjoy yourself."

Rawn bowed as Leif and his father headed for a side door, followed by his Kingsguard.

"Are preparations underway?" Leif asked one of his attendants.

"Yes, sire. Lord Karheim has chosen a spring date for the wedding. That is enough time to…" Their voices faded as they went into the hall, leaving him alone.

Or so he thought until a small pair of slippered feet came to stand in front of him.

"Rawn…"

His weary eyes closed at the sound of Aerina's soft voice. Her dynalya scent stirred around him. Rawn stood, but he didn't lift his gaze.

"I … I had a chest made for Nisa and Lowenna … for their ashes." Aerina handed him a polished box made of fine wood. It shone under the chandelier lights. It was gilded in gold, exquisitely carved with a horse galloping in a field of flowers. "They rest together now."

The emotion in her voice made his throat clamp and his vision sting. He accepted the small chest.

"I am sorry Nisa's life was cut short. It was not right."

It was the first lament that sounded genuine.

Not *"Sorry for your loss,"* or *"She is in a better place."* But sorry that she didn't live the life she was meant to.

Silence filled the throne room again as he waited to be dismissed, but she wasn't finished.

"Rawn…"

"Have you told him?" he asked flatly.

She fell silent.

Rawn shut his eyes tight, and the back of his eyes stung. "Have you seen a healer?"

Anon had placed a spell on her. One examination would confirm if she had been cursed as well.

"I have," Aerina admitted quietly, and her voice held the answer to his fears. In as little as two words, it fully struck him the magnitude of his failure. "Rawn, will you look at me?"

He had to swallow a few times before he could reply. "I cannot."

"Why?"

"Allowing myself such an indulgence is what led to me now carrying what remains of my sister in a box, Princess."

Rawn's reply had come out sharper than he intended. It wasn't Aerina he was angry with, but with himself. He let his guard down that night. If he had been on alert, instead of behaving like an infatuated fool, Nisa would still be alive.

"You are not to blame, Rawn."

He clenched his teeth. "Please, I cannot bear that lie. We both know I am."

"Merely because we enjoyed a night for ourselves? Prince Anon was already waiting for me. They had hidden in the woods. Whether they caught me while I-I had to—" She stuttered. "Relieve myself—or if they ambushed us on the road, the confrontation was inevitable."

"You were alone because I was not on duty as I should have been."

Her voice grew pained. "If you wish to blame someone, blame me. I didn't wake anyone to accompany me, and it led to my abduction—"

"No." He wouldn't let her take that from him.

"Rawn." Aerina took his arm. "Please look at me."

He inhaled sharply at the touch of her hand and stepped back.

"Why?" she asked desperately.

Because he loved her.

Because it was wrong.

Because he needed to let go.

"Do you know … I have watched you as often as you have watched me?" Aerina whispered.

Rawn stilled.

"You were a secret in my heart. I never dared to speak it aloud, knowing it could never be, but Nisa saw right through me." She laughed weakly. It was a breathy sound, and he fought back the choke of tears. He felt them burning behind his eyes at the sting gathering in his throat. Her confession left him astonished. To think this whole time, she had felt the same. "The night we danced was the first night I was not a Princess of Greenwood. I was only Aerina. But I am called back to my gilded cage. I am to marry soon and secure my brother's position. I will do my duty and leave my home ... if there is nothing for me here."

Rawn lifted his head and met her wet blue eyes. Aerina looked beautiful in a cream gown, her blonde hair woven up and adorned with a gold circlet encrusted with emerald gems.

Hope swam in her gaze as she searched his blank face that was empty of any emotion. She took a step forward. "Rawn—"

He stepped back and fixed his gaze on a point past her shoulder. "It was only a dance, Princess."

"You don't mean that..." Her hands shook. "My heart aches whenever I see your face. I have dreamed of you since we were children, praying for a future where we could be. Please tell me you feel the same for me. That I have lived in your thoughts as you have lived in mine."

Oh, how Rawn had wished to hear such words in the past. But they condemned him now.

Swallowing, he forced himself to say, "There is nothing I can offer you but my undying fealty, Princess. I wish you every happiness in your marriage with Lord Karheim."

Rawn's answer sliced through the threads of his heart. It rebuked him when delicate tears spilled down Aerina's cheeks.

He closed his eyes as she fled the throne room, leaving him with the weight of his remorse.

CHAPTER 45

Cassiel

Cassiel sensed her before he opened his eyes. His heart rate quickened as he peered through his lashes. His vision was unclear, his eyes heavy. He winced at the ache throbbing in his skull. Where was he? How long had he been unconscious?

He swallowed and licked his dry lips. The shift of his arm met resistance and the clink of metal. He was in shackles and fastened to a brick wall with much thicker chains.

Dyna's cool voice drifted from the shadowed corner. "Those are made with Skath metal, so don't bother attempting to break them."

His pulse immediately leaped at the sound. A single candle rested on top of a set of barrels, casting flickering patterns on the stone wall. His mate sat on a bench with her arms and legs crossed, her face draped in shadows.

She was a hallucination, had to be.

Because he couldn't fathom what it meant for them to be standing in the same room.

"I had time to think about what I would say if I ever saw you again," Dyna said. "But now that you are here, I find I have nothing to say except one thing." She was in front of him in an instant, and the icy touch of her blade met his throat. "Remove the barrier."

The weight in Cassiel's chest deepened, pulse racing in his veins at the sight of those emerald eyes as sharp as jagged gems. An invisible fist gripped his heart until he couldn't breathe. "Dyna…" Her name caught in his throat, and the back of his eyes stung. "You're real."

"As real as this knife. Now remove the barrier, Cassiel!"

He blinked at her shout, taking in the fury in her eyes, the burning against his throat, and her shallow breath on his skin. Her shield on the bond was so solid, he didn't feel any of her emotions through the fragments of their bond.

But he saw them on her face.

It carried the full force of her rage, and he finally realized that she knew exactly what he had done.

She remembered.

Everything.

"You're real," Cassiel said again with sudden clarity. "When did you regain your memories? I had no sign."

Dyna sneered. "You think I would give you one? Only so you would return to do it again?"

It was the hatred burning in her eyes that finally made everything fall clear for him.

Cassiel shook his head, his chest heaving. "Dyna, I ... I'm sorry. I—" His throat clamped shut, and he had to force himself to breathe. She was looking at him with such disgust he was desperate to say the right words, and terrified to say the wrong ones. "Your magic is a beacon. They would have kept coming after you until you were dead. I had to make them believe you already were. The barrier was for your protection. You were supposed to stay dead to the rest of the world, but you came to Nazar. You exposed yourself to everyone..." His voice caught as he felt a sudden fear for her safety. "Why would you do that?" he exclaimed. "Why would you show yourself?"

"Because I had to," Dyna said tightly. She looked away, as if she couldn't look at him, as if his presence offended her. "I wanted nothing to do with you anymore, but not even I could escape what you have become."

His eyes widened as he recalled what she had done to stop him. The things she must have seen him do...

Cassiel's quiet question fell in the silence. "What happened after you rendered me unconscious? Did they hurt you?"

"No one was keen on challenging me once they witnessed our *reunion*. I am now the Queen of Fire." Dyna retorted as though she found it absurd, but he couldn't think of a better title.

The way she had appeared in the smoke, encompassed in green flame as she walked through his Seraph fire—there existed no other way to describe her.

"Lord Gadriel was merely glad to be rid of you." Her hard gaze rose to him again. "As will I be once you return to me what you stole."

The day he constructed the barrier and erased her memories was still clear in his mind, carved into his bones. And as Cassiel looked at her, he found she was no longer within his reach.

"I—" He cut off at the ice-cold steel pressed at his jugular.

She lifted his chin with the tip of the blade. "You have three seconds to drop the barrier before I slit your throat."

Every word dripped with venom. She was a gorgeous fury, and he would have happily died in her arms if she were the last thing he saw. But at the tremble of the blade against his pulse, he knew that wasn't his fate today.

"You won't kill your mate," Cassiel sighed. "You can't."

"I am not your mate!"

The rejection punched him in the gut, yet he could only smile miserably. To simply be in the same room as her sent currents through the bond and the brittle remnants of his soul. It sang weakly in recognition and plea.

"This hum in my chest says otherwise."

Gritting her teeth, Dyna let out a frustrated groan that was part scream.

Cassiel didn't bother bracing. He was desperate to feel any other sort of pain other than the constant agony of the dying bond in his chest. "Do it," he whispered.

Backing away from him, Dyna's mouth trembled with shaky breaths. They stared at each other as she clenched her jaw tight.

Then she said, "As you wish."

Setting down the knife, Dyna tore off her corset and began to unbutton her tunic and kick off her boots.

His eyes widened. "What are you doing?"

The tunic dropped with a flutter at her feet. She pulled at the stays of her leather trousers next.

Dyna smiled shrewdly. "Torturing you."

His pulse climbed at the sight of her bare legs and the glimpse of soft cleavage from her white camisole and undergarments. Crimson locks fell in soft waves around her shoulders dusted with freckles. Cassiel swallowed, this throat drying.

Picking up the knife, Dyna returned to him and ran fingers up his chest over his racing heart. "Where should I start?"

He inhaled a ragged breath at her familiar honeysuckle scent. The bond burned with want. To have her so close after so long arousal instantly swam through him.

"Here?" Dyna traced the knife's cool hilt over his collarbone, making goosebumps sprout on his skin. "Or here?" She tapped the flat side of the blade against her thigh.

Cassiel blinked. "What—" She jabbed the knife into her flesh, stifling a scream. "Dyna!"

She ripped out the knife with an angry whimper. "Where else?"

Cassiel shuddered with panic breaths as her pain echoed through him. "What are you doing? Stop this!"

Holding his gaze, Dyna winced as she drew the knife above her belly button. Bright red rivulets dripped down her pale stomach.

"Dyna, stop!" The chains clanked as Cassiel jerked wildly against them to get to her. "Please, stop!"

He watched helplessly as the blade sliced down the outside of Dyna's left shoulder to the top of her wrist. Next, she cut herself from her ankle to her thigh.

His stomach churned when he realized she was cutting herself in every spot he had written a vow.

"No more!" He strained against the chains. "Please..."

She lifted the knife to her neck. "Do it!"

Cassiel winced from her scream. "All right," he said shakily. "You win. Come here."

Dyna hesitated to get any closer. She didn't trust him. How could she? The question only made him feel hollow inside.

"To remove the barrier, I have to touch you..." Cassiel lowered his gaze to the floor. "...in the same manner in which it was placed."

With a kiss.

Dyna recoiled. The distress in her body was so great he wanted to die.

"Upon my word, you have nothing to fear from me."

"Your word?" Her eyes became sharp as the jewels they resembled. "I have already seen what your word is worth."

He shut his eyes.

"Zev and the others are standing outside." She nodded to the wooden door beside him. "If I sense even a hint of your compulsion, they will come in here and finish it."

It was clear from her tone what she meant by that.

He nodded once.

Dyna watched him another second longer, then she took a staggering step towards him, and another until they were inches apart. "I am only doing this to recover what you stole from me. I will despise every second of it."

His gaze dropped to her lips. "I know."

Cassiel inwardly quivered at her nearness, taking in the flecks of gold in her irises and the constellation of freckles on her cheeks. She had changed. Her body was lean muscle and an aura of assurance in how she carried herself. The softness that had once been there was gone.

Rising on her toes, Dyna clutched the front of his coat and pressed her mouth to his. He inhaled sharply at the touch, even if it was hard and cold. Sighing, his lips moved over hers slowly. She was stiff and unresponsive, and he mourned the possibility she may never allow this again. His wings gently pulled her closer, and she finally leaned against him. Her arms snaked around his neck, melting into him as if she couldn't help herself, or perhaps for support.

She kissed him harder. It was wild and crushing and angry. It startled him because he didn't know she could kiss like that.

The frayed bond trembled, shaking awake. It rejoiced to be near his mate after so long that he didn't care. He would take any excuse to touch her ... when it may very well be the last time. The thought made the back of his eyes burn.

Cassiel soul searched, and her bright soul did not greet him as it used to. Its green light was dim, nearly swallowed in the darkness. It almost made him stagger to see the damage he had done. Dyna's nails dug into him, reminding him of her demand. He searched past her soul, coming upon the door of her shield, barred by steel and fire.

He dared not look at what lay there. Cassiel only searched for what he came to do. And he found it. A colossal wall that contained her magic. The barrier had several cracks across it, as though a giant had beaten against it, eager to break free. There was so much anger in each fracture, she eventually would have gotten through.

Because no matter how scared Dyna was, how helpless, or lost, she had a tenacity that didn't allow her to give up.

White light flared between their lips as Cassiel tore down the barrier brick by brick. Tendrils of green light danced in the edges of his vision as her Essence broke free like a river tearing through a dam. He felt warmth flood her body, coating her soft skin. He wasn't sure if it was due to her magic returning or because of him.

How he wished it was because of him.

Once the barrier vanished, Dyna wrenched herself off him, stumbling back, both of them panting. Her eyes were wild as she wiped her lips. Her hands shook, her complexion was horribly pale.

Cassiel felt the world tilt. The strength left his legs, and he almost fell back against the wall. But it wasn't him.

She made a sound before her eyes rolled, and she crumbled to the ground.

"Dyna!" Seraph fire flared at Cassiel's hands, and the chains snapped clean off. He gathered her small body in his arms, brushing away the single tear rolling down her temple. She had lost too much blood. This was how far she would go to get her magic back?

He buried his face in her neck, feeling like an absolute waste. "I'm sorry."

Standing, Cassiel gently laid her on the wooden bench before quickly fetching the knife. He sliced open his forefinger and spread his blood over her shallow wounds. The surface of his skin tingled with each touch as the slashes seamlessly healed. He waited, watching her face as he checked her pulse. Dyna's complexion gradually returned to normal, and her breathing evened out. With his awakened power, it didn't take long to heal others anymore.

There was a small cut above her eyebrow, but when he reached for it, Dyna's glowing eyes snapped open.

A blast of Essence hurled him back with a powerful force. He caught himself before he crashed into the wall.

Green light glowed off Dyna's skin, illuminating her eyes as her magic charged the air. She rose to her feet. "Never again, Cassiel."

There were so many declarations behind that statement.

Never to heal her.

Never to touch her.

Never to kiss her.

But he knew the main one of all.

Cassiel held up his hands to yield, making the manacles softly clink. "I was not—"

"If you ever use your power on me again, I will hurt you far worse than you have ever hurt me." They were biting words behind clenched teeth, laced with her anger. Beneath it all, he heard the well of hurt and betrayal.

His throat tightened.

"Lev sheli—" Cassiel took a step, but she jerked back with a hiss.

She didn't want him anywhere near her. That fact alone caved in his chest, and he felt like he couldn't breathe. His mate ... couldn't stand him anymore.

All his life, Cassiel had been despised and loathed. That had been due to what he was, and there was nothing he could change about that.

But Dyna despised him now for what he *did*. That truth hurt worse, knowing he had earned it. Cassiel forced himself to stay put, even if he was desperate to be closer to her.

But if he tried, she may kill him.

Vicious rancor came off her in waves so strong he felt it like a stifling summer heat.

Keeping her harsh gaze on him, Dyna retrieved her clothing. "Turn around."

He obeyed. Holding still, Cassiel listened to the wet peel of the bloodied fabric before it plopped on the stone floor. Followed by the soft whisper of cloth. The sound elicited memories.

White fabric sliding over her navel.

The graze of fingertips on his feathers.

Quiet words breathed against the curve of a neck.

"Where is Lord Jophiel?"

He stiffened at the sudden question. "Why do you ask?"

At the soft scrape of boots on the floor, he turned around.

Dyna stood across the cellar from him, now dressed, with her arms crossed. "Answer the question."

Cassiel's gaze dipped to the dried blood left on her fingers. They drummed against her arms, waiting. "He sits in a dungeon in Hilos where he awaits inquisition ... for conspiring against the crown."

The words made him sick.

Even his uncle had turned against him.

Dyna stared at him incredulously. "Surely, there must be some mistake. Did he plead his case?"

Leaning against the wall, Cassiel crossed his arms. "Of course, but his actions could not be denied. He claimed my father had ordered him to place the witch bangles on me, which was a lie. Thereafter, he insisted Zekiel had given them to him by royal command."

Her brow furrowed. "You believe Lord Jophiel was part of the coup? Or was it made to appear that way?"

"My uncle is no fool," Cassiel said tightly. The subject still stung, and he clenched his jaw to keep his ire from surfacing. "I cannot accept that he would not have seen through such a ploy. He had to be part of it. For why else would he subdue my power the night before I was challenged? Why bring Zekiel and Gareel to Skelling? Why did you have a matching bangle placed on you at the lake?"

Dyna fell quiet as she mulled over that. How he wished to have a glimpse of her thoughts. All that remained was empty silence where her presence used to be.

After a moment, she shook her head. "I simply cannot believe it."

"The evidence was irrefutable. He was part of the coup to see me dead."

His uncle had been his surrogate father, the only one who spared him any care. And yet to find none of it had been genuine only made him feel more worthless.

Dyna's expression flickered with something. "Whatever may have happened, I know one thing for certain. Lord Jophiel loves you like a son, and he told me so with a truth bell in the room. He couldn't have lied to me."

Cassiel shook his head, immediately dismissing that. Because he couldn't accept the possibility that he had been wrong.

Dyna leisurely walked to the other end of the room, passing him with a thoughtful frown on her face. "Could it be that his judgment was impaired because he feared you, Cassiel? You were not exactly in control of your power in Hermon. Perhaps he felt as if he had no choice."

The moon had shone on Jophiel's face in the room that night, his eyes pained with regret. *I wish I did not have to be the one. But you have left us no choice..."*

Had it been done out of fear?

"After what I heard of what became of Skath, and what I witnessed in Nazar, he had reason to be afraid." Dyna turned to face him with narrowed eyes. "Your uncle is not the only one with impaired judgment. A king should know better than to attack his people or contain them without trial."

She lifted her foot and took a deliberate step backward into the wall.

But there was no wall.

The room rippled with the luster of glamor, and the door behind him vanished, revealing a dingy wine cellar.

And him, standing within a cage.

Cassiel inhaled a sharp breath, and he ran for her. "Dyna!"

She yanked the cell door closed with a loud *clang*. Zev and Lucenna appeared behind her, their expressions cold. They lurked in a dark hallway leading to a shadowy set of stairs.

"What is this?" Cassiel gripped the bars. "What are you doing?"

"I may have lied about the chains, but this cell truly is constructed with Skath metal," Dyna said.

It was. He could feel the divine power within the craftsmanship of the steel. With a wave of her hand, green light coated the cell, imbuing it with her magic, assuring he couldn't break free.

Cassiel's chest compressed under the weight of shock, his lungs struggling for air as panic bubbled up his throat. "Don't do this."

"I did you the kindness of providing a window." She motioned to a small gap in the wall near the ceiling. It was level with the ground outside, the sky barely visible past a tuft of grass.

"No." Out of fury and desperation, Cassiel hit the bars, and they pulsed with green light, knocking him back. A shaky breath heaved from his lungs as he got to his feet again. He stared at her, still in disbelief that she would do *this* to him. "You don't understand the danger you're in now that the Realms know you're alive. I need to be free when they come!"

"I can take care of myself," Dyna said as Zev and Lucenna headed for the stairs. "If you want out of your cell, you will free Lord Jophiel of his."

She turned away.

"Dynalya." Her name trembled on his lips. He gripped the bars with shaking hands. "You ... you locked me in a *cage*."

She paused with her back to him for a moment. Turning slightly, she looked at him over her shoulder with pain shining in her teary eyes. "It's no different than what you have done to me."

Then she ran.

"Dyna? Dyna!" Cassiel's voice chased her down the hall until the wine cellar doors slammed shut behind her.

CHAPTER 46

Cassiel

assiel idled between waiting for Dyna's return and wondering if she ever would. His back felt cold and stiff where he sat beneath the slit of a window. He leaned over his folded legs as he watched the bars cast lined shadows on the floor.

There is a difference between justice and revenge, his uncle once told him. Perhaps he deserved to be here.

Cassiel circled the cell, testing that every bar was fused tight. It was recently built and made with enough space that it didn't feel stifling. But how did she acquire Skath metal? How did she know where he would be and what he had been up to? Someone had been feeding her information.

Where was he? There was nothing in the old wine cellar but bland stone, a bed, a blanket, and a chamber pot for his shame.

The only window near the ceiling was no larger than a brick, and it provided no hint of his location. He could see nothing but grass and a patch of sky. There was no telling how long Dyna had kept him unconscious or how far she had taken him from Nazar. Evening light made its way in, leaving patterns on the floor for his only company with the thoughts that were loud in his head.

His boots scuffed the stone floor as he paced. Now he was trapped here while she could be killed at any moment. Muttering a curse, he aimed a kick at the barred door but halted when he remembered the repercussions. Looking at his feet reminded him of the pins fastened into his boots. Cassiel yanked one off and felt around the gilded embellishments built into the counter above the heel, but he found nothing.

The pins were gone. Both of them.

Blinking down at the empty groves, half-manic laughter bubbled up his throat. He couldn't help it. Cassiel gripped his hair, pulling at his scalp until it stung. *Clever girl.*

He pitched his boot across the room, and it thudded violently against the wall across from him. Dyna knew him too well.

And she knew what this would do to him.

Clenching his shaking hands into fists, Cassiel forced himself to take a shallow breath. His chest felt too tight, and he was nauseous. It was an adequate punishment, he told himself. If she left him in here to rot, who could blame her?

Cassiel's legs buckled, and he slid down the wall with his back against it. His mind was a mess of memories from their past life and their present one. So many, some bright and some dark, some missing and so confusing, it made his head hurt.

He never did tell her the truth of who he was and why he did this. Cassiel had thought he could erase it all by erasing them. But he should have known his stubborn, maddening, incredible mate would never let him get away with that.

He should have told her the truth. But he couldn't, because her answer would be the same answer *Sheli* gave.

He heard an echo of two voices melding together, both sets of green eyes looking at him with complete love. One was spoken in spring and the other in winter. "*Through the darkness and through the flame, I'm with you, kohav...*"

Only one future waited at the end of that path. He couldn't bear to witness the consequences again, so he had convinced himself leaving was the best thing for them.

The only thing he succeeded in doing was making her hate him.

They all did, if Zev and Lucenna's cold expressions were any indication.

None of them realized what danger she was in now. He had to get out of here. His Valkyrie had to be nearby. Yelrakel wouldn't allow him to be taken, but the only one who could command her would be Dyna.

The Queen of Fire.

Never did she cease to surprise him.

She was a marvel.

Her power had held up against him, and Cassiel couldn't help feeling awed. It also gave him hope that she really could defend herself against what was to come. But *Sheli* had also been powerful, and it didn't prevent her death.

Cassiel winced at the horrid echo of the bond snapping in two. It was Kāhssiel's pain, embedded so deep in his soul, he still felt it.

He couldn't go through that again.

His entire body physically reacted at the thought. His stomach heaved, and his chest caved in as he struggled to breathe.

Cassiel pressed on his burning eyes as he recalled the day Dyna wept for him. He felt the shake in her hands, saw the shine in her wet eyes, pleading for him not to leave her. Over and over his mind plagued him with the image of betrayal on her face when he rejected the bond.

That agony lingered in his soul, like a wound that refused to heal. When he thought of her face that night, of all the cruel things he said, of how much pain he caused her, it strangled him. At the time, he told himself he could live with her hate, but he had not been prepared to see it.

And it brought him here.

Cassiel stared down at his hands blankly. A petal of Seraph flame wove through his fingers. Blue light glowed against the wall, making the shadows stretch. So many had fallen to his fire. That power had been easy to sink into. He could still taste it on his tongue and feel it like a current on his skin. It surfaced from within, rising like a feral creature of flame that urged him to eradicate all who defied him.

Maybe he had reason to fear you...

The way Lord Jophiel looked at him after Cassiel had nearly burned his brother alive had been one of fear.

Cassiel had been so caught up in righting wrongs and not allowing anyone to step on him anymore that he became the one who stepped on others.

Go on, Cassiel, Malakel had told him. *Show them who you are.*

And he certainly had.

Cassiel wrapped his arms around his knees and dropped his head over them. Like Kāhssiel, he had good intentions when he came to this world. He only wanted to do right, and to love who he was meant to love. But he had been deceived and lost too much. Was he wrong to try to prevent that from happening again?

This had all been for Dyna, and she put an end to it. Easily. Flawlessly.

He had often wondered why one Celestial would be given a True Bond while others weren't. It hadn't made sense to him before. What was the purpose of splitting a soul in two? *Elyōn* worked in mysterious ways, and not everything could be understood.

But he understood one thing.

The one to control your flame is not you.

They had been fused like steel, but he cut himself in half.

Half a man. Half a soul. Half a heart.

Without her to fill those places, what else could he become but a monster?

The tread of soft footfalls interrupted his thoughts, and shadows moved across the wall. He looked up at the tiny window with sudden hope.

"Little Prince."

Disappointment settled in the pit of Cassiel's stomach. "Sowmya."

Of course, it wasn't *her*. Dyna didn't want to see him. She could barely stand looking at him.

"How are you?"

"Well, I am trapped in a cage, Lieutenant. How do you suppose I am?" He narrowed his eyes at Sowmya's silence. "It was you, wasn't it? Your meddling brought Dyna to Nazar. You deliberately disobeyed a direct order. I commanded you to never show yourself."

Sowmya sighed. "You also commanded me to protect your mate at all costs, sire. It came to the point that exposing my presence required that."

There was something in her tone that made Cassiel pause. "Explain."

Taking a seat beside the small window, Sowmya told him of all she had witnessed while watching over Dyna since he left. Her nightmares. Her long, brutal days of training. Her spiral into depression and use of Witch's Brew. He felt sick as he silently listened to every danger she put herself in, from jumping through the Druid's portal to nearly getting herself killed on Tarn's ship.

"When did she break the compulsion?" Cassiel murmured.

"That very night."

He shut his eyes. Three months of living without each other, and neither of them had been spared the agony. He left so she could live, but Dyna hadn't been living. She had been merely existing.

Like him.

He did this to them.

How could he possibly think it was right?

Cassiel dropped his head against the wall. He didn't save her.

"I have been sent to ask if you have had enough time here," Sowmya said.

Enough time to decide if he would let his uncle go. Cassiel didn't know if Lord Jophiel was innocent, but Dyna was right. Sentencing required a trial. Honestly, he didn't have it in him to argue anymore.

He only wanted to see her. He couldn't do that while trapped here.

Cassiel sighed. "Do it. Notify Asiel of his father's location and send a squadron on the Pegasi to release him from the dungeons. My uncle can await my summons in Hilos."

"At once, sire."

"Will she come?" he asked, trying not to sound too anxious.

"I have not spoken to Her Highness. It is the wolf who sends her message. I was told you would be freed once she sees Lord Jophiel leave his cell."

How would she *see*? Unless Zev meant when Dyna received the news. Even with the speed of a Pegasus, the flight from here to Hilos would take a few days.

"For you, sire." Sowmya forced a small burlap sack through the window, and he caught it before it hit the floor. "Sustenance. To keep up your strength."

That alone told him he would be in here for a while more.

"Thank you, Lieutenant," Cassiel said, though he had no appetite for it. "Tell Zev I want to see her."

"I will attempt it, sire. He isn't exactly fond of me."

"Say it to her directly if you must."

If he could only speak to her. There was little chance Dyna would ever listen to what he had to say, but he had to at least tell her she didn't have to fear him. That was one thing he couldn't stand.

"Her Guardians keep her under guard," Sowmya said. "I am not permitted near the estate."

"Estate?" Cassiel blinked up at the window. "Where *are* we?"

That should have been his first question. He looked around the wine cellar for any clues, but it was all stone and dusty barrels stacked in the corner.

"Greenwood, sire. Sellav province. This appears to be the home of the elf."

"Rawn..." His brow pinched with further confusion. Suddenly, Cassiel felt as if he held only pieces of the story, and he was left to sort them through. "Why are they here? Tell me everything clearly."

Cassiel listened in dismay as the lieutenant described the encounter with the Red Highland soldiers in Dwarf Shoe and Lord Norrlen's capture. They had come here to notify his family, yet Dyna had been forced to step away from such a grave matter to deal with *him*.

As if she needed more reasons to despise him. Groaning, Cassiel rubbed the tension gathering in the center of his forehead. "Have you seen him?"

"Who, sire?"

"Yelrakel must have told you about my spy. He goes by Netanel."

Sowmya fell quiet, probably searching the sky or the branches for any winged forms. "I see no one," she whispered, lest someone hear.

"Netanel knows to remain out of sight, but he must be lurking somewhere about. If he arrives, allow him through. I must speak to him."

A drag of silence followed.

Cassiel wryly smiled. "Worried you will lose favor with the High Queen? I remember when you were once loyal to me."

Sowmya's boots shifted over the gravel as she stepped away. "I still am."

Then he heard the soft swish of wings as she flew away.

Cassiel spent the rest of the day blankly staring at the shadows slowly climbing the walls as the sun lowered into the evening. He sat there for hours, repeating everything that had happened in that cell.

Her words. Her expressions. Her movements.

Around and around, his mind spun with Dyna's face.

Never again.

He felt ill.

Maybe he needed to eat. Cassiel glanced at the small burlap sack with a sigh. Tugging it open, he found golden crumbles of manna bread wrapped in a cloth and a leather waterskin filled with rice milk. His favorites, yet he couldn't swallow more than a few bites.

His only thought was of the other half of his soul who had trapped him in a cage.

Dyna's voice hummed in his ear like the resonating ring of a bell. *It's no different than what you have done to me.*

A voice hissed his name. It startled Cassiel awake, finding the cellar dark and cold. He must have dozed off.

"Up here."

He glanced up at the tiny window above his head and smirked. "I knew you were near."

"I am the shadow at your side," Netanel said. The small opening only offered a view of his boots in the moonlight. "Having troubles with your queen, it would seem."

Sighing, Cassiel rubbed his aching temples. "I am, for a lack of better words, in confinement due to my misbehavior."

Netanel chuckled. "It may serve you to apologize. That is all they truly want."

He owed Dyna far more than that. "You are the last person who should advise me on my marriage."

"Perhaps you are right. Well, it wouldn't take much to free you of the wine cellar. We would be gone before anyone noticed."

Netanel could easily sneak in and pick the lock. But the moment Cassiel woke up in chains with his mate standing before him, he had already decided he was staying. "I have business here. I have another task for you."

"Of course, whatever you need."

Cassiel sighed. Logically, he should order Netanel to spy on Nazar, primarily Akiel. But he had other priorities. "Dyna's safety is your primary objective. Watch and listen for any who may attempt to come after her. I need you to help me keep her safe."

"It will be done."

"What's more, keep me informed on the situation with Lord Norrlen. I assume King Leif has the matter in hand, but I will lend my support if needed."

Netanel hummed. "It has been some time since Hilos and Greenwood have interacted. Since the reign of your grandfather, I believe."

"It may be time to reestablish the Accords. Meanwhile, guard the High Queen and this estate. If anyone comes near, I want to know. But you will *not* show yourself to her. She cannot know about you."

Dyna didn't trust him, and he didn't need to provide more reasons not to.

"Worry not, she will never see me," Netanel said as he stepped back. "However, I do not recommend keeping secrets from your wife, especially if you want to regain her affections."

Before Cassiel could reply, his spy left as quickly as he appeared.

CHAPTER 47

Dynalya

Odd how up until six months ago, the one thing Cassiel had feared was a cage. Now that he found himself in another once again, his old fear was drowned out by a new one.

That Dyna wouldn't return.

Two days passed in silence. Sowmya would briefly appear to bring him warm meals and water, provided by the estate, judging by the fine Elvish food. By the third day, he knew how many bricks made up the walls and how many bars lined his cage. With evening's arrival, Cassiel had grown restless. He paced back and forth, feeling as if the cell were shrinking.

Was this how his uncle felt? Locked away for months with nothing but his own thoughts?

Cassiel's pulse jolted at the sound of doors cranking open at the end of the hall. Halting in place, he stared at the main door, holding his breath.

The click of a lock sent his pulse racing. The cellar door opened—and his stomach dropped.

Zev stood in the doorway, his eyes bright yellow with his wolf. Cassiel wasn't sure what startled him the most. Zev's arrival or the indifference on his face. Not the anger, Cassiel expected that. It was a shock that they all clearly remembered him.

Dyna had broken his compulsion over everyone.

Cassiel couldn't help but feel astonished. But of course she repelled his power. The question of how was irrelevant. She had always been a wonder.

As he looked at his old friend, Cassiel braced himself for what would come next. "It's good to see you ... Zev."

The Lycan didn't answer. In his hand was a set of keys, and he used one to open the cage. At the motion of his chin, relief washed through Cassiel's stiff body. This must mean they were notified that his uncle was freed. He slowly stepped past the door into the hall. Zev walked on in silence, and he followed.

"How have you been?" he asked hesitantly.

"Be quiet," Zev rumbled. "I don't want to talk to you. I don't even want to look at you."

Well, he couldn't expect things to be the same. Yet it still stung.

As Cassiel watched his once friend walk away from him, something tightened in his throat. *I'm sorry.* He wanted to say so but knew it wouldn't be accepted. If anything, apologizing now would only provoke Zev.

Cassiel followed behind him in silence. They went up the stairs through another dusty storeroom, then through a set of heavy doors that opened to the side of a courtyard framed by trees. Storm clouds shrouded the sky and the fading light.

Their footsteps filled the silence as they continued around a massive building of white stone layered in green vines. From there, Zev took a path through the gardens until they finally reached the anterior of the estate.

But they didn't go to the front door. Zev turned his back to it, taking the wide gravel path to the wrought-iron gates. They were guarded by elves wearing the sigil of House Norrlen on their chest plates.

Beyond the gates, Yelrakel and a squadron waited for him.

"Wait," Cassiel slowed. "Where is Dyna? I wanted to—"

Pivoting back sharply, Zev grabbed his arm and hauled him away for the gates. The guards opened them, and Zev shoved him outside. "Go," he snarled through his bared fangs. "She relieves you of your service. You are a Guardian no more."

Cassiel shook his head, feeling a surge of panic. "But I—"

Zev turned away. "She has nothing to say to you."

"Wait!" Cassiel took his shoulder. "I can't go without seeing her first." Zev spun around with a feral growl. The Valkyrie rushed forward to defend him. At the raise of Cassiel's hand, they halted in their attack. "I know you're furious with what I did to her—"

"It wasn't only her, Cassiel. You betrayed all of us. You said you would be there. And you weren't." As they stared at each other, the anger wavered enough to see the hurt in Zev's yellow eyes. "We don't need you here now."

Cassiel lowered his gaze, knowing very clearly Dyna wasn't the only one he had hurt. "Please, can I see her?"

"No. You made a choice to turn your back on all of us. On *her!*" Zev jabbed a clawed finger at the estate. "*I* saw what it did to her. *I* witnessed her pain. *I* held her hand every night when she woke up screaming from the nightmares of you tossing her away!" Cassiel winced at each roaring accusation. Chest heaving with a harsh breath, Zev spoke evenly through his clenched teeth. "You broke her. You are too late to pick up the pieces. We did that."

Those words settled like bitter poison in Cassiel's stomach. He closed his eyes, because he couldn't withstand the disgust on his friend's face. "Please. I only need to speak to her."

"I don't care what you need." Zev's voice deepened with the rise of his wolf, and his claws grew. "Leave now, or you won't leave at all."

The threat was real.

Cassiel felt the force of his words and the anger seeping from his pores. The wolf was out, fangs bared. From the way Zev shook, he was seconds from tearing out his throat.

"I am not going anywhere," Cassiel said softly. "Hate me. I deserve it. Tear me apart if you wish. But I will leave when she commands it."

He stormed away. "Go. I won't repeat myself again."

"No."

Halting, Zev expelled a short, dry laugh at the sky. "Thank you," he said. "I was waiting for an excuse to keep *my* promise to you, after all."

He whipped around with a snarl. The Valkyrie moved in on swift wings like streams of gold. Their swords halted an inch from Zev's throat, and he froze, his chest heaving.

Cassiel fixed his sharp gaze on his general. "Did I say you could attack?"

Veins twitched on Yelrakel's forehead as she trembled against his compulsion. "But sire—" She cut off when her air did. "Forgive me..."

Utter disgust crossed Zev's face. "So this is the kind of king you have become. A tyrant who holds no bounds with how he uses his power. I don't know why I am surprised that you would take away their will when I watched you take away hers."

The words struck Cassiel deep in the pit of his stomach. He dropped his hold on the Valkyrie, and they retreated three steps, falling back into formation.

Tyrant...

It struck him more to hear Zev say it, and his next statement dismantled him. "I wonder what your father would think of you now."

Sharp pain clamped down on Cassiel's skull. The pressure was so strong, he nearly keeled over. A shallow breath passed through his lips, and he had the sudden urge to burn everything, including himself. If he became ash and faded with the next wind, would he have the chance to live life over again?

Cassiel pressed on his aching forehead. "Should he take my heart, let him keep it. He's not to be harmed—"

Zev grabbed him, claws poised at the center of his chest. Cassiel didn't fight it. His heart pumped steadily, unafraid.

Yelrakel tensed but didn't defy his order. Within the cover of the trees, Netanel watched him with a startled expression. Cassiel discreetly waved him back when he took a step forward.

Maybe he had been waiting for this. For someone to end his misery.

"Take it," Cassiel murmured. "It's useless, anyway."

"I should," Zev growled through his bared fangs. "Dyna survived a shattered soul. She would survive a broken bond, too."

That got a weak laugh out of him. "I know..."

Dyna was so undeniably resilient that if one day Cassiel left the world, she would undoubtedly muster the strength to go on without him. But surviving her loss?

He could never.

"Zev." The sound of her voice sent a current of energy through Cassiel's veins.

From the shadows of the estate's archway, two glowing green orbs appeared. Dyna stepped out into the evening light, and her bright gaze locked on the blood oozing from where Zev's claws had pricked his chest. "Remove your hand."

He did. *Immediately.*

Because they both sensed she was on the verge of attacking him. It was the instinct of a True Bonded mate to protect their other half. For her to still feel a sense of protection over him, however small, planted a kernel of hope.

"Leave us," Dyna commanded as she strode to the gates. Zev hesitated, but at her hard look, he headed for the estate with the Norrlen guards following. She glanced at the Valkyrie next. They sheathed their weapons and bowed to their High Queen, and Cassiel couldn't help but feel admiration.

"Sire, this area is not secured," Yelrakel said under her breath.

For her.

They were out in the open where an attack could fall any minute. His enemies wouldn't attack them on foreign soil and risk gaining Greenwood as an enemy. That didn't mean they wouldn't find a way around that. But Dyna didn't offer him to come inside.

"Form a perimeter in the sky," Cassiel said, not looking away from her.

The whoosh of wings and rush of wind was the only indication they were finally alone. His lungs constricted as he looked at her. Dyna stood only a short distance away with her arms crossed. She wore black trousers and a black corset over a white blouse. A short sword at her hip.

Cassiel had wanted to speak to her, but having her here now made his throat dry.

Dyna stared past him in stony silence, her red tresses flowing around her face with the breeze. "You wanted to be commanded, well, it's given. Leave and do not show yourself in front of me again."

Cassiel lurched forward when she turned. "Wait, please." He tried to take her arm.

"Don't," Dyna hissed, her eyes flashing with magic. "Go. I do not wish to speak to you."

"If I could only explain—"

"What is there to explain?" she snapped. "We went into this marriage with the promise that we would decide everything together. Nothing but the truth and our happiness as we made it. Yet you took back every single promise you made to me."

Cassiel shut his eyes. He had meant those promises, every single one. "I was trying to protect you."

"Gods, I am so sick of hearing that! I never wanted your protection, Cassiel. All I ever needed was you. Only *you*." Dyna's chest heaved with the tears she fought, her mouth bracketing with the words she wanted to scream at him. He felt them there, bubbling beneath the surface. Heaving a sharp breath, Dyna shook her head and backed away. "I have nothing else to say to you. Please go. I never want to see you again."

She turned around, and the panic set in.

"Wait, please. I must explain." Cassiel grabbed her hand out of pure desperation. And it was the wrong choice. Dyna whipped around so fast her palm struck him sharply across the face.

"I don't want to hear any more of your reasons!" Her ragged scream broke into a sob that he felt spear him through. "You were everything to me, Cassiel. I gave you all of me. I trusted you. I *believed* in you! Even after you stole my memories and abandoned me, I still waited all of winter for you." She pressed on her chest with a shaking fist as tears rolled down her face. "Some hopeless part of me still believed you would come back. And you never did."

His eyes welled, blurring his vision, because so many times he had dreamed of coming back. Of returning to her, only to wake and remember why he couldn't.

"Then I *hated* you," she said through a sob. "I hated you so much because you took away my choice. How could you do that to me?" She wept with every trapped emotion finally breaking free, and he bore it all. "What did I do to deserve that?"

He lowered his head, feeling the monumental weight of her pain fall on him.

Breath quivering, she said, "Why put a sword in my hand only to refuse to let me join you in battle? It was supposed to be us against the world. I didn't want to be protected and coddled. I wanted to fight by your side. That's what marriage is. A partnership. I would have chosen you no matter what. You were my heart, Cassiel, and you ripped it out of my chest with your own hands." The accusation tangled him in a web of thorns. Pain sank through his own withered heart in his hollow chest. She covered her face as she wept. "And don't you dare say you didn't have a choice. Because you did. You simply didn't choose me. Out of everything I have ever endured, nothing ever hurt as much as that."

Cassiel's face crumbled. To know that broke another piece of him. He gripped his hands to suppress the urge to reach out, because all he wanted was to hold her.

"I did choose you." His voice shook, taking everything to hold it together. "I'm so sorry, Dyna. I believed it was the only way to keep you safe."

"From what?" she demanded. "You didn't take the time to explain anything to me. You simply decided what *you* thought was best. I no longer have the heart to accept your apologies. It's far too late for that."

All the air left his lungs. Her pain was a mirror. It reflected the hurtful words he had flung at his father.

Was this his pain? His regret?

It was the life Cassiel lived because he had been blind to the truth. She also didn't know why he made those decisions.

"I felt like I was dying when Zekiel hurt you. Then I was fading when I pulled your frozen body from the lake." His voice broke. "They promised to keep coming for you until they cut you from my soul, and I could not bear that."

Again.

He couldn't tell her that part. That she had already died once because of him.

With desperation in his voice and tears in his eyes, he said, "Leaving you destroyed me. But I would go through whatever pain a million times over to protect you. That's how much I love you."

Dyna shook her head. She wiped her wet cheeks, and her face cleared of any emotion. "That's not love, Cassiel. That's fear, and I don't want it. I'm finished with fear. All it has done is take from me."

That's what fear did.

It stole. Lives. Hope. Futures.

And it hit him with a glaring realization of how much he had let it take from him.

"I'm sorry..." Cassiel took a step toward her, but she flinched back. "I'm so sorry I hurt you. I will never cease to regret that, Dyna." He took a small step toward her, and another. When she didn't attack him again, he gently took her in his arms, wrapping his wings around her. "You're right. Everything you say is true. Leaving you like that was the worst thing I could have possibly done. You were in so much pain I couldn't bear to leave you to suffer that. I thought if I erased your memories, you could start over. I thought you could be happy and safe if I was no longer plaguing your life." He murmured into her hair, burying his face in her neck. "I swear to you, it will never happen again."

For a split second, he hoped they could repair this, but she was stiff and motionless in his arms. Cold.

Cassiel lowered himself onto his knees and took her hands. "What can I do to earn your forgiveness?"

She stared past him impassively. "Did you reject our bond?"

"I did," he admitted faintly.

"Did you erase my memories against my will?"

He closed his wet eyes. "Yes."

When she spoke again, her voice had dropped to an impassive murmur. "How could you think I would ever forgive you?"

Cassiel's gut twisted into knots. He hugged her waist, pressing his face against her stomach. "Please," he wept. "Please."

She took a shaky breath. "I can't."

What those words did to him, they almost left him a mess in the mud.

Dyna removed his arms. All the emotion faded from her face with a low exhale. "What you did killed me, Cassiel. That girl you met in Hilos is dead. As far as I'm concerned, you are dead to me, too."

Like in the wine cellar, she took a deliberate step back across the threshold of the gates. With a flick of her hand, they slammed shut between them. Cassiel shook his head, reaching through the bars for her. The last time he was in a position like this, he had been a child. He was helpless to stop anyone from leaving.

A sob caught in his throat. "Dyna," Cassiel called to her retreating back. "I beg you."

"Beg?" Her next words were like ice on his skin. "Go on, then. *Beg me.*" Dyna looked him dead in the eyes, and the emptiness in them shook the foundation of his existence. "Beg me more than I begged you. But not even that will change my mind ... because you don't belong in my world. I don't want you in it. *I don't accept the bond.*"

Cassiel inwardly flinched at the attack of his own words. He bit back a groan as another strand in their fraying bond snapped. Only one remained. The main strand that tied them together, but everything that had constructed their bond was gone.

The shock of it stole all the air out of his lungs. Cassiel slumped back on his heels, watching the one who used to be his world walk away from him. Dyna went into the estate without looking back. The heavy doors shut behind her, and the shield dissolved away.

Tears rolled down his face as he thought of the sweet, innocent girl he once met in a forest. The one who smiled freely at him like he was *someone*. He was nothing to her anymore.

Part of Cassiel didn't want to believe this reality, yet he had no one to blame this time. Long ago, his mother once told him nothing lasts forever. Perhaps forever was a word meant for memories and not people.

But even memories didn't last.

CHAPTER 48

Dynalya

Dyna felt her strength vanish the moment Cassiel was gone from her sight. She was filled with such a keen sense of loss, it took all her will not to break down behind the front door. Her steps moved silently across the foyer, and worried eyes followed her. Her composure remained in place as she climbed the steps to her bedroom. Dyna walked through and shut the door. Her lungs spasmed with ragged breaths. A tear fell, then another, and she collapsed against the wall as she sobbed through it all.

Her body shook with it. Her legs gave out, and she dropped to her hands and knees. Her vision blurred, and droplets hit the floor beside her clenched fists.

It had been torturous to see him. Even more to say goodbye.

Lucenna knelt next to her.

A sob shuddered through Dyna's throat. "Why is it that I have my magic back, and yet I have never felt so helpless? It hurts. It hurts so much."

Lucenna hugged her tight, and she clung to her, trying to muffle her sobs. She cried uncontrollably, as if another part of her had died. It probably had. She didn't cry merely over the end of their marriage. It was everything that had happened since she walked out of the front door of her cottage.

Dyna wept for the girl she had been.

The day she left home, she was searching for the power to fight more than the Shadow, but the darkness within herself, believing somehow it would bring her happiness. Dyna thought she had found it when she met an enchanting prince in a glass tree who lured her into his life with a gentle melody.

But she was beginning to believe happiness was unattainable, and this was the extent of her life.

Twilight came and passed, draping the room in a dull darkness. Lucenna stood to light the hearth, but Dyna told her to leave it, and that she wanted to be alone. She didn't move from her spot against the wall or answer anyone coming to knock on the door. The storming skies rumbled with distant thunder. Eventually came the flash of lightning, and the glass doors of her balcony pattered with rain. For hours she sat on the floor, watching the deluge fall over Sellav.

Cassiel was still out there.

She could feel him.

Dyna shut her eyes. He said he would go if she commanded it. More lies.

A winged shape moved across her balcony, and Dyna braced, but it was only Sowmya. The Lieutenant slipped through the doors, her golden armor dripping wet.

Dyna sighed. "You're still here?"

"I am charged with protecting you, my lady." The lieutenant closed the balcony doors behind her. She paused by the curtains framing the south windows that faced the front of the estate. Her gaze flickered to Dyna, then to the floor.

She narrowed her eyes. "Speak your mind."

Sowmya hesitated before saying, "It's been raining all evening, my lady. This is unbecoming of a king."

"He decided to be out there, so leave him," Dyna said sharply. "You will not interfere."

Sowmya's mouth bracketed with disapproval, but she bowed her head at the command. It angered her. She was no one to bow to now.

"Why are you still here? Why didn't the Valkyrie leave? Why didn't *he* leave?" Dyna demanded. "Didn't you hear us?" She shut her eyes, feeling embarrassment and shame. The whole of Sellav must have heard her shouting. "I am not his queen anymore..."

"His Majesty cannot leave while you are not safe." Sowmya said. "I asked you to impede him, despite knowing it would put you in danger again. Now that the Realms know you are alive, so do his enemies. War is not coming, my lady. It has already arrived, whether you wish to be a part of it or not."

There was something in her tone that made Dyna stand. She walked to the window, keeping behind the curtains.

Cassiel was still on his knees, his gaze trained on her window. It was too dark inside for him to see her. Nonetheless, he sensed exactly where she was.

"You may not fight for him," Sowmya said, "but he will always fight for you."

Dyna followed her gaze to the shadowed forms moving through the dark trees that lined the main path. At first, she thought they were other Celestials, but they didn't have wings. Lightning flashed, exposing figures dressed in black armor. Their skin was gray, eyes reflecting yellow like reptiles in the night.

She gasped. "Are those elves?"

"Not elves," Raiden said quietly from her doorway. "Not anymore."

"What are they?" Dyna asked.

"May I join you?"

She nodded.

Entering her room, Raiden came to stand beside her and crossed his arms as they watched the shadows come closer. "Shades, we call them. They have walked through the veil of the Shadow God to embrace black magic, turning themselves into creatures of the night. They are fast and vicious assassins who lend their dark skills to those who would pay very highly for it."

A horrible chill swept down Dyna's back as she recalled what Rawn had told her. *There are elves who move through the shadows. They sever lives for the right price, and there is a substantial one for mine.*

"But why are they here?" she asked him. "Do they come because of your father, or because of the bounties on our heads?"

"No, my lady. They have come for *you*," Sowmya answered, and Dyna's breath caught. Cassiel had yet to move from his position. She had the urge to yell at him to run, but he stood, and his shoulders shifted with a deep breath. He already knew they were there. "My people do not have jurisdiction to enter Greenwood territory in any official authority without risking reprisal against the Realms."

It seemed Lord Raziel found a way around that. Akiel must have immediately notified him of her survival.

"You have enemies in high places," Raiden said.

Dyna swallowed, her pulse beginning to climb. "Forgive me, I never meant for this to happen. I have put Princess Aerina in danger." She moved to leave the room, but Raiden caught her arm.

"I hope you don't mean to go out there."

"I have to make sure they won't get inside," she said.

"There is no need."

A glowing gold light sparked outside the windows. It formed a line in front of the gates, and rapidly spread as it circled the entire estate. From it, a golden wall rose up until they were encompassed within an enormous, enchanted dome.

"Eldred has shielded the estate. No one will touch my mother—or you." At Raiden's definitive response, she glanced up at him, and he gave her an assuring nod.

Dyna was surprised he cared enough for her wellbeing as well, but it seemed Raiden had inherited his father's kindness.

They all watched the Shades creep forward like black ghosts to surround the only one standing between them and the estate.

"Your..." Raiden frowned, struggling to find the right word to label Cassiel. Not friend. Not husband. In the end he settled on, "Your Guardian would be better off flying away since he cannot call on reinforcements."

The Valkyrie couldn't join the battle on Greenwood land, yet Dyna didn't sense any disquiet from Cassiel. Her shield blocked all her emotions, but since they spoke, he had dropped his. Everything he felt was out in the open for her, and at the moment, the only thing he felt was calm.

"I wouldn't worry about him," Dyna said.

Cassiel's eyes flared to a vibrant blue, his flame glowing as bright as a forge. He faced the path, wind whipping his long black coat around his legs. Seraph fire blazed from his fists and wreathed his feet as he strode idly down the path.

Raiden murmured a shocked word in Elvish.

"His Majesty does not require reinforcements," Sowmya added, a hint of pride in her voice. "He is enough."

Two Shades flitted in a veil of black smoke, sighted only by the flash of steel of their blades. Dyna jerked instinctively closer to the window. They moved so fast, she blinked, and they were falling on him.

Cassiel vanished from view.

She gasped. Before she could ask where he went, Cassiel reappeared behind them, and his knife clashed against the blade of one of the Shades. He winked out of existence again, reappearing to parry the attack of another. It wasn't that he could teleport. Cassiel was moving too fast for her to see.

He hadn't done that in Nazar.

Sowmya nodded. "Witness the power of the true High King."

Dyna's brow furrowed at the way she put it.

What did she mean by *true*?

Cassiel's Seraph fire swept across the ground, dousing the area in flame. The firelight gleamed on his wings, lighting his silhouette. The Shades screeched and retreated beyond the smoke screen. But the fight wasn't over.

Blue embers hovered around Cassiel as he waited.

"Dyna." Zev rushed into the room with Keena on his shoulder. "Did you see?"

"Yes," she said, not looking away from the fight. "Where are the others?"

"Klyde and Lucenna are downstairs with Eldred, manning the front door. Von is with the guards."

She was pleased to hear of them working together, but Cassiel very well may not need any help.

They all huddled by the windows while watching in silence. She searched the dark trees. The dancing flames cast writhing shadows, making it difficult to distinguish anything.

Shades leaped through a black cloud and landed on either side of Cassiel. He parried their blades with incredible speed. His blade shoved through the stomach of one, and he turned to deflect the other. The wounded Shade leaped into the air with a wild screech as it came for him. Cassiel cast out his hand, and a torrent of Seraph fire turned the Shade to ash.

He faced the second one, drawing *Esh Shamayim* free. Beautiful blue flames spiraled around the divine blade. They ran at each other and flitted too fast for her to catch the moment they clashed. Cassiel reappeared as his sword swept down in a flash. His boots dragged through to the gravel, bringing him to a stop. The Shade stumbled a couple feet behind him, swaying on his legs before he dropped on the ground, and his body was engulfed in flames.

Minutes.

It only took minutes for him to kill them.

The way he moved, the agility and speed, it was unlike anything she had seen from him before. Every attack had been swift.

Instinctive.

Demise on wings of flame.

Cerulean fire wrapped around Cassiel as he shot into the sky for the Celestials flying his way. There were so many of them.

"You said they wouldn't come here," Dyna murmured to Sowmya.

"Assassins have no borders, my lady."

All this. To kill her.

"Should we help him?" Keena asked worriedly.

Dyna glanced at Zev, and he grimly looked back at her.

"No." The Lieutenant shook her head. "His Majesty would want you to stay here, where it's safe."

Dyna turned away from the window and sat on the edge of her bed, having no answer for either of them.

For three days, Cassiel was out there in the cold rain without food or shelter. Celestials came by day and the Shades came by night.

Cassiel slayed them all.

Why?

Why stay?

Why stay and fight for her after she tossed him out?

Dyna wondered as she stayed in her room, standing by the balcony. The estate was quiet. The guards stood on alert, nearly everyone watching Cassiel's battle from the windows.

Seeing all of this made her realize what kind of danger her life was truly in.

There was an inaudible awe in the air. All rendered speechless by the destructive beauty of his flame, turning everything to dust. Grass no longer carpeted the path. There were no more trees. No more *green*. Only smoke and ash.

But even the High King needed rest.

Cassiel stumbled as he cut down the last Shade. His legs wobbled, and he sank to his knees, breathing heavily.

Dyna moved to the balcony doors but halted with her hand on the knob. She closed her eyes. If she went to him now, she would never be—

Dyna gasped at the sudden tremble in her chest.

The bond.

Outside, on the charred path, Cassiel collapsed.

CHAPTER 49

Lucenna

Lucenna had little patience for pitiful things. Crossing her arms, she glowered at the matted High King covered in soot. His filthy clothes were torn, and he reeked of smoke. Curling her nose, she nudged his boot. He didn't stir, still unconscious where Zev had dumped him on the dusty bed last night.

Scowling, Lucenna kicked Cassiel's leg next. He woke with a jolt, looking around at the small cabin before noticing her.

"Lucenna..." He rubbed his forehead and winced. "What happened?"

"You collapsed. Exhaustion will do that to you." She tossed a waterskin and a dry bread roll onto his lap. "You're fortunate a part of her still cares. If it were up to me, I would have left you out in the rain."

Cassiel had nothing to retort back. Sitting up, he shifted his legs over the edge of the bed and raked the messy black hair out of his face. It was longer now, falling past his jaw. "Where am I? I half expected to end up in the cell again."

She would have liked that. But after he took down those Shades, it would be bad form to lock him up again. A tiny voice in the back of her head suggested perhaps Cassiel may have been justified, because the threat against Dyna's life was very real.

They all saw it.

And without him, they may not have been enough to protect her.

No more Shades came, though. Either because he had eradicated them all or they deemed the commission not worth risking their lives to collect. The Celestials were also being cautious.

"Lady Aerina was gracious enough to lend you the foreman's cabin," Lucenna said. "Even after you have destroyed her property. We haven't told her who you are yet. Do you realize why we are here in the first place?"

He nodded. "I heard about Rawn."

Her throat tightened as she thought of Lord Norrlen, dreading to imagine what he must have been enduring this past week. He must have arrived in Red Highland by now.

"We leave for Avandia tomorrow."

"The capital of Greenwood?" Cassiel blinked up at her. "Why?"

"We have a meeting with King Leif to discuss what can be done about Rawn's capture. And no, you are not welcome," she added when he opened his mouth to respond. "Rest here for today, but you need to be gone by first light." Lucenna pivoted on her heel for the door.

"I can't..." Cassiel rasped, his voice meek and defeated. "She's my mate, Lucenna."

She glowered at his reflection in the window. People who meant to be in your life would be. If it was so easy for him to leave, he gave up any right to be in Dyna's life. He had his chance.

"Not anymore." Maybe it was cruel of her to say, but Lucenna didn't care.

Still, she expected Cassiel to snap back, to be the Black Hearted Prince who used to argue with her over everything. But he looked more like a sad bird who could no longer fly. *Hmm, no demands today?*

His tired, red eyes blinked at the ground. "Let me see her. Please."

"Do you not understand?" Lucenna said. "She doesn't want to see you, Cassiel. Did you think taking out the Shades would absolve you? What you did broke her apart. Being around you now would only reverse everything she did to put her pieces back together." Even if they had not been put back in all the right places. Lucenna took the door handle. "Stay away from her, or we will hurt you."

She left the foreman's cabin, and Zev straightened where he had been leaning up beside the door with his arms crossed.

Klyde was on guard duty. He sat on a barrel on the other side of the door, sharpening his short swords with his sleeves rolled up, enjoying the spring breeze. The grinning skulls on the blue pommels glinted in the sunlight. "Don't you think you're being a little hard on him?" he said when they turned to go.

"Hard on him?" Zev growled. "We are being too soft on him. You know what Dyna endured."

"Aye, I do, mate. But I think we have forgotten how young Cassiel is. I was no wiser at his age, and I have done plenty of wrongs I wish I could take back. Can you stand there now and tell me you have never made a mistake you regret?"

The question left Lucenna stunned, because she could easily think of her greatest regret from two years ago, and she still carried those consequences. Zev was silent beside her, his fists clenched so tight blood seeped through his fingers. The scars from his manacles were waxy and horrid in the sunlight.

At one point or another, she knew he wished things had been different on that full moon night. To go back in time to change her mistakes was something Lucenna wished for every day, too.

Klyde nodded at whatever he saw on their faces and continued sharpening his blades. "We all have regrets. I think we can spare him a little kindness in that regard."

Sighing, Lucenna decided to let it go. She was mostly angry at what Dyna had gone through, but Zev's resentment ran deeper. He stormed away toward the garden. It would be harder for him to let go, because Cassiel had been his first true friend. And his betrayal had stung deep.

She frowned. "When is the King's escort going to arrive? It's been five days."

"Shouldn't be long now..." Klyde said, stilling when he noticed something past her shoulder.

Lucenna turned to see Dyna come out onto the terrace with Keena sitting on her shoulder and the former commander at her side. Tension immediately charged the air as Von and Klyde locked eyes.

Lucenna smirked. "I think you should also take your own advice, Captain," she said before going to join them. "All right?"

Dyna fleetingly glanced at the cabin. "There is a commotion at the gates."

Her heart leaped with hope. "Has the escort arrived?"

"I'm afraid not."

Frowning at the wariness in her tone, Lucenna and the others followed Dyna's quick stride through the courtyard to the front of the estate.

A mob of Elven nobles was gathered outside of the gates. All were dressed finely and handsome as most elves were, but they were arguing amongst each other and with the Norrlen Guards preventing them from entering.

"We have a right to see Her Grace!"

"I must know that she is safe and well!"

"Give her my name. That is enough to request an audience with her!"

Immediately, Lucenna was annoyed by their raised voices and demands. She might have thought them residents of Sellav, but the main path to the estate was lined with carriages and personal guards wearing the livery of the Houses they served.

Lucenna frowned. "Who are they?"

"Trouble," Dyna replied. She glanced at Klyde and Von. They nodded at her silent order, and headed for the estate, Keena fluttering after them.

"I take it these are the suitors Raiden had mentioned?"

"They must have heard about Rawn's capture and assumed Lady Aerina is a widow, or about to become one," Dyna said. "Now every eligible noble is petitioning for her hand. She was nearly taken by force once, and she is at risk of that happening again."

How dare they? Rawn was still alive, but they were already flocking around his wife and his land like vultures. Now they demanded to see her as if their nobility gave them that privilege.

They only saw Aerina's status as a means to raise their own. It reminded Lucenna too much of women in the Magos Empire being used as currency for power. They didn't have rights there as they did here.

"The others have gone to safeguard her in case anyone makes it past the guards," Dyna said.

Electricity crackled on Lucenna's skin. "I will flay anyone who takes a step past those gates."

They headed for the entrance at the same time Eldred appeared at the top of the stairs to the estate. He marched past them to the gate as Raiden galloped up the road on his white steed. He yanked on the reins, and the horse reared, making the nobles quickly draw back.

Raiden dismounted. "My mother is not available to see any guests."

"Until when?" one asked.

"Indefinitely," he gritted out. "I am the Lord of Sellav. If you come for a matter of trade or other relevant concerns, you may request an audience with me. Otherwise, get off my land."

Laughter broke out among the nobles.

"You? The Lord of Sellav?" The retort came from the tallest elf with light brown hair flowing down to his shoulders. A silver circlet on his forehead brought out the gray in his ashen blue eyes. He came to the front of the crowd, shadowed by guards dressed in armor, their chest plates marked with the same sigil of a sassafras leaf sitting above a half crescent of stars embroidered on his cape. "I have horses older than you, lordling. They would better serve to protect Sellav, as we all see the very poor state

your land is in." He curled his nose at the charred earth. "There have been rumors of all sorts of ... ill *guests*... stirring conflict in these parts." His gaze traveled over Lucenna and Dyna, his mouth curling. "Yet we are no more welcome than whatever miscreants you have allowed through your door."

Eldred gave them a look. "Stay here," he said before slipping past the gate.

Lucenna scoffed at the old elf, thinking he could give her orders. She followed him out with Dyna.

"The state of Sellav is none of your concern, Varden," Raiden said informally, foregoing his title. "What do you want?"

Smirking, the elf noble straightened the front of Raiden's tunic. "I came for the same reason these other fine gentlemen have. To court your mother." Varden patted Raiden's cheek hard enough to hear the claps, and Lucenna saw every muscle in his neck tense. The Norrlen Guards reached for their hilts but halted at Raiden's motion. "Now be an obedient son and run off to let her know the Karheim House has come to call. Whatever problems have befallen on Princess Aerina's lap, I will see them removed." Varden turned his back, chortling to the others. "After a score of celibacy, she must be pining for someone with the right vigor to share her bed."

Lucenna hissed under her breath. Oh, that vile—

Raiden jerked forward with his teeth clenched.

"No, my lord!" Eldred shouted.

Karheim Guards pointed their spears at them, and the Norrlen Guards immediately drew their weapons. Oh, well, if they wanted a fight, Lucenna filled her hands with electricity. A black wolf appeared at her side, snarling.

Everyone fell still, tension filling the silence.

Varden laughed. "Careful, lordling. You may look like your father, but we both know you're no warrior."

Shadows crossed Raiden's hard expression; his hands clenched so tight the knuckles turned white. Teal light crackled around his fist, charging the air with magic. Dyna placed a hand on his arm and tugged him back a few steps.

"If His Grace were here, you would never dare insult his House in this manner," Eldred said, moving to cover them. "He will hear of this."

"Will he?" Varden retorted. "All of Greenwood knows Rawn Norrlen is rotting beneath the Blood Keep, Magi Master. And well deserved. Princess Aerina was meant to marry into my Household before he stole her from me." Varden eyed Raiden with an air of superiority and disgust. "Your mother was forced to marry a lowborn castle guard when he seeded her with you, ruining her name and repute. Now that he is gone, she is free to right her name again. Would you not want that for her?"

Raiden ground out through his teeth. "Leave."

"Or what?"

Lucenna had enough. She struck the ground at Varden's feet with a bolt of electricity. The elves jumped back, startled. "That was your only warning. Go before *I* make you."

"Foolish woman," Eldred snapped at her. "He taunted us for a reason!"

Varden laughed as he stepped backward, and two of his company in green robes came forward. They had been looking for a reason to fight, and she gave it to them. His Magi Masters chanted in Elvish, and a violent force of magic charged the air.

"Cease this, Varden," Raiden said evenly as he looked past him. "Unless you wish to explain to *them* why you are here."

Everyone turned to see a calvary of soldiers in dark armor riding up the path, kicking up dust behind them. Their chests bore the gold dynalya sigil of Greenwood.

The King's escort had arrived. *Finally.*

Varden sniffed, curling his lip. "I see Her Grace is otherwise engaged today. I will call upon her at another time."

He headed for his carriage. It was a light blue with gold embellishments, flying the flags with his sigil. A footman stepped down to open the door. Once Varden went in, his guards mounted their horses. The other nobles followed suit and returned to their mounts and carriages. The ground rumbled as they rode away.

Dyna smirked. "The Royal Guard seems to have a formidable reputation."

"They are not the Royal Guard, but the King's elite unit of armed forces called the Ranger Regiment. They are the most lethal warriors in all of Greenwood," Raiden said.

"Rawn was once offered a position among them." They all turned at the sound of Aerina's voice. She stood behind them at the gate, and her eyes watered at the sight of Raiden's red cheek. She went to him, reaching for his face. "My dear boy, I'm so sorry."

He sighed and took her hand. "I'm fine, mother. You shouldn't be out here."

Keena flew around Lucenna's shoulders. "We tried to keep her inside, but she was determined to reach her son when that rude elf struck him."

Lucenna noticed Von and Klyde standing outside of the estate doors. She moved to join them, but Eldred took her arm and pulled her aside.

"The next time there is a confrontation, do not interfere. You are not suited for a battle against a Magi Master."

"Excuse me?" she hissed.

Eldred frowned at her. "The level of your magic is inferior."

She scoffed, purple electricity glowing on the surface of her skin and eyes. "That is easy to say when you have access to limitless Essence. But if you wish for a demonstration of my power, I will gladly meet your challenge."

He shook his head. "I do not say so to insult you. Yes, you have magic, but you are untrained and emotional, throwing out spells with no proper plan. It is clear you have never had a real teacher, have you?"

Lucenna blinked at him, feeling her face heat. No, she had never had a proper teacher. If only he knew simply using her magic was enough to get her killed where she was from.

"You still have much to learn." Eldred returned to Aerina and Raiden as the Rangers rode up. The ground rumbled with the stampede of their horses. They dismounted and bowed to Aerina.

A Ranger with short blond hair and green eyes stepped forward with a bow. Fine black leather armor fit his tall frame. The symbol of his rank was embossed on his shoulder pauldron. "Evening, princess."

She gave him a soft smile. "It has been sometime, Commander Camsen. Welcome to Sellav. I take it you are to lead my escort?"

Camsen handed Aerina a rolled-up scroll. "Yes, princess. My orders are to accompany you and your company to Avandia, where the King and Queen await your presence. We will see to your safety along the way."

"Thank you," Aerina said, taking the scroll. Everyone watched silently as her eyes swept across the letters on the page. They widened, and she looked up in surprise.

"What is it, mother?" Raiden asked.

"His Majesty has a message for the King of Hilos." Lady Aerina blinked at them. "What does he mean?"

Dyna stiffened beside Lucenna; her gaze locked on the scroll.

Then everyone else turned to the gardens where Cassiel stood.

CHAPTER 50

Cassiel

Cassiel's footsteps echoed in the quiet halls of the estate as he followed the guards. Green banners displaying the Norrlen sigil adorned the smooth stone walls. Sunlight spilled through the iridescent windowpanes, casting rainbow refractions on the polished floor.

Apparently, King Leif knew of his presence here. Perhaps his interference with the Shades was a government issue, as he had no authority here, but Cassiel didn't really care what the message was. He only cared that he had gotten another chance to speak to Dyna.

But they passed by the grand hall where such meetings would take place. Frowning, Cassiel continued following the silent guards until they brought him to a set of open doors of a library. The walls were full of books and hanging vines. Warm sunlight streamed in from the wide, circular windows above, where more greenery grew. The air was fresh here, carrying the scent of old parchment and the forest.

Gentle wind tousled Cassiel's hair as he followed the path of light on polished stone floors further inside the maze of shelves to an open area that faced the garden. The glass doors were wide open, letting in the steady stream of cool air. In the center of the library grew a tree, receiving its light from the glass ceiling above. Set before it was a leather chair where Rawn's wife waited with the old elf standing beside her. A Magi Master by view of his robes and staff. Lady Aerina's gown reminded him of soft moss. She wore her pale blond hair down, a delicate silver chain dangling on her forehead with a small gem.

The others had seated on the couches on either side of her, leaving him to stand in the center as if he were on trial. Cassiel flexed his stiff wings, feeling uneasy.

Dyna didn't look at him. Her tired green eyes fixed on the floor, purple shadows gathering under them. The male elf sitting beside her was watching him watch her. The son, Cassiel assumed, by how much he took after Rawn. He forced himself not to react to the sight of Klyde, Von and Keena among them. When had they joined?

It seemed much had happened while he was gone. It made him feel out of place, like he didn't belong. Not anymore.

Lady Aerina gave him a soft smile. "Welcome, Cassiel Soaraway of Hilos. My husband spoke highly of you in his letters." Her brow pinched with concern, and she wrung her hands. "I am very sorry your stay here was not suitable. If I had known, I would never have allowed it."

Cassiel shook his head. "No, Lady Aerina. It is I who should apologize for imposing during your time of need. Please forgive me for bringing my troubles to your door. I will pay whatever the cost to repair the damage I inflicted on your land."

"Please don't concern yourself with that. My gardeners will repair the landscape to its former beauty in no time. Lady Dyna has already explained the matters concerning the Realms. I can sympathize." Her gaze dropped for a moment, a distant sadness touching her features. But it was gone with her next question. "I'm given to understand that you did not intend to stay long?"

Cassiel cleared his throat. "Well, with your permission, I would like to stay if I could. Lord Norrlen was—*is*—a great man, and he became a good friend of ours in the short time we knew him. I will do all in my power to aid you in his release."

Her blue eyes filled with tears. She blinked them away, and a shaky smile touched her lips. "Your words do me a kindness, King Cassiel. I would be delighted if you would join our convoy across Greenwood to the capitol."

Zev and Lucenna didn't agree by the expression that crossed their faces as they sat in stony silence. The others looked uncomfortable. Dyna had yet to look at him. He was unwelcome; Cassiel could feel it in the air. No one wanted him to come along.

"My brother has requested for you to join us, as well," Aerina continued, bringing out a scroll. At Cassiel's confused frown, she said, "King Leif is my elder brother. He heard of your stay here somehow."

Before he could process that, the Magi Master interrupted. "That was my doing, Your Grace. I felt the need to share with His Majesty the occurrence with the Shades and the Celestial King's involvement."

"Why did you not bring this concern to me first, Eldred?" her son asked a tad tersely. "I do not need my uncle to interfere in what I can see to myself."

Eldred bowed his head. "Pardon me, my lord. It was a matter of your safety and that of Her Grace."

"His heart was in the right place, Raiden," Aerina said in a pacifying tone. She looked back at Cassiel apologetically. "As I was saying, the King of Greenwood would be pleased to meet you. He wishes to congratulate you on your ascension to the throne."

Scoffing under his breath, Raiden stood. "Mother, at least tell him the real reason Leif requests his presence. It's his *power* he wishes to make use of, since he has so little confidence in mine." He went out through the opening in the garden, disappearing past the bushes.

A blush colored Aerina's cheeks, and she sighed, watching her son go. She looked at Cassiel again and offered him the scroll that had arrived. "Forgive me. I did not wish to offend you."

Frowning, he unrolled the parchment. Elegant letters in black ink displayed a short letter addressed to him.

To Cassiel Soaraway, the High King of Hilos,

I hear you have unexpectedly found yourself in the quaint corner of Sellav. It would please me greatly to greet you in Avandia and properly welcome you to my kingdom. I have sent an escort to the Norrlen Estate for my sister. The capitol road can be quite perilous, foremost for a princess. I do hope you will honor me by joining Aerina and see her here safely.

I look forward to meeting the new ruler of Hilos. We have much to discuss, including the reaffirmation of the Accords.

Kindest regards,

Leif Silva, King of Greenwood

While a polite message, Cassiel read the tacit expectation for compliance.

"In truth, we are concerned for Lady Aerina's safety," Eldred said once he finished reading. "Not to mention, traveling through the ranges here is especially precarious during the rainy season. Your presence would be an added precaution."

Cassiel could see why she thought he would be offended. King Leif meant to use him. Yet he had been hoping for an excuse to stay, and they gave it to him.

"I see," he said nonchalantly, rolling up the scroll. "I would be glad to escort you to Avandia, Princess. And to reaffirm the Accords with King Leif, should he so wish. However, I must discuss this with my wife first."

Tense silence filled the library as all glanced at Dyna. Because Cassiel had already been looking at her, he noticed when she flinched. Dyna finally looked up. Not at him, but past his shoulder as if she couldn't care to meet his gaze. Her green eyes were tired and dull, but otherwise unreadable. Yet he didn't need to read Dyna's thoughts to know how she felt about his use of that word.

A tightness came over Cassiel's chest, making it feel heavy.

"Right, of course." Aerina stood. "Thank you. If you do decide to join us, we leave tomorrow morning."

She strode out of the library with Eldred as they discussed plans for the excursion. Dyna nodded to Zev and the others, and they silently stood.

"I will wait for you in the hall," Zev quietly told her, then they filed out of the room. The guards shut the doors behind them.

Cassiel stood there for a moment, not sure how to speak to her. His wings twitched as he opened his mouth, but his voice vanished. It had always been like this. Whenever he was in the wrong and wished to speak, the words never came when he needed them.

He was desperate to stay and try to fix what he had broken. But he had decided he would never force her will again. It had to be her choice. No matter what he wanted, even if his entire being was internally screaming, he would submit to whatever she chose.

He had no right to anything else.

He studied the way the sunlight streaming through the windows gilded Dyna's red hair that was braided back in loose waves. He took in the dark leather of her clothing and weapons at her hip. How different she was. The bright warmth that used to shine off her was gone, and in its place was mettle. Sharp and cold, like an iron sculpted to a fatal point.

Dyna's boots shifted as she rose to her feet with a sigh.

Fearing she would leave helped Cassiel work up the nerve to speak. *"Lev sheli..."*

Her jaw clenched.

"Dyna," he amended. "I know you are angry with me, and perhaps you hate me, but I would like your consent to stay to see this through. I care about Rawn as much as you do. For once, I have the power to help you and him."

Silence filled the library. He held his breath, waiting for her answer.

"Do as you wish," Dyna finally replied. When her gaze met his, she looked at him like a stranger. "I don't care what you do anymore."

Cassiel inwardly shook as she walked past him for the gardens, pretending that her response didn't carve out another piece of his soul. *"Ani ohev otach..."* His soft proclamation was so faint, he didn't think she had heard him.

Dyna halted in place with her back to him. *"Don't."*

The anger and harshness behind the single word dug into his chest like a needle. But he could no more stop loving her than he could stop breathing.

"You have no place to say those words to me."

And the rotten husk of his heart shriveled up further. It stirred a memory that echoed his past back at him.

"Let me make things perfectly clear." Her icy voice sliced away at him like a blade. "I am not your *lev sheli*. I am not your heart. I am not your sun. I am *nothing* of yours anymore. We ceased to be husband and wife the moment you left me. So don't hope for anything to change between us."

Dyna's footsteps carried in the library as she walked away. He didn't move. He couldn't, even if he had wanted to.

Cassiel waited until she fell out of sight. He waited until her footsteps faded. Waited until he was sure no one could see him break as her words cleaved into his skull. He had heard each one clearly, and the ones she didn't say aloud.

I hate you.

I hate you.

I hate you.

Cassiel looked up at the sunlight pouring in from the windows, letting it blind him until his vision burned.

He would give anything to go back.

To the life he once lived when he had been ignorant of what true suffering was. To the moment before everything went wrong. Before he understood what being there for someone truly meant. If he knew then what he knew now, would it have made a difference?

But it didn't matter how sorry he was.

He had realized too late the damage fear could do.

It still lurked around him like a poisonous fog, suffocating him with the thoughts of what could still happen.

Because leaving had changed nothing, and Dyna was in danger now more than ever.

Cassiel pressed on his aching temples. He refused to let history repeat itself because he wasn't strong enough or fast enough to prevent it. If she could only give him one more chance, he wouldn't make the same mistakes again.

Taking a deep breath, Cassiel walked outside and followed the faint link of their bond through the garden paths until he reached the stables. He found her there, speaking to the young lord on a white horse.

Noticing him, Dyna glowered and said to Raiden. "Would you be so kind as to take me away from here?"

Raiden glanced at Cassiel, then said, "Of course."

Taking her hand, he helped her mount the horse and sit in front of him. She was that desperate to escape him? Raiden placed his arm around her waist, holding her securely against him. The sight made Cassiel's jaw clench.

Tugging on the reins, Raiden maneuvered the horse to trot around him. "King of Hilos," he greeted in a reserved tone.

"I am sorry to hear about your father," Cassiel said, eyeing him warily. "I don't know another nobler than him."

"So I am told. However, I am yet to be told the same of you."

Well.

Cassiel frowned at Dyna. "Where are you going?"

"That no longer concerns you," she said without looking at him. "Don't follow me."

Raiden snapped the reins, and the horse broke into a gallop. Dust rose on the path as Cassiel watched another ride off with his mate.

He sat on a barrel and leaned forward with his throbbing head in his hands. These damn headaches.

"That one is encroaching on your territory. Shall I kill him? I could make it look like an accident."

Smirking, Cassiel looked up at Netanel. His spy leaned up against the stable with his arms crossed, the shadows of his dark cloak obscuring his face. "No, don't do that."

"Are you sure? The world has enough spoiled lordlings. No one would miss him."

Cassiel laughed dryly and rubbed his face. "I sometimes wonder if you're half mad. Why else follow a tyrant king who burned down a Realm, who curses everything he touches ... who lost..." *his queen*. He couldn't bring himself to say it aloud, because it meant he really did lose everything.

"Every night I see her face when she begged me not to leave her. I truly believed it was the only way. How wrong I was. I wish to go back. I wish to erase everything..." The back of Cassiel's eyes burned, and he pressed on his eyelids.

He had been unraveling these past months, tumbling through the sky with no end. When she appeared again, he finally stopped falling, as if he had reached the foundation of the world. But the ground had swallowed him whole.

She told him not to hope, yet hope was all he had left.

He clung to it like a disease.

"I want to believe somehow I can undo what I have done. But I am now on the other side of her shield of our dying bond, left in an empty void with no end. Fix this?" He retorted sardonically at his idiocy. "I am so far past delusional. Perhaps I am the mad one..."

There was a reason why he chose to do this, yet nothing made sense to him anymore. He swallowed back a thick knot of regret. The one that formed in his throat every time he pictured her face doused in tears.

Cassiel pressed on his chest, feeling as if his lungs had collapsed. He had ruined something precious, something that could never be repaired. He had shattered the delicate trust and love that had been the foundation of their marriage in the most devastating way.

Every waking moment was filled with the pain of their broken bond. It made him feel as though his life had been a waste. He had dreaded that his world would snuff out her light, but it was he who did it.

Maybe Malakel was right about him. He destroyed everything he touched.

A gentle pat fell on his back. "Life is a road of lessons, and you stand before another," Netanel said. "Relationships are seldom easy, and love can reduce even the wisest to lunacy. However, I have the utmost faith in you."

Cassiel wasn't sure how to accept this rare comfort. "Why?"

"Because I know who you are and who you are meant to be."

Smirking wryly, he sat up. "You're only saying that to make me feel better."

The spy chuckled. "Of course."

Cassiel looked out to the town where the other half of his soul was and spotted a pair of red wings flying in the distance. "Have you spoken with Sowmya?"

"She ignores me." Netanel shrugged. "I don't think she approves of my presence here."

Because Cassiel had chosen a pureblood instead of her as his spy, but he needed Sowmya to protect Dyna when he couldn't.

"Well, I will return to my patrols. I overheard your decision to join the convoy. I will fly ahead to scout the roads."

Netanel backed up a step, but Cassiel grabbed the end of his cloak. "Thank you ... for being here."

Even if it was only out of duty. At least there was someone here who didn't despise him.

The spy lifted his head enough to expose the warm smile crossing his face. "I am with you. Every step of the way."

"Do I have your word?" He had lost so much in his life. There wasn't much else he could lose now without losing more of himself.

Netanel patted his arm. "For as long as you need me."

The assurance in that statement eased his anxiety, only for embarrassment to replace it. He wasn't a child anymore.

Cassiel waved him off. "Go on. Be careful."

"I always am." Netanel spread his white wings as he turned to go. "Oh, and perhaps you should ask yourself why Dynalya keeps her shield up on the bond. For if she truly holds no affection for you, there would be no reason to hide."

Then his spy winked and flew away into the sky.

Cassiel was left to stare blankly after him, too stunned to do anything else.

CHAPTER 51

Dynalya

Dyna didn't care where they went. The only thing she wanted now was to flee the pressure in her chest. Raiden must have sensed it because he took her away from the estate without question. The road led to a stone bridge, and the sound of pounding hooves beat against her heartbeat. It was soon behind them, and she exhaled out a sigh of relief as they raced toward the meadow plains of Sellav with no sign of pursuit.

"Where would you like to go, my lady?" Raiden asked.

"Somewhere I can breathe."

After a pause, he said, "I know the perfect place."

Kicking his heels, they broke into a gallop off the road. Who knew where he was taking her. She was only grateful it was in the opposite direction of the estate. Blinking back her misted eyes, she gazed at the idyllic country of Sellav. Beyond opened the beautiful valley with a crystalline river running through, fluttering with dynalya flowers in the breeze. In another field, a herd of Elvish horses in all colors galloped together.

They reached the town and rode through the streets. Raiden rode faster, as though she weren't the only one running away. Dyna peeked behind her and spotted Sowmya flying among the clouds, following but keeping her distance.

No other winged form followed.

They rode up a foothill of the Anduir Mountains until Raiden brought her to a ridge that overlooked the province. It was a secluded little nook within a cluster of rowan bushes, and a smooth log was set a few feet away from the edge of the cliff, proving he had been here before.

"Here we are." Dismounting, Raiden took hold of her waist and lifted her off the saddle.

"Oh, thank you," Dyna said in surprise at how swiftly he did it. She smiled at the scenery with a sigh. "It's lovely up here."

He looked out at the horizon as the wind tousled his long hair. "We all need our own corner of the world to escape to. This one is mine."

Dyna heard a weight in his tone, and she looked up at the pensiveness in his eyes. "I am sorry for placing you in further bad standing today."

Their presence called into question his reputation. Those suitors were awful to him.

If Lucenna had not reacted, she certainly would have.

A bitter smile touched Raiden's lips. "Your being here has made no difference. Varden would have found another creative way to slight me. This is not the first nor the last time he will grace us with his company."

"Who is he?"

"Varden is heir of House Karheim and the Province of Erendor. An esteemed noble family. My mother was meant to marry him. Can you imagine?" Raiden scoffed wryly. "Perhaps I would have been better suited to have an arrogant father from a respected House, rather than an absent father from a soldier's House where I have to prove myself every blessed day."

Dyna knew Raiden didn't mean to say that by the way he stiffened. Red flushed through his cheeks. He grimaced, rubbing the back of his neck.

"Pardon me, my lady. Folly words from a folly son."

"No ... I understand." She looked out at the land, feeling her throat tighten. "I was once in a similar position where I felt the need to prove myself against others who had no regard for the title I once held. It's enough to make you feel..." Her brow furrowed. "As though perhaps they are right. You don't belong. No matter how much you wish for it."

Raiden's gaze slid to hers a moment, and they both looked away to the estate in the distance. The brittle bond in her chest faintly pulsed, letting her know where the other half of her was. Dyna shut the feeling away.

When would the stupid thing understand there was nothing left between them?

"And that caused the end of your marriage?" Raiden asked.

It was Dyna's turn to weakly laugh. "Cassiel made that choice."

"Which he seems to regret."

She thought of his teary face as he knelt in the rain at her feet, begging for forgiveness. Dyna shut her eyes. "It doesn't matter now."

"I agree," Raiden said. "Because you don't belong together."

The unexpected statement made something in her chest tighten, and it drew her attention back to him.

"A Celestial and a human..." Raiden's expression shifted as he gazed at the fog rolling over the mountains. "It is no better than a princess and a soldier of modest means. My parents didn't belong together either, yet they fought for their love and look at where it brought them. The king cast my mother away from the castle with her name besmirched. My father abandoned us in the name of glory simply to escape the judgment of his country. And it destroyed them." Anger painted each word, marked heavily by his resentment. "My mother was left *alone* in a place she didn't know, and I ... I was left to live in his shadow, born with the face of a man both admired and reviled for his deeds. Now he awaits death, and I ask myself what was it for? Why was this the future they chose? Had he done the right thing and let her go before it ruined their lives, perhaps they could have found some sliver of happiness."

Dyna was taken aback by his words because she wouldn't have expected him to have anything but respect for Rawn, as she did. But that respect came from the time she spent with him; time Raiden didn't have. "What makes you believe they were unhappy? Your father didn't leave to escape judgment, but to fulfill an oath he made to King Leif. That is the only thing he regrets. All Lord Norrlen has ever wanted was to come home."

Raiden's long fingers drifted to the wooden pendant he wore around his neck a moment before his brow tightened again and he stood. "Then it should not have taken him twenty years to return."

"Wait." She caught the end of his gray tunic, the fabric soft against her fingers.

His gaze drifted down to her hold. "You care for him, don't you?"

"Of course I do. We have been through a lot together, and it has bonded us as family." Dyna realized it was the wrong thing to say by the look on his face.

"Therein lies my contempt, my lady..." Raiden gently removed her grasp, holding her hand a few seconds before letting go. "He has formed a new family while he has forgotten his own."

"That's not true." Dyna moved in Raiden's way when he tried to leave. "Please don't think ill of him. I know Lord Norrlen's thoughts have always been full of you and your mother. Don't feel as though he went willingly."

"Know? How would you know this when I know nothing about him at all?"

Sighing, Dyna nodded at the wooden pendant. "Your father made that, didn't he?"

Raiden looked away.

"I recognize the carving style," she said. "In his spare time, I watched him carve little statuettes every night for his child."

"I have outgrown such things," Raiden murmured.

"Your father knew that, yet he carved them anyway." Dyna brushed her fingertips over the pendant resting over Raiden's heart. "But this one is significant, isn't it?"

For the fact that he kept it with him. It also looked older, smoothed from time. In the center of the pendant lay a single symbol she couldn't read.

"It's a … birth token." Raiden cradled it in his hand. "Meant to be made by one's father when Elven boys turn ten. It's supposed to symbolize the wish they hold for our future on the path we might take. Whether it be another soldier, a scholar, a Magi Master, or whatever aspirations they may have. Tokens are usually made of pearl or gold, or other precious stones, and they open with a gift inside. Mine is made of wood and it arrived with nothing but a rusted piece of metal and a message. The only one he ever wrote to me. All it said was that one day I would understand." Raiden's brow furrowed, and he let it drop. "The only thing I understand is *this* is the extent of what he truly thinks of me."

Dyna frowned, not understanding either. That didn't sound like Rawn at all. "What does the symbol mean?"

"Rey. It's the first syllable of my name in Old Elvish. I'm told it means primordial or beginning." Standing at the edge of the cliff, Raiden inhaled a deep breath and slowly exhaled.

He simply breathed, and all the tension in his shoulders melted away. She could almost see Lord Norrlen in his place, and she wondered if he had ever stood here, too.

Raiden turned to her, a little sheepish. "Pardon my ramblings, my lady. Thank you for lending an ear."

"Not at all. I am fortunate that you felt comfortable enough to share that with me."

Raiden's head canted as he looked at her, and the makings of a soft smile on his face. "Enough about me. Tell me about yourself instead."

"Me?"

"Yes, you. How did you come to be on this journey?" They strolled back to his horse, and he helped her mount the saddle before climbing up behind her with graceful ease. He felt warm and solid at her back. Taking the reins in his elegant hands, Raiden clicked his tongue, and they cantered down the mountain trail at a leisurely pace. "I assume you were on your way to Mount Ida with my father, as locating the island was part of his mission."

Right, his family would know about that.

"I am," she said."

"And what put you on that path?"

Dyna gazed at the land of Sellav, past the trees. "Your home reminds me of mine. North Star is a small village nestled within the mountains, secluded from the rest of the world. It's peaceful and lovely, with vast meadows and cascades adorning the range. A great threat comes to destroy that, so I am on my way to find the means to eliminate it."

Her vision misted as she thought of her family. She imagined Grandma Layla in the garden picking herbs for her tonics, while Lyra studied her books by the fire. Oh, how she missed them. Dyna missed the serene days of that time, when she had not been the person she was now. When she returned, she would carry the scars of her journey.

Raiden looked down at her and said softly, "It's a brave thing to step out your front door and go out into the unknown. Only those of stout heart would take on an arduous journey full of peril to protect something they love. I commend you for your courage, my lady."

Dyna had needed to hear that. For someone to tell her she was brave and strong instead of foolish and weak as she had been feeling. It served to remind her of all she had accomplished despite every hurdle that had come her way. Even when she had been knocked down, she managed to push herself up again. She faced death time and again and kept going.

Somehow, she had forgotten that it also took courage to find your worth.

"Thank you," she whispered, tears gathering on her lashes.

Sunlight streamed in through the branches as they left the trees. Its warmth fell over her, and she expanded her lungs with a breath, taking the weight that had been dragging her down and tossing it away.

And she finally realized *that* was her strength.

Her inability to give up.

Raiden handed her a handkerchief, and Dyna stifled a breathy laugh, because it reminded her of Rawn. He was more like his father than he thought.

Soft neighing carried to them, and she spotted the same herd galloping over the fields.

"We raise horses in Sellav," Raiden commented. "We are known for breeding the best in Greenwood. Most come here to select a horse to bond with."

Dyna heard the sense of pride in his voice and smiled. She petted the white mane of the stallion they rode. "Is this one yours?"

"Unfortunately, not. Sight here merely tolerates me. I think the stubborn brute is waiting for a better rider to come along."

The stallion nickered as if to agree, and she laughed.

They followed the road and passed through the town of Sellav. As they cantered along the cobblestone streets, it caught the attention of everyone they passed. Some waved to their lord, calling out greetings. Bright flowerbeds lined the streets, carrying the sweet scent of spring. Raiden stopped so they could stroll among the merchant stalls, and she could admire their wares.

"Do you wish to return to the estate?" Raiden asked her when the evening arrived.

Dyna sighed. "Not particularly."

"Because you wish to avoid the King of Hilos?"

She glanced back at the white structure set upon a hill, dreading seeing him again. It was too difficult. Whenever Cassiel was near, her chest ached like a lingering bruise. A constant reminder of who they used to be and what they would never be again.

"That will be inevitable now that he has joined the escort." Dyna brushed her fingers over the silky red petals of a dynalya flower. "Which I must admit he will offer more protection for Lady Aerina. However, I can't say I am overjoyed by his presence."

"Then may I be of assistance with that?" Raiden murmured, prompting her to look up at him. "I have been meaning to thank you, for being here and for helping my mother. What better way than by serving as a barrier between you and the one you wish to keep away?"

"What do you mean?"

The breeze picked up, ruffling the stall canopies and her cloak. Flower petals swirled into the air.

Taking her hand, Raiden bowed as he pressed a soft kiss on the back of her fingers. "Lady Dynalya of North Star, may I court you?"

Dyna lay in bed, staring up at the tracks of the evening light on her bedroom ceiling, replaying the moment in town. "It would be a *guise*," Raiden had quickly clarified when she blushed and stuttered over her words. "A means to merely keep him at bay by stating I am courting you now. None but us would know the truth."

Should she accept his offer?

She shook her head. No, that was silly.

There was no need to enter a pretend courtship simply to keep her former husband at bay. She made it clear they were over.

Sighing, her tired eyes slid closed. As soon as they rescued Rawn, her dilemma would be over, too.

Dyna jolted up in bed, stifling her scream. The sound of her racing heart hammered in her ears, her chest heaving with wild breaths and sweat slicking her skin. Her body shuddered with the remnants of her nightmare, and she touched the back of her head, feeling the phantom crack of her skull.

Her room was dark.

The candles had gone out.

Only faint moonlight trickled through the window curtains. She stumbled out of bed, quickly casting out her magic. The wicks lit, and she sagged against the bedpost. The light didn't diminish her trembling. It wasn't the dark she feared anymore.

A soft knock came at the door.

She knew who it was without him needing to speak. "Go away, Cassiel."

"Are you all right?"

Dyna glowered at her sweaty face in the mirror across the bed and quickly fortified her shield on the bond. Her exhaustion must have brought it down. She lay down again, giving her back to the door. If she ignored him long enough, he would eventually leave.

"May I come in?"

The gentle question made tears gather on her lashes. When she used to have nightmares, his simple touch was enough to keep them away. She was so tired of these relentless dreams she almost allowed him in purely to find rest. But she couldn't bear looking at him anymore. Because whenever Cassiel was near, she was highly aware of him and the way she fixated on the sound of his voice, on the heat of his presence, and over how much her broken heart ached with longing.

Dyna shoved the thought away.

She couldn't allow him to come near her again.

At her silence, Cassiel's sigh was heavy enough to slip through the cracks of her door. "Dyna, please talk to me."

Shutting her wet eyes, she drew the blanket over her head. "Leave me alone."

She didn't want to talk to him. His pleading only made her angrier. He did this to them. To her.

It was doubtful his touch would soothe her anymore. Nothing he did now would be enough to keep those hands from pushing her over the cliff.

She glanced at her satchel sitting on the vanity, imagining the purple wilted leaves inside that would banish away the nightmares and pain. But she decided not to embrace her monster.

She would be something *else*.

Dyna was glad she tossed the last of the Witch's Brew, or she may have been tempted to drink it.

Fatigue weighed over her body, and her heavy eyelids drifted closed. She would face everything until she rose above it. The ache in her chest gradually faded, probably with Cassiel's departure.

As she drifted off to sleep again, Dyna contemplated Raiden's offer.

CHAPTER 52

Rawn

The carriage cell lurched to a stop, startling Rawn awake. His heart jumped next at the sound of rushing water. Sitting up, he exchanged a look with Elon. Both looked out at the glistening lake of Naiads Mere. The vast body of water was so large it resembled the ocean.

The scent of algae carried on the wind, and his pulse quickened. They were thirty feet away from freedom. Rawn discreetly flexed his stiff limbs, and Elon did the same. The guards allowed them out of their cell once a day to relieve themselves.

This would be their only chance.

They stayed still, feigning disinterest, as a guard unlocked the carriage cell door. As soon as he heard the bolt click, Rawn lurched up and threw his body against the door. It knocked back the guard, and he bolted outside.

"Follow me!" Elon hissed, sprinting alongside him. Rawn followed close behind as shouts rang out behind them.

His heart sped wildly at the sound of horses and Bloodhounds giving chase. He kept his gaze on the water. All he had to do was jump in.

He was twenty feet away.

Fifteen.

Ten.

Please.

A blast of orange magic hit them. The air tore from his lungs as he crashed into the ground headfirst. His vision skewed and sound dulled.

But none of it compared to the devastation he felt. Rawn looked up, and Anon rammed a boot into his face.

Twenty-Five Years Ago

Within the castle's garden, Rawn pathetically attempted to drown himself in a bottle of wine. But he had chosen the worst place to do so, where he was surrounded by Aerina's scent. The dynalya blossoms in the castle garden seemed to mock him as the wedding bells tolled.

A shadow fell over him, and he looked up at Sylar's father.

"Master Eldred," Rawn slurred. He held up the bottle to him in a toast. "To love and prosperity and wishes unattained."

The old Magi Master sighed, and his sad eyes only saddened more. He sat beside Rawn and took a drink from the bottle. "Look at what grief has done to us."

Rawn's throat tightened. "I miss him."

"I know. I do, too." Eldred rested his staff on his lap. It was now woven with the wood that had once belonged to Sylar's staff. "I am afraid to ask why you are here, young master."

Rawn looked up at the many glowing windows of the castle. "I wanted to see her..."

Eldred shook his head. "You can't, Rawn. Not today. You have fallen into your drink and are in no position to speak to anyone. Where have you been?"

He had taken a leave of absence from his duties and spent most of his time at the bottom of a barrel, drowning in wild berry wine, searching for something to fill the hole in his chest. But he couldn't put Aerina out of his mind, or the last thing he said to her. In some drunken stupor, he had stumbled his way here because it was where his heart called.

"I need to tell her the truth, Eldred. I need to tell her—" Rawn's voice cracked, and he dropped in his hands. "That she has always had my heart."

Eldred's eyes widened, and he glanced fleetingly at the castle with alarm. "She is to marry Varden Karheim today," he hissed under his breath.

"I know," he choked.

"She is a princess, young master. This cannot be. The king would have your head."

Rawn shut his wet eyes. "How cruel the fates be, for she is so far out of my reach and beyond the dreams I am worthy to covet. I kept my distance and settled to only watch over her from afar. I tried to harden my resolve, yet I am weak, and I despise myself for it..." He pressed on his chest that seemed to cave beneath an invisible weight. It was crushing him. Maybe it was the wine, or maybe it was knowing he had a chance to confess and relinquished it for the sake of duty. "My love for her betrays my king and country. I know this; nonetheless, I cannot seem to let it go. My yearning is too great, beyond what I can bear. If I am to die for it, so be it. But I cannot ... I cannot go another day without telling her, as I should have the night we danced. That she had been my wish..."

"And you are mine."

Rawn's heart lurched to find Aerina standing in front of them. She wore a white gown, a crown of silver in her golden hair, a stunning beauty in the backdrop of the setting sun.

His breath caught. "Aerina..."

Her pretty eyes shone with tears, her lips trembling. And he knew she heard his confession. Every word.

"Forgive me." He looked away. "I..."

Leaning down, she cupped his cheek and made him look at her, fingers cool and gentle against his skin. "Do you think of me?"

Rawn swallowed, though it did nothing to dislodge the lump in his throat. "With every passing thought and breath," he whispered.

"Do you long for me?"

"With every beat of my heart."

"Then what more could you want, but to be in my arms, dreaming of more days where you are my own?" Aerina held out her hand to him, and his own shook as Rawn took it. He couldn't stop the tears that continued falling. She pulled him up to his feet and started leading him away. "Master Eldred, please tell the king I will no longer marry Lord Karheim."

Rawn stared at her. "What?"

"Wha-what do you mean?" Eldred stuttered, equally aghast. He quickly got to his feet. "What am I to tell him, Princess? The entire kingdom is here to see you wed!"

Aerina's eyes danced with joy as she pulled Rawn to his feet. "Tell him, I have chosen another."

She led him into a run, and they dashed toward Fair.

"Princess, are we really doing this?" Rawn gasped.

Aerina only laughed. He helped her climb onto the saddle and quickly mounted behind her. Eldred and guards rushed to them, shouting at them to stop.

"*Ralov, Osomreh,*" Aerina told Fair, encouraging him to flee. "*Ralov!*"

Wrapping an arm around her waist, Rawn snapped the reins, and they galloped away. The Royal Guard gave chase, but they made it past the drawbridge before anyone could stop them. This was the most foolish thing he had ever done. Rawn wasn't sure where he was taking his princess, but he kept racing away.

The only thing he cared about now was her. When they reached the road outside of Avandia, Rawn brought Fair to a stop. They paused there, looking back at the castle.

"It is not too late to go back."

"Yes, it is," Aerina whispered.

"It's wrong to steal you away in this manner. The king would never let this go." He shut his eyes, suddenly very sober. "I have tarnished your name."

Even if Rawn had not touched her, he took her away unescorted. Most, if not all, would assume what they had done.

"I care not what they say," Aerina said faintly. She turned her face to look at him. "Have me so no other will. Keep me so I will no longer suffer your absence. Take me away so no other will attempt it again, for I now belong to the Red Shade." She moved closer, her lips faintly brushing his. "The Vale will surmise its own story, but I know the truth. I am foolishly in love with you too, Rawn Norrlen."

Rawn breathed her in, shutting his eyes. "I must have fallen off my horse and lay now in a ditch half dead, imagining you say such things."

Aerina laughed and kissed his cheek. "Does that feel imaginary?" He stilled as she kissed his mouth. "How about this one?"

Rawn held her to him and deepened the kiss. She wrapped her arms around him and sighed against his lips.

"Will you do me the honor of becoming my wife?" he asked between kisses.

"I will."

They rode away together but when Aerina fell asleep in his arms, Rawn looked down at her serene face and knew stealing her away was no better than what Red Highland had done.

It was enough to know she loved him as much as he loved her. Even if it cost his life. Rawn took her back the next morning. Aerina woke as soon as they arrived at the castle, and wept as the guards dragged him to the dungeons.

Rawn waited for death during the week he rotted in his cell. His only company was the strip of sunlight from a single high window in the cold, weathered stones of his walls.

"You swore your allegiance to me," a harsh voice surfaced from the shadows.

Weak from a diet of only bread and water, Rawn's head lolled to where King Leif stood by the dungeon doors.

He worked his dry throat to speak. "If you did not have it, I would not have returned her to you, sire."

"I should have you executed for this."

Rawn closed his eyes. He knew what his chances were when he returned.

"I would put you to the sword if your blood would remove the stain on her name. Rumors have already begun to spread that you have bedded her."

A knot tightened in Rawn's throat, offended and angered to not only have his integrity tarnished, but also hers. "I swear before the God of Urn, I have not touched her."

"It matters not. Most already believe it. No one will have her now."

Brow furrowing, Rawn's shackles clinked as he straightened. "Should my blood be of no use to you, I fail to understand why I yet breathe."

The king was quiet a moment as they studied each other. "Aerina has told me the truth."

Rawn's heart sank into the pit of his stomach.

"She is now cursed and unable to bear children. The future of our kingdom is lost." Leif rubbed his face, suddenly looking so tired. "I suppose this is the end of our line." He shook his head at the cobwebs on the ceiling. "Could you still love her, knowing she would never give you a son?"

"There is no question, sire. I accept her as she is in any form, in any status, in any life. If she would have me."

Leif scoffed faintly. "I thought as much. Likewise, Aerina refuses to eat in protest if I do not terminate her engagement to Lord Karheim. I fear she will leap from her tower should I sentence you to death. Royalty bears the duty to marry for wealth and power. By which you have none." His steel eyes sharpened with anger, but Rawn sensed Leif wasn't truly here to kill him.

He held his breath, not daring to move or even blink.

"My reign hangs in the balance, now more than ever. It cannot be said that my own men betray me. Nor can I afford to lose those loyal to me. Your father, the most reserved elf I know, has offered his life in your stead."

The news left Rawn speechless. His father was never affectionate. He was a hard and cold elf, driven by honor and duty. He would lay down his life for the king, but Rawn never expected he would lay it down for him.

"Are you my enemy, Rawn Norrlen?"

"If you truly believed me to be your enemy, sire, I would not be alive to speak to you now." Shifting to his knees, Rawn bowed his head. "Whatever your verdict, my life is yours."

Leif's dark green eyes held his, the intensity behind them piercing a hole through his chest. "Yes, it is."

Thereafter, the King granted him a dukedom over the land of Sellav.

The previous lord had passed without an heir, thus it was given to Rawn as a reward for his deeds in preventing the capture of Greenwood's princess. At least that was the tale fed to the court. With such a title, he now had the status to marry Aerina.

It wasn't a reward well earned.

Rawn knew it as did the people. His family shunned him, and society scorned them. Making them the subject of gossip and malcontent. Even when he felt regretful for ruining her standing, Aerina held up her head through all of it.

Their wedding ceremony was small and private.

No fanfare. No guests.

Regardless, as Rawn spoke his vows, he could forget everything else, for at last, he could be with the one he loved. It was perhaps the best night of his life. So perfect, it felt like a dream.

But the morning after, when he woke to the golden light of dawn streaming in through their window, his bride tearfully stood in front of the mirror with a hand over her flat stomach.

Rawn thought he could live with never having any children. But he had not considered how his wife would feel. He saw the sadness in her eyes whenever a baby was in her sights. It was another secret wish neither of them dared to say aloud.

The best thing he could do was give her his heart and comfort hers, yet he could hardly give her that either. Henceforth, Leif named him Greenwood's Red Shade, forever bound to his control.

Payment for his bride.

Over the course of four years, Rawn was called away nearly every day on missions for the crown. He led many battles and won each one. The victories were sour. For they cost the lives of his estranged brothers and his father. Once becoming General of the Armies, he would endure several months without seeing his wife.

The more Aerina was left alone, the more her desolation grew. Rawn could see it in the effort of her smiles that no longer glowed, and in her eyes that always seemed on the verge of tears. This wasn't what he had envisioned for their marriage.

Relief came when Red Highland fell quiet again, and the fighting came to a standstill. There was no telling when he would have to pick up his sword again.

On a whim, Rawn took his wife on a short holiday away from the castle as an excuse to visit their appointed lands of Sellav. They traveled off the main roads and the change in scenery seemed to lift her spirits.

By the third evening, they arrived in a beautiful wood south of River Myst. The rush of water greeted them as they rode Fair onward until they reached a pool crowned by three cascades. Dynalya flowers glittered in the moonlight, petals floating on the surface. Their sweet scent filled the air.

Aerina's face lit up with a true smile he hadn't seen in months. "Oh, Rawn, it's beautiful. Where are we?"

Dismounting from his horse, he took hold of her waist and brought her down. "The Melodyam Falls."

They paused there by the shore, watching the water glisten beneath the moonlight.

"This place was all Sylar spoke about," Aerina said with a sad sigh. "It was the subject of his healer studies. He was convinced..." she trailed off and softly gasped, looked up at Rawn with wide eyes.

"He was convinced the water infused with the dynalya flowers may hold great healing capabilities." Rawn began to unbutton his tunic. "Beyond our understanding..."

Her eyes went wider when she saw his shoulder. Her fingers lightly traced the spot of where the spear had pierced him. The same spot Sylar had treated. The scar was gone.

"This is..."

"Impossible?" Rawn smiled.

Her eyes welled. "Are you saying...?"

Sighing, he pulled her to him and pressed his forehead against hers. "Aerina, I cannot promise to undo your curse, but I can promise I will love you and give you your heart's desire, even if we should adopt a son who does not bear our blood." He lightly kissed away the tears on her cheek and traced her trembling mouth with his own. Rawn's pulse danced, so highly aware of Aerina's warmth pressed against his chest. "You deserve the world," he murmured against her ear. "For you are the entirety of mine."

Lifting Aerina in his arms, Rawn carried her to the pool where he made love to her under the moon. Perhaps it was magic. Perhaps it was love. But after a month in Sellav, Aerina announced she was with child.

It was a miracle.

An impossibility.

But their joy quickly faded into distress. Neither of them had truly expected the healing waters to work, and now that it had, Rawn realized the birth of their child threatened the future of the throne.

The first matter was to extend their holiday by hiding away in their estate, for fear of what the king would do. After a month of giving excuses to circumvent his summons, Rawn had no choice but to bring a bottle of the healing waters to Leif and confess.

He was right, of course.

Lief was furious that they kept this from him.

It was only the fact that they had found the answer to undo his own curse that pardoned Rawn. By his command, they were to remain in Sellav and keep Aerina's pregnancy a secret. Their child wouldn't be acknowledged until the Queen herself had given birth first.

Rawn couldn't have hoped for anything better.

They found peace in their corner of Greenwood. Aerina was a glowing light of happiness as her belly grew.

"What shall be our child's name?" she asked one night in bed. "It must be a great name and one of meaning. So they will always know what they mean to us."

"I think you're right." He laid a hand on her perfectly round stomach and laughed at the little kicks against his palm.

She smiled. "Do you have one in mind?"

"I will ponder on it."

The sun was low on the horizon of red blooms when Rawn's son came into the world. Pink and screaming, with a tuft of blond hair and his mother's eyes. He was a fussy little thing, but Rawn had never seen anything more perfect.

"I'll take him now," he said softly when Aerina finished feeding him. "Rest."

"Oh, darling, the nursemaid can take him to the nursery," she said sleepily.

"Absolutely not. I'm here. He has no need of a nursery. This little one is staying with me." Rawn kissed her forehead and tucked her in before slipping outside onto the terrace. "Best we let your mother sleep, yes?" he murmured as he swayed their newborn in his arms. Rawn could only gaze at him in wonder, at his little miracle.

It seemed at last their wish had come true.

But Rawn only held his son for one day before the royal messenger came galloping up the road with a cryptic message.

The desert searches for an eye, and the forest lacks a fang.
Return to the castle at once.

It could only mean Red Highland had brewed a new scheme. Rawn had been a soldier most of his life, but at that moment, he abhorred it. His wife had given birth. He wanted to be home with his family, not on another mission for the crown.

But it wasn't as if there was another choice. He couldn't defy a royal command. Perhaps it was more punishment, for King Leif had yet to forgive him. Or perhaps it was retaliation, for the Queen had not yet fallen with child.

When he told Aerina the news that night, she wept as she held their newborn close. "It's not fair..." she told him. "I gained a son, but he may lose his father. If anything happened to you, I could not bear it."

Rawn curled with her on the bed, holding his family tight. "I have thought of a name," he said.

"Tell me."

He did.

Tears rolled down her cheeks. "It's perfect."

The day he had married the love of his life, Rawn had sworn to do whatever necessary to repay the gift he had been given. Even if the cost was the remainder of his life in service. So at dawn the next day, he left home for his mission.

If only he knew he would never keep what he had paid for.

CHAPTER 53

Zev

Zev splashed his face with cool water, soothing the itch on his skin. He stared at his reflection in the bureau mirror, yellow eyes looking back at him. After years with the Madness, sometimes his head felt too quiet.

Perhaps it was the stillness and unfamiliarity of his borrowed bedroom in the Norrlen estate that unsettled his wolf. A light breeze picked up and blew in through the open balcony, rustling the branches outside. On days like these, when all he heard was the whisper of the trees, he heard another voice. Zev glanced at his pack resting on the bed where he had tucked Lara's letter. The scent left on those pages seemed to linger, or it may have been simply imprinted on him.

The image of a beautiful white wolf arose in his mind. It was so clear that he could almost see her there, standing in front of him. But there was no room to think about what he wanted when Dyna needed him first.

Zev grabbed his pack off the bed and left the bedchamber. The others must already be awake. He could hear their voices drifting from the grand hall along with the chirp of birds outside of the hallway windows.

The sky was pink with the coming dawn, coating the land in a light dew. He could smell the dynalyas from here. A dark green carriage adorned with gold filigree waited on the path. The Rangers were already outside, and an entourage of servants loaded a wagon with luggage and supplies.

Zev strode down the hall for the east wing where Dyna was staying. He let the conversations of the passing servants swarm over him, ignoring the guards eyeing him uneasily. Most had seen him shift yesterday and were naturally wary of him now.

Reaching Dyna's hall, he clenched his jaw when he found Cassiel there. The newly appointed King of Hilos slept with his back against the wall, arms crossed, head hanging. What was he doing there?

Before Zev could ask, Dyna's bedroom door swung open. She came out with her disheveled hair still in yesterday's braid as she quickly tossed on a cloak.

Cassiel jolted awake, and she halted at the sight of him.

"What are you doing? Did you sit outside my door all night?"

Rubbing the sleep from his face, he rushed to his feet. "I only wanted to make sure you were all right. Were you able to rest?"

Dyna stared at him mutely. The color had returned to her face, and she appeared more rested than she had in days. She must have slept soundly enough to even wake up late. Zev frowned. It couldn't have been because Cassiel had simply been a few feet away from her.

"Your necklace…" Cassiel said when he noticed its absence. "Where is it?"

Dyna swept past him. "I tossed it in the rubbish where it belongs."

She quickly strode down the hall and vanished around the corner. Sighing heavily, Cassiel rubbed his face.

"You did that," Zev said from the shadows. "You filled her heart with hate. That was done by *you*."

Cassiel gazed lowered to the floor. "I know," he said faintly. His voice was tired, strung with emotion. Nowhere near the cold, black-hearted prince Zev was used to. "I know…"

"Why stay here when her indifference is the only thing you will receive? You said you could live with her despising you, so do it. Live with it, because that's what you've earned."

Sorrow creased his tired features. "If her resentment is all I am given, so be it. I can stand being nothing to her, even if it's only to serve as the source of her loathing." Cassiel tugged at a loose string on his cuff. It pulled away from the meticulous lacing, unraveling the fine cloth row by row. "I'm not entitled to her affection simply because she has mine…"

Zev didn't know what to say to that. It was pathetic, really. He had everything, then tossed it all away. For what? It infuriated Zev; it infuriated him more that some small part of him felt something akin to sympathy for the one who used to be his friend. And he couldn't stand the suffering on Cassiel's face.

He looked tired of life and so lost.

Zev hated it. He hated it so much because it reflected him when he had also lost his way. Despair hung over Cassiel like a dark cloud. It had only lifted for a moment yesterday when Zev noticed him conversing with someone out of view. Whoever they were had used a tall shrub for cover.

"I saw you by the stables yesterday," Zev said. "Who were you speaking to?"

Cassiel paused the unraveling of his cuff. "Don't concern yourself with that."

He grit his teeth. "Well, I am."

Taking the loose thread he'd undone, Cassiel wrapped it around his fingertip, turning it purple, until the thread audibly snapped. Sighing, he tucked his hands in his coat. "It's irrelevant."

Gods, he continued to disregard them as the day he left.

"Then tell me why?" Zev growled. "You owe me at least that."

Why did he hurt them?

Cassiel's lethargic gaze fixed on his reflection in the windows across from him. "I was willing to sacrifice everything, including my soul, if it meant our fate would be different..."

Zev clenched his teeth at the poisonous anger that roiled in his stomach. The cost had been Dyna's innocence and their friendship. "That's the thing about sacrifices, Cassiel. Someone always pays the price, but it wasn't you."

They shared a long look, and Cassiel's brow tightened. "Zev—"

"No, I have no interest in your apologies either. There is nothing for you here anymore." He turned in the direction Dyna had gone. "Give up and go home."

"I am not giving up on her."

Zev clenched his fangs, his claws sharpening. "I hope you are prepared for disappointment. None of us will ever forgive you."

After a faint sigh, Cassiel's footsteps retreated.

"To quell her deep well of scorn, it would take reducing yourself to the dust beneath her feet," Zev called after him. "Which a king would never do."

Cassiel paused by the opening of the adjoining hall. "And what makes you believe I am above groveling for my queen?"

He walked away and vanished down the next hall.

A question that Zev had wanted to ask was left to wither in a moment passed. Yet he whispered it to the empty hall for no one to hear. "Did you ever once think of me as your friend?"

That too was irrelevant now.

Turning away, Zev continued through the estate, following the sounds of voices and the scent of food. His senses led him to the dining hall where his companions were already seated as the servants served the morning meal.

Dyna sat quietly between Raiden and Von, drinking tea. Zev took the chair across from her, next to Lucenna and Klyde.

Keena grinned cheerfully when she saw him. She had been fluttering around the tiered plates filled with food. Piling a plate with pastries, fruit, and sausages, the fairy flew it over to him. "Let's share," she whispered.

The others were quiet as they listened to Lady Aerina, Eldred, and Raiden discuss the course of their journey across Greenwood with Commander Camsen.

"We would avoid unwanted attention if we took the game trail through the forest," Raiden said. "Our large party is sure to draw many eyes, and we know not who is watching the capital road."

Camsen pursed his lips. "Yes, but the season is a concern, my lord. It rains much in the mountains, particularly at this time of year."

"How did the roads look when you traveled to Sellav, Commander?" Lady Aerina asked him.

"Manageable, for the most part, princess."

"But very frequented, I imagine," Raiden countered. "The convoy bears a higher risk of attack. I will not risk my mother's safety."

Camsen straightened. "I admit, the capital road is quite active. For that very reason, the King sent us to escort you. I believe the hills and mountains hold a much higher peril."

"Then it's fortunate we are traveling south. We have not had a flash flood since two seasons ago, but when they do come, they tend to fall from the Anduir Mountains. The risk will diminish once we leave Sellav."

Zev paused eating at the mention of a flash flood. They had one in Lykos five years ago, and it wipes away a good portion of the land, and with it a third of the Pack. He glanced at Lucenna and Klyde. Their expressions were wary. Von glanced at him when sensing Zev's stare, his face unreadable.

Keena was the only one who looked frightened. Her golden wings tucked close against her back, she moved to sit on a saucer by Lucenna's arm. "I don't like the rain," she muttered to her. "Pixies can't fly when our wings are wet."

Lucenna conjured a tiny storm cloud above Keena's head, making her dash beneath a teacup for cover.

Eldred hummed, linking his fingers together. "I'm afraid the risk remains until we cross River Myst, young master. If the rains continue, the river may flood. Regardless, danger will follow us whether you choose to take the King's Road or the game trail. We will abide by whatever you decide."

Raiden sighed and looked at Dyna. "What do you think, my lady?"

She blinked and looked up at everyone nervously. "Oh, I am not the right one to ask. I am not familiar with Greenwood's terrain—"

The servants opened the doors to the dining hall, and Cassiel entered.

"Good morrow, King Cassiel," Lady Aerina called to him. "Please join us."

An uncomfortable silence fell over the table.

Straightening, he schooled his expression with a bow of his head. "Thank you, princess."

Cassiel took the empty seat at the end of the table. Away from the others, which he so clearly knew didn't want him near. It reminded Zev too much of their first time in Hilos.

"We were discussing the better route of travel for our journey," Aerina shared with him. "The main road is too exposed but the trail through the forest could face a deluge. We are weighing the risk of both. In your opinion, what do you think is best?"

Irritation fleetingly flashed across Raiden's face before he composed himself by taking a drink.

Cassiel paused, equally taken back by the question as Dyna had been. "Well, Lady Aerina, my kind prioritizes discretion. I would better serve you as an escort through the forest. However, I am compliant to whatever you decide." He glanced at Dyna. "If my wife agrees, of course."

Zev heard Dyna's pulse spike, but she didn't look in his direction.

"I find it amusing you should continue to use that word," Raiden said as he took another drink from his goblet. "As I understand it, she is not yours anymore."

The very clear jab invited a sudden tension over the table. Keena's head popped out from under the cup, her mouth gaping open. A look of either shock or discomfort crossed everyone's faces as they all stared between Cassiel and Raiden, who were locked in a stare. Zev heard Dyna's shallow inhale as she sat frozen in her chair. He didn't know whether to take her away or change the subject.

Cassiel's cool response cut through the silence. "I beg your pardon?"

Raiden cleared his throat and linked his fingers. "You left her. Therefore, she has no obligation to you, correct?"

Cassiel's jaw clenched, his silver eyes storming.

The young lord shrugged. "Pardon me if I offend. I simply wanted to assure myself that I did not misstep."

"In what regard?"

Raiden laid a hand over Dyna's on the table. "I intend to court Lady Dynalya." Her eyes widened, her face turning as red as her hair. Aghast silence fell over everyone. Lucenna nearly spat out her water, and Keena stifled a gasp. "In fact, I asked her yesterday, and she accepted."

She did? All eyes fell on Dyna again. Her mouth opened and closed, at a loss for words.

Raiden turned to Aerina. "Do you approve, mother?"

It was Lady Aerina's turn to blush under everyone's stares. "I-I don't know if this—they are—" She winced apologetically at Dyna. "Forgive me, dear, I don't wish to interfere, but while there is a marriage in place..." Her eyes flicked to Cassiel nervously. He had yet to say anything or react other than to stare at Raiden's hand over Dyna's. "I don't know if a courtship is possible, Raiden. The politics with you being a nephew of the king and she is a queen of a foreign kingdom ... and the ethics of-of-such a situation..."

The poor woman didn't know how to respond. Neither did Zev. Dyna didn't say anything about this to him, and she looked equally shocked as everyone else.

"It is a complicated situation," Raiden agreed nonchalantly, "But you yourself challenged principles and politics when you chose a soldier to love. Are you to deny me the same? Do you not want your son to be happy?"

Aerina's face softened. "Of course I do, darling."

Clever elf knew how to wrap her around his finger.

"Then I hope you will treat my intended kindly." He smiled at Dyna and brushed a crimson lock of hair from her cheek, tucking it behind her ear.

Dyna made a sound that was caught between a squeak and a faint gasp. But she didn't pull away, and Zev sensed whatever was going on, she had now silently agreed to it. Her green eyes flickered to Cassiel, and his gaze slowly lifted to her. There was no anger there. Whatever he was feeling was hidden behind a mask.

"This is so terribly awkward," Keena whispered to Lucenna, now sitting on her shoulder.

The sorceress quietly snickered. "Oh, this will be fun."

Klyde braced his elbow on the table, curling a fist over his mouth as though to hide a grin. Von merely continued eating, not interested in the spectacle at all. Well, whatever road they took to Avandia, it was going to be uncomfortable, to say the least.

Raiden raised his eyebrows at Cassiel's silence. "Well, I do hope you will provide Lady Dynalya with a divorce and a substantial alimony that she is rightly owed."

Cassiel's jaw flexed, and he laughed. It was a dry, harsh laugh, lined with ice. A spark of blue light fanned over the back of his fists resting beside his plate. "Celestials do not divorce." He smiled at him sharply. "Lordling."

Raiden's expression hardened. "How fortunate that she isn't a Celestial, wouldn't you say?"

He had a point. And that was the very reason that tore them apart in the first place.

Cassiel met Dyna's gaze across the table. "If Dynalya wishes to entertain this jest, I will not stop her." A white light began to glow through his tunic, from his chest and arms. It spread to his neck, taking the shape of foreign letters. "But our vows will forever remain, and they will always hold value to me."

Zev's wolf tensed as the silence in the room grew heavier while Cassiel and Dyna stared at each other. Those must be the vows she had painted on him during their wedding night. But what value could they hold now?

Their staring match was interrupted by the sudden commotion of voices in the hall. The dining room doors swung open, and the Norrlen Guards dragged in a boy by his arms, forcing him to kneel. He was tattered and filthy, his hair matted with leaves, but he wore a familiar dark blue coat and a harness at his waist.

Zev immediately recognized him.

Lucenna audibly sucked in a breath. The others stiffened in their seats. Von blinked up from his plate with a dazed frown, and he froze.

Klyde jerked up from his chair so abruptly, it toppled over and banged loudly against the stone floor behind him. His wide eyes were fixed on the boy with disbelief.

"Tavin?"

347

CHAPTER 54

Von

Many things happened at once. Klyde wrestled the boy free from the Norrlen Guards and pulled him out into the hall. The sorceress and the Lycan followed. Dyna profusely apologized to Lady Aerina and her son before following them.

Von didn't move. He couldn't.

His vision spun, and there was no air in the room. It couldn't be. It was impossible.

"That was strange," the fairy princess with butterfly wings asked. "Who was that?"

Von blinked at her, not able to form words yet.

Raiden glowered at them. "I take it you know this intruder?"

"Yes." Cassiel set his napkin down on the table as he stood. "Pardon us for the interruption brought to your home, Lady Aerina. The boy is Klyde's nephew. While his arrival is unexpected, I assure you it's not a matter of concern."

She smiled at him politely. "Oh, right, of course. It's all right."

"No, it's not." Raiden rose to his feet as well, his eyes narrowing on Cassiel. "I must be frank with you, King of Hilos. We have had more than enough interruption in our home as of late, and I do find it very concerning that a human found his way here past our borders."

Cassiel leveled him with a look. "Should you find his presence disagreeable, shall I pass on your complaints to my wife?"

Raiden's expression shifted, because he had him there.

"Please excuse me." Cassiel strode away from the table and went out into the hall.

A small swirl of gold dust swept into Von's vision as Keena flew up to him. "Shall we follow?" she whispered.

Without waiting for a reply, her little yellow wings carried her away.

Von had to consciously make himself stand and force one step in front of the other. His heartbeat was pounding loudly in his ears as he drew closer to the hallway. Distant voices echoed through it, leading him to the gardens.

Von came to the glass doors where Princess Keena lingered. He joined her side as they looked outside. Dyna, Zev, and Cassiel stood back, silently watching at the base of the stone steps.

Klyde had the boy by the fountain, his voice so strung with anger, he was nearly yelling. "What are you doing here? How did you find us?"

"I-I've been following you since the Bridge..." the boy replied in a small voice.

"The bridge?" Klyde's face went red, his fists bunched, his chest heaving as he struggled to speak. "You know how dangerous troll territory is, and you risked it anyway. I told you to stay home, and you deliberately disobeyed me! You could have been killed!"

The boy lowered his head. "I'm sorry, uncle."

"All right let's calm down," Lucenna said, placing a hand on Klyde's arm.

The mercenary rubbed his face, and his shoulders heaved with a deep breath.

Halder came forward and handed Klyde the reins of two horses. One with a black coat and the other was gray. Coal, Von's horse. He didn't think he would ever see it again.

"I found Onyx in Argos," Tavin said sheepishly. "The other in the White Woods. I brought them with me when hiking over the mountain."

Klyde shook his head. His next question came out ragged, his voice strained. "What if something had happened to you, Tavin?"

The name rang in Von's head, and he recalled an old memory, yet he remembered the details clearly. His sister sat in a chair by the open window with the sunlight gleaming over her brown curls. She smiled at him, resting her hands on her round belly. *"He will be called Tavin. A name to honor the two men I love the most in this world. His father and you."*

Von had to brace himself against the wall. How could this be?

Klyde took the boy's shoulders. "Can you imagine what it would have done to your mother if you never came home? She would be devastated."

Mother? But he had no mother...

Unless she somehow survived as well. Von's mind flashed with a memory of Aisling laying in a puddle of blood, her empty eyes staring at nothing. No ... she was dead. He couldn't make sense of it.

"I know, uncle. I'm sorry." Tavin lowered his head. "But I am ready to join the Skellings. I proved it."

"Gods, Tavin. This is not the right time."

"When will it be the right time? Sometimes I think you want to keep me hidden away. Why?"

The question stumped Klyde.

Dyna glanced back and met Von's gaze. Her expression saddened knowingly. The others turned to stare at him one by one. They had all known, hadn't they?

Von's feet moved on their own, stepping out slowly onto the terrace. As though getting any closer would somehow solidify this new reality. The movement drew the boy's attention, and he glanced up, fixing Von with those pale blue eyes.

The exact color of a brutal winter.

A chill washed through his body, and everything was suddenly all clear.

Klyde spotted him on the steps. His expression darkened, sharp and cold as the blades at his hip. It carried a silent but deadly warning to stay away. Tension wove through the silence in the garden as everyone watched.

"Who is that?" Tavin asked.

"No one," Klyde growled.

Those two words set Von back into place. He turned away and strode back into the estate, letting their voices fade behind him. They may share blood, but Klyde was right.

He was only a stranger.

Von wasn't quite sure why he was here. Still breathing. Why had he decided to follow Dyna to Greenwood? Tarn was dead. He had served his purpose by enacting his revenge, so why keep going now that he had none? Even if he went after Sai-chuen, that wouldn't bring Yavi back.

The waves had called to him, yet somehow, some impression beyond comprehension told him to stay.

Perhaps it was due to the boy he hadn't known existed until now.

Gripping the reins of his horse, Von squinted past the drizzle to the riders ahead of him. The Norrlen Guards flanked a fine carriage making its way on the forest game trail. The large wheels slogged through the mud, leaving tracks of puddles behind. The girls had taken shelter inside with Lady Aerina and her son.

Klyde and Tavin rode at the front with Eldred and the King's Rangers. The boy refused to go home. Even if his uncle dragged him back, he threatened to follow him again. Klyde had no other recourse than to allow the boy to stay.

Cassiel had flown off some time ago, presumably following from above. Like him, Von didn't exactly feel welcome, regardless of being a Guardian. He kept to the back of the procession. A flash of black in the thick green bushes reminded him of the large wolf following in their wake.

The drizzle changed into rain, pattering loudly on the leaves. The first couple of days spent on the road were wet and tense. While Von gave a wide berth to everyone, Dyna avoided Cassiel, and Zev avoided the wary elves who distrusted a wild Lycan. He had no opinion on anyone's business.

The rain let up when they at last reached the end of the province by the evening, marked by the view of a large river in the open clearing. The gray skies had at last cleared as well, casting the last rays of the sun over the glittering surface. Beyond it rose the distant silhouette of mountains and flowering knolls.

"Ah, now there is a sight," Eldred said as they came to a stop.

"God of Urn willing, may the rains allow us a reprieve, or we may have a problem," Camsen said as he studied the surrounding hills. "We will stay on high ground when we can, but it's best we reach Avandia as soon as possible." To his men he announced, "We will camp here tonight."

The carriage door opened, and Raiden stepped out. He helped his mother down first, then Dyna appeared at the opening.

She took Raiden's offered hand and stepped down. "Where are we?"

"The River Myst. It serves as a border between Sellav, Erendor, and Avandia."

"It's beautiful."

"Isn't it?" Aerina smiled brightly.

"Are we to cross the river tomorrow?" Lucenna asked as Keena came to sit on her shoulder.

"Yes, but not here," Raiden said. "There is an old bridge a day's ride up the river at the Melodyam Falls."

"The ruins there are lovely as well. It's quite a sight," Aerina told Dyna, taking her arm. "Come with us to the river. You simply must have a drink. There is no other water like it in all of Urn."

While they left to do so, the Rangers quickly set up a perimeter as the Norrlen guards unloaded supplies and built tents. The familiar activity reminded Von of his time as a Raider. He dismounted and began unbuckling the saddle from Coal's back. Best to find a dry place to sleep under a tree somewhere, far away from the others.

"It's incredible that he managed to track us all the way here on his own," Von overheard Keena say. The fairy and Lucenna lingered by the carriage, watching Klyde and Tavin gather wood.

"Tenacity runs in their family," Lucenna muttered, crossing her arms.

It certainly did.

Von passed by the camp, taking a roll of bread from the reserves as he wandered off into the woods. He found a dry enough spot beneath a tree and set down his bed mat with the rest of his belongings. A rattle came from the branches above him. Von looked up and a force flipped him onto his back. Gasping for the air knocked out of him, he met Klyde's glare.

The mercenary had him pinned to the ground with a knife at his throat. "Do you recognize me now?" he asked through clenched teeth.

Von sighed. "Aye, I know who you are ... Dale. I think I always knew."

The signs were all there.

Tarn's reaction to the description of the mercenary's fighting tactics had given it away. The mercenary fought like Lord Morken because he was his son.

Klyde grit his teeth, tilting the knife with enough pressure to make Von wince. "I no longer answer to that name."

There was enough venom dripping from his words to feel the utter hatred embedded in them. Years of anger and resentment had settled in the lines of his face. Von could see it clearly, and he didn't blame him.

"I thought you were dead. I thought everyone was."

Scoffing, Klyde rose to his feet. "Is that what Tarn told you?"

Von looked away, hearing an echo of the words that had haunted him since that day. *You did this. You. They are all dead because of you...*

"So you left without checking for survivors."

The accusation left him stumped. He *had* left without checking on Tarn's orders. Without thinking of anything else but all the death he had caused.

"I saw the bodies." Von sat up, rubbing his face to ban the memory away. It didn't work. "Or what remained of them. I didn't have the heart to search for more."

"Well," Klyde replied derisively, "If you had bothered, you would have discovered a slew of orphaned children in the manor—with your mother among them."

Von stared up at him. His throat dried, his voice a mere whisper. "She's alive?

"Aye." Klyde sheathed his knife. "If not for Edyth, perhaps many more of us would have perished."

Von worked up the nerve to ask the question circling in his mind. "Did he know?"

Tarn had returned to the manor that night for coin and food. Von hadn't inquired about it, and Tarn hadn't mentioned finding his brother alive.

At the long silence, Von glanced up. Klyde's blue eyes were the storm of a hurricane, and it was answer enough. "I'm sorry. If I had known..."

"If you had, would you have stayed?"

Von had no answer. He had been newly sworn to his Master. He couldn't say what he would have done, but they both knew.

Sneering with disgust, Klyde turned to go.

"The boy..."

Klyde halted with his back to him.

Von had many questions, but he dared to only ask one. "Did Tarn know of him, too?"

"No." Klyde met his gaze over his shoulder. "And I thank the Gods every day for that."

They both looked at the camp where Tavin was speaking with the Rangers. The last rays of the evening sun caught his hair, an excited smile on his face. It was the same smile of his mother. Bright and warm.

Untainted.

An echo of Aisling's laughter surfaced in the next passing breeze, and it made Von's chest ache. What would the boy have been molded into if Tarn had raised him?

"Stay away from Tavin," Klyde said as he turned to go. There was no anger in his tone this time, only a mere idle fact. "Approach him, and I will kill you."

With all the blood on his hands, it was logical to stay away. Von wasn't a good man, and he had served an evil one.

"I remember..." Von murmured, looking down at the knives strapped to his chest. "You asked me once if I remember the people I have slain for Tarn. I remember every life lost because of me. I remember when I close my eyes at night and every morning I wake up. They haunt me in the wind, and in the faces around me. Especially his." Von glanced at his nephew. "The boy doesn't need me in his life. And I have no interest in being a part of it."

Attempting to have any family would only end the same.

With death and regret.

Klyde studied him a moment before turning away. "Go have a wash. You're proper sour."

Von watched him walk away, sensing somehow that some of the hostility between them had diminished. Albeit only a little.

Sighing again, Von's nose curled his stink of sweat and wet mildew oozing from his clothes. He really needed to bathe.

Von went into the woods in search of a secluded stream. The chatter of wildlife and the rustle of leaves kept him company until he heard the trickle of water. He passed through the bushes and came upon a creek, but another had found it first.

Zev rose from the surface and wiped the water from his face. Von froze. He had evaded the Lycan since joining and didn't expect to run into him now. Seeing him wasn't the only reason that rooted Von in place. Many horrid scars marked his body. The burn of chains, bite marks, and the tracks of claws.

But the scar Von had expected to see on his abdomen wasn't there.

Zev's eyes flashed bright yellow when he spotted him, claws extending at his fingertips.

"Ah ... I ... pardon." Von quickly turned to go.

Water splashed as Zev climbed out. "It's fine. I was leaving."

Von hesitated at the gruff response. By the time he turned around, Zev had already dressed. "I can come back another time."

"Get in the water," he growled. "Your stench is becoming unbearable. I can hardly smell anything past it."

Blinking, Von let out a weak laugh. "I suppose I can't argue with that."

As he removed his coat and bandoliers, Zev sat on a boulder to put on his boots. Von placed several feet between them before stripping off his clothes and stepping into the chilly stream.

The sensation hit him with memories of a winter night, blazing flames, and screams.

Von's entire body jolted with the urge to retreat onto dry land. He hated the water now as much as he feared fire. But he forced himself to move towards the middle of the creek and sank beneath the surface. His world darkened. The two gold rings tied to the cord around his neck floated up and glinted against the last of the evening light.

You have always been free, Von.

If so, why did he feel trapped?

The dark ocean held him captive as much as his duty had. Yavi took all the brightness with her.

Von stayed beneath the surface until his lungs burned for air. He merely wanted to feel something. To feel alive. But half of him would have preferred to rot at the bottom and let the fish have him. Standing, he gulped in the air raggedly. He cradled the rings in his palm as water dripped from the wet tangles on his face.

If he had perished with Tarn fifteen years ago, what would have come of Yavi's life? Von tried to picture it, but all he could see was her tearful smile when he kissed her for the last time.

Zev was still there. Locked in place, his eyes fixed on Von's back. He was staring at the scars left over after Tarn had whipped him. His brow furrowed. "Why are you here?"

"I have nowhere else to go," Von answered honestly. Glancing down at his reflection, he didn't recognize the pale bearded man looking back at him. "I have no other use except to kill and fight. Perhaps Dyna could use that."

Nodding as if he understood, Zev looked away. "I left you some clothes there," he murmured, motioning to the folded pile on the boulder. "The other ones need cleaning."

"I owe you an apology," Von blurted before he could leave. "For nearly killing you."

Zev paused for a moment and seemed to find that amusing. "I suppose it was my turn to hear such an apology." He picked up his pack and headed in the opposite direction of the camp.

"Not staying with the others?"

"No, not tonight." Zev glanced up at the darkening sky. "Full moon is coming. I can feel it. Best to find a good tree far away from here."

"Right. I heard you use silver chains." Von stepped out of the water and began dressing in the offered clothes.

"Aye, I do—" Zev froze, and his eyes widened with horror. He yanked open his pack and stuck his hand inside. His arm flailed around inside wildly, searching for something. "No ... no, it can't be."

Von frowned. "What's wrong?"

Zev stared blankly at his bag. "I forgot them."

"What?"

His clawed hands shook, his chest heaving with ragged breaths, and Von felt his own pulse quicken.

"What did you forget?" But Von could already guess.

"Commander..." Zev's fangs grew, his claws extending as fur began to sprout on his skin. His frightened yellow eyes stared back at him. *"Run."*

CHAPTER 55

Cassiel

Night had fallen. From his perch in a tree, Cassiel overlooked the camp. A squadron of forty Valkyrie were also on watch within the trees. He left the Legion behind in Sellav to keep an eye on Nazar.

The time to deal with Lord Gadriel and Akiel would come later. The only thing to have his attention was pretending he didn't exist. The opposite of love wasn't hate. It was indifference.

When Dyna ignored him, it felt like dying.

Cassiel watched her sitting by the stream with Raiden, smiling about something. The sight made his stomach churn. She had been the first one to smile at him in both lifetimes.

When the lordling declared he would court Dyna, it had hit Cassiel like a hurricane. It took all of his will to keep his composure instead of enacting all the hundreds of ways he imagined killing the damn elf for uttering the words.

Lucenna walked past his tree and quickly spotted him. Noticing what he was looking at, she grinned wickedly and mouthed, *"Suffer."*

Cassiel ignored her.

He had to win his mate back, no matter how impossible. It wasn't too long ago that he had compared himself to a weed. The thing about weeds, they tended to be stubborn.

But Cassiel hesitated. He had faced impossible battles, rendered an entire Realm to ash, faced his enemies head on, and now commanded an entire legion of warriors. Yet he couldn't find the courage to approach his mate who wanted nothing to do with him now.

"Dyna!"

The desperate shout for her name coming from the woods startled Cassiel out of his thoughts. Von came stumbling out of the bushes beneath him, holding his bleeding arm. Cassiel leaped to his feet, and Dyna was already running toward them.

"He's turned!" Von shouted. "Everyone, flee now!"

Before Cassiel could react, the Other tore through the camp, roaring. The clouds parted, and Cassiel balked at the sight of the full moon. Silvery light filled the camp full of people like a waiting feast. Among them was his family. It was Zev's greatest fear realized. If he killed someone he loved, it would destroy him.

The Guards immediately armed themselves and loaded their bows, and Eldred's staff flared with magic.

"No, stay back!" Dyna told them, then to Raiden she said, "Take your mother away from here!"

Raiden hauled Lady Aerina onto a horse and rode away. Klyde grabbed Lucenna and Tavin, and they ran with those who fled.

The Other went after Von first.

Cassiel dove and intercepted, tackling the Other. They crashed on the ground. The beast snarled and snapped its teeth for the commander.

Cassiel wrapped his arms around his neck, holding him back. "You probably hate Von as much as you hate me, but he's not for dinner tonight."

The Other snarled and bit his shoulder.

Cassiel gritted his teeth, hot blood gushing down his back. "Yeah, I deserved that, but you won't bite anyone else. Do you hear me, Zev?"

The beast tossed him aside, and he crashed into a tree. The force broke Cassiel's arm, but he pushed himself up as his wounds instantly healed. He waved off Sowmya and the other Valkyrie.

"Stay out of this," he ordered.

He spotted Dyna on the floor, grunting in pain and gripping her shoulder in the same spot he had been bitten. She glared at him, and Cassiel winced apologetically. Whatever wounds he earned, she could still feel it through the bond.

The Other leaped for Von again. He was snatched away in a blaze of green light and dragged to Dyna's side. "Go, now," she told him.

Von scrambled to his feet and backed away. "Dyna, he mentioned not having his chains."

She exchanged a startled look with Cassiel. "All right. Go."

That left her in the Other's sights.

"Eyes on me," Cassiel called, hitting it with a small fireball. Enough to singe its fur.

Furious, the Other snarled viciously and stalked toward him.

"We have no chains to contain you this time," Cassiel said as he kept it in his sights. "I know you don't want any more innocent blood on your hands, Zev, so you can have mine."

The Other charged at him.

Cassiel flew out of the way and moved back, leading him away from the camp. The Other lunged and slashed at his chest. Claws tore through his flesh, and Cassiel stumbled back as hot blood seeped through his torn clothing.

Dyna hissed in pain behind him. "Are you trying to get hurt? You're fast enough to dodge him."

Cassiel was fast enough, but he had to let the Other hunt to hold its attention. And maybe because he felt it was only fair to bleed.

He braced his legs, watching the massive creature prowl toward him. His bright yellow eyes glowed with rage. No recognition in them.

Only hunger. And pain.

"I know you're angry with me," Cassiel said as the Other circled him. "I wasn't there when I promised to be, but I am here now. I am right here, brother." He filled his hands with fire. "So come on, then. Let's finish our fight."

The Other lunged, and those teeth nearly caught his arm. Cassiel whipped his wings, hitting the Other hard enough to throw it across the clearing.

"Use your compulsion," Dyna said, coming up beside him as the beast rolled to its feet.

Cassiel dithered. "I thought you said..."

"We can argue about the morality of it tomorrow." A flare of vivid green light filled her hands. The force of her power pressed against him like the heat from a forge. Dyna had been a candlelight he tried to shield against his chest, but unknowingly, that flame had grown to an incandescent flame befitting a queen.

He smiled at the confident power shining in her eyes, and the possibility that they would speak again. "What's your plan?"

"Keep him still for me."

Wind whipped Dyna's hair as she strode toward the Other. It charged for her with a bellowing roar. Calling on his compulsion, Cassiel wove the steel threads of his power through the Other's mind and body. The creature came to a halt a foot away from her, frozen in place. It growled and twitched, lips bearing angrily over its sharp teeth.

Lifting her glowing palm, Dyna gently laid it on his forehead. "Sleep, Zev." Its yellow eyes rolled closed, and the Other fell unconscious. "No more chains for you."

The containment dome glowed a soft gold over the sleeping creature inside.

Lady Aerina had retreated into her tent with her son, while the Ranger Regiment stood on watch. Their steady attention remained locked on the enchanted dome. Its light shone over Zev's black fur. He had the shape of a man, though with clawed hands and feet and the face of a wolf. Cassiel sat with him, keeping guard.

The camp was quiet save for the soft crackle of burning firewood from the braziers placed throughout the perimeter and the croak of toads from the nearby stream. Lucenna and Keena had already gone to bed. Only Klyde remained awake as he and Tavin ate at their own campfire by their tent.

Cassiel glanced over at where Dyna kneeled beside Von. Her hands glowed with magic as she healed the gash in his shoulder. The commander watched in awe. His skin slowly reformed itself, going through the stages of healing until fresh pink scars formed.

"It will be sore for a few days, but you will recover the full use of your arm," Dyna said as she finished.

Von smiled at her tiredly, and he slipped on his jacket. "Thank you."

"Go on and rest."

Nodding, Von got to his feet and strode away for a tent on the edge of camp.

Dyna took a seat by the dome. Not exactly beside him, but close enough that it stirred the frail bond in Cassiel's chest. Her emerald eyes stayed fixed on her cousin, clearly ignoring his presence. He had found himself in her eyes once, which made it all the more unbearable that she wouldn't look at him now.

"I didn't expect to see Von here," Cassiel commented tentatively. "Last I knew, he served Tarn."

"He serves me now. And I will hear no word against it. From anyone."

The sharp response silenced him on the matter, and he left it at that. He was in no position to argue otherwise. But nothing good could come of having that man here.

A breeze rustled the trees, blowing in the fresh scent of spring. Tension hovered over them like a weighted blanket. Cassiel tried to start another conversation, but no words would come. It was as though he had forgotten how to speak to her, or he had simply lost that right as well.

He returned to watching Zev and counted each breath. The scars had returned. They were visible through his fur, red and horrid at his wrists. Only three months, and there were so many burns. It doubled the weight over his shoulders.

I'm sorry...

He owed many apologies, but they were always difficult to say.

"You called him brother," Dyna murmured.

The unexpected statement made his pulse quicken. She was speaking to him. On her own. Unprompted.

Taking a breath, Cassiel rubbed the back of his neck, ignoring his blush. He hadn't known she'd heard him. "We have faced a lot together since we began this journey. I care more for Zev than those I share blood with."

Though, whatever kinship they once had was likely gone now. He was good at that. Ruining relationships.

"Including Lord Jophiel?" Dyna asked.

The question made something in his chest tighten.

Sighing, Cassiel rested an arm on his propped-up knee. He couldn't answer her yet. He still hadn't fully processed the possibility if his uncle had told the truth about the witch bangles. Perhaps he was afraid to find out that he was wrong and the immense guilt it would leave him with.

But he was also afraid to be right.

When Cassiel confronted him, he had been too angry and wracked with several other emotions to even hear what Lord Jophiel had to say. So sickened by all the deception, it was easier to believe his uncle had stuck another knife in his back, too.

"I don't know..." Cassiel replied faintly.

Another beat passed before Dyna asked, "Would you like to speak to him?"

He would need to muster up his wits for that first. "I will when all of this is over."

"I meant to say, would you like to speak to him now?"

Cassiel blinked at her, confused by her meaning.

Dyna reached into her leather satchel and pulled out a scalloped silver plate that glinted with an iridescent pearl finish. Lord Jophiel's water mirror. "I found it ... after."

After he left.

So, this was how she had confirmed his uncle's release. The mirror must have been left behind unnoticed somehow. Though Cassiel was sure he had checked the rooms when he had erased all traces of himself. Clearly, he failed.

He had to turn his head away so she wouldn't see the look on his face. Tentatively, Cassiel asked. "Have you ... spoken with him?"

"I have."

It took a few minutes to get a hold of himself to speak. "How was he?"

"Do you want the truth?"

There was something in her voice that made Cassiel look at her.

Dyna remained watching her cousin, but the expression on her face made his stomach drop. "He looked thin. Weary. He is resting in Hilos with Asiel there to care for him."

Cassiel lowered his gaze to the ground. A lump formed in his throat, drying the words in on his tongue. *I am despicable, aren't I?*

It was a raw question he couldn't bring himself to ask aloud. Even if Dyna had heard him, she would have told him the truth.

He was a sorry excuse for a person.

Dyna plucked a blade of grass and rolled it between her fingers. "Despite what he endured, Lord Jophiel does not hold you at fault. His first words to me were, 'Is he well?'"

Cassiel pressed on his burning eyelids. That sounded exactly like his uncle. He never felt more worthless and undeserving than in that moment.

It reminded him of the day he had arrived in Hermon as a boy.

Snow capped the mountains, so enormous they made him feel insignificant. Cassiel stood in the courtyard coated in ice as he took in the soaring castle before him. The frosty wind whipped painfully against his tender wings.

"Why did my father leave me here?" Cassiel asked. The wind stole the faint words from the air and his vision blurred. He didn't understand anything, except that he had been abandoned again.

Lord Jophiel crouched down, so that they were at eye level and draped a blanket over his shoulders. *"I would like you to live with me, Cassiel."*

"Why?"

Smiling, his uncle wiped away the tears that spilled down his cold cheeks. It had been the first genuine smile he received since his mother left. *"We all need someone on our side. Elyōn as my witness, I vow to always be on yours."*

Somehow, he had forgotten about that.

Cassiel knew then, how wrong he had been.

About many things.

"Thank you..." he murmured. "For pulling my head out of my arse. And for knocking me onto it, too."

Dyna's gaze at last met his. He stilled beneath the stare of those green eyes, flickering with the light of her magic. After three long months, he could inhale his first full breath. Even if she had not forgiven him yet, the fact that she was finally *looking* at him made him feel alive.

Dyna scoffed softly. "Someone had to."

Cassiel smiled. He couldn't help himself, and that earned her glare. This may be the only leniency she allowed him tonight, but he would take that morsel, for she had no idea how much he starved for them.

Clearing his throat, he nodded at the scalloped plate. "I take it the water mirror has come of some use?"

"I don't intend to relinquish it," she replied tersely. "It's mine."

"It is," he agreed. "The Element Mirrors belong to whomever finds them. They tend to be special in that way. Lord Jophiel found the water mirror several centuries ago, and now it has found its way to you." Cassiel frowned at it. "But you must be careful. While you can communicate with others through it and spy on them as well, they can also do the same."

Dyna slipped it back into her satchel. "Your warning is unnecessary. I have been careful."

"As careful as you were when speaking to Tarn?" Cassiel wasn't sure why he said that. He hadn't even been thinking of the man, but it slipped out, and he couldn't pretend otherwise.

A tense silence hovered between them as they studied each other.

Dyna's eyes narrowed. "You had Sowmya follow me."

"Her purpose was to only keep watch over you and to notify me if you were under threat again," Cassiel said, straightening his shoulders. "However, she overheard and saw many things while shadowing you, Dyna. Such as your deal with the Druid."

CHAPTER 56

Dynalya

The gentle patter of rain trilled on the leaves and containment dome. It filled the heavy silence between Dyna and Cassiel. He extended his wing above her head as they gazed at one another, but she broke eye-contact first.

It hurt to look at him.

The simple sight of that ethereal face that haunted her dreams and those silver pools in the night, soft and pleading, made her heart ache. Sparking it with a confusing mixture of anger and longing.

She detested it.

It was foolish to permit him to stay when he asked. Why did she allow it? Dyna reasoned his status, and power could be in their favor. He wanted to be used, so why not take advantage of it?

Yet it shouldn't surprise her that Cassiel continued to question her decisions. He never could help himself, could he?

"I take it you don't approve," Dyna replied curtly, moving out from under his wing. "Well, I don't require your permission."

Sighing, Cassiel shook his head. "Whether I approve or not, I know you well enough by now to know I cannot stop you," he said softly. *Even when I try.*

Gasping, Dyna lurched to her feet at the sound of his voice in her mind. Her boot caught on a stone, and she stumbled back. "No," she blurted desperately, nearly shrill when he reached for her. "Don't touch me. Don't mind-speak to me. I cannot stand it!"

Cassiel froze, a shocked breath slipping from his lips. His hand dropped, and he looked away as if the words hurt him. She hoped it did. May they crush him the way his words had once crushed her.

The animosity behind the thought almost startled her. She was once the person who could easily forgive any fault or wrong done against her. But she could never forget what he did.

Her *body* couldn't forget.

Cassiel's voice had been in her mind as he held her down and erased everything they were, burned eternally in her memory like a wound that wouldn't heal. It made her flinch whenever he neared, because that day had implanted a new fear that now plagued her.

The fear of being so utterly helpless again.

"You have nothing to fear from me, Dynalya..."

At the soft murmur of her name, she peered at him through her wet lashes. Cassiel had placed ample space between them, as if prepared to leave at her command.

"Never again." He repeated her fervent declaration in the wine cellar.

She could feel how much he meant it. How much he wanted her to know she was *safe*. Except she thought she had been safe with him before.

That trust was lost.

Dyna checked her shield on the bond, making sure it was solid.

Yet Cassiel didn't lift his shield, as if he didn't care to use it anymore. Everything he felt was there on the surface for her to feel, even when she didn't want to. But it was hard to ignore. His guilt hung around him like his very own storm.

Heavy and suffocating.

When they had discussed his uncle, she inadvertently found herself trying to comfort him, and it annoyed her. Showing him any sympathy was out of habit from the girl she used to be, not because she cared. They weren't friends anymore.

They weren't mates.

They weren't anything.

But no matter how much Dyna dissected his actions the day Cassiel left, she didn't fully understand why he would do such a thing as to bind her magic and seal away her memories in the first place. Whatever his promises now, it didn't change that she couldn't trust him to one day find another inconceivable reason to do so again.

"Tell me why you broke us apart," she said suddenly. "Tell me the truth for once. I am listening now."

Cassiel blinked at her, completely taken aback. The rain poured down harder, but neither of them moved for cover.

Dyna swallowed, forcing herself to face him. If she didn't confront him now with the questions that had fueled her nightmares for the past three months, she would never find any rest.

She needed closure to move on.

"You did this to us for a reason, right?" Dyna pressed when he didn't answer. "You broke us because you believed it was the best thing to do. Tell me why. And I mean tell me *everything*."

Because he was hiding something from her. Even with his shield down. Even with his sad eyes. Even with his soul pleading for another chance.

He was still afraid.

It had to be more than her simply being human.

Cassiel opened his mouth but closed it. His throat bobbed, and the silence thickened. He couldn't tell her. More like he wouldn't. Because in his mind, he was protecting her. Well, she never asked to be protected, and certainly not with secrets and lies.

Dyna faced the dome again. "Leave me alone."

"Dyna..."

"Leave," she hissed through clenched teeth.

"Very well." Cassiel yielded with a sigh, and he stood. "Someone should be here to watch over you and Zev. It will take a toll on your Essence to maintain the dome all night. Shall I call for Lucenna?"

"I'll be fine."

She may not have been able to train her magic all winter, but it was strong enough to keep a containment dome.

The soft swish of canvas drew her attention to Raiden slipping out of Lady Aerina's tent. Dyna waved him over, and Raiden nodded, but he paused in his approach when Commander Camsen stopped to speak to him.

"You may go now," she told him again in a low, clipped tone. "Raiden will keep me company."

Yet Cassiel lingered, and she felt his stare. "If you are entertaining this ruse of a courtship merely to keep me at bay, there is no need for it," he finally said.

She smirked. "What makes you believe it's a ruse?"

"You met him hardly a week ago. You expect me to believe you have already taken a liking to him?"

"Why should that be of any surprise? I was taken with you the first day we met." Heat flushed through Dyna's cheeks at what she inadvertently blurted. She looked away. "We bonded soon after, even if it was an accident. The heart wants what it wants."

Gods, why was she speaking about this?

Dyna closed her eyes, and her treacherous memories painted the day beneath the willow. It had taken some time before she could admit how hopelessly in love she had been.

"Your actions led to the dissolution of our marriage, Cassiel. Therefore, kindly grant me a divorce and find another to take my place. I will do the same."

Her demand seemed to clog up the air between them, and she felt the bond shudder. The angles of Cassiel's face caught the golden glow of the dome. He didn't disguise the pain in his eyes, and it made her heart ache.

"I will not chain you to me, Dynalya. If separation is what you desire, I will prepare a *ghet*. A contract which grants you an annulment." Cassiel turned to go, his wings spreading open. "But there will never be another who could take your place."

Then he soared away into the night sky and vanished behind the clouds.

There will never be another...

Did that mean he would be alone forever?

Groaning, Dyna pressed the heels of her palms against her achy eyes. She was exhausted, but her thoughts ceased to let her rest. She was sharing Lucenna's tent, leaving the flaps open to let in the light of the dome, but it gave her little comfort. Dyna glanced at where the sorceress slept beside her, Keena nestled in the pillows.

Slipping on her cloak, Dyna put on her shoes and went outside. Klyde was taking his turn to watch over her cousin. He sat silently by a small campfire with Tavin laying on a sleeping mat beside him. They exchanged a nod before she kept going.

The dark camp was quiet, with most asleep among the still tents and torches. Dyna tugged her cloak around her shoulders as she strolled through the brightly lit camp toward the river. A couple of Norrlen guards were posted outside Lady Aerina's tent, and the Rangers kept watch at the perimeter. She sensed their wariness as they watched her pass.

The atmosphere felt tense, and it may have to do with the whispered conversation Raiden had with the Commander of the Ranger Regiment. When he had joined her by the dome, he kept the conversation light. She had waited for him to ask about Zev, but he didn't.

Dyna glanced at the sky, catching a glimpse of a winged figure flying amongst the clouds. While Cassiel had left his army behind in Sellav, his personal guard had joined them, Sowmya and Yelrakel included. They must be keeping out of sight, as they prefer to do.

Her thoughts were interrupted by a soft rustle of leaves. Stiffening, Dyna glanced over her shoulder into the dark forest. A cool chill crawled over her skin as she studied the black shadows, but she felt no lingering eyes. Her hand relaxed around the blade's hilt at her waist when she caught faint voices. The wind made it hard to discern.

A flash of blue light briefly lit up the foliage deep within the trees.

Oh. It was *him*.

What was Cassiel doing in the forest?

Frowning, Dyna decided to investigate.

Trained to move silently, she slipped into the trees without a sound. The familiar prickle of goosebumps scattered down her spine as she moved through the darkness. Her heartbeat hardly reacted to her old fear. She focused on the faint blue light ahead and nothing else.

The light grew brighter, and Dyna moved slower until Cassiel came into view. He stood in a small clearing with a male Celestial kneeling at his feet. The male was dressed in dark red robes, his wide blue eyes filled with fear and disgust. The veins bulge in his face, his mouth caught in a silent cry. His back bent backward; arms held straight back as though an unseen force was slowly bending him.

Cassiel's eyes glowed like two blue torch fires in the night. "I will ask you one more time. Who. Sent. You?"

"*Lech la'azazel.*" The Celestial spat at him. "Death to you and your *zonah—*"

At the snap of Cassiel's fingers, Seraph flames erupted around the Celestial. He burst into ash instantly. So fast, there was no time to scream. Nothing was left but a few cerulean embers and scorch marks in the earth.

Dyna's chest heaved with a shuddering breath.

He executed him.

Without hesitation.

"How did that one slip through the perimeter?" Cassiel asked, his voice a low growl, laced with a wrath that sent shivers down her spine. It was the same voice she heard from him in Hermon when he discovered the bruise on her shoulder. His glowing eyes fixed on the tree branches above him. Dyna squinted at the spot, but it was too dark to see who he spoke to. "Have the others tighten patrols. I don't care how many assassins the Valkyrie have stopped. No threat should ever come this close to her."

Cassiel paused as he listened to a reply. The croak of frogs and the leaves rustling in the breeze muffled whoever answered. Who was he speaking to? Dyna would have assumed Sowmya, but the way he spoke seemed to imply they weren't part of the Valkyrie unit.

"There is no telling how many were sent after her," he said. "They won't cease until they succeed in taking her life, or until I take all of theirs."

Ice sank into her veins. The menacing statement made Dyna's heart race, and she was suddenly wary of her surroundings. They could have struck now, and she wouldn't have noticed. Someone had tried to strike tonight. How many more had come to kill her without her knowing?

Dyna inched closer to hear them better.

"I doubt she would turn back now, more so at my protest. Continue to watch over her and—" Cassiel cut off at a response she missed, and he laughed shortly, the sound weary and frustrated. "No, she wouldn't believe me. Not anymore."

Another pause.

He rubbed his face and scowled up at the branches. "Would it change anything if I told her the truth? Or would I condemn her to a life of paranoia and fear?"

There it was. The secret behind everything.

Dyna sensed it hanging in the air, on the tip of his tongue. She inched forward, desperate to hear it.

"Enough," Cassiel snapped sharply, making her halt. "Do not speak of this again. There are things that should stay in the past, and this is one of them. I will not subject her to that torture. She has suffered enough."

He still didn't learn.

Even when Cassiel had the chance to make things right, he still chose to keep his secrets. If he didn't trust her with the truth, how could she ever begin to trust him again?

Retreating into the shadows, Dyna turned back. Perhaps she should have confronted Cassiel, but she chose to walk away.

From him and any possibility of them.

CHAPTER 57

Rawn

Before Rawn opened his eyes, he knew where he was. The arid, warm air felt suffocating against his skin. It dried out his lungs and coated his mouth with sand. Thirst clamped his throat, making him cough. He winced at the pain throbbing in his jaw.

He didn't want to look. Because he knew when he opened his eyes, he would no longer see the waters of Naiads Mere, but the barren sands of the end.

Rawn had to blink several times to clear his vision. Elon sat across from him, his hands and ankles bound in chains and with a blackened eye. His amber gaze had fixed on something past the bars with dread on his face.

"We are here..." Elon said under his breath.

Those three words sent a chill through Rawn. He gathered his nerve and looked up at the Erdas Mountains, which marked the border of Red Highland. The sharp peaks rose like red fangs against the sunset, lipped by a massive wall of stone the color of clay.

"The West Wall..." Rawn rasped, his eyes growing wide.

That meant they were in the Covenant Pass between Red Highland and Greenwood. A barren stretch of land with nothing but rock and sand. The only place elves were protected beneath the law of immunity granted by the covenant between their kingdoms.

"Don't look," Elon warned next, but Rawn couldn't restrain himself.

He turned to the east, catching a hazy glimpse of another wall on the horizon. Constructed of gray stone, coated in a hint of green. He might have cried if not for not for his thirst.

The chains shackling his wrist and ankles made it difficult to sit. Rawn scooted closer to the bars, anguish swarming in his chest. His family was right there on the other side of that wall. Nearly a leap away.

He hadn't been this close to them in years.

"Norrlen," Elon hissed under his breath.

The carriage cell jerked to a halt, and the driver cursed. A snap of the whip punished the neighing horses, and the carriage jostled onward over the uneven earth.

"Rawn, listen to me." Elon kicked his leg, but he didn't want to look away from the only connection to his family. "When they take us to the Blood Keep, I will likely be the first to die." It was the resolve in his voice that finally caught Rawn's attention. "I betrayed the crown. There is no chance for me. But if you can escape, find the hollow at the end of the northern tunnels. It is hidden behind a stack of barrels. Once you go through, it will drop you into the cavern below. From there, it's a day's walk to the nearest waterway."

"Why are you telling me this?"

"Because I need to know you will find Sylar when you make it out."

Rawn read the resolve on his face. "We cannot give up yet, Elon."

Because freedom was right there, within reach. He could make it. All he had to do was wait until the guards opened the door again, and—

"Ah, there it is." Anon jeered outside the cell as he rode alongside them. Rawn hadn't noticed him there, and the prince laughed. "You have the same look every prisoner has when crossing this gorge—*hope*. Thirty miles between here and Greenwood. *So very close*. If only you could step foot on the Covenant Pass, and then you would be on no man's land, and we could not touch you. Well, gaze upon the East Wall, Norrlen. It will be your last glimpse of home."

Then Prince Anon waved a glowing orange hand over Rawn's face, and his vision went black.

When Rawn woke again, he found himself hanging from a pulley chain suspending him off the ground by his shackles. He was no longer in the cell. At least not one on wheels.

There was nothing significant about the room they put him in except it was round and carved out of red stone. The air was cold here. Sunless. No light, save for two torches on the walls on opposite ends and a lit brazier in the corner. They had stripped him to his torn trousers, leaving his chest and feet bare.

And he was alone.

Rawn's heart rate sped, and devastation hammered against his chest. He was beneath the Blood Keep. Fear seeded itself inside of him like a thorny weed. The chance of escape had been stolen away from him twice already.

His breath caught when his peripherals caught the sight of the wall on his left. Hundreds of pieces of desiccated flesh bearing tattoos of Greenwood's sigil were pinned there. Flesh of all those who fell before him.

Was he going to die here?

Rawn banished those thoughts. He had survived near death for the past twenty years, and he wasn't about to relinquish his life now. There was only one thing the Red Highland King wanted from him, and Rawn knew what they would do to him to get it. Elon was likely dead now. Whatever they did to him, he would suffer the same if he couldn't escape.

This was the first time they left him alone. No better time to break away than now.

He studied his shackles. It wouldn't be difficult to remove these at all.

"Are'bil," Rawn murmured. But the usual teal glow of his Essence didn't spark in response to the liberation spell. *"Are'bil,"* he said again, more insistent. *"Latem es'repmor are'bil!"*

No ... the air held no natural life-force for him to draw on. But even the dry earth should have had... Rawn's heart sank when he noticed the old warding spells carved into the walls.

"Magic will not work here."

Rawn stiffened. He hadn't been alone.

The scuff of boots over sand neared as another came out from behind him. It was an elf Rawn had never met before, but he recognized him all the same.

"King Altham..."

A gold circlet pinned back his dark hair, resting above his pointed ears. He resembled Anon, though his eyes were amber like tree sap. Fine, dark garnet robes embroidered in gold shrouded his lean frame.

Accompanying the red king was another elf. This one old, or perhaps he appeared older because of his hunched back, unsightly skin, and the few sparse strands clinging to his deformed head.

Altham watched Rawn intently with cool curiosity. "So you are the elusive Rawn Norrlen. I have heard much about you." He flicked a finger toward the hunched elf. "This is Grod, the warden of my Blood Keep. He will oversee your stay here. Which can be pleasant, or it can be very disagreeable." He shrugged, his tone light and friendly. "That will be up to you, Norrlen. Give me what I desire, and I vow not to harm you. As you know, an elf's word is his bond."

Rawn narrowed his eyes. Yes, to *his* people oaths were sacred. Making a promise was akin to making a covenant before the God of Urn. Breaking one was forbidden. But he doubted such things were as sacred in Red Highland. "I do not have the Dragon's Eye nor the Dragon's Fang. The blades are lost and have been for hundreds of years. Nothing you do to me will change that."

The king chuckled. "Oh, I know. Leif must be very disappointed that after twenty years of searching, his *Red Shade* has accomplished nothing but shame."

Rawn clenched his jaw.

"Nonetheless, you do know *where* the dragon blades are. As it happens, so do I."

He wasn't lying.

It was clear in the steady beat of Altham's heart. Nor could he contain the triumph from surfacing on his face. "We have long known they were hidden on Mount Ida. What I need is *access* to them."

Rawn frowned in confusion. "I don't understand."

Altham sighed boredly. "Already falling on lies?"

"I do not lie."

"Oh, but you do." Altham strode for the brazier and lifted the iron poker. The end glowed molten red, glinting against his eyes. "It is in your favor to end this quickly by simply telling me what I want to know." Returning, he held the poker, close enough to Rawn's cheek to feel its scorching heat, and he flinched back. "Where did you hide it?"

"I do not know what you speak of!"

All amusement faded from the red king's face. He handed the poker to Grod. "You lie so cleanly I almost believe you," he said, his tone cooling. "Yet I know you were in Xián Jīng for years, studying the history of the blades and how they were locked away, for my son nearly caught you there when you dropped *this*." From his pocket, Altham drew out an elaborate knot made of bronze metal, bluntly cut off at the end. "Where is the rest of the key?"

"Key?" Rawn stared at it. The metal piece did look like the top of a key, but it was missing the bit of teeth on the end. "I have never seen that before."

"Cease to play me for the fool. I know you found the bit ten years ago. Where is it now?"

Rawn shook his head. "As I said, I never found a key."

The only thing his studies in Xián Jing had produced was discovering where the blades were hidden.

Sighing, the red king tucked the broken key away and crossed his arms behind his back. "I see you will be difficult after all."

Grod jammed the iron poker into Rawn's stomach, and it hissed against his skin. He jerked back with a cry. The pain sent a flash of white behind his eyes, and he had to breathe sharply through his nose.

"Tell me where," the red king said again in a flat tone.

"I do not—" Rawn cut off when the iron poker seared against his thigh. He clenched his jaw. Whatever torture he endured, he refused to make a sound.

Bracing, he prayed to the God of Urn to give him strength before his feet were burned next. He violently shook, his teeth grinding so tight his face went numb. The scent of cooking flesh wafted in the cell. It made his stomach roll.

Regardless of whether he knew anything about a key, nothing would have changed. He would never betray his country. To betray Leif was to betray Aerina.

Closing his wet eyes, Rawn pictured the rolling green knolls of Sellav and the sweet scent of the crimson blooms on the fields. He pictured the path of his estate and his wife waiting at the gate holding their son. She waved at him, her smile as bright as any sun.

But the fire came again.

And again.

It blistered his flesh, striking him to the bone.

Rawn's resolve broke, and screams tore from his throat. They echoed through the dungeon until he couldn't scream anymore.

CHAPTER 58

Lucenna

It was hardly midday, and Lucenna was already restless. She shifted on the velvet green bench that did little in the way of comfort. After being cooped up in the carriage for three days, she would rather ride a horse than spend another moment inside.

Lucenna hardly listened to Aerina's story as she recounted how she and Lord Norrlen fell in love. She was busy watching Dyna.

Her distant cousin had been silent all morning. She stared blankly at the hills coated in fog outside. Shadows lined her exhausted eyes, her complexion pale. Dyna's Essence also seemed dim. Lucenna reminded herself to brew Azeran's tea whenever they stopped.

Keena giggled with a trilling sound, drawing Lucenna from her thoughts. The fairy's wings released a puff of golden pixie dust as she flew around the carriage. "Lord Norrlen sure knows how to woo a lady."

Lucenna smirked. "He does bear a certain charm about him."

"Do you have a beloved, Lady Lucenna?" Aerina asked her. "I see you have a lovely ring."

"Oh, uh, well—" Lucenna stuttered, caught off guard by the question. She glanced down at the pink diamond sitting on her finger. It once shone brightly, but somehow appeared dull to her now. "I suppose you could say I am promised."

The statement came out half-heartedly. She didn't know what to call Everest. Beloved? Love-mate? None seemed to fit.

"She is to marry the Crown Prince of the Magos Empire," Kenna announced cheerfully.

Lucenna shot the fairy a withering look.

Keena winced. "Oh ... forgive me. Was it a secret?"

Crossing her arms, Lucenna slumped back in her seat. "I suppose not."

Though she didn't think sharing her story with Keena last night meant it would be shared with others.

"I see." Lady Aerina's brows rose high with interest, but she courteously didn't press her further. She asked Keena, "Are you promised as well, princess?"

The little fairy's hazel eyes widened, and she shook her head, making the gold beads in her dark hair jingle. "Oh no. I am not fond of such entanglements."

"Have you ever been in love?"

"I am not sure I would recognize the feeling. Love is unusual for faeries. From what I have seen, I find it more trouble than it's worth. Though it's quite amusing to watch," Keena added with a laugh that sounded like a tinkling of bells. The petals of her dress fluttered as she flew over to sit on Lucenna's shoulder.

"I suppose it can be trouble," Aerina said with a sigh. "You find yourself on this precipice where everything begins and ends with this person. Then every thought of them has taken over your life, and there is this incredible feeling inside of you. Passion and desire are only a facet in the deep well of affection that exists for them. When they are gone, it feels as if one cannot breathe..."

Lucenna watched Dyna carefully for her reaction to the turn of conversation, but she hardly blinked, clearly not listening at all. In truth, Lucenna wasn't sure if she could understand love either. What she had felt for Everest didn't seem to match that description.

Affection, yes, but passion and desire?

Lucenna had shared his bed once, and while an enjoyable experience, she realized now it was done only to please him rather than herself. Her young, impressionable heart had convinced her it was love. Would she even know what true love felt like?

Movement at the carriage window drew her attention to Klyde as he rode past with Tavin.

"The time Rawn and I had together was very brief," Lady Aerina said, pulling her back to the conversation. "But each day was so wonderful."

"Even when your marriage became too difficult to bear?" Dyna suddenly asked, looking up at her. "Lord Norrlen is a soldier. You, Your Grace, are a Princess of Greenwood. Your statuses are so far apart, you may as well be from two dissimilar worlds. Was it worth all the pain and backlash you suffered for loving him? For the disrespect and danger you still endure to remain his wife?"

Lucenna and Keena exchanged a glance. She may have had the same thoughts, but to voice them aloud...

Lady Aerina wasn't offended. She smiled at Dyna, though it was a sad one. "When I married Rawn, I chose to bind myself to him completely. I saw my marriage not as a promise to love him so long as our life was perfect. But a promise to love him through every trial, for he is the one I chose to face this life with." Lady Aerina looked down at the emerald ring on her finger. "They say the God of Urn tied each soul to their soulmate with a thread. This thread is to represent the bond between two people. It may stretch and tangle, but it will never break. Even if they are separated by distance, time, or obstacles, they will eventually find each other and fulfill their destined love. It is often used to convey the belief that true love is predestined, and that fate plays a role in bringing soulmates together..." Her voice wobbled and her eyes grew wet. "And if I am not meant to be reunited with Rawn in this life, I fully believe I will see him again in the next one ... because he is mine."

"Oh, you poor thing." Kenna flew to her and patted her cheek.

Dyna heaved a breath and rubbed her face. "I am so sorry for my thoughtless question. I didn't mean to imply..."

"No, no, it's all right." Aerina laughed wetly and drew out a handkerchief from her dress to wipe her eyes. "I am quite emotional these days. Please forgive me for my endless bouts of tears."

"Please don't feel the need to hold up appearances with us," Lucenna said, taking her hand. "You miss your husband, and you're worried about him. You're allowed to cry."

Aerina's eyes welled with fresh tears. "Thank you, but I ... I must behave as a princess should. Each day is a burden knowing what he must suffer. I cling to the hope that my Rawn will make it home." Her hand went to her chest. "I dread the moment I no longer feel him."

They had a connection, Lucenna recalled. She had seen it in the *Essentia Dimensio* when helping Rawn with his tracking spell. Elves may not have bonds like Celestials, but they have their own form of a magical link, if only an awareness of their mate.

"I made a promise to Rawn that he would see his family again." Dyna took Aerina's other hand. "I assure you. Nothing will make me break my word."

The tears gathering on Aerina's lashes spilled over like drops of dew. She must have been containing all her worry and fear. They sat with her as she silently cried, watching the land roll by.

The carriage eventually rolled to a stop in the early evening. Horses knickered and voices called to each other.

A rap knocked against the ceiling. "We have arrived, Your Grace."

"Oh, yes." Lady Aerina straightened up excitedly, all smiles again, though her pale skin couldn't mask the redness around her eyes. "We are here."

"Where?" Keena flew to the windows.

"We have reached the Melodyam Falls. This is my favorite place." She giggled, a pink blush coloring her complexion. "It's where Raiden was conceived."

Dear Gods, Lucenna did *not* need to be privy to that information.

Raiden, having opened the door for them at that exact moment, turned bright red. He groaned at the sky. "Mother, please."

"There is nothing to be ashamed of, dear."

Raiden returned her smile, though his was sarcastically polite. "Yes, well, I would rather you not discuss the private matter of my *conception* with our guests." He glowered exasperatingly at Dyna. Lucenna was relieved to see her crack a smile.

Aerina accepted her son's waiting hand and stepped out of the carriage. "You should be proud," she told him. "Your conception is what led to the discovery of these sacred waters."

"Sacred waters?" Dyna repeated as the rest of them stepped outside.

At first, they only saw the forest and the cliffside south of the game trail. But they followed Aerina round the carriage, and Lucenna's mouth dropped in awe. They had arrived outside a set of ruins carved into the side of a foothill. It held many stone bridges and abandoned structures covered in moss and vines. It overlooked a beautiful arrangement of three cascades that fell into a crystalline pool. The crash of the water echoed through the empty ruins, making it seem as if the halls were singing.

But what Lucenna found most peculiar was the water itself.

From where she stood, it looked pink.

Red petals floated on the surface of the water. Dynalyas grew everywhere. On the rocky cliffs, the water's edge, and on the small island in the center of the pool grew a large bushel of them. So tall, it may as well be a tree.

"The dynalya flower symbolizes love, yearning, and devotion," Lady Aerina said. "What is more, they are also a source of healing. Somehow, its magic has transferred to the waters here."

As she spoke, Cassiel landed not too far from them. His gaze was already on Dyna, which she pointedly ignored. Klyde called him over to help with the unloading of the horses as the guards set up camp.

"That sounds fascinating," Dyna said, looking eager to study the water.

"I will tell you a secret," Aerina whispered to her. "Long ago, the royal bloodline of Greenwood had been cursed." Her hand came to rest on her flat stomach as she gazed at the cascades. "A King cursed a King to bear only barren children, so one day his line would end. My father's line. Leif did not believe it, until his wife could not bear sons. I, too, became sterile. It was a secret well-kept for fear my brother would lose the throne. Until one day, Rawn brought me here, and then there was you." She smiled up at her son. "You do not understand the significance of what that means."

Raiden rolled his eyes. "Mother, I have a rather *undesirable* understanding of what that means. I think you, however, fail to understand what hearing this story, an insufferable number of times, does to my mental fortitude."

Lady Aerina gave her son a look that Lucenna could only describe as loving. She patted his cheek. "All right, darling, forgive me. Come, I must stretch my legs. Would you like to see the ruins, Lady Dyna?"

"Oh, yes. I would be glad to."

Raiden held out his hands to both women. "I will escort you, if only to impede any more embarrassing tales on my behalf."

Dyna laughed, walking off with the young Elven lord.

"Princess, please be careful," Camsen said as he and Eldred followed. "We are below the base of the mountain, and far too close to River Myst."

Cassiel watched them go, his gaze on Dyna.

"I can see his mind working to figure out how to gain her trust and forgiveness again," Keena whispered to Lucenna. "I can't help but feel sorry for him. The pain and love in his eyes, it's almost—"

"Pathetic," Lucenna retorted under her breath.

Cassiel had always been skilled at maintaining pretenses, but he couldn't quite hide the misery on his face when it came to her.

Lucenna strode over to him and blocked his view. "You did it to yourself."

Cassiel only blinked at her idly. "I did."

She scowled. Being mean to him wasn't fun if he agreed.

Then Lucenna noticed the large tear on his shoulder where the Other had nearly taken his arm. Dried blood still stained the dark fabric. "Why haven't you changed yet?" Looking at him more closely, his face was gaunt, and his eyes were shadowed. "Have you even slept?"

"No…" Cassiel answered dismissively, glancing past her to Dyna again.

"Have you eaten?"

"I will later."

"What is wrong with you?" she snapped. "You drove yourself to exhaustion when the Shades came, then you put yourself in harm's way with the Other. It was reckless."

Lucenna had always known him to be the cautious sort. But yesterday he could have died.

Cassiel blinked at her outburst. "There wasn't much of a choice when people stood to be killed. My abilities were better served in that situation."

"Perhaps you think yourself invincible now, Celestial, but you are not immortal. Your actions fall on Dyna, and that includes your lack of self-care." Magic crackled around Lucenna's hands. "I won't have you disrupting her sleep any longer."

His brow furrowed with confusion. Dyna had not slept either and was hardly eating. It was clear why.

"I can feel how tired she is…" Cassiel looked back at where she was. "And her magic is spent. Why?"

"How do you think you survived your fight with the Shades?"

The question left him astonished. Of course, Dyna kept it from him. When Cassiel had collapsed, she ran outside to him without hesitation and unleashed a tidal wave of green fire upon the Shades, killing them all.

But Lucenna was too worried about her now to keep it a secret anymore. "She can't sleep."

"What do you mean?"

"She's having nightmares, Cassiel. They started after you left and became worse when you returned. The bond may be broken, but you are still connected. Rest, so she can rest, too." Lucenna jabbed a finger towards the cook's tent. "Now go eat something."

Cassiel stared at her mutely before walking off without a word.

Klyde chuckled. He was a few steps away, building a tent while Tavin gathered firewood. "Was that your way of saying you're worried about him, too?"

"She is ice cold on the outside, but soft as dough on the inside," Keena teased.

Lucenna ignored them. "Where is Zev?"

"He's keeping to the woods," Klyde said

That was probably for the best, though she hated to admit it. Lucenna searched the trees for any streaks of black. He needed to eat, too.

In the morning, Dyna had healed him before he vanished into the forest. To follow the convoy at a distance.

"I heard the elves whispering about him," Keena said worriedly. "They called him a demon."

"I am." They all turned at the rumble of Zev's voice.

Lucenna spotted his glowing yellow eyes first. He was a large shadow in the dim brush of the forest, wearing only his trousers. A sheen of sweat coated his chest, his dark hair windblown. He looked exhausted, but much better than he usually did after a full moon.

"Zev, how are you feeling?" Lucenna went to him. She handed him a waterskin, and he tilted his head back as he drank it all. Up close, it was clear he had not suffered any new scars since he had spent the night without his silver chains.

"Better," Zev said, wiping his mouth with the back of his arm. He fleetingly glanced at the camp.

"Von is fine, and no one else was hurt," she assured him. "Dyna and Cassiel stopped you in time."

The mention of Cassiel seemed to stump him. Zev nodded curtly and turned to go.

"You won't stay, mate?" Klyde called out from behind her.

"It's best I don't. I'll keep to the trees."

"Have a meal with us at least," she said.

"Plenty to hunt in the forest. Will you let Dyna know I came by?"

"Of course."

He ambled away.

"Zev..." Lucenna called, and he paused, glancing at her over his shoulder. "You're not a demon."

He smirked faintly, though it was resigned. "Our origins began with the bite of a warg. What else could I be but a demon?"

That little tidbit tied Lucenna's tongue. Wargs ... she remembered reading about them. They were demons that had roamed the Everfrost during the First Age.

Zev walked away, fading into the trees.

Sighing, she returned to the camp spot Klyde was putting together with his nephew. With a sweep of her purple Essence, she levitated some logs around the circle of stones already containing a pile of firewood. With a snap of her fingers, she lit them aflame and took a seat.

"Intriguing." Keena shifted to her full height in a puff of gold dust and took a seat beside her. "I heard his kind carried traces of demon blood, but I wasn't sure if it was merely a rumor."

Klyde took out a sleeping mat from his pack, laying it out. "Werewolves came into existence during the First Age. The first was once human until he had been cursed with magic from the God of Shadows and the God of Death. It had turned him into a monstrous, bloodthirsty beast."

Lucenna thought of the Other and shivered. "Zev isn't like that..."

"Except for last night," Keena stated. Lucenna shot her a glare, and the fairy smiled sheepishly. "Only a thought. I'll go about seeing if I can find us something to eat."

She shrunk again and flew off, zipping like a yellow butterfly through the camp.

"You're a tad short-tempered today," Klyde said, taking Keena's seat. "Though you're a ray of sunshine compared to his royal highness over there."

He motioned to where Cassiel spoke with his Valkyrie, his arms crossed and brooding.

"Klyde, I have very little patience today, so perhaps you can attempt not to be exasperating." Lucenna glowered. He sighed. "You're already doing it."

"Lass, not everyone knows Zev as we do."

She arched an eyebrow. "We?"

"You forget I had the privilege of knowing him over the winter."

"Right, and you are an observant bloke with an opinion on everyone," she said, flipping her silvery hair over her shoulder. "So what do you make of him?"

"I believe Zev is a good man with an unfortunate curse."

"Do you think he's a monster, too?"

Klyde fell quiet as he observed the dancing flames. The low sun caught his features, gilding them in a soft orange hue. "We all have a monster in us in individual forms. Most sleep and never wake. Others appear once a month. Sometimes ... they take over who we are."

Lucenna studied him, wondering if he was thinking of his brother. She tried to imagine Klyde's monster but failed in her imagination.

He caught her staring at him and grinned. "What? Are you thinking I look rather handsome in the golden hour?"

She rolled her eyes. "No. I was attempting to imagine what your monster would look like."

He laughed, the sound low and husky. "I meant it figuratively, lass."

"I know, but if you did turn as Zev does, I'd imagine you would look like a Skelling."

His grin widened. "Aye? And why is that?"

The answer caught in her throat, and Lucenna's face warmed. She didn't dare tell him because it would only encourage his ego. The world would freeze before she ever admitted that the blue of his eyes reminded her of the seas his ancestors once ruled over.

At the lack of her answer, Klyde's gaze roamed her face. "There you go again," he said. "Having me wonder what you could possibly be thinking."

"I think you can find a better use of your time," Lucenna murmured. They jumped at the sudden clatter of firewood dropping on the ground.

Tavin wiped his dirty hands on his shirt as he asked, "Who is that man?"

They followed his stare to Von walking away from the camp.

He had done well to leave the boy alone. Probably because Klyde looked ready to murder him if he came near. But Tavin had noticed Von's attention on him as well.

Klyde clenched his jaw. "I told you. He's no one."

Tavin's pale gaze studied his uncle for a long moment, and Lucenna found herself holding her breath. "Then why does he look like mother?"

His mother?

Lucenna stilled, and her eyes widened when it hit her. Gods, in the right light, Von looked like Edyth. She stared at Klyde, and his grim expression all but confirmed it.

"Stay away from him, all right?" Klyde said gruffly. "He's dangerous, Tavin. Go on now. Leave your gear and fetch water for the horses."

His nephew glowered. He yanked off his harness and tossed it on the ground before wordlessly storming away.

Lucenna shook her head. "You can't lie to him forever, Klyde. He'll eventually learn the truth. Secrets have a way of coming to light."

A strange look crossed Klyde's face as he watched his nephew go. "I fear what it will do ... to reveal the truth."

"I understand that. But take it from someone who was raised with secrets and lies. The truth is always better." Lucenna looked down at her ring. "Even if they cannot accept it and hate you for it. A life of lies is not a real life."

Klyde leaned forward with his head in his hands. She could see how much this secret weighed on him, because she felt that same weight.

It was about time she told Everest everything.

What if he hated her and called off the wedding? Strangely, it didn't bother Lucenna like she thought it would. If he cared about her, he would care about what she stood for.

Too many years had passed, and she wasn't the same girl who had been infatuated with a prince.

Dyna's voice echoed in her head. *Do you love him?*

At the time, she couldn't answer. Whether it was love or duty, Lucenna knew she had betrayed him a long time ago. She needed to speak to Everest and set things right.

But she had to arrange it with Lucien first. Today.

Klyde lifted his head, and blue eyes carried much as he looked at her. "You're right, lass," he said after a breath. "I need to tell the truth ... but that doesn't prevent me from being afraid."

"I know." She was afraid, too.

CHAPTER 59

Dynalya

After dinner, Dyna wandered away from the camp toward the cascades. Raiden had shown her the ruins earlier, and now she wanted to investigate the sacred waters that happened to cure infertility. She stopped by the edge of the embankment and kneeled to gaze at her reflection on the surface. Except brown curls fell around her face, and eyes from another time looked back at her.

Dyna's pulse pounded in her ears as she recalled the dream she had last night. She had found herself in a familiar forest, before a *Hyalus* tree. Its leaves glowed in the evening like twinkling stars.

"Allow me this, and I will grant you anything," the pleading words slipped from her mouth that didn't seem to belong to her. *"Whatever wealth or favor, I'll do it."*

She spoke to a man with his back to her. He wore fine white robes, his pearlescent white wings catching the light. Gold-spun blond hair fluttered around his face in the evening wind as he stood silent.

"Then what do you want from me?" she asked him desperately.

He turned, and her heartbeat raced at the sight of Cassiel. The Celestial had his face, and yet she knew he wasn't the same Cassiel she knew. His blue eyes softened. *"You already know the answer ... lev sheli."*

Dyna had woken from the dream with her heart pounding. It circled in her mind all day. What did it mean? She was so tired of these confusing dreams and her unanswered questions.

Whatever sleep she gained had been minimal and frustrating. She had little to say to anyone, and she ignored Cassiel completely.

Groaning, Dyna splashed her face with cool water, and like magic, it soothed her headache, banishing it away. Well, that was interesting. She removed a glass vial from her satchel and dunked it into the pool. Drawing it out, she held it up to inspect it.

The true color was difficult to distinguish. The water appeared pink, but that was either due to the twilight or another organic matter like the dynalya petals floating in the pool. Whether what they said about the Melodyam Falls was true or not, studying new remedies always helped clear her mind.

But she couldn't stop thinking about last night, her new dream, and all the ones that had taken over her life. Every night, she was falling to her death or stumbling upon another reality. None of it made sense. When would they stop? Dyna was afraid to sleep lest she be plagued with more nightmares that she didn't understand.

But maybe she wasn't simply dreaming anymore.

You already know the answer ... dream walker.

Exhaling sharply, Dyna thought back to her other strange dream in the White Woods. Did Leoake know something? If she could say anything about that dastardly Druid, he *always* knew something.

Dyna tucked away the vial in her satchel and thought of the scroll he had left her with. The case landed in Dyna's hand. Pulling it out, she briefly ran her fingers over the green leather. She took out the scroll and studied the faded illustration of the mysterious key.

How ironic that it was also the key to her freedom.

The geas faintly throbbed as if in agreement. Dyna pressed against her ribs. It was a beautiful key, archaic in its intricate design with a winding bow made of bronze. Whereas keys were now made of iron. That alone told her this one was very old.

Whatever lock the key belonged to, it had to be connected to Mount Ida.

"What do you have there?"

Dyna jumped up at the sound of Raiden's voice. He had been standing over her shoulder, frowning at the parchment. She quickly rolled it up and tucked it away.

"Raiden, ah, it is nothing, really." Dyna flushed at her lie. Guilt filled her chest, because frankly, she had been keeping this from the Norrlen family.

How could Dyna explain the key was another reason she had to go to Red Highland? Even if Leoake had planned for this, it was her actions that led to Rawn's capture and Fair's death.

"It's beautiful here," she said, changing the subject. "What happened?"

"These ruins were once a grand civilization in the Vale. It was lost during the first war that split the kingdom in two."

Oh. That only made her mood bleaker.

Raiden canted his head as he searched her face, clearly as perceptive as his father. Dyna held her breath. "How are you, my lady?"

"Me?"

"You seem troubled—or tired," he quickly amended. "Well, of course you are, with the constant rain and long travel. I, well, we haven't had a moment alone since..." Raiden ducked his head, and the tips of his pointed ears turned pink. "I have been meaning to beg your pardon."

Ah, now that she thought of it, it did seem as though he had wanted to speak to her last night. It must have been difficult with so many ears listening.

"Do you mean your declaration to court me?" Dyna raised her eyebrows. "I admit, I was taken aback."

"Forgive me, I could not help myself." Raiden worked his jaw. "You flinch every time he calls you his wife."

She did?

Well, it hardly surprised her. The very reminder of who they used to be was a constant pressure against an invisible wound.

Dyna brushed the hair out of her face, looking away. "There is a past between us, I suppose. But—"

"Before you say this is between you and him, I am aware I have no right to intervene. Nonetheless, I wish to continue the pretense of being your suitor."

Dyna stared at him. "Why?"

"Because he hurt you." A sharpness entered Raiden's tone, and his hands curled into fists. "He hurt you when he abandoned you, and he hurts you more so when he is near. I hear how much your heart races in fear that he will hurt you again." He loosened his fists and folded his arms behind his back. "It is against my honor to stand by while a lady is in need, most importantly one who is my guest."

Dyna didn't know what to say. Raiden wanted to help her because he felt indebted, but it was also more than that.

She canted her head. "Is this because of your mother? Because you believe her also abandoned?"

He opened his mouth to respond, then closed it with a resigned sigh.

Dyna nodded. "You have shared with me what it was like to watch her suffer because she was alone. How you must have hated not having the power to protect her."

Raiden looked back at the camp in the distance. "When you brought us the news of my father's capture, that was the first time I saw her break. Yet she didn't allow me to comfort her. She sent me away, so she could weep in private. Now the veil of the perfect princess is back in place, for the court watches." He scoffed faintly, but she heard the resentment behind it. "She suffers still but does so in silence."

His mother sat beneath a velvet canopy outside of her tent, speaking with Eldred and Camsen with a polite smile. Gone were the tears from the carriage or any sign of distress. Sensing his stare, she met her son's gaze, and her face brightened.

Seeing her struggles and how she faced it with such kindness, Dyna learned the definition of grace. "The reason she hides the vulnerable part of herself is not because of the court, but because of you. A mother's instinct is to protect her child before herself."

Raiden sighed dejectedly, and his shoulders slumped. "Am I a terrible son?"

She gave him a small smile, and they walked along the pool. "No, I wouldn't say so."

"As for my offer?"

"I appreciate it, my lord, but Cassiel is not someone to challenge."

He hummed thoughtfully. "Due to his abilities, you mean. I have come to wonder how he wields such power. Those blue flames, the might behind them is..."

"Catastrophic." Dyna remembered clearly the destruction of Cassiel's power when he defended the Estate. He was much stronger now. "Seraph fire is a detrimental force. It burns through anything."

"Except for the metal used in the wine cellar," Raiden reminded her.

Dyna kept to herself that she was also immune to it somehow. "Skath metal is the only kind that can withstand Seraph fire."

"And no other Celestial possesses this power? Or is it only because he is the High King?"

Dyna bit her lip, frowning. "The past kings didn't wield Seraph fire. Except one, long ago. The first High King..."

King Kāhssiel.

The name reverberated through her mind, and she felt her heart shake. The sense that she had forgotten something important came over her.

At the familiar flutter in her chest, Dyna looked up at the gray skies. They watched Cassiel slip out of the clouds like a drop of black ink. He was hundreds of miles above them, but she felt his gaze on her as well.

"He's dangerous."

"So am I," Raiden said.

Dyna smiled bemusedly. It was a rather bold statement, and not one she had much confidence in. Not because she doubted Raiden's abilities, but because she knew how powerful Cassiel was.

He nodded for her to follow him, and they walked further west. Still within sight of the camp, but far enough away from the ruins and cascades.

"Pick one." Raiden motioned to a cluster of tall boulders.

Curious, Dyna raised her brows. "Hmm, the one in the center."

With a soft incantation in Elvish, a teal glow filled the forest as Raiden conjured a bow made of pure magic. Dyna's mouth parted with a soft gasp. A glowing arrow formed at his fingers next. He drew it back with perfect form and aimed at the bolder. The enchanted arrow zipped away and shattered the boulder into pieces.

"Oh, that was remarkable!" Dyna laughed. "I see there is more than one expert marksman in the Norrlen family..."

She trailed off when Raiden took her chin, his fingers gentle as he had her look into his eyes. "I am not a soldier like my father, but I can protect you from him."

Dyna stilled beneath his stare, and her face warmed. She was flattered, but the way he was looking at her made her nervous. "Well, let us hope it does not come to that." Clearing her throat, she backed up a step. "Could you teach me?"

Raiden chuckled. "It will work differently for you, but it all begins with Essence." The bow vanished with a flick of his fingers. "You must create the image of the bow first. I believe mages call these impressions, correct?"

Dyna nodded. Lucenna had already taught her that spell. She was teaching her invisibility now.

"This will be much the same, except it is now called conjuring, for we are to make the impression corporeal. To do so, you must feed it tangible energy. While I draw from the energies of nature around us, you would use your life-force." Raiden positioned his arms and spoke the incantation. The tug of power he drew from the air prickled against her skin. His hands shone with teal light as a bow formed between them.

It filled Dyna with giddy excitement, and she bounced on her toes. "That's simply magnificent."

"Now you try."

Dyna positioned her hands as he did and called upon her Essence. Her body as well as her Essence channels were exhausted. Pulling on her magic briefly made her veins ache, but her power was strong. Essence instantly surfaced at Dyna's call, and her hands blazed green. The bow formed as she had pictured it in her mind. Made of pure magic but solid in her hands.

"Now the arrow," Raiden instructed. Once she conjured it, he moved to stand behind her and gently positioned her arms. "Focus on the target. Keep your elbow tight and relax your grip."

"Like this?" Dyna asked innocently, doing as instructed.

"Yes." Raiden adjusted her fingers and shifted the position of her feet. He moved closer, his mouth near her ear as they both looked out at the second boulder. "Now draw and release with your next breath."

Exhaling, she released, and the arrow flew. It hit the target, shattering the boulder.

"Well, I'd say you're a natural." Raiden arched an eyebrow. "Have you trained in archery before? I made assumptions like a fool again, haven't I?"

Dyna laughed, but it faded when her chest thrummed, signaling Cassiel's approach. Her heart began to pound. Raiden must have heard it, because his smile faded, too.

Straightening, he looked up at the sky, then at her again. He said nothing more but held out his hand.

When the young lord first offered to court her under a guise, she hadn't truly considered it. Even now, the idea seemed so silly. Her past with Cassiel had nothing to do with him, but she found herself taking Raiden's hand anyway.

She heard the whoosh of Cassiel's wings as he landed a few feet away from them. His wet hair fell in messy waves around his flushed face. His eyes were careful as he took in their linked hands, before he focused on her, completely ignoring Raiden.

"May I have a word?"

"As you can see, we are preoccupied," Raiden replied unceremoniously. With familiar ease, he placed an arm around her shoulders and pulled her close.

A muscle flexed in Cassiel's jaw. His expression remained neutral, though his wings snapped open and closed, betraying his agitation. "Forgive me, but I am not speaking to you." His sharp gaze met Raiden's. "Lordling."

Raiden laughed dryly. "Well, I am speaking to you, fledgling."

Dyna felt a potent charge of power in the air.

And it came from both.

Flames wove through Cassiel's fingers like live eels as magic lifted off Raiden's silhouette.

"If you wish to fight me, then let us do so further away from the falls. I will not have you destroy more of my land."

The Elite Guards were watching, Lady Aerina's hand on Camsen's arm as if to hold him back. Her friends were watching worriedly, too.

"Stop," Dyna hissed sharply to Cassiel.

His Seraph fire was immediately extinguished. "I am not here to fight."

"Why?" A cool smirk played on Raiden's lips. "Afraid you would lose? Or that you would lose her to me? Rather late for that."

Cassiel smiled, but nothing about it was kind. A menacing blue light spiraled in his eyes, making them glow eerily. "You truly are determined to find a patron for your funeral."

The air grew heavy with stifling heat, and magic crackled violently on her skin.

A bracelet of runes formed around Raiden's wrists as he positioned himself in front of her. "You may be king where you're from, but you have no power here, Soaraway."

Cassiel laughed shortly as he rubbed his jaw. "For someone who scorns those who attempt to court your mother while she is yet married, you have the gall to pursue my wife."

Raiden's expression hardened. "Cease to call her that."

"Until our annulment is finalized, she is very much my wife."

"That word holds no value anymore. I know it, as does she. So tell me, which will be more difficult for you? Letting go of something so beautiful, or watching me take her from you?"

Cassiel's eyes glowed like blue torch fires in the night. "Be very careful what you say next. They may be the last words you ever speak."

"Should I take that as a threat?"

"Continue to irritate me, and it will be."

"All right, that is enough." Dyna stepped in between them. To Raiden she said, "Would you give us a moment?"

He frowned at her questioningly.

"Please."

Raiden hesitated to leave, but eventually nodded. "Shall I stay nearby?"

She shook her head. "No need."

He reluctantly walked back to camp, glancing back every so often.

When he was far enough away, Dyna glared at Cassiel. "Really, Cassiel? You would threaten Rawn's only son? In front of his mother, no less."

He sighed and shut his eyes. "I have been more than cordial, yet he—"

Dyna waved away the subject. "Well? What do you want?"

Cassiel shifted on his feet, hesitation lining his features. "I ... I'm worried about you. I know you don't wish to hear it from me, but using magic may not be wise right now..."

"I beg your pardon?" Dyna hissed through her teeth. Essence crackled around her fist. "You stole my magic from me, and now you want to determine when I use it?"

Letting out a groan, Cassiel raked a hand through his hair. "I meant to say you're tired, Dyna. And your Essence is low. I can feel it. Perhaps resting would be best."

"Gods, you are the last person who should tell me what is best for me." Dyna stormed away toward camp.

"Lucenna mentioned you are having nightmares."

She halted with her back to him. "That hardly concerns you, Cassiel."

"Well, I am concerned. They must be unbearable ... if you find the need to rely on Witch's Brew to stave them."

Anger surged in Dyna's lungs, and she scowled up at the trees. "What else has Sowmya told you?"

Because no one else knew about her taking Witch's Brew other than Zev, and her cousin would never share that with him.

Cassiel ignored the question. "Are you taking it again?"

"Whether I am or not is no business of yours."

"Have your nightmares of the Shadow returned?" he pressed.

"No, Cassiel. I am not dreaming of the Shadow again. It so happens the dark is no longer my greatest fear." Conjuring a blade of magic, Dyna faced him. "You are."

CHAPTER 60

Cassiel

The Valkyrie swooped down from the trees and surrounded them. Dyna didn't react, though. Her eyes stayed on him, her grip tight on the glowing sword's hilt.

Cassiel was rooted in place by her words.

Her greatest fear was *him*.

"My lady," Sowmya whispered to her urgently. "It is treason to draw a weapon against the king."

"He is not my king." Dyna lurched forward and attacked.

Cassiel dodged the swipe. His personal guard instantly drew out their swords.

"Stay your weapons," he commanded without looking away from Dyna. "Do not interfere."

Yelrakel clenched her jaw. "If she draws blood, sire?"

"Then your Queen will draw blood."

Dyna was enraged. He felt it pulsing in the bond. He also felt other things that told him she needed this.

"Dynalya is your High Queen, equal to me in every way. From today her word is law as much as mine. Be this the last time you ever draw a weapon against her. Even to defend me."

The Valkyrie sheathed their swords in unison and clanked a fist over their hearts as they bowed. Dyna's mouth thinned.

"Do you wish to duel, *motek?*" Cassiel drew out his divine sword, and blue flames swiveled around the blade. "Let's duel."

Fury simmered in her glowing eyes. Magic pulsed around her, and green flames enveloped her blade. So fierce, his mate. There was a wildness about her he couldn't help but admire. Even if it was pointed at him.

Dyna attacked. Her moves were swift and brutal, and she wasn't holding back. Cassiel met her swing for swing. The clash of their weapons rang through the forest as they fought. Many eyes were on them, but they kept their distance.

"Your skill with a blade has improved tremendously," Cassiel said, panting heavily.

"It's amazing what you can accomplish with time and rage." She leaped off a boulder as she swiped for him.

He parried her blade's next attack, and she countered. "Why do you fear me?"

Dyna lunged, and their swords crossed, bringing them face to face. "You know why."

The blades screeched as she pushed back, breaking them away.

"I gave you my word."

"And that means nothing to me." She gritted her teeth and came for him again.

Cassiel faltered in his next move at her response, and her blade swept nearly caught his torso. "Am I the one who fuels your nightmares?" At the look on her face, his eyes widened. "Tell me what you see in your dreams."

"No," she hissed.

Catching her next swing, he brought their blades to cross between them again. "Was that the reason why you went after Tarn? For Witch's Brew?"

Dyna glared at him for a long moment. "What Herb Master can't brew a potion?" Her smirk was cold and cruel. It broke his heart, because he knew he did that to her.

"If so, why go to him?"

"For what other reason? I went there to kill that man, and I did!" Dyna spun away and slashed.

Cassiel deflected, retreating from out of range. She wanted him to see her bloodthirsty. But he saw past that to her pain and wrath. "No, you didn't."

She bared her teeth. "Yes, I did!"

Dyna pivoted around him and swung her sword. Cassiel parried the blow. With a twist of his wrist, he struck Dyna's hilt and disarmed her.

The enchanted weapon dissolved in the air. Her chest heaved with labored breaths, her flushed face turning redder. Growling, she snatched the sheathed sword at her waist.

Cassiel straightened out of his stance. "Sowmya was there, Dyna. Tarn was wounded, and you left him on that burning ship, but you didn't kill him. In fact, I don't believe you wanted him to die."

She barked out a sardonic laugh. "You know nothing about what I want. Tarn asked for my help, and I turned my back on my morals as a healer when I turned my back on him. I left him to burn."

"You left him *alive*. As much as you despise him for what he has done, you're not a killer. A part of you wanted him to survive."

Dyna shook her head, her eyes wide with outrage. "You're wrong. He's nothing to me."

She once said those same words about him.

Cassiel didn't mean to fall on this topic. Sowmya had told him about everything she had witnessed on that ship, but it hadn't been a surprise.

He could only look at his mate and accept the past for what it was. Dyna stared back at him angrily at first, then her expression switched to realization, and the flash of guilt crossed her eyes. Cassiel wasn't angry or resentful, though. He had no right to be.

That didn't avert the pang that had nailed him in the chest when he felt his mate kiss another man. It was so sudden, so unexpected, Cassiel had nearly dropped out of the sky.

He looked at his Valkyrie, and they bowed their heads before retreating into the woods.

Cassiel straightened out of his stance. "You forget, Dynalya. We share one soul. You cannot lie to me."

"I am not ashamed," she snapped.

It was inevitable, he had told himself. When he left his mate, Cassiel had not planned to return. He knew Dyna would start her life over without him, and that meant she would eventually find another to share it with. The last thing he had expected was for her to pick Tarn.

But he had never questioned why.

"You have nothing to be ashamed of. I am the one who drove you to it." He met her eyes, burning so ferociously with anger and the emotion she denied. "I'm sorry."

"I don't want to hear again how sorry you are!" Dyna cried. She swung her sword, and their blades clashed. "That useless word will not heal all the pain you have put me through. I hate it, and I hate you!"

Cassiel parried her next blow and brought her close with the next. "Good," he said. "Hate me."

It was another echo of words he once said to her before. In another forest. In another time.

She growled and came at him again. The clash of their blades rang sharply as Cassiel met each attack she gave.

"Did it ever occur to you to discuss your worries with me?" Dyna shouted. "To try and face this hardship together? You didn't give me the chance to fight beside you. Why was breaking our souls the best decision to make?" She swung again, but he captured her wrist, bringing them face to face. "I hate that you did this to us! To *me*. Did you believe yourself something gallant by sacrificing yourself to spare me?"

Her scream ricocheted against the chasm, louder than the roar of the cascade. She was nearly sobbing. The agony rolling from her left Cassiel immobile. He let go, and she tackled him. Landing on top of him, she whipped out a knife, bringing it to his neck.

Cassiel didn't fend off. He didn't move at all. His eyes stayed on her as the sky rumbled with distant thunder, and rain began to fall.

"No ... I do not believe myself gallant. There was nothing noble about what I did."

"It was cowardly!"

"Yes..." he admitted. "It was."

"Why did you do it?" Her eyes brimmed with tears. "Tell me why, Cassiel, or by the Gods, I will stab you again."

He wanted to tell her, but even now the words lodged behind his teeth. At his silence, Dyna's hand shook. A trickle of blood leaked down from where the knife nicked him.

He could bleed out on the wet ground, and he wouldn't care, because she was finally *looking* at him. Those fierce green eyes acknowledged his existence. They were angry and sad and shining with tears. But she *saw* him. The relief slammed into him like a stone wall.

Cassiel couldn't resist faintly brushing his fingertips across her cheek. She stiffened, but didn't move away.

"Stab me. Flay me. Torture me. I deserve it all in the end," he muttered. "Each night I close my eyes, I see your face and relive the pain I put you through. It's like dying over and over again, yet I accepted it because I thought that pain was worth keeping you safe, and it nearly killed us both. So I am finished standing in your way, Dynalya. I can do nothing more than follow behind you."

She stared at him wordlessly, her ragged breaths fogging in the air. There was only them, the silence and the rain.

Dropping her knife, Dyna climbed off him and stumbled back. "Each night I asked myself why you did this, but from the beginning it was clear I was no more than a stupid, weak human to you. Best to fake her death and leave her behind, trapped where she cannot get herself killed, right? I resented that so much…" Her voice broke, and she covered her face. "I spent so much time making myself stronger to prove to you that I'm not weak … but deep down, I knew I truly was. I am reckless, and I make stupid decisions. Fair was killed and Rawn was taken because I am so stupid."

Dyna shook with quiet sobs. She couldn't stand anymore and toppled to her knees, weeping on the grass. To hear the fault she carried triggered something in him, and Cassiel's vision misted. The reason he left had nothing to do with that.

All he wanted was to hold his mate. To undo all the cracks he left behind. But he couldn't stand it if she flinched away from him anymore, so all Cassiel could do was sit beside her and drape his wing over her like a blanket, shielding her from everything else.

"I never thought you were weak," Cassiel murmured, prompting her to look up at him. "I cannot help but protect you. It's an instinct which has turned me into an overbearing fool from the day we met. But I haven't for one moment forgotten the strength that you have, for not even I have that." Tears spilled down her cheeks like dewdrops in the twilight. "You are what my people call *Eishet Chayil*. A woman of valor. Not only for what you did in Nazar, but for the courage you showed me every day that I have known you." He cupped her face, gently wiping away her tears with his thumbs. "*Ahuvati … at mehamemet.*"

Dyna closed her eyes for a moment, pulling down his arm. "Don't speak so lovingly to me. Do you think I'll forgive you simply for saying such things?"

It worked before.

As if hearing his thoughts, she glowered at him, but surprisingly, didn't leave. They stayed right where they were, gazing at each other as the rain fell around them.

"You paint me as pure and good, but I'm not. Not anymore." Dyna brought up her knees and wrapped her arms around them. "I also took lives."

That was the last thing he ever wanted for her. He was supposed to be the one who took lives in her stead. "Do you refer to the Shades? Why did you do that?"

Because if he had perished, she would be free of him for good.

"I may hate you, Cassiel, but I don't want you to die." She looked out at the camp. "The one death I can't forgive myself for is Fair's. Yet I ... I can't bring myself to tell them..."

Cassiel sighed. He wanted to comfort her, but that wasn't what she needed from him. "They don't need to know. We will fix it."

"Is that what you tell yourself when you hide things from me?"

His tongue caught.

Narrowing her eyes, Dyna straightened up, slipping off his wing. "I heard you in the woods last night. What happened in the past? What are you keeping from me?"

Trying to mask his panic, Cassiel rubbed his forehead. "Dyna..."

"If we are ever to repair a shred of our friendship again, the secrets and lies end now."

Gods, to know there was even a possibility of that filled him with a desperate hope—and fear. He didn't want to lie, but he couldn't tell her the truth either. Speaking it aloud would do no one any good.

Cassiel amended by telling her part of the truth. "Do you remember when Lord Jophiel spoke of the first High King of Hilos who had turned on his people?"

She nodded. "King Kähssiel..."

He swallowed, lowering his gaze. "The reason he turned on them was because they turned on him first. Those in his circle both feared and coveted his power, and so they plotted to remove him. The only way to weaken Kähssiel was to kill his True Bonded Mate." Dyna sucked in a soft breath. "Now another seeks to do the same to me..."

Dyna fell quiet for a long pause. "You left me to prevent that?"

He met her wide eyes. "In my mind, if the Realms thought you were dead, no other assassin would come after you. But now they know you survived, and wherever you go, death will follow. For he will never stop."

Her chest heaved with a breath. "You speak of Lord Raziel."

It was his turn to be surprised that she knew.

"Zekiel confirmed it before he tossed me in the pond." Dyna's lips thinned. "What did you do to him?"

Cassiel felt his blood heat with his fire at the reminder of the Celestial who nearly took her life. "I tore out his heart."

She went still, and her throat bobbed. "Why?"

"Whoever dares lay a finger on you revokes their life. I will spare *no one*." His reply came out as a growl, as if the very thought of anyone hurting her awoke the entity of flame that lived inside of him.

A breath shuddered on Dyna's lips as she stared at him. The blue glow of his eyes reflected on her pale face, and she glanced down at where the grass smoked beneath his burning fists. Raindrops hissed as they landed on his skin. Cassiel forced himself to take a breath to calm himself.

"Was that the reason you destroyed Skath?" she whispered.

It was a weighted question that extinguished his ire and left behind the ashes of shame.

Cassiel searched for the right words, but there were none. "When I left Skelling Rise, my only thought was vengeance. I pursued the Vanguard into the north, set on finishing the fight they started. I thought if I eradicated them, I'd feel gratified ... but I didn't." He dug his fingers through the scorched grass into the earth, and it crumbled around his hand. "I was the last one standing in the Realm I razed, and I felt worse than when this all began. I felt ... empty."

Skath Celestials were warriors. Even those not in the Vanguard had joined in the battle. They fought valiantly for their lives. If he had been anyone else, they might have won, but against his power, they never stood a chance.

"I didn't pursue the survivors. There was no justification in hunting down females and children. I had taken so many lives at that point, the thought of taking innocent ones..." Cassiel's stomach churned.

He almost said it would damn him, but he already was. His people viewed him as a thing that shouldn't exist, and they may be right.

Silence lingered between them as she looked at him. "How did you learn of Lord Raziel?"

Cassiel had known who his enemy was ever since he regained the memories of his past life. He played with a petal of flame, weaving it around his fingers. "Lord Hallel confessed before the end."

"Then why go after Lord Gadriel next?"

"I intend to save the Lord of Edym for last. For the best way to alienate an enemy is by removing his supporters."

One by one.

Dyna's mouth pursed with disapproval. "And that included destroying another Realm?"

"That was not my intention. I only came for those who took part in the coup."

"Yet if I had not arrived, you would have demolished Nazar."

Cassiel didn't argue, because she was right. In his rage, he had lost himself to his Seraph fire, and Kāhssiel's wrath had arrived with it.

"Your people fear you for your abilities, and you have done nothing but prove them right. This cannot be the way your father wanted you to rule. What would he say about this?"

Cassiel pressed on the tension pinching his temples. "I doubt he would come to me with any complaints."

"Don't be morbid."

He frowned at her aghast expression. "I'm not."

She shook her head. "Cassiel, the Realms may no longer concern me, but—"

"They do."

She stared at him.

"They do concern you, as much as you wish to deny it. You came to Nazar not simply to foil my plans, but to protect them because you are their queen."

She had *always* been their queen.

Her brow furrowed as she let his statement sink in. Sighing, Dyna wiped the soaked hair from her face. "Cassiel, have you ever thought perhaps you should align yourself with the Lords instead of attacking them? Do not follow Kāhssiel's footsteps. We must find another way to make peace with Raziel."

Cassiel's first instinct was to declare he would never allow Raziel to keep his life, but she had said *"we"*.

Two letters more valuable to him than gold.

"If to rule means a constant battle against your people, perhaps you should pass the crown on to another," Dyna continued.

"To whom?" He shook his head. "Who could possibly take the crown and not use it to strike me down? There is no other I can trust to rule in my stead without fearing they would condemn us both. Like it or not, I will always be a threat to them ... as you will always be my only weakness."

Dyna looked at him in a way that made his chest ache. Her features softened with another sigh, and she laid her head on her arms. "What fate the Gods have given us. They must find this all rather amusing."

"They are certainly laughing at my foolery."

A small smile played on her lips. "I think I hear it."

They fell quiet as she simply looked at him, a river of crimson hair cascading over her cheeks. He drank her in, admiring everything about her and the deep emerald eyes glimmering with flecks of gold. They seemed to absorb what was left of him.

"I missed this," Cassiel admitted. "Talking to you." Their sparring match somehow cleared the muddled air between them, at least a portion of it. "Shall we go for a flight?"

It was the wrong thing to ask by the guarded expression crossing her face. He was reminded of the way she had recoiled away from him last night. This was as close as he could get without frightening her. But touching her in any way that made her feel confined was out of the question.

"I understand." Cassiel stood, stretching out his wings. "Perhaps another time."

He turned to go, because he needed some space to feel what he couldn't feel in front of her. But a violent rumble echoed over the land, shaking the earth. They froze.

"What was that?" Dyna whispered, slowly standing.

Cassiel motioned for her to quiet as he studied the forested hills. The rumble came again, and the hair stood on end on the back of his neck.

"We must leave. Now."

CHAPTER 61

Lucenna

Lucenna's taut fingers turned white from how tight she gripped her crystal orb. She was no longer listening to Lucien as he rambled on about all the reasons why she couldn't contact Everest. Lightning flashed overhead, and it may have been partially due to her. The wind picked up, blowing her white hair around her face as she glowered at the view beyond the cliffside.

Exhaling a sharp breath, Lucien linked his hands together on his desk. "Lucenna, I know this is not what you want, but you know how imperative your survival is to the future of Magos. It's not safe."

She paced along the edge of the cliff, feeling her frustration climb. "I will be careful and only speak to him, Lucien. Everest would never betray us. I must tell him the truth."

"No," his tone hardened. "You don't."

"What are you not telling me?"

"Lucenna, come quick!" Keena flitted to her. "Dyna and Cassiel are fighting, and I think it's serious."

"What?" She glanced over her shoulder to see Dyna and Cassiel sparring in the woods. But the Valkyrie were standing guard. Good, they probably needed to work things out this way.

"Keena, they're fine. Go keep watch if you're worried." Lucenna swatted a hand, and the fairy flew away with a huff. She glared at her brother. "I need to know what you are keeping from me, Lucien, because you have been alluding to the subject since I left. Does Everest know I joined the Liberation?"

Her brother's expression grew guarded. "Lucenna, simply take me for my word when I tell you we cannot trust him."

"Why? If you don't answer me, I will contact him myself."

Lucien closed his eyes and took a deep breath. When he looked at her, the expression on his face made her still. Whatever her brother had to say, he didn't want to speak the words.

"Lucien?" she whispered, afraid of his answer.

"Ava is no longer with child."

The strength left Lucenna's legs, and she sat on a large boulder. "What do you mean? What happened?"

Her brother's lilac eyes grew wet and looked away. "She was found at the bottom of the stairs in the west wing..."

Lucenna's chest heaved, and she covered her mouth. "Is she...?"

"Ava is alive, but only just. Her child didn't survive."

"Oh, Gods."

Whatever she thought of Ava, to lose a baby was horrible.

"Wait. What does this have to do with Everest?" The expression on Lucien's face made her blood run cold. "You cannot possibly think he had anything to do with it?"

"Lucenna, that child would have deposed him as heir apparent to the throne. Removing it would restore his position."

All obstacles in your path will be removed.

She sucked in a breath, her chest heaving with sharp denial. "Listen to yourself. Everest is kind. He would never—"

"Everest is to be the next Archmage," Lucien said tightly. "Like all those who came before him, his only goal is power. If you expose yourself to him, he will find you, and bring you back to Magos. He is not the person you think he is, Lucenna."

She continued to shake her head. It couldn't be. Not after everything they had been through together. Not after everything they shared.

"You were raised with him, Lucien. He was your closest friend. What you are telling me doesn't sound like the Everest I know."

Her brother leaned back in his seat, and his shoulders slumped. "I don't think we ever knew him at all."

It simply didn't make any sense.

"Do you have proof?"

He blinked at her. "What?"

"Do you have proof that Everest pushed Ava down the stairs?"

Lucien frowned. "No, but clearly this was intentional. He is the only one who benefits."

RISING DAWN

"Out of everyone in the castle, why do you insist he's the culprit?"

Her brother blinked at her, stumped by the question. He looked away from her and shifted in his chair.

She narrowed her eyes. "You are keeping something from me, Lucien. You have no proof of your claims, yet you refuse to allow me any contact with Everest. What are you hiding?"

Lucien's mouth pursed into a thin line. "You will *not* contact him, Lucenna. I forbid it. We will not speak of this again."

With a wave of his hand, the orb cleared. She gaped at it in disbelief. Lucien had never behaved in such a way before, where he strictly commanded her and expected her to obey.

Like a mage would.

Lucenna had the sudden feeling she was oblivious to much more than she realized. The cool orb sat still in her hand, catching the last of the evening light. Well, she was never one for obedience.

Crouching down, she placed the orb on the ground and drew runes in the mud with a stick.

"Lucenna?" She ignored Klyde's approach as she drew a circle around them. "What are you doing, lass?"

"I am breaking Lucien's warding spell on the orb," she muttered.

"Why?"

"So I can contact others." She waved her hand over it, and the runes blazed purple.

Klyde paused. "Others, or your prince?"

"I need to speak to Everest. My brother is hiding something from me, and I will find out what it is." Pressing her fingers together, Lucenna paused, questioning if she should do this.

She couldn't imagine Everest would ever hurt anyone. Not when she had so many sweet moments with him. Her first memory of him was when she was a little girl.

While chasing butterflies, Lucenna had tripped in the courtyard in Castle Ophyr and skinned her knee. Blood stained her dress, and she cried, but then Everest appeared like a god against the sun. It was the first time he had spoken to her, but she knew who he was. The prince she was meant to marry. He was older, seventeen at the time. Everest smiled at her with his golden amber eyes, as if she were the most precious thing in the world. Laying his hand over her knee, his gentle magic healed her. *"I cannot allow anything to harm my future."*

That was the mage she knew.

Lucien was wrong.

403

She snapped her fingers, and the warding spell broke. Closing her eyes, Lucenna reached out with her Essence and called on Everest.

When she found him, his awareness instantly flooded her mind with familiarity. She opened her eyes as the crystal orb glowed with light. The sphere filled her vision until the world had disappeared, until all she could see was spiraling white smoke. Her heart pounded with anticipation.

She was finally going to see him after four years.

Klyde's boot rammed into the orb.

She gaped at it in horror as it flew over the cliff and vanished from her sight. Lucenna sprinted to the edge, only to see it drop into the river below.

She whipped around to Klyde in disbelief. "What do you do?"

He stepped back, holding up his hands. "Ah, pardon me. I ... slipped."

"Slipped? You *slipped*?" Lucenna shrieked. "That was clearly deliberate!" She stormed at him and swung her fist. "Have you lost your mind?"

Klyde dodged the punch with a chuckle. "No, but I lost my footing. It's quite muddy around here. Come away from the cliff's edge before you slip, too."

Rain came pouring down, and she shook with anger. "That orb was the only means I have to communicate with my brother!"

"Oi, calm down, love."

"I am not your love! And don't tell me to calm down!" Lucenna beat her fists on his chest, though she may as well strike a wall. In their struggle, she slipped, and he caught her against him, which only enraged her more. "Honestly, you are the most infuriating, preposterously arrogant, inept man I've ever met!"

Klyde caught her wrists in his solid grasp. "Having encountered the caliber of men from the Magos Empire, I'll take that as a compliment."

Lucenna had the urge to strangle him, but he still hadn't released her. Purple electricity crackled across her skin. "I should kill you."

They both watched her magic merely fizzle out when it met his enchanted mercenary coat. Klyde cracked a smile. "I would find that more threatening if it were possible."

"Would you like to wager that?" She grabbed the blade strapped to his belt, but it vanished from her hold before she could do anything with it.

The blade twirled in Klyde's hand as he stepped back. "Lass, you know I have scruples against harming women. But I do admit I am at fault here. Allow me to replace your orb."

"That orb can never be replaced. I have put up with your exasperating candor, but this..." Tears sprang to her eyes, and she quickly turned away from him. "That orb belonged to my mother."

Klyde let out a long breath, softly cursing. When he spoke again, the amusement was gone. "I am so sorry, Lucenna..."

"Why did you do that?"

Because it was no accident. He intentionally kicked the orb.

He sighed again. "I—"

A loud rumble shook the earth, and she backed into him. He caught her waist.

"Did you feel something?" she whispered.

He chuckled. "Aye, I did."

"Ugh, pig." Lucenna elbowed him back.

The rumble came again, and she whipped around to see the trees break away from the hills, and the ground sunk in on itself. Water and mud rushed down like a wave. Cries broke out, and everyone fled. Cassiel snatched Dyna into the air with the Valkyrie. The Rangers ran for their horses, rushing Lady Aerina and Raiden to safety. Some elves tried to cast magic to obstruct the deluge, but it swept them away.

"No," Klyde breathed. "Tavin."

He sprinted toward the camp.

"Klyde, wait!" Lucenna ran after him.

Water flooded the camp as everyone ran. A large black wolf landed in a crouch beside her, skidding over the mud.

"Zev!" Lucenna shouted as she ran alongside him. "Find Keena."

He sprinted off.

She spotted Klyde ahead, quickly strapping on Tavin's grappling harness. "He's not here," he said urgently when she caught up to him. "The horses are gone."

Lucenna searched the running crowd and pointed. "There!"

Tavin was riding a horse and holding the reins of Onyx as he also desperately searched the chaos.

"Tavin!" Klyde ran for him.

The boy's face lit up with relief when he saw him. And in a blink, a rogue wave of mud swept him away from view. Before Lucenna could scream, another wave hit them next. She choked on muddy water, blinded and disoriented as she tried to breathe. She fought desperately to kick and flail, but the rogue current pulled her beneath the surface. A firm grip on her arm yanked her back up, and she coughed violently, sucking in air.

"I got you," Klyde said, his arm like a vice around her back. "Move with the current—"

A tree slammed into them. The force tore her from his hold at the same time pain shot up her arm. She bit back a scream. The wild current rushed everything toward the cliff, including her.

"Klyde!" she cried, choking on water. She flailed desperately, panic and fear smothering her.

His frightened voice yelled her name. He was several feet away, trying to swim toward her, but she was still too far.

Lucenna's scream echoed in the sky as she went over the cliff. Klyde leaped after her and caught her with a grunt. He twisted his body and shot grappling hooks out of his harness. They pierced the rock wall, and their fall down the ravine halted midway down.

"Hold on!" Klyde slung her onto his back without breaking a stride.

He scaled down the length of the cliff as the endless deluge poured over them. Lucenna fought to breathe. Her heart pounded wildly, and she dug her nails into him. They were several feet from the rushing river below.

The metal cables snapped.

She screamed as they dropped into the icy current. Klyde didn't let go. His bruising grip dug into her as waves and debris crashed into them. She choked on water. Branches and rocks sliced at her skin. Lucenna clung to him for her very life, but the harness weighed them down. Klyde yanked it off and grabbed onto her, keeping her head above water. But he was struggling to swim. The current was too strong, and he was growing tired.

"Head to land!" he told her.

She shook her head, tightening her grip on him.

"You can do it, Lucenna. Use your magic or you will drown, and so will I!"

"Not without you!"

"I can swim. I'll make it."

Arrogant mercenary. The riptide would eventually overpower him, and she wasn't leaving him behind.

Lucenna wrapped her arms around his neck and shut her eyes. She ignored the fact that she had no real training in water magic, because it was life or death, and she wasn't going to die here.

Her magic surged at her call, and she threw out her hand with a scream. A purple Essence Blast hurtled them from the water, throwing them up against the boulders lining the shore. Pain throbbed all over her body. She couldn't move. Klyde dragged himself out, then hauled her up onto the bank. They fell back, wheezing.

"You did it," Klyde rasped. He pulled her to him, holding her so tightly against his chest she could hear his heartbeat racing. Lucenna shut her eyes, her breath trembling. "I knew you could..."

Klyde laid there for a long moment. He stared blankly at the canopy of trees above them, probably contemplating how close they had come to death ... or the last moment he saw Tavin.

"He's alive," she whispered.

"The flood hit him head on..."

"Yes, but he lives."

"How do you know that?"

Lucenna hesitated before sitting up. "When I realized who Tavin's father was, I was curious to see if he had any magic in his blood." She looked away from the force of Klyde's stare.

"And?"

She flinched at his harsh question. "It's dormant ... but it's there."

Klyde didn't speak. She listened to his breaths as his chest expanded with each one until she felt his anger subside. "Can you sense him now?"

"Only that his presence is on this plane, as I know Dyna's is."

"Can you track him?"

"Perhaps once I gather my bearings."

Klyde roughly rubbed his face. "He's probably alone out there. Who knows where the current took him."

"You trained Tavin to survive. He traveled across Urn on his own to find us. Have more faith in him."

Klyde nodded. "Aye, you're right. We won't be of any use until we sort ourselves first." He looked her over. "I need to get you warm. Your lips are blue."

Lucenna trembled uncontrollably. They were soaked through, and the temperature had dropped, but she wasn't aware of being cold. Likely due to the adrenaline.

"Are you wounded?" she said, spotting the many red stains on his shirt. She tried to stand but cried out at the sharp pain shooting through her arm.

"I'm fine." Klyde made her sit down again. "Your shoulder is dislocated."

Lucenna whimpered at the sight of her arm hanging at an odd angle. It was suddenly hurting now that she noticed it.

"I need to push it back into the socket."

"Is that going to hurt?"

His mouth curled in bemusement.

She grimaced. Of course it would. "Perhaps we should wait for Dyna."

"It will only get worse, lass. Best I do it now." Klyde studied her for a bit, then reached in his coat and brought out a small leather wineskin. He took a drink and offered it to her next. "Here, drink this. It will help take the edge off."

Lucenna accepted it without question, and she took a sip. The ale burned down her throat and flushed her face with warmth. It was no use waiting for Dyna to heal her. She already felt faint, and her arm was throbbing terribly. Klyde raised his eyebrows when she tipped her head back and swallowed down the rest of the ale. It immediately rushed to her head, leaving her woozy.

She wiped her mouth. "I'm ready."

Klyde shifted to sit next to her. His large, warm hands took hold of her shoulder and elbow. It was in these moments when she noticed how much he dwarfed her.

Tightening his grip on her arm, he nodded. "Clench your jaw or you'll bite your tongue."

Lucenna snapped her teeth shut and closed her eyes. His breath brushed against her cheek.

"Look at me," he ordered softly. She tilted her head to look up at him, and he was watching her, his eyes as calm as a still sea. "Now breathe."

Bracing herself, Lucenna inhaled a sharp breath through her nose a second before he shoved her arm into its socket. She screamed through her gritted teeth and slumped against him, breathing harshly.

Klyde cradled her against his chest, lightly massaging her shoulder joint, encouraging the pain to subside. "It's over now, lass. You did well."

He rubbed her back, working the heat back into her body. Whenever his fingers brushed her lower spine, it bloomed electrical currents of warmth across her skin from her toes to her scalp. She shivered as her mind grew hazy. He was warm. She tucked her cold nose against his throat, and he stiffened.

"You smell nice..." Lucenna mumbled.

He chuckled. "You mean like mud and blood?"

"Like a winter forest at sea..." Why was she telling him this?

Klyde held her back by her shoulders and his eyes widened as she smiled at him lazily. The cool breeze felt good against her flushed cheeks. "Are you all right?"

"I'm grand." The pain was faint, pushed to the back of her mind. Lucenna blinked at him through her bleary vision, taking in the angles of his face and the moonlight falling over the worried knot between his brows. His wet hair fell in messy waves past his jaw. Reaching up she stroked his cheek, feeling the bristles of his stubble. She wondered what he looked like without a beard. "You're pretty."

"Ah, erm, well, I suppose I am." Klyde cleared his throat. Was he blushing? "Lass, you can't look at me like that. You have me stuttering like a fool."

She giggled at the befuddled look on his face and said in her best brogue accent, "Aye, lass."

"Gods, you're drunk. I shouldn't have given you the whole thing. We're in for a night."

Lucenna laughed again. There was something about his voice. She simply liked hearing him speak. "You're funny, Klyde Morken. Are you always this funny?"

She stood and slipped on wet stones, flailing backward toward the river.

"Oi!" He snatched her wrist and yanked her back to him. "Are you trying to be the death of me, woman?"

The question snapped her out of her haze. The last thing she wanted was to be the death of anyone.

Suddenly annoyed, she pushed off his grasp. "Why did you break my orb?"

"Come on." He moved her away from the bank. "You need to lie down. We should find somewhere to stay for the night."

"No." She jerked her arm free, whimpering at the throbbing in her shoulder. "I won't go anywhere with you until you tell me why."

Klyde ran a hand through his hair and groaned with exasperation. "I couldn't stand it, all right?"

Lucenna blinked at him.

"I know he's the one you want, but..." He stepped closer, and her pulse quickened. "Some arrogant, infuriating, inept part of me didn't want to share you with another man. When the orb began to glow, I reacted before I could think. I truly am very sorry about that."

Lucenna suddenly couldn't look at him. That was quite clearly a confession, if she understood him correctly. He had to be teasing her again. But she couldn't think clearly past her pounding heartbeat. "W-well, that is the most a-bsurd thing I ever heard. Fool."

He chuckled quietly. "Agreed."

She crossed her arms, heat radiating in her face. "You will acquire me another orb. Made of the finest quality."

"Of course. Nothing less than perfect." Lifting her chin, Klyde made her look up at him, sending tingles down her neck. He tilted his head, holding her gaze. "Come, I'll carry you on my back as we look for a spot to stay tonight. You'll get nowhere in this state."

"That sounds like an excuse to carry me," she mumbled.

One end of his lips curved, and a dimple appeared. He didn't deny it. With the way he looked at her, so tender and warm, she hadn't the will to protest.

Klyde crouched and motioned for her to climb onto his back. Ignoring her blush, Lucenna wrapped her arms around his neck and hooked her legs around his torso. He lifted her with ease. Her mind listed all the reasons she shouldn't allow this, but his steady stride through the trees and the warmth of his broad back soon had her body relaxing against him. It was absurd how easily he made her defenses drop. Her next inhale was filled with his scent, and it occurred to her why her glamor continued to fail when she was with him.

Because Klyde made her feel safe.

Gods. She needed to get a hold of herself.

Glowering, Lucenna rested her head on his shoulder. "I could have walked, Captain."

He chuckled, and the husky rumble tickled her ear. "With all the ale you drank, you'd only end up on your bonnie arse, love." Then he added in a murmur so soft she nearly missed it. "I can't have you falling if it's not for me."

CHAPTER 62

Cassiel

Cassiel's boots squelched in the mud as he strode over to where Dyna sat by a campfire. Voices swarmed around him, Camsen directing his men to either search for survivors or supplies. The new campsite was set only a couple miles down from where the flood had hit them. It was late into the night when they at last got a hold of Lucenna and Klyde through the water mirror.

Dyna nodded tiredly at the glowing plate on her lap as she said goodbye, and the light faded. She dumped the salted water in the grass.

He sat beside her, handing her a cup of warm vegetable broth. "Here."

"Thank you..." She blew on it before taking a sip.

"How are they?" Cassiel asked as he wiped down the mirror and put it away in her enchanted satchel.

"Fine, from what I could see. She's a little bruised, but that's the worst of it. Klyde gave her something for the pain. The current took them several miles west from here. Her location spell on Tavin puts him on the other side of the ridge, nearly fifteen miles away. I sent Zev to look for him and Von."

"That's good news."

She sighed heavily. "We needed some tonight."

He and the Valkyrie had pulled many from the water. Dyna had joined Eldred and Raiden in using magic to block most of the current before more lives were lost. And it had taken a toll on her. Cassiel could feel it as well as see it on her pale complexion.

"I told them to reunite with us in the City of Evos at the border of Avandia," she added. "Camsen said we will respite there before making our way to the capital."

Cassiel nodded hesitantly before saying, "Once you finish the broth, you should lie down."

Glowering at him, she downed the rest of it and set down the empty cup. "I will once I have checked on the wounded."

Cassiel sighed. "Dyna, Eldred can tend to them. Your magic is at its limit. I am worried about you."

"What you worry about holds no weight right now." Her voice was quiet, cold. Her eyes burned like a raging fire. She was furious. "What is most important?"

He knew the answer she wanted, but he could only tell her the truth. "You," Cassiel said. "The answer is always you."

Her anger wavered, and emotions crossed her face. So swift, he may have imagined them.

"Spare me your concern for my well-being. I will rest once I'm finished." She walked away toward the camp. "Don't follow me."

He halted mid-step and reluctantly watched her walk away from him again.

A chuckle drifted from the dark trees. Cassiel ignored Netanel as he came to stand beside him.

"I like her. She's stubborn, as are you."

"Did you see when she wielded her blade against me?"

His spy grinned. "I did. I feared for your life a few times there. She has my respect."

"I was holding back."

Netanel gave him a look. "Is that what you call it?"

"She may cut me all she wishes. I would rip myself apart if it would atone for what I've done." Cassiel sighed heavily and pressed on his aching forehead. "She keeps me at arm's length, and I know not what else to say to her."

"You mean short of revealing the truth?"

Cassiel glanced at him sharply.

Netanel gave him a desolate smile. "I have come to learn that words can only do so much. Dyna is far too hurt to hear anything you have to say right now. The best thing you can do is be there for her and show how much she means to you."

They looked at each other a moment, then Cassiel looked away. "How?"

"Your queen is made to quell your flames. Likewise, only you can quell hers."

Cassiel sighed and turned to Yelrakel standing a few feet behind him. "If you are here, I assume you have something to report, General?"

She fleetingly glanced past his shoulder to Netanel, then dropped to one knee, bowing her head. "I have received word from Nazar. Lord Gadriel wishes to speak with you."

Cassiel crossed his arms. "Does he? To lure me into another ambush, or to beg for his son's life?"

"He did not say."

Expelling another breath, Cassiel massaged the knots in his temples. He didn't have time for this. "Kindly send word to Lord Gadriel that I will not be summoned at his whim. He will see me at the hour I deem it so."

"As you command." Yelrakel stood, but she didn't leave.

"What is it?"

She hesitated. "Forgive me, but is it wise to delay this matter further? The Realms are unstable, and the Lords are revolting. Our people need their king—"

"I am needed *here*," Cassiel cut her off. "I cannot rule until I can be assured my queen will not be murdered behind my back. You forget. I cannot live without her. If she dies, so do I. Any more counsel you wish to give, General?"

Yelrakel bowed her head. "No, sire."

"Then do your duty."

Backing up three steps, she flew away.

Cassiel glanced at Netanel. "And you do yours. I told you not to reveal yourself unless necessary."

"It seemed you needed some encouragement."

He glowered at him. "I'm not a child."

"Certainly not."

But Cassiel read the hesitation on his face, too. "You agree with Yelrakel."

Netanel's wings stretched out as he flexed them. "Only you can decide the future of your reign, Cassiel. But whatever your plan, it must be made quickly. For you have many enemies, and too few allies. The throne of Hilos will not sit empty for long."

With that dire warning, his spy strode away toward the trees and slipped into the forest. They were right, of course. His responsibility as king was to put his people first. Yet how could he rule them when his sole focus was only on one thing?

He watched Dyna move around the open tent set up for the wounded. All he wanted was to take care of her, but it was selfish to impose himself on her. It was best to be nearby when she needed him.

Sighing, Cassiel turned toward his tent.

Nausea sank through him, and he fought a sudden spell of weakness as the world spun. Cassiel whipped around to Dyna in time to see her eyes roll. He was running before she tipped over, caught her before she hit the ground. But *that one* reached her at the same time, with his presuming hand cupping the back of her head.

"I've got her," Cassiel snarled.

"You did. Once," Raiden replied coolly. He shifted his position for a better hold. "I will take care of Lady Dyna from here."

They were locked in a stare, neither budging to let go. Whatever claim this fool thought he had on her, Cassiel was finished allowing it to continue.

"Do you like having hands, Raiden?" His eyes flamed blue. "Then I suggest you remove them *off my wife.*"

His Seraph fire swarmed up his arms and enveloped her in a cocoon of heat. Raiden immediately leaped back with a curse. Standing with Dyna in his arms, Cassiel tucked her against his chest. All eyes followed him as he took his mate away.

In that moment, he carried his whole world.

CHAPTER 63

Dynalya

D yna woke to warmth and a familiar scent. Her body seemed to sway, and she blinked up in confusion at the night sky speckled with stars. What happened?

Her heart jolted to find herself cradled in Cassiel's arms.

The sounds of the camp and firelight grew further away behind him. He was taking her away somewhere.

"What are you doing?" she asked, alarmed. "Put me down!"

Cassiel sighed as he looked down at her, and she sensed his relief mingled with annoyance. "You fainted, Dyna."

She fainted? It took her a moment to recall her vision tilting before falling over in front of everyone. That was rather embarrassing.

"I can walk."

"You have met your limit. I'm putting you to bed."

Dyna muttered another protest, but attempting to wiggle out of his hold hit her with a dizzying wave. Her vision tilted again. Groaning, she buried her face against his shoulder, eyes squeezed shut as she fought a wave of nausea. He was right. She was done for the night.

Her body settled back into his hold, and Dyna listened to his heart. He was warm, skin damp from the rain, but she didn't mind. It accentuated his ambrosial scent that inexplicably put her at ease. She had always liked how he smelled.

Like wind and divinity.

But it left her with awkward unease to accept his help after publicly spurning him. Now they watched him carry her away. It felt inappropriate. Too intimate. Even if that man was her husband.

Had been, she reminded herself.

Cassiel slipped in through the flaps of a tent and placed her on a bed. It was a very nice four-poster bed carved from a pale gray wood. The blue bedding felt soft against her palms. Not something one expected to find in the middle of the wilderness. And magic hovered in the air, she could sense it.

The tent was enchanted.

"Whose tent is this?"

"Mine." Cassiel went to the brazier, lighting it on fire. The blue flames turned to yellow and filled the space with warm light. "And yours, for as long as you need."

She took in the fine furniture: a desk with scrolls, a dining table, iron candle stands, the blue drapes adorning the canvas ceiling, and the dark blue rug embroidered with a filigree of gold. Behind her hung a banner with the sigil of Hilos—a flaming sword with wings. His scent was strong here.

Cassiel poured her some water and had her drink it before moving behind a privacy screen. Another flash of blue glowed against the walls. He returned. "Sowmya filled the bath earlier. I heated the water now so you may bathe."

Dyna only blinked at him, taken aback by all of this. "You enchanted the tent with stardust?"

"And pixie dust. I learned a useful thing or two from Lucenna." Cassiel rubbed the back of his neck. "Don't tell her I said that."

Dyna didn't know what else to say to him. She expected he would leave, but her eyes went wide when he lowered to one knee in front of her. Dark lashes shadowed his eyes as he took her boot and carefully released the buckles. Each deft movement of his fingers had her entranced, and her heart thrummed so hard in her chest that she worried he would feel the pulse all the way down her leg.

"You don't need to do this, Cassiel."

"I want to."

Her skin warmed. It reminded her of another night that mirrored this one.

I will always kneel for you.

Setting her foot down, Cassiel picked up the other boot to do the same thing, his hand supporting her calf gently. Heat bloomed from every contact of his touch, and her skin tingled despite the layer of clothing between them.

Finished, Cassiel looked up, close enough to her that she could see every fleck in his silver eyes. His expression was neutral, but tense. The bond may be meaningless now, a ghost of what it once was, but she felt the fire burning behind his wall.

"You're angry," Dyna stated.

His brow pinched, slight surprise crossing Cassiel's features before he rubbed his face and sighed. "Yes, well, that is a perpetual condition, it seems. Yours, however, can be fatal."

Ah, he was annoyed by her carelessness. Again.

Which only annoyed her in turn.

"Why do you continue to push yourself?" Cassiel scanned her face, as if he worried something about her had been damaged.

Her heart squeezed beneath the concern in his gaze, but she couldn't take it, because it made her feel things she didn't want to feel. "My well-being is no longer your concern," she said rather curtly.

A muscle shifted in his jaw. "Your well-being will always be my concern, Dyna." He stood. "Now, where did you leave your satchel?"

"My satchel?"

"I assume that is where the herbs for Azeran's tea are stored. I will brew a pot for you."

She shook her head but winced when that made her dizzy. "I don't have any more herbs. I used everything I had in treating the wounded." It had gotten to the point that Dyna even used the pink waters she gathered from the Melodyam Falls. She fainted before learning if it worked. "Replenishing my reserves will wait until we reach Evos."

Cassiel's eyes flashed, and she braced for his chiding, but he simply took a deep breath. "Will you be all right until then?"

"I'll be *fine*." He didn't need to hover over her, especially when she smelled like murky bog water. "Please, I am too tired to argue. I want to bathe and lay down."

He conceded with a nod. "Shall I have Sowmya assist you?"

"I can manage." Dyna missed her handmaiden, though. Noemi had long returned to Hermon.

"Very well. Leave your clothes by the entrance, and Sowmya will see them washed. Meanwhile, you may wear anything of mine." He opened the chest of clothing set by the bed. Inside were neatly folded tunics, coats, and trousers. Every single piece of clothing was black. The visual reminder that Cassiel was in mourning made her irritation fade.

Dyna was so tired of being angry. She could deal with pain, but anger was poison, and it was making her sick. Things would never be the same between them, but maybe they could find some sort of common ground. At least while he was here.

"Thank you," she sighed.

He paused, as if surprised by that. "The Valkyrie are positioned outside. No one and nothing will come near without your say. Are you sure you can manage until we reach Evos?"

"Nothing sleep won't mend." She didn't meet his gaze when she said it, because it would take more than a night's rest to recover the amount of magic she had used.

Cassiel turned to go but paused by the entrance with his back to her. She stilled, a sudden burst of currents dancing on her skin.

"Whenever you need me to take care of you..." he said. "I will come."

The low sound of his voice made her belly tighten in response. Heat sprouted in her cheeks because she knew exactly what he meant.

Herbs were not the only way to replenish Essence.

Cassiel strode out of the tent, leaving his words behind. It took a moment before she could sort her thoughts enough to wander to the bath. After stripping off her soiled clothing, she sank into the heated water and rested her head against the edge.

Dyna shut her eyes, trying to put her mind off him. It would be a lie to deny the thought had not fleetingly, *secretly*, crossed her mind. But no, she couldn't allow herself to ever be that close to him again. Yet the soft rumble of his offer repeated in the silence, thrumming on her skin, drawing out a desperate longing that left her too warm and too restless.

There would be no rest for her tonight.

Dyna fell into the endless dark, her cries echoing all around her. She hit the ground with a shriek. The sheets had tangled around her arms and legs. The tunic she'd borrowed stuck to her damp skin like a net. Her heart pounded wildly in her ears as she fought to recognize where she was.

The trilling of rain and Cassiel's familiar scent cleared her confusion.

The tent flaps parted, and a winged figure stepped in.

Her racing heart inexplicably sank. "Sowmya..."

"My lady," she crouched by her side. "What happened? Are you all right?"

"Yes..." Dyna sat up, embarrassed to realize she had fallen off the bed. "I'm fine."

Sowmya helped her up onto the bed again. "Another nightmare?"

Dyna laughed dryly and laid an arm over her eyes. "Of course you know about those as well."

"May I bring you anything?"

She shook her head. "I half expected Cassiel to burst in here himself."

Sowmya gave her a look.

Glancing at the entrance, Dyna lowered her voice. "He's outside, isn't he?"

"Can you blame him, my lady? His only desire is to protect you, even from what cannot be seen." Her guard rose. "If you command it, I will not allow him to enter."

"You would defy your king?"

Frowning, the Lieutenant said, "It is not defiance. It is compliance. When he declared you his equal, it was not for flattery, but to exalt your place. You are the High Queen, should you need me to remind you of that."

Dyna said no more as her guard marched outside. She stared at the entrance, sensing Cassiel on the other side. He wouldn't enter without her permission.

She was determined to stay awake with the candles for company. But sleep came swiftly, and the same terrors awoke her again. Dyna buried her face into the pillow and stifled her cries. Why wouldn't the dreams stop?

It was too much.

She was so tired, but too scared to fall into another nightmare. All she wanted was to feel safe. There was only one person who made her feel that way. She barely whispered his name, so faint she hardly heard it herself.

Yet Cassiel instantly swept in the tent as if he had been waiting for her call. Her vision blurred from relief, and in that moment, she didn't care how much he had made her cry.

She needed him.

Cassiel kneeled by the bed, his wings draping his back and the floor like a black cloak. "You had another nightmare."

"They never stop." Her voice broke. "I feel I am going mad."

"Then may I stay with you?" he murmured, brushing the hair from her sweaty temples. It was the only part of her he touched, yet his warmth filled her cold limbs and eased the racing of her heart. "I'll keep the nightmares at bay, so you may find rest."

The last of her tears rolled down her cheeks. "Do you swear to stay?" she whispered.

"I will not move until the sun rises."

Dyna scooted back to make room for him on the bed. He hesitated before lying beside her, careful to leave space between them. She lay flat on her back, and he did the same, both watching the candlelight shadows dance on the tent ceiling.

She didn't know what came after for them. Not only because he was here for Rawn and tonight for her. What was his plan after he conquered the Realms? Before all of this, at the beginning of their journey, his goal had been something else entirely.

"Cassiel?"

"Hmm?"

"Have you given up on Mount Ida?" Dyna asked quietly. The real question she couldn't voice was had he given up on his mother.

Cassiel was silent for a long minute, and she sensed he was sad. "I don't know." After another breath, he asked, "What are your nightmares about?"

Dyna shivered at the sensation of dropping through a dark chasm. "Falling..." she whispered. "They started after you left. It's always the same. I chase you out of our room, then I fall into a void..."

Cassiel rolled over to face her. Worry swam in his gaze, but she wasn't ready to say more, and he must have sensed that too. "Sleep, *motek*. I will be here."

The tender word tickled her mind, and she wondered what it meant. Knowing him, another endearment that would only make her cry.

Dyna closed her eyes again, fighting back the tightness in her throat. After several breaths, she tentatively reached over and linked her pinky with his. She didn't know why she did it. Maybe she simply missed touching him.

It rose above the fear of him hurting her again. Above her anger and fatigue. She simply wanted, for this one night, to feel close to him again. In the morning, she would remind herself why they were no longer together.

But for now, she needed this.

Cassiel looked down at where they touched. He gently slid his hand under hers and linked their fingers together. Soft currents of energy scattered over her skin. The heat radiating from his palm transferred into her body, and she slowly relaxed.

When her next nightmare came again, she didn't fall. She was caught and pulled from the darkness. Dyna woke wrapped in his wings with his arm around her waist and her head tucked beneath his chin. Cassiel's even breaths were steady in her ear as he slept.

Somewhere in the night, they had curled up together.

Dyna didn't fight it this time. He was the only thing that brought her rest. How ironic, for he had caused the lack of it before. Yet now she didn't have it in her to move away.

Completely warm and at peace, she fell into a dreamless sleep.

CHAPTER 64

Von

The morning fog rolling over the mountains appeared like waves crashing in the seas. Von shivered in his damp clothes and moved closer to the campfire. The skewered fish he'd caught hissed as they cooked over the flame.

Tavin slept across from him with a bandage wrapped around his head. The flash flood had hit them so fast it swept everything away, including the boy. Von had dove in after him without a second thought. He pressed against his ribs. They ached with every breath he took. He'd certainly taken a beating, but that was the worst of it.

It was a miracle they managed to make it out alive.

Dawn broke over the horizon, and birds chirped in the morning. No one had come looking for them yet. Either because no one had survived, or they were too far out in a land he knew no one in. If elves came across unescorted humans in their territory, it would be trouble.

His main concern was the boy. He had been unconscious all night, and Von was beginning to worry.

But then Tavin's brow furrowed, and he groaned faintly. Relief swam through Von. The boy's pale eyes blinked open, noticing him immediately.

"What happened?" He tried to sit but dropped back on Von's coat, pressing on his head. "Ow…"

"Easy now. How are you feeling?"

Tavin winced as he pushed himself up again to sit. "As though my skull has made its acquaintance with a boulder."

Von's mouth twitched. He may look like Tarn, but that humor belonged to his uncle. "Do you remember anything?"

His face scrunched. "I ... remember the flood and nearly drowning. You pulled me from the water..." Tavin blinked at him and at their surroundings. "Where are we? Where is my uncle?"

They were in an open field of rippling grass with a rushing river in the distance.

"We are somewhere south of the campsite, I take it. No telling how far the current took us. Once you gather your strength, we'll search for the others."

Worry and fear lined the boy's features. "Do you think he's alive?"

Von poked at the fire. "If I know your uncle, he's out there somewhere."

"Do you? Know him, I mean."

Von avoided his gaze as he busied himself turning over the fish. "We've only met twice before."

"Then why does Klyde say you're dangerous?"

Von ignored the question. He was dangerous.

"I noticed your accent," Tavin continued. "That tells me you're from Azure."

"All that tells you is that I'm from the north, laddie," Von said dismissively. "The food is ready."

Tavin snorted. "I'm no laddie." He took a skewer and blew on the fish before taking a bite. "I'll be fifteen summers old this year. Nearly a man now."

Fifteen...

Dried mud caked Tavin's clothing and face, but it didn't hide how young he was. Von watched him eat, finding it surreal to be sitting across from his sister's son. He'd only learned of the boy's existence days ago. It almost didn't feel real.

When he had found Aisling in her home, Von hardly looked. He didn't want to see. Maybe if he had looked closer, he would have realized someone had pulled the babe from her body.

Still, the question remained. Would that have changed anything?

Sensing his stare, Tavin looked up with those eyes that reminded him of winter. Beneath the fire's glow, his light brown hair nearly appeared white. He was the very image of Tarn at his age.

A sudden cold sensation crawled over Von's skin, but it faded when Tavin canted his head and scrunched his mouth to the side. The same way Aisling did when puzzled.

"What is your name?"

"Von." He grabbed the other skewer. "Most call me the Commander."

Tavin's eyes widened with awe as he stared at him for a long moment. "Are you an acquaintance of Lord Norrlen?" he asked next after taking another bite. "I assumed, since you've joined the escort for his rescue."

Von paused at the mention of Rawn. They had also only met twice before. It was unfortunate that the elf fell to Red Highland, but admittedly, Von was glad Elon wasn't around when it happened. He wouldn't have involved himself in the matter otherwise, if not for the Maiden. "I am here out of obligation to Dyna."

"Why?"

Ignoring the question, he focused on his meal.

"Do you owe her a debt?"

Von supposed he did.

"Oh, you must be another mercenary!" Tavin said as he admired the bandoliers of knives strapped to Von's chest. "I am one, too."

He arched an eyebrow. "Are you?"

"Aye." Tavin straightened his shoulders proudly. "I'm a Skelling Mercenary. We're known as the Skulls who bow to no one. Surely, you've heard of us." He flushed at the skeptical stare Von fixed on him and shrugged sheepishly. "Well, I haven't officially joined yet, but I am due to finish my training. My uncle Klyde is the captain. Many kings and lords have paid handsomely for his service."

Von kept eating. Best not to encourage this jabbering. Not only was he tired, but Klyde wouldn't like them speaking. Yet sweet silence only lasted half a minute.

"Are you part of a company, or do you work alone?"

Von inhaled a sharp breath. "Are you always this inquisitive?"

Tavin shrugged. "I'm curious. No one tells me anything."

For good reason, clearly.

"If you don't mind me asking—"

"I am not in the mood for conversation," Von snapped. "Eat and be silent."

The light dimmed from the boy's face. He murmured an apology and lowered his gaze to the dirt.

Von grimaced. He couldn't eat anymore. After handing Tavin the rest of his fish, he got up. "We should go. I must find the others."

Standing, Tavin wiped his hands on his trousers and handed Von his coat. "Thank you."

As they headed south, silence hung heavily between them. After hearing nothing but chatter for the last five minutes, the quiet wind and distant chirp of wildlife was awkward.

Von sighed. "What did you want to ask?"

"Well, I only wondered how Dyna paid your fee?" Tavin said sheepishly. "They lost all their gold when they tried to cross the Bridge, so she couldn't have paid my uncle for his service. They must have bartered for something else."

Grunting with disinterest, Von led them out of the woods and onto a vast field. Why was Klyde still with them? He didn't seem keen on collecting Von's bounty, and Tarn was dead, so why not return home?

"I know they're hiding secrets, them lot. They stayed with us for the winter, and I learned all sorts of things."

Von paused, frowning at the boy. Dyna hadn't mentioned she'd been in his old town. "What things?"

"Well, I have been able to gather that they carry large bounties on their heads."

Right ... Von had completely forgotten to remove those.

"They accused Klyde of planning to turn them in at one point," the boy continued. "Perhaps he should have for all the trouble they caused. I have seen the power they hold. They're dangerous folk. Especially the witch." Tavin glowered. "She must have cast a spell on my uncle. He's besotted with her. Now he's to escort them on their journey to only the Gods know where. He refuses to tell me."

Did that mean Klyde knew about Mount Ida?

"You must know where they are going."

Von frowned at him drily. "I'm not at liberty to discuss it, lad."

Tavin groaned. "Why? It can't be so dangerous since the company didn't join him. Klyde never kept secrets from me until they arrived. Honestly, it's insulting."

"So you decided to follow." Von paused by a creek and filled his waterskin. He passed it to Tavin to drink first.

"I'm ready to join the company on missions, but my uncle always leaves me behind. I had to prove to him I am not some feckless boy."

"Aye, instead you proved to be a stupid one," Von said tersely as they continued. "The world is foul, boy. You could have been killed. If not on the bridge, then in some back alley, leavin' your corpse to the worms. Most people out there would sooner see you dead if it was to their benefit. You should have obeyed and stayed in Azurite, where you belong."

They came upon a ridge that looked over the land. Not too far in the distance was a city. Thank the Gods.

"We need to find the main road and hope we find the others."

At Tavin's silence, he glanced back at the stunned look on his face. He must have scared him.

Von sighed. "Look, lad, you may think you're ready—"

"I never told you where I'm from," Tavin said, his eyes narrowing. "How do you know about Azurite? Who are you?"

Von slipped on his coat. "As Klyde told you, I'm no one. Carry on. I want to reach the city before nightfall."

He moved ahead to escape any more questions. They may share blood, but he was no one to him, and it needed to remain that way.

Gods willing, he would find Klyde and return the boy. It's not as though he knew how to take care of him. At fifteen, Tavin wasn't a helpless child, yet to Von he was.

His sister's child.

And Tarn's.

A pressure tightened around Von's lungs, making the hike more difficult. Gods, what was he to tell him?

Pardon me, lad, I am your other uncle, brother to your mother, who caused her death without intention. I am also the one who intentionally blew up your father's ship with him on it. A pleasure to meet you.

Sure, that would be the perfect introduction. If he wanted to traumatize the boy.

A sudden rustle disturbed the bushes. Von leaped in front of Tavin and whipped out two blades. They flew and hit a tree trunk, where two yellow eyes watched them. A large black wolf emerged from the trees, prowling forward with a slow, eerie grace.

And sitting on his head was a dainty fairy with golden wings.

"There you are!" Keena announced cheerfully. "We have been searching everywhere for you."

CHAPTER 65

Rawn

R awn lost count of the number of deaths he witnessed beneath the Blood Keep. Prisoners died by torture, starvation, or infection. The worst deaths came from the Bloodhounds patrolling the tunnels. Sometimes, the guards would leave a cell unlocked merely to feed the hounds, or perhaps out of boredom. They enjoyed it when prisoners attempted to escape.

They always tried.

They never succeeded.

Rawn listened to screams in the dark of another failed attempt. Their pleas to be saved cut off at the crunch of bone. The dark was welcomed then, sparing him the sight. The tunnel echoed with the hungry snarls and wet tearing of flesh as the Bloodhounds viciously fought over the elf's remains. Rawn clamped his shackled hands over his ears, desperate not to hear.

With no sun or moon, he could only mark the days when they dragged him out of his cell for questioning. Grod experimented with many ways to torture him. His favorite method was to shear pieces of flesh from Rawn's back and douse him in vinegar.

No matter how much he denied knowing anything about a key, the pain didn't stop. It lived in his bones, in the pores of his skin, and in every breath of his lungs.

How many times had it been? How many days?

He lost count when he had stopped speaking. He couldn't when his throat was raw from screaming and so dry from dehydration, it may as well have been filled with sand.

The act of nobility had been ingrained in him. It was the foundation of his House, But he didn't feel noble now. He felt resentful. Remorseful. And with it a horrid regret because he feared he would die in this place. Reprieve came only when he could sleep and dream of his family.

They should have come first.

If he had put them first, he wouldn't be here now.

Rawn lay curled within his small cell. It hardly had enough room to move, and it was so cold. The air was rank with the putrid scent of decay and filth. His back still throbbed where they had carved off a piece of him the first day he arrived.

The main tunnel gate clanked open, and Rawn flinched. He shook when guards arrived at his cell door. He internally begged for mercy, but his mouth only managed a weak moan.

They grabbed his ankles and yanked him out of his hole and dragged him away. God of Urn, how did it come to this?

Rawn had no more strength left as the guards brought him to the same carved out room he had first awoken in. The warden's torture chamber. The dried strip of his bloodied flesh with Greenwood's tattoo was pinned to the wall with all the rest.

Grod wandered to a stone table assorted with rusted weapons. The guards didn't attach Rawn's shackles to the long chain attached to the pulley on the ceiling this time. Instead, they hauled him over to a barrel filled with murky water reflecting his gaunt face.

"I think he needs a drink," Grod commented. "He looks thirsty."

A guard violently snatched a handful of hair at the base of Rawn's skull and shoved his head inside. The filthy water rushed up his nose and mouth. He gagged on it, spasming against the barrel. Panic and fear wrangled his heart as his lungs burned for air. They held him there, and his consciousness began to slip away.

The sun was warm on his face, the trilling of water soothing to his ears as he carved another piece of wood for his boy. It was a beautiful day by a quiet creek.

"What do you think? Will he like it?"

Fair paused his grazing and neighed in approval. Rawn smiled down at the birth token for his son. Raiden would turn ten years old soon.

They yanked his head out of the water, and he sucked in ragged gulps of air.

Grod hissed in his ear, "Where is the key?"

They shoved him back down before he could gasp a full breath.

Rawn sighed at the stack of books and scrolls set on the table. He was surrounded by rows and rows of shelves that filled the many floors of the Liánhuā Library. Stacked with so much knowledge, he would need a lifetime to read them all.

His research had made very little progress in ten years. He was beginning to fear he would never find it.

The Princess of Xián Jīng slid into the chair across from him. She wore a fine silk robe in the deepest of red, embroidered with flying dragons and lotus flowers. The sleeves slid down her arms as she linked her fingers together, resting her dainty chin on them. "Why do you continue to search for the blades, Lord Norrlen? You will find no answers here."

Rawn stood and bowed his head. "Princess, if you wish to revoke my access to your library, I will readily depart."

The gold combs pinning up her black hair glittered in the torchlight as she canted her head. "Sit, please. I merely wonder about your motivation. You have made every effort and have found nothing. Could your king not accept this?"

He sighed, making the dust collected on the old scrolls waft into the air. "Perhaps, princess, but I cannot. By oath, I swore never to return home until I have the blade in my hands."

"Would that be so terrible?"

"To do so would be to forsake my wife and son, who await my return. I can think of nothing more terrible than that."

"Even if continuing this pursuit may end in your death?"

"Even then."

The shock of the unfamiliar memory pulled Rawn back to reality. He had met the princess of Xián Jīng?

But the lack of air stole all focus. They let him up again, and he drew in ragged mouthfuls of air. His lungs spasmed with the effort, and he vomited all the foul water he had swallowed.

"Answer, filthy elf, or you will lose more than air."

"I..." Rawn rasped. "...know nothing."

"Lies! We know you're hiding it!" Grod lifted a club and beat him across the back of his head. Stars flashed in his vision, and Rawn dropped on the ground, a ringing piercing his ears. "The key, damn you! Give us the key!"

The club smashed into his skull.

The princess's warm brown eyes saddened. Reaching into her robes, she placed something on the table with a faint clink. "You will find what you need on the last floor, in the restricted section. I have approved your access there."

She rose from the table and strode away.

"I don't understand," Rawn said to her retreating back. "Why share this with me now?"

She paused and gave him a small smile over her shoulder. "Perhaps I can respect a father who would go to the ends of the earth for his family."

His eyes watered, and he deeply bowed. "Thank you, princess."

"Lord Norrlen, my friends call me Daiyu."

A foot rammed into Rawn's stomach. He gasped at the breath torn from him, and he choked on bile and sand.

"Enough." A sharp voice barked. There was a sudden thud, and Grod hit the ground next to him. "If you kill him before we get any answers, I will lop off your head."

Grod scrambled back, cowering into a low bow. "F-forgive me, Your Highness."

Rawn's sight skewed as the sound of his heartbeat thudded in his ears, and he looked up at the red prince.

Anon's mouth twisted with a snide smirk as he looked over the damage done to his body. "I am surprised you're alive, though you may not have long. You reek of rot." He pressed a finger into the hole burned into Rawn's thigh yesterday. He moaned, jerking against his chains. "You bear a strong will to live, it would seem, but everyone breaks beneath the Blood Keep, Norrlen. Eventually." Anon's red cape flared out as he marched for the door. "Put him with the others. He is not to be questioned again until I say. The king and that usurper past the wall are negotiating."

Usurper?

Rawn closed his eyes. He dared to hope that meant King Leif was bargaining for his release. Help was coming. A shudder sank through his body, and he had the urge to both laugh and cry.

"Don't think you're safe," Grod growled, jabbing Rawn's chin with his club. "I'll have you strung up here again soon, along with that pretty wife of yours." He bared his yellowed teeth in a sinister grin. "You will watch as I have my way with her before I split her in two."

Rage surged in Rawn's veins like poison. He snatched the club and rammed it into the warden's stomach. Grod's eyes bulged out, wheezing for air. Grabbing his neck, Rawn shoved him into the barrel. The hunched elf clawed at him frantically, sloshing water everywhere.

Rawn held him there with some primitive strength that had surfaced from the dark pit of his soul. He would slaughter him for nothing else but saying those words.

But guards stormed in, and a club struck the back of his head again.

He drifted in and out of consciousness as they dragged him over the dirt down an unfamiliar tunnel. He only knew it was different because the stench of Bloodhound droppings and decay wasn't as strong here. The hounds followed them, their growls and hot breath heavy on his neck. Prisoners murmured as the guards hauled Rawn past their cells and dumped him in front of another.

"Away from the door!" Grod bellowed. The Bloodhounds gutturally barked, and a shadowed figure inside moved back as he took out a set of keys and opened the cell. "Throw that sack of shit inside."

The guards did so unceremoniously, and Rawn hit the cold ground with a ruthless thud. He laid there, struggling to breathe. Pain radiated all over his body. The cell clanged shut loudly, making him wince. Grod hawked a wad of spit at his cheek. Their laughter echoed in the tunnel until their footsteps faded away.

Rawn shut his eyes, grateful for the momentary relief from his next bout of torment.

A voice surfaced from the dark. "I surely thought you were dead."

Rawn managed a weak smile. "I thought the same of you."

He heard the soft clink of chains and scuffs in the dirt as a figure moved closer. The single torch on the wall provided enough light to illuminate Elon's face. Unexpectedly, the red elf used his torn sleeve to wipe the spit from his face.

Rawn stilled at the sight of the bloodied cloth over his left eye. "What did they do to you?"

"I can live with one eye. You got the worst of it." He rolled Rawn on his side to examine his back and made a disapproving hum. "Your wounds are beginning to fester."

Rawn suspected as much by the smell.

"Once sepsis is in the blood, death comes swift," Elon said, moving toward the cell door. He reached through the bars and returned with something putrid. "Hold still."

Rawn shuddered at the horrid sensation of something crawling over his back. "I am afraid to ask."

"Maggots. They will eat away the rot."

Nausea rolled through his empty stomach. "I suppose I should thank you..."

Elon moved back to sit against the wall and closed his remaining eye. "I am only delaying the inevitable. Elves only come here to die."

"A wise man knows when his time has ended. This is not where we die."

Elon scoffed. "You are closer to death than I am, Lord Norrlen."

"Yet I still have faith." Rawn groaned as he laid flat on his stomach, tucking his arm under his head. He tried not to breathe in the scent of filth and urine. "I was given to understand that my king has been in contact with yours. They must be negotiating my release. I will put in a petition to take you with me."

That drew Elon to look at him again. "What?"

"We will leave this place."

"You are a fool if you believe Altham will allow that, more so if you assume Greenwood would give sanctuary to a red elf. This crypt will sooner be our tomb."

The declaration made Rawn's hands shake, but he curled them into fists. "I have a son, and you have two. When they were born, we lost the recourse to concede defeat."

The reminder weighed heavy in the silence.

Rawn didn't know if Leif would grant Elon sanctuary, but after everything he sacrificed for his country, he could ask this of him. "You saved my life more than once. I owe you a debt."

Elon studied him in the dark for a moment.

"You escaped this place once before. How?"

Elon's one eye moved up to the ceiling of their cell. By the faint light, Rawn could barely distinguish runes carved into the stone, but they were no longer active. "Sylar was the one who broke the warding spell in the prison. He said for one of this magnitude, the runes must be in perfect order to work. No flaw. No line out of place. He understood the fundamentals of magic in a way I didn't."

Well, of course. Sylar had been an apprentice to become a Magi Master before he was taken, and he was highly skilled.

"We planned our escape on a day Grod was distracted questioning another. I stood guard as Sylar chipped away one of the runes in his cell with a rock, and the warding spell broke. With his magic, he broke out, and we fled through the eastern tunnels to the waterways." Elon looked past him to the bars. "But they have adapted."

Rawn followed his gaze to the ceiling of the main tunnel, where runes faintly glowed yellow. Out of their reach. "What of the keys to the cells? If I could—"

Elon shook his head. "Grod never leaves them out of his sight. Short of removing the wards from the walls, these cells are also warded. As of now, there is no way out."

431

The matter appeared bleak, and Rawn felt his strength wane. "It's your prerogative to sit here and wait to die. But I will not join you."

"If they are truly negotiating, that means Altham desires a trade. What would he trade you for?"

Rawn hadn't thought about that until now, and he was suddenly anxious. What would they trade him for?

"They must have brought you here for something," Elon pressed.

"Altham wants a key..."

"A key?"

Rawn fell silent, thinking of the memory he had recovered during his torture. After Princess Daiyu had gone, he found what she left on the table. A small rectangular box made of ivory, carved with the design of a sprawling tree. No more than three inches wide and six inches tall. Inside, on a bedding of red velvet, lay a bronze key split in two.

"Rawn, what key?"

"It's a key to a door that should never be opened..." he said faintly, his pulse quickening as the words slipped from him. How did he know that? He sat up, his chest rising and falling with rapid breaths.

Elon grabbed his shoulders and made Rawn look at him. "Speak plainly. What door?"

"I know not."

Whatever lucid facet that had surfaced in Rawn's memory quickly swam away like a minnow into the depths of his mind. It was as though whatever he needed to remember had been purposely hidden.

But why and by whom?

Elon's grip tightened. "Where have you hidden the second half of the key?"

"I don't remember..." Rawn blinked at him. "How do you know there are two halves of the key?"

The question made Elon's expression impassive again, and he withdrew to his corner against the wall. "I overheard the guards talking."

On the back of his scarred hand was a fresh tattoo. The flesh was red and inflamed, but Rawn could distinguish very clearly the sigil of a maple leaf.

"They have placed us together for a reason, haven't they?"

Elon said no more.

They sat in silence for the rest of the day, listening only to the wails, snarls, and groans echoing through the prison. Rawn leaned against the wall to cool his sweaty face. The rest of his body was cold and trembling. The infection must be worsening.

Both stiffened when the gate to their tunnel clanked open. It was followed by the shuffle of footsteps. They both moved back to the darkest corners of their cell, not wanting to draw any attention. A soft female whimper echoed in the dark and Elon's head whipped up. Rawn's heart raced faster, and they slowly turned toward the cell door.

Grod appeared with a torch first. Then Anon slinked out of the shadows, gripping the arm of a she-elf. She wore a dark red dress, and a golden circlet adorned her waves of long, dark hair.

Elon inhaled a soft breath. "Garaea..."

Her amber eyes shone wet. "I'm sorry."

He snarled at the red prince detaining her. *"Damn you."*

Anon stroked her cheek, and she whimpered, recoiling away from him. "I caught a little mouse lurking about, perhaps searching for a way to break you free. Our sister always did favor you, Elon. She has certainly grown into a beautiful woman, hasn't she?"

Sister? Rawn's mind was reeling.

"Why have you brought her here?" Elon seethed.

"I thought you might need a little motivation to do what I asked. But if Garaea is not enough, I can acquaint myself with that other elf you love. Sylar, was it? We brought him to the keep last night. He's upstairs now, waiting for me. And he is certainly lovely. I can see why you chose to betray us for him."

Elon's one eye widened. "You swore..."

Anon laughed. "I swore I would not harm your family, and I kept my word. But that green scat is not part of our family, is he, sweet sister?" He kissed Garaea's head, and she flinched.

Elon slammed his fists against the bars, making his shackles clang loudly. "If you harm him—"

Anon straightened, washing all emotion from his face in a blink, as if he had none at all. "Oh, you are not in the position to make threats when I have the means to take everything from you. You should be on your knees begging for my forgiveness."

His voice dropped to a menacing pitch that made the sweat chill on Rawn's body. He remembered what Anon had done to his sister and feared now for Sylar.

Elon's loud breaths filled the silence as he sank to his knees. "Brother, please. Forgive me…"

A cruel, satisfied smile rose to Anon's face. "There, was that so hard? Alas, it's not my forgiveness you need to spare him, Elon, but father's." His dark eyes moved to Rawn. "At the moment, your prison companion cannot be touched, so I will propose another to take his place." He grabbed Garaea's throat, and she screeched as he yanked her close to the bars. "For each day he remains silent, I will mark the pretty flesh of everyone you love, Elon. Find out what I want to know, and it ends."

Garaea silently wept, and he clenched his shaking jaw.

"I don't know where the key is," Rawn exclaimed. "I have no memory of where it is hidden!"

He had tried for hours to remember, with nothing to show for it.

"I am sure my little brother can help with that." Anon sneered at Elon. "Do what you do best. You have three days, and today is day one."

The prince strode away into the dark, with the Bloodhounds following him. Grod grabbed Garaea, and she cried out.

"Unhand her!" Elon reached through the bars.

Grod yanked his sister away, tearing their hands apart. Her soft weeping echoed through the tunnels.

Rawn shut his eyes. He braced himself against the wall, pleading for his mind to remember, but it gave him nothing.

Elon's hands shook as he gripped the bars tight. His low, ragged voice filled the cell. "You must tell me where the other half of the key is, Rawn. Or I will be forced to tear the information out of you."

CHAPTER 66

Lucenna

Lucenna woke completely dry and warm beneath Klyde's mercenary coat, enveloped in his scent. Her pulse jumped when she opened her eyes to a view of his bare torso in the morning light. Remaining still, her gaze drifted across his smooth skin to the defined V line of his hips that disappeared beneath the fabric of his trousers.

The muscles in his arms shifted as he stretched, and she bit her lip. The sun highlighted the defined ridges and mounds of his preposterously perfect abdomen. A swoop of heat sank through her stomach and continued past her navel as her eyes traveled along his well-defined chest and up the column of his throat. Every beautiful muscle in his arms and back flexed as he bent, but he winced and muttered a soft curse.

Klyde turned, and Lucenna let out a horrified screech.

"Is that a stick in your thigh?" She rolled onto her knees and jerked his waist around to fully face her.

Yes, he did indeed have a stick pierced through his right leg. Dried, crusted blood had formed around it, leaving the skin there inflamed. The stick was at least half an inch in diameter and no telling how long.

She peeked around his back and found it hadn't gone clean through him. "Did you have this in you all night?"

Klyde stared at her a moment, and she looked down, realizing she wore nothing more than his white tunic. The hem ended right beneath her bottom, leaving her legs bare. The wide collar fell loosely around her shoulders, exposing a good deal of her cleavage.

She leaped to her feet with a yelp, covering her chest. "Where are my clothes?"

Klyde pointed to where her black dress hung from a tree branch, keeping his gaze pointed up at the sky. "You took it off last night. Apparently, you weren't keen on sleeping in wet clothes."

Lucenna's face flamed.

Her memory of last night was hazy, but she wanted to fade away from existence when she recalled peeling off her soaked dress and letting it drop with a wet splat at his feet, rambling on some nonsense about needing a warm bed.

"Oh, Gods..." She groaned, covering her face.

Klyde held out his mercenary coat. "Best you wear this too, love." He placed it over her shoulders and muttered under his breath, "For my sake."

She was smothered by another wave of mortification. Klyde had said something similar last night as he fought to wrestle her into his shirt while also doing his best not to look at her.

Lucenna snatched the coat shut, wrapping her arms tightly around herself. If only the ground would swallow her whole. "If you speak a word of this to anyone..."

"I will meet an untimely demise, I know."

"You still might," she said, arching an eyebrow at the stick. "Did that happen during the flood? Why didn't you say anything?"

"Well, lass, clearly you weren't in a sober state of mind." He shrugged. "I considered taking it out myself, but I might have bled to death in the night."

Lucenna groaned at the distant ache that throbbed in her head. "I need to sit down. So do you." She tugged on his wrist, and he took a seat on a large boulder. He already looked flushed with a mild fever, and a sheen of sweat shone on his forehead. Sitting beside him, Lucenna bit her lip as she studied the branch. "I will have you know I never did learn how to cast Essence Healing."

He grimaced. "Shite, I was hoping you wouldn't say that. Well, there's no helping it, then. You must cauterize it shut."

She recoiled. "What?"

"We're out in the wilderness with no Herb Master, bandages, or the like to stitch me up. I can't go on with this inside of me, so the best option is to pull it out and cauterize the wound."

Lucenna's stomach churned. "Must *I* do it?"

"You have threatened to flay me alive and remove my favorite appendage, yet this is out of the question?"

Trying not to gag at the churning in her stomach, she nodded. "All right. Give me a moment." She hesitantly took hold of the rough shaft of wood, but he winced, and she quickly let go. "No, I can't do it. I can't."

Klyde sighed heavily. "Well, I must admit, I'm rather disappointed. You're not as plucky as you pretend to be."

She narrowed her eyes. "Excuse me?"

He stood with a shrug. "I suppose all women do faint at the sight of blood. After all your threats, I wouldn't have taken you for the squeamish sort. Turns out your poised air of superiority was merely bravado—"

Lucenna ripped out the stick. Klyde hunched over with a strained grunt, bracing himself on her shoulder.

"See," he said with a labored wheeze. "I knew you could do it."

Yes, it only took angering her, oddly enough.

Lucenna held onto his hips so she could inspect the wound better. It seemed deep. Tearing off her sleeve, she pressed the cloth against it. "Hold here. Apply pressure." Picking up the bloody stick again, she frowned at it. "It's bigger than I expected."

"Thank you." He smirked down at her. "I am pleased to exceed your expectations."

Lucenna then realized her face was inches from his groin. Groaning with disgust, she tossed the stick at him, and it bounced off his head.

"Ow." He sat back on the boulder.

"Another word, and you will reach the bottom of this mountain quicker than it took you to climb it."

Klyde rubbed the pink welt on his forehead. "That is what I like about you, lass. Your boundless sense of empathy."

She threw the stick into the fire. "That thing was about eight inches long and at least half of them were inside of you."

He snickered.

"This is a serious matter, Klyde." Lucenna punched his arm, and he ducked for cover, still snickering. "Can you stop enjoying this so much? Why are you laughing?"

"Because I find you rather adorable when you're cross with me."

Lucenna rolled her eyes. "Well, let's get on with this. I will be beyond cross if we are caught without the escort before we ever reach Evos."

Klyde drew back the bloodied cloth and Lucenna's stomach roiled again at the sight of the dark hole in his leg. Blood steadily leaked out.

"I don't know where to start."

"I'll hold here." He pushed the skin around the wound together, forcing it shut. More blood and other substances spewed out. "You seal it with a bit of fire and give me a new scar. Simple."

She balked. Why was this so difficult? Looking at the wound, it made her sick ... and angry.

"You need a distraction, lass. Talk to me. Tell me about your mother."

"What? Why her?"

Klyde canted his head. "She's part of what made you. To know her is to know you."

That knocked the breath out of Lucenna, and she stood, moving back. "No, we're not doing this."

"Do what?"

"I won't tell you my sad story simply because you told me yours," she snapped. "I don't need a shoulder to cry on, and I certainly don't need a man to jump to my aid every time I'm in danger."

He stared at her for a moment, and his mouth thinned. "If I didn't jump after you, you would have drowned, Lucenna. You can't swim, need I remind you. Are you that confident in your magic?"

"I am confident in myself! I would have made it out. Now you have this horrid hole in you because you cannot cease to play the gallant knight."

Klyde's chest expanded with a heavy sigh, and he applied the cloth over his wound again. "I thought we discussed this already. It's all right to need help."

She clenched her teeth. "I don't *need* anyone."

He fell quiet for a long moment, his deep blue eyes observing her, seeing through her glare, through *her*. Always understanding more than she wanted him to.

"It's not that you don't need them," he murmured. "You're afraid to need them." Lucenna froze, her chest shaking. "Because the people you relied on let you down?"

Her fists clenched. "*No...*"

"Then why?"

Lucenna looked away from him to the fire. She stared into the flames until the heat dried her misted eyes. "Everyone who has ever helped me..."

"Has died?" Klyde guessed, so easily as he continuously seemed to do. "Beginning with your mother..."

Lucenna's throat tightened with the emotion she forced back.

Klyde reached for her hand, his skin warm and tan compared to her pale one. His thumb stroked the back of her fingers. "Lass," he called softly, prompting her to look at him. "Don't worry about me. Morkens are difficult to kill, if I haven't proven so already." His mouth lifted in a half smile. "But I may not have long with this hole in me."

That made her scoff faintly, if only to push back the knot in her throat. Kneeling down in front of him, Lucenna drew raw Essence into her fingertips. It heated the air like a torch. Klyde removed the bloodied cloth, and she cast out a thin beam of fire beginning at the top of the wound.

"I was eighteen when my mother died," Lucenna said. His skin sizzled as she slowly sealed it shut. Klyde's fists clenched tight on his lap, but otherwise, he didn't make a sound. His gaze stayed on her as she worked. "Her name was Lucilla, and she was extraordinary. She taught me not to be afraid of who I am or of my magic. I suppose that confidence … is what led to her death." Lucenna finished cauterizing the wound and stared at the fresh scab for a moment. "My father … he found us because I cast a stupid spell that revealed where we were." Her voice broke, and she struggled to make herself say the words. "My mother stayed behind to distract him, so I could run. We both thought he would simply take her back to Magos…" Klyde brushed away the tear she hadn't felt fall, and she looked up at him through her blurry vision. "But he siphoned her."

"You saw it?"

She shook her head. "I felt it. When Essence is torn from a body, it feels like the air is being pulled from the atmosphere, until their presence is simply … gone."

She had been powerless to stop it.

Klyde pulled her to him, holding her as though he knew she needed it. Lucenna's first instinct was to push him away, but she inexplicably sank into his warmth. "I'm sorry," he whispered. "You weren't ready to lose the one who raised you."

She shut her eyes. Was anyone ever ready for that?

A sudden spark of magic above their heads made them jump apart. From the small puff of smoke in the air came a torn piece of parchment fluttering down. Lucenna caught it. Quickly wiping away her tears, she read Lucien's scrawl in fresh ink.

I cannot reach you through the orb. Forgive me for yesterday. Please tell me you're safe.

"Your brother?"

She nodded. "I'll send him a message later. We need to find the road."

While Lucenna changed into her dry clothes, Klyde put out the fire. They gathered their belongings and headed south. Evos wasn't very far, according to her location spell on Dyna. They fell into an easy silence as they hiked down the mountain together.

Lucenna constantly glanced at the sky though, because she was worried about Rawn. He'd been captive for over a week now, and she shuddered to think of what he suffered. Each day they delayed his rescue was another day lost.

Klyde lifted a low-hanging branch out of her way, and she caught him looking at the Lūna Medallion. She had been absentmindedly twisting the chain around her fingers. He moved on ahead of her.

Lucenna stopped. "Why don't you pry into our business anymore?"

He raised his eyebrows. "Eh?"

"Before, you wouldn't cease to question us on our story and where we're headed, but you stopped."

"If I remember correctly, you did warn me to stay out of it."

"Klyde," she pressed.

"All right, what's the story behind your medallion?"

"No, it's my turn. I answered your question earlier. Now you answer mine." Lucenna crossed her arms. He tensed, and she narrowed her eyes. "You figured it out, didn't you?"

Taking a breath, he raked the messy blond hair out of his eyes. "I have been tracking Tarn's activity for many years, lass. Once he began collecting the Sacred Scrolls, it was clear he searched for Mount Ida. Then he put a bounty on your heads, and well, with how secretive you were, it was easy to guess you were headed there as well."

Lucenna eyed him carefully, wary of whether she should be worried about that or not.

Reading the suspicion on her face, Klyde frowned. "Where you were going didn't matter to me. I am no Relic Hunter in pursuit of treasure. The only thing I hunted for was Tarn."

"To protect Tavin?"

Klyde looked to the horizon on valleys and hills. His blue eyes caught the light of the sun, making them pale blue. And she read the worry in them. He may not have been Tavin's father, but he loved him as one.

"Tarn has the power of the Ice Phoenix now, and a right to the throne of Azure. It was no question what he would do if he ever learned there was another out there with Morken and Jökull's blood. Once I discovered he planned to become immortal on that Godsforsaken island, I was desperate. I was willing to do *anything*, by whatever means necessary, to protect Tavin against him. At whatever cost ... even if I came to regret it later." Klyde's gaze returned to her, and his brow furrowed as if it weighed on him.

Lucenna had seen the darkness that lurked beneath his jests and amusement. She could only assume what things he might have done to get answers, and how he must have felt when he decided the only thing he could do was kill his brother.

"You did it for Tavin's sake," she said. "You truly believed Tarn would have harmed his own son?"

"I wasn't going to give him the chance to try..." His expression creased, his gaze going distant. "When I was a boy, my mother would call me her wild Skelling. I assumed it was merely a term of endearment, since she called Tarn her Phoenix. I believe now she was telling me I was the only one who could defeat him."

Yet that didn't sound right to Lucenna. What mother would tell her son to kill her other son?

Klyde looked down at the pack he carried, and she pictured the Skelling talon inside. "Fortunately, I have the fates to thank for preventing me from having my brother's blood on my hands."

A mixture of resolve settled on his face, shadowed by distant sorrow. A twinge of guilt settled on her. She never did ask him how he felt, now that his brother was gone.

"A part of you mourns him."

"I mourn the memory of who he used to be." Klyde continued on. "He was dead to me a long time ago."

She watched him go and couldn't help thinking, even from the back, he looked sad. Tarn had committed many vile deeds, beginning with killing their father. But what had wounded Klyde was that the one person he had admired the most left him to die.

Lucenna caught up to him at the top of a hill, and he nodded at the view. Nestled within the forest below rose a small city.

"Not far now," Klyde said. "We should find the road soon. Meanwhile, tell me about how you came to join the others. I'd wager it has to do with your medallion. It's my turn to ask, right?"

Well, she didn't know they would be trading questions, but she didn't feel so mistrustful of him anymore. "It's missing a jewel that I need to find. A Moonstone."

"Which is on Mount Ida?"

"Yes. So when did you discover—"

"Wait," he laughed. "That is all I am getting? I expected a better tale rife with danger and all-powerful mages."

Lucenna scoffed as they made their way down. "What mages have you met that were all-powerful?"

He paused, blinking at her.

"You've mentioned meeting mages before."

"Ah." Klyde took her hand as he helped her down a rocky ledge. "I meant the Elite Enforcers in Dwarf Shoe."

She curled her nose. "Those mages were not all-powerful, Klyde. They would never hold a candle to Azeran."

So she told him about her great ancestor, and how he revolted against the Archmage to fight oppression. That he had created a Moonstone that helped him during the War of the Guilds. She told him of her life in Magos, the things women suffer there, then the Liberation enlisting her and her mother. Klyde listened intently, all of his attention absorbed by her story.

"War is brewing again. But the Archmage is untouchable as long as he has the Tellur Medallion. It's my mission to find the Moonstone that belongs to the Lūna Medallion so I can give my people a fighting chance." Lucenna looked up at the faint roll of thunder. A storm was gathering in the south. "I will finish what Azeran started."

They had finally left the woods and came out onto a paved road. Up ahead rose Evos within the trees, and she spotted a few of the Norrlen Guards waiting for them.

"Finally, we made it."

When Klyde didn't answer, she found him watching her steadily, the sea blue of his eyes glinting with something focused and intoxicating.

"What?" Lucenna asked.

"Even the most powerful people can be made to feel powerless. Yet, you found your strength regardless of when an empire declared you had none. And here you are, making a stand like a true force."

The way he was looking at her with such wonder, it made Lucenna's skin warm. Somehow, despite not knowing him for long, he always had a way of seeing through her in a way no other had.

"Is that to say you believe I have a chance of defeating the Archmage?" Klyde brushed the silvery locks from her face. "You are a storm, lass. May the Gods have mercy on whoever stands in your way."

CHAPTER 67

Dynalya

The City of Evos was nestled in the heart of the forest. Charming buildings of dark wood and stone stood among the elevated trees, blending in seamlessly with the greenery. Flowering bushes lined the cobblestone paths, illuminated by glowing lanterns. The elves had made a home here without disrupting the beauty of nature.

Magic glittered in the air, and it seemed to soothe the ache in Dyna's veins. While they were waiting for the others to arrive, the escort brought them to rest and eat at *Misty Hollow*, a tavern built within a semi-enclosed cavity of a massive tree. A singular round window above allowed in a natural stream of light. Vines and roots adorned the tree's walls, lanterns offering an orange glow. Every table on the stone floor was taken, elves murmuring softly to each other in Elvish or in Urnian.

Dyna smiled at Zev sitting across from her. He happily feasted on a rack of lamb. Keena sat on an overturned teacup, her feet swaying idly, as she chatted with Von and Tavin about fairy food.

A tingle swept through the bond. Dyna fleetingly met Cassiel's gaze. He sat at the next table with his Valkyrie, their wings hidden from sight. She looked away and cut into her blistered tomatoes roasted with herbs and cheese, resting atop a mound of wild rice.

Things had been awkward since the morning.

Well, for her.

Halder, the Captain of the Norrlen Guard, brought them two mugs of wild berry wine. It was added to the other gifts of food and drink that had already filled their table. He gave them a nod of approval, then rejoined Lady Aerina, Raiden, and Eldred at the table across from them.

"Aw, they are fond of you now," Keena said teasingly. Zev shrugged and chugged down the ale. "And all it took was saving most of their lives from the flood."

"We were fortunate to save the ones we could," Dyna said as she passed on her mug to Von.

Many of the Rangers and Norrlen guards had also thanked her for treating their wounds. The Melodyam waters had worked. She made a note to study the falls further.

"I hear that both of you are to be commended," Lucenna suddenly said from behind her. "The escort wouldn't cease to speak of your valiant deeds all the way here."

"Lucenna, thank the Gods you're all right." Dyna got up to hug her. "Where is Klyde?"

"He's outside tending to his horse. Commander Camsen had found him."

"Oh, that's wonderful."

Tavin suddenly put down his fork and grabbed his bag, making his way to the front door.

"Oi, boy, where are you going?" Von called after him.

"I'm off to find a scribe's shop." He waved over his shoulder. "I need parchment and ink to write to my mother. Don't worry about me. I can find my way back."

Von and Zev shared a frown, and both rose to follow.

"I better go with the lad in case he finds himself in any more trouble. Could you pass on word to Klyde that he's with me?" Von asked her.

Dyna nodded. She was glad to see Zev and Von were getting along now.

"Oh, I'm famished," Lucenna sank into Zev's chair, and her eyes lit up at the many plates piled with an assortment of food. "And this looks delicious."

"Help yourself," Keena said, cutting into a strawberry half her size. "The almond cakes are *delectable*."

Klyde soon joined them, and they ate their fill as they shared their experiences during the flood.

"Are we staying here for the night?" Lucenna asked as Dyna inspected Klyde's leg with a mist of Essence.

"I believe so. When we arrived this morning, Commander Camsen said the horses needed rest, and he needed to procure a new carriage for Lady Aerina. It's unfavorable for her to be seen on the open road." Nodding in approval, Dyna covered the fresh scab with a salve and wrapped a new bandage over it. "You did well, Lucenna. I don't detect any internal bleeding." She handed Klyde the salve container. "Rub this in twice a day for the next three days to clear up any infection and ease any pain. It's made from Echinacea extract and milk thistle. If you develop a fever, come see me."

"Right, thanks lass." Klyde tucked it into his coat pocket. "Has Tavin arrived yet?"

"Yes, not a short while ago with the others," Keena said. "He went to the market with Von and Zev."

Klyde's mouth thinned. "Where is the market?"

"I'll escort you, sir," a Norrlen guard volunteered.

He quickly made for the door with the elf, and Keena followed.

"I'll go with them too, in case he decides to murder Von," Lucenna said, but her expression shifted to worry as she looked her over. "All right? You look a little pale."

Dyna sighed. "I need to replace my herbs to make Azeran's tea, but the prices here are..."

"Past our means?" Lucenna muttered as she stood. "I noticed. I'm out of herbs, too. There may be more reasonable shops further in the market. I will ask around."

Trying not to grimace, Dyna pressed on the tension gathering on her forehead. She wasn't sure what annoyed her more. Her lack of funds, or her growing headache from lack of Essence.

Lucenna glanced past her shoulder with a sly smirk and added under her breath, "Though I doubt you would have trouble finding a wealthy admirer or two who would gladly acquire whatever your heart desires."

Dyna glowered at her. The sorceress winked and hurried on to catch up to Klyde.

There was no need to look. She more than sensed gazes of Raiden and Cassiel. A pretend suitor and a former husband who glared daggers at each other. It was beginning to become rather tiresome.

Glancing up, Dyna met Aerina's amused smile. She must have heard that. A blush washed through Dyna's face, and she inwardly groaned.

"Your lodging is secure upstairs, princess," Camsen said as he approached with his men. "The King has sent word that a carriage will arrive on the morrow. Shall we escort you to your room to rest?"

Aerina's brow furrowed slightly, the only sign of displeasure. She was anxious to reach Avandia, and so was Dyna.

"I think I would like to go for a stroll through the market." Aerina rose from her seat with graceful ease. The streams of her pale blue dress fluttered around her. "Lady Dyna, would you please join me? I wish to visit the apothecary, and I could use your expertise."

Dyna stood. "Oh, of course, Your Grace."

"Why? What's wrong?" Raiden quickly came to his mother's side.

"Are you feeling ill?" Eldred asked next.

Camsen said in alarm, "I will send for the royal Herb Master at once."

"It's nothing at all to fuss about." Lady Aerina waved them off and took Dyna's arm. "If you must know, I am in my season."

The men all turned pink and suddenly looked uncomfortable. They all seemed to understand what that meant, but it left Dyna confused.

"Would you be so kind as to allow me some privacy, please? It's a lady's business, after all."

Raiden cleared his throat. "Right, of course."

The market was at the center of the city. Elves watched curiously, and they passed by with a trail of Rangers and Valkyrie following at a distance.

"Season, Your Grace?" Dyna asked.

Aerina masked a giggle behind her hand. "To be in one's season refers to a female's fertile year, much like the mating season in spring. It comes every ten years and requires a special tonic to ease one's ... urges. A delicate subject the males are not prone to discuss."

Dyna flushed and smiled. "Oh, I see."

"Apologies. This way we can speak at leisure without the others listening. How are you, Lady Dyna?"

"Me?"

"You seem troubled and weary. I couldn't help but notice the shadows under your eyes. Though you do appear more rested today."

Dyna ducked her head. "I have difficulty sleeping, Your Grace. Nightmares, as it were. But I did manage to find some rest last night."

She tried not to think about sleeping in Cassiel's arms, but the memory hovered in the back of her mind like a swarm of bees. She had woken to his scent embedded in the sheets and her clothes, but he was gone with the dawn.

That's what he had promised.

To only stay for as long as she needed. Dyna knew he did so out of respect for her space, but for some reason, disappointment had tangled in her chest.

But it's what's best.

Keeping him near wouldn't do any good, yet why was she so bothered by it?

"Dreams have plagued me, too, as of late," Aerina said, her burrow furrowing with worry as she looked ahead. "They wake me up in the middle of the night with my worst fears. Most dreams are only due to our minds sorting through our memories and emotions and unconscious desires, fears, and wishes. Other dreams are forewarnings of the future. It is difficult at times to discern which type of dream they may be. That burdens me the most."

Aerina also had shadows under her eyes. What nightmares must plague her? Dyna didn't ask. It wasn't her place. But she knew they would all be about Rawn.

At first, her dreams seemed to reflect her lack of control, but they now felt more like a forewarning.

Her mind was trying to tell her something.

"We will arrive in Avandia tomorrow." Dyna gently squeezed Aerina's hand. "I am sure King Leif has not sat idle these past few days. The negotiations for Rawn's release are likely underway or perhaps complete. He may have already sent for him by the time we arrive. Have faith. You will see him again."

"Thank you, dear." Lady Aerina squeezed her hand back. "I have faith. For I believe those meant to be together will always find their way back to each other."

She gave her a knowing smile as they reached an apothecary and opened the door. Before following her inside, Dyna glanced behind her at the crowded market where Cassiel lingered by a merchant's stall. His gaze flickered up to her, and she quickly went inside.

The apothecary was much the same as the rest of the city, but familiar with a wall of many herbs. Dyna smiled as she breathed it all in.

"Good evening," Aerina greeted the Herb Master, and the male elf deeply bowed. "My friend here is in need of herbs, if you could fill her order please."

"Of course, Your Grace."

Aerina waved her over.

447

Dyna gasped. "I-I couldn't possibly."

"After what you have done for my family, it's the least I could do."

Her throat clamped shut, and she almost broke down there with horrid guilt. "Your Grace, I cannot accept—"

The door chimed with a tinkling of bells, and Cassiel entered behind her.

"Ah, you have arrived on time, sir," the Herb Master told him. "Your order is ready." He brought out a package wrapped in paper and twine. "Ten gold, please."

"Thank you." Cassiel placed a sack of cold coins on the counter. "I'll cover Her Grace's tab as well."

Before Aerina could answer, Raiden stormed in. "I will see to my mother, Soaraway.

"As you wish." He turned toward Dyna. "I have what you need."

Gaping, she pulled Cassiel back outside and moved him into a private nook between two trees. "What are you doing?"

He frowned. "I acquired the herbs for the tea. I believe they're the right ones. You're welcome to inspect—"

"I didn't ask you to buy them for me."

His silver eyes grew upset. "Dyna, please don't argue with me on this, of all things. You needed the herbs, so I placed the order as soon as we arrived. Take them."

"No, thank you."

Cassiel's chest heaved with a heavy breath. "Can we pretend for a moment you don't hate me?"

Dyna looked away. She needed to hate him because if she didn't, her heart would attach to the other emotion she tried to ignore whenever he was near.

"Do you refuse me because I paid for them?"

No, it was because if she accepted this gift, she would struggle to continue keeping a wall between them. Sleeping beside him had already made it worse.

"I recovered some Essence last night. I'm fine." Dyna was saved from having to say more by the chime of bells as Raiden and Aerina left the Apothecary. She joined them on the street. "If you are to continue in the market, may I come with you?"

Raiden offered her his arm. "I would be delighted."

As they strolled together, gentle music filled the market. Evos was holding a festival to celebrate spring. They paused to watch as elves stood atop rooftops or on balconies and lit up pieces of colorful paper on fire. They released them, filling the sky with a rainbow of glowing cinders as the paper dissolved away.

"The Hail of Embers," Raiden explained. "It's a ceremony we hold in the spring. We write down all our troubles, ill memories, and hardships from the previous year and burn them. It symbolizes leaving the past behind and starting anew."

Maybe she should write Cassiel's name on one.

I'm fireproof, ahuvati. His husky, amused voice passed through the bond, and Dyna flushed.

Her shield had dropped for a second at the most embarrassing moment.

Fortifying it again, Dyna tried to ignore him and what he called her. *My love.* Odd how she seemed to understand his language better now, as if she had learned it already. But the pitch of his voice had reminded her of last night, when he offered another way to replenish her Essence.

Heat churned in her lower belly, and her Essence Channels ached as if encouraging her to accept. Dyna hardly had the energy to pretend she was fine.

Cassiel must have sensed it though, because his eyes followed her wherever they went. She plastered a smile on her face, making sure to speak to Raiden energetically, attentive to whatever he said.

His brows quirked up. "I am glad to see you in better spirits, my lady. I was concerned about you last night when you collapsed."

"I had been neglecting my rest. I feel much better now."

Raiden swept away a lock of hair from her eyes. "I am pleased to hear that."

The unexpected touch caught her off guard. She looked away from his soft gaze with a nervous smile, shifting back on her feet. Their courtship was only pretend, or meant to be, but sometimes she wondered if Raiden wasn't pretending anymore. Or he was doing too well to uphold a performance in front of Cassiel.

Either way, it only made her feel guilty and uncomfortable.

"Perhaps we should return to—" She cut off with a soft gasp when a striking green gown within a shop's window caught her eye. It was made with sheer sleeves that hung off the shoulder and delicate gold embroidery on the trim, jewels sewn into the waist.

"Do you like it?" Raiden asked her.

"It's beautiful," she said in awe. "I don't think I have ever seen anything quite like it anywhere else."

"Perhaps since our dressmakers and tailors design their clothing from fabric woven of Goldseed. It is a root that grows only in Greenwood and takes form similar to silk. Gowns can be enchanted to never fade, to enhance the beauty of the wearer, or even improve your skill as a dancer."

Dyna laughed. "Surely, you jest."

"I do not." Raiden nodded for her to follow him to a stall selling baubles of rings and jewelry. "You will find all sorts of magic in Greenwood." He picked a simple wooden ring in the shape of a leaf and placed it on her finger.

A whoosh of magic tickled her skin from head to toe. The merchant held up a mirror, and Dyna gasped at the sight of her brown irises. "My eyes..."

"Elvish jewelry can be enchanted to change the color of your features to even your voice."

It must be why the elves had taken to tattooing themselves with their Kingdom's sigils. With these, it was easy to disguise who you were.

"Try this one." Raiden picked up another ring. He held her gaze as he slipped it on her ring finger. The tingle of magic crawled over her scalp, and Dyna laughed at her new blonde curls.

Cassiel appeared in the mirror's reflection, standing behind her. "What have you done to her?"

"Nothing but a mere illusion," Raiden said flatly.

Cassiel looked her over, lifting a section of her hair to inspect the roots. "If this is permanent—"

"They're merely enchanted trinkets, Soaraway. Calm yourself."

"I've had quite enough of your antics, Norrlen."

Dyna sighed. There they were, bickering again.

"Take it off." Cassiel reached for the ring.

Raiden moved to block him. The action wedged her between them, pressing her against Cassiel's chest.

"Mind yourself instead." Raiden tried to tug the curl of hair Cassiel was holding.

Cassiel jerked his wrist away from him, inadvertently pulling on her hair, and Raiden pulled it back in the other direction.

"Ow," Dyna hissed. "Would you please desist? Both of you."

But they weren't paying attention.

Cassiel clenched his jaw. "Remove your hand before I break it."

"I will do as I please, Soaraway."

The Rangers and Eldred rushed their way. Listening to them squabble like idiots and having the whole market stare at them both humiliated and angered her.

Snatching out her blade, Dyna slashed through the lock of her hair. Cassiel and Raiden watched speechlessly as the red strands floated down to their feet.

Dyna stormed away, never feeling more humiliated. She should have stayed at the inn and locked herself in her room.

Swift movement caught her eye, and Dyna looked up at Aerina standing alone at the end of the street. A male elf came up from behind and covered her mouth before she could scream.

"Aerina!" Dyna sprinted to them. "Put her down!"

Two hands rammed into her back, and the cobblestone came rushing to her. Her head cracked against something hard, and pain stole her vision. Dyna screamed, clawing at her skull. Warm blood seeped through her fingers.

She broke it. She broke it.

Someone grabbed her, and she screeched.

"Lev sheli!" Cassiel grabbed her face. "Look at me. Look at me."

Her wild eyes fixed on him, her chest heaving with harsh breaths. Blood leaked down her temple, and she reached for it with shaking fingers.

"Breathe," he said. "You're all right. You merely bumped your head."

Dyna forced herself to suck in a breath.

"There you go. Another."

She took several more mouthfuls of air until her heart stopped racing. The ringing in her ears dissipated, and slowly her surroundings came into focus.

A crowd had gathered.

Raiden held his weeping mother, shouting something at Halder and his guardsmen. Camsen pinned the elf that had grabbed Aerina under his knee. Beside them, Sowmya and Yelrakel had another elf at sword point. He must have been the one who pushed her. Though they may have not been needed, since he was unconscious. Blood leaked from his broken nose.

"I thank you for showing some restraint," Eldred said, a hint of sarcasm in his tone.

It took her a moment to realize he wasn't speaking to the Valkyrie.

"The fact that he breathes *is* showing restraint," Cassiel said coolly. She winced as he pressed a torn piece of his tunic against her temple.

Leaving Aerina with Halder, Raiden came to stand before the elf who had tried to abduct his mother. His eyes burned with ire, but he seemed to draw it back. "We will take them to the king for questioning."

"But who sent them?" Eldred asked.

"They wear no livery nor carry any proof of orders, my lord," Camsen said after riffling their pockets.

Raiden gritted his teeth and said to the Magi Master, "We both know who is responsible. Put them in irons, Commander."

"Yes, my lord."

He turned to her, and his expression softened. "My lady, I'm sorry you were hurt. Can you walk?"

"I am all right," Dyna said, forcing a smile. "See to your mother."

"Raiden," Aerina called shakily. He quickly went to her, and the Rangers escorted them away.

"Come, we need to clean you up," Cassiel told her. He helped her stand, and Dyna moaned at the pain throbbing on the side of her head. "I will take you to the inn."

"I can make it on my own." Dyna pushed off his hand but stumbled, and Cassiel lifted her in his arms.

"So stubborn," he sighed.

Dyna couldn't even argue from how much her head hurt. Yelrakel and Sowmya shadowed them as he marched through the streets, drawing several stares. They flew away once Cassiel reached *Misty Hollow* and carried her up three flights of stairs to the room that must be assigned to her. It was a small nook carved into the tree. A single window provided a view of Evos below.

There wasn't much in the limited space but a hammock, a table with stools, and a short chest of drawers with a basin and a mirror. A map of vines and glowing lanterns adorned the walls. Cassiel set her on a stool, and she heard water pouring into a basin. He returned to her, and she tried not to hiss as he carefully cleaned the dry blood from her temple.

"Gods, what hit me?"

"When you fell, your head hit the corner of a merchant's table." He searched her eyes worriedly. "Are you all right?"

"I'm fine..."

"What happened, Dyna? You panicked."

"I told you I'm fine," she snapped. "You can go now."

She was safe. Lady Aerina was safe. She had been through worse.

Cassiel laid his warm palm over her cold fists. "If you're fine, why are you still trembling?"

It took all her will to fight back the tears threatening to surface.

Dyna couldn't tell him that when those hands had pushed her, she had fallen back into the chasm of her nightmare. The blow against the table had shocked her mind into thinking she had cracked her skull. And it had left her helpless on the ground.

If he and the others hadn't been near, Lady Aerina would have been taken.

Shutting her eyes, Dyna stamped down a fresh wave of panic. She felt so stupid and pathetic to have been left vulnerable by such a simple thing. Pressure built in her chest, and she pushed a fist against it. Her breathing quickened as the world tilted.

"*Motek.*" Cassiel took her hands. The contact sent a tingling energy over her skin, and the spinning in her head faded at the soft foreign word. *Sweetheart*, he called her.

"Please don't ask me about it," she whispered. "I can't speak of it."

"When you do, I hope you will share it with me." Petals of Seraph fire unfurled from Cassiel's palms, casting steady heat over hers. She hadn't realized how stiff she was until her body sagged as soothing heat spread through her, and her trembling ceased. "May I heal you?" he asked next.

She shook her head.

Exchanging blood was intimate. The foundation of a mate bond. That held too much meaning to allow it anymore, because it would only confuse him ... and herself.

Cassiel's brow furrowed. She read the silent worry in his eyes. They were the gray of a coming dawn, and however angry or sad she was with him, she still found herself yearning for those skies whenever he was near.

Dyna dug her nails into her palms until pain washed the thought away.

"You are to meet the King of Greenwood tomorrow," he said. "It wouldn't do to arrive with your face bruised. What would the court say?"

It was merely an excuse to heal her, yet as Dyna looked at him, kneeling in front of her, she couldn't help but give in.

She nodded.

Taking out his white opal knife, Cassiel cut his fingertip and gently traced the gash. His thumb brushed against her jaw, sending shivers down her neck. Every contact of their skin sent a flush of warmth through her body she tried to ignore.

453

"Why do you continue to care for me?"

His expression tightened as if the question pained him, and he wiped away the rest of the blood from her face. "*At yekarah li.*"

Dyna told herself she didn't understand, but it was a lie. Regardless of how cold and cruel she was, no matter how much she hurt him and pushed him away, she was still precious to him. "But I am terrible to you..."

Yet I cannot deny what remains true.

The tattered strands of the bond danced in her chest at the sound of his soft voice passing through her mind. It wanted to reform itself, and Dyna couldn't deny a hidden part of herself wanted it too. Her heartbeat fluttered in her throat as they gazed at one another.

He was close enough to feel the heat of his body, and she still remembered what it felt like to have it on her. To feel the touch of his breath on her bare skin. Her throat dried.

Cassiel's eyes grew darker—heated. And she realized her shield had slipped again, exposing the desire that she had tried to hide since last night. His silver eyes dropped to her mouth. Her pulse drummed as his warm breath brushed over her skin, and her heart beat faster, air locking in her lungs. Taking her elbow, he leaned closer, enveloping her in his heat. He watched for her reaction, weighing ... deciding. She didn't move away because all of her burned with need.

And he knew it.

The inch of space between them closed, and his lips brushed hers. Lightly, tentatively. The sweet kiss made her insides glow. But it was too much like their first kiss. The memory of that innocent moment made her eyes well.

Because they were not those people anymore.

"Cassiel..." Dyna whispered. "We can't."

His lips grazed the shell of her ear, and her body trembled treacherously. "You deny me, but I know what you desire, *lev sheli*. I can feel it." His lips moved along her jaw, and each caress echoed in her bones. "Your Essence is spent. Let me help you restore it," he murmured, every word vibrating.

His mouth pressed another light kiss beneath her earlobe, and it sent her skin ablaze with need. But she stiffened, chest rising and falling with shaky breaths to resist him and the ache of her dwindled Essence.

Cassiel lifted his gaze to hers. "Dyna ... you're suffering needlessly. I can feel your physical need and your magical one." His brow furrowed with frustration, and his eyes became pleading. "I feel how much it hurts, and I hate knowing I can take it away. Let me help you. Not because I am a foul male who wants you, but because you need it."

"I don't need you," she snapped, feeling her face redden. "If I want to be bedded to restore my Essence, I can find anyone else equally capable."

He stared at her, taken aback by her blurted response. She didn't know why she said something so callous, but he didn't look angry.

Cassiel trailed his fingers along her collarbone, eliciting a current of heat across her flushed skin. His thumb traced slow circles over the pulse fluttering at the base of her throat. "As much as you detest me, no one else can illicit what you feel with me." His nose skated her cheek. *Only I know exactly how you liked to be touched, Dynalya.*

His husky voice in the bond sent a shock of heat through her body.

"Tomorrow you can return to ignoring me, and I can return to pretending that it doesn't kill me. But right now, let me take care of you."

Dyna trembled, every part of her wanting to give in. But the shattered pieces of her soul trembled within the confines of her being. If he hurt her again, she could not survive it. "Please ... go."

Cassiel pulled back with a faint sigh. His hand slipped away from hers, taking all his warmth. She already missed it. He didn't touch her again, and she was relieved, because her head was pounding, her body aching, and she needed air.

He turned to go, nodding to the package of herbs left on the table. "Please, drink your tea. Call if you need me."

"I won't." Taking Cassiel's arm, Dyna pulled him to the door and put him out into the hall. "That will never happen again."

Then she shut the door before he could say anything else.

CHAPTER 68

Cassiel

Cassiel was so afraid of widening the rift between them, he always seemed to make it worse. He couldn't make himself move from on the other side of Dyna's door. Every shred of him ached with longing and misery. He wanted to plead at her feet to let him in. Not only in the room, but in her heart and mind. After last night, he hoped it meant their bond could be mended, but for every step he took forward, he stumbled several more back.

"Is there a reason you stand there?" Cassiel glanced at where Netanel lingered in the shadows.

"I came to assure Lady Dyna's well-being."

Cassiel stiffened at Raiden's voice behind him. Netanel quickly retreated into the adjoining hall. "And why should her well-being be any of your concern?" Cassiel faced him. "See to your mother. That is where your attention should lie."

Raiden lifted his chin. "And yours is no longer required here."

At that moment, Lucenna, Zev, and Klyde arrived in the hall. They stilled, sensing the tension in the air.

Klyde crossed his arms and leaned up against the wall. "I wouldn't provoke him, mate. He can breathe fire."

"No," Cassiel said drily. "I don't."

"We heard there was an incident in the market," Lucenna said. "Is Dyna all right?"

"Yes, she's resting now," Cassiel told them, and fixed his glower on Raiden. "What is your strife with me? From the moment I arrived, you have been nothing but insolent."

"I cannot abide any man who would readily abandon his wife. Nonetheless, I think you made the right choice in this case. A human does not belong with a Celestial, especially when it endangers her life." Raiden mouth curled. "I am the better choice for her, Soaraway. You must see it. I could give her a better life. A good life free of danger."

That declaration stirred Cassiel's veins with his fire. He crossed the hall to Raiden until they were a mere two feet from each other. They stood at the same height, their eyes glowing with their power.

"Free of danger?" Cassiel repeated through his clenched teeth. "Was she not put in danger because of you and your mother?"

"An unforeseen circumstance that I will not allow repeating."

"Is that so?"

"Acknowledge that our courtship would not be possible if you had stayed by her side, instead of running off to do whatever else you deemed more important than her. The only reason she is at my side and not at yours is because of *you* alone."

Fire scorched through Cassiel's chest, and he felt it press against his being. His ears started ringing.

Raiden smirked. "No argument there? How frightening it must be to face a future without the one you planned it with."

The entity of flame awoke inside of him with a wrathful roar, ready to set everything ablaze. He shook. "Stop. Talking."

Cassiel couldn't see straight. The sound of his heart pounded in his ears. Sweat broke out on his back. *Protect and destroy.* That was all his flame demanded, and Raiden was in his line of sight.

"Thank you for stepping aside," the damned elf continued. "Now I will see that Lady Dyna is never abandoned again."

Cassiel slammed a flaming fist into the wall beside Raiden's head. It cracked from the force, spreading fissures across the surface. Blue light glowed in the hallway, bathing his startled face.

Grimacing, Raiden didn't move as he withstood the immense heat pressing into the side of his cheek. "You're so preoccupied with convincing her you're the hero, but we both know the truth."

Cassiel bit back a harsh laugh. "I never once claimed to be a hero. For you see, lordling, there is not a shred of nobility inside of me." His eyes flamed with his beast, and the first threads of fear crossed Raiden's face.

"You're no Celestial ... are you?"

Since he had been born, Cassiel knew what he was. He saw it in the disgust of his people. In their hatred and revilement. The truth was clear every time he looked in the mirror, and now in the reflection of his flame.

He was an *abomination*.

"You know nothing about who I am or the things I have done. As vile as you believe I am, you cannot possibly fathom how far I will go to protect that which I hold most dear." The wall cracked and blackened under Cassiel's fist as the flames spread up his arm. "Perhaps you are confused, so I will make it perfectly clear. I don't call Dynalya my wife merely to stake my claim, but because we are bound by blood. I feel her heartbeat in my soul, as she feels mine in hers. Therefore, go on then. Attempt to win her heart but know one thing. When you think you at last have her, you will come to realize who she belongs with will never be you."

Raiden stared at him mutely.

There was only silence in the hall and the crackle of burning wood. The others stood tense, ready to leap in if needed. But Cassiel took a breath and distinguished his flames. It took a lot of effort to make himself turn away.

"In the end, the choice will be hers, won't it?"

Snarling, Cassiel hooked his arm around Raiden's neck and flipped him over his shoulder, slamming him on the ground.

Zev shoved Cassiel into the wall, pinning him there by his chest. "Cease this now," he growled. "Do no more to tarnish yourself in her eyes."

That was when he noticed Dyna standing at her door. The startled look on her face made the air drain out of him.

One step forward.

Two steps back.

Raiden stood and straightened his tunic. He cleared his throat, his voice a little strained. "You dishonor yourself."

Cassiel swept past him and took the stairs down to the main floor.

His veins burned with the need to light something on fire, but he made it to the forest behind the inn without combusting. The trees gave way to a small glade peppered with clusters of bluebells. He dropped onto a boulder, resting his elbows on his knees.

"I made it worse, didn't I?"

Netanel slipped out of the trees with a grimace.

Cassiel groaned and rubbed his face. "Why does he infuriate me?"

His spy came forward and sat cross-legged on the ground. "Because you're afraid of the small voice in your head telling you he's right. That you're losing her."

Was he right?

"Learn to quell your temper, Cassiel. It does you no favors."

He knew that. But was it him or his flame that easily sparked his ire?

Maybe it was due to the lingering wrath seeded into his soul so long ago. It didn't really matter. No one else made his choices for him.

Cassiel lost track of how long he sat there. Next thing he knew, the sun was already setting, and Netanel had left him to stew in his thoughts. Or so he thought until he heard steps approach.

"I am in no mood for any more lectures."

"Clearly you need one." Zev's unexpected voice astonished him, because he was the last person Cassiel expected to come. Yet Zev stood at the edge of the glade, eying him with a mixture of disapproval and concern. "What is wrong with you? That darkness in your veins is turning you into a belligerent brute."

He let out a short laugh and dropped his head in his hands. "I had a moment of idiocy. Is Raiden all right?"

"You winded him, but he'll live."

If Cassiel had used his full strength, he might have truly hurt him. He stared blankly at a caught leaf fluttering beneath his boot. There was no honor in crushing someone weaker than you.

He wished these powers never came to him. Life had seemed so much easier before, when he was someone the Realms ignored instead of feared. Before he broke Dyna's heart. True power would be to live in a world where he didn't make any mistakes.

He had lost the ability to be happy in this one.

"Oi, what are you thinking about?"

Cassiel looked at Zev, recalling he was still there. "What?"

"What's lurking in your mind? You seem lost in there."

He tiredly shook his head. "Sometimes I think it isn't real."

"What isn't real?"

"This life I find myself in."

Zev gave him a strange look, but it wasn't something he could explain.

Cassiel released the leaf and let the wind blow it away. "Ignore me. I am merely accepting that life does not always go as I want. Most of the time, it's my doing."

Somewhere along the way, he had locked himself in a prison of his own making.

And he may never get out.

PART III: KEY

CHAPTER 69

Rawn

R awn called for his horse in the silence only to remember Fair wasn't there anymore. At times, he heard soft neighs, in others he heard Aerina's call. His memories were drifting, tangling with images of faces and the sound of voices, filling him with a sense of regret. There was only darkness in that hole, and all he smelled was death.

"How much did you torture him?" a female voice asked. "He stands before the Gates."

Aerina's blurry face rose above him, her features faintly lit by dim firelight, and Rawn was relieved. The God of Urn blessed him with a glimpse of her before he died. He tried to say her name, but it was a pained moan on his lips.

"He collapsed without my efforts," another said. "The fever is taking him. Did you bring what I asked?"

"Yes."

Aerina... Rawn reached out to her with a trembling hand. She took it, but it didn't feel like hers.

His vision waned, and the darkness took him to the meadows of Sellav.

Rawn was at peace laying in the tall grass, listening to it gently rustling. The warm sun and cool breeze landed over him, and he breathed in her scent.

Soft fingers stroked his cheek, making him smile. "You have laid here for a while. You must wake now, my love."

No. That was the last thing he wanted.

He looked up at his wife smiling down at him, his head resting on her lap.

Her blue eyes saddened. "You can't stay here."

Rawn took Aerina's soft hand and kissed her palm. "Grant me the wish of staying in this dream with you a little while longer."

Her lips brushed his forehead. "Return to me."

A passing growl startled Rawn awake.

It took a couple of tries to fully open his swollen eyes, but even that hurt. He lay face down on a thin sheet in the cold dirt. The smell alone told him he was still in the Blood Keep. Rawn wanted to scream, but he didn't have the strength. His back felt stiff, hot, and wet. He tried to get up, but a hand pressed on his shoulder.

"Don't move, Norrlen. You're still healing." Elon came into view and held a waterskin to his mouth.

He took a sip. At the first touch of water, he desperately gulped more, only to end up coughing violently.

"Easy. Not too much now." Elon took it away. "When you feel ready, eat this." He placed something beside him and returned to his corner at the back of the cell.

Rawn almost couldn't believe it when he caught the scent of bread. He grabbed the roll and ate it with eager bites. His stomach ached to at last have something solid. He drank a little more water. That was all the strength he could muster before laying back down.

"You nearly succumbed to your wounds last night," Elon said. "We're fortunate my sister could bring what I needed to treat the infection."

He attempted to thank him, but Rawn drifted away again. The next time he woke, he could finally sit up. But not for long; it made him dizzy. The best he could do was slump against the cold wall.

"Who is Aerina? You call for her in your sleep."

"My wife..." Rawn stared at the wall, seeing past it to the land of his home. "She is the one Anon came for..."

Elon made an incredulous sound. "The Princess of Greenwood?"

"I was never meant for her, yet that didn't prevent me from loving her all the same. I would have made an absolute fool of myself to spend merely one more minute with her..." Rawn weakly rambled on about the rest of the tale, from how Leif allowed them to marry, to the birth of his son, then leaving home and living as a vagrant for years until they caught him. They both fell silent, looking at their surroundings.

Rawn took a moment to work up the courage to ask. "Sylar?"

"Anon lied." Elon leaned his head back against the wall. "He doesn't have him. Only my sister."

Rawn allowed himself to feel relief. "Did he harm her?"

Elon didn't answer, and his relief faded.

"I'm sorry ... God of Urn knows I have no knowledge of the key. My memories were veiled somehow. The little I recollected came to me when they held me underwater."

Elon studied him thoughtfully. "Curious..."

From what Rawn knew of such spells, whoever placed it also locked it behind a trigger. Did he need to nearly die to remember what he'd forgotten?

"Regardless of who cast the spell, I will find no answers now." He exhaled a heavy breath, making the dust in the air stir. "If only I had known what it meant when I took up the sword for the crown."

"Do you regret it?"

Rawn leaned up against the wall with his shoulder, careful not to disturb the salve on his back. He thought of his sister, and his heart ached. "I had spent many years regretting my service, then I regretted my oath. I never intended to leave my family this long, but fighting for the future of Greenwood has been a noble choice. I must believe that it is worth something."

"Noble..." Elon retorted, staring blankly at the wall. "I have never understood the meaning of that word. Was it noble to torture elves not born of my country? Was it noble to serve my father's commands blindly, no matter the depravity of my deeds? I was one of many bastards vying for a place in his halls until I realized that wasn't what I wanted. But I left these sands soaked in the blood I spilled. If rotting here is the price of my sins ... may it be the first and last of my noble deeds."

The blood of elves also soaked Rawn's hands. It had colored his cloak and gave him a moniker by which he was ashamed. "It couldn't have been your first one," he murmured. Elon glanced at him questioningly. "You spared Sylar and chose to raise two sons with him. They're not yours by blood, I take it."

A faint sadness crossed Elon's face as his one eye stared blankly at the ground. "Four years ago, we found them within an overturned carriage outside the border of Dwarf Shoe," he murmured. "Their mother and father had defected and attempted to flee, but the Bloodhounds caught them..."

Rawn's stomach sank. Red Highland sent the hounds to hunt them down. How they must have felt to be steps from freedom, only to have it snatched away.

"They were babes. Hardly months old. Spared because of their mother's love. We only heard their cries, for Sylar had sensed them hidden behind her protection spell. 'They are ours now,' he said." A rare smile touched the edge of Elon's mouth. "Henceforth, they were. I never understood how that could happen. That something so small and helpless could become everything to you..."

Rawn understood perfectly, for he felt the same when his son was born. "To have a child, it's a peculiar kind of love. You would tear out a piece of you and consume any darkness to protect them. Including killing your mate's childhood friend."

Elon smirked. "And I would do so without hesitation, Norrlen."

He chuckled. "Then why save my life again when you believe this place will be our tomb?"

"*Sooner be*," he corrected. "I was not waiting here to die. I was only waiting for you."

He lifted a tiny leather pouch in his fingers.

Rawn recognized it as the same one Dyna had pinned to the inside of his cloak.

"I found it on you when we left Dwarf Shoe and I tended to your wounds," Elon told him. "I knew it may give us a chance, so I made sure that they wouldn't find it."

Rawn rubbed his chest where arrows had shot him over a week ago and found a fresh bandage.

Elon handed him the pouch. He turned it over in his palm and out fell the dried four-leaf clover. An amber bead with a black clover inside rolled out next.

"A gift from Garaea."

Rawn's heart hammered at the sudden spark of hope. "Will it work?" he whispered. "Can you break the wards?"

Elon nodded. "The black clover will absorb the magic embedded in our cell."

That would give them the ability to cast magic to defend themselves.

"The matter is staying alive. We only need to wait for the right opportunity to make our escape."

Growls echoed through the dark tunnels. The guards and Bloodhounds were constantly patrolling. It would be near impossible to fight their way out in his state, let alone without weapons.

A cynical thought suggested that even if they could somehow escape the Blood Keep, there were miles of sand between here and the wall. Hounds would hunt them down before they ever reached it.

But he had fought to survive all these years, and he didn't intend to make it easy for others to kill him.

Rawn returned the items to the pouch. "I take it you have a plan?"

Elon waited for a guard to pass by before saying faintly under his breath, "Garaea has been spying on Altham's negotiations, and she contacted your king to make negotiations of our own."

Rawn straightened. "What do you mean?"

"It was your suggestion we seek sanctuary in Greenwood. She's made it her task to persuade him."

"How?"

"By offering something valuable enough to allow two red elves past his borders."

Rawn sat back on his heels, attempting to guess what it could be. But the answer came easily. He shook his head. "Altham would never let him have it."

"If your king is daring enough to come here, Altham would never let him leave this place alive—or you."

Then it was a trap.

"I cannot leave my life to chance," Elon said. "When your king comes, I plan to break out of here and make for the waterways."

"When is he coming?"

"Day after tomorrow."

Rawn's pulse jumped. Then tomorrow was their day to escape.

He locked eyes with Elon.

"What say you, Norrlen?"

Faith was like a sword. Loyal to those who could wield it and cut the reckless who left too much to chance. But they both had a reason to fight their way out of here. He understood now why the prisoners attempted to escape. Dying for a chance to live was greater than dying here for nothing.

He would attempt it now too, even if it meant failing.

Rawn's split lip stung when he cracked a smile as he repeated what Nisa once told him. "We all die one day. A warrior's wish is to die well."

Elon smirked in agreement at that.

"I will help you reach the waterways, Elon, but I cannot leave my king to die."

The red elf took in his resigned expression. "Making your way out of here alone will be nearly impossible."

"I know." Perhaps he would be walking towards his death, but Rawn's honor wouldn't accept anything less, for he had more than one oath to keep. "But I will not die without taking Anon with me first. He mutilated my sister, and he killed my horse. His life is mine."

With an inaudible sigh, Elon gave him a small nod. He knew his brother had earned it. "Anon is not an opponent to take lightly."

"Neither am I."

Elon considered that, then his shackles clinked as he moved away from the wall and crouched in the middle of the cell. He studied the ground for a moment before he began drawing shapes in the dirt.

"What are you doing?" Rawn asked as he joined him.

By the low torch light, he could barely distinguish the runes Elon quickly formed within the rings of a circle. "How well versed are you in spell casting?"

"Enough to summon my Essence."

"Well enough. I am going to teach you a spell. A last resort if you are caught. It's not one I have dared to use myself, for it requires the very essence of your life. It could kill you."

"What spell is that?"

"The Blood Scythe."

CHAPTER 70

Zev

The scent of dynalyas was heady on the morning gust. Zev paused by the high rise as the wind tugged against his fur. The view of Avandia opened before them within the rocky hills coated in greenery. Cascades poured down into a crystal blue river below. Their winding path led to a large bridge made of white stone.

Before it rose a white castle, tall and proud at the highest point of the land. Its gleaming white walls reflected the light of the sun. Soaring turrets and towers reached toward the sky, flying the flags of Greenwood with a dynalya flower in full bloom.

Zev was both relieved and anxious to see it. In his experience, visiting castles in foreign lands hadn't gone too well for them. But they were here for Rawn, and by the fates, he hoped it meant something good.

The creek of the carriage wheels and the trotting of the horses arrived as the others caught up to him. Commander Camsen led the escort of Rangers and Norrlen guards. He nodded to Zev as he rode past. The carriage carrying Aerina, and the girls passed him next.

It surprised him to find Tavin riding in the back of the procession with Von, but only a little. The boy followed the Commander around like an excited pup, asking all sorts of questions about knife throwing and whatever held his interest. Watching Von now as he awkwardly tried to avoid the boy, yet couldn't help but care for him, was amusing.

Klyde had been furious at Von for following Tavin into the market yesterday. "I told you to stay away from him."

"If he did, Tavin wouldn't be here now," Zev had said. "He pulled him out of the water, Klyde. Perhaps you should thank him for that instead of holding onto that stick up your arse."

The mercenary didn't have much to argue. It wasn't for Zev to mettle, but he saw Von dive into the water without hesitation and risk his life to keep his nephew alive. Klyde should at least acknowledge that.

"There's the castle!" Tavin cantered to catch up to Klyde. "Uncle, did you see?"

Von's shoulders dipped with visible relief, but he stared after him with an odd look on his face. One Zev had seen on several faces as of late.

Cassiel briefly came into view as he soared above the clouds with his flock of Valkyrie warriors in golden armor.

When they crossed the bridge, another escort of Rangers was waiting for them. They saluted Commander Camsen and led them through the Capital of Avandia towards the castle.

Carriage wheels creaked and hoofs clomped as they crossed the gates and rode into the royal courtyard. A garden framed the castle, the smell of dynalyas and rain strong in the air. North of the courtyard grew a particular tree. It seemed to be an oak tree of some sort. It stood nearly thirty feet tall. The trunk had somehow split from roots in two and formed into a near perfect circle. Its branches had woven around the odd shape with a coating of moss and leaves.

Surrounding it were intricate carvings on the floor. Some of them were runes. Round grooves were also on the floor, eight of them, and each placed in a perfect circle around the odd tree.

"I have never seen anything like it," Lucenna murmured beside him in fascination.

Neither had Zev.

But no one offered them any explanation as to what it was.

Cassiel flew down on silent wings, landing in a graceful crouch. His wings brushed the ground as he rose to stand. He was dressed in all black, no color on him at all.

He looked to Dyna wordlessly, and she came to stand beside him. Poised, head held high. Despite their differences, they presented themselves as a united force for Rawn's sake.

Even without their crowns, Dyna shone of royalty, and Zev felt proud.

The King of Greenwood waited to greet them at the top of the stairs. The gentle wind tugged at his long, ashen blond hair as his gray eyes calmly took them in. A gold circlet rested on his brow. He wore elegant dark green robes embroidered with golden leaves. At his side stood his

BECK MICHAELS

Queen in a blue gown. A beautiful woman with pale blonde curls and soft features. Their five daughters took after her, their ages ranging from adult to perhaps ten years in age.

"Sire, thank you for having us." Lady Aerina and Raiden came forward, lowering into a deferential bow.

"Come now, sister, we haven't seen each other in so long to hold to such proprietary customs now," Leif said, holding out his hands.

Aerina rushed up the steps and embraced her brother. She tearfully smiled at him and the queen. "Ossenia!" She gasped when noticing the bundle in her arms. "Who is this little one?"

Queen Ossenia nuzzled her baby's cheek. "This is Lotham, the Crown Prince and heir of Greenwood."

Aerina gathered around her, bustling with excitement. "Oh, hello wee one. When did you come into the world?" She playfully glowered at Leif. "Your father kept you a secret."

"He was born a fortnight ago. I didn't wish to reveal his coming once we learned Lotham was a boy. I will announce his birth today, and we will hold a feast to celebrate."

"Today?" Aerina blinked at him and shared a confused look with Raiden.

King Leif moved past her and offered Cassiel a polite smile, dipping his chin slightly in greeting. "High King Cassiel of Hilos, welcome. Thank you for seeing my sister here safely."

"Of course," Cassiel politely dipped his head in the same manner. "I was pleased to receive your letter inviting us to Avandia. I have been meaning to greet the monarchs of Urn now that I have taken the crown. May I introduce—"

"Your High Queen?" Leif took Dyna's hand and kissed the back of it. "I have heard much about you, Dynalya Astron, and of your companions."

She curtsied. "We are honored to meet you, Your Majesty."

They hadn't expected him to be so well informed, but Zev had to assume the elves had spies everywhere.

"The pleasure is mine," King Leif said.

"Your correspondence mentioned political matters you wished to discuss in person," Cassiel said.

"Yes, and we will confer on that soon. That is tomorrow's business, however. I am honored that the King and Queen of Hilos could be here on our joyous occasion. All of you must come to tonight's banquet, of course."

470

Disquiet fleetingly crossed Cassiel's face. "Thank you for extending us an invitation. Perhaps another time."

"Nonsense. I will not accept no for an answer." Leif ushered them forward. "Please come in. Your rooms have already been prepared in the west wing. I am sure you are tired from your journey here. Take the afternoon to rest. The festivities begin at sundown. All of Greenwood will arrive."

The king moved on to join his wife again, but Aerina took his arm. "Leif, wait. I don't understand. I am happy for you, but we didn't come all the way here for a feast. We need to discuss how we are going to rescue my husband."

Leif patted her hand and wrapped an arm around her shoulders, leading her into the castle. "Be at peace, Aerina. I have spoken with Altham, and we have come to an agreement regarding Rawn's release. He has given me his oath that not a hair will be harmed on his head. He is *safe*. I promise we will discuss it come morning." Yet as he said it, Zev heard the beat of his heart rate briefly spike. "Greenwood has waited decades for an heir. The kingdom now has a future. Is that not something to celebrate?"

Aerina's shoulders slumped with both relief and defeat. She conceded with a sigh. "It is…"

Her brother smiled and brought her into the castle. Raiden was expressionless as he followed. They were led to the east wing with the royal family.

Zev glanced at the others, finding they were not as practiced in discretion. They all had expressions of confusion, annoyance, and shock. But they could say nothing while the Royal Guard stood near.

The servants led the rest of them through the elegant open hallways of the west wing. It provided a view of the gardens below, dynalyas climbing up the columns, filling the castle with their sweet scent.

They were provided an entire floor with private suites. The servants opened two large doors, leading them into the first suite for the girls. The many large windows spilled sunlight into the spacious drawing room. Sofas with velvet green upholstery were set near the fireplace.

"King Cassiel," a servant greeted with a bow of their head. "We have prepared your suite on the next floor for you and your wife."

Dyna flushed, looking away.

Cassiel cleared his throat. "Thank you. I will be up shortly. Meanwhile, please show my Valkyrie where I am to stay. They will inspect it for our security."

471

The servants went on their way with Yelrakel. Only Sowmya remained by the door. Castle Guards were posted in the hall. She exchanged a look with Cassiel and shut the door with her outside, at last giving them privacy.

Dyna nodded to Lucenna.

Purple Essence flared in her hands. With a wave of her fingers, a containment dome formed around them in a circle and enclosed them inside. No sound could be heard outside of it.

"This is ridiculous," Lucenna said. Crossing her arms, she plopped on a sofa. "He wishes to have a *feast* at a time like this?"

Zev found it odd, too. Rawn's life was on the line, so why delay? "King Leif seemed nervous," he told them. "When he was speaking to Lady Aerina, his heart rate had spiked for a few seconds."

Dyna looked to Cassiel. "What do you think it means?"

It surprised Zev that she cared to ask him, but he was raised in court life.

Cassiel crossed his arms behind his back as he studied the castle. "Leif is either stalling or something else is at work here."

"I find this very unbecoming," Keena said from where she sat on Von's shoulder. "Fae are always eager for revelry, but to put it above the life of an important member of his family seems rather cavalier. What if King Leif doesn't care about what happens to Lord Norrlen?"

The question left them in shocked silence. That was one thing they had not once considered. If so, why have them come all this way?

"I hate to be the one to say it..." Klyde said, sitting beside Lucenna with his silent nephew.

"Then don't." She jabbed his thigh, making him jolt. "Rawn isn't dead. I can still feel him."

Zev rubbed the back of his neck. He didn't like delaying this another day at all.

"What should we do?" Von asked.

They all looked to Dyna, and her shoulders straightened as she took a deep breath. "Oaths are binding to the elves. For the King of Red Highland to make an oath to do no harm, so he must honor it. Rawn cannot be touched."

For now.

It went unsaid, but they all seemed to be thinking it.

"We have no choice but to be patient and oblige King Leif today," Dyna continued. "Tomorrow, we will reconvene on what truly matters."

Once they settled in their rooms, they all bathed and dressed in the clothing left out for them. Zev eyed the soft fabric of his fine gray doublet and new trousers. If not for his worn boots, he could have passed for a lord.

The drawing room with blue upholstery that he shared with the others was quiet. Von and Klyde had already gone ahead. When Zev went out into the hall, Sowmya stood still and silent by the girl's suite across from him. The red-winged Valkyrie glanced at him impassively. She was always Dyna's shadow, even when he didn't see her. He had to acknowledge that loyalty.

Dyna and Lucenna stepped out into the hall, with Keena fluttering around them.

Zev bowed his head. "My ladies, you look enchantingly beautiful this evening."

Smiling shyly, Dyna took the skirts of her green gown and twirled, dipping in a curtsy. It was an exquisite dress adorned with a trimming of gold leaves at the neckline and jewels at the bodice. The gown Lucenna wore reminded him of a field of lilacs. Embroidered flowers and pearls as small as dewdrops embellished the bodice. A matching jeweled headpiece and purple ribbons pinned back her silver tresses. Keena wore a dress of crimson petals, and her dark curls glinted with tiny gold beads.

"Flattery will most certainly earn you my favor," Lucenna winked, giving his shoulder a pat as she passed him.

"Mine, too." Keena planted a tiny kiss on his nose. "Handsome wolf."

Dyna flashed him a smile as the girls walked ahead of them. She straightened out her skirts. "Raiden had it sent for me."

"Did he?" Zev held out his arm, and she took it. He heard Cassiel had also sent gifts with the servants, which she had all returned. "Your color looks better."

"Lucenna brewed us tea last night to replenish our Essence."

"Good."

"Have you spoken to him?" Dyna asked after a pause. He could tell she was worried about Cassiel.

"A little, only to make sure he wouldn't set Evos on fire." Though Zev sensed what she had really wanted to ask was if he was still angry. "I have already spoken my peace with him, Dyna."

She looked up at him with somber green eyes that matched his own. "Zev, Cassiel and I may no longer be together, but that doesn't mean you can no longer be friends. During the night of the full moon..."

"I remember what Cassiel did to stop me." Zev paused by the windows as they watched the procession of lords and ladies come to the castle. "But I don't know if it's enough to pay for all those nights that you suffered and every tear you cried. Even if I wanted to forgive him, how could I forget that?"

Dyna searched his eyes a moment in surprise. "You ... *remember*?"

He nodded.

"Why didn't you tell me?"

Because it was frightening. If he could remember what the Other did when it took over, it meant that something was changing.

"I have not told you this, Dyna, but I summoned the Other at will when fighting the Bloodhounds in Dwarf Shoe. The lack of a moon didn't keep it at bay. It's evolving, or I am. I don't know what it means."

He wished there was someone here with the answers. A question had been circling in his mind since it first happened. What if the next time the Other surfaced, he couldn't change back?

Dyna squeezed his hands. "Zev, if you can summon your Other at will, that must mean you're learning to control it."

"That type of belief is what led to my father's death. When I'm the Other, I don't have control of myself, and I'm not conscious of what I'm doing. I only remember after."

"But you will. I believe it." Dyna hugged him. "Oh, Zev, this is wonderful news!"

He couldn't say if it was. His greatest fear was hurting his family again.

"Once this is over, we are headed to Loup Garou next, you hear me? It's decided. Lara will know how to help you."

The mention of her name stirred something in Zev's chest. He could almost see himself there, running through a forest he didn't know, alongside a white wolf he wished he did.

A servant came by and called Dyna away to be presented with Cassiel. Sowmya followed on her heels.

Zev reached the main hall where gentle music flowed. He came to the entryway of the ballroom and found Lucenna standing there, frozen still.

Coming up behind her, he found what she was looking at. Klyde stood by adorned tables filled with tiered plates of food. He was mid conversation with an elf. His hair was no longer long but cropped short on the sides and slicked back. And he had shaved. Zev had already seen him, but to her, he must be nearly unrecognizable compared to how he had looked this morning.

Klyde noticed her and strode over to them.

"Close your mouth," Zev whispered, and Lucenna's jaw snapped shut. Keena shot him a grin, and they made their way inside.

"Lucenna," Klyde greeted when he reached them. His admiring gaze slowly roamed over the lilac fabric clinging to her curves. "You could start wars in that dress, love."

She flushed. "You-you shaved."

"I did." Klyde's mouth lifted in a half smile. "Do you like it?"

The question seemed to clear her head, and she fixed her expression into a flat glower. "I hate it."

"Do I at least look submissive and breedable?"

Lucenna rolled her eyes with a groan of disgust and strode away toward the tables.

Keena snickered behind her hand and fluttered around Zev. "She's absolutely smitten, isn't she?"

He chuckled as Klyde followed after Lucenna. "She's not the only one."

Zev flinched at the sudden fanfare of trumpets as the herald made an announcement. On the balcony overlooking the ballroom, King Leif and Queen Ossenia appeared with their newborn son in her arms. Only Lady Aerina wasn't present.

Guests quieted and faced the balcony.

"In the presence of King Leif and Queen Ossenia, presenting before the court, their first-born male, Crown Prince Lotham, heir to the throne of Greenwood."

Everyone in attendance dipped in a courtly bow.

"And presenting our guest of honor, the King and Queen of Hilos."

Awed murmurs passed through the crowd as Cassiel and Dyna entered the room with their personal guards. Guests once again bowed. The music commenced, and pairs took to the dance floor.

Cassiel had arrived dressed in an elegant black waistcoat. Luxurious gold filigree adorned shoulders and cuffs, matching his vest. But he kept crossing his arms and uncrossing them, shifting on his feet. He eyed the doors as if he wished to escape the ballroom immediately.

Raiden surfaced from the crowd, dressed in a fine green coat. He approached Dyna and crossed his arm over his chest with a bow. "Could I request the next dance? If you are not otherwise engaged."

Zev tensed, bracing for Cassiel's reaction. But he stared straight ahead as if he didn't care or didn't hear. A flex in his jaw was the only sign he did.

Dyna paused for a moment, maybe expecting he would say something, too. When he didn't, she took Raiden's hand.

The young lord pressed a kiss to the back of her hand. That drew Cassiel's gaze to Raiden's, and it burned like a forge.

"I can't stop staring," Keena whispered to Zev. "I think they are trying to kill each other with their eyes."

Cassiel probably could, but he stood by as Raiden led Dyna to the dance floor. Zev was impressed he could show some restraint after all. Cassiel remained by the doors, staring blankly at nothing. It was the same look he had last night. As though he were far away and lost in thought.

Or merely lost.

It's easy to shroud ourselves in lies while hiding the truth we ignore inside.

"Come try the food, Zev!" Keena tugged on his sleeve. He followed her to join the others.

Queen Ossenia retreated with the young prince as King Leif came down the steps and sat at the grand dining table. It had many open chairs reserved for them, but Zev lingered by the serving tables set up with wine and ale. Von kept to himself, drinking in a corner and eating whatever Keena offered him on a plate to try. Lucenna pointedly ignored everyone else.

"Tavin?" Zev asked Klyde as he poured himself a drink.

"I had the lad stay behind. I can't account for what may happen tonight, and I prefer he stays out of trouble."

"He wasn't happy about that, was he?"

"Livid."

Zev chuckled. That boy was certainly curious and had a habit of wandering.

"Hungry?" Keena brought him a small plate with a roll of bread. The top glistened with butter and a sprinkling of seeds. He took a bite, finding it stuffed with savory meat and mint.

"What about me, shimmer bug?" Klyde asked her.

Keena stuck up her nose. "I only feed my favorites, and you're not a favorite."

The mercenary clutched his chest. "You wound me."

It really did wound him when Keena flew off to bring Von something else to eat. Zev hid a grin at Klyde's pout. He wondered if she enjoyed feeding them because her stomach was too small to try all the delicious food.

"How long do you suppose we should entertain this incredibly dull affair?" Lucenna huffed, crossing her arms.

"For as long as needed without insulting the king," Cassiel replied tersely as he joined them at the table. He clearly didn't want to be here.

With an aggravated sigh, he grabbed a goblet of wine. Possibly out of habit to hold something since his kind didn't drink. Then again, he did have his fill of mead in Corron.

"Planning to get drunk?" Zev asked him.

Cassiel's silver eyes sharpened as he watched Dyna dance with Raiden. "Perhaps I should. It may help me endure the rest of tonight."

Zev exchanged a look with Klyde, and they braced themselves for another altercation. The moment Cassiel entered the ballroom, he had cared for nothing else but the beauty in the green grown. The golden chandeliers cast Dyna in a soft glow as she swayed on the dancefloor ... in the arms of another.

Zev could feel the irritation rolling off him in waves, but Cassiel had to endure this.

He clenched his teeth as Raiden's fingers trailed down Dyna's bare back to her waist. His only place now was to keep watch over her from a distance. The young lord pulled Dyna close, and she smiled at whatever he whispered in her ear.

Fire flared from Cassiel's hand, making the wine in his goblet boil over. He set it down with a harsh laugh. "The elf wants to die."

"Wait." Klyde grabbed his elbow. "You can't kill him. Need I remind you who he is?"

"Who said I intended to kill him?" Cassiel jerked free. "I am only going to *char* him a little."

"What's he going to do?" Klyde asked as they watched Cassiel stride toward Raiden and Dyna.

Zev smirked. "Something stupid."

CHAPTER 71

Dynalya

Dyna was relieved when Raiden led her away from the dance floor. It was difficult to maintain a smile on her face when her skin stung with every contact of his touch. The bond didn't like it, and neither did her mate by the heat of his stare on her back.

They reached the King's table and Raiden pulled out a chair for her. Once seated, he took the seat beside her, scooting his chair closer to hers. "Every beauty here pales in comparison to you tonight. That dress becomes you."

Dyna flushed beneath his stare. "It's a lovely dress, thank you..."

He straightened as he looked at something past her. She didn't need to turn to know who it was. The bond was already thrumming. "Did you need something?" he asked flatly.

"As a matter of fact, I do," Cassiel replied in an even tone. Dyna forced herself not to look up at him. She hadn't spoken to him since last night, and her lips still tingled with the memory of it. He sat in the other empty chair beside her and asked in a softer tone, "May I speak with you?"

She frowned. "Only if you send no more gifts to my room."

The servants had brought her a mountain of them.

Cassiel's mouth hitched on one end as his silver eyes swept over her. "At least you liked one of them."

Dyna blinked. *He* had sent her the dress. She had assumed Raiden had sent it because they had spoken of it, and the box it arrived in had stood out from the others. Wrapped in silk cloth rather than paper.

"As you can see, I am already having a conversation with Lady Dyna." Raiden leaned his arm across the back of her chair.

Cassiel's jaw clenched. "No, you're having a conversation with my queen, and it may be the last one you will ever have." He took the arm of her chair and slid her to him.

The sudden movement caused Dyna to knock her fork to the floor. She glowered at him and bent to retrieve it.

"Mind yourself, Soaraway. We are in the presence of the King."

As she straightened up, Dyna noticed Cassiel's hand covering the corner of the table. Done to protect her head. It inexplicably made her pulse thrum in time with the next song that began to play on a harp.

"It seems I need to remind you, Raiden. You are already in the presence of one." Taking her hand, Cassiel pulled her to stand. "Pardon us, King Leif," he announced to the rest of the table, drawing all attention. "We thank you for inviting us to your joyous occasion and may the God of Urn bless the next Heir of Greenwood. Forgive us for not staying longer, but my wife and I must retire early." He met Raiden's stare and added, "The journey to Avandia was quite trying."

"Of course, King Cassiel." Leif lifted his goblet. "Have a goodnight."

Drawing Leif's attention forced Raiden not to interfere as she was led away from the table. Cassiel made his way for the doors. Dyna held her skirts, nearly running to keep up with his quick pace. Her face heated beneath everyone's stares.

"Cassiel, what are you doing?" she hissed as they entered the hallway. "Where are we going?"

He pulled her into an empty library. The last of the evening light streamed in through the large glass doors that led to a garden. A light drizzle fell outside.

Cassiel stopped a few feet away from her. She could practically see the waves of heat hovering on his silhouette. His fire pressed beneath the surface, warming the room.

"I despise feeling this way…" he said quietly.

"Are you angry that I avoided you, or that I chose to dance with him in favor of you?"

Cassiel shook his head.

The veil of their shields thinned, and Dyna saw herself from his point of view. She looked happy dancing with Raiden, held close in his arms. Her big green eyes glittered under the chandeliers as she smiled at him.

Cassiel couldn't stand it, and she couldn't either, because secretly, a part of her had been doing it on purpose. To push him away, because she was trying so hard to let him go.

"Let us not pretend what this is," he said.

"The only one pretending is you," Dyna shot back. "You're jealous of him."

Cassiel prowled forward, and she stumbled backward until her spine became flush against the wall. Bracing his arm above her head, he leaned down, his silver eyes holding hers. "What I am is territorial." His low, gravelly voice sent a scatter of currents over her skin. "Jealousy is due to wanting something that isn't yours. And you, Dynalya, are *mine*."

Her breath caught, her pulse climbing at the possession in his gaze. She felt his want and desire, his anger that another dared hold her. It awoke an instinct in her that could only be described as thrilling.

"Cassiel—"

"No, I'm finished standing by. My tolerance with him has reached its limit. Whatever he touches you with will be removed from his person. His hands. His mouth. His co—"

"You have lost all right to dispute who touches me." Dyna shoved him off her and moved away from the wall. "If I want to be courted by Raiden, I will. That is *my* choice."

It wasn't as if she had any interest in a relationship with him or another man, but she wasn't going to tell him that.

Cassiel stared at her a moment and he chuckled, the low dark sound sending scatters down her spine. "Very well. Then it will be my choice in how I send him through the Gates. Do make sure he has a pleasant time before I do."

He turned to go.

After seeing him nearly fight Raiden last night, she wasn't sure if he was jesting anymore.

"Your arrogance is staggering. On what grounds do you have to harm him? Raiden has been nothing but kind to us. He's a good person."

Cassiel stopped by the door, his back to her. His quiet voice floated in the room. *"My heart will always be filled with none other than you…"*

The reciting of the vow she had made to him struck her chest. It reminded Dyna of how her lips had burned when she kissed someone who wasn't him, and how much her body hated it.

"'I will live each day worthy of you," she replied feebly in return, emotion rushing up her throat. "Maybe you should have kept your promises if you expected me to keep mine. Our *vows* were broken the moment you broke me."

Cassiel took a breath, and she knew her blow had landed.

"It hurts, doesn't it? Being lied to. Being betrayed by the one who swore to love you always." Dyna's chest heaved as tears stung the back of her eyes. "You're being selfish, Cassiel. *You* left *me*, remember? You told me to move on and I am trying to, but you won't let me. That's not fair."

"I did say that..." he murmured. "I thought I could let you go, but I can't stand seeing you with him or anyone else. When it comes to you, I am selfish, and it's maddening. The tether that binds us as mates is still there." Rain lightly pattered against the glass, storm clouds darkening the room as Cassiel turned to her. "I have told you once before, and perhaps you forgot or didn't believe me, but I will tell you again. I am not a good person. But you're right, Raiden is. And what do you think he would do if it came between choosing your life or his father's? Or better yet, his mother or his people? What if he had to choose between the greater good and you?" His black wings softly brushed the floor as he drew closer to her. Dyna swallowed, her voice trapped beneath the intensity of his stare. "He would do the right thing and save them, but not I." A faint blue glow spiraled in Cassiel's eyes, and he took a lock of her hair, entwining it around his fingers. "I would gladly render the world to ash and become whatever monster I needed to be. A good man would sacrifice you for the world. I would burn it for you."

She knew he would.

And the main sacrifice had been their souls.

The thought reached him, and his hand dropped. He closed his eyes, his long dark lashes brushing his cheeks. "Is it senseless to cling to the hope that I can mend what I destroyed?"

Her vision welled at the brokenness in his voice. The hollowness in her chest ached, and it was coming from him. Whatever shred of their bond that remained still allowed her to feel him.

She wrapped her arms around herself. "Cassiel..."

"Don't tell me it's over, Dyna."

Her jaw trembled, fighting to keep her tears from spilling. "It is."

"Then prove it." His eyes softened in a way that seemed to see right through her. "Drop your shield and show me there is truly no place for me in your heart anymore."

Her pulse hammered in her throat, and she curled her fingers tightly in her palms because all she wanted was to touch him and fall into his arms, but she couldn't.

"I don't need to prove anything to you. Gods, I don't want to speak about this anymore. I already said everything that needed to be said."

Dyna stormed for the glass doors and went outside into the gardens. Her heels crunched on the graveled path as she wandered in no particular direction until she found a stone bench enclosed in bushes of dynalyas. The cool evening breeze cooled her skin. Birds chirped in the coming twilight as she breathed in the scent of dynalyas. The garden was full of them, gleaming like rubies.

Cassiel walked around the bench and kneeled in front of her. That was always him. He never stood above her. Always eye to eye. "You asked me if it hurt," he murmured. "It hurts more knowing how much I hurt you ... and even more when I make you cry." He reached up, and she didn't flinch away as he wiped the tears from her cheek. "I'm so sorry, Dyna. I will say it to you every day for the rest of my life."

On his face were countless days of torment. Of shame. Punishment. She saw the racking guilt and bone-deep agony and stark regret. That's what pained her the most. That despite everything that had happened, that he was still choosing to suffer right here—for her.

As the sun lowered, a light shone from his pocket.

"What is that?"

Cassiel drew out her crystal necklace.

Dyna stared at it in disbelief. The last time she'd seen it had been when she threw it into the lake at Skelling Rise. "Where did you get that?"

His silver eyes dimmed a little, though he hid it with a soft smile. "Sowmya retrieved it ... for safekeeping." He looked down at the glowing crystal cradled in his palm. "I broke so many promises to you. I beg you to allow me to keep this one."

The gentle plea made her eyes sting. He made it too difficult to hold on to her anger when he treated her this way. A part of her couldn't help wanting to bridge the gap between them.

Shifting around, Dyna lifted her hair and exposed her neck to the cool air. Cassiel sat on the bench beside her. The chain gently grazed her neck as his hands fastened it at her nape. Her skin tingled at the graze of his fingers. It reminded her of Hermon as an indulgent warmth faintly flooded through her body at his proximity. He was so close she felt his every movement. When Cassiel finished, they remained still, simply breathing in the sweet air and each other.

"Thank you..." he whispered.

"For what?"

He expelled a soft sigh, and his breath drifted down her shoulders, making her shiver. There was no need to say it. He thanked her for allowing this small reprieve from her resentment. For allowing him to be here with her.

Dyna looked up and found him close. The wind picked up, carrying the hint of rain and his scent that made her heart race. A deep ache of longing sank through her. He was inexplicably beautiful, an entity not of this world. Oddly enough, the feeling was still there, a mix of familiarity and love and awe that dove deep.

For a moment, she lost herself in the depths of silver. His gaze silently begged her to close the remaining distance between them. To take the kiss he so desperately wanted to give her.

She wanted it.

She wanted so much to go back to who they were.

But her heart was still bruised from the last time she trusted him with it.

Dyna looked away. "I need to go."

She moved from the bench and stepped onto the garden path.

Cassiel caught her wrist. "Don't go to him," he pleaded softly. He stepped closer, his dark hair tangled across his eyes and dripping with rain. Long lashes framed his eyes, the flecks in them gleaming in the last rays of the sun. "Please don't run from me anymore."

"I need to … because it's easier than admitting that I…"

Cassiel shifted closer and wrapped her in the warmth of his wings. He cupped her cheek, stroking her lips with his thumb. *"Ani mitga'ah'ge'ah elayich."*

Dyna's vision blurred with tears, and she shook her head. He knew speaking to her so lovingly in his language always made her cry. "I miss you, too, Cassiel. All the time. But my heart is too broken."

He took her hand and placed it over the beating one in his chest. "Then take mine. Do with it as you wish. Tear it apart or shatter it to dust if that will right my wrongs. Without you, I have no use for it anyway."

His soft voice was so raw, so painfully open, she couldn't move away.

"Don't tell me those words when I am so angry with you," Dyna's voice caught.

Her heart longed to give in. She wanted to reach out and give him everything. But she was terrified. If he hurt her again, she may not recover from it this time. But his eyes grew pained, and she realized that he was as afraid as she was.

Afraid that he may hurt her again.

That he had already lost her.

Afraid that he couldn't call her home.

"Why do I hear your soul pleading for mine?" she asked.

Cassiel offered no reply. He didn't need to. The answer was right there in his watery gaze. Her heart squeezed into itself because he looked at her with so much love, it completely dismantled her.

"Stop it," her voice broke. "Please, stop."

Stop loving me.

Cassiel sighed as he kissed away the tears from her lashes. "Impossible." His lips drifted over her cheek, planting small kisses to the corner of her mouth. "You are asking me to stop breathing."

"Oh, I hate you," she said in defeat, pulling him toward her. "And I hate that I don't quite hate you enough."

Cassiel's arms immediately wrapped around her, capturing her mouth. He tasted of sheer divinity and salted tears. Her entire body was thrumming, and the bond glittered in her chest.

The rain picked up, pattering on the leaves in time with the beat of her heart. They broke apart with an exhilarated laugh. Standing, Cassiel grabbed her hand, and they ran back to the castle. Instead of the library, he brought her to a set of stone steps that led up a terrace adorned in more flowering bushes.

He kissed her again as they stumbled toward the doors and into his bedchambers. She knew they were his because his scent lingered in the air. His mouth came over her racing pulse as she tugged at the buttons of his vest. He moved backwards, pulling her with him, simultaneously tearing off his coat.

Cassiel tripped over a snag on the rug, and they stumbled against a wall. She giggled, and his warm hands came over her waist, hauling her to him. Their mouths cashed in an urgent kiss. She wrapped her arms around his neck, rising on her toes, simply drawn into him. He flipped her around and pinned her against the wall as his mouth planted heated impressions of his lips up her neck to the shell of her ear.

Desire unfurled deep in her stomach. There was a shift in the room. The air became thicker, the sound of their panting growing louder.

His fingers lightly trailed down her spine, making her prickle with goosebumps. He murmured soft foreign words against her skin, yet her heart understood him completely.

Heat traveled through her body as his mouth devoured hers. His hands were everywhere, holding her, caressing her in every way that reduced her to molten glass.

Gods, she needed this. Needed him.

Lifting her by her waist, Cassiel placed her on the table beside them, never breaking apart from her lips. He hitched her leg up as he leaned forward, his body invading her air. Dyna gasped at his sudden clutch of her hips. He hauled her closer against him and she felt the hard press of his arousal between her thighs. Her heart lurched into her throat, pounding faster, liquid heat building at the stroke of his fingers moving up her thighs beneath her dress.

Her arms wrapped around his neck, needing him. Closer. Deeper. Cassiel groaned against her lips as she stroked his wings. They were a tangle of fabric and hands as he pulled up her skirts and she yanked at his tunic, tearing the buttons. His skin was hot and pale in the dark room with nothing but the glow from her crystal necklace and the vows lighting up on his skin. She traced the shape of the letters she had written on his chest, feeling him shudder.

Her eyes drifted shut as Cassiel's mouth traced the one he had written on her throat. The bond was thrumming in the center of her with a soft glow. She leaned her head back as he made his way to her collarbone, and her heart pounded wildly, all of her warming beneath his touch.

Lips against hers, he faintly asked, "Can you forgive me?"

Dyna froze.

Her eyes flew open as a culmination of shock and a chill instantly washed the arousal from her system. The light faded from their skin ... and from the bond.

The question surfaced the night he broke her apart and every night she cried herself to sleep. That hollow in her chest was still there, filled with the pain he left her with. What he had done to them changed her, and only for the worst.

Feeling the change, Cassiel immediately stopped. He shifted back to look at her. By his torn expression, he knew whatever spell had come over her was broken.

"Dyna—"

She pushed him off and ran out of the room without another word, because she had to. Even if every part of her screamed to run back into that room. Because no matter how much she craved him, she hadn't forgiven him yet.

And Dyna feared she never would.

CHAPTER 72

Lucenna

I f there was one thing elves knew how to make well, it was cake. Lucenna intently scrutinized the glazed tarts and fruit pastries displayed on the fancy-tiered plates set upon the dessert table. She ignored her friends prattling on about the spectacle Cassiel was going to make of himself as he strode for the king's table. She might have stepped in his way in the past, but with so many guests in attendance, he stood to make a fool of himself all on his own.

She had no interest in making herself one, too.

"I suggest the lemon cake."

Lucenna stiffened at the sound of Klyde's voice behind her. "Why is that?"

"I find them to be the perfect amount of bitter and sweet."

Was that supposed to be a euphemism about her of some sort? Or was he toying with her again? She truly hoped he hadn't already seen her eat three of them.

"Sounds as if that would suit your tastes better," Lucenna retorted as she turned away from the table and took a sip from her goblet. She kept her eyes trained on the swaying elves moving across the dancefloor.

"It certainly does," Klyde murmured.

Lucenna's face warmed at the way his low reply seemed to rumble in her ear. She took another drink, and the cloying taste of wine settled heavily in her stomach. Gods, she refused to look at him. Which was completely ludicrous. This man should not have this much power over—

The moment Klyde stepped into view, all of Lucenna's thoughts vanished. Her heart dipped in her chest and fluttered wildly as she took in his face, free of the mangy beard he had had all winter. She visually traced the chiseled cheekbones and the fine angles of his perfect jaw.

He wore a fine waist coat in midnight blue, the collar detailed in gilded filigree, accompanied by pristine black trousers and boots. He'd been ruggedly handsome before, but this ... this was absurd.

Klyde's blue eyes gleamed in the low candlelight, and his mouth curved as he took in whatever expression was on her face, making his dimples appear.

She swallowed. *Damn it.*

"Do you need something?" Lucenna asked dismissively. She moved, so he was no longer in her view.

Klyde chuckled. "Well, I do have a request for you, love."

"Are you to ask me what I think of your hairless face again? Do you wish me to brandish you with praises of how handsome you *believe* you are?"

He flashed her a grin, and his finger trailed over her shoulder as he adjusted her fallen dress strap back into place. The unexpected touch left tingles on her skin. His gaze roamed over the thin fabric clinging to her body. "If I'm drunk enough, I may end up singing a ballad of praises about a moonlit lass."

Lucenna's cheeks flamed, and she looked away. She never knew what to say when he said such things. He was only attempting to get a rise out of her. "What do you want?"

The question seemed to weigh more than it should have. His lips curved in a half smile, small and rueful. There was an answer in his gaze that made her stomach tight. She suddenly felt hot all over.

Klyde took her goblet and set it on the table. "Well, could I interest you in a dance?"

"No." Lucenna snatched her drink back. The last time she allowed that, she'd almost fallen for his coquetry. Elvish music was too soft and slow—too intimate. To imagine herself dancing to such music while in Klyde's arms made her pulse leap. "Go find another mindless girl to dally with. I am busy enjoying my wine."

But before she could take another drink, Klyde downed the rest of it, his throat flexing as he swallowed. She gaped at him angrily.

With a smooth move, Klyde twirled her to the dancefloor. "Indulge me for a song before you lose function of your feet again."

"I think you would trip over yourself first. That goblet was nearly full."

"You'll find I have more practice holding my drink." Klyde dipped her with the next turn. Her heart lurched as he hauled her up with his easy strength and brought her close to his chest again.

Klyde's gaze flicked past her, and she followed it to the King's table as Cassiel excused himself and Dyna. Everyone stared as they left the ballroom.

Lucenna exhaled an annoyed breath and moved to follow, but Klyde stopped her.

"They need to resolve it for themselves."

"What is there to resolve? Cassiel betrayed her."

Klyde sighed. "He lied to protect her, and he unequivocally regrets it. There is nothing he wouldn't do to take it back."

Lucenna glowered. "As you said, he *lied*. And he has yet to tell her the truth as to why he hurt her in the first place."

His brow furrowed as he searched her eyes. "It's a terrifying thing to bear your heart to others and reveal every truth and lie ... because what if they can't forgive you for it? What if the truth is so unbearable, speaking it aloud will destroy everything you've come to love?"

Lucenna's chest hurt in a messy, confusing way as she considered that. Her gaze dropped to his gentle hold on her hand. She had witnessed too many betrayals in her lifetime. From Ava snubbing Lucien, her father siphoning her mother, the empire segregating sorceresses, and the injustices of life itself.

Perhaps the greatest betrayal was the way her heart reacted to the touch of a man who wasn't Everest.

Trusting others was another form of vulnerability.

But loving them tore off all armor.

She could never leave herself open to feel the inevitable pain of a knife in her back.

"Sometimes," Lucenna whispered. "The greatest testament to love is letting go."

After a breath, Klyde's hold slipped away. Lucenna strode quickly for the glass doors leading to the courtyard. She needed air. She needed space. She needed to not feel this way about a man she had no business wanting.

Lucenna's heels clacked on the paved ground as she ran alongside a glittering fountain toward the sunset. Light rain fell, trickling on the leaves. The view of the garden blurred with her stupid tears.

Why did she have to be this pathetic?

She arrived at a gondola made of stone. It sat beneath the cover of wisteria trees, enclosed in a curtain of purple petals.

"Lucenna!" Klyde called. His footsteps rushed up behind her. "What are you doing?"

She spun around and blurted, "Tell me something true."

"What?" His brow furrowed. He looked perplexed, worried, and so handsome in the rain.

"Tell me something true," Lucenna repeated, her voice breaking. "I have already lived a life of lies. For once, I need something real."

That wasn't what she had wanted to ask, at least not in those words, but a look crossed Klyde's face that told her he understood her anyway. Her heart pounded wildly as he stepped closer to her. The last rays of the sun shone like gold through the gondola, illuminating the edges of his face.

"I am possessed by you," Klyde admitted quietly, and her heart stopped. "From the very first moment I laid eyes on you, I was done for. You have occupied my mind every day since. When night falls, I wish on every star I see to have the girl who shines like the moon." He drew her closer, and his hand slid up her arm, making her shiver. Her pulse jumped at the way his eyes focused on her, yearning and unwavering. "When sleep takes me, I dream of losing myself in every inch of her and kissing her sweet lips that refuse me." His nose trailed across her cheek, and his mouth hovered above hers, so close she could feel them. "But I gave my word," he whispered. "That I wouldn't until she asked it of me."

All her hesitations evaporated, all her worries and uncertainties. Perhaps because she could feel it was the undeniable truth, or the way she simply felt safe with this man. So everything that held Lucenna back, she let go.

"Klyde..." she whispered.

"Aye?"

Her lips trembled. "Kiss me."

His hands curled around her waist, palms warm as they moved up her back, drawing her close. Leaning down, he brought his face close to hers. She closed her eyes as their lips came together, an exhilarated rush through her like a current of lightning. His hand slid to her face as his mouth moved over hers in a way that stole the last of her breath. Lucenna closed her fingers around his wrists and rose onto her toes, wanting more—and he responded in kind.

His hands slid to the small of her back as his lips crushed against hers with a demolishing kiss. Her mouth parted, moving with his, and he swallowed her gasp as she felt his tongue move smoothly over hers. Caressing. Tasting. Electricity shot straight through her to his grasp on her hips. Her pulse raced, molten heat expanding through her center. She had been kissed before, but this was something else.

It was deep. Insatiable.

Lucenna didn't realize he was pushing her backward until her back met the wet column of the gondola covered with leaves. She yelped, and Klyde's

489

boot slipped down a wet step, leaving her lips cold as his disappeared. He caught himself on the rail, and she stifled a laugh.

He looked so charming standing there in the rain, face flushed and amused. But she wasn't finished kissing him yet.

Lucenna was already reaching for him the same time he was. He lifted her off the steps as she wrapped her arms around his neck and yanked his mouth back onto hers. He hooked her legs up around his waist and carried her off deeper into the garden, out of sight and out of the rain, kissing her as they went.

They arrived in a secluded corner surrounded by flowering bushes and trees. Her feet landed on soft grass as he pinned her to the wall. His hands wove into her hair, holding her head as he explored the shape of her lips. A rough sound rumbled in his throat as she ran her hands up his chest. His heart raced beneath her palms, and she was glad not to be the only one barely holding on.

Lucenna tipped her head farther back as his mouth moved on to her throat. The stroke of his tongue and gentle nip of his teeth dazed her senses. His mouth returned to hers, taking what he wanted, and every part of her was ready to surrender to him and the fire he'd ignited.

Her fingers found their way under his tunic, her nails lightly gliding over his bare stomach. His answering shudder and deep groan filled her with a tingling thrill. Klyde paused, panting, heavy-lidded eyes gazing at her. It was a look of craving. Of undeniable desire that flushed heat through her body and fluttered in her stomach.

It made her wonder what kind of lover he was. If he was rough or gentle. Whatever the answer, it made her body tremble. It could be that sinking into him scared her, but by the Gods, did she want him.

More than she ever thought possible.

Biting her lip, Lucenna reached for the buttons of his tunic. His heady gaze held hers, and her pulse sped with each button she released until she exposed his chest to the cool air.

Good Gods. He may as well be sculpted from marble. It was suddenly very difficult to breathe as she admired the endless plane of strength and masculine beauty. Klyde's lashes drifted closed at the first graze of her hand. She lightly traced the scars over his chest, trailing her fingers over his perfectly honed abdomen to his navel.

"Lass." Klyde grabbed her hand. "I've had too much to drink tonight to maintain the pretense that I'm a gentleman. If you continue to touch me like that, there's no telling what I'll do."

Tremors fluttered on her skin with the warning. But any resistance she once held had long fallen away. There was only him, the gentle patter of rain, and his scent on the evening breeze.

"What will you do?" she whispered.

Taking her waist, he pulled her flush against him and his hips where she could feel very clearly the undeniable effect she had on him. She quivered at the flush of heat it sent through her.

Klyde's nose skated from her cold cheek to her neck, breathing her in. His lips met her ear, and the heated rumble of his voice sent an electrical current to the very center of her being with his confession.

"Every ungodly desire I've ever imagined doing to you."

Lucenna's pulse climbed with the ardent sincerity burning through his words. She playfully dodged his next kiss and moved around him toward the garden. Holding his heated gaze, she kicked off her heels. His chest heaved with a breath as she reached for the ties of her corset. She watched his eyes dilate as she tugged at the laces. He didn't make a move, but she felt his anticipation hovering on the surface. The strap of her dress loosened with the corset and slid down her shoulder.

Klyde swiftly cut the distance between them and caught her hands again. "Love, your beauty could topple a nation. If you remove that dress, I may not survive it."

"Hmm..." She smiled. "Tempting. Don't move."

He remained still, allowing her to slip the tunic completely off his shoulders and it landed at their feet. Lucenna canted her head, continuing her perusal. She heard his intake of breath as he watched her pale hand move over his tanned chest.

Klyde groaned faintly and lowered his nose along her shoulder. His hot breath wafted along her skin. "I am trying to keep my restraint, but you're making it very ... hard."

Lucenna laughed softly. She curled her fingers in his hair and brought his face to hers, holding her mouth a breath away from his. She held him there, not allowing him any closer.

Klyde growled in response, gripping her hips tightly. "Don't play with me, woman. Last warning."

His voice was strained. All of him shook, his body hot, and she knew he was on the verge of falling over the edge because of what she did to him. She felt it in the way he held her, undeniable in the press of his hips against hers. And Lucenna fed off that power. His chest rumbled as she slowly ran her nails across his back, and she pressed her mouth to his throat.

Klyde's control snapped.

He grabbed her possessively in his arms as he kissed her wildly. They ended up on the grass, a tangle of limbs and lips. His rough hands slipped up her thighs, roaming over her heated skin, leaving tendrils of fire in their wake. His mouth possessed her, demanding entry. She gave into him, accepting of his caresses and touches, clinging to him with as much desperation.

Her loose dress strap slipped down her shoulder. The cool air fell over her bare skin. His mouth brushed over the curve of her breast. Inhaling her. Kissing. Licking. Lucenna gasped and her spine arched, pressing against the length of him, wanting more of him and everything he could give her.

His knee pressed between her legs, and a rush of desire swept through her with a gasping moan. Klyde suddenly paused. He panted as he stared at her. Perhaps debating whether they should do this here.

"Don't stop." Lucenna pulled his face back to her. His grip on her dress was tight, possessive, and she heard the fabric tearing in his shaking fist. Yes, that's what she wanted, for him to tear it off and take her here and now. He kissed her, but it wasn't deep enough for her liking. She kissed him harder, only for him to pull away again.

"Wait..." Klyde blinked at her, slowly rising out of the fog of lust, and he sat back.

Lucenna rose up on her elbows, biting her lip. A ball of insecurity gathered in her chest. Had she done something to ruin the mood? "What's wrong?"

He shut his eyes. "I can't."

Her heart pounded, shock and confusion washing away the heat from her body. "Can't do what?"

Klyde moved away from her, and she wasn't prepared for how much the action stung. "I shouldn't have done this. We both had too much to drink tonight. This was a ... mistake..."

"A mistake?" she whispered.

Shame entered his eyes, and her breath caught.

Anger surged first, but it simmered beneath a surface of humiliation and hurt. The sharp emotions slapped her in the face, startling Lucenna so much she was horrified when her eyes burned. She tried to swallow it away. Tried to bury it because she *refused* to cry in front of him. Getting up on her feet, she turned away from him and adjusted her dress.

"Lucenna..."

She hated the sound of guilt in his voice and how utterly exposed she suddenly felt. That was the thing when one removed their armor. Without it, nothing else protected you.

She knew that. She *knew*, and she had stupidly let him remove it.

Klyde said her name again, and he took her face in his hands, making her look at him. His blue eyes shadowed further at the tears he found in hers.

"Did you mean everything you said to me, or were you simply attempting to bed me?" Lucenna asked. She hated how weak and pathetic she sounded.

"No." His expression tightened. "That's not what I meant. Listen, please, I am trying to explain."

"You already did." She took his wrists and pulled them down.

She grabbed her shoes, fighting to keep her damn tears from spilling over as she put them on.

"Lucenna, wait—" He reached for her hand, and she tore it away.

"Don't touch me!"

His face crumbled at her scream. "Lucenna I—it wasn't supposed to happen this way. I can't have you like this." His gaze dropped to her ring glittering in the moonlight. "I am trying to do what's right."

"Because of this?" She held up her hand and scoffed harshly. "When I attempted to contact Everest, I had planned to end the engagement. I felt so terribly guilty because I realized I never loved him. Some stupid part of me thought perhaps I might know what that felt like with you." She smirked airily, shaking her head. "*Thank you* for completely eradicating that absurdity. Gods, I don't even know why I wear this anymore." She grabbed the ring to yank it off, but Klyde stopped her.

"Don't take it off," he pleaded. "Not for me."

That infuriated her so much she slapped him. The sharp blow imprinted a pink handprint perfectly on his cheek. "Don't pretend to care now. The ring certainly didn't deter you from seducing me."

Klyde shut his eyes.

Her fists crackled with violent electricity. "If you come near me again, I truly will rip off your nethers."

Lucenna stormed away, and he didn't attempt to follow.

Good.

It wasn't as if she expected him to. She didn't need him or this. Her face burned, and an ugly feeling she couldn't name bubbled up her chest. How could she allow him to beguile her this way?

Casting an invisibility spell over herself, Lucenna found another set of courtyard doors into the castle and made her way through the winding corridors for the west wing. The only thing she wanted right now was a bath and a private place to cry.

Because damn him, his rejection truly cut deep.

But when Lucenna entered their shared bedroom, she found Dyna on the couch, arms wrapped around her knees, crying so hard she was gasping for air.

Lucenna rushed over. "What happened?"

Keena worriedly fluttered around Dyna's down turned head. "I don't know. I found her like this."

Dyna looked up, her face a mess of tears and snot. "Why must love hurt?"

Sighing, Lucenna sat beside her. She laid her head over Dyna's as her own eyes grew wet. "I wish it didn't..."

"I'm afraid of having my heart broken again. But how do I move on when I can't cut him out of me?"

Keena settled on a velvet cushion. "My mother once told me no relationship is easy. They come with deceits and qualms and other muddled things that hurt." She shrugged her tiny shoulders, scattering a sprinkling of gold dust on the upholstery. "You must decide if loving him is worth that."

Lucenna moved to sit on the floor with her back resting against the couch. "We can't tell you what to do about your relationship, Dyna, but I think I'm finished with men. The whole damn lot of them can piss off."

Dyna arched her brows at her. "Did something happen with Klyde?"

She blushed. "Why do you assume he has anything to do with it?"

Keena giggled like a tinkling of bells. "Lucenna, your squabbling was clearly flirting. Now there are leaves in your hair and your lips are flushed. You kissed, didn't you? It was bound to happen."

She groaned and dropped her head on Dyna's lap. "I allowed him to lure me in with those infuriating dimples and cocky charm. All he cared for was the chase. How much of an idiot can I be? I was never this blind."

"Are you all right?" Dyna asked as she brushed the silver tresses from her face.

"Of course." Lucenna scoffed, ignoring the lump in her throat. "I have more important things to do than brood over some *man*."

"Gods, you're right. We have lost sight of what's truly important. The only thing that matters right now is Lord Norrlen." Wiping her eyes, Dyna rose to her feet and marched toward the door. "Everyone else can piss off!"

"Where are you going?" Keena asked.

"To find some wine. We need a drink!"

Well, Lucenna wouldn't argue with that. Dyna stepped out into the hall with Sowmya, the door shutting behind her.

"Whatever happened between you and Klyde, I doubt it was only about the chase." Keena's tiny slippers padded on the velvet upholstery as she sat on the edge of the couch by her nose.

Lucenna arched an eyebrow at her. "You're defending him? I thought he wasn't one of your favorites?"

"Eh, I find him amusing, but I like to make him think he's not."

Lucenna smirked. That must really vex him.

Keena smirked back. "One benefit of being small is that no one notices me there when I'm paying attention to them. And he is always looking at you, Lucenna. I don't mean like a lustful fool, but like someone who worries and cares."

She didn't know what to think about that.

It didn't make sense because Klyde would say one thing and do another to contradict himself. Why kiss her merely to call it a mistake?

The lump in her throat turned to a burning that threatened to rush up her nose. It was too confusing and embarrassing. Regardless, he was right.

Involving herself with him was the most dimwitted thing she could've done.

The fairy princess canted her head, staring at the fireplace thoughtfully. "The world is so big, but at times it seems so small. Tarn is Dyna's sworn enemy and somehow you end up meeting his brother on Troll Bridge."

"Actually, I first met Klyde in the Port of Azure."

Keena's hazel eyes turned to her with astonishment. "Would you consider that coincidence or fate?"

Lucenna rolled her eyes. "Coincidence."

They simply had been in the same place at the same time. A witch's den, oddly enough.

"Klyde joined you to take out his brother for his nephew's sake, but Tarn is dead, right?"

Lucenna sighed. "Yes."

It was probably a good thing Klyde hadn't told Tavin about him. It would be too difficult of a conversation.

"With his brother no longer a threat, that means Klyde lost his reason to be here, Lucenna."

She blinked at her, realizing she was right. He had only joined them to hunt down Tarn.

"Haven't you wondered why he hasn't returned home?" Keena smiled at her startled expression. "What reason could he have now to stay except for you?"

Then the fairy flew away toward the plate of honey cakes on the sofa table, leaving Lucenna to stew over that.

CHAPTER 73

Dynalya

Come morning, Eldred arrived to escort them to the meeting the King of Greenwood at last called forth. Dyna took her place beside Cassiel as they walked together, with Yelrakel and Sowmya close behind. He didn't attempt to speak to her, but she felt his gaze on her hair. Last night, she cut it to her shoulders.

Out with the old and in with the new.

Eldred brought them before a set of tall doors. "It is not everyday outsiders are invited to the king's council meetings," he murmured. "Please do not interject unless addressed."

Dyna nodded.

The Royal Guards opened the doors, and they followed Eldred inside. Golden sunlight streamed through the tall open windows, gleaming on the polished surface of the long stone table in the center of the room. Many elves were already present. Their soft-spoken voices floated in the room as they waited to begin. Then conversations halted, and all eyes were on them.

King Leif sat at the head of the table with Lady Aerina on his left. Exhaustion shadowed her eyes, pink and swollen from crying. Raiden sat in the chair beside her, expressionless. Joining them at the table were advisors or warriors.

Camsen was also present. He and the Rangers stood silently against the north wall behind their liege lord.

"Welcome," King Leif called to them. "Please, take your seats."

Cassiel came forward and chose the seat on the opposite end of the table that was already set with two chairs. Dyna sat with him and the Valkyrie took their posts at his back. Her Guardians settled in the empty seats on either side of them. Their group sat away from the others. A position that displayed them as invited to the table, but not exactly a part of the discussion.

King Leif cleared his throat. "Now that we have all gathered, we can at last discuss a dire matter. First, allow me to properly introduce King Cassiel and Queen Dynalya of Hilos, and their companions. They are acquaintances of Rawn Norrlen, who he met while on his mission for the crown. They came all the way here to bring us the news of his capture. He is very fortunate to have such great friends."

He paused for a moment, letting that sink into the room. No one reacted to the news, telling Dyna that everyone already knew about Rawn's situation.

"The call of a soldier is not without its risks," Leif began. "They fight for their country, and at times, the battle ends with their lives. I value all who serve, but Rawn Norrlen has earned our respect with his many great deeds for his people. When I learned of his capture by Red Highland, I, of course, petitioned King Altham for his life. After much negotiation, I am pleased to announce we have settled on a peaceful trade. A delegation is to be dispatched to Red Highland to retrieve Rawn."

Aerina covered her mouth, stifling a soft whimper of relief. Raiden wrapped an arm around her shoulders.

An elf in deep blue robes cleared his throat. "A trade, sire? Since when has Greenwood capitulated with Red Highland?"

"When elves are initiated into the army, the first thing they are told is to never be captured by the enemy, for they are considered lost," a second counselor said. "Any intervention could instigate another war in the Vale."

The councilors murmured in agreement, but the warriors glared.

Dyna didn't like how they were speaking. Was this what it meant to be a soldier of Greenwood?

"Sire." An elf with ruddy hair pulled back in a braid stepped forward. He clanked a fist over his heart, the light catching on his green armor veined in silver. "Send me and my men. Our general fought with us. He bled with us. We will stake our lives to release him and bring down the keep as we do."

The warriors agreed with vivacious calls.

King Leif lifted his hand, silencing the room. "I admire your courage, Lieutenant Handuril. We have been at war with Red Highland for an age. I do not wish to start another."

"They hold a vital member of your army," Eldred stated thoughtfully. "Lord Norrlen has slain many red elves, and he has married to the princess they once tried to capture. Yet King Altham is willing to return him to us? He is notorious for his cruelty. I have never known him to be reasonable."

"What does he want in exchange for my husband?" Aerina asked.

"Altham searches for a key," Leif announced, and Dyna stiffened in her seat. "Well, the second half of a key."

She felt the shock of her friends, but her mind was racing. Here it was, the thing Leoake sent her for. If the red king searched for the second half, that confirmed he had the first.

"A key? A key to what?" a counselor asked.

"I know not what it opens, only that Altham wants it. He believes Rawn found it while he was in Xián Jīng, but I have received no news of it in his quarterly reports. Whether it be true, it appears he has no memory of it."

"For this to hold Red Highland's interest, this key is no ordinary key," Eldred said. "It must open something dire, an imaginable power to behold."

Dyna's mind flashed with the night she had jumped through Leoake's enchanted Door.

Azulo told her there was another door on Mount Ida. *Many dire treasures were hidden inside of it. The Gods wish them to remain hidden.*

Then she recalled the glowing rhyme that had appeared on the key's scroll when she had held it to the fire.

Seek a key and make your claim but beware the door untamed.

Cross into realms of old, in the loom its secrets unfold.

Once a bridge of finder's luck, now a curse to madness struck.

Dyna's pulse drummed, her ears ringing.

Lief studied his sister and nephew carefully. "Has Rawn mentioned anything about this?" When they shook their heads, he worked his jaw. "This is dire. I need to know about this key and what it opens."

"It opens a door…" All eyes turned to Dyna, and she realized she had said it out loud.

Leif's eyes narrowed. "What door?"

"A door to the In Between. The realm between worlds." As she said the words, Dyna knew they were true. "I think the Dragon Blades are there."

Stark silence fell over the table. Raiden's eyes locked on hers.

Leif leaned forward, his hands bracing on the table. *"Where is the door?"*

"Mount Ida."

Voices of alarm, shock, and wonderment swarmed the room. And she saw the glint in the king's gaze as he sat back in his chair.

"We need to get this key, sire," the first counselor now eagerly said. "It will at last assure our victory against Red Highland. They would never dare challenge us again."

"Only once I acquire both pieces. To discover where the second one is, Rawn must be returned to me. A trade is inevitable."

"Wait..." Aerina softly spoke up. "Altham wants the missing piece of this key, but you have no piece to trade. What have you agreed upon for Rawn's release?"

King Leif paused as he met his sister's gaze. "To broker peace, Altham has proposed an alliance. He would trade your husband for a Greenwood Prince to wed a Red Highland Princess."

A shocked silence once again filled the room.

"But it is forbidden," a councilor in bewilderment. "The kingdom would never accept a union between a red elf and a green elf."

Leif sighed. "Yes, it will be a difficult change, but it is a primitive law I aim to abolish to bring peace to the Vale. I tire of bloodshed, and so do our people. They will come to accept this."

Aerina's delicate features creased with disbelief and concern. "Leif, there was a time when you never would have contemplated that. You couldn't possibly consider giving up your firstborn son."

"I am not." He stared at her, and Dyna felt her body chill.

Aerina's chest heaved with shallow breaths as she glanced between Raiden and him. "What are you saying?"

"I told you once, sister. Those of royal blood must marry to serve the crown."

What he implied hit all of them at the same time.

Aerina's face went white. "No..."

"I am sorry it has come to this."

"You cannot ask me to give them my son," Aerina cried, leaping to her feet. "He is my son, Leif. Our *only* son. If you send him there, he will be a prisoner within their walls. My husband has served you loyally for years. Is this his reward?"

Dyna's chest tightened with emotion at her broken voice. Raiden stared at the king, motionless, too stunned to do anything else. His teacher who helped raise him was equally appalled, proving Eldred had no idea about this.

King Leif was indifferent to their reactions. "His reward was you."

Aerina's eyes welled, and she shook her head. "That was not a reward but a leash. Rawn is a noble elf, which you have exploited. He served your every whim to regain his honor. He removed the curse upon our family, and for that very reason, you are blessed with many children. My husband has held fealty to you for over twenty-five years. It is time that you show him the value of that allegiance."

"What do you expect me to do? Send more men to war?"

"I expect you to act like a king!" Aerina slammed her hand on the table, making them jump. Leif stared at her, taken aback by her outspoken behavior, but the princess no longer cared what the court thought. "Lieutenant Handuril and the others who served under him are willing to fight. Why not you?"

Leif straightened. "Some conflicts cannot be settled with a sword."

Her wet eyes shone with anger. "Some cannot be settled without one."

His steely gaze narrowed as his lips pressed into a thin line. "The decision is made. Raiden is to be crowned a prince today."

"You cannot do this to me!"

"I know this seems unjust, but how am I to leave Greenwood without a future?"

"What of *my* son's future?" Aerina cried. "When Raiden was born, we hid him away so your firstborn could be declared first. You shunned us to the country for fear his existence would threaten your throne. I went willingly to prove to you my son would never be a hindrance. I endured you taking my standing. I held my tongue when you took my husband. How much more can you demand of me?"

"Aerina," Leif said tightly. "You forget yourself."

"Mother..." Raiden at last spoke, his voice tired and resigned. "That's enough." He rose from his seat and met his uncle's gaze. "Is this your command?"

"It is."

"Then I will go," Raiden said, prompting Aerina's face to fall. "May it be the only time you acknowledge that my existence holds any value to you, even if it's merely to use me as chattel." He bowed. "Sire."

Raiden swiftly strode out of the room without looking back.

Aerina's fists shook as she looked at her brother, her marred face now stone. "I take your deeds as inaction and your caution for cowardice. I have never been more ashamed to share blood with you."

Leif blinked, his face flushing.

Her mouth pursed tightly. "You cannot have him."

"Aerina—"

"You cannot! Find another way to bring my husband home." Then she ran out after her son, leaving an awkward silence behind.

With a heavy sigh, Leif removed his crown and rubbed his temples. No one moved or spoke as they awaited his next response. "I must do what I can for the sake of Greenwood, and I do so with a heavy heart," he said tiredly. "We will conduct the trade at the Blood Keep tomorrow at high noon, and there Raiden and the red princess will be wed. The conditions of our exchange have already been settled by oath."

Dyna's heart sank into her stomach, and she closed her eyes. Even if Leif wanted to rescind Raiden's engagement, he couldn't.

"We have not crossed onto those red sands since the last war," Leif continued. "Therefore, this exchange is to happen under careful conditions. Altham has agreed that I may arrive escorted with seventy of my Kingsguard and my nephew."

"Sire, you cannot possibly consider going yourself," a counselor exclaimed. "With such little numbers, this would be the perfect opportunity to eliminate you."

Voices swarmed as the elves again argued.

"I am going," Leif said, silencing them again. "This exchange will happen between king to king with our guards in company. No Rangers." His gaze flicked to Dyna and Cassiel. "No outsiders. Altham will keep the same number of his own Kingsguard in the Blood Keep. That was our oath, and it must be followed to the exact terms agreed upon."

Dyna clenched her jaw.

"Does that mean we cannot go?" Keena whispered from where she sat on Lucenna's shoulder.

Zev's eyes glowed yellow when he met Dyna's gaze. They silently agreed those terms wouldn't apply to them. They didn't come all this way to stay behind.

Cassiel was quiet beside her, and for once she couldn't read him through their bond. It had been silent since last night. Sowmya and Yelrakel stood motionless like sentinels behind their chairs.

"Sire," Commander Camsen came forward and bowed. "I will step down as a Ranger, as will my company. We will join your seventy as part of the Kingsguard."

Lieutenant Handuril stood with the other warriors. "As will we."

King Leif nodded. "I expected nothing less. I am sure Altham is also searching for ways around our terms. See that your men are ready." He glanced at the old Magi Master next. "Eldred."

He stood. "Sire?"

"We will cross tonight when the moon is high. Prepare what you need for the Gateway Circle. Enough to reach the Covenant Pass."

"Yes, sire."

"Thank you, that is all. I will now speak to our guests." At Leif's dismissal, the elves bowed and began filing out of the room. Only Eldred and Camsen remained. Once it was empty, Leif linked his hands. "I am sure you have many questions."

"We do," Cassiel at last spoke, and his silver gaze fell on her. He was giving her the floor first.

Dyna straightened in her seat. Whatever their standing, in this moment, they agreed on what mattered. "My first question, Your Majesty, is due to my curiosity. What is a Gateway Circle?"

"It is magic of Greenwood," Camsen replied warily. Clearly something they did not readily share with outsiders, then.

"It is all right." Leif nodded. "Hilos is no stranger to secrecy."

"A Gateway Circle is a portal," Eldred told them. "It works similar to a courier portal, but it can transport people. They only open within what some would call a fairy door, or rather an Elder Tree."

Dyna inhaled a shallow breath. Gods, why didn't she realize it when they arrived yesterday? The strange round tree outside in the courtyard was an Elder Tree. There had been runes carved into the stone surrounding it, and one of them had been *Raido*.

The rune for journey.

"Fae that hold great power can open gateways within Elder Trees at whim," Camsen continued, and Keena nodded in agreement. "The rest of us rely on crystals."

Eldred placed two small stones on the table, one white and the other pale blue.

"Moonstone and Tanzanite," Lucenna murmured, her wide lilac eyes fixed on the stones. The white stone was no bigger than a pebble. It wasn't big enough to fit her Lūna Medallion, but it was fascinating all the same.

"Highly rare to find, yet they are the only crystals that can activate the Elder Tree," Eldred said. "The range with Tanzanite is limited and their magic lasts only once. The best are Moonstones. It has unlimited uses, and its range is substantial."

"How far can it take you?" Klyde asked.

"If we wait until the moon is at the highest point in the sky, far enough to reach the East Wall. It's our barricade that lies fifty miles west, within the gorge of our western borders."

Of course, that made sense. Moonstones were very powerful. Most had been lost or destroyed in the First Age, but something else tugged at the back of Dyna's mind. Something she struggled to remember.

"Only elves and fairies can activate Elder Trees?" Lucenna asked.

"Whomever wields Essence could." Eldred leveled her with his astute gaze. "However, it requires the power level of a Magi Master or a Grand Magus. Should any untrained attempt it, the force of creating a gateway would tear them apart."

Dyna's stomach flipped at that.

Von crossed his arms, his brow creasing as he studied the elves. "I take it you have a contact on the inside. Crossing enemy lines requires special planning, and I can only assume it wouldn't be wise to leave anything to chance."

King Leif linked his fingers together, a small smile playing on his lips. "You are correct. I do have a contact. Two, in fact. One of them is imprisoned with Rawn. They were captured together in Dwarf Shoe. A red elf named Elon."

Von's mouth parted, shock settling on his face.

It surprised Dyna to hear that, too. Elon wasn't the type to be subdued.

"We were separated during the skirmish." Zev's low, rumbling voice pulled her from her thoughts. He peered at Von. "I assumed he had escaped."

"I am not leaving him to rot," the Commander said under his breath.

"As for my second question." Dyna met King Leif's gaze. "This extraction for Lord Norrlen, is it out of care, or because you want the information he may hold on the missing key?" The question drew tension back into the room. "I know him well, and how much he loves his family. I am curious as to what you expect Lord Norrlen's reaction will be once he learns you have relinquished his son to Red Highland for his sake."

The rest of them stayed silent, because they agreed. Rawn would never abide by this.

"In peace, sons bury their fathers. In war, fathers bury their sons." Leif looked out the window. "It's unfortunate, but Raiden will buy Greenwood a modicum of peace for a time. I am no fool. Altham will find another way to instigate conflict. My hope is to have the Dragon Blades before he does."

"So you send your nephew to become a political hostage knowing it may be for nothing?"

"The most difficult part of being a king is sacrificing the few to save the most. Even if the few include those most precious to us." He looked at Cassiel. "You understand, don't you?"

Cassiel leaned back in his chair. He raked his long black hair back, his cool gray eyes sharpening. "The one thing I have come to understand is that it's kings who plan the fighting and the soldiers who do the dying. You were clear that outsiders would not be included in the delegation, yet you invited us to this meeting. So let us discuss what you have truly planned."

A cunning smile edged Leif's mouth. Camsen reached into his cloak and brought out a scroll with the Greenwood seal. Yelrakel stepped forward to take it and brought it to Cassiel.

They fell quiet as he opened it and read the page. A muscle jumped in his jaw, and Dyna knew it wasn't good. He placed the scroll flat on the table for her to read the elegant script.

"It says here, Greenwood will reaffirm the Accords with Hilos under the condition that we form an official alliance between our nations," Cassiel said. "Except I find an issue with that, seeing as the Vale is constantly at war."

"Red Highland will always seek ways to gain more power against Greenwood, and we must do the same. With his half of the key, Altham is one step closer to collecting the Dragon Blades. I need a weapon of my own."

Like Seraph fire.

Dyna ground her teeth. Eldred had borne witness to Cassiel's power when the Shades came for her and informed Leif of how powerful a weapon he could be.

"You cannot involve yourself in this matter any further without instigating Hilos into our age-old strife, Cassiel. However, if you wish me to sign the Accords, that is exactly what you will do."

Dyna clenched her fists under the table. Leif brought them here to use them.

"Does that not negate your oath?" Keena asked.

"No, for you are not part of the seventy."

Therefore, him mentioning outsiders were not to be involved was intentional. He expected them to disobey.

"You want to assure that Rawn is released, and I need to assure my people that their king will return alive." Leif held Cassiel's glowing gaze. "I may call upon your Valkyrie to aid us in the future, but we will assure that the secrecy of the Realms—like Nazar—are protected."

Cassiel let the silence linger a moment as he rolled up the scroll. His expression was unreadable, but she could feel the heat of his anger in the bond. "Thank you, Leif, for taking the time to consider the Accords. Five hundred years ago, your grandfather proposed the same when Hilos was ruled by my grandfather before me. I will give you the same answer Rael did." Lifting the scroll in his fist, Seraph fire flared out, and it instantly dissolved away, ash falling to the table. "Celestials will never again spill Celestial blood for the gain of others, but we will gladly spill yours to protect ours."

A shiver rolled down Dyna's spine. Yet in that moment, she felt proud.

The aghast expressions on Camsen, Eldred, and Leif's faces were almost comical.

"Would you end decades of peace with Greenwood?" Leif demanded.

She narrowed her eyes. "We came here in good faith. It's you who has broken it."

"If you have forgotten," Cassiel added. "The Accords protect our secrecy, and no monarchy who has signed it, past or present, can act against it with impunity. I assure you, should any threat be brought against Hilos and the Realms, we will respond—as we have done so before."

The reminder of Gamor's destruction and the occurrence in the Port of Azure were still fresh in Dyna's mind.

And in King Leif's, by the caution rising to his face. His mouth thinned. "I see. Thus henceforth, our pleasantries end here. I do not give you leave to interfere in this matter any further. When the delegation departs tonight, you will remain."

"With all due respect, Your Majesty." Dyna stood with her Guardians. "I am a Queen. I do not take orders. I give them."

CHAPTER 74

Dynalya

Dyna marched out of the council room as her thoughts raced to dissect all the new information she'd learned and form a new plan. The key was the center to it all. She had a sinking feeling they were being moved by the Druid's invisible hand like pieces of a game only he understood.

Her Guardians walked with her, silent and ready, awaiting her command. She looked to Cassiel as they came to a pause at a concourse of her hallway and the stairs that led to his chambers.

"Pack your belongings if you haven't already, and prepare whatever you need for tonight," Dyna told them. "I want to be ready to leave before that gateway is open. Lucenna, can your invisibility spell cover them?"

She nodded. "I will make sure it does."

"How will we cross unnoticed?" Zev rumbled. "Their hearing is as good as mine."

"I will speak with Eldred," Klyde said. "He wasn't too keen on the king's plan. I think I can convince him to help us for House Norrlen's sake."

Dyna nodded. "Make it happen. We must hope for the best and prepare for the worst."

Her Guardians moved on to do as she asked, leaving her alone with Cassiel.

"I hope you won't attempt to dissuade my decision," she told him. "I am going to Red Highland to bring Lord Norrlen home—including his son."

Cassiel crossed his arms behind his back as he looked over her face, his gaze falling on her short hair pensively. "I have long learned that when you set your mind to something, it would be futile to hinder you."

She almost smirked, relieved they could at least settle on that. "Cassiel, about last night—"

"Let's not speak about it now. Other matters come first, but I intend to continue that conversation when this is over."

Dyna nodded mutely, and he gave her a small smile. She almost told him she had admired how he dealt with Leif but thought better of it. "I will go find Raiden," she said instead. "He'll be apprehensive. I must tell him we won't let the trade happen."

"Agreed. Come see me when you are finished." Then Cassiel took the stairs to the next floor with Yelrakel, their wings moving like graceful veils of gray and black.

Dyna watched him go a moment but didn't allow herself to think about what she needed to say to him.

"What will you have me do, my lady?" Sowmya asked her.

"Observe the delegations' movements. Should anything change, report any findings to me."

Sowmya bowed and marched on.

Dyna hurried down the hall. Before seeking out Raiden, she needed to do something first. But when Dyna reached her bedroom, she found Tavin closing the door. He froze when he saw her.

"Tavin?" She frowned. "What were you doing in my room?"

Tavin flushed and lowered his head. "I'm sorry. I was searching for more of the salve you gave Klyde. The flood gave me a good throttling." He lifted his shirt for her to see. Large, dark purple and yellow bruises had flowered all over his back and she gasped. "It looks worse than it is. But if Klyde knew, he would only send me home." He gave her a sheepish grimace. "Please don't tell him."

Dyna could sympathize with that. Others had coddled her too much as well, and it was exasperating. She patted his arm. "I won't tell him. I gave Klyde the last of the salve, but I'll ask the castle healer to send for some."

He smiled with relief and turned to go.

"Wait. You mentioned wanting to write letters to your mother. How would you like to use the water mirror when I return? I am sure Edyth would be relieved to see you're all right."

He blinked at her. "Oh ... that would be grand." He hugged her abruptly. "Thank you!"

507

"Of course," she laughed in surprise.

Tavin pulled back with a timid grin and ran off. Well, she didn't expect an embrace, but it was better than having the boy point a crossbow at her.

Stepping into her room, Dyna quickly packed up her belongings into her satchel and changed into her fae armor. Once her weapons were strapped in place, she sat on the bed to slip on her boots as she thought of the gateway. Elf magic, they said.

It requires the power level of a Magi Master to open it...

Lumina surfaced in Dyna's mind. A pretty Magi Master who was too soft to be a Raider, yet still valuable to Tarn.

And it came to her suddenly.

The clear memory of a corded bracelet of white stones wrapped daintily around Lumina's wrist.

Dyna's heart pounded, and goosebumps sprouted on her skin. *Please don't let it be.*

Swallowing, she reached inside her satchel and summoned the water mirror. It landed in her palm, still wet from its last use. Dyna yanked it out. Snatching the carafe on her nightstand, she poured water inside and tossed salt in next. Her breathing grew heavier as she stirred the water with her finger and watched the surface ripple.

The water fogged a moment before clearing with the view of runes burned on a tent wall. His back was to her as he poured a cup of wine.

"Now, you must be patient. We will be reunited soon enough." Tarn paused and turned around to face her. A cool smile rose to his mouth, sending shivers down her back. "Maiden."

Dyna dropped the mirror with a scream. It hit the ground, splattering water everywhere. Its glow faded away. Gods, she had to tell the others.

Shoving the mirror into her satchel, she ran for the door and crashed into an elf. It took her a second to recognize the head Norrlen Guard.

"My lady, forgive me." Halder steadied her. "Are you all right?"

"Yes, but pardon me, I must go!"

"Wait, I have a message for you from Lord Raiden." The captain reached into his cloak and handed her a folded letter sealed with a dab of wax displaying the Norrlen sigil.

"Thank you." Dyna snatched it. "Please excuse me!" She ran for the stairs to the next floor.

She needed to tell someone Tarn was alive, and the first person was instinctively Cassiel. Her boots clacked sharply on the stone steps, her heart in her throat. She reached Cassiel's floor and sprinted for his room, bursting through the doors.

The chambers were dark inside. The windows faced the west, away from any morning sun, and the skies were gray with the coming of rain.

Dyna walked in hurriedly, calling for him. "Cassiel?"

But there came no response, and the Valkyrie were gone. Where was he? She needed him.

The fragments of their brittle bond shook in her chest at her hesitant tug. *Cassiel, where are you?*

Dyna felt a presence rush in from behind her. She whipped out a knife and spun. Steel clashed as she caught the blade coming for her throat. She stared at a pureblooded male Celestial. Not one she recognized at all.

He sneered. "I was waiting to get you alone, Sheli."

The statement rocked Dyna to her soul. That distraction was all he needed to knock the weapon out of her hands. He raised the knife, but it never came down.

The Celestial's eyes widened. His face went red, veins bulging in his face, grunting as if straining against a force holding him in place. Seraph fire bloomed from his chest like a flower. It spread out, consuming him in a bouquet of blue flames. Within seconds, he dissolved into ash, leaving nothing but a scorch mark on the rug.

Dyna's heart pounded wildly. From the dark, appeared blue eyes glowing with flame.

Cassiel came forward, and she flinched back. "Dyna, it's all right."

"You killed him..."

"I did."

"He was another assassin ... he-he tried to..." She was babbling, her spinning mind trying to clear after nearly dying. "He came for me..."

"Yes."

Dyna made herself take a shaky breath. "But he deserved a trial. At the very least, a questioning..."

Even as the words tumbled out of her mouth, she wasn't sure if there was another choice. The Celestial wouldn't have hesitated. He was ready to take her life.

Dyna couldn't stop shaking, and Cassiel took her arms. "He called me Sheli. Why did he call me that? Why did my body grow cold when I heard that name?"

The fire faded from Cassiel's eyes, and he grew guarded. "You misheard him. I am sorry. He had delivered a message on behalf of Gadriel, and I didn't realize he was still here—"

"No!" She shoved off his hold. "I heard him clearly. No more lies, Cassiel. Tell me the *truth*. Why did he call me Sheli?"

"Because that is your name," Yelrakel replied. They both snapped their heads to her standing at the threshold, Sowmya behind her. "Sheli was who you were ... in your first life."

Dyna's breath caught, and her satchel slipped from her fingers. "What...?"

"General, you are dismissed," Cassiel barked. "Close the door."

"She stays." Dyna stumbled forward. "I am not finished speaking to her."

"Yelrakel," Cassiel growled.

"She stays!" Dyna shouted, silencing him. Swallowing, she said to the Valkyrie, "I command you to tell your queen what your king cannot."

Cassiel shut his eyes.

She moved past him, fixing her hard gaze on Yelrakel. "Answer."

The general bowed her head. "Your Majesty ... you are the reincarnation of Sheli, the first High Queen of Hilos. Mate of High King Kähssiel."

Her legs wobbled, and Cassiel caught her arm.

The first High Queen...

Now it was clear why the title of princess never felt like it belonged to her.

"You were the first True Bonded mates amidst our people at a time when it was not fully understood," Yelrakel continued. "We came to this world to serve mankind as a penance to *Elyōn*. They saw your union as impure, and when you fell with child, it served to turn the tide against Kähssiel's reign. But he was too powerful. His generals could only remove him by removing you first."

She stumbled back a step, holding her stomach. Nausea churned through her, and she was afraid she may spew on the rug.

"Dyna, sit down." Cassiel tried to lead her to a chair, but she pushed him off.

"How did I die?" she asked him.

He struggled to say it, so she looked at Yelrakel again. Her heart hammered, the room growing colder and smaller. The general's expression became somber. Dyna knew the answer before she said it.

"You were thrown off a cliff ... and fell to your death."

510

CHAPTER 75

Cassiel

Cassiel felt the strength leave Dyna's body. Lurching forward, he caught her before she dropped to the floor and pulled her tightly against him. The erratic pounding of her heart echoed in his chest. She was cold and trembling. He cupped her cheek, but her wide-green eyes stared blankly past him at the wall, faint shallow breaths passing through her lips.

He wrapped his wings around her. "Look at me, *lev sheli.*"

But she was trapped in the moment.

She had to work through that revelation as he had.

"Your death led to the destruction of the Realms when Kāhssiel enacted his vengeance," Yelrakel continued. "They banded together and fought him. He died for you then, but you can spare him now, My Queen. Please, do not let history repeat itself."

Cassiel scowled at her in angry disbelief. "You have said quite enough."

"Only one of you can live, sire. Please, I must assure you of your future. If she loves you, she will sacrifice herself in your stead."

"General!" Cassiel roared, making Dyna flinch. He forced a breath through his lungs and said with a frightening measure of control, "I dismiss you from your duties here. Leave now before I do something I may regret."

Her gray wings went limp and Yelrakel expelled a stricken breath. Composing herself, she bowed deep. "Sire."

She stepped back into the hall with Sowmya and shut the door.

Picking Dyna up, Cassiel placed her in a chair at the dining table in his room and kneeled in front of her. She blinked at the ground slowly. He took her cold hands in his. "Dyna, look at me."

"My nightmares..." she mumbled. "Every night, for weeks ... I dreamed of falling, of someone pushing me into a chasm. I had been reliving my death..." Tears gathered on her lashes as she met his gaze. "And you knew."

At the hurt and anger swimming in her eyes, Cassiel lowered his head.

Dyna pulled her hands away. "*I cannot let you relive the same fate.* You said that to me ... before you left."

He stood and rubbed his face. "I thought the best thing was to leave, Dyna. To keep you safe."

"Were you ever going to tell me?"

Cassiel couldn't answer.

"You are incorrigible." Dyna pushed to her feet, her voice catching with emotion and resentment. "Why didn't you share your burden with me? Why did you run away instead of facing this with me? Why did you erase my memories? Why couldn't you simply be honest with me!"

"Because I was afraid!" he shouted, making her flinch back. The action tore at him. Cassiel immediately backed away, because he never wanted her to fear him. He kept putting space between them until his back hit the wall. He leaned up against it and closed his eyes. "I was afraid to speak the words ... and make them true."

His confession fell into the quiet room, filling the void between them. Dyna shook her head and stepped onto a balcony with flowering bushes. Her red hair fluttered in the wind as she leaned on the stone banister, watching the rainfall over the land.

"Am I to be killed for merely being your wife?" she murmured as he joined her outside.

"I will never let that happen," Cassiel said, coming to stand beside her. "I broke my soul to protect you. I left to wage war against anyone one who would harm you. I would spill any amount of blood, even my own, for there is nothing I wouldn't do for you, *lev sheli.* You are, without question, my only priority." He turned her face to look at him. "I know you're scared, but please trust me."

"Trust you?" She jerked her chin out of his hold. "That worked out so well for me before." Her bitter scoff fogged in the cool air and tears shone in her eyes. "I asked you more than once to tell me the truth. I gave you a chance, but you couldn't trust me with that. Instead, you selfishly hid everything and left me behind."

"I only wanted to give you the life you deserved," he said softly. "You didn't have one in our first life, but by all the Gods, I swore you would live in this one. I don't care what the cost is." He braced his fists on the banister, flames flickering over his fingers. "Because I'm terrified of what I will do to the world if you are gone. You died a horrible death that I couldn't save you from. I left to prevent that from happening again."

"No. You *ran away*. One thing I've learned is you can't run when you're afraid, Cassiel. That is not love."

How could that be true when she was his reason for living? He loved her so much, but maybe it was the wrong kind of love.

"I thought I understood you better than anyone, but I don't know you anymore." Dyna wrapped her arms around herself. "Worst yet … I don't even know myself."

Cassiel looked out at the Kingdom of Greenwood, searching for answers in the green hills and gray skies. "I don't know who I am anymore, either. I was once so certain of who I was. A third-born prince with sullied blood, unwanted and unneeded, and relatively … purposeless. Life had no meaning, and I didn't care. There was nothing to care about. I had no place in the world, or so I thought, until you arrived."

The wind picked up as they faced each other.

He reached for her hair, taking a short lock in his fingers. "I stumbled upon this delicate, reckless human, who became so precious to me, I was poisoned with a terrible fear that she would break. So I did the worst thing in my life by breaking her heart, because it meant she would live. In my mind, I thought I was keeping you safe from the darkness of our past, including my own."

Dyna's eyes glistened wet as she listened to his raw words. It reminded him of that day in the snow, when he shared everything he held inside. Because she was the one person he could show everything to, and he had forgotten that.

"Then my existence depended entirely on the future I fought to give you. I would kill for you, Dynalya. I have killed for you. I have done horrible things that make me unworthy of you. Agreed. I was never worthy of anything. But you are. Before you, I didn't understand what it meant to care for someone. To love them … because I couldn't remember what it felt to be loved. But the night we were wed, when you came down the steps in your white gown and chose me, I knew I would do anything for you." Cassiel took her hands in his as tears rolled down her cheeks. "Call me a coward if you must, and deem me terrible and worthless, but please do not deny my love for you. I hate that I hurt you, and I hate that you hate me." He pulled her into the shelter of his wings, holding her against his chest. "But I will endure it because everything I do, no matter how painful, will always be to protect you."

Dyna had told him his vows no longer mattered. But there was no other vow more valid than this one. It was chiseled in his bones, inscribed on his skin, woven through whatever matter that made up the threads of his soul.

They stayed that way for a moment, breathing each other in. She trembled in his arms, her tears soaking his tunic. Now that it was all out there, he clung to that last kernel of hope she could forgive him.

"Is there anything else I need to know?" she asked faintly.

Cassiel opened his mouth but closed it because he didn't want to lie anymore, but he couldn't bring himself to answer. Dyna stepped back holding the crumpled message that he had stuffed in his pocket. She retreated from him as she read it.

His heart lurched to his throat. "Ignore what it says. They are empty threats."

"Empty?" Dyna repeated, her hands shaking. "You call this empty?"

The message slipped from her fingers and landed on a pool of water at their feet, floating on the surface with dynalya petals. Raindrops smeared Gadriel's scrawled message.

As you deign not to honor me with your presence, I am forced to send my reply by messenger. Nazar will not stand with the High King while the witch queen lives. We refuse to be ruled by such abominable power, including your own. Do away with her and stunt your fire. Prove you are worthy of the throne, and you will have gained our allegiance.

Refuse, and the life in peril will be yours.

"Perhaps we cannot run from our fate." Dyna closed her eyes. "The past is intertwined in our future, but I alone will shape my fate. Not them."

He stilled, everything in him tensing as the bond fell quiet. When she looked at him again, her green eyes didn't shine with tears or trust anymore. They were resigned.

Shattered.

"It's over, Cassiel."

The foundation shook beneath his feet, and the air left his lungs.

"You were right to leave me. I should never have allowed myself to fall for you from the start. Staying together means I die—or you."

He lurched forward, "Dyna—"

She took a step back. "Your people need you. Mine need me here. Stage my death again if you must and return to the Realms where you belong. I will go to Red Highland as I came to do."

Turning away from him, she strode back into his room. Cassiel quickly rushed after her. She bent behind the table as she picked up her satchel.

"Please, I must stay by your side," he pleaded. "Separating now is too dangerous."

"Every day I risk my life, but I decided a long time ago I would no longer be afraid of death." Dyna recovered her satchel and checked her weapons, returning her fallen knife to the sheath on her thigh. A dour expression settled on her face that told him she had already made her decision. "I told you. The person I used to be is gone. I'm the one who is angry, violent, and who doesn't feel *safe*. The girl who used to believe in the goodness of others, who had faith that everything would be all right— she's gone. And I miss her." Dyna's eyes glistened wet for a moment, but they dried with her next breath. "I miss who I used to be, but that girl is never coming back."

It broke him to hear her say that.

He never wanted that for her.

"The only thing I care about right now is saving my friend. Whether going is right or wrong, it's my decision to make. I made a promise to Lord Norrlen." Her gaze hardened. "And I, for one, keep my word."

That line drove clean through his ribs and out through his spine.

Cassiel had to lean against the desk, because he thought his legs might give out. He wanted to speak, but the words were locked behind his teeth. *Please don't say you are finished with me yet. Even if you never forgive me, please.*

As if she heard him, Dyna's anger softened.

Her next words were so faint. Brittle. That little hope he had clung to withered away with it. "When you left, I tried so hard to rid myself of you, as if that would make a difference. I can't love you and hate you at the same time, Cassiel. It's splitting me apart." Dyna removed the crystal necklace around her neck and placed it on the table. "To live, I need to remove you from my heart. I need to not think about you or care about you at all. You must let me go. I need you to let me go."

It took everything he had not to show how much that destroyed him.

Cassiel curled his fingers around the crystal and turned away, because he had to. Because if he looked at her, she would know he was nothing now.

"At times ... I regret remembering us," Dyna said faintly. "I see now it's kinder not to remember. Maybe the memories you should have erased were your own."

Cassiel waited until his voice was clear before saying, "If it would ease my pain and yours, perhaps you're right. But I have already broken too many promises to you."

"There is no need to keep them anymore."

Then it was Cassiel's turn to watch his mate walk away from him.

He braced his hands on the table, feeling his body go numb. He couldn't breathe, he couldn't speak or move.

He wanted to say more, to plead for another chance.

But she was already gone.

Netanel quietly came through the terrace doors, sympathy lining his features. "I'm sorry, Cassiel. What will you do now?"

Inhaling a ragged breath, he found the strength to move to the desk in the corner. He laid out a piece of parchment on the table and dipped a quill in a well of ink.

"What I should have done from the beginning."

CHAPTER 76

Dynalya

D yna let the sound of her heels clacking on the steps fill the loud void in her mind. She had spent all last night deliberating about officially ending their marriage. Cassiel had nearly convinced her to give them another chance, but learning about her past life and Gadriel's message only confirmed that ending it was the right thing to do. The Realms had declared it so from the beginning.

They were not meant to be.

She inhaled a shaky breath and banished away the tears gathering in her eyes. The weak bond dimmed to near nothing, sending a sharp ache through her chest. Eventually, it would lose all its light, and the doors between them would seal.

She had to do this. For both of their sakes.

Dyna reached in her pocket as she continued down the steps, and her fingers wrapped around Raiden's message.

Except, she noticed now it wasn't flat.

Frowning, Dyna pulled it out of her pocket and broke the wax seal. She unfolded the page and read the short letter in an elegant script.

To Dynalya Astron, the High Queen of Hilos,

I have met many interesting individuals in my short life, but none as brave and sincere and with a greater sense of integrity as the girl named after a flower. Our short time together has changed my life, and it will save that of my father's. Before I go, I must pay my debts, and so I leave you this gift. It may not seem like much, but it holds great value to me. After today, I believe it was always meant to be in your hands.

Your grateful friend and humble servant,

Raiden Norrlen

Sucking in a breath, Dyna turned over the envelope. A piece of bronze metal landed in her palm.

The second half of the key.

Gasping, Dyna sprinted down the hall to the east wing, but Raiden wasn't in his room. She ran through the castle, asking the servants where he was. She finally found him in the empty grand hall, holding his mother as she wept in his arms. Noticing Dyna over her shoulder, he murmured something to his mother. Aerina released him and stepped aside, giving them a moment alone.

Dyna went to him, and her stomach tightened as she held out the missing key piece. "I got your message. How did you find this?"

"My father sent it to me a long time ago inside of this." Raiden laid a hand over his wooden token. "I didn't understand what it was at the time. I thought it perhaps a jest or a slight, before it became one of the few connections I had to him. Then you arrived. When I saw your scroll at the falls with an illustration of a key, I began to realize none of it was ever a coincidence." He gently closed her fingers over the broken bit. "Consider it yours now. Whatever happens onward, I am at peace."

Dyna's brow furrowed at his words that sounded like a goodbye. "You can't mean to leave yet."

He sighed. "I cannot defy a command of the King. If this will save my father, I will go willingly."

"Rawn wouldn't want this, Raiden. It would break his heart and your mother's."

Raiden's brow tightened as Aerina's soft weeping drifted to them from the corner of the room. "Dyna—"

"No, I won't let you go."

"Then marry me," he blurted.

She froze, and Aerina fell silent. "What?"

Flushing, he smiled at her. "I know this is all ever untoward. Truth be told, I was waiting for your hand to be free, and if it is, am I mistaken to ask? I have every intention of retrieving my father, but if you don't want me to stay in Red Highland, give me reason to return, my lady."

Dyna stared at him, at a loss for words. He meant it. Sometime during their pretend courtship, it ceased to be a guise to him anymore. Gods, this wasn't meant to happen. Her friends were standing at the doors, watching with silent shock. This was so unexpected she wasn't sure how to react or what to think.

Aerina walked over to them hesitantly, her eyes wide. "Raiden..."

He glanced bashfully at his mother. "If I am already promised to another, I cannot be forced into a marriage I do not want. This one ... I do want."

Aerina smiled tearily. She removed her emerald ring and handed it to him. "Then I suppose you should ask her properly, son."

Dyna struggled for air, her mind spinning. The last thing she wanted was to be married again. But what gave her pause was the fact Raiden wouldn't be taken from his family if she accepted.

Before she could say a word, Raiden took his mother's ring and knelt in front of her. Her heart leaped into her throat.

"Dynalya, I know we have not known each other long, but when I look at you, I see a beautiful and valiant woman to face every tomorrow to come. Therefore I, Raiden Norrlen, the firstborn son of Rawn Norrlen, the Lord of Sellav, would beg for your hand in marriage under the eye of the God of Urn. Would you do me the great honor of becoming my wife?"

Dyna took a gasping breath. Every fiber of her being was against this. She couldn't speak the word that would have been a lie. But in her satchel, rested Fair's ashes. It was her fault Rawn lost his horse. She owed it to him to protect his son.

It didn't have to be real. She could continue the ruse and accept the engagement until both were safe in Sellav. But her voice caught on her tongue. It took several seconds before Dyna could work up the nerve to speak.

"Yes..." she said, so faint it was barely a whisper.

A smile lit Raiden's face, and he slipped the emerald ring onto her finger. It was a little tight and a little cold.

It looked wrong.

Motion on her left drew her to meet Cassiel's eyes standing at another set of doors. He stood motionless. Silent.

He looked as if his soul had been pulled from him

Dyna almost blurted that it wasn't what it looked like, but she stopped herself because she had to. The bond trembled inside of her, and it took everything not to break down in front of him. They couldn't be together, no matter how much she wished for it. She couldn't bear it if her mate died simply for loving her.

Noticing him, Raiden stood. "I will give you a moment."

He and Aerina quickly left the grand hall through the set doors her friends stood at, leaving her with Cassiel.

His silver eyes lifted to hers. They were dull, as if all the light had left them. After a breath, he came to her. For a moment, he said nothing. His brows curled, and he rubbed his mouth, shifting a step. His fingers tightened around the folded parchment in his hand. "So ... this is what you want?"

Dyna meant to answer firmly, but no words came out, so all she managed was a weak nod.

His throat bobbed. "I see..."

Dyna couldn't look at him. Her hands shook as she made sure her shield was in place, hiding the way her heart was breaking all over again. She told herself this was a good thing. Now he could move on with his life, and she could go on with hers, no matter how much it was breaking her apart.

"I'm glad." Cassiel offered her a feeble smile. One that was trapped between pain and acceptance. Clearing his throat, he handed her the folded parchment. "The *ghet* I mentioned. A contract of annulment. Once you sign it, our marriage is dissolved, and you are free to marry again."

Dyna's eyes stung with unshed tears as she took it, masking the great effort needed to swallow the lump lodged in her throat. As the parchment passed into her hands, she felt the moment Cassiel gave up on the possibility they could ever recover what they had lost. In its place was regret and sorrow, but beneath it lingered a relief that she would be all right now.

His gaze lowered to her new ring. "Can I ask only one thing of you?" he asked quietly. "Don't go on in life merely existing. Promise me you will live."

His voice cracked on that last word, and it made her vision blur. Standing on her toes, Dyna pulled him into her arms and held him tight. She needed one last embrace.

And so did he.

"Goodbye..." she whispered, tears filling her eyes.

Cassiel's hands quivered on her waist, and he planted a light kiss on her temple. "Be happy, *lev sheli*. That's all I've ever wanted for you ... even if it's not with me."

Then he slipped out of her hold and walked away. He passed through the courtyard doors, going into the garden without looking back. Clenching her teeth, Dyna forced herself not to call out to him.

She had to let go, too. But she would never fall in love again.

Not the way she did with him.

Dyna opened the scroll and the tears she fought spilled. The letters were jagged and smeared, as if written by a shaking hand. Cassiel had left her everything he owned. Enough wealth to live the rest of her life without wanting for anything.

Why would he leave her everything?

Lucenna came to her with Keena fluttering at her side. "Are you truly going through with this?"

Pressing over the ache in her heart, Dyna made herself turn away from the direction her mate left. "I already caused Rawn to lose Fair. I will not let him lose his son, too."

"Do you think Cassiel will be all right?" Keena asked her.

The question made her heart squeeze. Gods, she hoped so.

"Dyna ..." Zev murmured. He had moved to the windows that faced the garden. "He's not all right."

Her throat tightened. She blinked away her wet eyes and tucked the parchment in her satchel. "It's only natural for him to pretend he's fine with this."

"No. I mean, something is wrong. I don't think *he* is fine."

Frowning, Dyna and the others joined Zev by the windows. Cassiel was only in the garden, sitting on a bench beneath a tree. There wasn't anything out of place with that. She couldn't see what was wrong.

Until she did.

CHAPTER 77

Cassiel

The world skewed on its axis. Cassiel's lungs seized with the tightening in his chest, and he struggled for air. But he kept his composure until he was out of view. He stumbled into the garden and pressed a shaking fist over his racing heart. Sweat beaded on his face as he fought to breathe.

There was no fighting through the attack. He merely had to let it pass.

His vision swam, and the sound of his pounding heartbeat thudded in his ears. Cassiel heaved ragged breaths, but his ribcage splintered open, and there was no sewing it shut.

He thought he knew pain.

But he was served an incomparable kind when his mate chose another. It was a new sort of loss. One that stole the solidity of the ground.

Cassiel leaned up against a tree and shut his eyes, fighting back the burning rushing up his throat. But it lodged there, closing all his airways, stealing his air.

It felt like drowning.

He shut away the image of her taking Raiden's hand. He buried it. He quickly threw up a shield and then another, slamming each one down, barricading himself and every shred of his misery from her.

He was alone now.

Everybody leaves.

Netanel was suddenly there, and he took him under his wing. "Breathe. You must breathe."

Cassiel focused on his voice. He grabbed Netanel's arm and grounded himself in the solidity of his presence. His throat became raw as he sucked in ragged breaths.

"That's it," Netanel said as he made him sit on a stone bench beneath the tree. "Keep breathing, Cassiel. I'm here."

He shut his eyes and slowly filled his lungs with more air. His heartbeat slowly steadied, and his hands stopped shaking. The gray skies cleared as the rain stopped. Sunlight streamed through the low-hanging branches dancing in the soft breeze, but he couldn't feel it.

Hope was for fools.

Wishes and dreams and second chances were only found in stories with happy endings. His story was already written.

But this ... there was no fate to blame for this.

It was his doing alone. He placed her hand in another's. He was the only one to blame.

And damn, did it hurt.

The pain tore open his previous wounds when he had shattered their souls.

Cassiel willed the wet sting in his eyes to dry. He couldn't afford to be weak now.

"Crying does not make you weak," Netanel said, taking the spot beside him. "But sitting here sulking does."

No, he didn't sulk. He mourned. Dyna turning him away meant he must leave. It was time to continue with his plans and go to Edym to finish what he started. Even if it ended in his death. "There is no reason to follow me anymore. Return to Hilos."

"Where will you go?"

Cassiel only wanted to fly away. In any direction. He leaned back and looked up at the open sky. He had the urge to disappear so completely in it that he would simply fade into oblivion. No feelings. No memories. Simply gone. To a place no one would ever find him.

"You cannot give up now." Netanel laid a hand on his shoulder. "You have a long life ahead of you yet to be lived."

"What good is my life when I have lost the one person I want to share it with?"

Sighing, Netanel said, "I cannot say it will be easy, for I know the weight of that pain well." Cassiel looked at him somberly. "Dynalya may one day forgive you, Cassiel, but whether she does or not, perhaps in time, you can learn to forgive yourself."

His chest constricted under a sudden sharp ache, and he shook his head. "I can't."

"You can."

"I cannot."

"Cassiel—"

"Stop." He dropped his throbbing head in his hands. "Please."

Netanel placed a gentle hand on his back, and Cassiel exhaled a trembling breath. The one thing he knew was that there was no forgiveness for what he had done. Living with that guilt was his punishment.

He looked down at his shaking fingers, stained with ink and blood where his nails had dug into his palms. He had held sunshine in his hands. It was gone now, leaving him in the cold dark.

As it had years ago, when he stood in Hermon's courtyard, watching a pair of white wings fly away.

"Life is like a garden," Lord Jophiel had told him. *"We cultivate what we plant, so be mindful of what seeds you sow."*

Fate must laugh at him now for wishing he had heeded those lessons. It was too late, though. Here lies the result of what he planted.

"The damage is too great to atone for what I've done," Cassiel murmured. "My selfishness cost me everything. I can no longer hold on, regardless of how much it kills me. The only thing I want for her is to find happiness … and it begins with setting her free."

He had left because he was afraid of losing her.

In the end, he lost her anyway.

But could he go on like this? Could he survive with only the memory of what they had? The thought of leaving her in the arms of another was unbearable. He should forget, but he couldn't bear to do that either.

Netanel mussed his hair. "Well, that may be the first wise choice you have made since becoming king. I'm proud of you."

Cassiel grunted halfheartedly, warmed by the gentle praise. "I don't know if I can go on, let alone be a wise king, but maybe I can, as long as you're here. You will stay with me forever … won't you?"

Netanel's smile saddened. He didn't reply, but Cassiel already knew what he would say.

Nothing lasts forever.

"Cassiel?"

He jumped at the sound of Dyna's voice behind him. She looked at him strangely, and searched the garden, but Netanel had already slipped into the foliage without making so much as a sound.

Her eyes returned to him. Cautious. Concerned. "Who were you speaking to?"

Cassiel's first instinct was to lie. It came out of habit now. But he had built a mountain of them, and it was about time he was finally honest.

"Netanel," he called. "It's fine. Come out and greet Dyna."

Her brow furrowed with confusion. "Who?"

Bracing himself with a deep breath, Cassiel got to his feet. "That's the name he goes by now. Please don't be angry. I should have told you about him before, but I didn't want to give you another reason to fear me."

Her eyes widened. "What do you mean? Who is Netanel?"

He took another breath. "...My father."

Dyna stilled. "What...?"

He scratched the back of his neck uneasily. "Well, it was best to keep it a secret. I needed him to work for me from the shadows. Only a few know about him..." Cassiel trailed off when her shock hit his chest like the sudden splash of ice-cold water. It hovered between them for a moment, chilling his skin. Sorrow filled its place.

Dyna stared at him with dismay. "Oh, Gods ... I think..."

He frowned. "Why are you looking at me like that?"

She took his hand. "Cassiel ... I think you erased your memories after all."

He blinked at her, because he didn't understand. The ache in his skull returned, and it made his ears ring. Suddenly, everything seemed jumbled.

Tears gathered on her lashes. "Cassiel, your father is dead."

He dropped her hand, putting several steps between them. "No, he's not," he said defensively. "I saved him. I stopped his soul from passing through the Gates and gave him half my lifetime."

Her voice became muffled, trapped behind a curtain. "You couldn't have."

"You weren't there."

Dyna took a careful step toward him, as if she worried he would bolt. "That's not possible."

"You're *wrong*," he retorted. They were all wrong. She tried to approach him again, but he backed away. "Yoel is here, Dyna. I brought him back. He's been with me all this time." Cassiel spun toward the bushes. "Father, come out and show her."

Only the wind answered with a gentle rustling of the still trees.

His chest heaved with the breath he struggled to inhale. "I don't find this amusing," he said shakily. "Where did you go?"

Dyna reached for his arm. "Cassiel—"

"Don't." He moved closer to the bushes, waiting for the one who had held him together for the past three months to appear. "Father, please come out. I need you to come out." But no winged shadows came forward, and his hands shook. "He-he was right here. He's *alive*. He didn't leave me. He didn't."

Dyna covered her mouth as more tears welled in her eyes. Zev, Lucenna, and the others came outside. They all looked at him in that same strange way. The same way his Valkyrie had.

With sympathy and remorse.

You cannot return a life that was given, son.

"No..." Cassiel shook his head, backing away. Pain lanced through his skull, and he clutched his head.

He had saved his father in time.

He gave him youth and a new name.

He had ordered him to hide and cover his face so no one would know... That he had lost his mind.

Memories he had buried away bombarded him, tearing into his mind. Shattering glass. A blade of flame plunging through his father's chest. Blood pooling on the floor.

I am sorry that I have to leave you again...

"Please!" Cassiel pleaded, his voice breaking. "I'm not ready for this!"

The crushing weight of reality set in, and it splintered like glass. His chest rose and fell with gasping breaths, each one growing smaller. Reality struck him so hard, Cassiel had to lean forward on his knees. His heart raced wildly as the world caved in.

No, it's not true. It's not true.

He desperately tried to erase it all away, but memories of the past and the present he created were surging together and taking over every corner of his being. The pressure built in his head. It grew and grew until it burst, shattering his delicate world. Cassiel simply buckled and collapsed among the shards.

"No. No. *NO!*" The word turned into a wretched cry as he screamed.

Seraph fire flared out and encompassed him, scorching the earth. He rocked on the ground, grasping his head as he fell apart. Gut-wrenching sobs tore from his throat and blue flames roared around him, spiraling out of control, destroying everything it touched—including him.

It was too much.

It was tearing him apart.

Someone stepped into the maelstrom and knelt beside him on the blackened earth. She gathered him in her arms and held him as he sobbed.

"It's all right, *kohav*," she murmured in his ear, caressing his hair. "I'm here with you. I'm here."

He locked onto her voice, onto the shelter of her hold. With each soft assurance, his flames began slowly to extinguish. The last of his strength faded with them, and his body went limp.

Not once did she let go.

He didn't fight when her power wove into his being, cradling the scattered fragments left of him in the ash. His eyes grew heavy and drifted shut as he breathed in the sweet scent of honeysuckle.

And Cassiel knew only relief as she gently put him to sleep.

CHAPTER 78

Dynalya

How could she have not seen it? Dyna asked herself that many times over as she watched Cassiel rest in his bed. He didn't move or make a sound, but he was at peace in the dreamless sleep she had put him in. It seemed to be the only way to end his torment.

"I didn't know. This whole time, I never noticed something was wrong." She clenched her fists on her lap, wrestling with a terrible guilt, because she had only been focused on her own anger. "This was what you meant. When you said that he was not well. That he needed me..."

Dyna looked at Sowmya, where she stood at the foot of the bed. Yelrakel remained silent by the door like a dismal shadow as she watched over her king.

The red-winged Valkyrie lowered her head. "There is no punishment worse than living with the fact that you killed someone you love."

"He didn't kill Yoel."

"That blade was meant for Cassiel, my lady. His father took the blow, and he couldn't forgive himself for it."

Emotion lodged in Dyna's throat. When she had learned Amriel had assassinated Yoel, she didn't know it was because he had shielded his son.

"Losing his father and rejecting the bond on the same night broke him. He couldn't accept both losses. The burden was tearing his soul apart." Sowmya's voice wavered, and she took a breath. "He couldn't bear to forget you, and he couldn't bear to remember Yoel's death ... so he erased it."

Because Cassiel had promised to never forget her...

"I think a part of him knew it wasn't real," Sowmya looked down at him. "Black clothes, refraining from revelry, and not cutting his hair are customs of *aveilut*—the year of mourning for a parent. Then there is the name he gave the illusion. Netanel means 'a gift from *Elyōn*.' For what else could his father be but a divine gift the Heavens had granted him. It was the only way Cassiel could accept the new reality he conjured."

Dyna's mouth wobbled. His mind created it, not only to cope with the loss, but because Cassiel had finally had Yoel back. He had lived all his childhood without a father. He couldn't bear not having him after losing so much.

Dyna laid her hand over Cassiel's. He felt so cold. "How could he do this to himself? Why reject our bond and go through all this pain alone? I don't understand."

"I think it was Yoel's death that drove him to it, because he had already suffered failing to protect someone he loved before."

"Do you mean ... because of Sheli?"

Sowmya's brown eyes held hers a moment, then dropped to the *Hyalus* crystal left on the bedside table. "What Cassiel feels for you is what my kind call *ahava nitzchit*. A deep and eternal love that goes beyond duty and obligation. Beyond the threads of the universe and time itself."

Dyna's brow furrowed. She didn't know what that meant.

"The depths of which his soul is bonded to yours could never be comprehended by another without feeling it for themselves. I know how much he hurt you and the anger you carry. But my wish, should *Elyōn* grant it, is for you to understand how much he truly loves you. I suppose only time will tell."

With that, both Valkyrie bowed and silently stepped out of the room.

Dyna leaned her arms on the edge of the bed, watching Cassiel sleep. To understand everything, every reason behind every lie, she would need to live his life. Both lives.

Only time...

Would it be possible?

Taking Cassiel's cold hand in hers, Dyna closed her eyes. She breathed in and out as her magic stirred. The *Essentia Dimensio* opened before her. Dark with the two blue bulbs of light. The aura of a Celestial's divinity. One was Cassiel's and the other...

Dyna reached out to it with her Essence and cradled them both.

And she sank.

She found herself in a new dark void. Similar to the *Essentia Dimensio*, but it felt ... different. A faint green light appeared ahead, and Dyna walked toward it. The ground beneath her feet turned into the reflection of water as she came out onto a trickling stream with shores of moss. Magic glittered in the air like green rain.

Her magic.

Did she pass through a new dimension? Perhaps within herself. She kept walking, and memories flashed around her, distorted with color and voices and sounds of music.

Memories of two lives.

Dyna didn't sort through them. She let the past come to her as she dream walked through Kāhssiel's life, letting him decide how to tell his story.

The first memory halted abruptly and opened to darkness and the clash of steel. Blades of white flame cut through demons as a battle raged around her.

It was the Dark War against the God of Shadows.

Seraphim and humans fought and died as creatures of shadow tore into them. It was a brutal slaughter.

A bright blue ball of fire tore through the demon ranks. Dyna whipped around in search of him. And there he was.

Kāhssiel in gold and silver armor, flying ahead on six white wings. "Here we stand!" he bellowed, and his familiar voice shook Dyna's soul. "Cut them back!"

His army of Seraphs followed his lead, but demons came in an endless stream. Shadows writhed and sprang from the earth. They were darkness personified, with horns and talons of smoke. Each Seraph they cut down littered the ground with feathers, ash, and blood. Screams and the clash of blades rang in her ears.

The largest Shadow demon with red eyes she recognized fell upon Kāhssiel. With a swipe of its claws, he lost hold of his divine blade. His hands flared with Seraph flame, but the Shadow slashed at him. The blow tossed him, and he crashed into a dead tree. Groaning, Kāhssiel slumped against the roots, wincing in pain. Some of his wings hung at odd angles. They were broken. His wounds struggled to heal.

All around him, Seraphs continued to fall.

The air was ripe with sulfur and blood. With death and hopelessness.

They were going to lose the war, and Kāhssiel knew it.

A soft sigh passed through his bloodied lips as he pushed himself back on his feet.

"If I am to fall here … so be it." He smiled wryly at the skies churning with black clouds. "But let it not be this day."

His eyes flared blue, and he gritted his teeth as he faced off with the Shadow demon. It charged for him with a roar. Kāhssiel roared back, Seraph fire engulfing his fists. Ready to fight. Ready to die. Here was his last stand.

A blast of green power erupted between them. The powerful blast knocked Kāhssiel to the ground.

The Shadow screeched as it was thrown across the battlefield with streaming remnants of green stars.

The roots of the dead tree blazed, and from it sprang a new magnificent tree. One made of pure white light and leaves like glass. It cast its brilliance across the battlefield like a blazing sun, and the demons fled from its light.

Seraphs rejoiced and cried out to the Heavens, thanking *Elyōn* for this miracle.

But Kāhssiel stayed on the ground, gaping up in awe at the young woman in armor standing beside him. The wind whipped her dark brown hair around her face.

Dyna's face.

Her green eyes, glowing with magic, met his, and she scowled. "Are you attempting to lose your head, or is there simply nothing in it? Stupid Seraph."

She ran off into the throng.

"Wait!" he called, staring after her with a dumbfounded look on his face. "What is your name?"

Was it possible to fall in love at first sight?

Such a thing begged to question as Kāhssiel was enthralled by the human who had saved his life. Once he learned Sheli's name, he invited her into his circle of generals. For her power, Kāhssiel said, but he and Dyna both knew it was because she intrigued him.

In their time together, Sheli became his emissary with the humans, fortifying his army with more allies. Her influence encouraged him to establish the first Valkyrie. She found a way for his smiths to forge divine steel for their armor that could protect them when Kāhssiel unleashed his Seraph fire. Later called Skath metal, Dyna realized.

Sheli rode with Kāhssiel to battle on the Pegasi, and they fought side by side during the Dark War. They learned how to combine their fire in an ultimate attack that turned the tide against the God of Shadows and his demons.

Dyna's heart swelled as she watched them argue with each other, protect each other, and fall completely in love. Even if they never said it aloud.

They were made for each other.

Together, they banished the darkness and brought forth the sun.

The dream smoke brought Dyna to that same *Hyalus* tree during the golden hour. She at last recognized it as the one she came across in Hilos months ago.

Kāhssiel was there. The gentle breeze tugged at his white robes, his pearlescent wings catching the light. Gold-spun hair shadowed his face as he silently faced the tree.

Dejection contorted his features as he asked, "You wish to leave?"

Behind him, Sheli clutched her arm to herself, dropping her gaze to the ground. Her gown was woven from all shades of gold. "I should return to Magos with my family. There is nothing for me here."

"You are one of my generals. *I* need you here."

"The war is over, Kāhssiel." Her eyes filled with tears, though her voice remained steady. "And so is our time together. Now you must live your life. Be a king and rule your people. I should be with mine." She looked away. "Allow me this, and I will grant you anything. Whatever wealth or favor, I'll do it."

But he didn't answer.

Sheli choked on a sob and shouted desperately. "What do you want from me?"

Kāhssiel turned to her, and his blue eyes softened. "You already know the answer ... *lev sheli.*" He took her chin, lifting her face to him. "I want you to choose me, because I have already chosen you."

Tears rolled down her cheeks. "But I'm a sorceress. Your people would never approve."

"I care not," he breathed. "From the moment you arrived, your light was a gift in the darkness. *At hazricha v'hashkia sheli.* You are my sunrise and my sunset. The one I choose. In this life and in the next one."

Kāhssiel kissed her beneath the glow of the *Hyalus* tree, and Sheli stayed.

Dyna bore witness as they were wed and crowned before the court. The Seraphs secretly whispered that such a union was blasphemy. She overheard plotting from the shadows of the halls and felt the antagonistic stares of his three generals that secretly reviled them.

The third general was the one who led the scheme to remove them. He looked exactly like Lord Raziel. His past life, Dyna assumed, but he had the same name, and those cold blue eyes had not changed.

It left her with an unsettling feeling as the memory faded away, and the dream smoke darkened.

Yet Kāhssiel and Sheli were too happy, or perhaps too oblivious, to notice the displeasure of their people, for they awaited a child.

Dyna found them in their chambers within the Hilos castle, laying together in bed on a sunny evening. He kissed her belly that was beginning to round as they laughed at the responding flutters. As the sun descended, the crystal necklace on her chest began to glow.

"I remember the first time I saw you," Sheli murmured as she ran her fingers through his hair. "I was there when the Heavens opened, and the Seraphs fell to this world. You were a bright blue light in the sky like my very own shooting star. Then I found myself wishing I could fly through that sky with you." Sheli smiled sleepily and placed a hand on her belly. "Once that wish came true, I dared to wish for another, and *Elyōn* granted it. What do you wish for, my star?"

Kāhssiel looked at her with so much love, Dyna felt it. "*Ahuvati*, I already received my *mish'alah*." He curled his body around hers. "Do you know what your name means?"

Sheli's green eyes danced with happiness as she snuggled closer to him. "It means meadow."

"In my language, your name means *mine*." He kissed her languidly, speaking against her lips. "As in belonging to me..."

If only that wish had been enough.

The low drone of a horn rang outside, announcing the alarm. Both leaped up and someone banged on their door.

Kāhssiel opened it to reveal Raziel. "Sire, we are under attack. Your generals ... they have mounted a coup against you."

He was in disbelief. "What? Why would they do this?"

Raziel shook his head, his expression creasing with anguish. "They deem you unworthy to rule us for choosing a mortal queen, sire. Now that you have begot a child with her, they are calling it an abomination and have chosen to take your throne by force."

"That is treason!" Kāhssiel said angrily, exchanging a frightened glance with his wife. She trembled in her white nightdress, placing a hand on her belly. The clash of swords and screams outside snapped him into action.

"Come quickly," Raziel said in alarm. "The men don't know who our enemies are, and they are falling quickly!"

Kāhssiel grabbed up his weapons, and his wife helped him put on his armor. "I cannot leave Sheli here. She cannot use magic while pregnant."

"Allow me to see to the Queen's safety, sire." Raziel clamped a fist over his heart and bowed. "I will guard her with my life."

No... Dyna gasped. *Don't let him take her!*

Raziel quickly ushered Sheli out into the hall, and Dyna dashed after them, but the dream smoke took her away to a battle in the Hilos courtyard.

Celestials fought Celestials, and Kāhssiel was forced to strike down many. Valkyrie rallied to his side, but by the time he realized who was friend from foe, it was too late.

Kāhssiel! Sheli called out to him through the bond.

He whipped around and met Raziel's sneer where he stood with his struggling mate at the edge of a cliff. And before his eyes, Raziel shoved her off.

"SHELI!" Kāhssiel tore into the air with wings of flame and raced to them like a comet. He dove through the free air down the chasm for his mate. His splayed hand stretched for her as he screamed.

Sheli's wet eyes looked up at him, her dark hair and dress rippling in the roaring wind. There was only sad knowing on her face. The sound of her voice passed through their connection and Dyna's heart. *This is not the end, kohav. We will be together again. Wait for me.*

Dyna shut her eyes.

She couldn't watch her past-self die, but she felt it when Sheli hit the ground. Her entire body spasmed with agony.

The Blood Bond brutally shattered, and Kāhssiel's horrible screams echoed through the sky.

At the bottom of the chasm, he clutched Sheli's broken body. All fighting ceased as his cries rendered across the kingdom. The loss of a True Bonded mate should have killed him, but mad with grief and rage, Kāhssiel transformed into an entity of flame. Sheli's body dissolved away, and he was left holding only ashes in his empty hands.

"They took her from me," he growled like a monstrous beast of annihilation. "They will all *burn.*"

Dyna watched helplessly as Kāhssiel filled the Realms with flame. Their screams of fear filled her ears. His people either fought or fled. Armies rose against him by the thousands, and each met a sea of pure flame. It struck them down, swarming into their armor, their eyes and mouths, smothering their screams as they turned to ash. All that remained of them were fields of blackened earth, cinders glowing within empty helmets. The skies darkened with smoke as he banished the sun once more.

All fell to his power.

For he was unstoppable.

So Dyna was confused when the dream smoke cleared to a memory of Kāhssiel in chains. He sat on his knees beside the *Hyalus* tree. His armor and face were stained with soot. All that was once green was now charred to ash. Scattered fires lit the brush and charred feathers floated in the breeze.

The dried blood on his lips cracked with a cough. Wind rattled the translucent leaves softly, and he briefly closed his eyes, as if remembering a past moment in this very place.

A brokenness lined the shadows of his face.

Exhaustion.

Surrender.

"All this death and bloodshed, only to end defeated. To what end?" Lord Raziel said. "For some witch?"

Kähssiel lifted his dull gaze to him. "Am I defeated?"

"You are in Skath chains, Kähssiel. Your Seraph fire is useless now."

He chuckled sardonically. "They will not hold me for long, Raziel. As soon as I am free of these chains, I will come for you. For all of you." He snarled at the traitors standing with him and lurched at them. The guards held onto his chains, jerking back his manacled arms. "Each of you has betrayed me, and nothing will inhibit me until I have melted the flesh off your bones. I will return you to the Gates and raze the Realms to the ground. As soon as I am free, I will fill this world with a sea of flame and consume it all until there is nothing left of it!" His eyes blazed with flame. *"I WILL BURN IT ALL!"*

His roar echoed his promise over the land, and they grimaced from the force. Fear stole their confidence as they realized the truth.

"I am invincible." Kähssiel chuckled. "You cannot stop me. Not with these chains. And not with your army. In the end, you will be naught but dust."

Raziel's mouth thinned, but he smirked, only cold amusement on his face. "I questioned why *Elyōn* chose you to remain a Seraph and wield the pure flame. Why did he choose you to hold such a power when it has only created a monster? It was not made for this world, and it shall not remain."

He nodded at the guards holding the chains. They forced Kähssiel forward and yanked out his six white wings.

His eyes widened. "What are you doing?"

"Ending your reign," Raziel said as they drew their swords. "Kähssiel, we hereby denounce you as our High King and as a son of the Heavens. Your wings will be sheared from thy back and with it your power. Thus, your soul shall be eternally damned, cast away to *Gehenom* for eternal punishment. Never to return to the Heavens again."

"Stop!" He fought against the chains. "You cannot do this. It's sacrilege!"

"It is no less than you deserve."

Dyna cried out in horror as swords of flame raised above him. But she caught the moment he strained forward, fanning out all six wings, exposing the margins. The blades sliced clean through them. His scream of pain tore through her ears, and he fell flat on the ground. The power that had hovered off him like a wave of heat vanished from the air.

Kāhssiel shuddered on the ground, surrounded by his sheared wings. White feathers floated on the surface of his blood.

His speed. His strength. His fire.

They were gone.

All that was left were the six stumps of exposed muscle and bone on his back. His mortal weakness and terrible agony crashed over Dyna as she cried. His pain almost matched the pain he endured when Sheli had been taken from him.

Almost.

Kāhssiel choked on a dry chuckle. He rolled onto his back and his body shivered as he bled out. Yet he laughed and laughed, the crazed sound filling the stunned silence.

"What is so amusing?" Raziel demanded.

"You never defeated me," he murmured, looking up at the gray skies. "You merely assured that I would return to finish what I started."

They all stared at him in stunned silence. Dyna's heart pounded wildly.

"My soul is now mortal, but not truly human and no longer a Seraph. It will belong nowhere. I will go to *Gehenom*, but you forgot one thing." Kāhssiel met his eyes and smiled. "Lost souls are always reincarnated."

All the color drained from Raziel's face, his eyes growing wide as he realized what he had done. "You wanted this..."

"You have my gratitude. As my thanks, I curse you with a long life. You will live to see my return, Raziel. Perhaps you shall sire your own demise."

Raziel's roar of fury filled the field. Kāhssiel's laughter mocked him, because they both knew only one of them had truly won.

Tears filled Kāhssiel's eyes as he continued laughing. The sun rose on the horizon and fell over the *Hyalus* tree. The translucent leaves rattled gently, gleaming like stars of gold.

Enraged, Raziel shoved off the guards and wrenched out his sword.

Dyna covered her mouth, her vision blurring as the burning blade lifted above Kāhssiel's neck. She reached out to him desperately, wishing she could stop it.

His dried lips parted with a soft exhale as he gazed at the beautiful sunrise. Tears rolled down his temples. He whispered his last words into the wind, as a soft wish for only her.

"I will find my way to you ... in every lifetime."

The sword came down, and Dyna fell backwards off the chair with a shriek. She was back in Greenwood. Cassiel was still there, sleeping soundly in the bed.

Dyna stifled her sobs.

They had been killed for loving each other. For bearing a child that was different. Yet they called him the monster?

Taking Cassiel's hand in her shaking palms, Dyna finally noticed the bracelet wrapped around his wrist. Braided out of crimson hair.

When the Vanguard had come for her, he must have seen the past repeating itself again. The fear had strangled him. He saw no other choice but to cut out his heart and shatter their souls to erase himself from her life. There was nothing left to do but once again go to his death for her.

Because her life was more precious to him than his own.

Dyna's tears landed on the bed beside his fingers, soaking through the cloth. She had been so angry with him. So furious and spiteful without ever stopping to consider that he had been suffering, too. She never felt more wretched than at that moment.

Her shaking hand pressed on her stomach where his lips had once kissed. The vow he had written there had burned when he left.

Everything I do, no matter how painful, will always be to protect you.

Laying her head over Cassiel's heart, Dyna wept.

When night fell, she stepped out into the hall. Yelrakel and Sowmya straightened.

"Watch over him," Dyna told the General.

Yelrakel clanked a fist over her heart.

Then she faced her other Valkyrie. "Lieutenant, I have another task for you. A mission for the crown."

Sowmya lowered to one knee and bowed her head. "My Queen, I am yours to command."

CHAPTER 79

Lucenna

"I don't understand why I cannot go with you!" Tavin's angry voice filtered into the hallway as Lucenna reached Klyde's chambers. The boy's face was flushed, his fists clenched as he yelled at his uncle. "You are always leaving me behind!"

Closing his eyes, Klyde pressed on the knot between his brows. To her surprise, he wore a Ranger uniform. The black leather armor fitted his tall form like a second skin, making Lucenna's eyes linger on his broad back and strong arms. Instead of the twin short swords that he usually carried, a new sword was strapped to his hip. It bore an elegant black hilt, with gold plated vines. Forged by Elven smiths, no doubt. A hint of magic hazed the air around it like heat rising off stone.

A tired frown settled on Klyde's features. Von and a black wolf stood in the room with him, waiting to leave. "I've told you, lad. This mission is far too dangerous. I cannot take you to Red Highland."

The Blood Keep, rather. A prison fortress guarded by Bloodhounds, red elves, and rife with other untold dangers Lucenna could only imagine. It was the last place Tavin should be. She didn't know what to expect, but they were certainly risking their lives in going. This would most certainly end in bloodshed, and possibly not all of them were coming back.

Lucenna's hands shook, but she clenched them into fists and buried all dread in the back of her mind. Lord Norrlen needed them.

She exchanged a look with Keena, who fluttered at her shoulder as the arguing continued. They really didn't have time for this.

Lucenna rapped her knuckles on the door. "The delegation is about to depart."

Klyde sighed, and he nodded. "Aye, we're coming, lass."

Tavin scowled. "Why can the witch and dainty fairy go, but I must stay behind? That's a load of bollocks!"

"Dainty?" Keena huffed and crossed her arms. She wore tiny iridescent armor, gilded plates protecting her neck and wings. Her black curls had been braided away from her pointed ears, a quarterstaff in her hands. Lucenna wouldn't have pegged her for a warrior, but pixies were prominently strong.

Klyde sighed. "Tavin—"

"Aye, he's right," Von interjected with a shrug. "The lad may be ready."

Tavin's face lit up. "There, see. The Commander thinks I can go."

Klyde glowered at Von. "I don't care what he thinks."

"If he is old enough to hold his drink, he's old enough to fight with us." Reaching into his maroon coat, Von handed Tavin a small wineskin. "Go on, lad. Show him."

Tavin snatched the wineskin and chugged it all. His mouth pursed with disgust, but he forced himself to swallow and flashed them a grin.

Well, now what?

Klyde grabbed Von's coat and snarled, "What do you think you're doing?"

"Putting him out of harm's way."

Before either of them could question what that meant, Tavin stumbled back.

"Why do I ... feel strange?" he garbled, pressing on his head. His eyes rolled. Klyde caught him as he fell unconscious.

"What did you give him?" Lucenna asked.

"Dreamshade oil." Von tucked the wineskin back into his coat pocket. "Don't worry. He will sleep it off by tomorrow."

With that, he strode out of the room. Klyde stared after him, then down at the boy. He may not have liked it, but this assured Tavin would be safe—and that he wouldn't follow them.

Klyde tucked his nephew into bed, and Zev's paws lightly scraped on the floors as they went into the dark hall. The Castle Guards sent to make sure they didn't follow the delegation were now slumped against the wall, sleeping soundly where Lucenna had left them.

"Nice work," Von said.

She nodded at the room. "Likewise."

Once Klyde joined them, Lucenna had them gather. With a wave of her hands, she cast an invisibility spell over all of them. It fell like a tickling electrical mist on her skin, and they vanished from view. She had spent the evening practicing to expand the spell to cover more than herself, and it had blessedly worked.

They followed the sound of Zev's paws as he led them out the side of the castle. The empty gardens were lit with torches, the clear night cold and free of rain. Raiden had left saddled horses for them behind a wall of tall hedges.

Lucenna's pulse thrummed nervously as they climbed their mounts and snuck around the castle to the courtyard. They kept to the soft grass, careful not to make too much noise. The rushing winds were in their favor tonight.

King Leif, Raiden, Eldred, and seventy armed elves on horseback lined up in front of the Elder Tree. The bright moon shone down on them as the old Magi Master began to chant in Elvish.

"Gateways are tricky," Eldred had explained to her earlier in private. *"The one who opens the gate should direct its course. I will aim for the East Wall, but the brief seconds between us crossing could cause our groups to be separated. If that comes to pass, you will be near. Make your way to the West Wall at the borders of Red Highland. It lies across the Covenant Pass. You cannot miss it. Should you not arrive at the wall by dawn, you will need to find a way into the Blood Keep on your own."*

If luck was on their side, they wouldn't be separated too far apart.

She glanced up at the rooftop of the castle where Dyna and the Valkyrie surely lurked, already cloaked from view. The moment Dyna had regained her magic, Lucenna had been training her to learn *invisibilis*—the invisibility spell. Clearly, she learned it well.

Lucenna smiled. The red king didn't know what awaited him.

We're coming, Rawn.

Eldred's voice rose as he chanted, and his spell power charged the air like static. He placed glowing Moonstones into the grooves within the stone circle on the ground, and runes lit up across it. Energy hummed in the air, sending currents against Lucenna's Essence, and goosebumps sprouted on her arms. Light spiraled from the center of the Elder Tree, filling the opening with a brilliant white glow.

The gateway was open.

Raiden switched his reins from the left hand to the right.

"That's the signal," Lucenna whispered to the others. "Eldred will keep the gateway open for only fifteen seconds once they cross. Be ready."

The Greenwood King and his delegation cantered into the spiraling light. Lucenna's heart pounded, and she gripped her reins tight.

When the last elf passed through, she shouted, "Now!"

Hooves clopped on stone as they galloped across the courtyard toward the glowing light. The wind whipped against them with the sound of beating wings. They leaped in, and the gateway whisked them away.

Lucenna's vision flashed white, and the air left her lungs as the universe hauled her through an unseen void.

For a split second, she feared getting lost in it, but the next thing she knew, her horse cantered onto hard earth. The temperature had shifted to warm and arid. It was dark with nothing but the moon and stars to light her way. Dropping her invisibility spell, Zev, Von, and Klyde appeared beside her on their mounts.

"That was a rush," Klyde said with a nervous clearing of his throat. "But I'd rather not do that again."

Zev stretched, shaking out his fur.

"Where are we?" Keena asked from Von's coat pocket.

Lucenna studied the rocky terrain below them. There wasn't much, but some sparse vegetation. A far cry from the fruitful knolls of Greenwood.

"I think we landed on the tail end of the Anduir Mountains," Klyde said. "North of East Wall."

"How do you know?" Lucenna asked.

"We're on a ridge. Then there is that." He pointed ahead. She wasn't sure what he was pointing to at first until she noticed the peak of an obelisk catching the moonlight in the far distance.

"What is it?"

"That's what the elves call the Covenant Pass. Thirty miles of barren desert between Red Highland and Greenwood. We will need to cross it tonight to reach the Western Wall by morning."

"And the Maiden?" Von asked.

Lucenna searched the night sky but saw only stars amongst the wispy clouds. If they had landed with them, Dyna would have dropped her spell by now. "The gateway must have dropped her somewhere else when she crossed."

Zev trotted behind a cluster of bushes and shifted on two feet. "Don't worry," he said, his voice caught in a growl of his wolf. His yellow eyes reflected in the dark as they fixed on the horizon. "We expected this to happen, so we will follow Dyna's plan. Wherever she is, her task is to fly ahead to the Blood Keep."

He had confidence in his cousin, and Lucenna did, too. Dyna could do anything she set her mind to.

"She *will* get the other half of the key," Lucenna stated, internally wishing her luck. "We will take care of our part."

Dyna had wanted to go after Rawn, but they all agreed she was the best one to sneak into the Blood Keep and steal the key while the red elves were distracted.

For the Druid to choose her, it meant he had seen it in his visions.

The plan had to succeed. Not only to release Dyna from his geas, but the key also opened a door on Mount Ida. They were going to need it.

Zev nodded. "Von and I will steal into the dungeons and break Rawn free."

"And the rest of us will make sure his son isn't traded," Keena chimed in as Zev shifted back on all four paws. "What could possibly go wrong?"

Klyde chuckled. "Let's not curse ourselves with bad luck quite yet, shimmer bug."

"I am not a bug!" She tossed a tiny ball of gold dust at his cheek and flew away with a huff, following the black wolf down the mountain.

Grinning, he wiped the dust off. "I think that means I'm one of her favorites."

He would assume that.

"Off we go then," Von said, tugging on his reins.

"Hold a moment," Klyde called to him. From his saddlebag, he drew out a knife studded with an amber bead in the pommel. "It's yours, right? You forgot it in the Blue Capital."

Von's brows shot up as he returned it to him. "Aye, it is."

They looked at each other for a moment. Perhaps it was Klyde's way of unofficially thanking him for helping Tavin ... and forgiving old grudges. The Commander nodded and rode onward, leaving them alone.

Lucenna fleetingly glanced at Klyde, and his gaze met hers. She didn't mean to. It was instinct, really. She had nothing to say to him, though.

"Wait." His horse cut hers off before she could go. He motioned at the loose belts of her greaves. "May I?"

She wasn't used to wearing armor, much less practiced in putting it on properly.

At her stiff nod, Klyde dismounted, and her pulse quickened as he marched toward her. She stayed silent as his deft fingers tightened the belts, adjusting the greaves on her forearms properly. He secured her leather chest plate and checked the armored plates on her hips, making her face warm.

"Now is not the time to speak of it," Klyde murmured as he worked. "But I want you to know my intentions with you were never impure. When we return, I plan to explain myself for last night. If you will permit me..."

The moonlight caught his blue eyes as they rose to hers.

Gods, why did he have to look at her like that? As if only she existed for him in this pocket of time.

It was wrong.

Lucenna studied the angles of his face, annoyed that even the night favored him. Honestly, she shouldn't want him as much as she did. Let alone fantasize about him taking her in his arms and continuing what they started in Avandia. She wanted his lips on hers again. Wanted his lips all over her. How could she let him affect her like this?

Lucenna hated that she wanted him.

Hated even more that he knew.

He frowned as he looked her over. "You're not armed."

"My magic will do fine."

Reaching for the scabbard at his hip, Klyde drew out a long Elvish dagger with a polished black hilt engraved with swirling gold leaves. "Here. Take this."

Lucenna arched an eyebrow at the glinting blade. "You're not very bright, are you? Give me a weapon, and I am likely to stab you with it."

A faint smile edged his mouth. "If you manage to cut me, I'm not worth my own merit, lass." The knife flipped to his other hand with graceful speed. "We have been in situations where magic has failed you before. It is better to have the dagger and not need it, than need it and be left wanting."

Lucenna snatched the dagger from him.

"Oi, hold it like that and you'd sooner hurt yourself." Klyde corrected her fingers for a firmer grip on the hilt. "If you're ever cornered and have no other choice, slash here, here, or here." His finger stroked her neck, the side of her waist, and across her torso. Each touch sent scatters across her skin. His gaze locked on hers as his expression grew serious. "Go for the heart through the ribs. Stab straight up with enough force until you see the light leave his eyes."

The severity of his low voice made Lucenna's skin prickle. She had taken down many mages; there was no other choice when the outcome was having her Essence siphoned if she failed. She fought her opponents within a given space, separated by spells across a battlefield. Stabbing someone was up close and much more personal.

"What if I miss?" she asked quietly.

"Then go for the eyes. Your enemies can't hurt what they can't see. I'll take care of the rest." Klyde's rumbling reply sent an inexplicable warmth through her chest.

"Hmm." Lucenna crossed her arms and nodded at the new weapon strapped to his hip. "And what have you got there?"

"Oh, this?"

Stepping back, steel sang as he drew the sword free. The black blade shone like ink in the moonlight. It was inscribed with glowing Elvish runes she couldn't read. Lucenna felt her Essence react with the magic imbued into the steel, and faint shimmers of white light glittered off the enchanted blade, like smoke infused with stardust.

"Lothian steel." He wielded it expertly, the blade whirling as it sliced through the air. "Courtesy of Eldred. It's called Shadowbane."

She smirked. "You named it?"

"All great swords have a name, lass." Sheathing the enchanted weapon, Klyde mounted Onyx's saddle. "So their deeds are forever remembered."

It was a jest, as was his way, but that last word made her think of that morning. It must have done the same for him, because his smile faded.

"Are we bad people," Lucenna whispered, "for not noticing how far gone he was?"

Shame and guilt weighed on her for kicking Cassiel down when he was already on the ground. The way he screamed had made her cry, because she felt how much pain he bore. They all felt it.

"No." Klyde sighed, looking out at the sea of rock and sand. "Sometimes, that sort of despair can be easily hidden away. They can drown right in front of you, and you wouldn't know until they sank too far beneath the surface to pull them out."

None of them had noticed anything wrong. Except for Zev. Perhaps because he, too, had lived with a voice in his head.

The wind picked up, and Lucenna shivered. "That's why Cassiel left, didn't he? The guilt of losing his father and fearing he would lose her too, it must have..."

"Aye, it haunted him." Klyde looked up at the stars. "I don't say he did the right thing, but I don't think we realize how much we love something until we have to give it up."

As Lucenna looked at Klyde, she realized she could easily be in Cassiel's position, too.

Perhaps that's why she overreacted yesterday. She had been waiting for any sign not to involve herself with him, because it would put him in danger. Which was ludicrous, really, that she would care that much about a man. *This* man, this preposterous handsome man who meandered into her life by some unexpected chance.

Because she highly doubted it was fate.

Klyde turned to go. "Come, lass. We have a long night's ride ahead of us."

"When we ran into each other in the witch's den, why were you there?" Lucenna asked.

He paused, and the moon shone in his eyes as he gazed at her. "I was searching for answers."

"Did you find them?"

A soft smile touched his lips. "I found you."

CHAPTER 80

Cassiel

Cassiel opened his eyes to find the world was not as he left it. He sprang out of bed, and his feet caught on the sheets. It sent him stumbling to the floor. His hands shook against the cold stone as he *remembered*. As if he had not endured enough.

Why this?

He had spent years hating his father. Hurting him with his anger. Years of simply wasting time.

All that time lost when he could have used it to be a son.

"Where am I supposed to go from here?" Cassiel looked up at the version of Yoel who had been with him all winter.

He sat on the windowsill against the sunrise, smiling at him tenderly. So young and carefree. A soft white light hovered off him and his wings. He no longer seemed solid anymore.

"I can't tell you where to go. Only to keep going."

He shook his head. "I should have been faster. I should have been stronger. If I had reached you in time, you would still be here. We were supposed to have more time. I'm sorry. I'm so sorry."

"I am here, Cassiel. Didn't I say I would be with you for as long as you needed me?"

His throat tightened. "But I have to let you go now, don't I?"

Yoel stepped down and came over to him. "There is a time for everything, son. What is coming is far better than what is already gone."

Cassiel lowered his head to hide the way that hurt. "You should have lived..."

"I do." His father laid a hand on his shoulder, yet he could no longer feel it. "I live in your memory."

His shoulders shook with silent sobs. How was he supposed to go on without him? His father's presence was the only thing that had provided any guidance in the void of his life. "I feel lost."

"I know. But now it's time to find your way back."

"What if ... what if I can't go back?" he asked in a broken whisper.

Smiling gently, his father held out a hand to him. "Then we will find our way back together."

He took it, and Yoel pulled him up. When he blinked his eyes again, Cassiel found himself still in bed. He had been dreaming. But it felt too real to be a dream.

His father had come to say goodbye.

"Sire?"

He turned his head, noticing Yelrakel standing guard at his door. Her shoulders slumped with relief, and she rushed to his bedside.

"My king, how are you feeling?"

Cassiel looked at the empty windowsill. The moon had replaced the bright sun and the last traces of that assuring presence faded away like a breath on a breeze.

Alone.

There was a hole in his chest, and he didn't know how to fill it. How did he get here?

Cassiel missed the days when he didn't know who he was, when he was a stupid boy taken with a girl he met in the forest, learning what it meant to love. How could he find his way back to who he used to be?

Without his father and mother, without his mate, what was there to live for anymore?

Sometimes he thought death would be easier. Life was much harder. But Cassiel reminded himself he had returned to this world for a reason.

"Dyna?" he asked.

"My Queen and her Guardians departed Greenwood through the Elder Tree," Yelrakel said. "They are on their way to Red Highland."

"I am going after her." Cassiel sat up and began dressing in fresh clothes. He had been too late to save her in their first life, but *Elyōn* gave him a second chance. He wasn't wasting it. "Have the squadron prepare to depart."

"I have already sent them ahead with her, sire." Yelrakel put on her helmet. "My ride awaits me on the roof."

She looked back at him steadily, ready to serve. With her Pegasus and the speed of his flame, he could recall the rest of his Valkyrie from Sellav and catch up to Dyna.

"I will see you there, General."

She clanked a fist over her heart and marched out of the room.

Stepping out onto the balcony, Cassiel climbed up onto the banister. Crimson flowers rustled gently in the wind. Closing his eyes, Cassiel breathed in the fresh air, filling his lungs. The moon called him west and promised to light his way.

CHAPTER 81

Dynalya

The hooves of Dyna's Pegasus cantered on the hard ground as she landed. The air was warmer and drier than in Greenwood. It was night now, but she sensed it grew hot here beneath the sun. Before them was an immense obelisk made of stone.

The gateway had brought her to the Covenant Pass.

Sowmya and the squadron formed a perimeter around her as they quickly surveyed the area. Other than the forty female warriors, there was no one else nearby but them.

"The others must have landed elsewhere," Dyna said, looking toward the east.

It was too dark to see the East Wall. That was where King Leif and Raiden surely had arrived with his delegation. She sensed Lucenna a little further up north.

That put her ahead. Good, it gave her a head start.

Dyna nodded to Sowmya. "You know what to do."

"The Valkyrie await your command." The Lieutenant clanked a fist over her heart and bowed her head. "Be safe, Your Majesty."

Tugging on the reins, Dyna rode for the west, kicking up sand. The muscles of her Pegasus shifted, and she stretched her large white wings.

Dyna crouched low, her gaze fixed on the horizon. *"Lashamayim, Shira. Lashamayim."*

The wind rushed to meet them as they galloped faster. Shira's wings caught the wind and carried them off into the air. Dyna looked back to the east, where she had left a piece of her soul in the care of another. She would return to him when this was over.

Dyna faced ahead and focused on what she came to do.

They flew into the night. Time passed swiftly until the sky lightened with the coming of dawn. The sharp peaks of the Erdas Mountains rose before her, the border of Red Highland. With a command, Shira soared over the crest and the Blood Keep appeared in the far distance among the sea of red sand.

She was close.

Shutting her eyes, Dyna cast an invisibility spell over herself and her Pegasus.

As the sun rose over the horizon, the desert heat came with it. It blazed down on her, sprouting sweat on her skin beneath her armor. She felt relief when she at last reached the Blood Keep. It was an odd name since the tower was made of a pale stone. But as Dyna grew closer, she saw the bodies of long dead prisoners hanging from the ramparts. Their blood and the blood of many others had stained the walls a dark red.

Her empty stomach churned.

Dyna shut her eyes and looked away. In the middle of the keep's courtyard was another Elder Tree. This one had pale bark and crimson leaves.

That would serve for a good escape.

She made it to the roof and landed. Dismounting, she petted the Pegasus's muzzle. "You did well, Shira. Now return to Sowmya. It's not safe for you here."

Shira nickered softly. Turning, she cantered for the edge of the tower and took off into the sky.

Dyna surveyed the land. Many miles of sand dunes and rocky formations in all directions. On one side, if she squinted enough, she could see a hint of the hazy silhouette of Agarmon, the Capital of Red Highland. On the other side of the keep, the rising sun illuminated a stone barricade in the mountains.

The West Wall.

The delegation would have reached it by now. Her Guardians, too.

She had to sneak into the keep and retrieve the key before the trade for Raiden took place. They would not allow Rawn's son to be taken.

Removing the ring of rope attached to her hip, Dyna quickly tied a knot to the battlements of the tower she landed on and scaled down the side. She was careful to go slow and step lightly. The invisibility spell may keep her hidden, but elves had keen senses and would catch her at the slightest sound.

She made it to a narrow window and climbed inside. Voices and faint wailing cries echoed off the walls. It was difficult to tell from which direction. The narrow windows created a constant stream of wind that passed air through the tower, carrying ventilation and sound with it. Which may work in her favor.

Dyna stole along the walls, keeping alert. Guards patrolled below, along with large creatures. Their brown hides twitched, the growls rumbling in the keep. Bloodhounds, Zev had called them. If they caught her scent, no magic would be able to hide her.

She continued, searching for the warden's quarters. It was her best guess on where to begin searching for the other half of the key. Leoake said it would be here, but he didn't say where. If it was with King Altham, her plan would prove more difficult.

Voices neared, and she ducked into an alcove.

"To leave your elevated sanctuary, you must surely be desperate to be rid of him if you are willing to align yourself with elves."

"Desperation is an overstatement. Think more of it as ... *eager*."

Dyna's pulse jumped at the sound of Lord Gadriel's voice. She carefully peered past the edge of the wall and spotted the pureblooded Celestial striding down the hall with a male elf in elegant red robes and a gold crown sitting on his head.

King Altham, she had to assume.

But what was Gadriel doing here?

"He wields Seraph flame, you say," Altham mused as they went into a room, and Dyna's chest caught with a gasp. "I'm intrigued. A rare phenomenon I would be glad to study, but as such, I am aware of the might behind such power. If your army cannot obstruct him, why should I place mine in his line of fire?"

Gadriel followed him in. Dyna slipped into the room behind him, keeping her steps soundless. Her training served her well. She slinked behind a sofa for a better view of the room.

"Your soldiers are skilled in magic," Gadriel said as he took a seat across from Altham at his desk. "Paired with the divine weapons I provide, your force stands to defeat him. Strike his weaknesses, and victory is guaranteed."

Dyna's heart pounded. *Weaknesses?* But she was supposed to be the only one.

"When the time comes to confront the threat beyond your walls, you can expect our support."

Altham canted his head. "Nazar would wage war against Greenwood?"

"If it means my people will flourish beneath a new king, my sire pledges you will have the might of Hilos and the Four Realms on your side. We will ensure you win your war."

Chills scattered down Dyna's arms.

They were planning to depose Cassiel, even if that went against the law of never spilling Celestial blood for the gain of others. And Dyna had the sinking feeling of who Gadriel's sire was.

She should have known killing Cassiel was only part of his plan.

Raziel intended to sit on the throne, too.

A slow smile sharpened on Altham's face as he leaned back in his chair. In his fingers, he turned a bronze piece of metal. It flickered in Dyna's eyes as it caught the light.

The other half of the key.

Her heart pounded in anticipation, and she forced herself to stay still.

"If all goes according to plan today, it may not come to that," Altham said. Trumpets sounded outside, and his grin grew. "You are not invited to today's occasion, but I suppose I have no control over what others choose to do, do I?"

That was a strange way to put it.

Gadriel's wings whooshed as he rose to his feet. "We await your signal."

With a slight bow of his head, the Lord of Nazar strode for the open terrace and took off into the sky.

What did that mean? Did they bring Celestials here? Altham had given his oath that the trade would go peacefully, but it was clear he found a way around it.

Gritting her teeth, she prayed the others would be ready. She kept her eyes on the key piece, and her body tensed as she waited for the right moment to snatch it.

King Altham looked up. "I know you're there."

Dyna froze.

The door opened and another male elf strode in. His dark hair was held back by a silver circlet on his head. He bore similar features as Altham. It had to be his son. She held her breath, careful not to make a sound with him so near.

Altham pursed his lips. "Well?"

"They're here, father."

Her pulse spiked. No. She didn't have the key yet.

Glee crossed the red king's face. "Is Garaea ready?"

"I will send for her."

"She should already be here, Anon. Find her." Altham slipped the key into his pocket as he stood.

"It may be best to leave that behind," the prince said indifferently.

"I never leave it off my person."

"As I am sure the green scat would have predicted. Now that you have revealed the key to that usurper, he will want it for himself. Why risk the chance he could take it from you?"

King Altham paused, narrowing his eyes. "Leif gave me his oath."

"Rather foolish of us to believe they have not found a way around their oaths as we have." Anon strode back out into the hall, his red cloak flowing behind him as he took the stairs.

Shutting the door, Altham paused there a moment. Dyna watched, waiting. He returned to the bureau behind his desk, opened a set of small doors, and placed his half of the key inside. With a short incantation and wave of his hand, a glowing gold dome fell over the key. Then the red king swept out of the room. Dyna internally groaned. Crossing the room to the bureau, she opened the set of doors and frowned at the dome. It was some sort of protection spell. But she wasn't skilled in spell breaking yet, and this was elf magic.

The door jingled behind her. Dyna quickly shut the doors and held still beneath the invisibility spell as another elf came in. A female this time, with a delicate golden crown. She was beautiful. Long dark hair framed her heart-shaped face, eyes like honey and sun-kissed skin. She wore a sheer white dress with an exposing neckline, a filigree of gold adorning her chest and waist. Elegant yet practical for the heat.

Princess Garaea, Dyna assumed. The pretty elf glanced around before rushing to the bureau. Opening the doors, her face lit up, and so did Dyna's.

Garaea had snuck in here to steal her father's key.

They came to save Rawn and to intercept Raiden's engagement, but Dyna couldn't help but think the princess would have made him a good match.

With a glowing finger, Garaea drew the spell for dissipation on the enchanted dome, along with other runes in a complicated array. She murmured a spell, and the sphere burst. Smiling, she snatched up the key.

"Well done," Dyna said.

The princess gasped, and her amber eyes snapped right at her. *"Alever."*

The revelation spell peeled Dyna's invisibility away. Dropping, she swept out her foot, knocking Garaea off her feet. She snatched the key. "Thank you, princess."

Garaea rolled to her feet with a hiss, and two yellow blades of magic appeared in her hands. "I need that."

"So do I." Dyna knocked her back with an Essence Blast and bolted for the doors.

"Intruder!" Garaea shouted behind her. Her voice echoed through the keep like a rising tide. "There is an intruder in the Blood Keep. She stole my father's key!"

CHAPTER 82

Rawn

Torch fire broke through the darkness. Clamoring voices rang through the dungeon as guards ran about in alarm. Rawn crouched within the shadows of his cell, listening. Elon's one eye flickered to him, conveying the same thought. Something had happened.

Rawn's pulse quickened, and he prayed that this was the moment they had been waiting for.

Guards rushed into their tunnel and began inspecting each cell. One stopped by theirs, lifting a torch as he briefly peered at them. "The prisoners are still here, warden," the guard called, moving on.

"Then who is the intruder wandering the keep?" Grod barked. "Find him! Set the Bloodhounds loose."

More armed elves marched past in a steady stream of red cloaks. Their voices faded as the search moved on to other tunnels. Rawn glanced at Elon, and they exchanged a silent nod.

Whoever this intruder was, he sent his thanks.

Now was the time to run.

"We have to move quickly," Elon whispered as Rawn took out the small pouch from his pocket. "I will take point."

He quickly dumped out the amber bead and passed it to Elon. "I will guard your back."

Making sure the tunnel was empty first, Elon skulked to the cell door and pressed the bead against a bar. The black clover inside glowed, and the metal hummed. Energy pulled from the air, and Rawn heard a static pop.

A triumphant smirk crossed Elon's face. The confinement spell that made the iron indestructible had broken, trickling enough life-force into the air to allow him to gather a sliver of Essence.

Taking hold of the bars, magic ignited beneath Elon's palms, and veins of blue light snaked up his arm. His lips moved in a soft murmur—an incantation in Elvish tongue. *"Ep'mores yalbod esoreca—are'bil."*

The cell door popped open with a loud *clang*, and their shackles broke clean off their wrists, thudding to the ground at their feet. God of Urn. Rawn's chest heaved with a disbelieving laugh. They were free.

They leaped up and ran out into the passage. Prisoners desperately cried out to them. Their bony hands waved through the bars, begging for release.

Elon turned away. "Make haste. The guards will soon return."

Rawn stared at his retreating back. "Wait, what of the others? We cannot leave them here."

"We don't have time to break all these cells open, Norrlen." He continued onward. "The hounds will soon catch our scent."

The wailing voices of the prisoners filled the tunnel. He couldn't walk away from this. It wasn't right.

Rushing to catch up to Elon, Rawn grabbed his shoulder. "We must help them. You regretted soaking these sands with the blood of others. Here is your chance to prevent more from spilling."

"You're an honorable elf, Norrlen, but we can't save them all. Most will likely die down here if they run."

"They will surely die if they don't. We owe them the chance to fight their way out of here or die trying." Because Rawn would want that chance. For the possibility of ever seeing his family again, he would face Death itself.

Sighing, Elon looked at the gaunt faces pleading to them, and confliction tightened his brow. "We cannot break open each cell."

"Nor do we have to." Rawn nodded up at the softly glowing runes carved into the stone ceiling. Why break small spells when they could break the main one?

Elon's mouth hitched. He tossed the amber bead up, and it shattered against the ceiling. A crack split the stone through the runes, and their light winked out. Stunned silence filled the tunnel.

Rawn held still. "Did it work—"

The earth violently rocked beneath their feet. Voices cried out, and the Blood Keep groaned. They stumbled, bracing themselves against the walls. But the quake soon settled, and Rawn gasped when life-force flooded into the stale air, falling over him like a soft blanket, warming his skin. He drew on his Essence, and his palm gently glowed teal blue.

"The wards are broken," Elon announced. "Free yourselves!"

They ran as chants and spells were called out. Cell doors began to crumble or burst open with a flash of colors. Rawn felt a surge of elation.

They weren't out yet, but he was one step closer to home.

"The prisoners have escaped!" a shout echoed behind them, and that elation quickly vanished.

More guards came running. The sounds of growling hounds and screams filled the tunnels as everyone fled.

"This way!" Elon panted as they skidded around the bend into another tunnel. "We can still make it to the waterways."

The dungeon was a maze. Rawn couldn't pinpoint north from south, but Elon seemed to know exactly where to go.

Until a Bloodhound cut off their escape.

They skidded to a halt. The enormous hound filled the tunnel, blocking the way. Its short ears folded back, lips pulling back from its sharp fangs that could easily tear them in two. Elon cursed, and they slowly retreated.

Rawn's mind raced to calculate how to take it down, but it would be difficult without a weapon. He drew what Essence he could from the dry air and Elon did the same.

The Bloodhound snapped its teeth, reflective eyes glowing in the dark as it stalked toward them. Their only choices were to run toward the clamor of voices or face the Bloodhound. One opponent was better than many.

Rawn clapped his hands together with a call. *"Erb'mul."* A petal of flame flickered in his palm. *"Eria."* He blew into his hands, and a cyclone of fire hit the hound. The blow launched it back, but it landed with an enraged snarl. A patch of scorched fur was the only damage in its hide. Rawn panted, catching his breath. He hadn't regained enough strength yet, but he had enough Essence for one more spell. *"Orum ed erb'mul!"*

A wall of fire flared up between them and the Bloodhound, keeping it at bay.

But now the way to the waterways was blocked.

"We need to find another way out, Elon."

"Rawn," he alerted him.

He heard the charge of running boots as guards flooded the tunnel with Grod in the lead.

"I can hold off the Bloodhound," Rawn said. "But not for long."

"Then allow me." Elon's eyes and hands spiraled with blue light as he faced the elves. His low voice dropped into an eerie hum. *"Arreit ratrep'sed. Ahcucseim adamall."*

Runes of the elements flared out within a hexagon beneath his left palm, tangling with symbols and circles. The glowing magic shone brightly within the tunnel. Rawn reared back, shielding his eyes.

Elon aimed at the guards, his words rising in a chant. *"Ot'neiv. Az'reuf ed erb'mul, et'neirroc ed auga, ojulf ed otneiv, esab ed arreit."* The pentagram blazed. The pressure of his magic filled the air and pulled at his being. It was the same explosive spell Elon had tried to cast against Lucenna. *"Ranib'moc yriuit'sed!"*

The spell shot forward with a roaring blast. Grod dove out of the way. The explosion of light tore through the guards, and the tunnel violently shook. Coughing, Rawn stared at what remained of their charred bodies wafting with smoke.

He shuddered. *God of Urn...*

Scrambling to his feet, the warden punched a lever on the main cell door and bolts shot out of holes in the walls. Rawn tackled Elon, losing hold of his firewall. They crashed together on the hard ground. The freed Bloodhound snarled, prowling forward.

"Get up!" Rawn leaped back to his feet, but Elon staggered.

A bolt had pierced his thigh.

Grod bared his yellowed teeth in a grin as more guards and Bloodhounds filled the tunnels. "Hinderance bolts. Nullifies the magic."

Elon cursed, ripping it out.

To his reinforcements, the warden shouted, "Seize them!"

The guards drew their weapons and charged.

"I cannot cast any more spells, Norrlen," Elon said, watching them come.

The Bloodhound slashed at Rawn, claws tearing into his side. He cast another cyclone of fire, throwing it back, but the creature was too large for the spell to do any real damage. "This is the limit of my skill with magic."

Enemies surrounded them on all fronts. There was no tunnel to escape into and no time to cast a spell strong enough to fight back.

They failed.

"Well, it appears our endeavor ends here," Elon sighed as they stood back-to-back. "Couldn't say I expected to die beside a green elf."

"Perhaps not," Rawn said, faintly smiling to himself. "But it's an honor to die beside a friend."

He shut his eyes and exhaled slowly. May his family forgive him.

The guards and hounds fell on them.

The tunnel exploded with a cacophonous roar, hurling everything away.

Rawn hit the wall hard, and dust billowed through the tunnel. The blast left his ears ringing painfully, skewing his vision. He choked on the smoke clogging the tunnel. It swirled, blinding him.

He didn't see what hit them. Another spell? Whatever it was, he barely survived it.

"Elon?" he rasped.

Only one torch at the end of the tunnel remained, casting very little light. The guards and Bloodhounds had been buried beneath the rubble. All that was seen of Grod was his twitching arm.

"Elon!" Rawn called out, his heart pounding.

Then he heard something coming.

Something big. Another Bloodhound was hunting them.

Rawn scrambled to his feet. He wildly searched for Elon as he heard footfalls near.

A massive black creature emerged from the darkness like a beast of shadow. Eyes reflecting bright yellow in the faint light.

Rawn laughed in utter disbelief. "Zev?"

The wolf whined softly at the sight of him and rushed to his side.

"I am so incredibly relieved to see you, my friend. But how...?"

Another, in a maroon coat with a mask covering the bottom half of his face, stepped through the smoke.

Commander Von.

The last person Rawn would have expected to see.

Von reached into his coat and handed Rawn a sword. "I'm told this belongs to you."

Rawn blinked at the weapon a moment before accepting it, recognizing the Elvish hilt. It had once belonged to his father. He took the sword, and its familiar weight filled him with a sense of courage he hadn't felt in days. "Thank you." He glanced between him and Zev. "How did you come to find this place? Are the others with you?"

"It's quite the tale. The others wait for us above." Moving past him, Von crouched by Elon's still form among the broken rock and shook his shoulder. "Oi, are you dead, mate?"

Elon groaned. He rolled over and stared at him incredulously. "I must be if you're here, Commander." Then he winced in pain. "No, most certainty alive."

"By the grace of the fates." Von chuckled and helped him stand. "You're missing an eye."

"Clearly. I take it this is a rescue?"

"Clearly," Von retorted back as he surveyed the area. The tunnel to the waterways had caved in. They wouldn't be able to go that way anymore. "Dyna has tasked me with breaking you out of the keep before they begin the trade, Lord Norrlen."

"Trade?" Rawn asked warily. "What trade? Who has come?"

"Everyone, including your king." Von went to a guard who stood up off the ground with a groan, swaying. "Sorry, no time to explain." He smashed the elf's skull into the wall, leaving him to drop unconscious at his feet. "We need to leave."

The wolf growled in warning, staring ahead with glowing eyes.

"More of those hounds are coming." Von handed Elon two long knives. "Our only option is to go out the main entrance."

Elon expertly whirled them, testing their weight and balance. "Yes, this will do."

"I brought enough *huyao* powder to blast our way out of here. We're bringing down the keep."

"Good," Elon said, turning away. "If I fall here, swear that you will bury me beneath the rubble when you blow this damn place to kingdom come." That was an unexpected, morbid request. They stared at Elon, but he ran ahead without waiting for an answer.

Zev ran onward, paws lightly touching the ground, moving with a smooth grace. Sword at the ready, Rawn kept his gaze ahead on Von and followed.

Their chances of escape had significantly increased, and hope hung above him anew.

They were going to make it out. They had to make it out.

Aerina's face surfaced in his mind, and his heart ached.

Wait for me.

Elon stopped at a crossway between four deviations. He studied them a moment, perhaps not sure which one to take. Cries and the clashes of metal echoed around them.

"Which way?" Von pressed.

"Patience, Commander."

"Which we cannot afford right now, Elon."

He turned in place, and his amber eye settled on the right tunnel with warmer air. "This way—"

Zev crouched and bared his teeth at a dark tunnel on the left, sharp canines gleaming. A Bloodhound's answering snarl rumbled from the darkness as it stalked forward into the crossway. With a savage growl, the wolf leaped on the hound's back, tearing into its neck.

Guards rushed in from another tunnel. Elon and Von drew their weapons and charged at them, attacking in a practiced formation of soldiers who knew how to fight together. Rawn parried a guard's blade, slashing through him and spinning for the next. The clash of steel rang out as they fought.

But for every red elf they killed, more flooded the passageways in a steady stream. No matter their skill, they would soon be overwhelmed.

As if in answer to an unspoken plea, a stampede of elves in tattered clothes swarmed the tunnels, shouting spells and attacking the guards with their own weapons. The prisoners they had freed.

Chaos broke out, and magic rendered through the air. Rawn ducked, but no rogue spells touched him. The four-leaf clover, he realized. It brought him good luck, after all. Trusting the clover to protect him, he fought through the barrage of guards. The fallen piled on the ground. Flashing spells invaded his vision, stealing the oxygen as more and more bodies compacted in the crossway.

Rawn's heart hammered with a growing panic as he struggled to breathe. They needed to get out. But he lost sight of the others. Where did they go? Which way was out?

Slipping on a puddle of blood, Rawn fell out into another dark tunnel. Stumbling back, he sucked in ragged breaths. He searched the swarm for his companions, but it was impossible. He needed to go in and pull them out.

A violent spell flashed orange in the darkness. It vaulted off the protective force field around him, but the force threw him down.

Rawn rolled to his feet, grasping his sword. The air stirred behind him. He whipped around and white-hot pain impaled his ribs.

It tore the air out of him. His legs gave out, and he sank to his knees. Rawn's sword slipped from his fingers, clattering on the ground. Shakily, he clutched onto the spear lodged in his side and looked up at Anon.

No.

The red prince ripped out the spear, along with all shreds of hope. Anon beat him across the face with the other end of the shaft and Rawn hit the ground, choking on sand and blood.

Crouching next to him, Anon smirked. "You truly thought you would escape this place, Norrlen?" He rifled through Rawn's pockets and snatched away the leather pouch with the clover, tossing it to a hound to eat. The last of his hope evaporated with it. "Well, I'm impressed you made it this far. Bring him."

Anon strode away, crimson cloak fluttering in his wake. Two guards grabbed Rawn by his arms and dragged him behind their prince. His strength sank beneath the well of pain throbbing against his lungs.

His vision blurred. *Aerina...*

No, this couldn't happen.

Sand became hard stone as they carried Rawn up a set of stairs and dumped on the ground. He reached for Anon's spear, but a boot rammed into his stomach, knocking the air out of him.

"Now, now, don't be rude, Norrlen. Many guests have come a long way to see you."

The guards took hold of him again and hauled him along Anon's footprints, leaving a trail of his blood. They went through a door, and Rawn was hit with fresh air and a bright light that burned his eyes. He squeezed them shut with a strangled moan, but he felt heat on his skin. The sun. He was feeling the sun.

They hauled him up a short set of steps and dumped him on his knees. He slumped forward.

"Oh, no, you need to see this." Anon snatched a handful of Rawn's hair and violently yanked his head up. His eyesight stung against the bright daylight. Having been in the dark for countless days, it took a moment for his aching vision to clear. They had brought him to a wooden dais adorned with yellow flowers overlooking the courtyard below. "Revere the valiant souls who came for you."

King Leif rode in with an entourage of soldiers. Rawn's chest hitched sharply with relief to see him, Eldred, and the many soldiers he fought with in the last war.

Anon then hissed in his ear, "Not a single one of them is leaving here alive, Norrlen. After today, your blood will mark the walls of this keep." He forced Rawn to look at a young elf dressed finely as a Prince of Greenwood. With his face and Aerina's eyes. "As will your son's."

CHAPTER 83

Lucenna

Lucenna kept close to the tail end of King Leif's delegation as they entered the Blood Keep's courtyard. They dismounted from their horses and the elves fell into formation behind their king. She kept close to Raiden. Klyde couldn't be seen beneath her invisibility spell, but she sensed him beside her, and Keena was doing well to stay quiet in her pocket. They had caught up with them at dawn at the West Wall, and it had been a long tense morning as they rode the rest of the way to the Blood Keep in silence.

Being here now made her magic react to the tension in the air. An Elder Tree with red maple leaves stood out in the center of the courtyard.

The soldiers of Greenwood were on high alert. Lucenna's stomach rolled at the many bodies hanging from the keep's walls. The blood of many had stained the brick as if dripped with dark russet paint. Black flags with the red sigil of a maple leaf fluttered from the Blood Keep's tower. A dais of wood adorned with yellow flowers was the only thing in the courtyard.

And she sensed magic there, too. They were being watched.

"Welcome!" A red elf with a gold crown and crimson robes greeted them as he climbed down the main steps of the tower. "I hope the journey here wasn't too difficult, Leif."

The King of Greenwood smiled, though it didn't reach his eyes. "Not at all, Altham. I thank you for allowing this treaty between our kingdoms. It is time peace has been brought to the Vale, and it can only start with unity."

"I cannot agree more." Altham approached with his Kingsguard in black armor. Only a few for a sense of protection or decorum. He glanced at Raiden, and his smile widened. "This must be your nephew. He takes after his father, doesn't he?"

"He does."

Raiden's expression remained blank and apathetic.

Altham chuckled. "Well, my daughter is beautiful, Raiden, I assure you. I believe this is the first union between our kind since the separation of the Vale some ages ago."

"And where is the princess?" King Leif asked.

"Garaea should join us soon." Altham shot a look at the guards standing by the main doors, and they disappeared inside the Blood Keep. He went on to say, "I think you will be pleased with my desert flower."

"I care nothing for your desert flower," Raiden said tersely. "I want Rawn Norrlen returned. For which we rode in haste across the desert, yet he is not present as well."

Leif laid a hand on Raiden's shoulder, giving him a look. "Forgive his comportment. He is anxious to be reunited with his father, as are we all."

King Altham chuckled. "Well, you need not wait any longer. He is right here."

He waved a hand at the dais set up for a wedding, and the illusion magic there rippled as it faded away, revealing Rawn.

Lucenna stifled a gasp.

He sat on his knees in only torn trousers with many wounds and scars on his chest. He was thin, pale, and gaunt. Barely alive as blood spilled from a fresh wound on his side. Lucenna could feel the power hovering off the red prince standing beside him.

Must be at the level of a Magi Master.

Curses and growls surged from the Greenwood soldiers. Raiden stared at his father, frozen in place. And Rawn stared back at him. He made a strangled sound that was caught in a weak groan.

King Leif's jaw clenched. "You gave me an oath not to harm a single hair on his head, Altham."

"And I did not." At Altham's nod, the prince holding Rawn captive pulled up a golden strand, and he laughed. "There, see? A strand unharmed."

"You're despicable," Raiden growled.

"Now, now, let's not be tetchy. Your father is alive to bear witness to your blessed union with my daughter."

Rawn's eyes widened, and he tried to say something, but Anon kicked his wounded ribs, making him wheeze with pain.

Lucenna hissed under her breath, snarled curses coming from the green elves.

"Ah, there she is." Altham announced as a beautiful she-elf in a white dress was escorted to his side. One guard murmured something in his ear, and Altham's delight faded. His hard eyes glanced at the keep before saying, "What do you think, Garaea? Are you pleased with your intended?"

The Red Highland princess briefly glanced at Raiden, and dipped in a curtsy, keeping her gaze lowered. "Yes, father."

But when she straightened, her amber eyes flickered to King Leif. They exchanged a look, and her head shook slightly. So subtle, Lucenna almost missed it. Leif's expression shifted.

"I will not marry her," Raiden repeated. "I am already promised to another."

All heads snapped to him, including Garaea's.

"What is the meaning of this?" Altham asked Leif narrowly.

King Leif shrugged. "I know nothing of what he speaks. Be that as it may, I must agree, for I find you have not kept up your end of our agreement." He said this while looking at the princess, and she grew anxious. Leif rested a hand on his sword, facing Altham. "You have broken the oath that you have made before the God of Urn; thus, our treaty ends here. I do intend to take Rawn with me. Let us go peacefully, unless you wish to start another war."

The Greenwood soldiers behind him drew their weapons, and Lucenna braced.

But Altham didn't look perturbed by the subtle threat. He didn't even seem angry that the wedding would no longer take place. He was ... pleased.

Prince Anon tossed a flare of orange light into the sky. It burst like a firework.

No ... like a signal.

"I have not broken my oath, Leif," Altham said, resting his hand on his sword's hilt as well. "For it was not by *my* hand your Red Shade was harmed, and *I* was not the one who ordered for more armed forces to the Blood Keep." He sneered, enjoying his ability to find ambiguity around his promise. "Regardless, I never did intend to allow you to leave. For alas, I have always chosen war."

Red elves took aim at them from the tower. There were three times as many guards as Altham agreed to bring.

Shadows passed overhead. Lucenna's heart sank at the sight of Lord Gadriel and an armed host of Celestials.

King Leif looked almost relieved until he recognized the sigil of Nazar on their breastplates.

Altham laughed, drawing his weapon. "They are not here for you."

"No," Raiden said. "But they are."

Lucenna dropped the invisibility spell. The squadron of Valkyrie soared over the Blood Keep and clashed into the Nazarians. She couldn't help but grin at the sight of a bright blue comet speeding toward them in the far distance.

With it came a legion of gold.

Altham snarled and swung at Leif. Their swords clashed. An onslaught of steel and magic broke out as arrows rained down from the keep. Lucenna and Eldred threw up golden shields, blocking most of them.

"Go for Rawn!" Klyde shouted at her.

Lucenna blasted a red elf swinging for her head and sprinted for the dais, following on Raiden's heels.

"Cover me," he told her.

Raiden conjured a bow in his hands, made of pure magic. She watched in awe as he aimed an arrow of teal light at Anon. Lucenna threw out a volt of purple electricity, striking down every elf and arrow that came their way.

Seeing they were closing in, the red prince grinned. "Little Norrlen." He chanted a spell, and an orange pentagram filled with runes flared out beneath his palm. Rawn tackled Anon, but that didn't prevent him from shouting, *"Arreita revlov!"*

Orange light blasted toward them. In the instant before it struck, Raiden called up a lightning-fast spell of his own. *"Ramrased!"*

He released the arrow, and the two enchanted forces collided—and exploded. The blast catapulted them away, simultaneously shattering the atmosphere.

Lucenna hit the sand with a grunt. She gaped at Raiden. The magnitude of power behind that spell—he was a Magi Master, too.

Anon began to sit up, but Rawn rammed his elbow into the prince's face, and he dropped unconscious.

They ran to him. Raiden reached him first and cut through the enchanted bindings at his wrists.

Rawn stared up at him in confusion and concern. "Son..."

Raiden fleetingly met his gaze. "We must make haste."

He and Lucenna helped his father stand, bringing Rawn's arm over his shoulder.

Then Rawn looked at her, and Lucenna gave him a watery smile. "At last we found you, Lord Norrlen."

He smiled tiredly. "It is good to see you, my lady."

"Talk later," Raiden said. "Let's move!"

She caught sight of Keena's tiny form flying in front of them with her quarterstaff. Every elf she hit was thrown out of their way with a burst of gold dust.

"Where are we taking him?" Lucenna asked as they stumbled down the steps with Rawn.

"The Elder Tree. It's the only way to escape here quickly."

"Do you have the Tanzanite stones?" she asked.

"Eldred must have them."

The old elf was battling back the red elves and protecting his king from any rogue spells. They seemed to be making their way toward the tree, too.

Klyde and Keena caught up to her. "Zev and Von haven't left the tunnels yet," he told her, striking down another elf.

Lucenna searched the chaos for a black wolf among the swarming bodies, or for a man in an auburn coat. All she saw were elves fighting elves.

"They must be caught down there," Keena said in alarm.

Eldred appeared with Princess Garaea at his side. "Head for the tree."

"What is she doing here?" Lucenna demanded.

"The king is granting her immunity, and she also has the stones we need."

Klyde grunted, "That means she's coming with us, lass."

They fought their way through the courtyard as scorched feathers rained down. The Celestials battled each other overhead. Eldred led the way, clearing their path with earth shaking spells. Klyde's blade of smoke cut down spells raining down, staying by her side as she cast out spears of electricity. Garaea conjured two yellow blades of magic and covered Raiden's back as he dragged Rawn with him.

They were swarmed as they fought to stay alive.

Lucenna's heart hammered as she followed the others. But smoke veiled her vision as spells flashed across the battlefield. Cries and clashes of steel rang all around her. She nearly tripped into Lieutenant Handuril as he cut down a red elf, making her lose sight of her group. Searching for them wildly, Lucenna crashed into a red elf, and they fell into the sand. Snarling, he chanted a spell and struck her chest with his glowing palm. She screamed at the pain shocking her veins. She called on her Essence to defend herself, but only a weak sputter of purple light sparked in her fingertips.

Whatever he did, it snuffed her Essence.

BECK MICHAELS

The elf snatched her throat and squeezed. Lucenna gasped for air, kicking and flailing. Twitching, she grabbed the dagger strapped to her waist and slashed him across the eyes. He dropped her with a shout. It cut off at the black sword swiping through his neck. The elf dropped, revealing Klyde standing behind him.

"On your feet, lass!" He grabbed her arm and hauled her up.

They ran through the chaos together. She cast spells on her right as he cut down enemies on their left. But the enemy had them surrounded. They slowly began backing away and the green elves retreated with them toward the Elder Tree. Regardless of their efforts, the red elves outnumbered them.

And losing.

A blast of blue fire tore through the atmosphere, throwing the Nazarian army across the sky. The Legion of Valkyrie hit them next. The air turned into fire as both Celestial forces clashed into each other.

Altham snarled a curse. "That coward."

Cassiel arced through the air for the courtyard and landed with a *boom*. A wave of blue flame broke across the sand and incinerated half of Altham's forces. It was instant. They didn't even have time to scream.

Lucenna muttered to Eldred, "If you were looking for your chance, now is the time."

Eldred and Garaea began inserting the Tanzanite crystals into the grooves carved into the stone circle surrounding the Elder tree.

Cassiel walked through the scatters of fire, his eyes molten blue. Embers drifted off him with every flap of his wings. His face didn't betray a hint of emotion, while his palpable power coated the air.

The three kings faced off.

"High King of Hilos, I assume," Altham stated tightly. Glass shattered from a high window in the Blood Keep, and elves fell screaming. A flash of green light flickered inside. "That must be your little queen." He sneered. "Yet I am the oathbreaker?"

Cassiel nodded to Leif. "Do you need further assistance here?"

The King of Greenwood chuckled as he readied his sword. "You have leveled the field, Cassiel. I can take it from here."

Crouching, he blasted like a flare of flame for the keep.

"Are you almost done?" Lucenna asked Eldred urgently.

He glowered at her and continued the incantation. The center of the Elder Tree began to glow. Leif launched at Altham, and their fight continued. Spells and swords rang out as green clashed into red once more.

"There, look!" Keena pointed at the south end of the keep. Zev came out of the smoke, covered in blood, with Von and Elon on his shoulders.

568

"Oh, they made it." Lucenna sighed in relief, and they ran to him.

"We need to go," Zev said when he caught up to them. "Where is Dyna?"

"She's still up there."

"What do you mean?" he exclaimed in alarm. "The explosives are set to blow any minute!"

Her breath caught, and they all looked up at the Blood Keep.

"She must have been delayed," Klyde said. "Cassiel went after her. He'll get her out, mate."

A flash of orange from the corner of Lucenna's eye had her whipping around. Anon had regained his consciousness, and he was conjuring a spell. His voice rose in an eerie wave as a hexagon of runes flared around his palm.

He pointed it at the Elder Tree.

"Oh, Gods," Lucenna gasped, and she ran back to Eldred, waving her arms. "Get down!"

The world ripped away with a massive explosion.

A force struck her. Brick, stone, magic. She didn't know. The world spun, and she slammed into a solid surface. Whatever it was, agony shattered through her entire body.

Lucenna twitched on the sand, gasping for the air that had been torn from her lungs. Someone shouted her name, but she hardly heard it past the ringing in her ears. Something was wrong. She called for Klyde but gagged on the blood coating her mouth. Tears sprang to her eyes. Why couldn't she move? In her mind, she tried to crawl, but pain invaded her consciousness, and her sight blurred.

She couldn't feel her legs.

"Lucenna!" Klyde's voice cleared, and he took her face. "Can you hear me?" He looked her over, and his face crumbled. "Oh, love..."

She whimpered, afraid to ask why she couldn't move. Blood leaked from her lips. "It hurts."

"It's all right," he said, his voice breaking. "I've got you."

Was she going to die?

Her vision waned, but she managed to look down at her legs. They were twisted in the wrong direction. The smoke cleared away from the field.

The Elder Tree was gone.

CHAPTER 84

Dynalya

"**S**eize her!" Red elves charged at Dyna from all fronts. Sprinting forward, she slid on the ground on her knees, passing beneath their swords. She sprung to her feet and swung her blade of Essence, parrying an incoming spear. Swerving another attack, she ran for the stairs, only to meet another unit of guards. Gods, they never stopped coming.

Dyna fought down a spiraling flight of stairs, cutting her way through a barrage of elves. There were five floors between her and escape. Dodging a guard's blade, she shoved a knife into his chest and slammed a palm against the hilt, driving it home.

An arrow zipped past her nose. Another elf was perched on the steps across from her, an arrow aimed at her. A black-winged figure knocked him over the railing, and he fell screaming.

Relief swam through her at the sight of Cassiel. He cast out a torrent of fire at the elves charging at her from above. Parrying another attack, Dyna leaped up onto the railing and jumped.

Cassiel dove and caught her raised hands.

She grinned up at him, unable to hide how immensely relieved she was to see him.

Cassiel returned her smile. "Sorry I'm late—"

An explosion ripped through the keep.

The force threw them off trajectory and Cassiel yanked her against him, protecting her from the blast. His wings wrapped around her before they hit the second landing. He groaned, and she winced, wheezing for the breath knocked out of her. Pushing up, she looked him over.

"Are you all right?" they asked at the same time.

Cassiel laughed tiredly and brushed the hair from her face, cupping her cheek. "I am now."

Dyna stayed there with him for a moment. His eyes were a little sad, but clear. There was so much she wanted to tell him, but a sudden gust of wind had them both looking out at the massive hole in the Blood Keep.

The explosion had killed the remaining guards, most of their bodies crushing beneath the debris on the bottom floor. Dyna and Cassiel made their way to the opening, providing a view of the courtyard below.

Her Guardians scattered in the sand, some wounded and others unconscious. Rawn and Raiden pushed off the ground as Prince Anon strode out of the smoke, his hands flaring with magic. He shouted out spells, making the earth shake.

"Help them," Dyna told Cassiel. "I can make it out."

His brow furrowed with worry. "But—"

"It's all right." She picked up her weapons. "Go!"

Cassiel leaped through the hole and flew for them. Spells flared all around as the elves battled for the upper hand. Klyde and Zev fought to protect their fallen friends, too wounded to fight. The Valkyrie were far off into the sky, battling Gadriel's army.

She needed to get down, but the stairs had crumbled from whatever blast had hit them. The battle outside caught her attention at the charge of searing magic in the air.

Power bloomed from Anon's hands in an orange haze, and a glowing hexagon spiraled from beneath palms. Runes flickered through it, the air crackling at the power building. The flowing spell swelled, and he barked a command. An orange beam shot at Cassiel like cannon fire. He winked out of view in a flare of blue as he dodged every attack.

A tide of Seraph fire came for Anon. Snarling, he threw out a shield and slid across the sand, flinging up his hand at the Blood Keep. With a barking command, a large piece of the keep's broken wall catapulted at Cassiel with frightful speed. It knocked him out of the air and pinned him on the ground with his wing beneath it. Anon yanked down another arm and more boulders piled onto it.

Cassiel cried out in pain. Dyna fell against the wall as she felt his strength seep away with the agony of his broken wing. That was where their power lied.

His weakness.

Cassiel had told her what it was from the beginning of their journey. Without their wings, they were human.

Her chest caught with a frightened breath. *No.*

A spell circle flashed around Anon's wrist, power pulsing. Gritting her teeth, Dyna conjured a flare of pure green flame and took aim. She cast it with a scream, and the blast blazed through the air. Anon threw up a shield. It blocked her spell, but the force knocked him off his feet, throwing him to the sand. Anon glared at her, furious.

He rolled to his feet only to block Raiden's glowing sword made from magic.

"Get him out!" Dyna shouted frantically to the others.

Zev, Klyde, and Keena ran for the boulders pinning Cassiel, but red elves swarmed them. Raiden and Anon fought across the battlefield, their enchanted weapons and violent spells tearing through the atmosphere with their power.

Dyna quickly took a rope out of her satchel. Tying it to a beam, she tossed it out of the opening in the wall.

"Enough!" Leif roared.

She froze, and her heart sank. Cassiel was still trapped, and Anon had Raiden on his knees, a glowing blade at his neck.

King Leif clutched Garaea to him, a knife pressed to her throat. "We end this now, Altham. Either your son stands down, or you lose a daughter."

Immediately, Altham held out his hands in surrender and dropped his sword. "All right," he said warily and nodded at his son. "It ends here."

"On your knees."

Gritting his teeth, the King of Red Highland slowly lowered to the sand.

Everyone lowered their weapons, but Anon didn't surrender.

The red prince sneered at Rawn on the ground. He was on his hands and knees, his wide eyes fixed on his son. "You're right. We end this here, father. Beginning with the Norrlen line."

"Put the knife down!" Altham shouted at both his son and Leif. "I command it!"

"Why? We have the upper hand. You have daughters and sons to spare. But this one," Anon sneered as he pressed the blade's edge against Raiden's throat, making it bleed. "He is precious to them." Anon laughed at Rawn as he shook on the ground, fingers digging into the sand. "Your son will bleed out the way your sister did, Norrlen. And I will carve my name into him next."

Raiden glanced at Dyna from the corner of his eyes, and she read the message. She was the only one who could do anything now.

Taking a breath, she conjured a bow in her hands and aimed with a special arrow she had saved in her quiver. One with a hindrance rune carved into the arrowhead. Exhaling a breath, she released. The arrow flew across the field and pierced Anon's thigh. He staggered back with a curse. Raiden twisted free and ran back to his father's side.

With an enraged curse, Anon ripped the arrow out at the same time a ring of red runes blazed around Rawn. It wasn't his Essence. The crimson veins of power streamed from the wounds in his body.

Blood.

They crawled over his hand and raced along his arm in twisting trails that glowed as Rawn chanted. The blood magic snaked over his shoulder, up his neck, and across his face. The glow in his teal eyes brightened as his power streamed out, shining through his skin.

"Still clinging to hope, Norrlen?" Anon laughed and strode toward him confidently, chanting a spell of his own. But none responded. He halted, staring at his hands.

Dyna smirked. Her arrow had nullified his magic. By the time Anon realized he couldn't call on his Essence, Raiden had conjured bindings of teal light around his legs, trapping him in place.

The prince's eyes widened. He grew panicked, flailing to break free as the crimson spell circle around Rawn bloomed with light and lifted into the air above him. The lines of blood flashed brighter. Pressure built against Dyna's Essence so powerfully, and she felt fear.

The Red Highland elves fled.

The Greenwood elves ducked.

The wind went still, and all fell silent.

Rawn lifted his hand. A red glow lit up his bleeding fingertips, palm aimed at Anon. "You should have run." Then he calmly cast his spell with two eerie words. *"Anadaug Erg'nas."*

The spell blazed out in a sharp wave. A crimson blade swept clean through Anon and every red elf standing—like a scythe. The mist of blood sprayed into the air.

The prince froze, his eyes wide in disbelief.

In denial.

His spear and torso split in two, toppling in the sand. Red elves dropped all around them like broken pillars.

Rawn's eyes rolled. Raiden lurched forward and caught his limp body. He pressed fingers to his father's throat and nodded that he was alive. The green elves cheered as they got to their feet.

It was over. They won.

Dyna's shoulders slumped, and she allowed herself to breathe.

Cassiel looked up at her and smiled as the others began to remove the boulders off him. *Nice shot,* he said through the bond.

She smiled at the sound of his voice, simply so happy he was there. Now everything would be all right now. *Cassiel, I—*

The earth ruptured with a detonation beneath the keep. The violent quake knocked her onto the floor and Dyna gasped. She had forgotten about this part of the plan. The Blood Keep groaned, cracks splintering through the bricks.

It was coming down.

The ceiling caved in as the walls began to collapse. Dyna leaped out of the way of falling bricks. She dove for the broken stairs as dust and boulders rained down. Her Guardians shouted for her outside, Cassiel's frightened voice ringing in her head. She missed a step and dropped through a hole. Her body slammed into the main floor, bricks hitting her. She bit back a pained whimper. Rolling to her feet, she ran outside onto the front steps, but there was no more ground to run onto.

A massive fissure split the earth between the courtyard and the Blood Keep, swallowing elves and horses. Shouts cried out as everyone fled. The rift grew too wide for anyone to jump, including Zev. He shouted for her on the other side, Von and Elon holding him back.

"Dyna!" Cassiel yanked desperately to break free from the boulder that still pinned him. "Raiden, get to her!"

Raiden's wide panicked eyes looked between her and his father being carried off by the sand that was falling down the chasm. He had to make a choice, and they both knew the right one. She nodded that it was all right.

The ground gave away.

Raiden dove and caught Rawn's arm.

"No!" Cassiel shouted.

The earth trembled, the building crumbling above her. Dyna exhaled a shaky breath, knowing she couldn't escape this. Tears streamed down his face as those shattered eyes met hers. He was trapped, but a decision crossed his face.

"Don't," Dyna whispered in horror, suddenly understanding what he was going to do.

Cassiel shoved against the boulder with a pained roar. He tore himself free with a spray of blood and feathers. She screamed with him at the terrible agony washing through her body. He crawled on his hands through the sand, pushing himself to his feet.

Sprinting to her, Cassiel leaped across the chasm with the last of his Seraph fire. He crashed into her, and in the same momentum, he tossed her. She sailed away from his crushed, starlit eyes, and she landed in Zev's arms. Pushing off him, Dyna spun to her mate. He stumbled back, blood streaming profusely from his back.

His wing.

It was gone. He couldn't fly to her anymore.

Cassiel gave her a watery smile. *You're right, lev sheli. I can't run away from our fate. So I'm changing it.*

Dyna screamed as the building came crashing down, and he fell out of view. She flailed against Zev, kicking to break free. He yanked her away from the chasm as it spread, and they fell back into the sand.

Then all fell still. Dyna trembled with ragged breaths, staring at the crumbled building her mate was buried under. The bond shook and cracked, and after so many months of silence, she felt him. It started as a vicious twisting in her gut and spread to her whole body. An unbearable weight crushed her, squeezing all the air out of her lungs, her throat clamping with cries she couldn't make.

Pain. She felt his pain.

And the last beat of his heart faded.

Dyna's broken cry echoed in the skies as the rest of her being split open.

"CASSIEL!"

CHAPTER 85

Cassiel

It all came down to this moment. To the end of all things. Cassiel couldn't even be angry, because what else would he deserve? There was no controlling how his life began, but he could control how it ended.

The darkness swallowed him. Thin strips of faint light spilled from cracks in the debris. Cassiel's chest ached with his crushed ribs, his body trapped beneath the earth. It was crushing him alive, and he had no way to breathe. As death drew near, all else faded.

No pain.

No fear.

Only remorse for what should have been.

On the other side of his consciousness, Dyna was there. Soft and warm. Beautiful, gentle, foolish, safe. Alive.

He made sure she would live, even if it meant he didn't. In that he could rest, because there was no greater miracle than that.

But as Cassiel began to fade, a force burst through his soul, and he felt her. The bond surged to life with Dyna's scream that rendered through the earth. The power behind her cry brought one last gulp of air to his lungs and feeling back to his body.

Her magic ripped through the atmosphere with a powerful wave so strong it blew the darkness away. The building shook again, and boulders cracked as they lifted off him, leaving smoke and green embers falling like rain. His broken chest rose with a gasping breath as he blinked up at the opening several feet above him. Dull gray light filtered in.

"Cassiel!" came Dyna's cry again, closer this time. His waning vision fought to stay at the sound of her voice. "Cassiel, where are you?" she sobbed. "Answer me, please!"

Here... He lifted his hand or tried to. He couldn't move his body anymore. *I'm here...*

Scuffing footsteps echoed in the cavern. Shimmering green light followed.

"Cassiel?" Dyna's face stained with tears and dust appeared in the opening above him. "Oh, Gods. I'm coming!"

She vanished from the opening

Don't come down. His eyes grew heavy, and he took a shallow breath, coughing up blood. *It's too dangerous,* he tried to say, but his voice came out raspy and tasted wrong. He couldn't move or sit up. Nothing worked.

Everything hurt.

The air burned his lungs and darkness filled his vision.

"Cassiel! Oh Gods, please!" A hand gently patted his cheek, and pain yanked him to consciousness. A blurry face surrounded by red hair hovered above him. "Please wake up." Dyna's voice broke on a panicked sob. Her small hands closed over his face. "Cassiel!"

He stared up at the most beautiful emerald eyes glistening with tears. His chest struggled to rise with shallow breaths. Dyna sobbed as she looked over him because she knew he wouldn't be getting up. His ribs must have punctured a lung. He coughed up blood, struggling to breathe. Pain. There was so much pain, but he could take it, because she was there.

"Oh, *kohav.*" She sobbed as she looked over him, and he knew it must be bad. "Can you heal with your divine blood?"

His back throbbed painfully. Cassiel felt the hole there, the emptiness of where his wing used to be. "I can't heal myself anymore," he rasped faintly.

"Then use your fire."

His fingers twitched, and the flames flickered, sputtering out. He knew what it meant, and so did she. "Dyna..."

She shook her head, weeping. "No."

He smiled faintly, remembering they had been here before. They say one saw their life in their last moments, but all he saw was her.

"You can't do this to me now." Dyna angrily wiped her cheeks. "You will not die here." She placed her hands over his heart, and her warm magic swept over him. It sunk into his cold body, easing the last of his pain. But he was broken beyond repair. He would bleed out faster than she could heal him. She shut her eyes tight, and green light flared around them as she pushed herself beyond the safe parameters of Essence Healing.

"Dyna..." Cassiel took her hand. "Stop..."

"No, I am not giving up. You must hold on. The others are coming." She looked up at the opening at the distant call of voices. "We're here!"

"Dyna, listen..." Cassiel murmured, making those pretty green eyes look at him. "I should never have taken your choice. No one can decide your life's direction but you." Every word cost him, and he struggled to take another breath to finish what he should have said from the beginning. "I will no longer beg for your forgiveness, because it was never mine to have." Cassiel's shaking hand reached for her wet cheek, but he had no more strength left. She caught his falling hand. "For what I have done, and I have failed to do, I am sorry..."

"Stop it," she wept, holding his palm gently against her cheek. "You will not die. I will not let you. Because I love you. Even when I hated you, I still loved you."

He smiled. "I know."

Her tear landed on his face, and his vision waned with the soft press of her lips on his forehead. Blinding light lit the cavern as the heat of her magic flared through him. She continued trying to heal him. But without both wings he couldn't heal. It was too late for him.

Lev sheli...

"No, you must hold on," she cried. "Hold on to me, Cassiel. Please don't give in."

Cassiel tried. He really tried. But white light was streaming from him like a bright star. He didn't have the strength to keep his eyes open anymore. He could no longer speak, so he let his thoughts float to her through the bond.

Maybe in another world, in another lifetime, there is a version of us that survived. I see us together on a hill evergreen, watching the sunrise...

The light carried him away on a veil of peace. The world ebbed, and the cry of Dyna's voice faded with it.

CHAPTER 86

Dynalya

Dyna sobbed over Cassiel, pressing her face to his cheek stained with blood. She sank all of her power into his body. Her Essence wove into his bones, into his flesh, into the cells that made his blood. He was so broken. So many holes and tears, so many shattered bones. And he was dying.

All of Essence Channels opened as she poured her raw life-force into him.

"Don't take him," she begged *Elyōn*. "Please don't take him."

The light of the Heavens slowly faded from his body as she fought to keep his heart pumping. But it was taking all her magic to keep him here with her. She couldn't keep him alive this way for long.

Dyna stifled her anguished cries as she grew weaker. "No, please."

In his last moments, Cassiel had looked at her like he knew he would never see her again. Because they both knew her abilities couldn't reverse the damage done to his body. The power that created him was beyond her skill to heal. Even if she gave him all of her Essence, it wouldn't be enough.

It would require powerful magic to heal powerful magic.

Dyna gasped when she realized what she needed to do.

She flooded Cassiel's wounds with enough Essence to halt the bleeding, if only for a few minutes, and quickly gathered stones into a circle and tossed the key pieces inside.

"Leoake!" Dyna cried out into the cavern, choking on a sob. "I need your help!"

"No need to shout, clever mortal."

Gasping, she looked up at the opening above them. The Druid sat on the rim, arm resting on his propped knee. She didn't bother wasting time to ask how or when he got there.

He tutted his tongue at Cassiel. "Oh, dear. He stands at Death's Gate. Healing him yourself would take more than all your Essence, and you would surely die."

"I know that. I need to use your Door to take Cassiel to Melodyam Falls. It's the only way I can save his life. Please, he is succumbing to his wounds, and I can't stop it."

"Hmm." The Druid curled his fingers and examined his gold rings with a pout. "It may have escaped your attention, Dyna, but our deal ends here. You know I do not work for free. Unless..." His gold eyes glowed as they fixed on her, a mischievous smile curving his lips. "You intend to make another deal with me."

Of course. She shouldn't have expected anything less.

Dyna clenched her jaw, shaking with anger and desperation. "What do you want?"

Leoake chuckled and tapped his chin as if in pensive thought, but she knew he had already decided. It only infuriated her more as precious seconds passed. "Your greatest wish, perhaps? A precious treasure."

"What treasure? I don't have any treasure."

He smiled at her slyly. "You will."

Because she had begun this journey in search of one. The Sōl Medallion. The only thing that could save North Star from the Shadow Demon.

"But I need it."

He shrugged. "And you need him. You must decide which you want more."

Dyna trembled with indecision and anguish. Arguing with the Druid would only delay more time, and she could feel Cassiel slipping.

"Fine, the treasure is yours!" she blurted, "but only after I have saved my village."

Leoake's quiet chuckle floated to her. "Agreed."

He reached out his hand, and Dyna took it before she could change her mind. She winced as a new geas marked her once more. It took the shape of a brown leaf on the inside of her wrist.

Not an oak leaf, but of sage.

A twin symbol marked Leoake in the same spot.

She ignored the shaking in her chest and turned back to her mate. Out of sight of Leoake, she slipped the key pieces back into her pocket. "Take us there."

Dyna carefully lifted Cassiel's body into the air and wrapped him in a swath of her green Essence, layering it with a shield. Climbing out of the hole, she quickly made her way through the cavern with him and the Druid.

Zev waited for her by the opening at the top with Keena. He helped her climb outside. Leif and the surviving soldiers of Greenwood had Altham and any red elves that remained kneeling in the sand. Von waited for her on the other end of the chasm with Elon. But Klyde held Lucenna's limp body in his arms. Her limbs were broken, and blood leaked from her mouth. Raiden sat beside Rawn's unmoving body.

Dyna gasped, "No..."

"They are all right," Zev murmured.

"Quickly now," Eldred called out. He had built a bridge of floating stones over the chasm for them.

Dyna and Zev ran across it, Cassiel pulled closely along in her Essence.

Leoake strolled over the bridge without a care to hurry. Once he was on solid ground, the stones crumbled away. Everyone stared at the Druid as he walked past them and the scattered bodies to the charred stumps where the Elder Tree used to be.

"It's gone," Dyna said, devastated. She would never be able to keep Cassiel alive long enough to reach the falls in time. Maybe if they flew on a Pegasus! She looked to the sky, but Leoake crouched down and placed his hands on the stumps.

"The roots are still there, clever mortal. All they need is *time*."

His eyes glowed and gold light spiraled into the air from his hands and sank into the stumps. The tree began to grow.

Fae that hold great power...

The elves exclaimed in awe as the trunk rose up and curved to form a new Elder Tree. The center glowed with light. Not white, but gold.

"Come," she told the others. "Hurry!"

Leoake shook his head. "Our agreement is only for you and your mate, Dyna."

"But I can't leave them here."

"Go on. We have enough Tanzanite to make it to Avandia," King Leif said as Princess Garaea came forward with a handful of blue gems in her hands.

"Why are you helping them?" Altham shouted at her, enraged. Handuril held him back. "You traitor!"

His daughter flinched, but she wouldn't look at him.

581

At that moment, Yelrakel flew down and landed in a crouch. "My Queen, Gadriel's forces have retreated..." Her wide eyes fixed on Cassiel, and she yanked off her helmet. "Sire!"

"I am taking him to Melodyam Falls," Dyna told her. "I will save him, General. I leave my friends in your care. Please escort them home."

Leoake stepped through the gateway, vanishing from sight. Dyna followed with Cassiel. She looked back at the boulder where his wing was still pinned, blood soaking the sand. Zev met her gaze and nodded.

Dyna slipped into the Elder Tree. It whisked her away, stealing all direction. She opened her eyes at the cool ail on her skin.

The hot sands of Red Highland vanished, leaving the misty forests of Greenwood before her. It felt like stepping into another world.

Save for the gentle patter of a drizzle, the ruins were still. The destruction of the flash flood was still apparent. The sound of water crashed within the waterfalls, the scent of dynalya flowers strong in the air.

Dyna ran for it.

The cold water splashed as she waded inside and brought Cassiel with her. She released her hold on him, and he sank into the water. Leaning him against her chest, Dyna staggered under his weight. She could feel the stump where his wing used to be.

What he did for her ... that was an undying sacrifice she could never repay.

A sob caught in Dyna's throat. She sat on the shallow end and wrapped her arms around Cassiel, bringing him to rest on her lap. Red petals in the water lapped around them.

"This will work, won't it?"

Leoake stood by the bank, surveying the area with disinterest. "These waters will aid you in healing what remains of his body, but not his mind."

"What do you mean?"

"Not only is his body broken," the Druid looked back at her. "But also his spirit. He doesn't wish to stay in a world where he has lost everything. If you want to save him, you must show him he still has something to live for, *dream walker*."

With that, Leoake strode away for the trees, still singing that same tune that tugged at somewhere deep in her soul. Because her soul was connected to Cassiel's, and the song meant something to him.

Shutting her eyes, Dyna followed the melody into his mind. The whistle turned into a gentle hum as the dream smoke took her away. There were no flashes of memories or muddled voices.

The next blink of her eyes opened to a scene of a little boy with black wings. He was perhaps three or four, standing on a terrace with a beautiful woman. She wore her black hair pinned up, her gray eyes glittering as she chased her son. Cassiel's small wings flapped excitedly as he laughed.

"I've got you!" Elia caught him up in her arms. He squealed with laughter as she nuzzled his cheek with kisses.

He tried to wiggle out of her arms, but she tickled him, and he gasped with laughter. "No fair!"

"Well, if you wish to escape me, I suppose you will have to learn how to fly, won't you?"

Cassiel's giggles faded.

Setting him down, Elia kneeled in front of him. "You can do it, Cassiel."

"Papa said he would be with me the first time."

She sighed and smiled at him sadly. "Your father is a little busy now. But I am here, and I think you're ready."

He looked up at the sky anxiously, his eyes welling up. "What if I fall?"

"Oh, darling." She hugged him tight. "I promise I will catch you."

Dyna then stood with Elia as Cassiel drew the courage to climb onto the banister and leap. His mother cried tears of joy as he soared across the sky painted with a sunset, and yet, they were tears of sadness, too.

Elia watched him grow in that sky, and every year he flew further and further away. His mother would often sit by the window with a book on her lap. On the cover was the image of a volcanic island, and Dyna sensed she was dreading the day she had to say goodbye.

When night came, Cassiel cuddled with her in bed. He was only six years old. His little fingers clutched her dress as if afraid she would disappear.

"Mama..." Cassiel mumbled as his sleepy closed. "Don't go."

Elia's lip quivered, but her voice was steady. "It will only be for a little while, darling."

"Don't leave me behind. I want to be where you are."

Her face crumbled, and she took him into her arms, rocking him to sleep as she hummed. Dyna went still at the sound. She recognized it.

It was the same tune the Druid whistled, and it was the roots of the song Cassiel played on his flute.

Silent tears rolled down Elia's face. It was all she could do but hold him close to her heart. Dyna cried as she listened to a mother gently hum to her son. His mother held him, knowing it would be for the last time, and in that heartrending song was the sound of love and grief.

Cassiel's memories grew darker after she left.

He wandered the cold halls of the Hilos castle searching for something he couldn't find. Yoel wandered them, too. But the absence of Elia rendered him a ghost, and he seemed to have forgotten about his son.

Dyna found Cassiel sitting on his balcony, staring at the horizon day after day, season after season. And the light in his eyes dimmed.

He had lost both parents.

Abandoned by one.

Ignored by the other.

Terrorized by the ones who did acknowledge his existence. She could feel the hurt left by the hollowness in his heart.

I was so angry with him. Cassiel's voice filtered around her. *For so long. I blamed him for my mother leaving. For the way they treated me. I blamed him for everything.*

Memories flashed around her of Cassiel much older. A fourteen, perhaps. Yoel came to realize what he had done to his son and tried to mend their relationship. But Cassiel turned his back on his father each time.

I wanted nothing to do with him.

She appeared in Hermon during the winter. Cassiel stood in the courtyard, watching Yoel fly away. *Whenever he came to visit me, I would elude him until he left. Then I would stand here and blame him for abandoning me once again.*

The dream smoke dropped her in Skelling Rise, within the manor. Cassiel held him in his arms as Yoel faded away into light. All that remained was the blood on his hands.

Everything darkened, leaving him alone on his knees on that bloodied floor.

When I finally let go of my anger, he was gone before I could say I was sorry. Before I could say goodbye. His body didn't stay long enough to grow cold. To even accept that it happened. It didn't feel real. So I made it not real. Because I still ... I still needed him.

She nodded, her lip quivering. Yes, he had still needed his father. As she had still needed hers.

Dyna tried to approach him, but her foot went through the floor, and she was falling among the stars. She landed in a dark corridor. Little Cassiel ran past her, and she followed, calling his name. But she lost sight of him, and the world seemed to stretch no matter how fast she ran.

Everyone I love leaves. They die because of me. My father. My mother. You.

I'm still here! She called out. *Cassiel, I'm here!*

Dyna at last reached the end, and she found herself in a garden with an Azure tree. Hilos again.

The sound of distant laughter lured her to a scene with Elia holding up a baby boy against the sun, laughing as she nuzzled his little face. Yoel was with them, watching with a smile not yet burdened by it all.

Of all people, she deserved happiness.

Cassiel, a six-year-old boy again, now sat in the garden by himself. He stared at the empty spot where his family used to be. *Before I knew it, everyone was gone, and I was left in the silence.* His head lowered, dark hair curtaining his face. *There will never be a day where we will be together again. We will never be happy like that again ... because of me. And I couldn't take it. I couldn't bear to remember what I had done to them. I was alone, and I didn't know what I lived for anymore.*

Dyna went to him and knelt in front of that little boy. She reached for his cheek, and it was solid against her palm. Tears rolled down his face as he looked up at her. "'You are only a memory I wish to forget'. I said those words to him ... and then I killed him."

"Oh, no. You didn't, Cassiel. You didn't." Dyna pulled him into her arms. His entire body shook with sobs, and he clutched onto her with trembling arms.

"They're gone." The broken words tumbled out of him. "No one is home."

As he cried in her arms like a lost child, Dyna finally understood why Cassiel left. Because he had the utter, mind-numbing fear she would die because of him, too. And no part of him could ever endure that. It tore at her heart, and her tears joined his.

Closing her eyes, Dyna let her shield fall.

She reached in through the bond and shoved aside all the darkness, all the blame and guilt, and held the little boy who had no one. Who was rejected for being Nephilim. Who lost his mother and father. Who grew up into a young man too afraid to trust others or to love until he found it. Then he loved so much that he gave up everything out of fear of losing it, even when it destroyed him.

The pieces of his soul lay scattered on the ground around him like shards of glass. That very soul already died for her once before because they had promised to find each other again.

And they had.

"You're not alone, Cassiel," Dyna murmured to him, stroking his hair. "I'm home."

CHAPTER 87

Dynalya

Dyna kept her fingers over Cassiel's pulse, counting each steady beat. He was so still. He didn't dream anymore. When she attempted to dream walk again, there was nothing there. She told herself it was simply because his mind was resting at last. So she could only pray that the life force she had given him had been enough.

She had poured everything into him. Found reservoirs of Essence she didn't know she had, and she was nearly drained. Dyna leaned back in her chair, blinking tiredly at Cassiel's enchanted tent. The rush of the falling cascades was all that kept her company as she waited.

It had been two days without change. If he didn't wake, Dyna didn't know what she would do.

Something soft brushed against her ankles, and she yelped. A blue fox with a gem on its forehead yipped at her.

She smiled tiredly. "Oh, hello, sweet one. What are you doing here?"

Azulo scampered outside. Dyna followed and found Leoake outside by her campfire, sampling the vegetable broth she'd been cooking.

Dyna frowned. "I was wondering when you would return for the key."

"You were successful, I take it."

She didn't answer, aware of the weight in her pocket.

Leoake returned the ladle to the pot and took a seat in the nook of a tree, reclining back as if it were a comfortable chair—or better yet, a throne. He crossed his legs. The light glinted on the gold rings adorning his fingers and pointed ears. "And now you are contemplating ways to keep it."

"It's certainly a thing of value to hold the key to Mount Ida's door. Primarily given that said door opens to the In Between." Dyna reached into her pocket and pulled out the two broken pieces in her palm. "I know what you plan, Leoake, but I will sooner destroy this key than allow your schemes to be realized."

He laughed. "Is that so?"

"You were shifty with your words when we made our first deal, and I listened to them carefully when you came to initiate it. Our agreement was that I *retrieve* the key. You said nothing about returning it to you."

His golden eyes narrowed. "Clever."

"I thought you might think so. It's unlike you to make a mistake.

"Who said it was a mistake?"

Dyna stilled at the smirk playing on his lips.

"As it happens, I no longer have a need for the key. For you see, what you traded to save your mate's life gives me exactly what I need."

"What do you mean? The Sol Medallion can open the door to the In Between?"

The Druid canted his head, and that same smile slithered across his lips. The smile that told her she was a fool. "I never mentioned a medallion. In your panic, you failed to listen carefully the second time we made a deal."

She stared at him, her body growing cold.

"You traded your greatest wish, which is indeed a treasure, but not the kind you would think. And not one that would come to be … if your mate had died."

Her insides twisted with muted horror.

I care nothing for gold and jewels. He had told her that before, and the fae couldn't lie.

"I was referring to a precious treasure you had a long time ago, in another life."

Dyna's heart pounded, her chest rising and falling as she fought to breathe. She stumbled back, her vision skewing. "No."

Leoake tutted, shaking his head at her. "Not so clever after all, are you?"

Dyna looked back at the tent. Cassiel had already lost so much, and she had now taken a part of his future from him before they ever knew what it was. She pressed her shaking fists into her stomach, feeling the urge to vomit.

"No need to fret yet. You won't give birth to my prize for several more years." He shrugged. "Well, given that you survive the island. There is plenty of time before you need to tell your mate you have bargained away his firstborn son."

Son. Her *son*.

Dyna stifled a sound that was between a scream and a whimper that tore from her gut. She sank to her knees in the wet grass facing the tent, too shocked to do anything but stare at the canvas.

"Why?" she asked shakily. "Why do you want my child?"

"Why do you think your son's first life ended before he could be born? A half-breed is one thing, but can you imagine what power the progeny of a sorceress and a Seraph would have? Your son will wield unimaginable power unlike anything this realm has ever beheld before." Leoake grinned, eyes eerily glowing. "Like his mother who can cross into dreams, he will cross into *worlds*."

Dyna shook. "You already knew this would happen."

"Of course. I *see* everything." Leoake cackled. "You have the same look in your eyes the first time you unintentionally bargained your son's life away. Sheli wasn't so clever." With an exaggerated sigh, he slumped back as if he were exhausted. "It took very careful planning to ensure every piece fell into place exactly as needed for this moment. Beginning with leading Rawn to Xián Jīng and veiling his memories, to influencing every step you and your Guardians took after that, until now. So try to stay alive in the meantime, fair maid. If you or your mate die, I will be forced to wait another age to try again."

Dyna's fingers tightened over the bronze pieces in her hand, and it burned in her shaking fists.

He did this to her. To them.

All to merely to steal her unborn child.

"Well, not all is lost if you do die." Leoake tapped his chin thoughtfully. "I have other progenies out there who may serve me fine if you do. Consider it my contingency plan."

"You are truly evil, aren't you?"

A mischievous smile spread across his delicate features as he rose to his feet. "How can you expect me to be anything short of *wicked*? If you thought the end of this journey would have a happy ending, well, then you haven't been very heedful."

Goosebumps prickled her skin with his insinuation.

Soft fur rubbed against Dyna's arms, and Azulo looked up at her, whining. Conveying something he couldn't say with words.

The Druid can see all fates but his own.

Dyna opened her fist. The bronze key had reforged itself into one piece again, mended by her broken heart and her rage.

Leoake approached to pick up Azulo, running his fingers through his blue fur. "Sometimes, the strings of fate cannot be unwoven from the web. Yet there are times when all we are left with are choices. When the time comes to relinquish your greatest wish to me, I will remind you again that you chose this." He turned to go. "Until then."

Taking a breath, Dyna rose to her feet. "You keep mentioning the way of fate," she said. "I am continuously told how my life is meant to be, but in this life, I have already decided I alone will shape my fate."

She spun around and jammed the key into Leoake's right eye.

Screams tore from his mouth, and he flailed back, dropping Azulo.

"You didn't foresee that coming," Dyna hissed. She tore out the key, letting it drop to the ground with a dull thud.

The Druid blindly stumbled for the forest, his screams echoing through the trees. His blood glistened on the grass like drops of rubies, surrounding his golden eye and the key.

The geas throbbed painfully on her wrist. It bound her throughout the known universe, but she swore to find a way to break it.

"Tell your master my son is not his to have," Dyna said, meeting the blue fox's frightened gaze. "The next time he comes, I will take his other eye."

CHAPTER 88

Rawn

The gentle patter of rain against glass drew Rawn to consciousness. Cool wind brushed against his cheek. The air. He knew this air. It smelled like rain and freshly cut grass. It smelled like the trees he once climbed as a boy. Sweet like the flowers that filled the castle gardens. He blinked blearily at the open window, curtains billowing in the breeze.

Distant voices drew him to look at the door cracked slightly open.

"Have the castle send more fresh linens and clean water."

The sound of that voice rocked Rawn's chest. He was dreaming again, as he had hundreds of times before.

"If the healer is available, please send him to see his lordship again. He needs more tending..." The door opened, and a lovely woman stepped in with a servant, carrying a tray.

She halted when she saw him. His wife. His Aerina. The tray dropped from her hands with a crash, and she bolted for the bed with a cry.

He reached out and caught her, wincing as he did.

"I feared I would never see you again." She wept. "Then I feared you would never wake."

Rawn held her tight, breathing her in, feeling how solid she was. "I fear this is another dream."

Her wet eyes looked up at him, and she laughed wetly. Aerina kissed his cheek, his forehead, his nose. "Does that feel real to you?"

Rawn nodded, his vision blurring.

"I was there with you beneath the keep," she said, weeping. "Not only in spirit, but in your dreams. I called out to you, my love."

The whole time he thought they had been dreams he conjured to stave off the madness threatening to consume him in that pit. But she had been the one saving him.

"I heard you, Aerina. Your voice saved me from the darkness." Rawn pulled her to him, his arms trembling. He pressed his forehead to hers, trying and failing not to pathetically weep. "I carried your absence within the hollow of my bones. There was not a day that went by where you have not occupied my thoughts. However far I was across the world, my heart remained here with you."

Aerina didn't speak. How could she when she shook with heaving sobs? Half of him still feared it was a dream. But she was in his arms, solid and warm, sharing the air he breathed. Nothing else felt more real than this.

Rawn thanked the Gods and thanked the fates. He thanked every star in the universe for this gift.

Then he broke down, too.

It took another day of rest before Rawn was well enough for visitors. First came Zev and Keena. The Lycan was quiet in his relief. He took a seat in the chair beside him and filled him in on everything that had happened from the moment of his capture to the events of their excursion across Greenwood, and coming to his rescue in Red Highland.

"The prisoner with me," Rawn murmured, his voice still a little weak. "Elon. Did he make it?"

Zev nodded. "He crossed with us to Avandia."

"His sister came as well," Keena chimed in. "It's the talk of the castle. Apparently Garaea was King Leif's second contact. She petitioned for immunity for herself and her brother, in exchange for the other half of the key. They wanted a safe place to escape their father. But the key was lost when the Blood Keep came down." She and Zev exchanged a look, and Rawn nodded that he understood. When he had nearly died from casting the Blood Scythe, he remembered exactly what he had done with the second half of the key. "Regardless, King Leif has allowed Elon and Garaea to stay. I suppose he isn't so terrible, after all."

"Eldred went to Dwarf Shoe to find Sylar," Zev mentioned. "With Elon to accompany him. He was beside himself with the news of his son's survival, let alone that he's with a red elf. But I think Eldred was pleased to learn he's a grandfather."

Rawn chuckled tiredly at that. "I'm certain he was."

"Von has joined us, too. Dyna has finally gathered all her Guardians." Zev looked pensive about that. Not against it as he once was, and Rawn wondered what changed.

"He came to your aid, if you recall," Keena said.

Rawn nodded. He would have to thank him.

"Lucenna wanted to come visit you, but she was hurt during the battle. The healers are doing well to treat her. Klyde hasn't left her side. And Cassiel..." Keena's smile faded, and her wings drooped. "He was terribly wounded. Dyna took him to the Melodyam Falls."

Rawn looked at Zev worriedly. "What happened?"

Zev's brow tightened, and he lowered his gaze. "Cassiel ... lost a wing during the battle. He was bleeding profusely. Taking him there may have been the only way to save him, but I don't know if they made it. It's been a few days. I haven't heard from her."

Which was alarming, because Dyna had a water mirror. Was there a reason she had not contacted them yet? Rawn could see from Zev's worried expression that he was anxious to leave and search for them.

"I will speak with the king," Rawn said. Out of decorum, he had to await his dismissal first.

Aerina entered with a tray of food, and Zev stood.

"That is enough for today, Keena. We should leave Rawn to rest." He gently scooped up the fairy in his palm and placed her on his shoulder.

Taking the petals of her dress, she curtsied. "It was a pleasure to see you again, Lord Norrlen."

"And you, princess." Rawn chuckled. When they turned to go, he called, "Zev."

The tall Lycan paused.

Rawn smiled, feeling so immensely grateful as he took Aerina's hand. "Thank you."

With a bow of his head, Zev quietly slipped into the hall.

Drawing back the covers, Rawn invited Aerina to bed. She lay beside him, curling into his chest as he held her in his arms. There was one who had not come to see him yet, and he was afraid to ask why. But his wife, his bonded soul, looked up at her with her big blue eyes, and she knew.

"Give him time."

He couldn't have expected a perfect reunion. After leaving them for so long, what else could his son feel but disgruntlement and resentment?

"Can you forgive me, my love?" Rawn murmured, cupping her face. "For not caring for you as a husband should. For leaving you to raise our son alone. For leaving you without my protection. My greatest regret was placing my oath to my country above our vows. All these years I despised myself for leaving, knowing there was a chance it could be forever." Her eyes welled as his did. "I am not worthy of being your husband or his father. I deserve your scorn and his aversion. I deserve to have my name stricken from your lips. But I still beg you to forgive me. You must have wished to have never married me, but without you, I am nothing at all."

"Oh, Rawn." She buried her face in his chest. "In all my years, there is only one thing I have ever been sure of. And that was the day I chose to spend my life with you."

He held her close, feeling so undeserving of her. Yet so thankful to finally be reunited again. "How have you and Raiden been in my absence?"

She lowered her gaze and hid her face against his chest.

"Aerina?"

"I have much to tell you."

By the third day, Rawn was well enough to move from the bed, though it was painful and difficult. The wounds on his feet were mending. He frowned at the small round table by the window, calculating how many steps it would take to walk to it. He wouldn't regain his strength by lounging in bed all day.

A knock came at the door.

He looked up as a guard opened it, and King Leif entered.

"There is no need to stand," Leif said, offering him a polite smile. "I am pleased to see you in better health, Rawn. It has been some time. How are you?"

Rawn shifted his head in a slight bow. "Alive, sire. I cannot ask for more than that."

"You have not changed." Leif chuckled and went to the windows, gazing out at the city of Avandia. "Do you remember anything?"

"I remember many things, the most prevalent being the blade held at my son's *throat*." Rawn's voice came out low, tight. "You used him in your ploy against Altham. Do not say it was for me when you have only held an interest in pursuing your own aims."

Lief faced him, his expression cool. "I understand your ire, Rawn, but mind your tongue when speaking to your king. The trade was a ruse. Altham was careful in his oath, as I was in mine. If he hadn't been so eager to fool me, he would have seen through my oath. I promised to bring your son to a wedding for the princess, not that Raiden would marry her. God of

Urn as my witness, I never intended it to pass." His shoulders slumped a little, the only sign of his guilt. "I am sorry I had to keep it from Aerina. I couldn't risk the chance it would reach Altham."

Rawn took a breath, taming the spark of his anger, but only a little. "You put our son in danger."

"I did, and I am sorry."

"I am told there was an issue with the Accords as well."

An unexpected sheepishness crossed Leif's face. "I suppose I may have intentionally angered the High King and Queen of Hilos in hopes they would defy me and arrive as reinforcements. Nonetheless, they made that decision on their own without my knowledge."

Leif found a way around his oath without breaking it. As Rawn's oath was not broken, for he had not returned to Greenwood by choice, they brought him here.

But Rawn wasn't sure if he could believe that was the extent of Leif's plans. "To what end? To get a hold of Altham's half of the key?"

Leif studied him carefully. "Do you have the second half?"

"I do not." And he could say so confidently.

His gray eyes narrowed. "The key opens the door which contains the Dragon's Fang and the Dragon's Eye. Keeping it from me would renege on your oath."

Rawn's lips pursed tightly together. He was no oathbreaker, and such an insinuation insulted everything he had done for the crown. "Sire, I have sworn my fealty to you for the good of the kingdom. I gave you an oath to not return until I found the Dragon's Fang, and I paid for that promise with years of my life. However, I never promised you a key. Greenwood does not need such dark power. It would only corrupt all that is pure here. There is a reason it was broken, for no one is meant to open that door."

Leif became pensive and crossed his arms as he watched the fire burn in the hearth for a long moment. "Red Highland was not always sand. It was once an oasis with many maple trees which turned red in the Autumn, giving the highlands the illusion of crimson seas. Their greed for power killed their land. Thank you for reminding me of that." He turned to him. "Be that as it may..."

Rawn inhaled a breath. "I must still find the Dragon Blades."

"Unfortunately, Altham still lives. Auxiliary forces arrived as we were crossing through the Elder Tree, and I was forced to release him." His cool eyes met Rawn's. "You killed his son and heir. Red Highland will never forget. Greenwood must prepare for their reprisal."

That meant war was coming.

It had always been inevitable, but his capture had accelerated it.

Leif moved from the window to stand before him. "You have served more than enough time on this mission, Rawn. Thus, I am permitting you to bequeath your oath to another."

Rawn blinked. "Another?"

"Raiden has endeavored to go to Mount Ida in your stead."

He sucked in a shaky breath, swallowing to control the outrage building in his chest. *"No."*

"Of course, I assumed as much. No respectable father would burden his son with his duties. Be that as it may, you have done plenty for the crown, and there is no dishonor in stepping down. As I understand it, you became great acquaintances with Elon. He declares to owe you a great debt and has proposed to inherit your oath once he returns."

"Thus giving you ownership of his life as you have owned mine?"

Leif raised his chin. "I think it is time that you stay with your family, Rawn. I am setting you free."

And chaining others.

"By all means ponder it," Leif said at his silence. "Take the remainder of the season for a holiday. Rest and decide what you want."

"At the moment, I wish to return home, sire." Rawn stood. "I have been away from Sellav for too long, and there are matters I must settle. All I ask is one favor from you. Spread the rumor of my demise."

Raising his eyebrows, the king gave him a nod. "You have my leave."

"I'm told two had attempted to capture my wife in Evos. I would like to question them before I go."

"I'm afraid that is not possible," Leif said as he strode for the door. "They quietly passed through the Gates the day after their arrest. No one harms my sister and keeps the privilege of life." He paused there, a slight smile hovering on the edge of his mouth. "Do give Lord Karheim my regards."

Rawn could have asked to be sent home through the Elder Tree, but he had not been in his country in so long, he was content to travel the land and see how much it had changed. And perhaps, he secretly hoped to bond with his son on the journey.

Yet he and his wife had to travel by carriage for discretion, and Raiden chose to ride with the escort instead. Joining them were his friends, the Ranger Regiment, and a handful of Valkyrie.

As they left the castle, Aerina glanced outside and softly gasped. The path was lined with Greenwood soldiers in decorative armor. As they passed them by, Lieutenant Handuril called, "*Order arms!*" The men saluted by drawing their blades and resting them diagonally across their hearts.

Emotion stirred in Rawn's chest, and Aerina laid her head on his shoulder. "Greenwood honors you."

But Rawn questioned if he was worthy of such honor. He had yet to complete his mission. To return home now with so much time gone, it made those years lost seem pointless.

Rawn stole glances of Raiden from the windows when he could. His son was strong, healthy, and handsome, if he could be so proud to say. Raiden had also wielded magic at an admirable level. Rawn spent the journey asking Aerina about him, and she told him everything. Raiden's schooling, his likes and dislikes, his habits that were so similar to his.

"He favors magic," she murmured to him on the night they had left Evos behind. "Eldred was his teacher, and he proved to be very proficient in all he set his mind to. Like his father." She ran the back of her fingers over Rawn's cheek, his head resting on her lap. "Raiden completed his apprenticeship at fourteen. He became the youngest Magi Master in the kingdom. Thereafter, he dedicated his time to overseeing Sellav and all its holdings. He did his duty to represent our House while you were away. Your subjects never wanted for anything."

Then Rawn was truly glowing with pride. "Of course he did. He's a Norrlen."

They reached the Melodyam Falls the following day. The ruins had been half buried in a mudslide, but the cascades remained.

A lonesome tent waited by the cascades.

The carriage wheels creaked as they rolled to a stop. Riders dismounted outside, and voices called out for Dyna.

Rawn quickly stepped down out of the carriage. The tent flaps parted, and Dyna rushed outside. Her wide eyes took them all in and when she saw him, her eyes welled with tears.

"Lord Norrlen, you made it."

"I did, my lady." He held out his arms, and she rushed into them. Dyna cried as he and the Guardians hugged her between them. "Thank you for bringing me home."

CHAPTER 89

Lucenna

Lucenna locked her gaze on the straw target set out in the open field not far from the Norrlen Estate. A sheen of sweat coated her forehead as she drew on her Essence again. A crackle of purple light gathered between her hands, and she winced. The light winked out.

Lucenna groaned up at the sky.

"Do they still hurt?" Dyna asked from where she sat on a blanket in the grass, Azeran's journal on her lap.

To her complete embarrassment, Lucenna had broken her right arm and both legs during the battle at the Blood Keep. Elvish medicine had mended her well in Avandia, and Dyna mended her bones once they reunited. It had been two weeks since they arrived in Sellav, but her limbs still ached.

"It's becoming a nuisance now." Lucenna scowled at herself. She stretched her arms and bent to touch her toes.

"It will take some time for your body to fully heal. It's fortunate you weren't left with a limp."

They all had a lot of healing to do. Some more than others. Dyna's green eyes lifted to the estate, a forlorn look on her face.

"He still hasn't woken?" Lucenna sat beside her.

She shook her head. "I think after living for more than three months carrying the weight in his heart and the illusion in his mind, his body is forcing him to rest."

But Lucenna could tell that's what Dyna had to tell herself. The truth was, Cassiel might not wake anytime soon—if at all.

"And his wounds?"

"They have finished mending." Dyna took a breath and stared down at the journal. She wanted to be strong for him, because if Cassiel woke, he would have to deal with the loss of his wing.

He would never fly again.

Lucenna could only imagine how painful that would be for him. Without magic, she would have lost use of her legs. She wouldn't have been able to cope with the anger and misery if she couldn't walk again.

"Perhaps I did something wrong when I dream walked into his memories," Dyna said. "The place I crossed through ... it was something divergent. Has Lucien discovered anything yet?"

It was a mystery Lucenna and her brother had spent many nights discussing since Dyna described it to them.

"Not yet. You dreamed walked into his past life, which has never been done before. Lucien's theory is that you may have crossed into another level of the *Essentia Dimensio*. It's already a subconscious dimension we know very little about. He will continue researching."

Dyna nodded thoughtfully. Lucenna was excited about what this discovery could mean.

And what's more, Lucien informed them that the Liberation was ready to begin sending refugees to Skelling Rise. The ships were set to make their voyages in the summer.

"Lucenna, what does *ianua* mean?" Dyna asked, frowning at the journal.

She perked up at the old tongue of Magos and scooted closer to her, observing the faded script written by Azeran's hand. "*Ianua* means door."

"I read this before, but I didn't understand what Azeran meant because I was wrong in my translations. I thought he meant a vault or gate, but he was talking about a locked doorway! This must mean Azeran saw the door to the In Between on Mount Ida." Her wide green eyes met hers. "Azulo told me this door leads to other worlds. That is exactly what Leoake is after."

Lucenna's mind spun at the concept of other worlds. It was both unimaginable and startling. To think the universe was so much bigger than she imagined made her feel insignificantly small. And she also worried what the Druid could be scheming.

"How did you come to that conclusion?"

Something fleetingly crossed Dyna's eyes, and she looked away. "What else could he want with that door?"

"Then why did he leave the key with you?"

"Perhaps he forgot to ask for it."

"Hmm." Unlikely. That Druid schemed as much as Tarn. They were all devastated to learn of his survival. But while they were in Greenwood, they wouldn't worry about him yet.

Dyna handed her the journal. "These lines here. I can't make sense of them. They almost seem like incantations."

"What?" Lucenna studied the words on the page, and they did seem like spoken spells. "That can't be right. Mages don't use incantations."

"Except I use one to unlock the journal," Dyna reminded her. *"Tellūs, lūnam, sōlis."*

"That's a passphrase, not an incantation."

"I spoke an elf incantation on Tarn's boat when I fought Lumina."

Lucenna gaped at her. "Dyna ... we can't wield elf magic. That could have been dangerous."

She shrugged. "My Essence was locked away. Even if it was free, there was no intent behind the words, and as you said, we cannot cast incantations. But I do wonder what these are." She tapped on the page.

Lucenna frowned. "I will speak to Lucien about this as well."

A new orb had arrived for her last week. It was made of the highest quality crystal and matched the purple of her eyes. There was no note with the package, but she knew who it was from.

Clearing her throat, Lucenna brushed her silver hair away from her face. "Azeran filled these pages with many learnings and secrets. I suppose it may be difficult to decipher what it means." She flipped through the journal. "Where is the map?"

She had passed it on to Zev, then lost track of who held it now.

"Klyde has it."

Lucenna's jaw dropped. "What?"

Dyna shrugged with a small chuckle. "Von had it for a time, and well, you told Klyde about Mount Ida, so it seemed fitting."

"Have you also told him about the prophecy?" At her nod, Lucenna groaned. "What happened to the ill-tempered girl who trusted no one?"

Dyna cracked a smile. "She reminded herself what integrity meant and who her true friends are."

Which, of course, was such a relief. Tetchy Dyna was so unbearable. She had her old friend back, her very *trusting* friend.

"I think after all Klyde has done, he has earned our trust, don't you think?"

Frowning, Lucenna glanced at the estate.

That ridiculous man aided them in many ways. Then Klyde took care of her when she had fallen unconscious at the Blood Keep. He had been there every day of her recovery, helping her learn how to walk again—even when she yelled at him and told him to leave her alone. She later discovered that when Anon's spell hit, Klyde had shielded her with his body.

The only reason he survived it was due to the four-leaf clover in his pocket.

He had heard their trust.

"I think he feels guilty," Lucenna muttered. "I keep finding that damn clover everywhere, no matter how many times I return it."

A teasing smile rose to Dyna's face. "I think he feels more than that, Lucenna. And so do you."

It would be a lie to say she hadn't imagined kissing him again, but it was pointless. They couldn't be together for many reasons. Even if she proposed a tryst with no commitment, she would be in denial to believe it didn't mean anything.

"How long are you going to keep avoiding him?" Dyna asked.

"For as long as Raiden keeps avoiding Rawn."

They exchanged a frown.

"Have you spoken to him?" Lucenna asked.

Dyna sighed at her hands, empty of any rings. "He hasn't been around, and well, I have been busy as well." She glanced at the Estate. "I must go check on Cassiel."

She never left him alone for too long.

Rising to her feet, Dyna tucked the journal back into her satchel. She took a step to go but paused. "Lucenna, I lent Klyde the map because he wanted to mark a path for us to best reach the train station in Ledoga." She hesitated, biting her lip. "He's leaving."

Lucenna inhaled a faint breath.

Of course he was.

When they had all reunited again, Dyna told them Tarn was alive. That meant Klyde had to take Tavin back to Skelling Rise for his protection. She didn't expect him to stay as long as he did, yet the news settled like stones in her stomach.

"Good," Lucenna retorted, as she looked away. "Now I will no longer have to suffer his countenance and crude jests."

But the statement sounded flat even to her own ears. Dyna said nothing more, and her soft steps faded away.

Getting back to her feet, Lucenna stretched as she eyed the targets again. She tried and failed to push Klyde from her mind. Who cared that he was leaving?

Her veins hummed with her pent-up Essence, and her hands flared purple with coils of electricity. She was glad he was leaving. He would only get in her way.

Volts shot out of her hands and obliterated the target, scorching a large hole in the field. She cringed. Oops.

"Was that intended to be a spell?"

Lucenna rolled her eyes and glowered at Eldred standing behind her. To her surprise, two little Elven boys with dark hair held his hands. Sylar's children. She recognized them from Dwarf Shoe. The grumpy old mage beamed with a rare smile.

"Oh, you're back."

He gently patted his grandsons on their heads. "Go on and return to your father. I have a lesson to teach."

The boys ran off giggling toward the estate where Sylar, Elon, and Garaea were speaking to the Norrlens. Rawn had graciously invited them to live in Sellav. It was a peaceful and secluded place to raise a family.

Eldred came to her side. "You have much to learn, young one."

Pursing her mouth, Lucenna crossed her arms. "I told you. I already know how to use magic. Clearly, you see I'm powerful."

"Wielding magic is not what makes you powerful. True power lies in mastering yourself. I have observed you since your arrival, Lady Lucenna. Yes, you are quite strong, but what you lack is finesse."

Gray light spiraled around Eldred's hand as he pointed it at the next target, and he murmured soft words under his breath. Lightning speared out like a rapid snake and pierced the target perfectly. The spell burned a hole clean through it without destroying the target or the field.

Such a simple but effective example of what he had been trying to tell her before. Lucenna was used to casting her magic in a raw, uncontrolled blast. Powerful, yes, but compared to him, clearly untrained. She'd been fortunate to win her battles by sheer power alone.

"How much you despise your enemy does not make you stronger or weaker, for a battle is not only won by strength but by strategy," Eldred said. "When you are to attack or defend, one must consider the individual elements of the spell and your intent. Something yet to be learned." He folded his arms behind his back as he canted his head, studying her pensively. "Have you considered speaking your spells?"

She frowned in bemusement. "I'm not an elf, Eldred. We do not cast incantations. Whatever spells you've mastered are Elvish spells I cannot wield. Mage magic and elf magic are dissimilar. You know this."

601

Eldred chuckled. "And yet the same. We draw Essence from nature, and your kind draws it from yourselves. Our magic cannot mix, for energies change once it passes through us. Yet the same type of power created it—life force. Which is found in all living things." With a soft murmur in Elvish, a handful of leaves at his feet fluttered up into the air, leisurely spinning above his palm. "Have you wondered why mages can levitate with a thought and elves with a word?"

"Our intent is directed by our minds," Lucenna said, watching the leaves spin. "Elves speak their spells to direct their intent."

"Yes, to direct it *precisely*. To build the spell with one finite purpose with word and rune, and to execute this purpose without error." Turning away from her, she felt the pull of power as Eldred chanted, *"Sajoh noi'cativel, es'recah sadapes yat'roc."*

A hexagon built around his hand, blazing with runes. Instead of aiming at the target, he aimed at a boulder. The leaves shot forth, piercing stone.

Lucenna gaped at the small green blades and imagined them slicing through a body. He had done that with *leaves*.

The presence of his Essence charged the air. His power was on a different level than she had ever felt before. It surpassed her father's and her uncle's.

"There was a time when your kind once did the same," Eldred said.

"Mages?" she asked in bewilderment.

"*Sorceresses.*"

Lucenna's breath caught. No one outside of Magos used that word. "When?"

"Before Magos relied solely on thought and the crutch of crystals. Before the spoken spell was replaced by enchanted artifacts." He glanced at her hands clenched in shaking fists. "Before the women of Magos were bound."

Lucenna's eyes widened, her heart racing. "How do you know this?"

"A long time ago, when the Vale of the Elves was under one kingdom, your people used to come here to study incantations in our schools. It was organized, structured magic. Not spells thrown at a whim like a child splashing in a pool. This was a discipline lost to your people when they lost their way."

The mere thought of women being allowed to study magic made her eyes sting. Lucenna could almost picture it. Sorceresses within schools, creating incredible spells with only their words. "Why did we stop?"

Mages could have kept coming even if women were no longer allowed to study magic.

Eldred cast another spell, and a glowing pentagram formed on the ground around them, spreading with rings of several runes. More than she had ever seen before. "Merely speaking a spell is not enough. The practice begins with learning to form the array in your mind and carefully placing the runes. Not one can be out of place, or the spell will falter. Perhaps this is the most difficult. It takes many rigorous years of study to master such complex magic, but never could a mage hold to the caliber of a sorceress. They were talented in this somehow, surpassing to a level they could not reach. Most never needed to use a staff."

Therefore, Mages removed the practice of incantations because they would have indeed never gained control of them if sorceresses could fight back with a single word.

Her pulse was drumming in her ears, her veins heating with rage. Electricity sparked around her clenched fists. The empire had bound them in so many ways, they never had a chance.

"Why are you telling me this?"

Eldred turned to her with a smile. "It has been quite some time since I have had the opportunity to teach a student with the means to surpass their potential. You have the makings to become a great sorceress, Lucenna. I would be honored to teach you."

CHAPTER 90

Von

"You decided to go, then?" Von asked as he took a drink from his mug.

"Aye," Klyde replied. He looked up at the windows of the estate that glowed with candlelight. The croak of frogs and the chirp of nightlife filled the garden. "Now that I know Tarn is still out there, I need to take Tavin back to the one place he can't reach him."

Because Tavin had both Morken blood and blood of the Ice Phoenix. That put his life in danger.

Zev tossed another log into the stone fire pit they sat around. The flames hissed, scattering embers into the chilly night. "If the worst comes to happen, and Tarn learns about the boy, what will you do?"

The firelight gleamed in Klyde's stony eyes. "There is nothing I wouldn't do for Tavin. No sin I wouldn't commit."

Including spilling the blood of his kinsmen. There was no need for it, however, because Von had already decided it would be his blade that would pierce Tarn's heart.

"When the time comes, I will not hesitate," he said.

They shared a long look, and Klyde nodded. The mercenary leaned forward on his knees, and Von glimpsed the Skelling sigil on his shoulder pauldron. Dyna mentioned to him the mercenary had a Skelling talon. A last resort if Tarn succeeded in becoming immortal. Von prayed it didn't come to that.

"Tarn can't enter Greenwood," Keena said as she fluttered above them. "Tavin is safe for the time being if you want to stay a little longer."

The king had given Rawn permission to remain in Sellav until the end of the season, and the rest decided they would stay as well. To heal and to give him time with his family.

A pensive expression crossed Klyde's face as he glanced at the estate again. It was the sorceress he thought of. Von had noticed their lingering looks braided between each moment they were together.

"I think you should go," Von said, because he felt Tavin's safety should come first. "Though it would be a lie to say I won't miss the lad. He's quite the pest."

They chuckled. Over the days, he had grown fond of the boy who always seemed to follow him around with his endless questions and curiosity. At first it was too hard to be around Tavin. He had his father's eyes and features, but that was where the likeness ended.

"He's exactly like her," Von murmured. The moon reflected off the surface of ale in his mug, and he looked up at the night sky. "To know that a piece of Aisling lives on is a gift. Thank you..." His voice wavered, and he met Klyde's gaze. "For doing what I couldn't."

"I ... never did thank you for saving his life."

"Don't." Von fixed wet eyes on the fire, hearing distant screams. "Saving him doesn't repay all the lives lost because of me."

He knew many last words, but he would never know Yavi's. She haunted him in the ocean wind and in the flare of flame. Dalton and Geon, they haunted him in Tavin's laughter, in the shine of his youth.

I stole many lives, it gave no value to mine," Von told them. "When I try to imagine my future, I see none. Somehow, I think you understand me, or I am merely a rambling drunk fool."

Keena flew down to land on Zev's shoulder. Klyde fell still as they looked at him. They didn't answer, but their expressions said they understood.

Von rubbed the tightness in his chest, feeling weightless without his bandoliers. He had spent many years carrying the weight of his knives and the blood they spilled. "At the end of this journey, I don't know what comes next. I don't think anything does. But if the lass finds her medallion, and I end Tarn like I plan, I will have fulfilled my part in this prophecy. What comes after? What else is there?" He smiled sardonically, and Keena gave his cheek a little pat of comfort. To Zev, he said, "You asked me why I am here. I came because I plan to die, be it with Tarn on that island if it comes to it." He finished his drink and set it down as he stood. "If I survive, that will be the end of my purpose, and likely my life. I have no use for it."

"Don't say that," Keena said sadly when he made for the path. Her yellow wings drooped. "You may think you don't have anything left, Von. But we are still here."

He paused for a moment, taking in the Guardians who fought to be there for each other. They were a strong circle of friends.

And maybe ... his friends too.

Von continued walking down the gravel path lit by lanterns. His chest clenched at the sight of them because it reminded him too much of his last night on that ship. He thought of that night many times and what he could have done differently to save Yavi and Geon. But he had made too many mistakes. Starting with going into Tarn's quarters.

His mind flashed with a memory of the golden Xián Jīng chest and teapot that had rested within.

Von rushed inside the estate to find Dyna. His search ended in the library where he spotted her sitting at a table buried by a pile of books. Her belongings were scattered around her, along with the bronze key and the pearlescent water mirror. The candles flickering on the stands shone over her short red hair.

Glowing lanterns hung from the ceiling, illuminating the walls full of books and greenery in the alcoves. The open glass doors allowed for fresh air and the sweet scents of the garden.

Von walked past the tree that grew in the center of the library and approached Dyna's table. "Up for late reading, lass?"

"Oh, good evening, Commander." She sighed tiredly and shook her head at the tome open in front of her. "Nothing here can help me wake Cassiel. I have tried mugwort, clematis, and bach flowers. Nothing works. I am a Herb Master. I studied everything there is to know but this. So why can't I..."

Von sat in the empty leather chair across from her. "You're worried he will never wake?"

"I have to hold faith he will." Dyna sighed again and rubbed her eyes. "Sorry, you came here to tell me something, not to hear me ramble. What's on your mind?"

"Tarn."

Closing the book, Dyna straightened in her seat.

"When I was planning our escape, I had discovered something among his belongings. A Xián Jīng teapot containing ashes. I had forgotten about it until now."

Her brow furrowed. "Ashes?"

Von's knee bounced as he wrung his hands. "I knew Tarn was the bastard son of the Azure King. That made him the only heir to the throne. I assumed that was the reason the crown wanted him dead. Tarn seeks immortality to keep himself alive, but it never occurred to me the reason King Lenneus hunted Tarn was because he had inherited Jökull's power. Now I believe those are the ashes of the Ice Phoenix. Tarn wants to bring Aisling back to life."

Dyna's eyes widened. "What do you mean?"

"There are many versions of the tale of the Ice Phoenix. In one of them, Jökull was resurrected from the ashes of his pyre, because his queen had given up her life for him. The night Yavi died, Tarn mentioned for life to be given, it must be taken. A sacrifice. I think he was speaking about you, lass." Von paused at her shudder. "I wasn't privy to all his plans, but I know he was planning something more than simply becoming immortal and usurping the Azure throne."

Dyna took a deep breath and pressed on her forehead. "This is a lot to take to mind. But if he does intend to resurrect your sister ... could it be this is the prophecy coming to pass?"

Von had briefly forgotten about that. Probably because they had assumed Tarn was dead, but the words came to him fresh now. Particularly the last line.

Be not swayed by love, lest it be thy undoing.

But it didn't make sense.

"Perhaps we are missing something." Von rested his chin on his fist as he pondered. "Tarn's only priority is preserving his life. Resurrecting my sister for love would go against the prophecy's warning."

"What else would he want to sacrifice me for?"

Von shook his head. He didn't know.

"You loved Yavi so much," Dyna said softly. "If you had the chance to bring her back, even if it meant you might not live, would you do it?"

Von didn't answer. He didn't need to. Because they both knew they would die for the ones they loved without a second thought. The back of his eyes stung as he recalled the day they had decided to run away. *If we fail and these are our last days together, then I will break open every Gate and take on the Gods if it means finding you again.*

The only way he would ever find Yavi again would be to leave this world. He had no other reason to stay in it, other than enacting his revenge on the man who took her from him.

"Whatever Tarn is planning, he now needs a new sacrifice and much more than ashes to do it. A power source of some sort." Dyna wandered to the bookshelves and began examining titles. "If he truly wanted to resurrect Aisling from the ashes, he must replicate the pyre. He has Jökull's ashes. Sunnëva burned with him, and she was a Morken, so he would need Morken blood, which he has. And there were flowers of some sort. I don't quite remember what it was."

"Roses and Azure leaves..."

She turned to him.

Von stood. "I remember the story because my mother used to read it to me when I was a child. Tanzanite Keep was once covered in enchanted roses of Jökull's making. They burned him with a rose along with a branch from an Azure Tree."

"Enchanted roses..." Dyna stared at the wall as if recalling something. "Are they blue?"

"Yes, but they no longer exist in this world. Without the rose, it's not possible to perform the resurrection."

She glanced down at Mount Ida's key set on the table, working out something in her mind. "If I know Tarn, he will find a way, even if he must wish it into existence."

Wish into existence...

Von had said something similar to Yavi not too long ago when he feared losing her. *If one day it was all devoured in flames, I would give up everything to wish for you back.*

"The Lost Well," he whispered.

"Pardon?"

"That's where Tarn is going," Von exclaimed. "There is a wishing well located in the Hashell Ruins of Harromog Modos. A means to wish what he wants into existence."

Dyna sank back into her chair, a hundred thoughts flashing behind her eyes. "I suppose that is where we must go next and stop him."

Coming around the table, he lowered to one knee in front of her. "What will you have me do? Command me, and I will do it."

She leaned back. "Von, you're not a slave anymore."

"Then make me one again."

"What?"

He lowered his head. "Yavi, Geon, Dalton—they are dead because of me, Dyna. Dalton tried to escape after you did, but Tarn wouldn't let him go. And I couldn't let that boy suffer his wrath ... so I..." Von couldn't make himself say it.

608

Tears welled on her lashes once she understood his confession. Sometimes he still heard Dalton's neck breaking, and each time he still flinched.

Von took a breath. "I ... sometimes dream of what their lives should have been like. Geon, somewhere discovering the world, with Dalton as a free mage. But *I* took that from them. Take what is left of my life in service to you so I can repay my sins."

She glowered at him, wiping her wet cheek. "I am not your master, Von."

"You're the Maiden, and I'm one of your Guardians."

"That does not make you my slave." Dyna sighed heavily. "Von, it wasn't your fault they were killed. You do not owe me a debt nor to anyone else. I know you also blame yourself for Azurite, but the viceroy opened the gates and let the trolls in at the Azure King's command. Tarn let you believe it was your fault to control you. I will not do the same."

Von sat back on his heels, feeling his body go numb. For years, he had carried that suffocating guilt. Tarn used it to enslave him. Knowing that made him feel so empty, adrift in a sea of purposelessness.

"You told me to keep going," he said with a shaky breath. "But my Yavi is gone. I can't keep waking up day by day without a reason. If serving you is not my purpose, what is?"

Dyna's eyes softened, and she laid a hand on his shaking shoulder. "I think we both know what your purpose is, Von."

His chest tightened at the sound of his nephew's voice calling for him in the hall, and his vision blurred.

"Tavin carries Jökull's magic in his blood. It's dormant now, but if it ever surfaces ... if Tarn ever learns that his son is alive, he will come after Tavin as the Azure King came after him. To keep his power, he would never let him live."

Von's fists shook on the cold floor at that appalling thought. The boy may even become the sacrifice for his very own mother. His stomach rolled. "What if ... the worst happens to him because of me?"

"It won't, because this time you will not fail," Dyna said firmly.

Maybe this was why he wasn't finished with this world yet. There had to be a reason why he continued to survive against all odds. It was for this.

When he rose to his feet, Dyna reminded him of something he had forgotten. "You are my Guardian of Vengeance, Von. But it wasn't Tarn who threw that lantern."

Sai-chuen's face surfaced in his mind, along with the proverb on how to strike his enemies.

609

Now there were two names on his list.

Exchanging a nod with Dyna, Von left the quiet library and went out into the hall.

Tavin spun around. "There you are, Commander. I was looking for you."

"What for?"

The boy grabbed Von's arm and pulled him through another set of glass doors that led out into the courtyard.

"Look!" Tavin took out two throwing knives from his blue coat, whirling them in his palms and threw them one after the other at a tree. They perfectly hit their mark with soft thuds. He grinned at him. "I did it."

Von crossed his arms. "Are those my knives?"

Tavin gave him a sheepish smile, scratching the back of his neck. "Ah, I borrowed them."

"Hmm. Show me again. This time, hit that other tree."

An excited grin returned to the boy's face, and he snatched up the knives again. With perfect form, the knives flew and landed.

Von chuckled. "Well done. You must get it from your uncle."

"I do..." Tavin's pale blue eyes met his. "I get it from you."

The air left Von's lungs for a moment, stealing his voice.

"I wondered why Klyde wanted me to stay away from you, but it was plain to see. You look like my mum. Well, my grandmother, but she raised me. Her name is Edyth, and she also had a son ... named Von."

The boy had known all along.

Tavin gave him a timid smile. "Hello, uncle."

Von swallowed back the knot in his throat. "Hello, laddie."

Tavin laughed shyly at that and scuffed his boot in the dirt. "Why did you leave Azurite?"

He looked like an unsure child then, a little sad and confused about the way of his life. A sentiment Von recognized from when he had been a boy.

Von sat on a stone bench and leaned forward on his knees. "Well, after the Horde came, there were too many bad memories for me in that place. I had to go and try to ... forget."

And to repay a heavy debt.

Tavin sat beside him. "Can I ask what happened that day? It's too painful for Klyde and mum to speak about. Everyone who fought the Horde is dead. I am only told stories, but I want the truth. What happened to my real mother and father?"

Von could see the question had plagued him. Tavin was ready to learn about his past, but he hesitated to answer. "What does Klyde tell you?"

"That my mother died giving birth to me, and my father died defending the town."

That was the best version Klyde could have given him.

If only it were true.

Von looked up at the sky, letting his mind drift to the screams and stench of death. "Tarn ... fought through the masses, even as he bled from grave wounds. He led his company and cut down every troll that came until he was the last man standing."

"That ... sounds true."

"It is," Von insisted.

Tavin frowned. "But you have the same look on your face when Klyde tells me the same story."

"What look is that?"

His pale eyes grew sullen. "That it's only part of the truth."

"Lad, it's the only part that matters." Von mussed his nephew's messy brown curls, making him snort. "I see your mother in you. You have her smile, her freckles, her unruly hair. You have her laughter and kindness. Her spirit shines in you." As he spoke, Tavin's eyes grew wet, and Von pulled him into an embrace. "Thank you for existing."

Von had lost much in his life, but he was grateful for this. His nephew arrived at a time when he needed some proof that not all was lost. The town still stood, his mother lived, and he had family.

But Tavin had a target placed on his head the day he was born. Von decided right then he would die before ever failing him. And if he lived merely to protect his sister's sweet boy, it was the greatest purpose he could have found.

CHAPTER 91

Lucenna

Lucenna watched the sunset at her bedroom window as she towel-dried her wet hair. Her long soak in the bath helped ease her stiff muscles, especially after a long day of training with that old elf. Once she slipped on a casual dress, she left to join the others for dinner but heard a clattering when she opened her door.

On the doorknob hung a thin gold chain with a small glass vial containing a four-leaf clover.

Growling to herself, Lucenna snatched the chain and stormed to Klyde's room.

She barged in and tossed it on his pillow. "I don't want it!" she snapped. "Have I not already made that clear?"

Klyde paused by the bed, in the middle of packing his clothes into his bag. She froze at the sight of it.

Crossing her arms, Lucenna focused on her irritation to regain her composure. "I have lost count of how many times I have returned that clover to you. Why do you insist on giving it to me?"

He looked at her steadily, his expression subdued. "You need that more than I do." Picking it up, he held it out to her. "Take it. At least so my conscience is clear."

Lucenna clenched her fists. "Klyde, I don't need you to save me. I can take care of myself. Neither I nor anyone faults you for what happened at the keep. Going there was my choice. I knew the risks. Getting wounded in battle, especially one of magic, is inevitable."

He clenched his jaw. "It doesn't have to be."

"Gods, you are infuriating!"

"I can say the same about you, lass." He tossed his mercenary coat onto his bed. "You are stubborn, haughty, tempestuous—"

"Excused me?" she hissed.

"It means—"

"I know what it means!"

Sighing, Klyde rubbed his jaw shadowed with stubble. His blue eyes stormed as he looked at her in a way that made her heart twist. "I am leaving tomorrow, so I won't dance around it any longer. You reject my gift not because you don't need it, but because you need to refuse anything having to do with me. That is the only way you can persuade yourself that you don't feel for me the way I do for you. And it frightens you."

Lucenna stared at him, her chest heaving.

Klyde closed the distance between them. "So insult me all you wish. Threaten me. Throw things at me. Hit me. I'll take anything you give me but stop lying to yourself."

She tried to speak, tried to shout, but all she could manage was a faint whisper. "It's not a lie."

"Say that again and mean it."

Hot tears built up behind her eyes and threatened to spill over. This man got under her skin. He challenged her. Confused her. Provoked her. Made her skin heat with anger and longing.

And she loathed it.

Lucenna clung to that anger and made it her boat to stand on. "I don't want *you*. I never wanted you. Not a ridiculous man who never cared for anything but his own selfish desires. I *despise* you. You are an infinite source of irritation, and once you're gone, I will be glad of it."

Klyde took a shallow breath, and it was the only indication that the blow had hurt. But he didn't fight her as she wanted. He didn't even raise his voice. He only reached out and gently wiped away the tear that had escaped.

Because they both knew it was a lie.

"Why?" Lucenna weakly hit his chest. "Why must it be you? I don't understand it at all. You're the fool that maddens me every day with your ways and stupid dimples. I can't stand that you see through me, that you hear what I don't want to say. When I finally gave in, you pulled away and left me to sit in my own humiliation. You accuse me of lying to myself, yet I sense you're afraid, too." She moved away from him, shaking her head. "You should never have kissed me, Klyde. For not even you know what you want."

Lucenna stormed out of his room for hers and slammed the door shut behind her. Leaning against it, she shut her eyes. Gods, why did she tell him that? It didn't matter. Tomorrow he would be gone, and she could move on with her life.

Yet why did she feel lonely at the thought of him leaving? She didn't want him to go. Her trembling hand lingered on the doorknob. She likely wouldn't ever see him again after today.

Could she let that be the last thing she ever said to him?

Maybe life came down to more than wants. If anything, this part of her journey had shown her it was awful to live with regrets.

Lucenna swung open the door.

Her heart lurched to find Klyde standing right there, his eyes burning. "I was never confused about what I wanted."

Then he grabbed her face and kissed her.

She wrapped her arms around his neck and rose on her toes, kissing him back. Her heart surged in her chest. With thrill. Relief. And complete, utter surrender. They stumbled backward into her room, and he kicked the door closed.

Klyde leaned her against a dresser, claiming her mouth with his. His heated hand slid to her waist, sparking a rippling current along her spine. Gripping her thigh, he hooked it up his waist. Her pulse throbbed as his tongue slid against hers, devouring her mouth. She couldn't hold in the small moan, and his hands tightened around her waist.

This wasn't like their first kiss.

This one was hungry.

Starved.

"What I want," he panted against her mouth. "Is your today and your endless tomorrows. I want to tear this off you." He gathered a handful of her dress in his fists so tight she heard the fabric tear. "And forget all else as I lose myself in the wonder of you. I want to feel your heart race in time with mine. To breathe in your scent and swallow the sound of your voice calling my name. I want you. Every blessed inch of you."

His voice vibrated through her being. Each ardent word stripping her to her bones. Lucenna kissed him heatedly. Challenging. Damn him for knowing exactly what to say to make her defenses fall.

"Tell me to go if you don't want this," Klyde said, so close she felt the brush of his low plea on her lips. "Give me a reason not to touch you.

Convince me you still belong to another, so I don't take you to bed and kiss you until I can't breathe. I've lost the will to fight against what I want."

There wasn't another. No other man who stirred her like him. No other touch she wanted but his.

Lucenna was done denying what she wanted, too. "Stay."

He shuddered. "Thank the Gods."

The roughness of his reply made all of her warm. His mouth captured hers again and she melted into the sweep of his tongue and the grip of his hands on her waist.

"It would be irresponsible of me not to address an important matter first," he said, and she already knew what he would ask. "Are you—"

"Yes."

"You won't—"

"No."

The shortest conversation she ever had about contraceptives, but Klyde understood her perfectly.

He pressed her into the wall as he continued to kiss and explore her neck, coursing down to the soft plush of her cleavage. With every press of his lips, her sighs tangled in a moan. She gasped softly at the stroke of his hand tracing up her leg still wrapped around him. Her pulse sped with each caress, warming her skin.

"This changes nothing," she said between kisses. "I still despise you."

Klyde's fingers threaded through her hair as he cupped her head to him, gripping tight enough to make her shiver with delight. "I love it when you lie," he ground out, slowly rocking her against him. "Your eyes always tell me the truth."

Lucenna really couldn't hide from him anymore, and she didn't care.

She tugged up his shirt, and he lifted her arms as she pulled it off him, dropping it at their feet. His lashes drifted closed at the first graze of her hand on his chest. She lightly traced his scars, exploring every hard inch of warm skin, savoring the chiseled ridges of his body. She nipped his neck and the rumbling sound he made vibrated in her pulse.

He reached up her dress, and she heard fabric tear as he dragged off her undergarments, exposing her to the air.

His firm hands traveled up her thighs to the source of her need. Her breath caught at the first stroke of his fingers, and she dug her nails into his back. Her breath came in soft pants as he created a building demand she couldn't take anymore. She tugged at his britches, and they were gone in her next breath. Klyde hoisted her up onto his waist. Wrapping her legs around him, he pulled her close, and she felt how much he craved her.

He carried her to the bed without releasing her mouth. Sitting on the edge, he scooted back with her still straddling him. He grabbed the hem of her dress, lifting it up and off over her head. There was nothing between them but this moment. His dark, heavy-lidded gaze trailed over her body, his chest rising and falling with shallow breaths.

"Gods, you're beautiful..." His husky voice, so laden with desire in the dimly lit room, made Lucenna shiver.

Klyde held her waist as he kissed the sensitive curves of her cleavage languidly. Every press of his heated mouth made her body hum with electrical currents. His lips moved on to her neck, and she leaned her head back as he learned the beat of her pulse.

The purple light of her Essence flickered around them, dancing like fireflies. His every touch pulled on threads of her heart, lacing them with his own. Breath trembling, she ran her hands over the hard lines of his forearms to his shoulders, feeling the muscles flexing with movement as his hands slid up her back.

Klyde panted a breath before saying faintly into her ear. "Tell me what pleases you."

"I have a feeling you already know."

Because even when she tried to deny it, when she lied to him and to herself, he always could see through her.

Lucenna wanted him to take her tenderly. Then wildly. To tangle his fingers in her hair and lose himself in the arches of her skin. She wanted his teeth to mark her with his need. For him to tame the tempest inside by taking her breath away. She had enough of his wavering and restrained desire. She wanted to feel the crash of his waves and know that she wasn't drowning alone.

Klyde flipped her onto the bed beneath him. Her eyes rolled closed as his mouth slowly made its descent over her body. He trailed kisses over her heartbeat, down her stomach to her thighs, and lower, until he had her writhing. Lucenna gasped and clutched the bedding in tight fistfuls. With every touch of his lips, he imprinted webs of stars across her body and made her his. Pressure rose in her, building and building until she was crashing on his shores.

Klyde's lips returned to hers, and he breathed her name mid-kiss. Each vowel curled up her spine. Whenever he spoke her name, everything else seemed to stop. Lucenna couldn't decipher what they were anymore. She didn't know what she wanted them to be. Only that she had to hold on for as long as she could.

He rose on his arms above her, and she saw the storm in his eyes. "Should you come to regret this tomorrow, know that none of what I feel for you is a lie."

She shook her head and wrapped her fingers around the back of his nape. "Klyde, shut up and kiss me."

He did. Deeply, tenderly. As his body joined hers, filling her so perfectly, Lucenna decided tomorrow didn't matter.

Only now.

The first roll of his hips dragged out her whimper. The sound seemed to snap something inside of him and Klyde picked up the pace in a measured, powerful rhythm. Lucenna pulsed at the sudden fire building inside of her. He pulled her hips up, burying himself so deep, pleasure rolled through her in waves. A low sound rasped from Klyde's throat as he rocked into her, extracting her every panting gasp and convulsing moan. Each swell was more intense than the last until she cried out and her entire body arched.

Lucenna sagged into the bed, and he sank down beside her, breathing hard. She quivered with soft ripples of pleasure.

Klyde brushed the silver locks from her eyes. "I take it that smile means I did indeed exceed expectations?"

Smirking lazily, Lucenna said, "That depends, Captain. Are you already conceding?"

Rolling over, he hooked her leg over his thigh, and she found he was nowhere near finished. "Moonlit-lass, I wouldn't dream of it."

Lucenna lay nestled into Klyde's side, as if the cradle of his arms were meant for her. His presence was a warm sensation she wanted to wrap herself in and never leave. It would be easy to fall asleep like this, listening to his chest rise and fall with even breaths as he slept. She breathed in his familiar scent of leather and sea salt, and something primal she couldn't get enough of.

Slowly, she traced his scars and the curves of his abdomen, memorizing the feel of his skin. The Gods took their time making him. He was the most beautiful sight she'd ever laid eyes on.

She was going to miss him.

It was still dark outside, but she sensed it was early morning. The low candlelight glinted over the pink diamond on her finger. The ring no longer belonged there.

Perhaps it never did.

Lucenna took hold of the band and began to slide it off, but a warm hand fell over hers.

"Keep it on..." Klyde murmured sleepily, and his blue eyes met hers through his lashes. "At least until I can replace it with my own."

She stared at him, her chest catching with a breath. "What did you say?"

Seeming to realize what came out of his mouth, he sat up. "I suppose something foolish by how terrified you look right now."

Swallowing, Lucenna struggled to sort her thoughts and looked away.

"Oi." Klyde turned her chin, making her look at him. "I am merely in a blissful mood and said something I shouldn't. Don't think anything of it."

"But you meant it."

He sighed and rested his arms on his crossed legs. "Are you so worried that I want a life with you? Or is it because I am not a mage?"

Her heart shook. "I am worried you would die because of it."

A somberness crossed his face. Her future was uncertain, but it most certainly held a war to come and a life constantly on the run. Elite Enforcers were always on her tail, and so was her father.

Lucenna shut her eyes, seeing her mother. "My greatest fear is having a dream in this wretched world. I fear I will grow weak because of that hope and lose those I don't wish to lose because I wasn't strong enough to protect them. If I allow myself to fall into you, I am putting a target on your back, Klyde. I won't do that."

Wrapping the sheets around her, she rolled out of bed and went to sit in the chaise by the fire. A knot of emotions tangled within her throat. Now she was the one pulling away, because she reminded herself why she had to be alone.

She heard the rustle of the bedding as Klyde rose. What else could he do but leave?

"I knew the risks that came with choosing this," he said a few steps from her, now dressed in only his trousers. "I told myself nothing good would come of it, but there was no ignoring what you did to me. I always asked myself the same question." He gazed at her, his eyes glistening. "Why ... why can't I stop?"

"Stop what?" Lucenna whispered as he stepped closer.

"Wanting you."

"Don't say those things to me," she begged as he kneeled in front of her. "When you do..." He made her feel like the world was no longer on her shoulders, and it tore down her walls. "You draw out parts of me I never show anyone."

"Show it to me, Lucenna. Every part." He brushed the hair from her eyes, cupping her face. Her pulse drummed beneath the tenderness in his gaze. "I wasn't ready for this. I don't think anyone ever is. I didn't know what I was looking for when I found you, but I found exactly what I needed in you."

"What are you saying?"

"You know."

Lucenna's heart beat so fast it was hard to breathe. "Don't," she whispered. "Don't say it when you're leaving."

"I always planned to come back, lass." Klyde drew her close, his nose trailing over her cheek, and her eyes stung with relief and fear for wanting this. "If you don't want to hear it, then in place of it, I will tell you that when I close my eyes, you're all I see." His voice vibrated through her. "My life started the moment I laid eyes on you."

She flushed. "When I was an old hag in a witch's den?"

"I saw you before that, in the city. In your leather redingote, silver hair swaying like streams of stars, and eyes that reminded me of twilight. Once you yelled at me, I was completely, irrevocably done for."

She cracked a smile. "Why?"

Klyde's mouth hitched on one end, and his fingers stroked down her arm. "Apparently, I am a fool for a woman who can destroy me with a snap of her fingers or a lashing of her tongue. Regardless of whatever consequences entering your life has brought to mine, I will never once regret it."

Lucenna warmed under his touch. He leaned in, but she slipped out of his range, eyeing him slyly as she backed away. "You say that now, but what if we wake up one day and realize last night was a mistake?"

"What is living without making a lifetime of mistakes?" Klyde rose to his feet and prowled toward her, forcing her to retreat until he cornered her against the wall. He dipped down, and the low rumble of his voice purred against her ear, sending a little shiver down her spine. "I suggest we continue making several more."

Her body tingled with delight at the thought.

"If we are going to be together, promise me one thing." Lucenna pulled out the chain holding the four-leaf clover from his pocket. She slipped it over his head, laying it over his heart. "Never take this off."

Because the Magos Empire would come for her again, and she needed to make sure he wouldn't be another casualty in her life.

"I promise." Klyde buried his hands in her hair, rendering her molten beneath the demanding press of his mouth. Gods, she loved the way he kissed her. She wanted to keep kissing him, to lose herself in him. To feel safe and warm for as long as possible.

"Stay," she breathed. "Stay in Sellav until the end of spring."

He paused, pulling back a little to meet her eyes.

Lucenna looked up at him, never feeling more vulnerable. "I know you must return to Skelling Rise. It's selfish of me, but I can finally admit to myself that I want something. And I don't want you to go."

He groaned as if it were torture. "Don't look at me that way, lass. The last thing I want is to leave."

"Then don't. Not yet."

The way he beheld her, with such soft adoration. It made her feel like she had reached a turning point in her life. When things would change into something new.

Klyde's fingers curled around her chin and gently lifted her mouth to his with a defeated sigh. "Then I will stay right here with you a little longer more."

CHAPTER 92

Dynalya

Dyna listened to Cassiel's steady breaths as she watched him sleep. She kept her fingers on his wrist, constantly checking for a pulse. *Come back to me,* she sent through the bond. *Please.* But there was no answer. Her mind felt heavy and her body tired. She needed rest, but Dyna was afraid if she looked away, he would disappear.

A soft knock came at the door, and Zev poked his head in. "Dyna," he called softly. Concerned lined his eyes at the sight of her. "You haven't slept yet, have you? It's nearly dawn."

She glanced tiredly at the windows. The darkness had shifted to a dull gray with the imminent arrival of morning. She had lost count of how many mornings it had been.

Dyna's throat tightened. "Why won't he wake?"

"He will," Zev said, coming to her side. But even he watched Cassiel worriedly.

"How do you know?"

"Because for all of his efforts, Cassiel could never stay away from you." Zev patted her shoulder. "I can sit with him. You haven't eaten since yesterday morning. Go have a cup of tea at least. I will let you know if anything changes."

Dyna sighed and pressed on her aching eyes. Tea might help her nerves.

"I'll be back soon," she whispered to Cassiel, brushing her lips on his forehead.

Stepping out into the hall, Yelrakel silently bowed her head. She loyally kept guard by their door. Dyna wandered through the quiet estate until she reached the kitchens.

Raiden looked up from his seat at the cook's table. "My lady, trouble sleeping?"

She nodded. "You as well?"

He offered her a slight shrug. "Many thoughts occupy my mind as of late."

Dyna took the chair beside him, and he poured her a cup of tea. She took a sip, letting the warm hints of honey, mint, and lavender soothe her stomach. "What thoughts?"

Raiden looked down at the loose leaves in his cup. "I suppose I question what is to come next, now that my father has returned ... and what is to come for you and I."

Dyna met his eyes, and whatever he found in hers seemed to give him an answer.

He nodded. "I understand."

Swallowing, she reached into her pocket and gently laid his mother's ring on the table. "I'm sorry."

Raiden sighed and shook his head. "Please don't apologize. I should never have dared to reach for the impossible." He laughed a little and looked out at the kitchen windows to the shadowed silhouette of the Anduir Mountains. "When you came here, I was taken with your kindness. Your resilience. You came from another land past the mountains, untainted by my memories of this place. When you cried in my stead by the fountain, you looked so lovely to me. Like the crimson fields in the spring beneath the sunset's gleam." His eyes grew wet, and so did hers as he met her gaze again. "I thought if I could somehow win your heart, I would know what love meant, but a part of me always knew yours was never meant for me. From the moment you first spoke of him, despite the pain he caused, and the anger he left you with, your light and your heart had only ever belonged to him."

It wasn't ever a question, was it?

Dyna lowered her head, not wishing to burden him with the sight of her tears. There was never a plan to go through with the marriage. Her acceptance had only been to save his life, but she felt awful for causing his first heartbreak.

Raiden brushed her cheek and caught one of her tears in his fingers. "I will keep this, though. To remember you by."

"You will find your light one day, Raiden. When you least expect it."

He nodded, though it was more out of politeness than in agreement.

"Who knows?" Smiling, she wiped her eyes. "Perhaps she is not a crimson bloom, but a desert flower from other distant fields."

He blinked at her, bewildered. "Surely you jest."

Dyna laughed a little, but it wavered at the reminder of the desert. They saved and lost things in those sands. "Raiden, speak to your father. Rawn isn't one to impose, so he will give you the time you need, but don't let too much time pass. Go on and air your grievances if you must. The only reason you can is because he is alive to hear them. We don't know what tomorrow will bring, but you will regret it if you lose this chance."

The weight of that regret was crippling.

Raiden lowered his gaze to the table.

Dyna meant to say more, but she cut off with a gasp and whipped around to the door, pressing a hand to her heart. The threadbare bond, it stirred.

"What is it?"

"He's awake," she said shakily. "He's awake!"

Bolting through the kitchen, Dyna flew through the halls, nearly tripping over the carpet runner.

The bond hummed through her chest, and oh, it was so beautiful. Like the twinkle of stars at twilight. She sprinted up the stairs with her heart in her throat, but she found Zev in the hall, chatting with Yelrakel.

"Zev?" Dyna rushed to him. "Where is he?"

"Who? Cassiel? He's still—"

She ran past him and burst into their room.

The bed was empty.

"No, where did he go?" she cried, searching the room. "You were supposed to watch him!"

"I'm sorry. I only stepped out for a moment!"

"Your Highness," Yelrakel exclaimed, looking out of the open windows. "He's outside."

Dyna rushed over. In the grayness of early morning, she spotted him walking away from the estate toward the dynalya fields. Barefoot, his single, limp wing hanging down his back.

"Cassiel!" she called, but he didn't stop.

He was leaving.

The last time they spoke, she had told him they were finished, and he was honoring her wishes. So he left again—without saying goodbye.

"Dyna, we are each born with our own fate," Zev said behind her. "He's yours. Go get him."

That was all the encouragement she needed to climb out of the window and jump. Green Essence flared around her before she hit the ground, softening her fall. Stumbling to her feet, Dyna sprinted across the courtyard to flowering fields. But he had already disappeared on the other side of the hill.

No, she had to reach him.

She had to stop him.

Because after days of telling him to leave, she didn't want that anymore. She never truly wanted that.

"Cassiel!" Dyna gasped, her voice hoarse. She slipped on the wet grass as she raced up the hill. She kept running, keeping her eyes on the sky turning pink and orange, praying and hoping that he had not left yet. "Cassiel!" Her cry echoed over the red fields. "Cassiel, wait!"

A form appeared at the top of the hill, and her heart swelled at the sight of him. The wind tugged at his long black hair, rippling across his white tunic. He blinked at her sudden appearance, staring at her in surprise. He was still here. She choked on a sob, slipping and sliding on the wet grass, reaching out to him with splayed fingers.

His silver eyes widened. "Dyna—?"

She tackled him, and he caught her with an *oomph*. They fell backwards on the knoll together. His hands were warm on her waist and the back of her head.

Cassiel's chest rose and fell against her ear. His heart, how perfect each solid beat sounded. "What—"

"I don't want you to go," Dyna blurted breathlessly. She sat back on her heels and clutched his arms. "Please, don't go."

Cassiel blinked at her a moment, and his brows curled, his mouth parting with a faint breath. He searched her face with soft eyes, confusion embedded on his pallid features. The wind brushed against his single wing, and her face crumbled.

"I hated what you did to us," she wept. "But in truth, you were hurting too, weren't you? From the beginning, you were hurting so much. Yet I didn't even try to see things from your perspective at all. I am so sorry. I know you're afraid of me dying again, but that wasn't because of you. Leaving doesn't protect me, and staying won't kill me. But you leaving..." She nodded through her tears. "That would kill me. When you were gone, I couldn't breathe. Then when you were dying, I was ready to die with you. There is no living if you're gone. I want to face this life with you because I love you. *So much.* So please don't run away again. You're not alone. Not anymore. *Stay.* With me."

Cassiel's silver eyes welled, and his warm hand cupped her cold cheek as he caught the tears rolling down her face. "Dynalya," his voice broke. "I am not going anywhere. Each dawn was a reminder of a life without you. Every sunset held a silent wish for your voice. It took everything I had to walk away from you the first time. I don't have the strength to ever do that again. Whatever darkness may come our way, I will be with you. Always."

His promise fell over the withered threads of their bond, and it pulsed between them, trembling with faint light.

"I was wondering..." Dyna reached into her pocket and held out her palm to him. His silver *Hyalus* ring glinted in the morning. "Would you like to wear this again?"

Cassiel blinked at it. "When did you...?"

Through her blurred vision, she saw the realization cross his face. She had found his ring in her enchanted satchel months ago, right where he had left it. At the time, she thought it was simply another thing he had abandoned, until she finally understood. He couldn't help but leave a piece of himself behind with her.

"Will you be mine again?" Dyna asked, her voice quivering.

Maybe because a part of her was still afraid to trust him again, but she had no reason to be. There was nothing but pure, devastating, world-shattering joy in his wet eyes.

Cassiel reached in his pocket and took out her small ring, the pair to his. She let out a wet, bubbly laugh. He had carried a piece of her with him, too.

His trembling reply came out hoarse. Breathless. "I never stopped being yours, *lev sheli.*"

Cassiel slipped on his ring. Gently cradling her hand, he slipped her ring back onto her finger, where it always belonged. And the bond, the brittle thing that had been dying, blazed with new life as it reformed itself.

Instantly.

Flawlessly.

So strong and as bright as every star in his eyes. As if all it took was this.

The spring breeze drifted over the hill of dynalyas, filling the air with their sweet scent and red petals. While he gazed at her, appearing as ethereal as the first day she saw him, she knew the only thing the bond needed was her forgiveness. Because love, that had never left.

Even in her anger and resentment that felt like hate, she had never—not once—stopped loving Cassiel.

Dyna didn't know who reached for who first. In the next breath, she was in his arms. Crying with him. Embracing him. Touching him. Exchanging wet kisses that tasted like tears and faith.

Home, her soul sang. She had come home.

His arms shook around her as he cradled her in his arms. His single wing wrapped around her in a way that vowed there would be no more letting go.

"If you weren't leaving me again, why did you come here?" she asked.

Pulling back, Cassiel smiled at the vast field of red blooms as the first gold rays of daylight peeked over the horizon. Bright and gentle and warm.

Those starry eyes welled as they met hers once more. "I was waiting for the sun."

Then she was crying all over again, as he had the power to make her do. Her chaotic emotions were free and wild, and she didn't care.

"*Ahuvati*." Cassiel took her face in his hands and rested his forehead against hers, breathing her in. "How I have missed you."

His warm lips kissed away the tears from her lashes and cheeks, leaving little impressions of heat behind, like the caress of feathers against her skin.

"My heart. My queen. My dawn."

In the privacy of their bedroom, Dyna bore witness to Cassiel cutting out another piece of his rib bone. She watched him burn it until it was charred black. He meticulously ground it into a powder with a special oil Yelrakel had provided, and it became sacred paint. Dyna tossed the *ghet* into the hearth, letting the flames dissolve it away. She sat by the fire as he knelt before her again and wrote new vows on her skin.

One on the inside of her right arm: *My mind's might and fire, I lay at your feet to never rise against you.*

Over her heart, his fingers painted: *Wherever you go, in life and in death, I will follow.*

Dyna was blinded by tears by the time he finished the last letter. Cassiel slowly kissed away each one that fell. His lips brushed over hers and traced the column of her throat. Her head lolled back to give him better access, and his teeth grazed across the spot where her neck and shoulder joined.

Languid heat uncoiled inside of her, anticipation tingling across her skin. He kissed his way back up her neck to the shell of her ear as his hand slid up her side, teasing her sensitive flesh over her nightgown. Her breath quickened as her pulse climbed. Then Cassiel swept her into his arms and carried her to bed. Their clothes slipped away and none of her was hidden from him anymore.

He explored every inch of her as though for the first time, his hands and mouth insatiable. His every touch, every soft kiss, was sweet and slow. Worshiping.

Cassiel held her in his arms as they joined, and Dyna merged into him. Her body fit every inch of his like two pieces cut from the same cloth. The new vows lit up on her skin, alongside the first ones. They shimmered in the bond between them, glowing like a dance of stars.

With every roll of his hips, her heart called to him, and his replied as it always did.

I love you, it said. *I love you. I love you. I love you.*

CHAPTER 93

Cassiel

"Does this mean you will not return to Hilos?"

Cassiel sighed and gave his uncle a nod. "I will return one day. Perhaps in a year's time, but right now, I choose my wife. With her is where I belong."

Lord Jophiel's expression creased on the surface of the water mirror as he searched his eyes. "Cassiel..."

"I am sorry for doubting you, uncle. I lost my way for a time, and it was difficult to find the way back. In my fear, all I could see were enemies around me while forgetting those who have stood with me. I hope one day you can forgive me."

Emotion crossed Lord Jophiel's face, and his voice wavered. "There is nothing to forgive, Cassiel. I should have realized Raziel was using me in his ploy. I suppose I didn't see it because I was consumed with worry for you. I feared you were committing Kāhssiel's wrongs and history would repeat itself once more. When I saw the hurt in your eyes, I knew I had lost your trust. But never would I ever intentionally harm you or your mate."

How monstrous he must have appeared when he let his ire rule him and his flame. Jophiel could only feel fear, and Cassiel had learned how terrible fear could be.

"Whatever my word is worth now, my only aspiration for you is the same as your father's. We wish for you to live the life you should have with the one meant for you."

Cassiel nodded. "Thank you. I have much to atone for. To you and to the Realms. For now, can I count on your support?"

Lord Jophiel's throat bobbed, and he blinked away his wet eyes before standing and bowing deep. "Before the witness of *Elyōn* and the Heavens I swear my fealty to you, Cassiel."

"Then I leave Hilos and the Realms in your capable hands until my return ... Lord Protector."

His uncle's mouth parted with shock, and Cassiel chuckled as the water mirror cleared. Rising with a sigh, he poured the salted water into another bowl and wiped down the mirror before putting it away.

"Is this how you apologize to your uncle?"

Cassiel glanced over at Dyna by the entry of their bedroom, her arms crossed as she leaned against the door frame in nothing but his tunic. Her red hair fell in rumpled waves a little past her jaw, skin softly glowing with divinity.

He visually traced the line of her body from her bare feet to her shoulder, exposed by a fallen sleeve. Residual desire coursed through his veins. He didn't think he wouldn't ever not have that reaction when it came to his mate.

Cassiel sat back on the couch and gazed at her with a soft smile. "Did I wake you?"

"Not feeling you beside me woke me." Dyna smiled back, but he felt the last threads of her anxiety fade now that she was in the same room as him.

He held out a hand to her. Her feet softly padded across the floor to him, and he pulled her onto his lap. Cassiel fed her a piece of fruit from the platter of food left for them on the sofa table. "I have given Jophiel a full pardon and made him my regent. What else should I give him?"

She wrapped her arms around his neck, playing with a lock of his hair. "You mean other than an immense responsibility?"

"He has experience lording over a realm. What are four more?"

Dyna laughed. "I think you're shirking your duties, High King of Hilos."

Chuckling, Cassiel ran his fingers through her hair. "The Realms will be waiting for me once this journey is over. In the meantime, I intend to stay right by your side."

The bond hummed with her happiness.

"Promise?" She meant to sound playful, but her tone wavered, and he felt a tiny echo of her apprehension. That was one thing he had to make disappear. Cassiel reached for the opal knife on the sofa table. Dyna grabbed his wrist when he tugged open his tunic. "What are you doing?"

"Sealing that promise along with any others you need."

Dyna stared at him. "You would cut out a piece of you every time you make a promise to me?"

"If that is what you need to believe in me again, I would bear that and anything else I must do to atone for my wrongs and earn back everything I lost. Including your trust."

"No, Cassiel." She took away the knife and set it on the table. "We have hurt each other and ourselves far enough."

His shoulders slumped, and his throat tightened. "Then tell me what you need to feel safe with me. How can I quell your fear that I will leave you again?"

"It's not that I am afraid that you will leave me again. I am afraid of losing you because I nearly did. You have nothing to atone for." She looked at the space where his left wing used to be, and her eyes welled. "You gave far more than you needed to, Cassiel. You shattered your soul for me. You went to war for me." Her voice cracked, and her tears spilled. "You sacrificed for me..."

"*Motek*, please don't cry." He took her face and wiped her tears with his thumbs.

His shadow on the wall looked strange. Incomplete. He didn't know who he was anymore without his missing wing. It was a miracle he survived its loss. He felt unworthy of it and that he still had her.

But he had the chance to make things right and earn her forgiveness.

Dyna leaned into his palm. "I have already forgiven you, Cassiel. I forgave you the moment I realized why you did what you did. It wasn't because you gave up your wings for me in both of our lifetimes. It's because I finally understand how much you love me."

"I do." He brushed the tears from her cheeks. "I think far more than I can understand."

Dyna curled against his chest and rested her head over his heart. It was her comfort, he realized. To hear it beat in time with her own. He held her there, brushing his lips against her temple and stroking patterns on her back as he wondered where their path would go from here.

"I have something for you." Dyna climbed off him. She went into the room briefly before returning with a rectangular box wrapped in brown paper. Taking a breath, she brought it to him and sat beside him again.

"This is a gift from your father. He entrusted it to me before… he said it was for your birth-date."

On top was an envelope addressed to him, sealed with a white wax seal embossed with the sigil of Hilos.

But he couldn't make himself take it.

Dyna placed the box on the table and brushed his arm. "You don't have to open it yet. It will be waiting for you whenever you are ready."

"I wonder what he would think of my deeds and my failures. I wish to have a shred of his wisdom now that I am in dire need of it." There wouldn't be a voice to guide him now. All Cassiel had left of his father was this box, and that was a hard truth to bear. "When a High King dies, all the Realms gather in Hilos the next day for a funeral. But I didn't go, because I didn't want that to be my last memory of him." He swallowed back the tightness in his throat, ashamed of himself for not honoring his father. He laid back on the sofa, and Dyna curled up beside him. "When I left you, I dove into the sky and held my breath until I couldn't breathe. I was lost for what felt like hours in the void, searching for something to pull me from this. All I found was my pain staring at me, daring me to fight back. But pain was all I have known, so I let it feed and consume me. Then I truly was alone in a darkness of my making. The only way out was to convince myself that my father lived. He had to be alive, because if he wasn't, it meant I was the reason he died. And it meant … I couldn't save you either."

Dyna buried her face in his chest and held him tight.

"Everything feels different. I am different…" Cassiel lifted his hand and only a thin layer of blue flame coated his fingers. "My fire has dimmed to embers, to a point I hardly feel it at all. The wrathful need for destruction is gone, the compulsion is gone, and perhaps my divine blood, but none of those things made me a good king and much less of a good mate. Perhaps I was meant to lose a wing. It's my penance for my wrongs."

Like doing the same to his own brother.

"But you loved to fly…" she said brokenly, silent tears falling. "I am sorry I wasn't there to protect what I vowed to protect. I am so sorry I put you in a position where you had to make that choice."

Cassiel took her hands in his and traced his thumb over her ring. "*Lev sheli*, I can bear a future without flying, but not one without you. I would tear off my other wing if it meant saving your life again. You already saved mine. Before the keep. Before the bond. Before this life. You were the light in the darkness. You were there when no one else was. When I least deserved it. I have loved you from the beginning of this world, and it was agony when I lost you. I only ask that you outlive me, so I never have to live another day like that again."

She cried harder, and he silenced her with a kiss. Cassiel couldn't withstand her apologizing when it was he who could never find all the ways he needed to apologize to her.

If that day comes, I will make the same promise to you that you made to me. Dyna closed her eyes and breathed him in, branding their souls with another vow. *I will find my way to you, kohav. In every lifetime.*

He kissed the tears from her lashes, then kissed her lips, holding her close until they were both warm. Soft currents ran along his skin wherever they touched, and their True Bond thrummed. Linking their fingers together, Cassiel opened himself to her soul. He surrendered himself as the electrifying colors of green and gold filled his vision.

Perfect. It was perfect.

They didn't make it to the bed that time, or the time after that.

But neither had any complaints. The bond danced to their song as he willingly lost himself in her again, because there was nothing else he cared about but this.

Cassiel dozed with Dyna on a mound of blankets in front of the hearth, listening to her breathe as the rhythm of her heartbeat moved through his soul. They were safe here in Sellav, where they could ignore the rest of the world, but only for now. Dangers waited past the mountain. He would be ready for them this time.

Dyna woke in his arms as a new morning shone into the room.

Her green eyes blinked sleepily at him, and her brow furrowed. "I can hear you plotting, *kohav*. Before you attempt to change my mind, you should know I will not let you face Raziel alone."

He cracked a smile "Well, *ahuvati—*"

"No." Sat up on her knees, letting the sheets fall. "Don't attempt to delude me with your sweet nothings. I have already decided to face this with you. It's not only you and me anymore. It's *us*. Whatever comes our way, we will fight together. And if..." She took a breath. "If I die again—"

"Dyna." He placed a finger on her lips. "I was going to say, what do you have in mind? For I have every intention of facing every trial of our lives with you."

She searched his eyes. "You mean it?"

"I am finished attempting to control you merely for the sake of my sanity. I made that mistake once before, and it cost me everything. It will never happen again." Running his fingers up her side, she shivered, her breath catching as he trailed his nose up her neck and nipped her skin. "If you've not yet surmised, there is nothing I wouldn't do for you."

"Hmm. Would you shave your head if I asked?"

Cassiel nodded in all seriousness. "Of course, after my period of *aveilut* ends. I will shave my eyebrows for you as well."

A smile tugged at her lips. "How about Zev's tail?"

"I may need help to hold him down."

Dyna laughed, and he loved the sound.

"I hear you already sent Sowmya on a mission to Edym."

A cunning smile graced her lips. "I did."

Rising to his feet, Cassiel scooped up his mate and strode for the bathing chamber. "While we take a much-needed bath, you can tell me what grand scheme you have conjured and whatever other secrets you haven't told me yet." The light of her smile faded, and he felt the bond shake. "What is it?"

Dyna couldn't look at him. Her voice became small and brittle. "I did something terrible, Cassiel."

Trembling, she turned over her wrist, exposing a new geas in the shape of a sage leaf. And he sensed the first trial of their future was already here.

CHAPTER 94

Rawn

Rawn jolted up in bed. His chest heaved with ragged breaths, a layer of sweat coating his skin. It took him a moment to recognize his bedchambers in the estate. So starkly contrasting from the bowels of the dark Blood Keep that plagued his dreams. His pounding heart slowed when he saw Aerina sleeping beside him, nestled within the covers. The morning sun streaming through the windows fell over her bare back and the golden strands of her hair.

The remnants of his nightmare faded with each of her faint breaths. Rawn kissed her cheek. This was real, he reminded himself. She was real. He was home.

A month had passed in Sellav.

It was a month of healing for everyone, though it may not have been enough. Some wounds ran too deep.

On the right side of his chest was a new tattoo with the Greenwood sigil of a dynalya in full bloom. He rubbed the pink scars on the left side that still dully ached. Perhaps because they reminded him of Fair.

Above his mantle was a box of white wood. It held Fair's ashes that Dyna kept for him. She had broken down in his arms as she begged for his forgiveness, but Rawn didn't hold her to blame. The spear wasn't thrown by her hands.

A twinge gathered in Rawn's chest as he blinked back his tears. His dear friend was gone, and he would always miss him.

Distant neighing came from outside, and he stilled at the familiar sound. The morning breeze tousled the sheer curtains framing his open terrace.

Picking up his clothes off the floor, Rawn dressed and went outside. He leaned against the terrace's column as he watched his son train a white stallion in the pen far below. The horse looked a lot like Fair.

Aerina wrapped her arms around his torso from behind. He brought her hand to his lips.

"Good morrow, wife." Rawn pulled her around and met her beautiful smile.

She wore only a white sheet around her, and he was glad of the sight. Messy blonde curls fell around the face he had only seen in his dreams for the past two decades.

"I will never grow tired of hearing you wish me good morning." She sighed happily, but her smile was also sad. "Did you have another nightmare?"

Rawn trailed his nose over her bare shoulder, relishing the feel of her soft skin. Memorizing it anew. "At times I am half convinced I am still in that dark pit, and this is only the weavings of my imagination." He planted a light kiss over her jaw to her lips. He sighed and looked out at the fields again. "Yet I know this is not another perfect dream..."

Aerina laid her head on his shoulder. "Rawn, I was without you for twenty long years. I suffered your absence, but I did not begrudge you. I held faith you would return, for I know the man you are, and what lengths you would go for your family. Nonetheless, our son was denied his father, often reminded it was due to our past transgressions and duty to the crown. It is not aversion, my love. Raiden feels aggrieved."

Rawn shut his eyes. "As he should."

He should have been here to raise him and protect him from the world.

"When Raiden was a boy, I would often find him in your study, admiring your badges, your armor, and weapons. He would spend hours gazing at your portrait, wondering who you were. Yet as he grew, the other nobles slighted him for being the son of a soldier, one the court both acknowledged and reviled. Then your prominence became a shadow he could not escape. Now that you have returned, he is at a loss for how to perceive you." Aerina took Rawn's hand, placing his palm against her cheek. "Yet I have no doubt Raiden will come to see what a noble father he has before you go."

Rawn's hand shook slightly. He had tried not to think about having to leave again, but each day brought that reality nearer.

"My courage fails me," he admitted. "I have at last come home after so long. I cannot bear the thought of leaving you now."

Aerina's blue eyes glistened with tears, and she wrapped her arms around him. "Nor I, but I know why you must."

Rawn embraced her tightly. He had decided not to pass on his oath to another. Not that it had ever been a choice he would consider. All he could do was seize the time left with his family.

Once he had bathed and dressed for the day, Rawn went in search of his son. The estate was quiet in the morning, his guards and servants greeting him with welcoming smiles and deferential bows. He took his time strolling through the halls, admiring the refractions of light streaming through the tall windows. Beyond them rose a town nestled within the rolling hills. His son had done well in overseeing Sellav.

Raiden's bedroom was in the east wing, past the library, on the highest floor. The door was made of a rich chestnut, carved with the intricate design of a forest.

At his knock, there came no answer.

Hesitating, Rawn opened the door, calling his son's name. But he halted there at the threshold, staring at the back wall of shelves. Each one was filled with wooden carvings set neatly in rows.

"What are you doing in my chambers?" Raiden demanded behind him, and he yanked the door shut.

Rawn blinked at him. "You kept them ... I didn't realize there were so many."

His son looked away, his face flushing. "You sent 1,561 to be exact. What else was I to do with them? Why send so many?"

The sunlight coming from the windows fell over the token hanging around Raiden's neck and Rawn couldn't help smiling faintly. "I carved each one while I was thinking of my boy."

Raiden's flush deepened, and he shifted on his feet. "I ceased to be a boy a long time ago..."

"Right, of course. Then what would you prefer I send to you next time?"

Raiden drew back, disbelief widening his eyes. "You're leaving *again*?"

The question had weighed on Rawn since he came home. But the distress in his son's eyes made it truly unbearable.

"I must..."

"This is intolerable." Raiden shook his head. "You were gone for *years* on that wretched mission. You left everything behind, and for what? Many died to pull you from that desert, yet you plan to continue?"

Rawn reached for his shoulder, but he stepped back. "Raiden—"

"No, I refuse to accept this. The king gave you leave to stay. That red elf volunteered to go in your stead. *I* volunteered!" His pained shout echoed in the hall. He turned away, clenching his fists. "How can you be so selfish? Does Mother know?"

"She does," Rawn said softly.

Inhaling a shaky breath, Raiden's wet eyes met his, simmering with anger and resentment. His reply was a soft whisper, yet as sharp as any blade. "Merely admit that marrying her was a grievous error, and you're ashamed of what my birth did to your honor. If your ambition was to die to regain it, you shouldn't have returned. For I would have rather believed you left us because you had no choice at all."

They stared at one another for a moment. The despondency on his son's face made a terrible remorse sink into Rawn's stomach.

Eldred appeared at the end of the hall and cleared his throat. "My lord?"

"Yes?" Both Rawn and Raiden replied.

Eldred glanced between them. "Ah, pardon me, Your Grace. Lord Varden Karheim is at the front gates, accompanied by a collection of lords from noble Houses. They have come to call ... upon Her Grace."

Raiden growled a low curse. "You tell that Godsforsaken craven, we are not—"

"Open the gates, Master Eldred." Rawn swept past him. "Have them welcomed into the dining room."

The Magi Master bowed his head and went on his way.

Rawn continued, with his son following close behind. When they reached the estate's main hall, the captain of his guardsmen stood at attention. "Guests have arrived, Halder. See that they are shown proper Norrlen hospitality."

"As you command, Your Grace." Halder bowed his head. He motioned to the men, and they quickly marched on. Rawn went in the opposite direction.

"What are you doing?" Raiden asked. "Why are you welcoming them in?"

"What are the standards of this House?" Rawn said as they reached the back stairwell.

"Respect and honor."

"Words by which we live by. When a guest comes to call, we answer as etiquette demands."

Raiden's mouth twisted with disgust. "Then are we to be cowards who turn the other cheek? I was here to witness them insult my mother and smear our name. I stopped them from attempting to capture her. Not you. Do not speak to me of respect and honor when you have none for her."

Pausing, Rawn met his eyes. Whatever Raiden saw on his face made him shift back a step. "A man's duty is to protect his family. A son's duty is to show respect." Raiden reddened and lowered his gaze. "Are you armed?"

The question made Raiden's brow furrow. He had no scabbard at his waist, but with a murmured spell, he conjured a blade of teal light.

Rawn nodded. "Good. Now escort your mother and host our guests. I will join you presently." He climbed the shadowed steps to the third landing. His bow and quiver waited for him by the alcove that overlooked the dining room.

Dyna and the others were already there. They kept quiet and to the shadows, only to watch. This was something he had to deal with on his own.

Voices swarmed as many lords filed into the large dining room. All doors were open, leaving the curtains to billow gently from the wind coming through the courtyard. Eldred motioned for their guests to please be seated. They sat at the long table, laughing and conversing as servants set out platters of food and decanters of wine.

Rawn searched the crowd until he spotted a tall elf dressed in blue robes with a silver circlet pinning back his light brown hair. Varden's ashen blue eyes swept the dining room as he entered with his guards. The sigil of a sassafras leaf sitting above a half crescent of stars embossed their breastplates.

Quite expectedly, Varden chose to sit himself in Rawn's chair at the head of the table, directly across from the alcove.

Fifty feet of distance.

Giving him the perfect angle.

Rawn lowered to one knee and nocked his bow with an arrow.

"Your Grace!" Varden called pleasantly when Aerina and Raiden entered. "At last, you bless me with your presence. I was beginning to believe you were snubbing me."

638

"I would never, Lord Karheim," Aerina's voice floated to Rawn from below his perch. "I am pleased you could join us today."

His wife came into view with her hand on Raiden's arm. She wore a lovely pine-green gown with the bodice embroidered in gold. Silver brooches pinned up her hair.

"Forgive me, Mother, but I really must protest," Raiden whispered to her. *"I find this cordiality far too generously given."*

"Hush and trust your father."

Perhaps trust was a lot to ask. Rawn was a stranger to him, but they were family. And no harm would ever befall his family.

He watched as his wife and son moved to sit on the opposite end of the table from Varden.

"I am told you traveled to Avandia regarding the concern with Red Highland and Lord Norrlen's capture," Varden commented. "I am sorry to hear of his passing."

It was said with enough sympathy, yet he couldn't quite disguise the satisfaction from his gaze.

Raiden stiffened in his chair at the assumption.

Aerina lowered her head. "Thank you for your sympathies, Lord Karheim."

"Let us toast to his valiant achievements." Varden raised his golden cup. "Rawn Norrlen was a renowned soldier who inspired many with his leadership, selflessness, and conduct. Greenwood will mourn his loss."

Well, that brief speech almost sounded genuine.

Varden drank the rest of his wine, as did the other lords, offering their feigned praises. He motioned his empty cup to Aerina. "I seem to be out of wine. If you would be so kind, Your Grace."

Aerina paused at the ill-mannered request, and the room quieted. Then she gracefully stood up. "Of course."

"Mother," Raiden hissed in disbelief.

Taking a decanter from a servant, she walked around the table to him. Rawn's pulse thrummed as he kept his gaze on his wife. Varden eyed her with a leering smile while she poured more wine into his cup.

Rawn's bowstring creaked as he took aim.

"You must surely be in mourning for a time," Varden said, taking her hand. "However, once that time has passed, I hope you will consider taking another husband. An exquisite woman such as yourself should not be left to wither in this hovel. I will be honored to take you as my wife."

"You are kind in your proposal, Lord Karheim," Aerina replied politely. "Yet I am afraid I must decline." She placed his hand flat on the table and took a deliberate step back. "For I already have a husband."

Rawn released his arrow. It flew and pierced Varden's hand, pinning him to the table.

His scream filled the dining room. With a wave of Eldred's hand, the doors slammed shut. The lords jumped out of their chairs, and Karheim's guards immediately drew their weapons. Conjuring his sword, Raiden rushed to his mother's side.

"Get this out of me!" Varden yelled at his men. He braced his other hand on the table and Rawn shot a second arrow, pinning that one, too. Varden could only scream and helplessly thrash.

The fifty Norrlen guards that had secretly positioned themselves on the second landing drew their bows and aimed at their guests. Karheim Guards froze with their hands on their hilts and the lords halted mid-step for the door.

Everyone fell still.

Grabbing hold of the velvet curtain framing the alcove, Rawn slid down and landed lightly below. All eyes fixed on him as he strode through the quiet room. None dared to move. At his nod, Raiden moved Aerina back to join Eldred.

Rawn's cloak dragged through the blood leaking on the floor as he took a seat beside Varden. "Lord Karheim," he greeted.

Sweat beaded on Varden's pallid complexion and his throat bobbed. "Lord Norrlen..."

"I have been given many noteworthy reports regarding your endeavors with my family as of late. Certainly unfortunate, for such a thing cannot be left unaddressed."

"N-noteworthy?"

"Perhaps I need to remind you. First," Rawn took hold of the left arrow. "You accosted my home." He wrenched it out. Varden bit back a cry, squirming against the table. "Then you struck my son." He tore free the right arrow, and Varden fell back into the chair with a gasping whimper. "What punishment should I dispense for attempting to abduct my wife? The last time she was taken from me, well, there is a reason I earned my name."

Varden's wide eyes glanced down at Rawn's bloodied cloak.

"You dare to threaten him?" the head of Karheim's guards shouted in indignation. "He is the heir of Erendor!"

"And you stand in the presence of the Princess of Greenwood, sister to your king. He who has given me leave to resolve this matter," Rawn replied idly. "Halder."

"Yes, Your Grace?" Halder replied from the landing across from him.

"Should he open his mouth again, shoot him."

"Gladly." Halder aimed his bow at the startled guard.

Rawn returned his attention to Varden. "I am a sensible man, but I would sooner kill you simply for laying your hands on my pride."

"For-forgive me, Lord Norrlen," he stuttered, his throat bobbing. "I mean, Your Grace. I assumed she was—If I had known—I would never— Please forgive me. I never wished to offend you."

Rawn narrowed his eyes. "No, you wished for something that was not yours to covet."

"Could I not petition for your great mercy? I give you my sworn oath. I will never be so bold as to disrespect you or your House again."

"So it is sworn before the God of Urn and the souls present here today." He looked to the lords. "Who should state witness?"

"I," every elf in the room replied in unison.

Rawn stood. "Be glad of my mercy, Lord Karheim. For I will not spare you a second time." He leaned down, bringing them eye to eye, and he said ever so calmly, "Should you ever step foot on my land again, I will bury you where you stand."

Varden shrunk back.

"Do we have an understanding?"

"Y-yes, Your Grace."

"Thank you for this pleasant meeting." Rawn motioned, and the doors swung open. "Kindly see yourselves out."

The chairs screeched and boots skidded over the floors as the lords promptly departed. Varden's guardsmen helped him stand, quickly leading him out. Leaving Rawn and his family alone.

Once they were gone, Aerina took his offered hand and laughed as he spun her into his arms. "If I did not already love you as much as I do, that display would have left me irrevocably besotted, Lord Norrlen."

Smiling, he dipped his wife back and kissed her. That earned them whistles and cheering from the alcove and the second-floor landings. But he glanced over in time to see Raiden slip outside.

There was still one more matter to attend to. Perhaps the most important one.

Excusing himself, Rawn went in search of his son. He had lived a long life and lived through many experiences. None could tell him how to be a father, but he did know what it felt like to lack the affection of one.

Rawn found Raiden leaning against the fence of the horse pen. He came to stand by him, both merely watching a white stallion gallop through it. Soft whinnying carried on the wind.

"You did in one hour what I could not accomplish in years," Raiden muttered. "They fear you, and yet they respect you. All of Greenwood knows your name. I can only presume that is why she named me after you."

"It was not your mother who named you," Rawn said. "I did."

"Oh, how presumptuous of you. Even in name I am to stand in your shadow."

Rawn met his son's glower and couldn't help but chuckle. So stubborn. So free to speak his mind in ways he hadn't been able to at his age. As if his son could fulfill everything he couldn't. And that alone made him smile. With wonder. With love. With elation to be here to see it.

Raiden frowned. "Does that amuse you?"

"I did not name you after myself. In Old Elvish, your name would be *reydoner*. It means miracle. The first of many. A miracle we have prayed for with such yearning, the fates sought to grant it."

Raiden stared at him, his breath trembling.

"You are our miracle. There are many regrets I have in my life, but never would you be one of them." Rawn cupped Raiden's cheek, warming the spot where he was struck. "I chose to continue my journey, for I cannot put that responsibility on the shoulders of another. Especially my son's, who I love so much. There is no burden I would not carry for you and your mother. No mountain I would not cross to find my way home again."

His son looked at the Anduir peaks, his eyes growing wet. There was no longer any resistance as Rawn pulled Raiden to him and held his child for the second time.

CHAPTER 95

Zev

That evening, Rawn held a feast as his thanks and to celebrate a second chance at life with his family. He had dressed finely in an elegant coat worthy of a duke, a brooch in the shape of a horse pinning his silken cloak. By some blessing of the Gods, Lucenna was in a pleasant mood for once, though Zev guessed it had something to do with Klyde's hand in hers. Von and Tavin laughed as Keena threw grapes at them for teasing her. Everyone cheered when Cassiel and Dyna arrived.

It warmed Zev to see his friends together again.

He soaked in their cheerful faces glowing in the candlelight and the sound of their laughter. Secretly, he prayed it would last this time.

Aerina gave them colorful pieces of paper and ink to hold their own Hail of Embers. But burning away the past had dimmed the little merriment Cassiel could manage. He slipped away into the garden when he thought no one was watching. Zev could tell Dyna wanted to follow, but she looked at him pleadingly instead.

Zev didn't know what he could say to him. They hadn't really spoken since he woke.

But he knew what Cassiel needed right now.

The scent of moss and rain greeted Zev as he followed Cassiel's trail to the far reaches of the estate. He found him sitting by the edge of a pond, staring down at the crumbled green paper in his hand.

"Working up the courage to fill it?"

Cassiel glanced up at him. "More so wondering if I have the strength to do it."

Zev sat down beside him with his own paper. His was blue. He hadn't been able to write down what ill memories and past hardships he wished to burn away either. Because they would all be about losing his father.

Both quietly watched the silhouette of their friends on the roof of the estate. Flickers of fire flashed, and a shower of colorful embers rose into the sky.

"There is no strength for loss," Zev murmured, and his chest tightened with a familiar ache. "We're never prepared when it comes. Our lives are constructed of moments with them, that we couldn't ever imagine there would be moments without them. Then you're living in those moments, and it dawns on you that a part of you died with them."

Cassiel pressed a fist over his heart. "Does that feeling ever go away?"

"I am the wrong person to ask."

His madness may be gone now, but he still grieved. Perhaps he always would.

"I think I will carry the weight of my guilt with me everywhere," Cassiel said, his voice breaking. "That death was mine. I should have died that day, not him. I don't think I can forgive myself." The page crinkled in his fist. "What am I to do with that? Where do we put our regrets? They are not small enough to fit on this paper."

A burning rushed up the back of Zev's eyes. "We don't put them anywhere," he said as the embers faded into the clouds. "We carry them with us until we are ready to let them go. There will be days you will doubt you can do it. The journey is exhausting. You will pretend to be all right while the rest of the world moves on and leaves you behind to sit in the hole you fell in. But I climbed out of it, and I believe you will, too."

Cassiel pressed a shaking fist to his chest. "It's agony to remember."

It certainly was.

Twilight arrived with the breeze, casting soft ripples across the pond. The last of the sun's gleam turned the surface gold. It reminded Zev of the many times he used to camp at Lake Nayim with his father. And those wonderful memories hurt as much as the bad ones.

"I'm scarred, Zev. I don't mean the mark on my back. I mean those other scars you can't see but feel them there inside. That day cut out parts of me, and other parts I cut out myself. Those holes run so deep there's no ridding myself of them. I wish I could take it back. I would give anything to go back to who we were, to the morning before I ruined everything."

It was difficult to hear that from Cassiel. Zev recognized that familiar pain, because it had plagued him for so long, too.

The day he lost his father was the day he lost himself.

Zev traced the scars on his arms, left by his own grief. "We can look at scars as evidence of our pain, or we can look at them and see healing. I think we all wish to go back and change the past at some point. But there is no going back, and the fear of moving forward will plant you in the ground." A gentle breeze passed over them, and he breathed in the scent of spring that always came after a harsh winter. From the bushes came a white butterfly. It briefly landed on Cassiel's finger, then flew away into the open sky. "Perhaps the most difficult thing about saying goodbye is having to say it every day. Because it means that life is fleeting, and our time in the world is short. To honor them, we can't hide from life. Eventually you must live it."

Cassiel shut his tired eyes and simply breathed. Sadness hovered over him like a storm, but Zev hoped he understood they would part one day.

When Cassiel looked at him again, his gray eyes looked lighter. "I'm sorry I left."

There was a time Zev wouldn't have been able to hear that, but he wasn't angry anymore.

"We all do things we regret, Cassiel. Sometimes it's done out of fear or ignorance. Sometimes out of anger and resentment. We can't take those things back, but we can learn from them." Zev leaned forward on his folded knees as he took in the knolls of Sellav. "So don't hurt her anymore, not even with lies. Because those wounds hurt the most."

Cassiel looked back at the estate where the other half of him waited. And Zev could see no matter how much it pained him, he wouldn't let himself stay stuck anymore.

Zev was ready for that, too.

So he decided to let go of his fear of the Other and to forgive himself for the past. It would take time to heal. But they would walk through the journey of living with scars together.

Taking a breath, Cassiel lifted his page in his palm. Small petals of Seraph fire unfurled in the center. Zev added his page on top and they watched them blacken and burn away. The embers left behind were carried by the next breeze, rising into the sky like wishes in the clouds.

"If I made you feel as though our friendship didn't hold any value," Cassiel murmured. "I want you to know it means a lot to me, and so do you."

Grinning, Zev laid his head on Cassiel's shoulder. "I know. I've always sensed you were secretly in love with me."

Cassiel groaned and shoved him off. "I take it back."

"No, I consider that a confession. Don't worry though. I won't tell Dyna."

"Oh, sod off!"

He laughed, then they said no more. Nothing else needed to be said. Being here was enough. Because when grief had broken Zev, all he had wanted was for someone to sit with him. To understand his pain and tell him it wouldn't hurt this much forever.

What better place to be than with his brother?

CHAPTER 96

Cassiel

assiel studied his reflection in the mirror, and the velvet patterns of his new black coat. He stretched out his right wing, still feeling the phantom sensation of where the left one used to be. Like a missing limb. Two months had passed in Sellav, yet he still felt off balance. But Cassiel was at peace with that, because the alternative was so much worse.

This was merely a new challenge to overcome, rather than a disability.

An aching sadness seeped into the bond, and he met Dyna's despondent gaze in the mirror. She entered the room in a gown that resembled the starry night. Decorative gold plating embellished her shoulders and chest. Her sword, with a hilt of wings and an emerald on the langet, casually rested at her hip.

"Every time I feel its absence, I will remember who it was for," Cassiel said, turning to her. "Please don't be sad."

As Dyna came to him, a long veil streamed behind her black dress, glittering with embroidered stars. Thin gold chains adorned the back, falling against her bare spine. She took his hand. "I cannot help it. I feel regretful when I see it, and I wish I had taken your offer to fly once more with you."

A lump formed in his throat. Cassiel had to admit he wished they had, too. He would miss flying in those skies with her, but he was grateful they had memories to remember.

He nodded to the Pegasus waiting outside in the garden. "We have other ways to fly, *lev sheli*. Before we go, I have something for you." Picking up a polished square box off the mantle, he opened it and showed her. Inside lay a gold tiara set with emeralds the deep green of a forest. It glittered in the candlelight. "A crown befitting a queen."

"Oh, Cassiel, I have no words..." Dyna inhaled a soft breath of awe and arched an eyebrow at him playfully. "Are you to bestow me with such elaborate gifts each time you anger me?"

"And each time I am fortunate enough to make you happy." Removing the crown from the box, Cassiel placed it on her head. It couldn't have fit her more perfectly. He turned her to face the mirror, and she shyly stared at her reflection as the last of the evening light glinted on the emeralds. He wrapped his arms around Dyna's waist from behind and she leaned into him. "This one, however, is a present for your birth-date. I do remember the first night we met you mentioned you were born in the spring."

Which was fitting for her. She continued to rise through the harsh and cold temperate of life. Forever blooming.

Her green eyes widened. "I completely forgot."

"When was it?"

Dyna's expression softened and she brushed his cheek. "The day you woke up."

Lifting her chin to him, Cassiel kissed her. That day was a gift for them both. "I have a confession," he said. "I had many crowns and gowns made for you. Only the best, as I said."

She smiled against his lips. "Is that so? And do you have any more secrets you wish to confess?"

"That day in the wine cellar, it wasn't true that I needed to kiss you to remove the barrier. The look in your eyes told me I may never have the chance to do so again, so I lied. I couldn't help myself."

"I know." She laughed. "Your wings always twitch when you're nervous or when you lie."

"Yet you allowed me to get away with it?"

"Cassiel, I was so angry with you, but I missed you more." Dyna turned to face him, placing her hands on his chest. Her smile faded and traces of guilt hummed through the bond. "I am sorry I put you in a cage..."

He tucked a lock of hair behind her ear. "I deserved it."

It was where he had needed to be to begin finding himself again. Even with the discomfort of being trapped, he had never felt unsafe because he knew she held the key.

A knock came at the door, and Yelrakel peeked her head in. "Sire, it is time."

Cassiel nodded to Dyna. "Ready?"

She nodded back. With a fluid motion of her hand, the warmth of her Essence fell over him like a soft mist. The illusion of a flawless wing appeared over his shoulder.

Where they were going, he couldn't arrive without it.

They strode out of the estate, hand in hand, to the waiting Pegasus in the courtyard. Cassiel helped her mount the saddle, then climbed up behind her.

With a murmured command, they took off into the sky. Ever their shadow, the Valkyrie followed behind. Dyna's hair was like flames in the wind as they ascended higher, following the setting sun.

The Citadel of Nazar emerged from the clouds.

They circled above it where many Celestials waited. Dressed in white, blue, yellow, and a small group in purple. All looked up at them, and Cassiel inwardly prayed for wisdom and strength.

Dyna sent her gentle encouragement through the bond. *I'm with you.*

He didn't wish for anything else but that.

Directing the Pegasus with another command, they flew down and landed on the extended platform. They dismounted and climbed up the steps to the circular planform that held Nazar's *Hyalus* tree.

The court was quiet.

All waited for the commencement of what they came to do.

Lord Jophiel was dressed in white as a representative of Hilos, and with him was an unexpected arrival. His brother Tzuriel gave him a small nod. Now Lord of Hermon, Asiel represented those in blue. Cassiel was curious about the young male in gold representing Nazar. Yelrakel's most recent report informed that his name was Nuriel Nephele, the youngest son of Lord Gadriel, and now the Lord of Nazar. Lastly, was Skath, represented unexpectedly by a female.

"I have called you here today to at last address the Realms, as I should have done the day of my ascension," Cassiel said. "Yet I failed you when I allowed my anger and grief to turn me against my people."

"You decimated our entire Realm," the female of Skath said scathingly.

"Lord Hallel staged a coup and violated the sacred law to never rise against the crown, Katriella," Lord Jophiel interjected. "Which led to High King Yoel's death. *Alav Hashalom.*"

"Alav Hashalom," the court repeated in the name of the dead.

"Our people have lived through a coup before, and the Realms will never suffer such a thing again," Jophiel continued. "Regicide deserves of only one sentence. A swift passage through the Gates."

"If it had been a true decimation, who were the survivors I granted sanctuary to in Hermon?" Asiel added. "We opened our doors to Skath. That which brought you the opportunity to speak here today."

Katriella glowered and shut her mouth.

"You are right to feel betrayed," Cassiel told them.

"You tore the Realms apart," Nuriel said, his eyes red with unshed tears. "My father was not part of the coup, but he felt forced to join it when you attacked Nazar. Then he returned wounded with burns by your Seraph fire two moons ago, and Akiel wasted no time slaying him for his Realm. My elder brother died defending me."

The court murmured the blessing for the dead upon hearing the news of Gadriel's passing.

"If my Vanguard had not supported me against Akiel," Nuriel continued. "He would have sent me through the Gates as well. That is what your reign has brought. The ruination of families."

Angry murmurs filled the Citadel. Cassiel was at a loss for what to say, because that was true.

He ruined families, beginning with his own.

Dyna brushed his arm and stepped forward. "Sons and daughters of *Elyōn*," she called, quieting them. "The ruination began when the Lord of Edym plotted to take the throne. Lord Raziel pulled the strings, which brought about the fall of King Yoel, Lord Hallel, and Lord Gadriel. From his very line came the conspirator who betrayed your first High King for his own gain. He seeks to do so again."

They had decided not to divulge that Raziel was the same General from the First Age. It may be too much for the court to believe.

"Perhaps Lord Raziel should take the throne," Katriella said, her pale blue eyes flashing. "High King Kāhssiel turned on his people, and so has the descendant of his line! Who is to say he will not do so again? With such a magnitude of power of Seraph fire at his hands, we are not safe." She shouted to the others. "My people live in fear of his flame. The Realms have sacrificed our peace for a king who rules with his fury rather than his insight." She glared at him. "You expect us to trust the one who came to destroy us? No one would follow a tyrant. If you are not the same Kāhssiel from the past, prove it. Until then, I will never bow to you."

Voices merged, most agreeing with her.

"And if I would sacrifice that power, would that earn your pardon, Lady of Skath?" Cassiel asked her.

She blinked at him. "Lady?"

"To defend your Realm so fiercely and advocate for your people. It could only be yours."

Katriella's mouth parted, and she cleared her throat. "Yes ... Skath would pardon he who would see fit to acknowledge his wrongs. But you speak of subduing your flame, and to do such a thing is..." She swallowed, her own wings twitching.

"Unimaginable?" Cassiel finished. An uncomfortable stillness fell over the court. No Celestial would ever relinquish their wings. Taking a breath, he nodded at Dyna, giving her permission to unveil his disgrace. *It's all right.*

How could he lead if he lived in hiding? To start over, he had to be honest with his people.

Biting her lip, his mate reluctantly waved her hand. The illusion fell away, and the court gasped. Lord Jophiel's face was a mixture of dismay and sorrow.

"Unpleasant sight, isn't it?" Cassiel said with a heavy breath. "When I first sprouted my wings at three winters old, it was perhaps the most frightening day of my short life. I didn't find the courage to fly until I was nearly four. Thereafter, flying became my solace and every day since I lived in those skies." He looked up at the clouds bathed in the colors of the sunset. "My father told me that our wings are a gift from the Heavens to fulfill our purpose. His wish was to leave behind a ruler who would bring a change for the betterment of our people. But in one night, in an instance of minutes, he was gone, and I forgot what was important. Instead of protecting the Realms, I have taken actions unworthy of my father's seat or the legacy he entrusted me with." His throat tightened a moment, and Dyna gently squeezed his hand. "I come to you now ashamed and regretful for all I have done. I am ready to serve you as I should, beginning with removing that which you feared the most. To give up our wings ... It is a great loss, but it's a sacrifice I made to protect what I hold most dear. I failed to keep my integrity in a time when it was needed most. I am deeply sorry for that, and for every wrong I have committed against you. Before the eyes of *Elyōn*, I swear it will be the last." Closing his eyes, Cassiel bowed to his people. "I am far from worthy to be your king, but I will beg you for another chance to fulfill my father's wish."

Losing his wings may not be enough to repay what he had done. He accepted whatever consequences that may come. Should the Realms demand it, he was ready to step down, for he would no longer rule by force.

Silence filled the courtyard.

Then came the first flutter of fabric and wings as Lord Jophiel, Tzuriel, and the Celestials in white lowered to one knee, bowing their heads. "Hilos swears fealty to the High King."

Grinning, Asiel lowered to one knee with his people, and they bowed as well. "Hermon swears fealty to the High King."

Cassiel's hand shook around Dyna's.

Lady Katriella and the fierce females with her followed suit. "Skath swears fealty to the High King."

Lord Nuriel studied him for a moment, and Cassiel saw the mirror of grief in his eyes. Exhaling a heavy breath, the young lord lowered to his knee, and every Celestial in the Citadel bowed. "Nazar swears fealty to the High King."

Either due to the coming of twilight or the blessing of the Heavens, the *Hyalus* tree glowed with the purest of white light. Upon Cassiel's head appeared a crown of Seraph flame. Looking out at his court, he felt his chest stir.

He hoped it meant that somehow his father approved.

"We hereby stand with the true High King of Hilos and the Three Celestial Realms," Lord Jophiel announced, gazing at him with moving joy. "Long may he reign."

"This is how you chose to play your hand?" Lord Raziel's sharp blue eyes gleamed with mockery on the surface of the water mirror. His private study in Edym was dark, nightfall visible on the open terrace behind him. In the shadows of the room lurked Akiel.

"Oh, I am only getting started," Dyna replied as she sat beside Cassiel on the sofa.

Raziel ignored her. "I really am disappointed, youngling. You are repeating the same senseless mistakes. Sullying the sanctity of the Realms and yourself by once again choosing a weak mortal." His mouth twisted with a snide smile. "Whatever you hope to accomplish will fail. I have had a thousand years to prepare for your coming."

Cassiel merely flipped through a book on local flora and the lord scowled at his lack of interest.

"You are foolish if you believe I am not ready for you this time, Raziel," Dyna said, crossing her legs. His face twitched at her informal address. "You can plot, but you forget, I can do the same. The Realms now know you have taken part in the coup against King Yoel. They have dubbed you an oathbreaker and rebuked your name. Edym is no longer under the cover of Hilos, and you are proclaimed an enemy of the crown, for their High Queen deemed it so." Fury simmered in his gaze, his face reddening. She canted her head and her eyes ominously glowed. "Do you see how much power a mortal has?"

Cassiel smiled to himself and continued turning the pages. He loved it when his mate behaved this way. Commanding. Strong. The embodiment of a true warrior. Sheli's spirit hadn't changed.

"You shoved me off a cliff," Dyna continued. "You killed my child, and you killed my mate. So you will contend with me now. I am coming for you, Raziel. When you least expect it, I will come."

The Lord of Edym stared at her, at last truly listening. From the shadows, a figure moved swiftly past Akiel. So fast, it was there a second, then gone. He stumbled forward with a gasp, pressing a hand over his heart. Crimson seeped through his fingers. Raziel reared back as Akiel fell at his feet and faded away into light.

He whipped around, his chest rising and falling with sharp breaths as he searched the room. But Sowmya had already vanished.

"I will fill your days with fear," Dyna said, her voice dropping to a pitch that sprouted goosebumps on Cassiel's back. Her glowing green eyes held Raziel captive. "And I will not stop until I take everything from you. Your kingdom. Your House. Your head."

The image in the mirror faded away.

Cassiel tossed the book aside and hauled his mate onto his lap. "I do not deserve you," he groaned, planting kisses all over her face. *"At mehamemet. At yafa. At mushlemet."*

She smiled against his lips. "You do, but you can always convince me again with more praises like that."

His mouth skimmed hers as he translated through the bond. *You are amazing. You are beautiful. You are perfect.*

"Cassiel." Dyna rested her head on his chest. "I am not perfect. I've hurt others, and I've hurt you. So much..." Her voice broke. "Then I bargained away our unborn son."

"I hope you know that I do not fault you for any of that, *lev sheli.*" He felt her trembling, and he wrapped her in his arms, covering her in a shroud of feathers. "We will not allow Leoake to take him."

She shut her eyes, both glimpsing the wispy image of a boy with dark hair and green eyes. The vision couldn't be any clearer when the future was so uncertain. Cassiel never expected such a thing to be possible for his life, and now that he knew it was, he already loved that little soul. He would do anything, tear down any wall, walk through any trial to assure they had a future.

At first, it seemed to be a miracle that he had survived. But he finally understood that miracle wasn't for him. It was for *them*.

All three of them.

"I will fight with you to the very end," Dyna murmured. "So don't forget that you have someone on your side. Don't carry your worries and burdens alone. If you ever try to leave me again, I will knock you onto your arse."

Chuckling quietly, he ran his fingers through her short hair. "You are probably the only one who can."

They had come a long way since they left Hilos, but he was ready to face whatever came next with her at his side.

Beginning with a letter.

They both looked at the sofa table, where the rectangular box his father left him waited with an envelope on top.

"I am afraid to open it," Cassiel confessed. "What if I can't withstand it again?"

"Loss is particular that way," Dyna said, placing a hand over his heart. "There are days where it leaves you defeated on the ground, and other days where it's a passing guest. The pain is always there, but our lives change and expand around it. One day, you may hear something, see something, or smell something that will remind you of them. And for a moment, you will grieve all over again. When those days happen..." She cupped his cheek. "Come to me."

Cassiel smiled wistfully. "So you may either embrace me or attack me, I assume."

"Which one do you prefer right now?" Dyna asked, and the vow she had written on his arm tingled.

It really wasn't a question when they both needed the same thing.

He tightened his arms around her, and she held him tightly, too. There was warmth in that embrace and pure, unconditional love that promised she would be right there to catch him when he fell.

"I may not always have the words to pull you from the dark, but I will always be here to sit with you in it."

And that was enough to give him the courage he needed to take the first step of living with this loss.

"I think I am ready to open it now..."

"Would you like me to give you privacy?"

Cassiel shook his head. He took a breath and another, before he could make himself open the envelope and read his father's last words.

My son,

If you're reading this letter, it means I have left you again, and I am so sorry for that.

I mourn all the days lost when I sent you away to Hermon. It was done to protect you from harm, yet I failed to protect you from the harm I caused. I made so many mistakes, but please know I loved you through all of them.

Forgive me for not being there when you needed me. For I wish I had been there when you felt alone. I wish I had been there when you soared into the sky for the first time. I wish for so many things I cannot have now. My greatest wish is for you not to fear tomorrow.

The past was painful, yet the future does not have to be. It may bear moments of pain, as well as moments of joy. Each one you will gather until at the end of your life, you are full of them. Living is the most arduous thing souls must do, but it's worth it.

I promise you it's worth it.

Whatever path you take, no matter what comes or what failures you face, know that I have great faith in you. Fly, Cassiel. Lead, and all else will follow. When we see each other again, I expect to hear about the marvelous life you lived.

With all the love in the world, your father,

Yoel Soaraway

The words on the page blurred together by the time Cassiel finished reading the last line. He closed his wet eyes and simply breathed.

This was one of those moments. It glowed there in his chest as he came to accept this was the way of life. It was filled with happiness and with pain. With loved ones who may not stay forever. But the impression of them, and the light they brought, was left behind in the map of his memories.

There would come a time to move on. A time to let go.

But only of the pain. Not of those moments.

Cassiel would gather them all and remember each one.

Something lifted off him then, and his lungs expanded with a full breath. He was better. Not good, but better. The weight of his loss was still there, but a little lighter. A little more bearable. His father was gone, and he was grieving, but it would be all right.

As Cassiel returned the letter to the envelope, he felt something inside. Turning it over, two silver cuffs landed in his palm. The bands were in the shape of wings coming together.

"What is that?" Dyna asked softly.

Cassiel didn't think he could cry anymore, but a burning clamped his throat. "Wing cuffs..." He swallowed, struggling to speak. "These are given to Celestial children when their wings first sprout. They fit over the margins where the shoulder blade meets the wing. The sacred steel draws out the divinity in our blood to ease the growing pains and to help us fly..."

He turned over the cuffs in his palm. They were hardly an inch in circumference, made to fit a three-year-old's wings. Polished and still new. They wouldn't fit him, not that he could use them anymore.

With a shaking hand, Cassiel opened the box, and inside lay golden plates.

Wing armor that he couldn't use either.

That was a bit much.

Rising, Cassiel went out onto the terrace, letting the cool air ease the tightening in his chest. He looked out at the skies that he would never be able to reach again. It was a choice he made and would readily make again, but he could admit it was another loss he mourned.

"My father must have had these made when I was a child," he said when Dyna joined him outside. She rubbed his back. "Why give them to me now?"

Cassiel placed the cuffs on the banister, and they glinted in the moonlight. He could have used them as a boy.

"Perhaps he wanted to make up for lost time," Dyna said. "You can still wear them to remember him by. They are small enough to fit as rings."

She took the cuffs and slipped each one onto his thumbs. No sooner had she done it, all the remaining divinity inside of him whoosh through Cassiel's veins to his back. Heat burst on his skin and blue light washed through the terrace. Gasping, Dyna covered her mouth, tears springing to her eyes.

Cassiel fell still, staring at her face. His hands trembled, his breath catching. Slowly, he looked up at his reflection in the glass doors and his heart lurched. There were two wings rising above his shoulders.

One as black as the night, and another made of pure flame.

Cassiel looked out at the horizon. How … how could his father have known?

Then it occurred to him then, these cuffs weren't made to train his wings, but made specifically to help control his Seraph fire. Yet they came to be exactly what he needed.

His power didn't vanish when he lost his wing. Here's what remained.

"Does this mean what I think it means?" Dyna asked shakily.

Sighing, Cassiel tearfully smiled at her and held out a hand. "Why don't we find out, *lev sheli.*"

Dyna didn't hesitate. She rushed to him, and he swept her into his arms. Her green eyes gleamed beneath the glow of his fire. They both looked up at the night sky, twinkling with stars and the pinnacles of the impossible.

And he soared.

CHAPTER 97

Dynalya

The days passed too soon for Dyna's liking. Before she knew it, spring came to an end, and it was time to leave the Valley of Sellav. They gathered outside the gates of the Norrlen estate in the early morning to say goodbye. The sun rose over the horizon, golden light bathing the land like a new beginning.

Rawn looked like a knight in his new armor and sword gifted to him by the king. Kneeling before his wife, he pressed his lips to her hand. "My lady, I give you my sworn oath to return to you again."

Aerina said tearily, "I will hold you to your word, Rawn Norrlen. Do not keep us waiting long." She lay a hand on her flat stomach, smiling happily. His eyes widened, and they all burst with cheers as he kissed her.

Raiden crossed his arms when he turned to him. "You have nine months to complete your mission. If you miss the birth, I will denounce you as my father."

A gentle smile rose to Rawn's face, as it always did when he looked at his son. "I will not fail you."

"That remains to be seen," Raiden retorted, but he couldn't help smiling back. Their relationship had grown over their stay, and it warmed Dyna to see it. "I have taken the liberty of choosing a horse for you."

He motioned to a servant coming up the path, holding the reins of a stallion. It had a beautiful white coat with eyes the color of a clear sky. Rawn stared at the horse, for it was an exact mirror of another they once knew.

"This is Sight," Raiden told him. "The last offspring of Fair. He was meant for me, but our bond never took place. I believe he was waiting for you."

So many emotions crossed Rawn's face, and they walked together toward the horse. He stroked Sight's muzzle, murmuring in soft Elvish. With a soft nicker, the stallion bumped Rawn's shoulder in the same manner Fair used to do.

Dyna squeezed Lucenna's hand, fighting the emotion swelling in her throat.

"The loss of a bonded horse is as painful, if not more, than the loss of family," Aerina said beside them. "They give their entire lives to loving us, and we spend the rest of ours missing them."

And she would. Dyna carried Fair's loss the same way she mourned losing a friend.

Lev sheli? At Cassiel's call in the bond, she went to him, and he gave her shoulders a gentle squeeze. *Fair now grazes in peaceful fields in the Heavens. His spirit rests.*

The image made her eyes well up. *I know.*

Eldred approached them with items in his hands. "The Accords," he said, passing Cassiel a scroll sealed with green wax embossed with the sigil of Greenwood. "It is signed and free of any instigations. Greenwood stands with Hilos. As our thank you for your great aid, King Leif grants you gemstones from his coffers." Eldred handed Dyna a velvet pouch in the same color, and something shifted inside. Opening it, she found small shards. Crystals. A handful of both Tanzanite and Moonstones. "There are Elder Trees across Urn in the unlikeliest of places. The closest one is a few miles north of the Anduir Mountains. Rawn knows where."

They both gave the Magi Master their thanks before he moved on to speak to Lucenna. Eldred had spent the spring training them on how to activate the Elder Trees.

They now had the means to travel more efficiently.

Yelrakel and the Valkyrie came forward and bowed, accepting their next mission. Dyna and Cassiel agreed it was best to send them to Skath to overlook the rebuilding of the Realm. Where they would be near when it was time to confront Raziel.

"My lady," Raiden approached her. He held out the reins of a graceful Elvish mare with a golden coat. "I have a horse for you as well. Her name is Solaya."

Dyna gasped softly and stroked her silky mane. "Oh my, she is magnificent, Raiden. But I don't know if I..."

"I will beg you to allow me this. Solaya is also unbonded, but I think you both are kindred spirits." Raiden's smile turned to a cool frown as he met Cassiel's gaze past her shoulder. "I will only surrender Dynalya to you this once, Soaraway. Break her heart again, and I will take her away from you for good."

Dyna tensed, but Cassiel only smirked. "Surrender? You never had her, Norrlen."

Smirking back, Raiden returned to his family. Well, that may be as close of a truce between them as there could be.

Once all goodbyes were said, Dyna nodded to her Guardians that it was time.

Zev shifted into his wolf, and Keena took her place on his head. Von mounted Coal, Lucenna and Klyde rode on Onyx, and Tavin climbed onto his own mount.

Lady Aerina held her son's hand as she gazed upon her husband. Her watered eyes went to them pleadingly. "Bring him home to me."

Each gave their word.

Then they rode across the valley for the next part of their journey.

"So Raiden can freely bask you with gifts, but I am limited?" Cassiel asked when they reached the foothills of the Anduir Mountains.

Dyna patted his arm securely wrapped around her waist. "Are you vexed that he threatened to steal me away if you broke my heart again?"

He huffed indignantly under his breath, making her smile. His possessive growl passed through her mind. *That will never happen again, lev sheli.*

Breaking my heart or stealing me away?

Both.

And that promise settled on the bond with all the others.

Their group reached a familiar ridge secluded within a cluster of rowan shrubs that overlooked the province of Sellav. Rawn paused there as he gazed at his home. Perhaps to memorize it until he saw it again.

Their hike up the Anduir Mountains took two days.

They came to rest within a range of cascades for the evening and set up camp. Dyna watched all her Guardians together, her friends, laughing as they shared a meal around a fire, and felt her circle was at last whole.

The journey was far from over yet. Many things still hung over her head, but she would live now and not fear tomorrow, or what she may come to regret. Everything at last seemed to be right again.

She was happy.

Safe.

And completely warm as she fell asleep in Cassiel's arms. So when a cold breeze brushed her cheek, Dyna instantly woke. She frowned sleepily at the canvas flaps undulating in the breeze, exposing the strip of pale morning sky.

Didn't she tie those shut?

Keena dashed inside in a flutter of gold dust. "Dyna, wake up!" she whispered urgently. "Tavin is leaving."

She blinked at her and sat up. "What do you mean?"

"I saw him ride away," the fairy said, her hazel eyes stretching wide. "And he had the key."

"What?" Dyna exclaimed, startling her mate awake.

"What is it? What's wrong?" Cassiel asked groggily.

Her satchel that she had left on a chair last night was now open on the table.

"He took it," Dyna gasped. "Tavin took the key!"

She threw off the blankets, instructing Cassiel and Keena to wake the others before running outside. Three tents circled the campfire where a black wolf soundly slept, and only three horses were tied to a tree.

She ran to Lucenna's tent, finding her and the captain curled together, fast asleep. "Klyde! Lucenna!" She shook them awake. "Tavin is gone."

That instantly woke them up. They rapidly threw on their shoes and coats as she blurted out what he had done. They ran outside as Zev darted into the forest.

He must have caught the scent.

"He went north," Von said, already on his horse with Keena in his pocket. They ran to mount their saddles.

"I'll search from above," Cassiel told her and leaped into the sky.

Klyde took point, galloping so fast through the trees, the rest of them struggled to catch up.

Cassiel called out from above, pointing north. "There!"

They broke out of the forest onto a hillock, and the boy had reached the top of it.

"TAVIN!" Klyde bellowed.

His nephew turned and watched them race across the field for him. Klyde reached the base of the hill first.

"Stay there, uncle," Tavin called. "Don't follow me."

Klyde jerked on his reins, coming to a halt. "What are you doing?" he exclaimed.

"I'm leaving. I can't be with you anymore." Tavin's jaw clenched. "I left Skelling Rise because I needed to know who I am. So I followed you to ask why you didn't tell me the truth. But I realized even if I did ask, you would never tell me."

Klyde stared at him, his chest rising and falling sharply.

"I heard what you said to them that day in your room ... about my father."

Dyna sucked in a breath, and they all fell still. Cassiel landed beside her.

Tavin's pale blue eyes shone with angry, unshed tears. "For the entirety of my life, you lied to me. You told me my father was dead."

Agony crossed Klyde's face, and he moved a little closer. "I'm sorry, lad. I chose to tell you he died because I couldn't admit to you that he had abandoned us."

"He didn't abandon me. If he knew I was alive, he would have stayed."

Klyde shook his head. "No, Tavin. Your father..." His face crumbled. "He doesn't care about anyone but himself. I told you he was a hero, but that's not him."

"How would you know?" he demanded angrily. "You haven't seen him in fifteen years. You don't know anything about him. You don't know what he would have done if you told him I was alive. You kept me from him, and I can't forgive you."

"Tavin—"

"You're a liar!" Tavin shouted. "Mum, Von, and the lot of you all lie to yourselves and to each other. You're all *liars!*" He took a gasping breath, and all emotion melted away to a familiar frosty indifference that sent a shiver down Dyna's spine. "It's only fair that I return the favor."

Then a new rider joined Tavin on the hill, and horror stole the ground from under her.

A cool smile crossed Tarn's face. "You've grown, Dale."

Klyde's breath shuddered at the sight of his brother. "Tavin, get away from him!"

But the boy simply reached in his coat and handed his father the bronze key to Mount Ida, along with a scroll.

Pocketing the key, Tarn unrolled the scroll, and his mouth hitched with a cool smile. His pale eyes fixed on Dyna. He showed her the page with a drawn copy of her map. "Thank you for your contributions, Maiden. They will serve me well."

Her heart pounded wildly against her ribs. *When did he...?*

"Well done." Tarn nodded at Tavin. "I am proud of you ... son."

"He's not your son," Klyde growled.

"Quick to temper, as always, little brother." Tarn rolled up the scroll and tucked it away into his coat. "You have no right to feel angry about this when it was you who hid something precious from me. Imagine my surprise when he pulled me from the sea after my ship went down."

That's how Tarn had survived? Tavin must have followed her to Argent.

"Would it have made a difference if you knew about him?" Klyde demanded. "Would you have stayed to raise him?"

Tarn didn't answer. A unit of Raiders on horses rose up on the hill with him, all armed. Tarn merely glanced at his son wordlessly, giving some signal. Obediently, Tavin mounted onto his father's horse.

He trusted him. That had to mean Tavin had been communicating with Tarn all this time. The water mirror, she realized. He had been in her room...

"I raised him, Tarn," Klyde said shakily. "He's *my* boy. Please don't take him with you."

Traces of sadness briefly crossed Tavin's face, but it faded beneath his resolve. "I am choosing to go with my father, uncle. Let me go."

"No, you can't go with him!" Klyde rushed the field, but ice sprouted from the earth, creating a blockade of frozen spears.

"Thank you for seeing to his well-being," Tarn said, tugging on the reins. "But my son will stay with me now."

Dyna exchanged a look with Von, and he nodded. "How did you find us?" she asked. To Cassiel she said in the bond, *Be ready.*

As if he couldn't help himself, Tarn smirked at her over his shoulder, "You really should learn how to properly use a water mirror, Maiden. It's a tool that could easily be turned against you."

You never know who is listening.

A cold rush crawled over her skin. Her mind flashed with a memory of Cassiel dumping out the water and wiping down the mirror after using it. A habit she had never practiced. She was supposed to clean out the salt. This whole time the mirror had been activated even when it didn't glow.

Tarn had heard every conversation and sound when the mirror was in the room.

Her weeping over the abandonment by her mate.

Her screams when she woke from her nightmares.

Her schemes.

He had heard *everything.*

Including the secret of Tavin's dormant magic.

"He knows..." Dyna said in horror. "He knows!"

Snapping the reins, Tarn galloped down the side of the hill with Tavin.

Cassiel cast out a wave of blue flame, instantly melting the ice. Throwing out her Essence, Dyna cleared a path through the fire. Klyde and Von charged ahead. The Raiders rode to meet them on horseback. A battle broke out on the hill, magic, fire, and steel clashing. Zev tackled his targets, teeth and claws slashing through flesh.

They easily broke through the barricade of Raiders, but it wasn't meant to hold them. Only to stall.

Von and Klyde made it over the hill by the time Dyna made it to the top. And she was once again struck with dismay.

Further past the bottom of the hill in another field were Sai-chuen and Lumina. They stood beside an Elder Tree. The pink light of Lumina's Essence gleamed in her eyes. The moon shards on her wrists glowed with her rising chant, and the gateway glowed with a spiral of light.

Klyde and Von were nearly at the bottom, but too far to stop them.

"Oh, Gods," Lucenna gasped when she and Rawn reached the top. "He's going to get away."

"No, he won't." Dyna kicked her heels, and they galloped down the hill after them.

But it was too late.

Tarn and Tavin rode through the gateway. His Xián Jīng spy and Magi Master strode in next.

Klyde and Von raced side by side across the field for the Elder Tree, galloping so fast they appeared to fly on will alone. They were only a few feet away.

"They're going to make it," Dyna said breathlessly, clenching the reins in her shaking fists. "They will."

Light exploded with a roar and tore everything away.

The force threw Dyna off her horse. Her body slammed into Cassiel's arms as he caught her and Lucenna. They hit the ground hard. The blow wrenched the air from her lungs. She gasped, staring up at the smoke billowing in the sky.

"Lev sheli, can you hear me? Are you hurt?" Cassiel's voice sounded dull beneath the ringing in her ears.

I'm all right... She assured him. With his help, Dyna sat up, and her vision slowly cleared. Smoke and clusters of flickering flame spotted the scorched field.

Lucenna sat up where she had been thrown beside her, and her eyes widened with terror. "Klyde!" She scrambled to her feet, vanishing into the smoke.

"Oh, no." Dyna stumbled to her feet, clutching Cassiel's arm as she frightfully searched for the others. "Lord Norrlen? Zev? Where is Keena?"

"She was with Von..." Cassiel said, his eyes widening.

And Von had been right at the Elder Tree when it exploded—along with Klyde.

Dyna shook as she continued searching for her cousin. "Zev!"

"Here!"

Dyna ran toward the sound of Rawn's voice. She found him kneeling beside a black wolf, motionless in the grass.

Rawn looked up at her, his face distraught. "He was right in front of me when it blew, my lady. He took the brunt of the blast."

Dyna slid to Zev's side and checked for a pulse. She sucked in a breath when she found his steady pulse. The glow of her Essence seeped into him and revealed a few broken ribs but nothing fatal. "He's alive. Stay with him."

She ran to search for the others, with Cassiel on her heels. A sobbing cry led them to Lucenna. She appeared within the smoke, holding Klyde on her lap. Dyna ran over to them and quickly examined him. He was unconscious but bore no burns or wounds. Only a little blood leaked from his ears.

Repercussion from the blast.

Dyna cast out her Essence and searched for any internal damage, but found none that should have been there. Only burst eardrums.

"Lucenna, he's all right." Dyna told her once she healed them. "It's a miracle he's alive. His mercenary coat must have protected him."

"It wasn't only his coat." She opened the lapels, revealing the small glass vial containing a four-leaf clover hanging from his neck.

Nature's charm that repelled attack magic.

"What happened?" Cassiel asked, inspecting the charred stumps in the ground. It was all that was left of the Elder Tree.

"They destroyed it so we couldn't follow," Dyna said as she got to her feet. But she paused, looking around the field. "Where is Von? I don't see him."

"He was right here when it blew. Do you think they…?"

She gripped her shaking hands, her breath catching with a wave of sorrow for her lost Guardians. But her assumption of the worst quickly faded because there was no sign of Von's body in the field. Not even his horse.

"No, they're alive." Dyna smiled with relief. "Von made it through—and Keena is with him."

EPILOGUE

Lucenna

Lucenna's magic moved through the *Essentia Dimensio*. The glowing purple net spread into the darkness far and wide, but for the third time, it faltered and faded away.

It was no use.

Sighing, she opened her eyes. "I can't find him. He's been veiled."

Klyde stood with his arms crossed at the edge of the cascades flowing over the cliff. He was quiet, simply staring out at the sun setting on the horizon. The ends of his blue tunic rippled in the wind. Without his mercenary coat, he seemed vulnerable, like his armor had been removed.

It was neatly folded with her satchel beside her. Along with his weapons. The emblem of a bird's skull stood out on the dark blue fabric. It was once a symbol of what united his family.

"I'm sorry, Klyde."

"It's not your fault, love." He rubbed his face. "I am the only one to blame. Tavin's right. I am a liar. I should have told him the truth a long time ago."

Everyone lied at some point, but she couldn't fault him for lying to protect his nephew. The one thing Klyde had always been honest about was how much he loved his family.

His clenched fists trembled. "I fear what he will do to him..."

"We will get him back, Klyde." Lucenna brushed his cheek, his tired eyes meeting hers. "We know where Tarn is headed, and the gateway could only take them so far. It's a long road from here to Harromog

Modos. The Elder Tree is gone, but if we take the train, there is a chance we'll stop him before he ever reaches the Lost Well." She sighed.

Klyde's eyes lightened with a sudden awareness. "There is an Elder Tree at the heart of Naiads Mere."

Lucenna gasped excitedly. "Gods, are you sure?"

"Aye, it's deep below in those waters. I've seen it. Well, I'm certain I did. I was a little distracted by the beautiful half-naked nymphs attempting to drown me."

She arched her eyebrow. "Are you trying to make me jealous?"

He grinned. "Is it working?"

She swatted his arm. "If we reach it, we could use that Elder Tree to jump to the Lost Well rather than trekking across the desert."

"My thoughts exactly."

She pivoted on her heel toward the direction of the forest where their camp was set up. "I'll tell the others."

But Klyde took her hand and spun her back to him and kissed her. It was an aching kiss, one that felt like goodbye.

Lucenna pulled back a little to search his eyes. "You're going after him alone, aren't you?"

It wasn't really a question, because he had already decided.

Klyde looked down and his brow furrowed. "On the day Tavin was born, I swore to never abandon him. He doesn't know what kind of man Tarn is or what he would do for his own gain. I must find him as soon as I can, and I can only move fast if I'm alone."

Sighing, Lucenna nodded reluctantly, but she knew this was the right call. "How will you cross through the Elder Tree?"

"I have friends in Naiads Mere." Klyde cupped her face. "Once Tavin is safe, I will return to you, love. Then I will help you find your Moonstone and take down the Archmage."

Lucenna gasped softly. "What?"

The speckles in his eyes gleamed like sunlight glimmering on the ocean. "My wicked storm. You will blow through the empire, and I plan to be right by your side, watching as you do."

Merely hearing that gave her courage. She would return to Magos one day, and knowing he would be there, gave her all the strength she needed.

But it also scared her.

After thinking he had died yesterday, she never wanted to feel that crushing weight in her chest again.

"It's too dangerous, Klyde. That mage battle in Dwarf Shoe is nothing compared to a full out war."

He tucked a lock of silver hair behind her ear and said in a voice as warm as a summer breeze, "I have faced many dangers in my life, Lucenna. This one is no different, except in only one thing. I am fighting to protect someone I love."

Her eyes watered, and she whispered, "I told you not to tell me that..."

His sea-blue gaze softened. "You have bewitched me, lass. How could you expect me not to fall hopelessly in love with you?"

As she looked at this wonderfully ridiculous man, Lucenna knew she wanted him forever. It was a frightening feeling, but for once she wasn't afraid of the future anymore. Because she was ready to have him.

To be with him. To call him hers. Whatever fear she had of opening her heart to him had been washed away beneath the gentle tide of his gaze. She had never expected her heart to choose him either, but it did.

She was completely, insanely in love with Klyde.

With the cunning, playful, protective, deadly, patient, gentle man who intruded into her life. It didn't matter that he wasn't a mage. In many ways, they were completely unalike, but her heart *chose* him. Not because he was absurdly handsome or because of those damn dimples that appeared every time he smiled at her. And certainly not because he had a mouth that made her see stars.

It was because Klyde looked at her like she was the very moon of his sky, and he didn't expect anything more than that.

Clutching his shirt, Lucenna rose on her toes and pressed her lips to his. He kissed her, softly at first, gentle and sweet, but she gripped his forearms because she had never wanted sweet.

His hands tangled in her hair, and his mouth responded urgently, with a need they had both been starving for. His groan against her lips rumbled all the way down to her center. He may not have had any magic, but he knew exactly how to make her lose herself blissfully and utterly in him.

She will miss him and the way he kissed her, as though he intended to memorize the very shape of her mouth.

Why had she resisted him for so long?

Lucenna laughed.

"What's so amusing?" Klyde asked, resting his forehead against hers.

"You were right."

"I normally am, but what about this time?"

She leaned back a bit and brushed her fingers over the stubble on his jaw. "About what would happen if you shaved."

Klyde's lips curved in that sly, cocksure grin that she thought she had hated. "I did say you would fall for me."

"That it wouldn't be fair." She smiled. "I wonder who fell first."

"Love, I was mad for you the moment you held a knife at my throat, and all I could do was beg the Gods. Whether it was for mercy or for thanks, I still do not yet know. You have me by the bollocks, woman. They're yours now."

She squealed with laughter. "How romantic. I suppose I will keep them as long as I have everything else attached to them."

Klyde grinned at that, but as he gazed at her it wavered, the first sign of the worry she knew had been building inside of him. He sighed and cradled her hands in his. "Lucenna, there is something I need to—" He froze, staring down at her fingers. "What happened to your ring?"

"I took it off."

His eyes widened. "Why?"

Lucenna smiled at him timidly. She had removed it last night after nearly losing him. It was the moment she knew she loved him. "Because of you."

But Klyde didn't look happy. All she saw on his face was pure panic. And fear.

"When did you remove it?"

She stared at him, confused by his alarmed tone. "I'm not going to marry him anymore, Klyde. I don't need the ring."

"Yes, you do!" He riffled through her satchel frantically. "Where is it? Put it on, Lucenna. I need you to put it on!"

"Klyde, stop it. You're scaring me."

The orb in the grass by her feet pulsed white, and her temple throbbed with Lucien's alarm. Something was wrong. Klyde glanced past her, and his breath shuddered.

Lucenna whipped around.

Amber eyes looked back at her. The shade belonged to a face she had nearly forgotten and had wished to forget entirely. The sight of him froze her on the spot.

Her mind stuttered, not sure if what she was seeing was real. She didn't want to believe the one in black robes standing a few feet away from them was real, even as the immense might of his power pressed against her very being like a wall of stone.

His name fell from her lips in a soft gasp. "Everest..."

The Crown Prince of the Magos Empire smiled at her the way he always had. But now she recognized it for what it was—cruel and heartless. And Lucenna felt the ire behind it. A spike of dread sent a chill rushing through her entire body. So cold that her skin prickled with goosebumps.

Red Essence bled into Everest's eyes as magic spiraled from his hands, and she knew why he had come.

And what he was going to do.

Klyde shoved her roughly out of the way, and she hit the ground. The next seconds stretched into minutes. Breaths stretched into infinity. Time slowed with only the streak of red light blazing past her—because the attack wasn't meant for her.

A grunt whooshed out of Klyde.

They both stared at the crackling spear of magic that pierced straight through his stomach and out his back. Blood bloomed from his tunic like a crimson rose, soaking through the fabric.

A whimper caught in Lucenna's throat. She couldn't speak, couldn't breathe.

That spell shouldn't have been possible. At the cold touch of glass on her chest, she found the four-leaf clover now hanging around her neck instead of his.

"Thank you for returning her to me, mercenary," Everest said. "But I'm afraid your services are no longer required."

Seventeen words.

Seventeen knives that cleaved into her heart.

Lucenna shook with cold horror and disbelief.

Blood leaked from Klyde's trembling mouth as his wet eyes lifted to hers. They shone with remorse and so much he wished to say. But a sad smile tugged at his lips as he told her only one thing.

"On your feet, lass..."

The crackling spear wrenched him through the air. He sailed over the cascade and his body fell through the mist. Gone to where she couldn't follow.

Lucenna's mouth opened with a soundless scream.

No sound tore from her throat.

No air passed through her lungs.

Pain demolished her from the inside as every part of her shredded apart. She couldn't do anything as Klyde vanished from her life. Her chest burned for lack of air. Her vision blurred as all grew dark. She hardly felt the crackle of red Essence envelope her limp body.

"There you are, my sweet," Everest said with a pleased smile. His red eyes glowed with cold satisfaction, and he caressed her tear-stained face. "Who knew that damn ring would be such a hindrance to me, but alas I found you. As promised."

With a wave of his fingers, a containment sphere formed around her, and it lifted her into the air. Then came the terrible declaration Lucenna had been running from for the past four years.

"It's time to return home."

ACKNOWLEDGMENTS

Of all the books I have written, *Rising Dawn* broke me and healed me at the same time. I have never cried as much as I did while writing this book.

It's no secret that *Rising Dawn* was a struggle for me.

THIS BOOK KICKED MY BUTT.

When I got to the middle of it, my mind stopped working. No inspiration would come. I had no urge to write, and I lost all motivation to keep going. It was like the magic had simply run out. I fell into a depressive fog, and I feared I would never write again. I eventually noticed it was Cassiel's chapters that left me stumped, which didn't make sense, because I love writing from his point of view. But I finally understood how much weight of his grief I had placed on my heart.

I lost my father when I was a teenager, but I never let myself grieve that loss. I was subconsciously running away from writing this book because I didn't want to feel that pain. I didn't want to grieve. Yet somehow, I had begun that process through Dyna and her Guardians, beginning with the first book. But for *Rising Dawn*, I needed to go through the five stages of grief with Cassiel.

It was as though, after over a decade since my father's passing, my soul was telling me it was time.

So I sat down and wrote those scenes that left me falling apart all over again and accepted that my best friend was gone. The chapters of Cassiel facing his father's loss were one of the most heart wrenching things I've ever written.

I sobbed over each word.

Broke over every line.

They are forever embedded in my heart.

Those last pages on the hills of Sellav, when the sunrise broke over the horizon, put a part of me back together. To the pieces I left behind between these pages, may you find peace.

Here's to you, daddy. Thank you for being my knight when I needed one, and for being the voice of wisdom when I was lost. You were a great dad, and everything you taught me has made me who I am. I wish you were here. And I wish you could have met my Mr. Right. I think you would have really liked him.

Thank you to my husband, my love, for always supporting me through every journey I take. And for carrying me when I needed it. I don't know what I would do without you, Michael. You're the other half of my soul.

Massive thank you to my incredible team, who without their help, this book may not have been released this year—or possibly at all. My PA Sarah Chance, you are an absolute godsend who appeared at the right time. Katie Ryan, you go above and beyond, and I am eternally grateful for your kindness. And to the rest of my beta readers: Mimi Corpus and Madeeha Idrees, I cannot thank you enough for continuing to give your amazing feedback to my stories when they are in dire need of polishing. They shine because of you.

Thank you to Shayna Alexa for sharing more of the Hebrew culture with me, so it could be shared through the characters in these books. Your kindness and insight have been a blessing.

A special acknowledgement to Kiely and her late grandfather, William Hardy. It means more than you know that my series held a special memory for you both.

Thank you, Guardians, for being so patient and offering me grace when I needed more time to finish this book. I am very sorry for all the delays with *Rising Dawn*. I promise to do better with the next one.

Forever within your debt,

Beck Michaels

CELESTIAL LANGUAGE
(HEBREW TRANSLATION):

Ahava nitzchit: eternal love
Ani ohev otach: I love you
Ahuvati: my love (for girl)
Lev sheli: my heart
Motek: sweetheart
Kohav: star
Mish'alah: wish
At mehamemet: you are amazing
At yafa: you are beautiful
At mushlemet: you are perfect
At yekarah li: you are dear to me (for girl)
Eishet Chayil: woman of valor
Gehenom: a place of cleansing for souls
At hazricha v'hashkia sheli: you are my sunrise and my sunset
Ani mitga'ah'ge'ah elayich: I miss you
Aveilut: mourning
Lashamayim: To the sky
Alav Ha-shalom: May he rest in peace
Ghet: divorce contract
Lech la'azazel: Go to hell
Zonah: bitch

FOR MORE ON THIS VAST WORLD VISIT:
WWW.BECKMICHAELS.COM/WORLD-GUIDE

The adventure continues in...

WICKED STORM

GUARDIANS OF THE MAIDEN: BOOK 5

ABOUT THE AUTHOR

BECK MICHAELS is the bestselling author of the enchanting epic fantasy series *The Guardians of the Maiden*. Beck lives in Indiana with her husband and two children, where she spends her time reading and daydreaming of stories in faraway lands.

WWW.BECKMICHAELS.COM

Made in the USA
Middletown, DE
18 September 2024

60603056R00409